The Pursuit of Happiness

The Pursuit of Happiness

Douglas Kennedy

W F Howes Ltd

Copyright © Douglas Kennedy 2001

The right of Douglas Kennedy to be identified as
the author of this work has been asserted by him
in accordance with the Copyright, Designs and
Patents Act 1988

A CIP catalogue record for this book is available
from the British Library

ISBN 1-84505-825-2

W F HOWES LTD

This large print edition published in 2003 by
W F Howes Ltd
Units 6/7, Victoria Mills, Fowke Street
Rothley, Leicester LE7 7PJ

1 3 5 7 9 10 8 6 4 2

First publi~~shed in the United Ki~~ngdom in 2001
by Hutchinson

Copy~~right © Douglas Kenn~~edy 2001

A CIP catalogue record for this book is available
from the British Library

ISBN 1-84197-652-0

Typeset by Palimpsest Book Production Limited,
Polmont, Stirlingshire
Printed and bound in Great Britain
by Antony Rowe Ltd, Chippenham, Wilts.

PART ONE

KATE

CHAPTER 1

I first saw her standing near my mother's coffin. She was in her seventies – a tall, angular woman, with fine grey hair gathered in a compact bun at the back of her neck. She looked the way I hope to look if I ever make it to her birthday. She stood very erect, her spine refusing to hunch over with age. Her bone structure was flawless. Her skin had stayed smooth. Whatever wrinkles she had didn't cleave her face. Rather, they lent it character, gravitas. She was still handsome – in a subdued, patrician way. You could tell that, once upon a recent time, men probably found her beautiful.

But it was her eyes that really caught my attention. Blue-grey. Sharply focused, taking everything in. Critical, watchful eyes, with just the slightest hint of melancholy. But who isn't melancholic at a funeral? Who doesn't stare at a coffin and picture themselves laid out inside of it? They say funerals are for the living. Too damn true. Because we don't just weep for the departed. We also weep for ourselves. For the brutal brevity of life. For its ever-accumulating insignificance. For the way we stumble through it, like foreigners without a map,

3

making mistakes at every curve of the road.

When I looked at the woman directly, she averted her gaze in embarrassment – as if I had caught her in the act of studying me. Granted, the bereaved child at a funeral is always the subject of everybody's attention. As the person closest to the departed, they want you to set the emotional tone for the occasion. If you're hysterical, they won't be frightened of letting rip. If you're sobbing, they'll just sob too. If you're emotionally buttoned up, they'll also remain controlled, disciplined, correct. I was being very controlled, very correct – and so too were the twenty or so mourners who had accompanied my mother on 'her final journey'. – to borrow the words of the funeral director who dropped that phrase into the conversation when he was telling me the price of transporting her from his 'chapel of rest' on 75th and Amsterdam to this, 'her eternal resting place' . . . . right under the LaGuardia Airport flight path in Flushing Meadow, Queens.

After the woman turned away, I heard the reverse throttle of jet engines and glanced up into the cold blue winter sky. No doubt several members of the assembled graveside congregation thought that I was contemplating the heavens – and wondering about my mother's place in its celestial vastness. But actually all I was doing was checking out the livery of the descending jet. *US Air. One of those old 727s they still use for short hauls. Probably the Boston shuttle. Or maybe the Washington run . . .*

4

It is amazing the trivial junk that floats through your head at the most momentous moments of your life.

'Mommy, Mommy.'

My seven-year-old son, Ethan, was tugging at my coat. His voice cut across that of the Episcopalian minister, who was standing at the back of the coffin, solemnly intoning a passage from Revelations:

God shall wipe away all tears from their eyes;
And there shall be no more death, neither sorrow
Nor crying, neither shall there be any more pain;
For the former things are passed away.

I swallowed hard. No sorrow. No crying. No pain. That was not the story of my mother's life.

'Mommy, Mommy . . .'

Ethan was still tugging on my sleeve, demanding attention. I put a finger to my lips and simultaneously stroked his mop of dirty blond hair.

'Not now, darling,' I whispered.

'I need to wee.'

I fought a smile.

'Daddy will take you,' I said, looking up and catching the eye of my ex-husband, Matt. He was standing on the opposite side of the coffin, keeping to the back of the small crowd. I had been just a tad surprised when he showed up at the funeral chapel this morning. Since he left Ethan and me five years ago, our dealings with each other had been, at best, businesslike – whatever words spoken between us having been limited to our son, and the usual dreary financial matters that force even acrimoniously divorced couples to answer each other's phone calls. Even when he's attempted to be conciliatory, I've cut him off at the pass. For some strange reason, I've never really forgiven him for walking right out of our front door and into the arms of *Her* – Ms Talking Head *News-Channel-4-New-York* media babe. And Ethan was just twenty-five months old at the time.

Still, one must take these little setbacks on the chin, right? Especially as Matt so conformed to male cliché. But there is one thing I can say in my ex-husband's favor: he has turned out to be an attentive, loving father. And Ethan adores him – something that everyone at the graveside noticed, as he dashed in front of his grandmother's coffin and straight into his father's arms. Matt lifted him off the ground and I saw Ethan whisper his urination request. With a quick nod to me, Matt carried him off, draped across one shoulder, in search of the nearest toilet.

The minister now switched to that old funeral favorite, the 23rd Psalm.

Thou prepareth a table before me in the presence of mine enemies; thou anointest my head with oil; my cup runneth over.

I heard my brother Charlie choke back a sob. He was standing in the back of this sparse congregation of mourners. Without question, he had won the award for the Best Surprise Funeral Appearance – as he arrived at the chapel this morning off the red-eye from LA, looking ashen, spent, and deeply uncomfortable. It took me a moment to recognize him – because I hadn't seen him in over seven years, and because time had worked its nasty magic, rendering him middle-aged. Okay, I'm middleaged too – just! – but Charlie (at fifty-five, nearly nine years my senior) really looked . . . well, I guess mature would be the right word, though world-weary might be a little more accurate. He'd lost most of his hair, and all of his physique. His face had become fleshy and loose. His waist bulged heavily at both sides – a spare tire that made his ill-fitting black suit appear even more of a sartorial misjudgment. His white shirt was open at the collar. His black tie was dappled with food stains. His entire countenance spoke of bad diet and a certain disappointment with life. I was certainly on cordial terms with the last of these concepts . . . but I was still stunned at just how badly he had aged, and that he had actually crossed the continent to say goodbye to a woman with whom he had only maintained nominal contact for the past thirty years.

'Kate,' he said, approaching me in the lobby of the funeral chapel.

He saw my face register shock.

'Charlie?'

There was an awkward moment when he reached

to hug me, then thought better of it and simply took my two hands in his. For a moment we didn't know what to say to each other. Finally I managed a sentence.

'This is a surprise . . .'

'I know, I know,' he said, cutting me off.

'You got my messages?'

He nodded. 'Katie . . . I'm so sorry.'

I suddenly let go of his hands.

'Don't offer me condolences,' I said, my voice curiously calm. 'She was your mother too. Remember?'

He blanched. Finally he managed to mumble, 'That's not fair.'

My voice remained very calm, very controlled.

'Every day for the last month – when she knew she was going – she kept asking me if you had called. Towards the end, I actually lied, and said you were phoning me daily to see how she was doing. So don't talk to me about fair.'

My brother stared down at the funeral home linoleum. Two of my mother's friends then approached me. As they made the requisite sympathetic noises, it gave Charlie the opportunity to back away. When the service began, he sat in the last row of the funeral chapel. I craned my neck to check out the assembled congregation – and briefly caught his eye. He turned away in acute discomfort. After the service, I looked around for him, as I wanted to offer him the chance to ride with me in the so-called 'family car' to the cemetery.

But he was nowhere to be found. So I traveled out to Queens with Ethan and my Aunt Meg. She was my father's sister – a seventy-four-year-old professional spinster who has been devoted to the destruction of her liver for the past forty years. I was pleased to see that she had remained sober for the occasion of her sister-in-law's sendoff. Because on those rare occasions when she was practising temperance, Meg was the best ally you could have. Especially as she had a tongue on her like a pissed-off wasp. Shortly after the limo pulled away from the funeral home, the subject turned to Charlie.

'So,' Meg said, 'the prodigal *schmuck* returns.'

'And then promptly disappears,' I added.

'He'll be at the cemetery,' she said.

'How do you know that?'

'He told me. While you were pressing the flesh with everyone after the service, I caught him on the way out the door. "Hang on for a sec," I told him, "and we'll give you a ride out to Queens." But he went all mealy-mouthed, saying how he'd rather take the subway. I tell you, Charlie's still the same old sad asshole.'

'Meg,' I said, nodding toward Ethan. He was sitting next to me in the limo, deeply engrossed in a Power Rangers book.

'He's not listening to the crap I'm talking, are you, Ethan?'

He looked up from his book. 'I know what *asshole* means,' he said.

9

'Attaboy,' Meg said, ruffling his hair.

'Read your book, darling,' I said.

'He's one smart kid,' Meg said. 'You've done a great job with him, Kate.'

'You mean, because he knows bad language?'

'I love a girl who thinks so highly of herself.'

'That's me: Ms Self-Esteem.'

'At least you've always done the right thing. Especially when it comes to family.'

'Yeah – and look where it's gotten me.'

'Your mother adored you.'

'On alternate Sundays.'

'I know she was difficult . . .'

'Try genteelly impossible.'

'Trust me, sweetie – you and this guy here were everything to her. And I mean *everything*.'

I bit my lip, and held back a sob. Meg took my hand.

'Take it from me: parents and children both end up feeling that they're the ones who landed the thankless job. Nobody comes out happy. But at least you won't suffer the guilt that your idiot brother is now feeling.'

'Do you know I left him three messages last week, telling him she only had days left, and he had to come back and see her.'

'He never called you back?'

'No – but his spokesperson did.'

'*Princess?*'

'The one and only.'

'Princess' was our nickname for Holly – the

deeply resistible, deeply suburban woman who married Charlie in 1975, and gradually convinced him (for a long list of spurious, self-serving reasons) to detach himself from his family. Not that Charlie needed much encouragement. From the moment I had been aware of such things, I always knew that, for a mother and son, Mom and Charlie had a curiously cool relationship – and that the root cause of their antipathy was my dad.

'Twenty bucks says Charlie-boy breaks down at the graveside,' Meg said.

'No way,' I said.

'I mightn't have seen him in . . . when the hell did he last pay us a visit?'

'Seven years ago.'

'Right, it may have been seven years ago, but I know that kid of old. Believe me, he's always felt sorry for himself. The moment I laid eyes on him today I thought: poor old Charlie is still playing the self-pity card. Not only that, he's also got hot-and-cold running guilt. Can't bring himself to talk to his dying mom, but then tries to make up for it by putting in a last-minute appearance at her planting. What a sad act.'

'He still won't cry. He's too wound tight for that.'

Meg waved the bill in front of me.

'Then let's see the color of your cash.'

I fiddled around in my jacket pocket until I found two tens. I brandished them in front of Meg's eyes. 'I'm going to enjoy taking your twenty off you,' I said.

11

'Not as much as I'm going to enjoy watching that pitiful shithead weep.'

I cast a glance at Ethan (still buried in his Power Rangers book), then threw my eyes heavenward.

'Sorry,' Meg said, 'it just kind of slipped out.'

Without looking up from his book, Ethan said, 'I know what *shithead* means.'

Meg won the bet. After a final prayer over the coffin, the minister touched my shoulder and offered his condolences. Then, one by one, the other mourners approached me. As I went through this receiving-line ritual of handshakes and embraces, I caught sight of that woman, staring down at the headstone adjoining my mother's plot, studying the inscription with care. I knew it off by heart:

John Joseph Malone
August 22, 1922 – April 14, 1956

John Joseph Malone. Also known as Jack Malone. Also known as my dad. Who suddenly left this world just eighteen months into my life – yet whose presence has always shadowed me. That's the thing about parents: they may physically vanish from your life – you may not have even known them – but you're never free of them. That's their ultimate legacy to you – the fact that, like it or not, they're always there. And no matter how hard you try to shake them, they never let go.

As my upstairs neighbor, Christine, embraced

12

me, I glanced over her shoulder. Charlie was now walking towards our father's grave. The woman was still standing there. But once she saw him coming (and evidently knowing who he was), she immediately backed away, giving him clear access to Dad's plain granite monument. Charlie's head was lowered, his gait shaky. When he reached the gravestone, he leaned against it for support – and suddenly began to sob. At first he tried to stifle his distress, but within a moment he lost that battle and was sobbing uncontrollably. I gently removed myself from Christine's embrace. Instinctively, I wanted to run right over to him – but I stopped myself from such an outward show of sibling sympathy (especially as I couldn't instantly forgive the pain that my mother silently suffered about his absence over all those years). Instead, I slowly walked towards him, and lightly touched his arm with my hand.

'You okay, Charlie?' I asked quietly.

He lifted up his head. His face was tomato red, his eyes awash in tears. Suddenly he lurched towards me, his head collapsing against my shoulder, his arms clutching me as if I was a life preserver in high seas. His sobbing was now fierce, uninhibited. For a moment I stood there, arms at my side, not knowing what to do. But his grief was so profound, so total, so *loud* that, eventually, I simply had to put my arms around him.

It took him a good minute before his cries subsided. I stared ahead into the distance, watching

Ethan (having just returned from the toilet) being gently restrained by Matt from running towards me. I winked at my son, and he repaid me with one of those hundred-watt smiles that instantly compensates for all the exhausting, endless stress that is an essential component of parenthood. Then I looked to the left of Ethan, and saw that woman again. She was standing discreetly in an adjoining plot, watching me comfort Charlie. Before she turned away (again!), I momentarily saw the intensity of her gaze. An intensity which made me wonder: how the hell does she know us?

I turned back to look at Ethan. He pulled open his mouth with two fingers and stuck out his tongue – one of the repertoire of funny faces he pulls whenever he senses I am getting far too serious for his liking. I had to stifle a laugh. Then I glanced back to where the woman was standing. But she was no longer there – and was instead walking alone down the empty graveled path that led to the front gates of the cemetery.

Charlie gulped hard as he tried to control his sobbing. I decided it was time to end the embrace, so I gently disentangled myself from his grip.

'Are you okay now?' I asked.

He kept his head bowed.

'No,' he whispered, then added: 'I should've, I should've . . .'

The crying started again. *I should've.* The most agonizing, self-punitive expression in the English language. And one we all utter constantly throughout this farce called life. But Charlie was right. *He should've*. Now there was nothing he could do about it.

'Come back to the city,' I said. 'We're having some drinks and food at Mom's apartment. You remember where it is, don't you?'

I immediately regretted that comment, as Charlie began to sob again.

'That was dumb,' I said quietly. 'I'm sorry.'

'Not as sorry as me,' he said between sobs. 'Not as . . .'

He lost control again, his crying now ballistic. This time, I didn't offer him solace. Instead, I turned away and saw that Meg was now hovering nearby, looking dispassionate, yet waiting to be of assistance. When I turned towards her, she nodded in the direction of Charlie and arched her eyebrows, as if to ask, 'Want me to take over here?' You bet. She approached her nephew, and said, 'Come on, Charlie-boy,' linking her arm through his, 'let's you and I take a little walk.'

Matt now relaxed his grip on Ethan, who ran towards me. I crouched down to scoop him up in my arms.

'You feeling better?' I asked.

'The toilet was yucky,' he said.

I turned towards my mother's grave. The minister was still standing by the coffin. Behind him were the cemetery's grounds-keepers. They were keeping a discreet distance from the proceedings, but I could still tell they were waiting for us to leave so they could lower her into subterranean Queens, bring out the earth movers, plug the hole, then head off to lunch . . . or maybe the nearest bowling alley. Life really does go on – whether you're here or not.

The minister gave me a small telling nod, the subtext of which was: *it's time to say goodbye.* Okay, Rev., have it your way. Let's all join hands and sing.

Now it's time to say goodbye to all our
  company . . .
M-I-C . . . See you real soon . . .
K-E-Y . . . Why? Because we like you . . .
M-O-U-S-E . . .

For a nanosecond, I was back in the old family apartment on 84th Street between Broadway and Amsterdam. Six years old, home from first grade at Brearley, watching Annette, Frankie and all the Mouseketeers on our crappy Zenith black-and-white set, with the round picture tube and rabbit-ears antenna, and the imitation mahogany cabinet, and my mom staggering towards me with two Welch's grape jelly glasses in her hand: Strawberry Kool-Aid for me, a Canadian Club highball for her.

'How's Mickey and his pals?' she asked, the words slurring.

'They're my friends,' I said.

She sank down next to me on the couch.

'Are you my friend, Katie?'

I ignored the question. 'Where's Charlie?'

She suddenly looked hurt.

'Mr Barclay's,' she said, mentioning a dancing school to which adolescent prep school boys like Charlie were dispatched, once a week, screaming.

'Charlie hates dancing,' I said.

'You don't know that,' Mom said, throwing back half of her drink.

'I heard him tell you,' I said. '*I hate dancing school. I hate you.*'

'He didn't say he hated me.'

'He did,' I said, and turned my attention back to the Mouseketeers.

Mom threw back the rest of her drink.

'He *didn't* say that.'

I think it's a game.

'Oh yes he did.'

'You *never* heard him . . .'

I cut her off. 'Why is my daddy in heaven?'

She went ashen. Though we'd been down this road before, I hadn't asked about my dead father for nearly a year. But this afternoon, I had arrived home with an invitation to a Father/Daughter evening at my school.

'Why did he have to go to heaven?' I demanded.

'Darling, as I told you before, he didn't want to go to heaven. But he got sick . . .'

'When can I meet him?'

Her face now betrayed despair.

'Katie . . . you *are* my friend, aren't you?'

17

'You let me meet my daddy.'

I heard her stifle a sob. 'I wish I could . . .'

'I want him to come to school with me . . .'

'Tell me, Katie, that you're my friend.'

'You get my daddy back from heaven.'

Her voice was weak, tiny, diminished.

'I can't, Katie. I . . .'

Then she began to cry. Pulling me close to her. Burying her head in my small shoulder. Scaring the hell out of me. And making me run out of the room, terrified.

It was the only time I ever saw her drunk. It was the only time she ever cried in front of me. It was the last time I asked her to get my father back from the celestial beyond.

'Are you my friend, Katie?'

I never answered her question. Because, truth be told, I never really knew the answer.

'Mommy!'

Ethan was squeezing my hand. 'Mommy! I want to go home!'

I snapped back to Queens. And the sight of my mother's coffin. I said, 'Let's first say goodbye to Grandma.'

I led Ethan forward, sensing that all eyes were on us. We approached the shiny teak coffin. Ethan knocked on it with his small fist.

'Hello, Grandma. Goodbye, Grandma.'

I bit hard on my lip. My eyes filled up. I glanced at my father's grave. *This is it. This is it. An orphan at last.*

I felt a steadying hand on my shoulder. I turned around. It was Matt. I shrugged him off. And suddenly knew: it's me and Ethan, and no one else.

The minister gave me another of his telling glances. All right, all right, I'll move it along.

I put my hand on the coffin. It felt cold, like a refrigerator. I pulled my hand away. So much for grand final gestures. I bit my lip yet again, and forced myself to stay controlled. I reached for my son. I led him towards the waiting car.

Matt was waiting by the door. He spoke quietly.

'Katie, I just wanted to . . .'

'I don't want to know.'

'All I was going to say . . .'

'Do you speak English?'

'Would you please listen . . .'

I started grabbing the car door. 'No, I will not listen to you . . .'

Ethan tugged my sleeve. 'Daddy said he'd take me to the IMAX movie. Can I go, Mommy?'

It was then that I realized just how shipwrecked I was.

'We have a party . . .' I heard myself saying.

'Ethan will have a better time at the movies, don't you think?' Matt said.

Yeah, he would. I put my face in my hands. And felt more tired than I had ever felt in my life.

'Please can I go, Mommy?'

I looked up at Matt. 'What time will you have him home?'

'I was thinking he might like to spend the night with us.'

I could see that he instantly regretted the use of that last pronoun. Matt continued talking.

'I'll get him to school in the morning. And he can stay the next couple of nights if you need . . .'

'Fine,' I said, cutting him off. Then I crouched down and hugged my son. And heard myself saying, 'Are you my friend, Ethan?'

He looked at me shyly, then gave me a fast kiss on the cheek. I wanted to take that as an affirmative answer, but knew I'd be brooding about his lack of a definite response for the rest of the day . . . and night. And simultaneously wondering why the hell I'd asked that dumb question in the first place.

Matt was about to touch my arm, but then thought better of it.

'Take care,' he said, leading Ethan off.

Then I felt another hand on my shoulder. I brushed it off, as if it was a fly, saying to whoever was behind me, 'I really can't take any more sympathy.'

'Then don't take it.'

I covered my face with my hand. 'Sorry, Meg.'

'Say three Hail Marys, and get into the car.'

I did as ordered. Meg climbed in after me.

'Where's Ethan?' she asked.

'Spending the rest of the day with his dad.'

'Good,' she said. 'I can smoke.'

While reaching into her pocket book for her Merits, she knocked on the glass partition with one hand. The driver hit a button and it slowly lowered.

'We're outta here, fella,' Meg said, lighting up. She heaved a huge sigh of gratification as she inhaled.

'Must you?' I asked.

'Yeah, I must.'

'It'll kill you.'

'I never knew that.'

The limo pulled out on to the main cemetery drive. Meg took my hand, locking her thin, varicose fingers with mine.

'You hanging in there, sweetheart?' she asked.

'I have been better, Meg.'

'A couple more hours, this entire fucking business'll be over. And then . . .'

'I can fall apart.'

Meg shrugged. And held my hand tighter.

'Where's Charlie?' I asked.

'Taking the subway back into town.'

'Why the hell is he doing that?'

'It's his idea of penance.'

'Watching him break down like that, I actually felt sorry for him. If he'd just picked up the phone towards the end, he could have straightened out so much with Mom.'

'No,' Meg said. 'He wouldn't have straightened anything out.'

As the limo approached the gates, I caught sight of that woman again. She was walking steadily towards the cemetery entrance, moving with fluent ease for someone her age. Meg saw her as well.

'Do you know her?' I asked.

Her answer was a couldn't-care-less shrug.

'She was at Mom's grave,' I said. 'And hung around during most of the prayers.'

Another shrug from Meg.

I said, 'Probably some kook who gets her giggles loitering in cemeteries.'

She looked up as we drove by, then lowered her eyes quickly.

The limo pulled out into the main road, and turned left in the direction of Manhattan. I fell back into the seat, spent. For a moment there was silence. Then Meg poked me with her elbow.

'So,' she said, 'where's my twenty bucks?'

CHAPTER 2

After the cemetery, fifteen of the twenty graveside mourners returned to my mother's place. It was quite a squeeze – as Mom had spent the last twenty-six years of her life in a small one-bedroom apartment on 84th Street and West End Avenue (and even on those truly rare occasions when she entertained, I can't remember more than four people in her home at any given time).

I had never liked the apartment. It was cramped. It was badly laid out. Its southwest position on the fourth floor meant that it overlooked a back alleyway, and was rarely in contact with the sun. The living room was eleven feet by eleven, there was a bedroom of equal size, there was a small en-suite bathroom, there was a ten-by-eight kitchen with elderly appliances and scuffed linoleum. Everything about the apartment seemed old, tired, in desperate need of updating. Three years ago, I'd managed to convince Mom to get the place repainted – but, like so many old West Side apartments, this new coat of emulsion and gloss simply added another cheap veneer to plaster work and moldings that were already an inch thick with decades-worth of bad paint. The carpets were getting threadbare. The furniture was in need of recovering. What few so-called luxury items she owned (a television, an air-conditioner, an all-in-one stereo unit of indeterminate Korean origin) were all technologically backward. Over the past few years, whenever I had a bit of spare cash (which, it has to be said, wasn't very often), I'd offer to update her TV or buy her a microwave. But she always refused.

'You have better things to be spending your money on,' she'd always say.

'You're my mom,' I'd retort.

'Spend it on Ethan, spend it on yourself. I'm fine with what I've got.'

'That air-conditioner is asthmatic. You're going to boil in July.'

'I have an electric fan.'

'Mom, I'm just trying to help.'

'I know that, dear. But I am *just fine*.' She'd give the last two words such pointed, tetchy emphasis that I knew it was useless to pursue the issue. This topic of conversation was closed.

She was always denying herself everything. She hated the idea of turning into a burden. And – being a genteel, yet fiercely self-respecting WASP – she loathed the notion of being a suitable case for charity. Because, to her, it implied personal failure; a collapse of character.

I turned around from where I was standing in

the living room, and caught sight of a cluster of framed family photos on an end table next to the sofa. I walked over and picked up a snapshot I knew all too well. It was of my father in his Army uniform. It was taken by my mother at the base in England where they met in 1945. It had been her one overseas adventure – the only time in her life that she ever left America. Having volunteered for the Red Cross after college, she'd ended up as a typist, working at an outpost of Allied Command HQ in suburban London. That's where she encountered the dashing Jack Malone, cooling his Brooklyn heels after covering the Allied liberation of Germany for *Stars and Stripes* – the US Army newspaper. They had a fling – of which Charlie was the byproduct. And they suddenly found their destiny spliced together.

Charlie approached me. He looked down at the photograph I was holding.

'Do you want to bring this back with you?' I asked.

He shook his head. 'I've got a copy at home,' he said. 'It's my favorite photo of Dad.'

'I think I'll take it then. I don't have too many pictures of him.'

We stood there for a moment, wondering what to say next. Charlie chewed nervously on his lower lip.

'You feeling better?' I asked.

'Fine, yeah,' he said, averting his eyes as usual. 'You bearing up?'

'Me? Sure,' I said, trying to sound unfazed by having just buried our mom.

'Your son's a great-looking kid. Was that your ex?'

'Yeah – that's the charmer. You've never met him before?'

Charlie shook his head.

'Oh yes, I forgot – you missed my wedding. And Matt was out of town during your last trip here. Nineteen ninety-four, wasn't it?'

Charlie ignored that question, and instead posed another:

'He's still something in television news, isn't he?'

'He's now something very big. Like his new wife.'

'Yeah, Mom did tell me about the divorce.'

'Really?' I said, sounding surprised. 'When did she tell you? During your annual phone call in nineteen ninety-five?'

'We spoke a little more than that.'

'Sorry, you're right. You also called her every Christmas. So, it was during one of your bi-annual phone calls that you discovered Matt had left me.'

'I was really sad to hear about that.'

'Hey, it's ancient history now. I'm over it.'

Another awkward silence.

'The place doesn't look very different,' he said, glancing around the apartment.

'Mom was never going to make it into the pages of *House and Garden*,' I said. 'Mind you, even if she'd wanted to do up the apartment – which she didn't – money was always rather tight. Thank God the place was rent-stabilized – otherwise she wouldn't have been able to stay on.'

'What's it now a month?'

'Eighteen hundred – which isn't bad for the neighborhood. But it was always a scramble for her to meet.'

'Didn't she inherit anything from Uncle Ray?'

Ray was Mom's well-heeled brother – a big-deal Boston-based lawyer who maintained a starchy distance from his sister. From what I could gather, Mom was never particularly close to him when they were growing up – and they grew even further apart after Ray and his wife, Edith, voiced their disapproval of the Brooklyn Mick she had married. But Ray did live according to the WASP code of Doing the Proper Thing. So after my dad's premature death, he came to the financial aid of his sister by offering to pay for the education of her two children. The fact that Ray and Edith had no kids of their own (and that Mom was Ray's only sibling) probably made it easier for them to foot this hefty bill over the years – even though, when we were younger, it was pretty clear to Charlie and me that our uncle didn't really want anything to do with us. We never saw him. Mom never saw him. We each received a twenty-dollar savings bond from him every Christmas. When Charlie was at Boston College, Ray never once invited him over to his Beacon Hill townhouse. I also got the cold shoulder while I was at Smith and dropping into Boston once a month. Mom explained his aloofness away by telling us, 'Families can be odd.' Still, fair credit to the guy: thanks to him, Charlie and I were able to attend private schools and private colleges. But as soon as I graduated from Smith in '76, Mom saw no more money from her brother – and she was always short of cash for the rest of her life. When Ray died in '98, I expected Mom to come into a little money (especially as Edith had pre-deceased her husband by three years). But she received nothing from his estate.

'You mean, Mom never told you that Ray left her zilch?' I asked.

'All she said was that he had died.'

'That was during your nineteen ninety-eight phone call, right?'

Charlie stared down at his shoes. 'Yes – that's right,' he said quietly. 'But I didn't know she'd been cut out of his will like that.'

'Yeah – Ray left everything to the nurse who'd been looking after him ever since Edith went to that big Episcopalian church in the sky. Poor old Mom – she always got shortchanged on everything.'

'How did she manage to pay the bills?'

'She had a small pension from the school. There was social security . . . and that was it. I offered to help her out, but, of course, she refused me. Even though I could have afforded it.'

'You still with the same ad agency?'

'I'm afraid so.'

'But you're some senior executive now, aren't you?'

'A senior copywriter, that's all.'

'Sounds pretty okay to me.'

'The money's not bad. But there's a saying in my business: a happy copywriter is an oxymoron.

Still, it passes the time and pays the bills. I just wish Mom had let me pay some of *her* bills. But she was adamant she wanted nothing from me. The way I figure it, she was either running an illegal canasta game, or she had a lucrative Girl Scout Cookie racket going on the side.'

'You planning to close up this place now?' Charlie asked.

'I'm certainly not going to maintain it as a museum.'

I looked at him squarely. 'You know you're out of the will.'

'I'm, uh, not surprised.'

'Not that there's much in her estate. Just before she went, she told me there was a bit of life insurance and some stock. Maybe fifty grand tops. Too bad you didn't make contact with her six months ago. Believe me, she didn't want to cut you out – and she kept hoping against hope that you'd make that one call. After they told her the cancer was terminal, she *wrote* you, didn't she?'

'She *never* mentioned in the letter that she was dying,' he said.

'Oh, that would have changed things, would it?'

Another of his evasive over-my-shoulder glances. My voice remained level.

'You didn't answer her letter, and you didn't answer the messages I left for you when she was in her final days. Which, I have to say, was strategically dumb. Because had you shown your face in New York, you would now be splitting that fifty grand with me.'

'I would never have accepted my share . . .'

'Yeah, right. *Princess* would have insisted . . .'

'Don't call Holly that.'

'Why the hell not? She's the Lady Macbeth in this story.'

'Kate, I'm really trying to . . .'

'Do what? "Heal wounds"? Achieve "closure"?'

'Look, my argument was never with you.'

'I'm touched. Too bad Mom's not here to see this. She always had these far-fetched romantic notions about everyone making up, and maybe seeing her West Coast grandkids again.'

'I meant to call . . .'

'*Meant* isn't good enough. *Meant* means shit.'

My voice had jumped a decibel or two. I was suddenly aware that the living room had emptied. So too was Charlie, as he whispered, 'Please, Kate . . . I don't want to go back to the coast with such bad . . .'

'Charlie, what the hell did you expect today? Instant reconciliation? *Field of Dreams?* You reap what you sow, pal.'

I felt a steadying hand on my arm. Aunt Meg.

'Great sermon, Kate,' she said. 'And I'm sure Charlie now completely understands your point of view.'

I took a deep steadying breath. And said, 'Yeah, I guess he does.'

'Charlie,' Meg said, 'why don't you go find yourself something alcoholic in the kitchen.'

Charlie did as commanded. The squabbling children had been separated.

'You okay now?' Meg asked.

'No,' I said. 'I am definitely *not* okay.'

She motioned me towards the sofa. Sitting down next to me, her voice became conspiratorially quiet:

'Back off the guy,' she said. 'I had a little talk with him in the kitchen. It seems he's been juggling some very major problems.'

'What kind of problems?'

'He was downsized four months ago. Fitzgibbon was taken over by some Dutch multinational, and they immediately canned half their Californian sales force.'

Fitzgibbon was the pharmaceuticals giant which had employed Charlie for the last twenty years. Charlie had started out as a San Fernando Valley sales rep, then gradually worked his way up to being Regional Sales Director for Orange County. And now . . .

'Exactly how bad are his problems?' I asked.

'Put it this way – he had to borrow money from a friend to buy the plane ticket back here.'

'Jesus.'

'And with two kids in college, financially speaking, things are hitting critical mass. He's in really grim shape.'

I suddenly felt a pang of guilt. The poor idiot. Nothing ever seemed to work out Charlie's way. He always had this unerring talent for making the wrong call.

'From what I gather, the marital front is also pretty choppy. Because Princess isn't exactly being the most supportive of spouses . . .'

Meg suddenly stopped talking and gave me a fast nudge with her elbow. Charlie had re-entered the room, his raincoat over his arm. I stood up.

'What's with the coat?' I asked.

'I've got to get back to the airport,' he said.

'But you just arrived a couple of hours ago,' I said.

'I've got a big meeting first thing tomorrow,' he said sheepishly. 'A job interview. I'm, uh, kind of between things at the moment.'

I caught Meg's glance – imploring me not to let on that I knew about Charlie's unemployed status. Isn't it amazing how family life is an ever-widening web of petty confidences and 'please don't tell your brother I told you . . .'

'I'm sorry to hear that, Charlie,' I said. 'And I'm sorry I boxed your ears before. It's a bad day and . . .'

Charlie silenced me by leaning forward and giving me a fast buzz on the cheek.

'Let's keep in touch, eh?' he said.

'That's really up to you, Charlie.'

My brother didn't respond to that comment. He simply shrugged sadly and headed to the front door. When he got there, he turned back towards me. A look passed between us. It only lasted a nanosecond, but it said it all: *please forgive me.*

In that sad nanosecond, I felt a surge of pity for my brother. He appeared so bloated and battered by life; as trapped and cornered as a deer staring straight into the oncoming headlights. Life had not worked out for him – and he now radiated disappointment. I could certainly sympathize with his sense of letdown. Because, with the serendipitous exception of my son, I was not exactly a walking advertisement for personal fulfilment.

'Goodbye, Katie,' Charlie said. He opened the front door. I turned away from my brother and disappeared into the bathroom. When I came out two minutes later, I was relieved to see that he'd left.

Just as I was also relieved that the rest of the assembled mourners began to make their goodbyes. There were a couple of people from the building, and some old friends of Mom – increasingly frail women in their seventies, trying to make pleasant chit-chat, and appear reasonably spirited, and not think too much about the fact that, one by one, their contemporaries were vanishing.

By three, everyone had gone – except for Meg and Rozella, the large, cheerful, middle-aged Dominican woman I had hired, two years ago, to clean Mom's apartment twice a week. She ended up being a full-time nurse after Mom checked herself out of Sloan-Kettering.

'I'm not dying in some beige room with fluorescent lighting,' she told me the morning her oncologist informed her the cancer was terminal.

I heard myself saying, 'You're not dying, Mom.'

She reached out from the bed and took my hand.

'You can't fight City Hall, dear.'

'The doctor said it could be months . . .'

Her voice remained calm, strangely serene.

'At the very outset. From where I'm sitting, I would say three weeks maximum. Which, quite frankly, is better than I expected . . .'

'Must you always, *always* look on the bright side, Mom?' Oh Christ, what am I saying here? I grasped her hand tighter. 'I didn't mean that. It's just . . .'

She stared at me critically.

'You've never really figured me out, have you?' she said.

Before I had a chance to offer up some weak refutation, she reached out and hit the call button by her hospital bed.

'I'm going to ask the nurse to get me dressed and help me pack up my things. So if you wouldn't mind giving me fifteen minutes . . .'

'I'll get you dressed, Mom.'

'No need, dear.'

'But I want to.'

'Go get yourself a cup of coffee, dear. The nurse will take care of everything.'

'Why won't you let me . . . ?' I suddenly sounded like a whiny fourteen-year-old. My mom simply smiled, knowing she'd checkmated me.

'You run along now, dear. But don't be longer than fifteen minutes – because if I'm not gone by noon, they charge another full day for the room.'

'So what?' I felt like yelling. 'Blue Cross is picking up the tab.' But I knew what her response would be.

It's still not fair to take advantage of a good, dependable company like Blue Cross.

And I would then wonder (for around the zillionth time) why I could never win an argument with her.

You've never really figured me out, have you?

Damn her for knowing me too well. As usual, she was right on the money. I never understood her. Never understood how she could be so equanimous in the face of so many disappointments, so many adversities. From the few hints that she had dropped (and from what Charlie told me when we used to talk), I sensed that her marriage hadn't exactly been happy. Her husband had died young. He'd left her no money. Her only son had estranged himself from the family. And her only daughter was Ms Discontented who couldn't understand why her mom refused to scream and shout about life's many letdowns. Or why, now, at the end of her life, she was so damn accepting, and would think it bad manners to rage against the dying of the light. But that was always her fortitudinous style. She never showed her hand, never articulated the inherent sadness which so clearly lurked behind her stoical veneer.

But she was certainly right about the timetable of her illness. She didn't last months. She lasted less than two weeks. I hired Rozella on a twenty-four-hour care basis – and felt guilty about not being with Mom full time. But I was under insane pressure at work with a big new account, and I had Ethan to look after (being pigheaded, I also didn't want to ask Matt for any favors). So I could only squeeze in three hours a day with her.

The end was fast. Rozella woke me at four a.m. last Tuesday, and simply said, 'You must come now.'

Fortunately I had already worked out an emergency plan for this exact moment with a new-found friend named Christine – who lived two floors above me in my building, and was a fellow member of the Divorced Moms Club. Though Ethan loudly objected, I managed to get him out of bed and delivered him to Christine, who immediately put him back to bed on her sofa, relieved me of his school clothes, and promised to deliver him to Allan-Stevenson that morning.

Then I raced downstairs, got the doorman to find me a cab, and told the driver that I'd tip him five bucks if he could make it across town to 84th and West End in fifteen minutes.

He did it in ten. Which was a good thing – as Mom went just five minutes after I walked through the door.

I found Rozella standing at the foot of her bed, sobbing quietly. She put her arms around me, and whispered, 'She's here, but not here.'

That was a nice way of saying she had slipped into a coma. Which, honestly, was something of a relief to me – because I was secretly terrified of this deathbed scene. Of saying the right, final thing. Because there is *no* right or final thing to say. Anyway she couldn't hear me now – so any melodramatic

'I love you, Mom!' proclamations would have been for my benefit alone. At a momentous moment like this one, words are less-than-cheap. And they couldn't assuage the guilt I was feeling.

So I simply sat on the bed, and took Mom's still-warm hand, and gripped it tightly, and tried to remember my first recollection of her, and suddenly saw her as an animated, pretty young woman holding my four-year-old hand as we walked to the playground in Riverside Park, and thought how this wasn't a significant or crucial memory, just something ordinary, and how back then she was fifteen years younger than I am now, and how we forget all those walks to the park, and the emergency trips to the pediatrician with tonsillitis, and getting picked up after school, and being schlepped around town for shoes or clothes or Girl Scout meetings, and all the other scheduling minutiae that comes with being a parent, and how my mom always tried so hard with me, and how I could never really see that, and how I hated my neediness towards her, and wished that I could have somehow made her happier, and how, back when I was four, she would always go on the slide with me, always sit in the adjoining swing, rocking back and forth, and how, suddenly, there we were, mother and daughter swinging higher into the sky, an autumn day in '59, the sun shining, my world cozy, secure, loving, my mother laughing, and . . .

She took three sharp intakes of breath. Then there was silence. I must have sat there for another fifteen minutes, still holding her hand, feeling a gradual chill drift into her fingers. Eventually, Rozella gently took me by the shoulders and stood me upright. There were tears in her eyes, but none in mine. Perhaps because I was just too paralyzed to cry.

Rozella leaned over and shut Mom's eyes. Then she crossed herself and said a Hail Mary. I engaged in a different sort of ritual: I went into the living room, poured myself a large Scotch, threw it back, then picked up the phone and dialed 911.

'What kind of emergency do you want to report?' asked the operator.

'It's not an emergency,' I said. 'Just a death.'

'What sort of death?'

'Natural.' But I could have added: *'A very quiet death. Dignified. Stoic. Borne without complaint.'*

My mother died the way she lived.

I stood by the bed, listening to Rozella wash up the dishes from the wake. Just three days ago Mom lay here. Out of nowhere I suddenly remembered something that a guy named Dave Schroeder recently told me. He was a freelance magazine writer: smart as hell, well-traveled, but still trying to make a name for himself at forty. I'd gone out with him twice. He dropped me when I wouldn't sleep with him after the second date. Had he waited until the third date, he might have gotten lucky. But anyway . . . he did tell me one great story: about being in Berlin on the night the Wall was breached, then coming back a year later to find

38

that that monstrous structure – the defining, blood-stained rampart of the Cold War – had simply vanished from view. Even the famous Customs Shed at Checkpoint Charlie had been dismantled, and the old Bulgarian Trade Mission on the eastern side of the Checkpoint had been replaced by an outlet of Benetton.

'It was like this terrible thing, this crucial corner-stone of twentieth-century history, never existed,' Dave told me. 'And it got me thinking: the moment we end an argument is the moment we obliterate any history of that argument. It's a basic human trait: to sanitize the past, in order to move on.'

I looked down again at my mother's bed. And remembered the soiled sheets, the sodden pillows, the way she would almost claw the mattress before the morphine kicked in. Now it was neatly remade, with laundered sheets and a bedspread that had just come back from the dry cleaner's. The idea that she died right here already seemed surreal, impossible. A week from now – after Rozella and I packed up the apartment, and the Goodwill Industries people hauled off all the furniture I planned to give away – what tangible evidence would be left of my mom's time on the planet? A few material possessions (her engagement ring, a brooch or two), a few photographs, and . . .

Nothing else – except, of course, the space she would permanently occupy inside my head. A space she now shared with the dad I never knew.

And when Charlie and I both died . . . *ping*. That would be it for Dorothy and Jack Malone. Their impact on human life rubbed right out. Just as my lasting imprint will be Ethan. For as long as he's here . . .

I shuddered, and suddenly felt very cold, and in need of another Scotch. I walked into the kitchen. Rozella was at the sink, dealing with the final dishes. Meg was at the little formica kitchen table, a cigarette smouldering in a saucer (my mom had no ashtrays in the house), a bottle of Scotch next to a half-filled glass.

'Don't look so disapproving,' Meg said. 'I did offer to help Rozella.'

'I was thinking more about the cigarette,' I said.

'It doesn't bother me,' Rozella said.

'My mom hated smoking,' I said. Pulling back a chair, I sat down, then reached for Meg's packet of Merits, fished one out, and lit up. Meg looked stunned.

'Should I alert Reuters?' she said. 'Or maybe CNN?'

As I laughed, I exhaled a lung full of smoke.

'I treat myself to one or two a year. On special occasions. Like when Matt announced he was leaving. Or when Mom rang me up in April to say that she had to go into hospital for tests, but she was sure it was nothing . . .'

Meg poured me a large slug of whiskey, and pushed the glass towards me.

'Down the hatch, honey.'

I did as ordered.

'Why don't you go off with your aunt,' Rozella said. 'I'll finish up here.'

'I'm staying,' I said.

'That's dumb,' Meg said. 'Anyway, my Social Security check just cleared yesterday, so I'm feeling flush, and in the mood for something high in cholesterol . . . like a steak. So how about I book us a table at Smith and Wollensky's? Have you ever seen the martinis they serve there? They're the size of a goldfish bowl.'

'Save your money. I'm staying here tonight.'

Meg and Rozella exchanged a worried look.

'What do you mean, *tonight?*' Meg asked.

'I mean – I'm planning to sleep here tonight.'

'You really shouldn't do that,' Rozella said.

'Understatement of the goddamn year,' Meg added.

'My mind's made up. I'm sleeping here.'

'Well, if you're staying, I'm staying,' Meg said.

'No, you're not. I want to be here by myself.'

'Now, that's nuts,' Meg said.

'Please listen to your aunt,' Rozella said. 'Being by yourself here tonight . . . it is not a good idea.'

'I can handle it.'

'Don't be so sure about that,' Meg said.

But I wasn't going to be talked out of this. After paying off Rozella (she didn't want to accept any additional money from me, but I shoved a hundred dollars into her hand and refused to take it back), I finally managed to dislodge Aunt Meg from the kitchen table around five. We were both just a little bit tipsy, as I had matched Meg

Scotch for Scotch . . . and lost track somewhere after the fourth shot.

'You know, Katie,' she said as I helped her into her coat, 'I really do think you are a glutton for punishment.'

'Thank you for such a frank assessment of my shortcomings.'

'You know what I'm talking about here. The last thing you should do tonight is be alone in your dead mother's apartment. But that's *exactly* what you're doing. And it baffles the hell out of me.'

'I just want some time by myself. *Here*. Before I clear the place out. Can't you understand that?'

'Sure I can. Just like I can understand self-flagellation.'

'You sound like Matt. He always said I had a real talent for unhappiness.'

'Well, fuck that social-climbing bozo. Especially as he has a proven talent for *creating* unhappiness.'

'Maybe he has a point. Sometimes I think . . .'

I trailed off, not really wanting to finish the sentence. But Meg said, 'Go on, spill it.'

'I don't know. Sometimes I think I get things really wrong.'

Meg threw her eyes heavenward.

'Welcome to the human race, sweetheart.'

'You know what I mean.'

'No – actually I don't. You're successful at what you do, you've got a great kid . . .'

'The *best* kid.'

Meg pursed her lips – and a momentary flicker

42

of sadness crossed her face. Though she rarely spoke about it, I knew that her childlessness had always been a quiet source of regret for her. And I remembered what she said after I announced I was pregnant: 'Take it from me. I mightn't have tied the knot, but I've never been short of guys. And the vast majority of them are useless, weak-kneed assholes who run a mile when they work out you're an independent broad. In fact, the only good thing a guy can ever give you is a kid.'

'Then why didn't you get yourself knocked up?'

'Because back in the fifties and sixties – when I could have done it – the idea of a single-parent family was about as socially acceptable as supporting the Russian space program. An unmarried mom was immediately labeled an outcast – and I just didn't have the balls to handle the heat. I guess I'm a coward at heart.'

'I think the last thing I'd ever call you is a coward. I mean, when you get right down to it, I'm the coward in the family . . .'

'You got married. You're having a kid. From where I sit, that's brave.'

She immediately changed conversational tack. We never spoke about her childlessness again. In fact, the only time she let down her guard on the subject was at moments like this one – when mention of Ethan would be accompanied by a hint of ruefulness, which she would then banish in a New York second.

'Damn right, he's the best kid,' she said. 'And,

okay, the marriage tanked. But hey, look what you got out of it.'

'I know . . .'

'So why get so down about things?'

Because . . . oh God . . . I don't know how to begin explaining that most ambiguous, yet all-encompassing of emotions – a pervading frustration with yourself, and with the place you've landed yourself in life.

But I was too tired – and too blotto – to get into this issue. So I simply nodded in agreement, and said, 'I hear ya, Meg.'

'Too bad your mother didn't raise you a Catholic. You'd make one hell of a penitent.'

We headed downstairs in the elevator. As we crossed the lobby, Meg slid her arm through mine, and leaned on me for support. The doorman hailed a cab. He opened the door and I helped her inside.

'I hope the hell all that Scotch will knock you out cold,' she said, ''cause I really don't want you to be sitting up there, thinking, thinking, thinking . . .'

'There's nothing wrong with thinking.'

'It's dangerous to your health.' She clutched me. 'Call me tomorrow – when you've emerged from the Twilight Zone. Promise?'

'Yeah – I promise.'

She looked at me straight in the eye.

'You're my kid,' she said.

I went back upstairs. I must have stood in front of the apartment door for at least a minute before my nerve returned. Then I let myself back in.

44

The silence inside was overwhelming. My initial thought was, *flee*. But I forced myself to go into the kitchen and put away the last of the dishes. I wiped down the formica table twice, then dealt with all the kitchen surfaces. I got out some Comet and gave the sink a good scrub. I found a can of Pledge and dusted every item of furniture in the apartment. I went into the bathroom. I tried to ignore the peeling wallpaper and the large damp patches on the ceiling. I picked up a toilet brush and went to work. Then I turned my attention to the bath, scouring it for a good fifteen minutes, but was unable to lift the deeply ingrained rust stains around the drain. The sink was even more rusted. I must have spent another quarter of an hour manically scrubbing it . . . . oblivious to the fact that I was doing all these domestic chores while still dressed in a really good black suit (an absurdly expensive, absurdly chic Armani number with which Matt surprised me five Christmases ago – and which I later realized was a major guilt gift, as Matt hit me with Surprise Number Two on January second by announcing he was in love with a certain Blair Bentley, and had decided to terminate our marriage, effective immediately).

Eventually I could take no more of this washerwoman act, and slumped against the sink, my white blouse drenched, my face beaded with sweat. The heating in Mom's apartment was always turned up to sub-sauna levels, and I suddenly felt in desperate need of a shower. So I opened her medicine chest to see what soaps and shampoos I might purloin. I was suddenly confronted with around ten bottles of Valium, and a dozen vials of morphine, and packs of hypodermic needles, and boxes of enemas, and the long thin catheter which Rozella had to insert in Mom's urethra to draw out her urine. Then I noticed the packages of Depends Adult Diapers stacked in a corner under her vanity table, on top of a plastic bedpan. I found myself thinking: somebody, somewhere, manufactures and markets all this stuff. And, Jesus, their stock price must always be buoyant. Because if there's one great certainty to life, it's this: if you live long enough, you will end up in a Depends. Even if you get unlucky and, say, contract uterine cancer at forty, chances are that, towards the end of your terminal drama, you too will need a Depends. And . . .

I was suddenly doing what I swore I wouldn't do all day.

I can't remember just how long I cried – because I was inconsolable. The emotional brakes were finally off. I had surrendered to grief's unbridled rage. A relentless deluge of anguish and guilt. Anguish because I was now all by myself in the Big Bad World. And guilt because I had spent most of my adult life trying to dodge my mother's clutches. Now that I had permanently escaped her, I wondered: what the hell *was* the argument between us?

I gripped the sink tightly. I felt my stomach surge. Falling to my knees, I just managed to reach the toilet in time. Scotch. More Scotch. And a surfeit of bile.

I staggered to my feet, brownish drool dripping from my lips on to my good black suit. I returned to the sink, turned on the cold tap, shoved my mouth under it, and rinsed it free of vomit. I grabbed the king-sized bottle of Lavoris mouth wash on the vanity table – why is it that only little old ladies buy Lavoris? – unscrewed the big plastic cap, poured around half-a-pint of that astringent cinnamon-flavoured gargle into my mouth, swirled it around, spat the lot into the sink. Then I lurched to the bedroom, pulling my clothes off on the way.

By the time I reached Mom's bed, I was down to my bra and tights. I rifled through her chest of drawers, looking for a t-shirt . . . but then remembered that my mom wasn't exactly a member of the Gap generation. So I settled for an old cream-colored crew-necked sweater: very Going-with-Tad-to-the-Harvard/Yale-Game-Fall-'42 vintage. Pulling off my underwear, I pulled on the sweater, stretching it down to just above my knees. It reeked of moth balls, and the wool felt itchy against my skin. I didn't care. I threw off the bedspread and crawled in. Despite the Florida-like heat of the apartment, the sheets felt eerily cold. I grabbed a pillow and clutched it against me, clinging on to it as if it was the only thing on earth right now that could give me ballast.

I suddenly had an overwhelming need to hold my son. I suddenly started to cry. I suddenly felt

47

like Little Girl Lost. I suddenly loathed myself for this burst of self-pity. I suddenly wondered why the room was beginning to tilt and keel like a boat in choppy waters. I suddenly fell asleep.

Then the phone started to ring.

It took me a moment or two to drift back into consciousness. The bedside light was still blazing. I squinted at the elderly digital clock by the bed – so 1970s that it had mechanically flipping numbers. 9.48 p.m. I had been asleep for around three hours. I lifted the phone, I managed to mumble . . .

'Hello?'

. . . but my voice was so thick with groggy sleep that I must have sounded semi-comatose. There was a long pause on the other end. Then I heard a woman's voice.

'Sorry, wrong number.'

The line went dead. I put the receiver down. I turned off the light. I pulled the covers over my head. And called an end to this fucking awful day.

CHAPTER 3

I woke at six. For about ten seconds, I felt curiously elated. Because, for the first time in around five months, I had actually slept for eight unbroken hours. But then everything else flooded in. And I found myself wondering: what deranged, grief-stricken despondency made me want to stay in Mom's bed overnight?

I got to my feet, careened into the bathroom, took one look at myself in the bathroom mirror, and decided not to make that mistake again. I peed, baptized my face with cold water, and gargled with Lavoris: three basic ablutions that enabled me to leave the apartment without feeling like a total fire sale.

My suit stank of vomit. As I dressed, I tried to ignore the smell and paid no notice to its trashed condition. Then I made the bed, grabbed my coat, turned out all the lights, and slammed the door behind me. Meg was right: I really was a glutton for punishment. I decided: the next time I see this apartment again is the time I pack it up.

The early hour meant that I didn't run into any of Mom's neighbors in the elevator or the lobby.

49

This was a relief, as I don't think I could have handled another heartfelt expression of condolence (I was also worried that people might think I was auditioning for a female remake of *The Lost Weekend*). The night doorman – slumped in an armchair by the lobby's fake electric fireplace – didn't even seem to notice me walking briskly by. There must have been two dozen empty cabs cruising West End Avenue. I hailed one, gave the driver my address, and collapsed across the back seat.

Even to a jaundiced native like myself, there is still something wondrous about Manhattan at dawn. Maybe it's the emptiness of the streets. Or the commingling of street-lamp light and the emerging sunrise. Everything's so tentative, so hushed. The city's manic rhythms are momentarily stilled. There's a sense of equivocation and expectation. At dawn, nothing seems certain . . . yet everything appears possible.

But then night drops away. Manhattan begins to shout at the top of its lungs. Reality truly bites. Because in the harsh light of day, possibilities vanish.

I live on 74th Street between Second and Third Avenues. It's an ugly, squat, white brick apartment building – of the sort favored by developers in the 1960s, and which now grimly define that bland Upper East Side cityscape between Third and the River. Being a West Side girl (born and bred!), I always considered this part of town to be the urban equivalent of vanilla ice cream: dull, insipid, devoid of edge. Before I got married, I lived for years on 106th Street and Broadway – which was anything but monotonous. I loved the exuberant grime of the neighborhood – the Haitian grocery stores, the Puerto Rican bodegas, the old Jewish delis, the good bookshops near Columbia University, the no cover/no minimum jazz at the West End Café. But my apartment – though insanely cheap – was tiny. And Matt had this rent-controlled two-bedroom place on East 74th Street, which had been in the family for years (he'd taken it over after his grand-father died). It was a steal at $1600 a month, not to mention a hell of a lot more spacious than my single cell up in Jungleland.

But we both hated the apartment. Especially Matt – who was seriously embarrased about living at such an unhip address, and kept telling me we'd move to the Flatiron District or Gramercy Park as soon as he left lowly paid PBS and got his senior producer gig at NBC.

Well, he got the big NBC job. He also got the big Flatiron pad – with that cropped-blonde talking head, Blair Bentley. And I ended up with the much-hated rent-controlled apartment on 74th Street – which I now cannot leave, because it is such a bargain (I have friends with kids who can't even find a two-bed place in Astoria for $1600 a month).

Constantine, the morning doorman, was on duty when I got out of the cab. He was around sixty; a first-generation Greek immigrant, who still lived with his mom in Astoria, and who really didn't like the idea of divorced women with children . . . especially those vulgar harpies who actually have to go out and earn a living. He also had the proclivities of a village stoolie – always checking up on people, always asking the sort of leading questions which made you understand that he was keeping tabs on you. My stomach sank when he opened the door of the taxi. I could see that he was interested in my trashy state.

'Late night, Miss Malone?' he asked.

'No – early morning.'

'How's the little guy?'

'Fine.'

'Upstairs asleep?'

Yeah, that's right. He's been home alone all night, playing with my collection of hunting knives, while working his way through my extensive library of S&M videos.

'No – he's staying with his dad tonight.'

'Say hi to Matt for me, Miss Malone.'

Oh, *thank you*. And yeah, I did catch the way you stressed *Miss*.

There goes your Christmas tip, *malacca* (the only Greek profanity I know).

I took the elevator to the fourth floor. I unlocked the three deadbolts on my door. The apartment was appallingly silent. I went straight into Ethan's room. I sat on his bed. I stroked his Power Rangers pillow case (okay, I think the Power Rangers are totally dumb – but try having a discussion about aesthetics with a seven-year-old boy). I looked at all the guilt gifts Matt had recently bought him (an iMac computer, dozens of CD-Roms, top-of-the-line roller blades). I looked at all the guilt gifts I had recently bought him (a walking Godzilla, a complete set of Power Ranger action figures, two dozen jigsaw puzzles). I felt a stab of sadness. All this booty, all this crap – all given in an attempt to ease parental remorse. The same remorse I feel when – two or three times a week – I have to stay late at the office or go out to some business dinner, and am therefore forced to get Claire (the part-time Australian nanny who picks up Ethan from school and looks after him until I come home) to stay on. Though Ethan rarely chides me for these evening absences, I always feel lousy about them . . . a mega-guilt fear that, if Ethan turns out to be a sociopath (or develops a taste for crack at the age of sixteen), it will be due to all those nights I was out working late. Working, I might add, to pay the rent, to meet my half of his tuition, to meet the bills . . . and (I also might add) to give my own life some definition and purpose. I tell you, women like me can't win these days. You have all these post-feminist 'family values' creeps playing the 'kids need stay-at-home moms' card. Then you have the depressing example of certain members of my generation who have decided to do the Soccer Mom thing in the 'burbs, and are silently going ga-ga.

When you're a *divorced* working mom, you have stereophonic guilt . . . because not only are you *not* at home when your son comes back from school, but you also feel partially to blame for undermining your child's sense of security. I can still see Ethan's wide-eyed confusion, his terrified bewilderment, when, five years ago, I tried to explain to him that his daddy would now be living elsewhere.

I glanced at my watch. Six forty-eight. I was tempted to jump a cab downtown to Matt's place. But then I saw myself loitering like a deranged stalker outside of Matt's building, waiting for them to emerge. I also feared running into *Her*, and maybe losing my much-heralded cool (ha!). Anyway, Ethan might be rattled to see me outside his dad's building – and might think (as he has intimated recently on several occasions) that Mommy and Daddy were getting back together. Which is not going to happen. Ever.

So I went into my bedroom and stripped off my disgusting suit, and stood under a very hot shower for around ten minutes. Then I put on a bathrobe, wrapped my hair in a towel, and went out to the kitchen to make coffee. As I waited for the kettle to boil, I rewound the answer phone and listened to yesterday's accmulated messages.

There were nine altogether – five from assorted friends and people at work, offering solace and all finishing up with that standard what-do-you-say-to-a-bereaved-person line: *if there's anything we can do*. (Which, though formulaic, was still rather touching to hear.) There was a message from Matt

– at eight thirty last night, telling me that Ethan was just fine, that they'd had a great day out, and he was now tucked up in bed, and . . . 'if there's anything I can do'.

It's too late for that, chum. Far too late.

Naturally enough, there was a call from my aunt. It was classic Meg.

'Hi, it's just me, thinking you might have finally gotten some sense and come home. I thought wrong. Now I'm not going to bother you at your mom's place, because (a) you might chew my ear off, and (b) you probably want to be left the hell alone. But if you have decided that you've done enough penance for one evening, and *have* come home, give me a call . . . as long as it's a reasonable hour. Which, for me, means anytime before three a.m. Love ya, sweetheart. Kiss Ethan for me. And keep taking the medicine.'

Medicine being a Meg synonym for whiskey.

Finally, there were two messages where the caller failed to leave a message. The first came (according to the answering machine, which electronically tags the time of the call) at 6.08; the second at 9.44 p.m. Both were marked by an eerie moment or two of silence . . . when it was clear that the person on the line was deciding whether or not to say something. I hate it when people do that. Because it makes me feel vulnerable, spooked. And on my own.

The kettle began to whistle. I turned down the gas flame, grabbed the cafetière and a vacuum jar of freshly ground, extra-strength French Roast, and shoveled enough coffee into the cafetière for seven cups. I added the boiling water and pushed down the plunger. I poured out a large mug. I drank it down quickly. I poured out another cup. After one more charring gulp of coffee (I have an asbestos mouth), and a quick glance at my watch (7.12 a.m.), I decided I could face calling Matt's place.

'H . . . e . . . l . . . l . . . o . . . ?'

The voice at the end of the line sounded half awake, and female. *Her.*

'Uh, hi . . .' I said, stumbling badly. 'Is, uh, Ethan there?'

'Ethan? Who's Ethan?'

'Who do you think Ethan is?'

That woke her up. 'Sorry, sorry, sorry. *Ethan.* Of course I know who . . .'

'Could I speak with him?'

'Is he still here?' she asked.

'Well, I don't really know the answer to that question,' I said, 'because I'm *not* there.'

She now sounded totally flustered. 'I'll just see if . . . Is that you, Kate?'

'That's right.'

'Hey, I was going to write you . . . but now that you're here, like, I just wanted to say . . .'

Cut to the chase, dufus.

'Like . . . I was real, real sorry to hear about your mom.'

'Thank you.'

'And, well, uh, if there's anything I can do . . .'

'Just put Ethan on, please.'

'Uh . . . sure.'

I could hear *Her* whispering in the background. Then Matt picked up the phone.

'Hi there, Kate. I was just wondering how the rest of yesterday went.'

'Terrific. I haven't had such fun in years.'

'You know what I mean.'

I took another sip of coffee. 'I got through it. Can I speak with Ethan now, please?'

'Sure,' he said. 'He's right here.'

I heard Matt pass the phone over to him.

'Sweetheart, you there?' I asked.

'Hi, Mom,' Ethan said, sounding half awake. My heart immediately lifted. Ethan, for me, is instant Prozac.

'How are you doing, big guy?'

'The IMAX movie was cool. These people were climbing a mountain, and then it started to snow, and they got into trouble.'

'What was the name of the mountain they were climbing?'

'I forget.'

I laughed.

'And after the movie, we went to the toy shop.' Figures.

'What did Daddy get you?'

'A Power Rangers CD-Rom.'

Great.

'And a Lego spaceship. Then we went to the television station –'

Wonderful. Just what I needed to hear.

'– and Blair was there. And she brought me and Dad into the room where they talk to the cameras. And we watched her on television.'

'Sounds like a terrific afternoon.'

'Blair was real cool. Then we all went out to a restaurant afterwards. The one in the World Trade Center. You could see all the city at night. And this helicopter came by. And a lot of people came to our table to ask Blair for her autograph . . .'

'You missing me, sweetheart . . . ?' I blurted out.

'Yeah, sure, Mom,' he said, sounding deflated. I suddenly felt like a needy idiot.

'I love you, Ethan.'

'Bye, Mom,' he said and hung up.

Jerk, jerk, jerk. You should never expect a child to make you feel wanted.

I stood by the phone for several minutes, willing myself not to break down again (I had done enough of that in the last twenty-four hours). When I felt myself under control again, I refilled my mug of coffee, walked out into the living room, and flopped down on the big cushy sofa – the last major domestic purchase that Matt and I made before his dramatic exit.

But he hasn't really vanished from my life. That's part of the problem. If we didn't have Ethan, the breakup would have been far easier. Because – after the initial period of shock, anger, grief, and mourning – I could have at least taken solace in the fact that I would never have to see the guy again.

But Ethan means that, like it or not, we must continue to *interact, co-exist, acknowledge each other's presence* (take your pick). As Matt said during that pre-divorce horse-trading process known as 'mediation': 'For everyone's sake, we really have to establish a little détente between us.' By and large, this détente has been achieved. Five years after the event, we've long since stopped screaming at each other. We deal with each other in (more or less) a correct manner. I have decided that the marriage was, from the outset, a huge mistake. But, despite my best efforts at so-called 'closure', the wound still remains curiously raw.

When I recently mentioned this to Meg during one of our weekly drunken dinners, she said, 'Sweetheart, you can tell yourself over and over again that he wasn't the guy for you, and that it was all one big blooper. But the fact remains that you're *not* going to totally get over it. It's just too big, too consequential. The pain will always be there. It's one of the many rotten things about life: the way it becomes an accumulation of griefs, both big and small. But survivors – and, sweetheart, you definitely fall into that category – figure out how to live with all that grief. Because, like it or not, grief is kind of interesting, and kind of essential. Because it gives things real import. And it's also the reason why God invented booze.'

Trust Meg to articulate a cheerful Irish-Catholic view of life.

'*For everyone's sake, we really have to establish a little détente between us.*'

Yeah, Matt – I do think that. But after all this time I still don't know how to pull it off. Whenever I sit in this living room, the thought strikes me: everything is so random, isn't it? Take the interior decor of this apartment. A large, cushy Pottery Barn sofa in stylish cream-colored upholstery (I think the name of the actual shade was Cappuccino). Two matching armchairs, a pair of smart Italian floor lamps, and a low-slung coffee table with a collection of magazines fanned across its beech-wood top. We spent a significant amount of time deliberating about all this furniture. Just as we also debated the veneered beechwood floors that we eventually had installed in this room. And the high-tech grey-steel kitchen units we chose at IKEA in Jersey City (yes, we were so serious about this life we were building together that we actually made a trip to New Jersey to size up a kitchen). And the oatmeal-knit carpet which replaced that dreadful aquamarine shag which your grandfather lived with. And the Shaker-style four-poster bed which set us back $3200.

That's why the sight of the living room still astonishes me. Because it's a testament to a lot of rational discussion about that thing known as 'a joint future' even though the two people involved secretly didn't believe in that future. We just happened to meet up at a certain juncture in time when we both wanted to be attached.

60

And we both quickly convinced ourselves that we were compatible, worthy of being spliced together.

It is extraordinary how you can talk yourself into situations which you know aren't durable. But neediness can make just about anything seem right.

The house phone rang, interrupting my reverie. I jumped up from the sofa, crossed over to the kitchen, and answered it.

'Hi there, Miss Malone.'

'Yes, Constantine?'

'I've got a letter here for you.'

'I thought the mail didn't arrive until eleven.'

'Not that kind of a letter . . . a hand-delivered letter.'

'What do you mean, hand-delivered?'

'What I mean is: a letter that was delivered by hand.'

Urgh!

'That part I get, Constantine. What I'm asking is: when was it delivered, and by whom?'

'When was it delivered? Five minutes ago, that's when.'

I looked at my watch. Seven thirty-six. Who sends a messenger around with a letter at this hour of the morning?

'And by whom, Constantine?'

'Dunno. A cab pulled up, a woman rolled down the window, asked if you lived here, I said yes, she handed me the letter.'

'So a woman delivered the letter?'

'That's right.'

'What kind of woman?'

'Dunno.'

'You didn't see her?'

'She was in the cab.'

'But the cab has a window.'

'There was a glare.'

'But surely you caught a glimpse . . .'

'Look it, Miss Malone – I saw what I saw, which was *nothin'*, okay?'

'Fine, fine,' I said, wanting to put an end to this Abbot and Costello routine. 'Send the letter up.'

I stalked off to the bedroom, pulled on a pair of jeans and a sweatshirt, then ran a brush through my tangled hair. The doorbell rang, but when I opened it (keeping the chain on in true New York paranoid style), there was no one there. Just a small envelope at the foot of the door.

I picked it up and shut the door behind me. The envelope was postcard-sized and made of good-quality paper. A greyish-blue paper with a ridged surface that made it exceedingly tactile. My name and address were written on the front. The calligraphy was small, precise. The words *By Hand* were written in the upper right-hand corner of the envelope.

I opened the envelope with care. As I lifted up the flap, it revealed the top part of a card with an embossed address:

346 West 77th Street
Apt. 2B
New York, New York 10024
(212) 555.0745

My first thought was: that's close to home. Then I pulled out the card.

It was written in the same precise, controlled handwriting. It was dated yesterday. It read:

Dear Ms Malone,

I was deeply saddened to read of your mother's death in The New York Times.

Though we've not met face-to-face in years, I knew you as a little girl, just as I knew both your parents back then . . . but sadly fell out of touch with your family after your father died.

I simply wanted to express my condolences to you at what must be a most difficult juncture, and to say that I'm certain someone is watching over you now . . . as he has been for years.

Yours,
Sara Smythe

I read through the letter again. And again. Sara Smythe? Never heard of her. But what really threw me was the line 'someone is watching over you now . . . as he has been for years'.

'Let me ask you something,' Meg said, an hour or so later when I woke her up at home to read her this letter. 'Did she write *he* with a capital *H*?'

'No,' I said. 'It was a lower-case *h*.'

'Then we're not dealing with a religious nut here. A big *H* means the guy upstairs. Mr Almighty. The Alpha and the Omega. Laurel *and* Hardy.'

'But you're sure you never heard Mom or Dad mention a Sara Smythe?'

'Hey, it wasn't my marriage – so I wasn't exactly privy to everybody your parents met. I mean, I doubt if your mom or dad ever knew Karoli Kielsowski.'

'Who was Karoli . . . how do you say his name?'

'Kielsowski. He was a Polish jazz musician I picked up one November night in fifty-one at Birdland. A catastrophe in bed – but good company, and not a bad alto sax player.'

'I'm not following this . . .'

'My point is a simple one. Your dad and I liked each other, but we didn't live in each other's pockets. So, for all I know, this Sara Smythe was one of their best friends. Of course, as it was all around forty-five years ago . . . .'

'Okay, point taken. But what I don't get is, why did she drop the letter off by hand at my apartment house? I mean, how did she know where I live?'

'Do you have an unlisted number?'

'Uh, no.'

'Well, that answers that question. As to why she dropped it off . . . I dunno. Maybe she saw the funeral announcement in yesterday's *Times*, realized she'd missed the planting, didn't want to appear overdue with the condolence note, and therefore decided to drop it off on her way to work.'

'Don't you think there's a lot of coincidence at work there?'

'Sweetheart, you want a hypothesis, I'm giving you a hypothesis.'

'You think I'm over-reacting?'

'I think you're understandably tired and emotional. And you're blowing this perfectly innocuous card out of all proportion. But hey, if you need to know more, call the dame up. I mean, her phone number's on the card, right?'

'I don't need to call her up.'

'Then *don't* call her up. While you're at it, promise me you won't spend another night alone at your mom's apartment.'

'I'm ahead of you on that one.'

'Glad to hear it. Because I was starting to worry that you might turn into some deranged Tennessee Williams character. Putting on Mommy's wedding dress. Drinking neat bourbon. Saying stuff like, *'His name was Beauregard, and he was the married boy who broke my heart . . .'*

She cut herself off. 'Oh sweetheart,' she said. 'I am one dumb big mouth.'

'Don't worry about it,' I said.

'Sometimes I just don't know when to shut the hell up.'

'It's a Malone family trait.'

'I'm so damn sorry, Katie . . .'

'Enough. I've forgotten about it already.'

'I'm going to go say three acts of contrition.'

'Whatever makes you happy. I'll call you later, okay?'

I refilled my coffee cup, and returned to the big cushy sofa. I downed half the coffee, then parked the mug on the table and stretched out, putting the heels of my hands against my eyes, in an effort to black out everything.

His name was Beauregard, and he was the married boy who broke my heart . . .

Actually, his name was Peter. Peter Harrison. He was the guy I was with before meeting Matt. He also happened to be my boss. And he was married.

Let's get something straight here. I am not a natural romantic. I do not swoon easily. I do not fall head-over-heels at the drop of a dime. I spent most of my four years at Smith without a boyfriend (though I did have the occasional fling whenever I felt in need of some body heat). When I hit New York after college – and picked up a temporary job at an advertising agency (an alleged one-month gig which accidentally turned into a so-called career) – I was never short of male company. But several of the mistakes I'd slept with during my twenties accused me of First Degree Aloofness. It wasn't that I was a cool customer. It was just that I had not met anyone about whom I could feel truly, madly, deeply passionate.

Until I met Peter Harrison.

Oh, I was so stupid. Oh, it was all so damn predictable. I was edging towards my mid-thirties. I had just joined a new agency – Harding, Tyrell and Barney. Peter Harrison hired me. He was forty-two. Married. Two kids. Handsome (of course). Smart as hell. For the first month at the office, there was this curious unspoken thing going on between us; a sense that we were both aware of each other's presence. When we did meet – in the corridors, in the elevator, once at a departmental meeting – we were perfectly pleasant with each other. Yet there was an undercurrent of nervousness to our trivial chat. We became shy around each other. And neither of us was, by any means, the shy type.

Then he poked his head into my office late one afternoon. He asked me out for a drink. We repaired around the corner to a little bar. As soon as we started talking we couldn't stop. We talked for two hours – gabbing away like people *destined* to be gabbing to each other. We connected, spliced, fused. When he eventually threaded his fingers through mine, and said, *Let's get out of here*, I had no second thoughts on the matter. By that point, I wanted him so desperately I would have jumped him right there in the bar.

Only much later that night – lying next to him in bed, telling him just how much I'd fallen for him (and hearing him admit the same to me) – did I raise the one question which I hadn't wanted to ask earlier. He told me that there wasn't anything terribly wrong between his wife, Jane, and himself. They'd been together eleven years. They were reasonably compatible. They loved their girls. They had a nice life. But a nice life doesn't mean a passionate life. That part of the marriage had ebbed away years ago.

I asked him, 'Then why not accept its cozy limitations?'

'I had, sort of,' he said. 'Until I met you.'

'And now?'

He pulled me closer. 'Now I'm not going to let you go.'

That's how it started. For the next year, he didn't let me go. On the contrary, he spent every possible hour he could with me. Which, from my standpoint, was never enough . . . but which also fueled the intensity of the affair. I actually loathe that word, 'affair' – because of its cheap, sordid connotations. This was love. Pure, undiluted love. Love that took place between six and eight p.m., twice a week, at my apartment. And frequently at lunchtime in a midtown hotel, three blocks away from our office. Of course I wanted to see more of him. When he wasn't with me – especially late at night – I actually pined for him. The longing was insane. Because I knew that I had found the one person on the planet destined for me. Yet I was determined to remained outwardly disciplined about my feelings for Peter. We both knew what a dangerous game we were playing – and how everything could fall apart if we became the hot subject of office gossip . . . or worst yet, if Jane found out.

And so, at the office, we remained rather formal with each other. He covered his tracks carefully on the home front – never arousing suspicion by staying out later than expected, keeping at my place the same toiletries he used at home, never letting me dig my nails into his back.

'That's the first thing I'm going to do on the first night we move in together,' I said, gently caressing his bare shoulders. It was a December evening, just before Christmas. We were lying in bed, the sheets askew, our bodies still damp.

'I'll hold you to that,' he said, kissing me deeply. 'Because I've decided to tell Jane.'

My adrenalin went into overdrive. 'You serious?'

'As serious as I've ever been.'

I took his face between my hands. 'Are you absolutely sure?'

Without hesitation he said, 'Yes, absolutely.'

We agreed that he wouldn't break the news to Jane until after Christmas – which was, after all, just four weeks off. We also agreed that I'd start apartment hunting for us straight away. After wearing out a lot of shoe leather, I actually found us a really cute two-bedroom place with a partial river view on Riverside and 112th. It was a few days before Christmas. I decided to give Peter a big surprise the next night (when, per usual, we were due to meet at my apartment around six) by bringing him to see our future home. He was over an hour late getting to my place. As soon as he walked in, I was scared. Because I could see that something was very wrong. He slumped down into my sofa. I immediately sat down next to him, and took his hand.

'Tell me, darling.'

He refused to meet my eye. 'It seems . . . I'm moving to LA.'

It took a moment or two to register. 'LA? *You?* I don't understand.'

'Yesterday afternoon, around five, I got a call at my office. A call from Bob Harding's secretary, asking if I could pay our company chairman a little visit. Like *tout de suite*. So up I went to the thirty-second floor, and into the great man's office. Dan Downey and Bill Maloney from Corporate Affairs were both there. Harding asked me to sit down, and cut straight to the chase. Creighton Anderson – the head of the LA office – just announced that he was off to London to run some big division of Saatchi & Saatchi. Which meant the job of LA boss was now open, and Harding had had his eye on me for some time, and . . .'

'They offered you the job?'

He nodded. I took his hand. 'But this is wonderful, darling. This is, in a way, what we wanted. A clean break. A way to establish our own life. And, of course, if there's a conflict about you hiring me to work in the LA office, no problem. It's a big market, LA, I'll find something. I can do LA . . .'

He interrupted this manic, scared rant. 'Katie, please . . .'

His voice was barely a whisper. He finally turned toward me. His face was drawn, his eyes red. I suddenly felt ill.

'You told her first, didn't you?' I said.

He turned away from me again. 'I had to. She is my wife.'

'I don't believe this.'

'Bob Harding said that I had to give him a decision by the end of today – and that he knew I'd need to talk things over with Jane first . . .'

'You were about to leave Jane, remember? So why didn't you talk first to the person with whom you were planning to start a new life? *Me*.'

He just shrugged sadly and said, 'You're right.'

'So what exactly did you tell her?'

'I told her about the offer, and how I felt this would be a great career move . . .'

'You said *nothing* about us?'

'I was about to . . . but she started to cry. Started saying how she didn't want to lose me, how she knew we'd been growing apart, but was terrified of even talking about it. Because . . .'

He broke off. Peter – my confident, secure, dauntless, always articulate man – was suddenly tongue-tied and sheepish.

'Because *what*?' I asked.

'Because –' he swallowed hard, '– she thought there might be someone else in my life.'

'So what did you say?'

He turned away – as if he couldn't bear to look at me.

'Peter, you have to tell me what you said.'

He stood up and walked to the window, staring out into the black December night.

'I assured her . . . that there was no one else but her.'

It took a moment or two for this to register.

'You didn't say that,' I said, my voice hushed. 'Tell me you didn't say that.'

He kept looking out the window, his back to me. 'I'm sorry, Katie. I'm so damn sorry.'

'Sorry's not good enough. Sorry is an empty word.'

'I am in love with you . . .'

That's when I stormed off into the bathroom, slammed the door, bolted it, then sank down to the floor, crying wildly. Peter pounded on the door, begging me to let him in. But my anger, my grief, were so volcanic that I blanked him out.

Eventually the banging stopped. Eventually I regained a modicum of control. I forced myself back on to my feet, unbolted the door, and staggered back to the sofa. Peter had gone. I sat on the edge of the sofa, feeling as if I had just been in a major car crash – that same weird, extraworldly shock, during which you find yourself wondering: *did that just happen?*

Operating on auto-pilot, I remembered putting on my coat, grabbing my keys, and leaving.

The next thing I knew, I was in a cab, heading

southbound. I didn't remember much of the ride. But when we arrived at 42nd and First Avenue – pulling up in front of a large elderly apartment complex called Tudor City – it took me a moment or two to recall why I was here, and who I was planning to visit.

I got out of the cab, I walked into the lobby. When the elevator reached the seventh floor, I marched down the corridor and pressed the bell by a door marked 7E. Meg opened it, dressed in a faded light blue terrycloth robe, the usual cigarette plugged into the side of her mouth.

'So, to what do I owe this surprise . . . ?' she said.

But then she got a proper look at me, and turned white. I walked forward, and laid my head against her shoulder. She put her arms around me.

'Oh, sweetheart . . .' she said softly. 'Don't tell me he was married?'

I came inside. I burst into tears again. She fed me Scotch. I recounted the entire stupid saga. I spent the night on her sofa. The next morning I couldn't face the office, so I asked Meg to call up work and tell them I was out sick. She disappeared into her bedroom to use the phone.

When she emerged, she said, 'You'll probably call me a meddlesome old broad after I tell you this . . . but you'll be pleased to hear that you're not expected in the office again until the second of January.'

'What the hell did you do, Meg?'

'I spoke to your boss . . .'

73

'You called Peter?'

'Yeah, I did.'

'Oh Jesus Christ, Meg . . .'

'Hear me out. I called him and simply explained that you were a little under the weather today. Then he said that, "under the circumstances", you should not worry about coming in until January second. So there you go – eleven days off. Not bad, eh?'

'It's especially not bad for him – as it gives him a real easy out. He doesn't have to see me before he vanishes to LA.'

'Do you really want to see him?'

'No.'

'The defence rests.'

I hung my head.

'This is going to take time,' Meg said. 'A lot of time. Longer than you think.'

I knew that. Just as I knew that I was heading into the longest Christmas of my life. The grief hit me in waves. Sometimes dumb, obvious things – like seeing a couple kiss on the street – would trigger it. Or I might be riding uptown on the subway (in reasonably cheerful form after happily squandering an afternoon at the Museum of Modern Art, or engaging in some retail therapy at Bloomingdale's) – and then, out of nowhere, I'd feel as if I was falling into this deep abyss. I stopped sleeping. I lost a lot of weight. Every time I castigated myself for over-reacting, I quickly fell apart again.

What disturbed me most was the fact that I swore, vowed, pledged never to lose myself to a man – and was always less than sympathetic (if not downright contemptuous) of friends and acquaintances who turned a break-up into an epic tragedy; a Manhattan *Tristan and Isolde*.

But now there were moments when I wondered how I would get through the day. And I felt like such a stupid cliché. Especially when – in the middle of a Sunday brunch at a local restaurant with my mother – I suddenly burst into tears. I retreated to the Ladies' until I got the Joan Crawford melodramatics under control. When I returned to the table, I noticed that Mom had ordered coffee for us.

'That was very worrying, Katherine,' she said quietly.

'I've been having a bad week, that's all. Don't ship me off to Bellevue yet.'

'It's a man, isn't it?' she asked.

I sat up, blew on my coffee, and eventually nodded.

'It must have been serious if it's causing you this much upset.'

I shrugged.

'Do you want to tell me about it?' she asked.

'No.'

She bowed her head – and I could see how deeply I had just hurt her. Who was it who once said that mothers will break arms and legs to remain needed?

'I wish you could confide in me, Kate.'

'I wish I could too.'

'I don't understand why . . .'

'It's just how things between us have turned out.'

'You sadden me.'

'I'm sorry.'

She reached over and gave my hand a quick squeeze. There was so much I wanted to say just then – how I could never penetrate her protective coating of gentility; how I'd never been able to confide in her because I always felt that she sat in judgment on me; how I did love her . . . but there was just so much baggage between us. Yes, it was one of those moments (much beloved of Hollywood) when mother and daughter could have reached out to each other over the divide, and after shedding some mutual tears, reconciled. But life doesn't work that way, does it? We always seem to balk, hesitate, flinch at these big moments. Maybe because, in family life, we all build protective shields around ourselves. As the years evaporate, these defences solidify. They become hard for others to penetrate; even harder for us to tear down. Because they turn into the way in which we protect ourselves – and those closest to us – from assorted truths.

I spent the rest of my week-off in movie theaters and museums. On January second I returned to work. Everyone at the office was very solicitous about my 'terrible flu' – and did I hear about Peter Harrison's transfer to LA? I kept to myself, I did my work, I went home, I laid low. The outbursts of grief lessened; the sense of loss didn't.

In mid-February, one of my copywriting colleagues, Cindy, suggested lunch in a little Italian place near the office. We spent most of the meal talking through a campaign we were still fine-tuning. As coffee arrived, Cindy said, 'Well, I guess you heard the big gossip from the LA office.'

'What big gossip?'

'Peter Harrison just left his wife and kids for some account executive. Amanda Cole, I think her name was . . .'

The news detonated in front of me like a stun grenade. For several moments I really didn't know where I was. I must have looked shell-shocked, because Cindy took my hand and said, 'Are you all right, Kate?'

I withdrew my hand angrily and said, 'Of course I'm okay. Why are you asking?'

'No reason,' she said nervously. Turning away, she scanned the restaurant, made eye contact with the waiter, and motioned for the check. I stared down at my coffee.

'You knew, didn't you?' I asked.

She poured Sweet-and-Low into her coffee, then stirred it. Many times.

'Please answer the question,' I said.

Her spoon stopped its manic agitation.

'Honey,' she said, *everybody* knew.'

I wrote three letters to Peter – in which I called him assorted names, and accused him of upending my life. I sent none of them. I stopped myself (on several occasions) when the urge to ring him at four a.m. was overpowering. In the end I scribbled a postcard. It contained a three-word message:

Shame on you.

I tore up the postcard around two seconds before I mailed it . . . and then broke down – sobbing like an idiot on the southwest corner of 48th and Fifth, becoming an object of nervous, fleeting fascination for the passing lunchtime horde.

Matt knew that I was still in brittle shape when we started going out. It was eight months after Peter had moved to the coast. I'd switched agencies – moving to another big shop, Hickey, Ferguson and Shea. I met Matt when he invaded our offices one afternoon. He was accompanied by a PBS crew, filming part of a feature for the *MacNeill-Lehrer News Hour* on advertising agencies that were still hawking the demon weed, tobacco. I was one of the copywriters he interviewed – and we got schmoozing afterward. I was surprised when he asked me out – as there had been nothing flirtatious about our banter.

After we'd been seeing each other for around a month, I was even more surprised when he told me that he was in love with me. I was the wittiest woman he'd ever met. He adored my 'zero tolerance for bullshit'. He respected my 'strong sense of personal autonomy', my 'smarts', my 'canny self-assurance' (ha!). Game, set and match – he'd collided with the woman he'd always envisaged marrying.

Naturally, I didn't capitulate on the spot. On the contrary, I was deeply confused by this sudden confession of love. Yeah, I liked the guy. He was smart, ambitious, knowing. I was attracted to his metropolitan acumen . . . and to the fact that he seemed to get me – because, of course, we were both cut from the same urban cloth. A fellow native Manhattanite. A fellow preppy (Collegiate, then Wesleyan). A fellow wise-aleck – and, in true New York style, a possessor of a world-class entitlement complex.

They say that character is destiny. Perhaps – but timing plays one hell of a big role too. We were both thirty-six. He had just been evicted from a five-year relationship with an uberambitious CNN correspondent named Kate Brymer (she dumped him for some big network talking head) – so we both knew a thing or two about romantic car crashes. Like me, he hated that inane neurotic dance called dating. Like me, he dreaded the idea of flying solo into forty. He even wanted kids – which made his attractiveness increase one hundred fold, as I was beginning to hear predictably ominous ticking noises from my biological clock.

On paper, we must have looked great. An ideal meeting of worldly equals. The perfect New York professional couple.

There was just one problem: I wasn't in love

with him. I knew that. But I convinced myself otherwise. Part of this self-deception was brought about by Matt's persistent entreaties to marry him. He was persuasive without being gauche – and I guess I eventually bought his flattery. Because, after the Peter business, I needed to be flattered, adulated, wanted. And because I was secretly scared of ending up alone and childless in middle age.

'A lovely young man,' my mother said after first meeting Matt. 'I think he'd make you very happy' . . . which was her way of saying that she approved of his WASP credentials, his preppy sheen. Meg was a little less effusive.

'He's a very nice guy,' she said.

'You don't exactly seem overwhelmed,' I said.

'That's because *you* don't seem exactly over-whelmed.'

I paused, then said, 'I am very happy.'

'Yeah – and love is a wonderful thing. You are in love, aren't you?'

'Sure,' I said tonelessly.

'You sound very convincing.'

Meg's sour comment returned to rattle around my head four months later. I was in a hotel room on the Caribbean island of Nevis. It was three in the morning. My husband of thirty-six hours was asleep beside me in bed. It was the night after our wedding. I found myself staring at the ceiling, thinking, *what am I doing here?*

Then my mind was flooded with thoughts of

Peter. Tears started streaming down my face. And I castigated myself for being the most absurd idiot imaginable.

We usually mastermind our own predicament, don't we?

I tried to make it work. Matt *seriously* tried to make it work. We cohabited badly. Endless petty arguments about endless petty things. We instantly made up, then started squabbling again. Marriage, I discovered, doesn't coalesce unless the two parties involved figure out how to establish a domestic détente between themselves. The will needed is huge. We both lacked it.

Instead, we dodged the growing realization: we are a bad match. On the morning after fights, we bought each other expensive presents. Or flowers would arrive at my office, accompanied by a witty, conciliatory message:

They say the first ten years are the hardest.
I love you.
Matt

There were a couple of let's-rekindle-the-spark weekends away in the Berkshires, or Western Connecticut, or Montauk. During one of these, Matt drunkenly convinced me to dispense with my diaphragm for the night. I was seriously loaded too – so I agreed. And that is how Ethan came into our lives.

He was, without question, the best drunken

accident imaginable. Love at first gasp. But after the initial post-natal euphoria, the usual domestic discontentment reappeared. Ethan didn't believe in the restorative virtues of sleep. For the first six months of his life, he refused to conk out for more than two hours at a time – which quickly rendered us both quasicatatonic. Unless you have the disposition of Mary Poppins, exhaustion leads to excessive crankiness. Which – in the case of Matt and myself – turned into open warfare. As soon as Ethan was weaned, I wanted us to establish a rota for night feeds. Matt refused, saying that his high-pressure job demanded eight full hours of sleep. This was battle music to my ears – as I accused him of putting his own career above mine. Which, in turn, sparked further confrontations about parental responsibility, and acting like a grown-up, and why we always seemed to fight about everything.

Inevitably, when it comes to kids, it's the woman who ends up carrying the can – so when Matt arrived home one night and said that he'd just accepted a three-month transfer to PBS's Washington bureau, all I could say was:

'How convenient for you.'

He did promise to hire (and pay for) a full-time nanny – as I was now back at work. He did promise to come home every weekend. And he hoped that the time apart might do us some good – lessening the bellicose atmosphere between us.

So I was left holding the baby. Which actually

pleased me hugely – not simply because I couldn't get enough of Ethan (especially as my time with him was limited to after-work late evenings), but also because I too was debilitated by all the constant bush-fighting with Matt.

Intriguingly enough, as soon as he moved to Washington, two things happened: (a) Ethan began to sleep through the night, and (b) Matt and I began to get along again. No – this wasn't an 'absence makes the heart grow fonder' situation; rather, a mutual lightening of tone. Freed from each other's constant presence, our ongoing antagonisms de-escalated. We actually started talking again – talking, as in: being able to have a conversation which did not eventually veer into angry exchanges. When he returned home at weekends, the fact that we only had forty-eight hours together kept us on good behavior. Gradually, a certain collegial rapport was re-established – a sense that we could get along together; that we did enjoy each other's company; that there was a future for us.

Or, at least, that's what I thought. During the final month of Matt's Washington bureau stint, a breaking story (the early days of the Whitewater scandal) kept him in DC for three straight weeks. When he finally made it back to Manhattan, I sensed that something was seriously askew as soon as he walked through the door. Though he strived to act naturally in my presence, he became cagey and vague when I asked a couple of innocent questions about the long hours he was working in

Washington. Then he nervously changed the subject. That's when I knew. Men always think they can mask these things – but, when it comes to infidelity, they're as transparent as Saran Wrap.

After we got Ethan to bed and collapsed in the living room with a bottle of wine, I decided to risk bluntness.

'What's her name?' I asked.

Matt turned the sort of chalky color I associate with Kaopektate.

'I'm not following you . . .' he said.

'Then I'll repeat the question slowly: *What . . . is . . . her . . . name?*'

'I really don't know what you're talking about.'

'Yes you do,' I said, my tone still mild. 'I simply want to know the name of the woman you've been seeing.'

'Kate . . .'

'That's my name. I want to know *her* name. Please.'

He exhaled loudly.

'Blair Bentley.'

'Thank you,' I said, sounding totally reasonable.

'Can I explain . . . ?'

'Explain what? That it was "just one of those things"? Or that you got drunk one night, and the next thing you knew, you tripped and found this woman on the end of your penis? Or maybe it's love . . .'

'It is love.'

That shut me up. It took me a moment or so

to regain the power of speech. 'You're not serious?' I finally said.

'Completely serious,' he said.

'You asshole.'

He left the apartment late that night. He never slept there again. And I became bitter. Maybe he wasn't the love of my life – but there was a child involved. He should have considered Ethan's stability. Just like he should have recognized that the separation had actually done us some good – that we had laid down our weapons of mass destruction and established an armistice with each other. An affectionate armistice – to the point where I had actually started to miss Matt. They always say the first year or two of marriage is hell. But, damn it, we'd turned the corner. We had started to become a common cause.

When I discovered that Ms Blair Bentley was twenty-six – and a leggy cropped blonde with perfect skin and a cliff of capped white teeth (not to mention a local news anchor on the leading NBC-affiliate station in DC, about to be transferred to big-time New York) – my bitterness quadrupled. Matt had found himself a trophy wife.

But, of course, the real bitterness I felt was toward myself. I had blown it. I had done everything I vowed never to do – from falling for a married man, to obeying the imperatives of my goddamn biological clock. We all talk about 'building a life' – finding the fulfilling career, the fulfilling relationship, the fulfilling balance between the professional and the personal. Glossy magazines are full of spurious strategies for *constructing* this perfectly synchronized, made-to-measure existence. But the fact is, when it comes to the big stuff (the man who breaks your heart, the man with whom you end up having children), you're just a hostage to fortune like the next jerk. Say I'd never joined Harding, Tyrell and Barney? Say I hadn't agreed to that after-work drink with Peter? Say I'd never changed agencies, and Matt had never walked into our office? A chance meeting here, a hasty decision there . . . then one morning you wake up in early middle age, a divorced single parent. And you find yourself wondering: how the hell did I ever end up in this life?

The phone began to ring, jolting me out of my extended reverie. I glanced at my watch. It was nearly nine a.m. How had I managed to lose so much track of time?

'Is that you, Kate?'

The voice surprised me. It was my brother. It was the first time he'd phoned my home in years.

'Charlie?'

'Yeah, it's me.'

'You're up early.'

'Couldn't sleep. Uh, I just wanted to, uh . . . it was good seeing you, Kate.'

'I see.'

'And I don't want another seven years to go by . . .'

'As I said yesterday, that's up to you, Charlie.'

'I know, I know.'

He fell silent.

'Well,' I said, 'you know my number. So call me, if you like. And if you don't like, I'll live. You broke off communication. If you want to get it started again, it's over to you. Fair enough?'

'Uh, yeah, sure.'

'Good.'

Another of his damn nervous silences.

'Well then . . . I'd better be going, Charlie. See you . . .'

He interrupted my goodbye by blurting out, 'Can you lend me five thousand dollars?'

'What?'

His voice became shaky. 'I'm, uh, real sorry . . . I know you probably hate me for asking, but . . . you know that I mentioned I was up for a job . . . sales rep for Pacific Floral Service. Biggest flower delivery company on the West Coast. Only thing I could find out here where they'd even consider a guy in his mid-fifties . . . that's how bad things are in the job market these days, if you're well into middle age.'

'Don't remind me. Isn't the job interview today?'

'It was supposed to be. But when I got back home last night, there was a message from someone at Pacific Floral's Human Resources department. Telling me they'd decided to fill the post internally, so the interview was off.'

'I'm sorry.'

'Not as sorry as me. Not as goddamn sorry as

me, because . . . because . . . it wasn't even a managerial job . . . it was a fucking sales rep . . . it was . . .'

He broke off.

'Are you all right, Charlie?'

I could hear him take a deep steadying breath. 'No. I am not all right. Because if I don't find five thousand dollars by Friday, the bank is threatening to take my house.'

'Will the five grand solve the problem?'

'Not really . . . because I actually owe the bank another seven.'

'Jesus, Charlie.'

'I know, I know – but you start building up those kind of debts when you're out of work for six months. And, believe me, I've tried borrowing money everywhere. But there are already two mortgages on the house to begin with . . .'

'What does Holly say?'

'She . . . she doesn't realize how bad things are.'

'You mean, you haven't told her?'

'No . . . it's just . . . I just don't want to worry her.'

'Well, she's going to be a little worried when you're evicted from the house.'

'Don't say that word, *evicted*.'

'What are you going to do?'

'I don't know. What little savings we had . . . and some stock . . . it's all spent.'

Five thousand dollars. I knew that I had eight grand in a savings account . . . and that Mom had a money market account with around eleven-five, which was part of the estate I'd inherit once the will was probated. Five thousand dollars. That was serious money to me. It didn't even cover a term's tuition for Ethan at Allan-Stevenson. Or it was nearly three months' rent. I could do a lot with five thousand dollars.

'I know what you're thinking,' Charlie said. 'After all these years, his first proper phone call to me is to bum money.'

'Yes, Charlie – that is exactly what I'm thinking. Just as I'm also thinking how badly you hurt Mom.'

'I was wrong.'

'Yes, Charlie. You were very wrong.'

'I'm sorry.' His voice was barely a whisper. 'I don't know what to say except, I'm sorry.'

'I don't forgive you, Charlie. I can't. I mean, I know she could be overbearing and just a little interfering. But you still cut her off.'

I could hear his throat contract, as if he was stifling a sob. 'You're right,' he said.

'I don't care whether or not I'm right – it's a little late to be arguing about that anyway. What I want to know, Charlie, is why.'

'We never got along.'

This was, indeed, true – as one of my abiding memories of childhood was the endless arguments between my mother and brother. They could not agree on anything, and Mom had this habit of being endlessly meddlesome. But whereas I figured out a way of deflecting (or even ignoring) her encroaching tendencies, Charlie was constantly threatened by her intrusions. Especially as they underscored the fact that Charlie so desperately missed (and needed) his father. He was almost ten when Dad died – and the way he always spoke to me about him let it be known that he idolized him, and somehow blamed Mom for his early death.

'She never liked him,' he once told me when I was just thirteen. 'And she made his life so miserable that he was away most of every week.'

'But Mom said he was away every week working.'

'Yeah – he was always out of town. It meant that he didn't have to be with her.'

Because Dad died when I was just eighteen months old, I was denied any memories (let alone knowledge) of him. So whenever Charlie spoke about our father, I hung on to every syllable . . . especially as Mom constantly skirted the subject of the late Jack Malone, as if it was either far too painful to deal with, or she just didn't want to talk about him. In turn, this meant that I bought Charlie's view on our parents' fractious marriage – and silently attributed its unhappiness to Mom and her meddlesome ways.

At the same time, however, I never understood why Charlie couldn't work out a strategy for dealing with her. God knows, I also fought with her constantly. I too found her maddening. But I would never have shut her out the way Charlie did. Then again, I did get the sense that Mom was a bit ambivalent about her only son. Of course she loved him. But I did wonder if she also silently resented him for being the reason why she ended up in an unhappy marriage with Jack Malone. Charlie, in turn, never got over Dad's death. Nor did he like being the only man in the house. As soon as he could, he fled – straight into the arms of a woman who was so controlling, so autocratic that Mom suddenly seemed libertarian by comparison.

'I know you never got along, Charlie,' I said. 'And yeah – she had her pain-in-the-ass moments. But she didn't deserve the punishment you and Princess meted out.'

Long pause.

'No,' he said. 'She didn't deserve it. What can I say, Kate? Except that I allowed myself to be wrongly influenced by . . .' He cut himself off, and lowered his voice. 'Put it this way: the argument was always presented in *"It's either her or me"* terms. And I was so weak, I bought it.'

Another silence. Then I said, 'Okay, I'll Fedex you a check for five thousand today.'

It took a moment to sink in. 'Are you serious?'

'It's what Mom would have wanted.'

'Oh God, Kate . . . I don't know what to . . .'

'Say nothing . . .'

'I'm overwhelmed . . .'

'Don't be. It's family business.'

'I promise, *swear*, I'll pay it all back as soon as . . .'

'Charlie . . . *enough*. You'll have the check tomorrow. And when you're in a position to pay

91

me back, you pay me back. Now I need to ask you . . .'

'Anything. Any favor you need.'

'It's just a question I need answered, Charlie.'

'Sure, sure.'

'Did you ever know a Sara Smythe?'

'Never heard of her. Why?'

'I've received a condolence letter from her, saying she knew Mom and Dad before I was born.'

'Doesn't ring any bells with me. Then again, I don't remember most of Mom and Dad's friends from back then.'

'That's not surprising. I can't remember who I met last month. Thanks anyway.'

'No – thank you, Kate. You don't know what that five grand means to all of us . . .'

'I think I have an idea.'

'Bless you,' he said quietly.

After I hung up, a thought struck me: I actually missed my brother.

I spent the balance of the morning tidying the apartment and dealing with domestic chores. When I returned from the laundry room in the basement of the building, I found a message on my answering machine:

'Hello, Kate . . .'

It was a voice I hadn't heard before; a deeply refined voice with a noticeable New England twang.

'It's Sara Smythe here. I do hope you received my letter and I do apologize for calling you at home. But it would be nice to meet up. As I said in my letter, I was close to your family when your father was alive, and would very much like to renew contact with you after all these years. I know how busy you are, so whenever you have a chance please give me a ring. My number is five-five-five oh-seven-four-five. I am in this afternoon, if you're around. Once again, my thoughts are with you at this difficult time. But I know you're tough and resilient – so you'll get through this. I so look forward to meeting you face-to-face.'

I listened to the message twice, my alarm (and outrage) growing by the second. *I would very much like to renew contact with you after all these years . . . I know how busy you are . . . I know you're tough and resilient* . . . Jesus Christ, this woman was sounding like she was an old dear family friend, or someone on whose knee I climbed when I was five. And didn't she have the decency to realize that, just having buried my mother yesterday, I wasn't exactly in the mood for socializing?

I picked up the letter she had hand-delivered earlier today. I walked into Ethan's room. I powered up his computer. I wrote:

Dear Ms Smythe,

I was enormously touched both by your letter and by your kind message.

As I'm certain you know, grief affects people in such curious, singular ways. And right now, I simply want to withdraw for a while and be alone with my son and my thoughts.

93

I appreciate your understanding. And, once again, my thanks for your sympathy at this sad juncture.

Yours,

Kate Malone

I read the letter twice through before hitting the button marked Print, then signing my name at the bottom. I folded it, placed it in an envelope, scribbled Smythe's name and address on the front, then sealed it. Returning to the kitchen, I picked up the phone, and called my secretary at the office. She arranged for our courier service to pick up the letter at my apartment and deliver it to Ms Smythe's place on West 77th Street. I knew I could have posted the letter, but feared that she might try to call me again tonight. I wanted to make certain I didn't hear from her again.

Half-an-hour later, the doorman rang me to say that the courier was downstairs. I grabbed my coat and left the apartment. On my way out the front door, I handed the letter to the helmeted motorcycle messenger. He assured me that he'd deliver it across town within the next thirty minutes. I thanked him, and headed up toward Lexington Avenue. I stopped by our local branch of Kinko's on 78th Street. I removed another envelope from my coat pocket and placed it inside a Federal Express folder. Then I filled out the dispatch form, requesting guaranteed next-day delivery to a certain Charles Malone in Van Nuys, California. I tossed it in the Fedex box. When he opened the letter tomorrow, he'd find a five-thousand-dollar cheque, and a very short note which read:

Hope this helps.
Good luck.
Kate

I left Kinko's and spent the next hour or so drifting around my neighborhood. I shopped for groceries at D'Agostino's, arranging to have the order delivered to my apartment later that afternoon. I walked around Gap Kids, and ended up buying Ethan a new denim jacket. I headed two blocks west and killed half-an-hour browsing in the Madison Avenue Bookshop. Then, realizing that I hadn't eaten a thing since yesterday afternoon, I stopped at Soup Burg on Madison and 73rd Street, and ordered a double bacon-cheeseburger with fries. I felt immense high-caloric guilt as I gobbled it down. But it was still wonderful. As I nursed a cup of coffee after-wards, my cellphone rang.

'Is that you, Kate?'

Oh God, no. That woman again.

'Who is this?' I asked, even though I knew the answer to that question.

'It's Sara Smythe.'

'How did you get this number, Miss Smythe?'

'I called the Bell Atlantic cellphone directory.'

'You needed to speak with me that urgently?'

'Well, I just received your letter, Kate. And . . .'

I cut her off. 'I'm surprised to hear you calling me by my first name, as I don't seem to remember ever meeting you, Ms Smythe . . .'

'Oh, but we did. Years ago, when you were just a little . . .'

'Maybe we did meet, but it didn't lodge in my memory.'

'Well, when we get together, I'll be able to . . .'

I cut her off again. 'Ms Smythe, you did *read* my letter, didn't you?'

'Yes, of course. That's why I'm calling you.'

'Didn't I make it clear that we are *not* going to be getting together?'

'Don't say that, Kate.'

'And will you please stop calling me Kate?'

'If I could just explain . . .'

'No. I want to hear no explanations. I just want you to stop bothering me.'

'All I'm asking is . . .'

'And I suppose that was you who made all those message-less phone calls to my apartment yesterday . . .'

'Please hear me out . . .'

'And what's this about being an old friend of my parents? My brother Charlie said he never knew you when he was young . . .'

'Charlie?' she said, sounding animated. 'You're finally talking to Charlie again?'

I was suddenly very nervous. 'How did you know I hadn't been speaking to him?'

'Everything will come clear if we could just meet . . .'

'No.'

'Please be reasonable, Kate . . .'

'That's it. This conversation's closed. And don't bother calling back. Because I won't speak with you.'

With that, I hit the disconnect button.

All right, I over-reacted. But . . . the intrusiveness of the woman. And how the hell did she know about the breach with Charlie?

I left the restaurant, still fuming. I decided to squander the rest of the afternoon in a movie. I walked east and wasted two hours at the Loew's 72nd Street watching some cheesy action film, in which inter-galactic terrorists hijacked an American space shuttle, and killed all the crew – bar some beefcake astronaut who naturally foiled the baddies and single-handedly brought the damaged shuttle back to earth, landing it on top of Mount Rushmore. Ten minutes into this stupidity, I asked myself why on earth I ended up walking into this movie. I knew the answer to that question: because everything's out of synch today.

When I got back to the apartment, it was nearly six o'clock. Constantine the doorman was thankfully off. Teddy, the nice night guy, was on duty.

'Package for you, Miss Malone,' he said, handing me a large bulky manila envelope.

'When did this arrive?' I asked.

'Around half-an-hour ago. It was delivered by hand.'

I silently groaned.

'A little old lady in a taxi?' I asked.

'How'd you guess?'

'You don't want to know.'

I thanked Teddy and went upstairs. I took off my coat. I sat down at the dining table. I opened the envelope. Reaching inside, I pulled out a card. The same greyish-blue stationery. Oh God, here we go again . . .

346 West 77th Street

Apt. 2B

New York, New York 10024

(212) 555.0745

Dear Kate,

I really think you should call me, don't you?

Sara

I reached back into the envelope. I withdrew a large rectangular book. On closer inspection, it turned out to be a photo album. I opened the cover and found myself staring at a set of black-and-white baby photos, carefully displayed behind transparent sheeting. The photos were pure fifties – as the newborn infant was shown asleep in one of those huge old-fashioned strollers that were popular back then. I turned the page. Here, the infant was being held in the arms of her dad – a real 1950s dad, with a herringbone suit, a rep tie, a crew cut, big white teeth. The sort of dad who, just eight years earlier, was probably dodging enemy fire in some German town.

Like my dad.

I stared back at the photos. I suddenly felt ill.

That was my dad.

And that was me in his arms.

I turned the page. There were pictures of me at the age of two, three, five. There were pictures of me at my first day of school. There were pictures of me as a Brownie. There were pictures of me as a Girl Scout. There were pictures of me with Charlie in front of Rockefeller Center, circa 1963. Wasn't that the afternoon when Meg and Mom brought us to the Christmas show at Radio City Music Hall?

I began to turn the pages with manic rapidity. Me in a school play at Brearley. Me at summer camp in Maine. Me at my first dance. Me on Todd's Point Beach in Connecticut, during summer vacation. Me with Meg at my high school graduation.

It was an entire photographic history of my life – including pictures of me in college, at my wedding, and with Ethan, right after he was born. The remaining pages of the album were taken up with newspaper clippings. Clippings of stories I wrote for the Smith College newspaper. Clippings from the same newspaper, showing me in a college play (*Murder in the Cathedral*). Clippings of my assorted print ad campaigns. There was the *New York Times* announcement of my wedding to Matt. And the *New York Times* announcement of Ethan's birth . . .

I continued flicking wildly through the album. By the time I reached the penultimate page, my head was reeling. I flipped over the final page. And there was . . .

No, this was unbelievable.

There was a clipping from the Allan-Stevenson newspaper, showing Ethan in gym clothes, running a relay race at the school gymkhana last spring.

I slammed the album shut. I shoved it under my arm. I grabbed my coat. I raced out the door, raced straight into an elevator, raced through the downstairs lobby, raced into the backseat of a cab. I told the driver, 'West Seventy-Seventh Street.'

CHAPTER 4

She lived in a brownstone. I paid off the cab and went charging up the front steps, taking them two at a time. Her name was on the bottom bell. I held it down for a good ten seconds. Then her voice came over the intercom.

'Yes?' she said hesitantly.

'It's Kate Malone. Open up.'

There was a brief pause, then she buzzed me in.

Her apartment was on the first floor. She was standing in the doorway, awaiting me. She was dressed in grey flannel pants and a grey crewneck sweater that accented her long, delicate neck. Her grey hair was perfectly coiffed in a tight bun. Up close, her skin appeared even more translucent and smooth – with only a few crow's feet hinting at her true age. Her posture was perfect, emphasizing her elegant stature, her total poise. As always, her eyes were sharply focused – and alive with pleasure at seeing me . . . something I found instantly unsettling.

'How dare you,' I said, brandishing the photo album.

'Good afternoon, Kate,' she said, her voice

controlled and untroubled by my outburst. 'I'm glad you came.'

'Who the hell are you? And what the hell is this?' I said, again holding up the photo album as if it was the smoking gun in a murder trial.

'Why don't you come inside?'

'I don't want to come inside,' I said, now sounding very loud. She remained calm.

'We really can't talk here,' she said. 'Please . . .'

She motioned for me to cross the threshold. After a moment's nervous hesitation I said, 'Don't think I'm going to stay long . . .'

'Fine,' she said.

I followed her inside. We entered a small foyer. On one wall was a floor-to-ceiling bookshelf, heaving with hardcover volumes. There was a closet next to the shelf. She opened it, asking, 'Can I take your coat?'

I handed it to her. As she hung it up, I turned around, and suddenly felt as if the wind had been knocked out of me. Because there – on the opposite side of the foyer – were a half-dozen framed photos of myself and of my father. There was that picture of my dad in his Army uniform. There was an enlargement of that photo of Dad cradling me when I was a newborn baby. There was a picture of me at college, and holding Ethan when he was just a year old. There were two black-and-white photos showing Dad in a variety of poses with a younger Sara Smythe. The first was an 'at home' shot: Dad with his arms around her, standing near a Christmas tree. The remaining shot was of the happy couple in front of the Lincoln Memorial in Washington. From the age of the photos and the style of clothes they were wearing, I guessed they were taken in the early 1950s. I spun around and stared at Sara Smythe, wide-eyed.

'I don't understand . . .' I said.

'I'm not surprised.'

'You've got some explaining to do,' I said, suddenly angry.

'Yes,' she said quietly. 'I do.'

She touched my elbow, leading me into the living room.

'Come sit down. Coffee? Tea? Something stronger?'

'Stronger,' I said.

'Red wine? Bourbon? Harvey's Bristol Cream? That's about it, I'm afraid.'

'Bourbon.'

'On the rocks? With water?'

'Neat.'

She allowed herself a little smile. 'Just like your dad,' she said.

She motioned for me to sit in an oversized armchair. It was upholstered in a dark tan linen fabric. The same fabric covered a large sofa. There was a Swedish modern coffee table, on top of which were neat stacks of art books and high-end periodicals (*The New Yorker, Harper's, Atlantic Monthly, New York Review of Books*). The living room was small, but immaculate. Bleached wood floors, white walls, more shelves filled with books, a substantial collection of classical CDs, a large window with southerly exposure, overlooking a small back patio. Directly off this room was an alcove which had been cleverly fitted out as a small home office, with a stripped pine table on which sat a computer, a fax machine and a pile of papers. Opposite this alcove was a bedroom with a queen-sized bed (bleached headboard, a quilted old Americana bedspread), and a Shaker-style dresser. Like everything else in the apartment, the bedroom exuded style and subdued good taste. You could tell immediately that Sara Smythe was refusing to embrace the muted dilapidation of senior citizenship – and live out the final part of her life in an apartment that was, stylistically speaking, two decades out of date, and reeking of shabby gentility. Her home hinted at a quiet, but ferocious sense of pride.

Sara emerged from the kitchen, carrying a tray. On it was a bottle of Hiram Walker bourbon, a bottle of Bristol Cream, a sherry glass, a whiskey glass. She set it down on the coffee table, then poured us each a drink.

'Hiram Walker was your father's favorite bourbon,' she said. 'Personally I could never stand the stuff. Scotch was my drink – until I turned seventy, and my body decided otherwise. Now I have to make do with something dull-and-feminine like sherry. Cheers.'

She raised her sherry glass. I didn't respond to her toast. I simply threw back my whiskey in one gulp. It burned my throat, but eased some of the serious distress I was feeling. Another small smile crossed Sara Smythe's lips.

'Your dad used to drink that way – when he was feeling tense.'

'Like father, like daughter,' I said, pointing to the bottle.

'Please help yourself,' she said. I poured myself another slug of bourbon, but this time restricted myself to a small sip. Sara Smythe settled herself into the sofa, then touched the top of my hand.

'I do want to apologize for the extreme methods I used to get you over here. I know I must have seemed like an old nuisance, but . . .'

I quickly withdrew my hand.

'I just want to know one thing, Ms Smythe . . .'

'Sara, please.'

'*No*. No first names. We are not friends. We are not even acquaintances . . .'

'Kate, I've known you all your life.'

'How? How have you known me? And why the hell did you start bothering me after my mom died?'

I tossed the photo album on to the coffee table, and opened it to the back page.

'I'd also like to know how you got this?' I said, pointing to the clipping of Ethan in the Allan-Stevenson school newspaper.

'I have a subscription to the school's newspaper.'

'You *what?*'

'Just like I had a subscription to the Smith College paper when you were there.'

'You're insane . . .'

'Can I explain . . .'

'Why should we be of interest to you? I mean, if your photo album is anything to go by, this hasn't been a recent fixation. You've been tracking us for years. And what's with all the old pictures of my dad?'

She looked at me straight on. And said, 'Your father was the love of my life.'

PART TWO

SARA

CHAPTER 1

What's my first memory of him? A glance. A sudden over-the-shoulder glance across a packed, smoky room. He was leaning against a wall, a glass of something in one hand, a cigarette between his teeth. He later told me that he felt out of place in that room, and was looking across it in search of the fellow who had dragged him there. As his eyes scanned the guests, they suddenly happened upon me. I met his gaze. Only for a second. Or maybe two. He looked at me. I looked at him. He smiled. I smiled back. He turned away, still seeking out his friend. And that was it. Just a simple glance.

Fifty-five years on, I can still replay that moment – nanosecond by nanosecond. I can see his eyes – light blue, clear, a little weary. His sandy hair, buzz-cut down to short-back-and-sides. His narrow face with sharply etched cheekbones. The dark khaki Army uniform which seemed to hang so perfectly off his lanky frame. The way he looked so young (well, he was only in his early twenties at the time). So innocent. So quietly preoccupied. So handsome. So damn Irish.

A glance is such a momentary, fleeting thing, isn't it? As human gestures go, it means nothing. It's perishable. That's what still amazes me – the way your life can be fundamentally altered by something so ephemeral, so transitory. Every day, we lock eyes with people – on the subway or the bus, in the supermarket, crossing the street. It's such a simple impulse, looking at others. You notice someone walking towards you, your eyes meet for an instant, you pass each other by. End of story. So why . . . *why*? . . . should that one glance have mattered? No reason. None at all. Except that it did. And it changed everything. Irrevocably. Though, of course, neither of us knew that at the time.

Because, after all, it was just a glance.

We were at a party. It was the night before Thanksgiving. The year was 1945. Roosevelt had died in April. The German High Command had surrendered in May. Truman dropped the bomb on Hiroshima in August. Eight days later, the Japanese capitulated. Quite a year. If you were young and American – and hadn't lost anybody you loved in the war – you couldn't help but feel the heady pleasures of victory.

So here we all were – twenty of us, in a cramped third-floor walk-up apartment on Sullivan Street – celebrating the first Thanksgiving of peace by drinking too much and dancing too raucously. The average age in the room was around twenty-eight . . . which made me the kid of the group at twenty-three (though the fellow in the Army uniform looked even younger). And the big talk in the room was of that romantic notion called the Limitless Future. Because winning the war also meant that we'd finally defeated that economic enemy called The Depression. The Peace Dividend was coming. Good times were ahead. We thought we had a divine right to good times. We were Americans, after all. This was our century.

Even my brother Eric believed in the realm of American possibility . . . and he was what our father called 'a Red'. I always told Father that he was judging his son far too harshly – because Eric was really more of an old fashioned Progressive. Being Eric, he was also a complete romantic – someone who idolized Eugene Debs, subscribed to *The Nation* when he was sixteen, and dreamed about being the next Clifford Odets. That's right – Eric was a playwright. After he graduated from Columbia in '37, he found work as an assistant stage manager with Orson Welles' Mercury Theater, and had a couple of plays produced by assorted Federal Theater Workshops around New York. This was the time when Roosevelt's New Deal actually subsidized non-profit drama in America – so there was plenty of employment opportunities for *'theater workers'* (as Eric liked to call himself), not to mention lots of small theater companies willing to take a chance on young dramatists like my brother. None of the plays he had performed ever hit the big time. But he wasn't ever aiming for Broadway. He

111

always said that his work was 'geared for the needs and the aspirations of the working man' (like I said, he really was a romantic). And I'll be honest with you – as much as I loved, *adored*, my older brother, his three-hour epic drama about a 1902 union dispute on the Erie-Lakawana Railroad wasn't exactly a toe-tapper.

Still, as a playwright, he did think big. Sadly, his kind of drama (that whole *Waiting for Lefty* sort of thing) was dead by the start of the forties. Orson Welles went to Hollywood. So too did Clifford Odets. The Federal Theater Project was accused of being Communist by a handful of dreadful small-minded congressmen, and was finally closed down in '39. Which meant that, in 1945, Eric was paying the rent as a radio writer. At first he scripted a couple of episodes of *Boston Blackie*. But the producer fired him off the show after he wrote an installment where the hero investigated the death of a labor organizer. He'd been murdered on the orders of some big-deal industrialist – who, as it turned out, bore more than a passing resemblance to the owner of the radio network on which *Boston Blackie* was broadcast. I tell you, Eric couldn't resist mischief . . . even if it did hurt his career. And he did have a terrific sense of humor. Which is how he was able to pick up his newest job: as one of the gag writers on *Stop or Go: The Quiz Bang Show*, hosted every Sunday night at eight thirty by Joe E. Brown. I'd wager anything that nobody under the age of seventy-five now remembers Joe E. Brown.

And with good reason. He made Jerry Lewis appear subtle.

Anyway, the party was in Eric's place on Sullivan Street: a narrow one-bedroom railroad apartment which, like Eric himself, always struck me as the height of bohemian chic. The bathtub was in the kitchen. There were lamps made from Chianti bottles. Ratty old floor cushions were scattered around the living room. Hundreds of books were stacked everywhere. Remember: this was the forties . . . still way before the beatnik era in the Village. So Eric was something of a man ahead of his time – especially when it came to wearing black turtlenecks, and hanging out with Delmore Schwartz and the *Partisan Review* crowd, and smoking Gitanes, and dragging his kid sister to hear this new-fangled thing called Bebop at some club on 52nd Street. In fact, just a couple of weeks before his Thanksgiving party, we were actually present in some Broadway dive when a sax player named Charles Parker took the stage with four other musicians.

When they finished their first set, Eric turned to me and said, 'S, you're going to eventually brag about being at this gig. Because we have just witnessed ourselves a true revolution. After tonight, rhythm is never going to be the same again.'

S. That was his name for me. S for Sara or Sis. From the time Eric turned fourteen, he called me that – and though my parents both hated the nickname, I cherished it. Because my big brother had bestowed it on me. And because, in my eyes, my big brother was the most interesting and original man on the planet . . . not to mention my protector and defender, especially when it came to our deeply traditional parents.

We were born and raised in Hartford, Connecticut. As Eric was fond of pointing out, only two interesting people ever spent time in Hartford: Mark Twain (who lost a lot of money in a publishing house that went bust there), and Wallace Stevens, who coped with the tedium of being an insurance executive by writing some of the most experimental poetry imaginable.

'Outside of Twain and Stevens,' Eric told me when I was twelve, 'nobody of note ever lived in this city. Until we came along.'

Oh, he was so wonderfully arrogant. He'd say anything outrageous if it upset our father, Robert Biddeford Smythe III. He fit his portentous name perfectly. He was a very proper, very Episcopalian insurance executive; a man who always wore worsted three-piece suits, believed in the virtues of thrift, and abhorred flamboyance or mischief-making of any kind. Our mother, Ida, was cut from the same stern material: the daughter of a Boston Presbyterian minister, ruthlessly practical, a triumph of domestic efficiency. They were a formidable team, our parents. Cut-and-dried, no-nonsense, reluctantly tactile. Public displays of affection were rare events in the Smythe household. Because, at heart, Father and Mother were true New England Puritans, still rooted in the nineteenth century. They always seemed old to us. Old and forbidding. The antithesis of fun.

Of course we still loved them. Because, after all, they were our parents – and unless your parents were savage to you, you *had* to love them. It was part of the social contract – or at least it was when I was growing up. Just as you had to accept their manifold limitations. I've often thought that the only time you truly become an adult is when you finally forgive your parents for being just as flawed as everyone else . . . and then acknowledge that, within their own boundaries, they did the best they could for you.

But loving your parents is far different from embracing their world-view. From the time Eric was in his teens he worked hard at infuriating Father (yes, he insisted we address him in that Victorian manner. Never Dad. Or Pop. Or anything hinting at easy conviviality. Always *Father*). Sometimes I think Eric's radical politics were less rooted in ideological conviction, and more to do with raising Father's blood pressure. The fights they used to have were legendary. Especially after Father discovered the copy of John Reed's *Ten Days that Shook the World* under his son's bed. Or when Eric presented him with a Paul Robeson record on Father's Day.

My mother stayed out of all father/son arguments. To her, a woman had no business debating politics (one of the many reasons why she so hated Mrs

Roosevelt, calling her 'a female Lenin'). She was always lecturing Eric about respecting Father. But, by the time he was ready to enter college, she realized that her stern words no longer carried any import; that she had lost him. Which saddened her greatly. And I sensed that she was always a bit baffled as to why her only son – whom she had raised so correctly – had turned into such a Jacobin. Especially as he was so astonishingly bright.

That was the only thing about Eric which pleased my parents – his exceptional intelligence. He devoured books. He was reading French by the age of fourteen, and had a working command of Italian by the time he entered Columbia. He could talk knowledgeably about such abstract, abtruse subjects as Cartesian philosophy or quantum mechanics. And he played a mean boogie-woogie piano. He was also one of those maddening whizkids who got straight As in school with minimal work. Harvard wanted him. Princeton wanted him. Brown wanted him. But he wanted Columbia. Because he wanted New York, and all its ancillary freedoms.

'I tell you, S, once I get to Manhattan, Hartford won't see me ever again.'

That wasn't exactly true – because, despite his rebelliousness, he still remained a reasonably dutiful son. He wrote home once a week, he made brief visits to Hartford at Thanksgiving and Christmas and Easter, he never shoved Mother and Father out of his life. He simply reinvented himself completely in New York. To begin with, he changed his name – from Theobold Ericson Smythe to plain old Eric Smythe. He got rid of all those Ivy League Rogers Peet clothes that my parents bought him, and started shopping at the local Army/Navy store. His skinny frame got skinnier. His black hair grew thick, bushy. He bought himself a pair of narrow rimless spectacles. He looked like Trotsky – especially as he took to wearing an Army greatcoat and a battered tweed jacket. On the rare times my parents saw him, they were horrified by his transformed appearance. But, once again, his grades silenced them. Straight As. Elected to Phi Beta Kappa at the end of his junior year. High honors in English. Had he wanted to go to law school, or get a doctorate, he could have waltzed into any graduate program in the country. But instead, he moved downtown to Sullivan Street, swept floors for Orson Welles for $20 a week, and dreamed big dreams about writing plays that mattered.

By 1945, those dreams were dying. No one would even look at his plays anymore – because they belonged to another era. But Eric was still determined to break through as a playwright . . . even if it meant writing hack jokes for Joe E. Brown to keep a roof over his head. Once or twice, I dropped hints about maybe finding a teaching job in a college – which struck me as more worthy of Eric's talents than churning out one-liners for a game show. But Eric refused to entertain such notions, saying things like, 'The moment a writer starts teaching his trade, he's finished. And the moment he enters academia, he slams the door on the real world . . . the place about which he's supposed to be writing.'

'But *The Quiz Bang Show* isn't the real world,' I countered.

'It's more rooted in reality than teaching English composition to a bunch of prim little women at Bryn Mawr.'

'Ouch!' I said, having graduated from Bryn Mawr two years earlier.

'You know what I'm saying here, S.'

'Yes – that I am a prim little woman who probably should be married to some dreary banker, and living in some prim little town on the Philadelphia Main Line . . .'

Certainly that was the life my parents envisaged for me. But I was having none of it. After I graduated from Bryn Mawr in '43, Mother and Father hoped that I would marry my steady back then – a Haverford graduate named Horace Cowett. He'd just been accepted into U. Penn law school, and had proposed to me. But though Horace wasn't as prim and humorless as his name (he actually was a rather bookish fellow who wrote some halfway decent poetry for the Haverford literary magazine), I still wasn't ready to impound myself in marriage at a premature age – especially to a man I liked, but about whom I felt no overwhelming passion. Anyway, I wasn't going to squander my twenties by sequestering myself in dull old Philadelphia, as I had my sights set on the city ninety miles north of there. And nobody was going to stop me from going to New York.

Predictably, my parents tried to block my move there. When I announced – around three weeks before my graduation – that I had been offered a trainee job at *Life*, they were horrified. I was home for the weekend in Hartford (a trip I made deliberately to break the job news to them, and also to inform them that I wouldn't be accepting Horace's marriage proposal). Ten minutes into the conversation, the emotional temperature within our household quickly hit boiling point.

'I am not having any daughter of mine living by herself in that venal, indecent city,' my father pronounced.

'New York is hardly indecent – and *Life* isn't exactly *Confidential*,' I said, mentioning a well-known scandal sheet of the time. 'Anyway I thought you'd be thrilled with my news. *Life* only accepts ten trainees a year. It's an incredibly prestigious offer.'

'Father's still right,' my mother said. 'New York is no place for a young woman without family.'

'Eric's not family?'

'Your brother is not the most moral of men,' my father said.

'And what does that mean?' I said angrily.

My father was suddenly flustered, but he covered up his embarrassment by saying, 'It doesn't matter what it means. What matters is the simple fact that I will not permit you to live in Manhattan.'

'I am twenty-two years old, Father.'

'That's not the issue.'

'You have no legal right to tell me what I can or cannot do.'

'Don't hector your father,' my mother said. 'And I must tell you that you are making a dreadful mistake by not marrying Horace.'

'I knew you'd say that.'

'Horace is a splendid young man,' my father said.

'Horace is a very *nice* young man – with a very *nice*, dull future ahead of him.'

'You are being arrogant,' he said.

'No – just accurate. Because I will not be pushed into a life I don't want.'

'I am not pushing you into any life . . .' my father said.

'By forbidding me from going to New York, you are stopping me from taking control of my own destiny.'

'Your *destiny*!' my father said, with cruel irony. 'You actually think *you* have a *destiny*! What bad novels have you been reading at Bryn Mawr?'

I stormed out of the room. I ran upstairs and fell on the bed, sobbing. Neither of my parents came up to comfort me. Nor did I expect them to. That wasn't their style. They both had a very Old Testament view of parenthood. Father was our household's version of The Almighty – and once He had spoken, all argument was silenced. So, for the rest of the weekend, the subject wasn't raised again. Instead, we made strained conversation about the recent Japanese activity in the Pacific – and I stayed button-lipped when Father went into one of his jeremiads about FDR. On Sunday he drove me to the train station. When we arrived there he patted my arm.

'Sara, dear – I really don't like fighting with you. Though we are disappointed that you won't be marrying Horace, we do respect your decision. And if you really are that keen on journalism, I do have several contacts on the *Hartford Courant*. I don't think it would be too difficult to find you something there . . .'

'I am accepting the job offer at *Life*, Father.'

He actually turned white – something Father never did.

'If you do accept that job, I will have no choice but to cut you off.'

'That will be your loss.'

And I left the car.

I felt shaky all the way to New York – and more than a little scared. After all, I had directly defied my father – something I had never attempted before. Though I was trying to be dauntless and self-confident, I was suddenly terrified of the thought that I might just lose my parents. Just as I was also terrified by the thought that – if I heeded Father's wish – I would end up writing the 'Church Notes' column in the *Hartford Courant*, and ruing the fact that I had allowed my parents to force me into a small life.

And yes, I did believe I had a destiny. I know that probably sounds vainglorious and absurdly romantic . . . but at this early juncture in so-called adult life, I had reached one simple conclusion about the future: *it had possibilities* . . . but only if you allowed yourself the chance to explore those possibilities. However, most of my contemporaries were falling into line, doing what was expected of them. At least fifty per cent of my class at Bryn Mawr had weddings planned for the summer after they graduated. All those boys trickling home from the war were, by and large, just thinking about getting jobs, settling down. Here we were – the generation who was about to inherit all that postwar plenty, who (compared to our parents) had infinite opportunities. But instead of running with those opportunities, what did most of us do? We became good company men, good housewives, good consumers. We narrowed our horizons, and trapped ourselves into small lives.

Of course, I only realized all this years later (hindsight always gives you perfect vision, doesn't it?). Back in the spring of '45, however, all that concerned me was doing something interesting with my life – which essentially meant not marrying Horace Cowett, and definitely taking that job at *Life*. But by the time I reached Penn Station after that horrible weekend with my parents, I had lost my nerve. Despite four years away at college, Father still loomed large in my life. I still desperately sought his approval, even though I knew it was impossible to receive it. And I did think he really would carry out his threat to disinherit me if I went to New York. How could I live without my parents?

'Oh, *please*,' Eric said when I related this fear to him. 'Father wouldn't dare cut you off. He dotes on you.'

'No, he doesn't . . .'

'Believe me, the old fool feels he must play the stern Victorian *paterfamilias* – but, at heart, he's a scared sixty-four-year-old who's about to be put out to pasture by his company next year, and is terrified of the horrors of retirement. So do you really think he's going to slam the door on his only beloved daughter?'

We were sitting in the cocktail lounge of the Hotel Pennsylvania, opposite Penn Station. Eric had arranged to meet me off the train from Hartford that Sunday afternoon (I had a two-hour wait for my connection back to Bryn Mawr, via Philadelphia). As soon as I saw him on the platform, I threw myself against his shoulder and started to weep, simultaneously hating myself for behaving so weakly. Eric held me until I calmed down, then said, 'So, did you have fun at home?'

I had to laugh. 'It was wonderful,' I said.

'I can tell. The Pennsylvania's nearby. And the bartender there makes a mean Manhattan.'

That was the understatement of the decade. After

two of those Manhattans, I felt like I was under anaesthetic – which, I must admit, isn't a bad thing to feel on occasion. Eric tried to get a third drink into me – but I dug in my heels and insisted on a ginger ale. I didn't want to say anything, but I was a little concerned when my brother downed his third Manhattan in four fast gulps, then called for another. Though we'd been in regular contact by letter (long-distance calls – even from New York to Pennsylvania – were expensive back then), I hadn't seen him since Christmas. And I was genuinely taken aback by his physical state. His lanky frame had thickened. His complexion was pasty. A small, but noticeable roll of fat hung beneath his chin. He was chain-smoking Chesterfields and coughing loudly. He was only twenty-eight, but he was beginning to have that puffy look of a man who had been prematurely aged by disappointment. Of course his conversation was as fizzy and funny as ever, but I could tell that he was worried about work. I knew from his letters that his new play (something about a migrant worker revolt in southwest Texas) had just been rejected by every possible theater company in New York, and he was paying the rent by reading unsolicited scripts for the Theater Guild ('It's pretty depressing work,' he wrote me in March, 'because it's all about saying no to other writers. But it's $30 a week – which just about pays my bills'). And when he threw back his fourth Manhattan in five gulps, I decided to stop being silent about his chain-drinking.

124

'One more of those Manhattans, and you'll stand up on the table to sing "Yankee Doodle Dandy".'

'Now you're being a puritan, S. After I see you off to beautiful Philadelphia, I shall take the subway back to my Sullivan Street *atelier* and write until sunrise. Believe me, five Manhattans is nothing more than creative lubrication.'

'Okay – but you should also think about switching to filtered cigarettes. They're much kinder to your throat.'

'Oh God! Listen to the Bryn Mawr ascetic! Ginger ale, filtered cigarettes. Next thing you'll tell me is that, if he gets the nomination, you're going to vote for Dewey against Roosevelt in the next election.'

'You know I would *never* do that.'

'I think I was making a joke, S. Though I must say Daddy would be boggled beyond belief were you to vote Republican.'

'He'd still insist that I return to Hartford like a good little girl.'

'You won't be returning to Hartford after graduation.'

'He's given me a pretty stark choice, Eric.'

'No – what he's doing is playing the oldest poker ruse in the world. Putting all his chips into the pot, pretending that he holds a straight flush, and daring you to see his bet. So you're going to call his bluff by taking the job at *Life*. And though he will grump and groan about it – and probably do a little of his Teddy Roosevelt sabre-rattling – in the end he's going to accept your decision. Because

125

he has to. Anyway, he knows that I'll look after you in the big bad city.'

'That's what's scaring him,' I said, and immediately regretted that comment.

'Why?'

'Oh, you know . . .'

'No,' Eric said, sounding unamused. 'I don't know.'

'He probably thinks you'll turn me into a raging Marxist.'

Eric lit up another cigarette. His eyes were sharply focused, and he looked at me warily. I could tell that he was suddenly sober again.

'That's not what he said, S.'

'Yes it was,' I said, sounding unconvincing.

'Please tell me the truth.'

'I told you –'

'– that he didn't like the idea of me looking after you in New York. But surely he explained *why* he thought I might be a bad influence.'

'I really don't remember.'

'Now you're lying to me. And we *don't* lie to each other, S.'

My brother took my hand, and quietly said, 'You have to tell me.'

I looked up and met his stare. 'He said he didn't think you were the most moral of men.'

Eric said nothing. He just took a long, deep drag on his cigarette, coughing slightly as he inhaled.

'Of course, I don't think that,' I said.

'Don't you?'

'You know I don't.'

He stabbed the cigarette into the ashtray, and threw back the remainder of his drink.

'But if it was true . . . if I wasn't "the most moral of men" . . . would that bother you?'

Now it was his turn to meet my gaze. I knew what we were both thinking: this was an issue that we've always dodged . . . even though it has always been lurking in the background. Like my parents, I too had had my suspicions about my brother's sexuality (especially since there had never been a girlfriend in his life). But, back then, such suspicions were never discussed. Everything was closeted. Literally. And figuratively. To openly admit your homosexuality in forties America would have been an act of suicide. Even to the kid sister who adored you. So we spoke in code.

'I think you're about the most moral person I know,' I said.

'But Father is using the word "moral" in a different way. Do you understand that, S?'

I covered his hand with mine.

'Yes. I do.'

'And does that trouble you?'

'You're my brother. That's all that matters.'

'Are you sure?'

My hand squeezed his.

'I'm sure.'

'Thanks.'

'Shut up,' I said with a smile.

He squeezed my hand back.

'I'll always be in your corner, S. Know that. And don't worry about Father. He won't win this one.'

A week later, a letter arrived for me at Bryn Mawr.

Dear S,

After seeing you last Sunday, I decided that a fast day trip to Hartford was long overdue. So I jumped the train the next morning. Needless to say, Mother and Father were just a tad surprised to see me on their doorstep. Though he refused to listen at first, eventually Father had no choice but to hear me out on your behalf. For the first hour of our 'negotiations' (the only word for it), he stuck to his 'She's coming back to Hartford, and that's the end of it' line. So I started playing the 'It would be a pity if you lost both your children' card with great finesse – making it less of a threat, more of a tragic potentiality. When he dug in his heels and said that his mind was made up, I said, 'Then you're going to end up a lonely old man.' With that, I left, and took the next train back to New York.

The next morning the phone rang at the ungodly hour of eight a.m. It was Father Dearest. His tone was still gruff and inflexible, but his tune had definitely changed.

'Here's what I will accept. Sara can take the job at Life, but only if she agrees to reside at the Barbizon Hotel for Women on East 63rd Street. It comes highly recommended by one of my associates at Standard Life, and operates according to strict rules, with nightly curfews and no visitors after dark. As Mother and I will know she is being carefully looked after at the Barbizon, we will therefore accede to her demands about living in Manhattan. As you seem to have cast yourself in the role of go-between, I will leave it to you to put this proposition to Sara. Please inform her that, though she has our love and support, we will not negotiate on this issue.'

Naturally I said nothing – except that I would pass on his offer to you. But, as far as I'm concerned, this is a near-capitulation on his part. So drink five Manhattans in celebration and kiss Pennsylvania goodbye. You're going to New York . . . with parental blessing to boot. And don't worry about the Barbizon. We'll check you in there for the first month or two, then quietly transfer you to your own apartment. And then we'll figure out a way of breaking the news to Father and Mother without reactivating hostilities.

Peace in our time.

Your 'moral' brother,

Eric

I nearly screamed with delight when I finished reading this letter. Racing back to my dorm room, I grabbed a piece of stationery and a pen, and wrote:

Dear E,

I'm writing FDR tonight and nominating you to run the League of Nations (if it's reconstituted after the war). You're a diplomatic genius! And the best brother imaginable. Tell all the gang on 42nd Street that I will soon be there . . .

Love, S

I also scribbled a fast note to Father, informing him that I accepted his terms, and assuring him that I would do the family proud in New York (a coded way of letting him know I would remain 'a nice girl', even though I was living in that Sodom and Gomorrah called Manhattan).

I never received a reply from Father to my letter. Nor did I expect to. It simply wasn't his way. But he did attend my graduation with Mother. Eric took the train down for the day. After the ceremony, we all went out for lunch at a local hotel. It was an awkward meal. I could see Father glancing between the two of us, and pursing his lips. Though Eric had put on a tie and jacket for the occasion, it was the only jacket he owned (a battered Harris tweed he'd found in a thrift shop). His shirt was Army-surplus khaki. He looked like a union organizer – and chain-smoked throughout the lunch (at least he kept his liquor intake down to two Manhattans). I was dressed in a sensible suit, but Father still regarded me with unease. Having dared to stand up to him, I was no longer his little girl. And I could tell that he was finding it difficult to be relaxed around me (though, if truth be told, my father was never relaxed in the company of his children). Mother, meanwhile, did what Mother always did: she smiled nervously, and followed my father's lead on anything he said.

Eventually – after much strained talk about the prettiness of the Bryn Mawr campus, and the bad standard of service on the train from Hartford, and which neighbor's boy was serving in which corner of Europe or the Pacific – Father suddenly said, 'I just want you to know, Sara, that Mother and I are most pleased with your *cum laude* degree. It is quite an achievement.'

'But it's not *summa cum laude*, like me,' Eric said, his eyebrows arching mischievously.

'Thanks a lot,' I said.

'Anytime, S.'

'You have both done us proud,' Mother said.

'Academically speaking,' Father added.

'Yes,' Mother said quickly, 'academically speaking, we couldn't be prouder parents.'

That was the last time we were ever together as a family. Six weeks later – returning home to the Barbizon Hotel for Women after a long day at *Life* – I was stunned to see Eric standing in the lobby. His face was chalky, drawn. He looked at me with trepidation – and I knew immediately that he had something terrible to tell me.

'Hi, S,' he said quietly, taking my hands in his.

'What's happened?'

'Father died this morning.'

I heard my heart pound against my ribcage. For a moment or two I really didn't know where I was. Then I felt my brother's steadying hands on my arms. He led me to a sofa, and helped me down into it, sitting next to me.

'How?' I finally said.

'A heart attack – at his office. His secretary found him slumped over his desk. It must have been pretty instantaneous . . . which is a blessing, I guess.'

'Who told Mother?'

'The police. And then the Daniels called me. They said Mom's pretty distraught.'

'Of course she's distraught,' I heard myself saying. 'He was her life.'

I felt a sob rise up in my throat. But I stifled it. Because I suddenly heard Father's voice in my head: *'Crying is never an answer,'* he once told me when I burst into tears after getting a C+ in Latin. *'Crying is self-pity. And self-pity solves nothing.'*

Anyway, I didn't know what to feel at this moment – except the jumbled anguish of loss. I loved Father. I feared Father. I craved his affection. I never truly felt his affection. Yet I also knew that Eric and I meant everything to him. He just didn't know how to articulate such things. Now he never would. That was the realization which hit me hardest – the fact that, now, there would never be a chance for us to breach the gulf that was always between us; that my memory of Father would always be colored by the knowledge that we never really talked. I think that is the hardest thing about bereavement – coming to terms with what might have been, if only you'd been able to get it right.

I let Eric take charge of everything. He helped me pack a bag. He got us both into a cab to Penn Station, and on the 8.13 to Hartford. We sat in the bar car, and drank steadily as the train headed north through Fairfield County. Never once did he seem stricken by grief – because, I sensed, he wanted to remain strong for me. What was so curious about our conversation was how little we talked about Father, or Mother. Instead we chatted idly – about my work at *Life*, and Eric's Theater Guild job, and rumors emanating from Eastern Europe about Nazi-run death camps, and whether Roosevelt would keep Henry Wallace as his Vice-President during next year's Presidential campaign, and why Lillian Hellman's *Watch on the Rhine* was (in Eric's unrestrained opinion) a truly terrible play. It was as if we couldn't yet bring ourselves to deal with the profundity of losing a parent – especially one about which we both had such complex, ambivalent feelings. Only once during that journey was the matter of family mentioned . . . when Eric said, 'Well, I guess you can move out of the Barbizon now.'

'Won't Mother object?' I asked.

'Believe me, S – Mother will have other things on her mind.'

133

How dreadfully accurate Eric turned out to be. Mother wasn't simply grief-stricken by Father's death; she was inconsolable. During the three days before the funeral, she was so despondent that the family doctor kept her under sedation. She got through the actual service at the local Episcopal church, but came completely unstuck at the graveside. So unstuck that the doctor recommended admitting her to a rest home for observation.

She never left that rest home again. Within a week of her admission, a form of premature senile dementia had set in – and we lost her completely. A variety of specialists examined her – and they all came to the same conclusion: in the wake of Father's death, her grief had been so intense, so overwhelming, that she suffered a stroke which gradually attacked her speech, her memory, her motor control. For the first few months of her illness, Eric and I traveled back together every weekend to Hartford, to sit by her bed and hope for some sign of cognitive life. After six months, the doctors told us that it was unlikely that she would ever emerge from her dementia. That weekend we made some difficult, but necessary decisions. We put the family home on the market. We arranged for all of our parents' possessions to be sold, or given away to charity. Neither of us took much from the family home. Eric laid claim to a small writing table which Father kept in his bedroom. I held on to a photo, taken in 1913, of my parents on their honeymoon in the Berkshires. Mother was seated in a stiff-backed chair, wearing a long-sleeved white linen dress, her hair gathered up into a tightly constricted bun. Father was standing by her. He was in a dark cutaway suit, with a vest and a stiff high-collar. His left hand was behind his back, his right hand on Mother's shoulder. There was no glimmer of affection between them; no sense of ardour, or romantic animation, or even the simple pleasure of being in each other's company. They looked so stiff, so formal, so unsuited to the century in which they found themselves.

On the night Eric and I were sorting through their possessions – and we came upon this photograph in the attic – my brother burst into tears. It was the only time I ever saw him cry since Father had died and Mother took ill (whereas I had been regularly locking myself in the Ladies' room at *Life*, and blubbering like a fool). I knew exactly why Eric had suddenly broken down. Because that photograph was the perfect portrait of the formal, constrained face that our parents presented to the world . . . and, more tellingly, to their children. We always thought that their austerity extended to each other – because there were never any public displays of affection between them. But now we realized that there was this hidden passion between them – a love and a dependency so profound that it killed Mother to be without Father. What astonished us both was that we never saw this passion, never detected it for a moment.

'You never really know anybody,' Eric said to

me that night. 'You think you do – but they always end up baffling you. Especially when it comes to love. The heart is the most secretive – and confounding – part of the anatomy.'

My one antidote at this time was my job. I loved working at *Life*. Especially since, within four months, I had graduated from trainee status to the post of junior staff writer. I was researching and writing at least two short articles for the magazine every week. I was assigned the stories by a senior editor – a chain-smoking old-school journalist named Leland McGuire, who used to be the City editor on the *New York Daily Mirror*, but had moved to *Life* for the money and the gentler hours, and really missed the rough-and-tumble of a big raucous daily newspaper. He took a shine to me – and, shortly after I joined his department, took me out to lunch at the Oyster Bar in the basement of Grand Central Station.

'You want a piece of professional advice?' he asked me after we worked our way through two cups of chowder and a dozen cherrystones.

'Absolutely, Mr McGuire.'

'Leland, please. Okay – here it is. If you really want to become a properly seasoned journalist, get the hell out of the Time and Life building and find a reporter's job at some bigdeal daily. I'm sure I could help you there. Find you something at the *Mirror* or the *News*.'

'You're not happy with my work so far?'

'On the contrary – I think you're terrific. But

face facts: *Life* is, first and foremost, a picture magazine. Our senior writers are all men – and they're the ones who get sent out to cover the big stuff: the London blitz, Guadalcanal, FDR's next campaign. All I can give you is the arts-and-craft stuff: little five-hundred-word pieces on this month's big new movie, or a new fashion craze, or cookery tips. Whereas if you went to the City desk of the *Mirror*, you'd probably find yourself out on the beat with the cops, covering the courts, maybe even getting a real juicy assignment like an execution at Sing-Sing.'

'I don't think executions are really my sort of thing, Mr McGuire.'

'*Leland!* You really were raised far too well, Sara. Another Manhattan?'

'One's my limit at lunch, I'm afraid.'

'Then you really *shouldn't* go to the *Mirror*. Or maybe you should – because after a month there, you'll know how to drink three Manhattans at lunchtime, and still function.'

'I really am very happy at *Life*. And I am learning a lot.'

'So you don't want to be some hard-as-nails Barbara Stanwyck lady reporter?'

'I want to write fiction, Mr McGuire . . . sorry, *Leland*.'

'Oh, brother . . .'

'Have I said something wrong?'

'Nah. Fiction's fine. Fiction's great. If you can cut it.'

'I am certainly going to try.'

'And then, I suppose, it's a hubby and kids and a nice house in Tarrytown.'

'That's not really high on my list of priorities.'

He drained his martini. 'I've heard that one before.'

'I'm certain you have. But, in my case, it's the truth.'

'Sure it is. Until you meet some guy and decide you're tired of the daily nine-to-five grind, and want to settle down and have someone else pay the bills, and figure this nice Ivy League type is a suitable candidate for entrapment, and . . .'

I suddenly heard myself sounding rather cross. 'Thank you for reducing me to the level of female cliché.'

He was taken aback by my tone. 'Hell, I was just talking out of the side of my mouth.'

'Of course you were.'

'I didn't mean to offend you.'

'No offence taken, *Mr McGuire*.'

'Sounds like you're pretty damn angry to me.'

'Not angry. I just don't like to be pigeonholed as some predatory female.'

'But you are one tough cookie.'

'Aren't cookies meant to be tough?' I said lightly, shooting him a sarcastically sweet smile.

'Your brand certainly comes that way. Remind me never to ask you out for a night on the town.'

'I don't date married men.'

'You don't take any prisoners either. Your boyfriend must have a fireproof brain.'

'I don't have a boyfriend.'

'Surprise, surprise.'

The reason I didn't have a boyfriend was a simple one: at that juncture in my life, I was simply too busy. I had my job. I had my first apartment: a small studio, on a beautiful leafy corner of Greenwich Village called Bedford Street. Most of all, I had New York – and that was the best romance imaginable. Though I'd visited it regularly over the years, living there was another matter altogether – and there were times when I literally thought I had landed in a playground for adults. To someone raised within the sedate, conservative, meddlesome confines of Hartford, Connecticut, Manhattan was a heady revelation. To begin with, it was so amazingly anonymous. You could become quite invisible, and never feel as if anyone was looking over your shoulder in disapproving judgment (a favorite Hartford pastime). You could stay out all night. Or spend half a Saturday losing yourself in the eight miles' worth of books at the Strand Bookshop. Or hear Ezio Pinza sing the title role of *Don Giovanni* at the Met for fifty cents (if you were willing to stand). Or grab dinner at Lindy's at three a.m. Or get up at dawn on a Sunday, stroll over to the Lower East Side, buy fresh pickles from the barrel on Delancey Street, then fall into Katz's deli for the sort of pastrami-on-rye that bordered on a religious experience.

Or you could just walk – which I did endlessly, obsessively. Huge walks – from my apartment on

Bedford Street all the way north to Columbia University. Or across the Manhattan Bridge and up Flatbush Avenue to Park Slope. What I discovered during these walks was that New York was like a massive Victorian novel which forced you to work your way through its broad canvas and complicated sub-plots. Being an impatient sort of reader I found myself compulsively caught up in its narrative, wondering where it would bring me next.

The sense of freedom was extraordinary. I was no longer under parental supervision. I was paying my own way in life. I answered to nobody. And thanks to my brother Eric I had a direct entrée into Manhattan's more esoteric underside. He seemed to know every arcane resident of the city. Czech translators of medieval poetry. All-night jazz disc jockeys. Emigré German sculptors. Would-be composers who were writing atonal operas about Gawain . . . in short, the sort of people you would never meet in Hartford, Connecticut. There were also a lot of political types . . . most of whom were either teaching at assorted colleges around town, or writing for small left-wing journals, or running little charities that supplied clothes and food to 'our fraternal Soviet comrades, valiantly fighting the forces of fascism' . . . or words to that effect.

Naturally, Eric tried to get me interested in his brand of leftwing politics. But I simply wasn't interested. Do understand – I did respect Eric's passion for his cause. Just as I also respected (and agreed with) his hatred of social injustice, and economic inequality. But what I didn't agree with was the way his political friends treated their beliefs as a sort of lay religion – of which they were the high priests. Thank God he left the Party in '41. I'd met a few of his 'comrades' when I'd visited him in Manhattan during college – and, my God, talk about dogmatic people! They really thought that theirs was the true way, the only way . . . and they would not broach any dissenting views. Which is one of the many reasons why Eric got fed up with them and left.

At least none of his political friends ever asked me out . . . which was something of a relief. Because, by and large, they were such a grim, glum bunch.

'Don't you know any *funny* Communists?' I asked him one Sunday over a late lunch at Katz's deli.

'A "funny Communist" is an oxymoron,' he said.

'You're a funny Communist.'

'Keep your voice down,' he whispered.

'I really don't think J. Edgar Hoover has agents stationed in Katz's.'

'You never know. Anyway, I am an *ex*-Communist.'

'But you're still pretty hard left.'

'Left of center. A Henry Wallace Democrat.'

'Well, I promise you this: I'd never go out with a Communist.'

'On patriotic grounds?'

'No – on the grounds that he wouldn't be able to make me laugh.'

'Did Horace Cowett make you laugh?'

'Sometimes, yes.'

'How could anyone with the name of Horace Cowett make *anybody* laugh?'

Eric had a point – though, at least, Horace didn't look as preposterous as his name. He was tall and gangly, with thick black hair and horn-rimmed glasses. He favored tweed jackets and knit ties. At twenty he already resembled a tenured professor. He was quiet, bordering on shy, but intensely bright, and a terrific talker once he was comfortable with you. We met at a Haverford/Bryn Mawr mixer, and went out for all my senior year. My parents really thought he was a splendid catch – I had my doubts, although Horace had his virtues, especially when it came to talking about novels by Henry James or portraits by John Singer Sargent (his favorite writer, his favorite painter). Though he didn't exactly exude joie de vivre, I did like him . . . though not enough to let him take me to bed. Then again, Horace never tried very hard on that front. We'd both been brought up far too well.

But he still proposed marriage a month before graduation. When I broke it off with him a week later, he said,

'I hope you're not ending it because you simply don't want to commit to marriage now. Maybe, in a year or so, you'll change your mind.'

'I do know how I will feel about this matter a year from now. The same way I am feeling now. Because, quite simply, I don't want to marry you.'

He pursed his lips, and tried not to look wounded. He didn't succeed.

'I'm sorry,' I finally said.

'No need.'

'I didn't want to be so blunt.'

'You weren't.'

'Yes, I was.'

'No, really – you were just being . . . informative.'

'Informative? *Direct* is more like it.'

'I'd say . . . *instructive*.'

'Candid. Explicit. Frank. It doesn't really matter, does it?'

'Well, semantically speaking . . .'

Before this exchange, I'd had a few nervous little qualms about rejecting Horace's marriage proposal. After this exchange, all lingering doubts had been killed off. To my parents – and to many of my friends at Bryn Mawr – I had bucked convention by rejecting his offer. After all, he was such a safe bet. But I was certain I could meet someone with a little more sparkle and passion. And, at the age of twenty-two, I didn't want to buy myself a one-way ticket to *wifehood* without stopping to think about other options along the way.

And so, when I reached New York, the idea of finding a boyfriend was low on my list of priorities. Especially as I had so much to grapple with during that first year.

The family house was sold by Christmas – but almost all the proceeds went on Mother's medical bills and residential care. Eric and I greeted 1944 in a grubby hotel in Hartford, having rushed back on New Year's Eve afternoon when the nursing home called, saying that Mother had contracted a chest infection which had suddenly mutated into pneumonia. It was touch and go whether or not she'd pull through. By the time we'd reached Hartford, the doctors had stabilized her. We spent an hour at her bedside. She was deeply comatose, and stared up at her two children blankly. We both kissed her goodbye. As we'd missed the last train back to Manhattan, we checked into this slum of a hotel near the railway station. We spent the rest of the evening in the hotel bar, drinking bad Manhattans. At midnight, we sang 'Auld Lang Syne' with the bartender and a few forlorn traveling salesmen.

It was a grim start to the year. It got grimmer – as the next morning, just when we were checking out, a call came from the nursing home. I took it. It was from a staff doctor, on call that morning.

'Miss Smythe, I regret to inform you that your mother passed away half-an-hour ago.'

Oddly enough, I didn't feel an overwhelming rush of grief (that came a few days later). More a sense of numbness, as the thought sank in: my family now is Eric.

He was also caught off guard by the news. We took a cab to the nursing home. En route, he started to sob. I put my arms around him.

'She always hated New Year's Day,' he finally said.

The funeral was the next morning. Two neighbors and our father's secretary showed up at the church. After the cemetery, we took a taxi back to the railway station. On the train back to New York, Eric said, 'I'm certain that's the last time I'll ever set foot in Hartford.'

There wasn't much of an estate – just two insurance policies. We ended up with around five thousand dollars each – quite a bit of money in those days. Eric instantly quit his Theater Guild job, and took off for a year to Mexico and South America. His portable Remington came with him – as he was planning to spend twelve months writing a major new play and maybe gathering material for a *journal de voyage* about travels in Latin America. He said he wanted me to come along – but I certainly wasn't going to quit my job at *Life* after just seven months.

'But if you come with me, you'll be able to concentrate on writing fiction for a year,' he said.

'I'm learning a great deal at *Life*.'

'Learning what? How to write five-hundred-word articles about the Broadway première of *Bloomer Girl* or why chokers are this year's fashion accessory.'

'I was rather proud of those two pieces,' I said, 'even if they didn't give me a byline.'

'My point exactly. As that editor guy told you, you'll never be assigned the big stories – because they all go to the senior male writers on the staff. You want to write fiction. So, what's stopping you?

145

You have the money and the freedom. We could rent a hacienda in Mexico with the money we have between us . . . and both write all day, unencumbered.'

'It's a lovely dream,' I said, 'but I'm not going to leave New York having just arrived here. I'm not ready to be a full-time writer yet. I need to find my way first. And the job at *Life* will also give me some necessary seasoning.'

'God, you're far too sensible. And I suppose you're planning to do something ultra-practical with your five thousand dollars.'

'Government bonds.'

'S, *really*. You've turned into Little Miss Prudent.'

'Guilty as charged.'

So Eric disappeared south of the border, and I stayed on in Manhattan, working at *Life* by day and trying to write short stories by night. But the pressures of the day job – and the vicarious pleasures of Manhattan – kept me away from the Remington typewriter in my studio apartment. Every time I sat down at home to work, I found myself thinking: *I really don't have much to say, do I?* Or that same doubting voice in the back of my head would whisper: *There's a great double-feature at the RKO 58th Street:* Five Graves to Cairo *and* Air Force. Or a girlfriend would ring up, suggesting Saturday lunch at Schrafft's. Or I'd have to finish a story for *Life*. Or the bathroom needed cleaning. Or . . . I'd find one of the million excuses that would-be writers always find to dodge the tyranny of the desk.

Eventually I decided to stop fooling myself. So I moved my Remington off the dining table and into the closet. Then I wrote Eric a long letter, explaining why I was putting my writing ambitions on hold:

I've never traveled. I've never seen anywhere south of Washington, DC . . . let alone the world. I've never been in mortal danger. I've never known anyone who's gone to prison, or has been indicted by a federal grand jury. I've never worked in the slums, or in a soup kitchen. I've never hiked the Appalachian Trail, or climbed Mt Kathadin, or paddled across Saranac Lake in a canoe. I could have volunteered for the Red Cross and gone to war. I could have joined the WPA and taught school in the Dust Bowl. I could have done around a thousand more interesting things than I'm doing now – and, in the process, found something to write about.

Hell, E – I've never even fallen in love. So no wonder nothing happens when I sit down at the typewriter.

I sent the letter c/o Poste Restante, Zihuantanejo, DF, Mexico. Eric was temporarily living in this corner of the Mexican tropics, having rented a house on the beach. Seven weeks later, I received a reply – scribbled in dense tiny print on a post-card, date-marked Tegucigalpa, Honduras.

S,

What you're really saying in your letter is that, as yet, you don't think you have a story to tell. Believe me, everybody has a story to tell – because all life is narrative. But knowing that is probably of little comfort to somebody suffering from writer's block (a condition of which I have ongoing experience). The rule of the game is a simple one: if you want to write, you will write. And know this: if you want to fall in love, you will find someone to fall in love with. But take it from your older, battle-scarred brother: you should never set out to fall in love. Because those sort of romances always seem to end up as the stuff of cheap melodrama. Real love, on the other hand, sneaks up on you unawares . . . then gives you a kick in the head.

I should never have left Mexico. The best thing about Tegucigalpa is the bus out of Tegucigalpa. I'm heading south. Will write again when I've unpacked somewhere.

Love,
E

Over the course of the next ten months – as I worked hard at *Life* and spent every free moment roaming New York – I tried not to rue too much my stalled literary career. And I certainly met nobody with whom I felt like falling in love. But I did receive plenty of postcards from Eric, date-marked Belize,

San Jose, Panama City, Cartagena, and eventually Rio. He returned to New York in June of '45, dead broke. I had to lend him two hundred dollars to see him through his first month home, during which time he moved back into his apartment and scrambled for work.

'How'd you manage to run through all that money?' I asked him.

'Living the high life,' he said, sounding sheepish.

'But I thought the high life was against all your political principles.'

'It was. It *is*.'

'So what happened?'

'I blame it all on too much sun. It turned me into a very generous, very dumb *loco gringo*. But I promise to resume wearing a hairshirt immediately.'

Instead, he landed a job writing a few episodes of *Boston Blackie*. When he was fired off of that show, he talked his way on to *The Quiz Bang Show*, churning out gags for Joe E. Brown. He never mentioned the play he was supposed to be writing during his year away – and I never asked. His silence said it all.

But he dropped right back into his wide circle of arty friends. And on the night before Thanksgiving of '45, he threw a party for all of them.

I had already been invited to an annual soiree given by one of *Life*'s senior editors. He lived on West 77th St between Central Park West and Columbus – the street where the balloons for next

149

morning's Macy's Thanksgiving Parade were being inflated. I promised Eric that I would drop by his bash on my way home. But the editor's party ran late. Thanks to the Macy's balloons (and the crowds who had come out to watch them being pumped up), all the streets around Central Park West were closed, so it took over half an hour to find a cab. It was now midnight. I was dead tired. I told the driver to take me to Bedford Street. As soon as I walked into my apartment, the phone rang. It was Eric. In the background I could hear his party in full swing.

'Where the hell have you been?' he asked.

'Playing office politics on Central Park West.'

'Well, get over here now. As you can hear, the joint is jumping.'

'I think I'll pass, E. I need to sleep for a week.'

'You have the rest of the weekend to do that.'

'Please let me disappoint you tonight.'

'No. I insist you hop a fast cab, and present yourself *tout de suite* at *chez moi*, ready to drink 'til dawn. Hell, it's the first Thanksgiving in years without a war. Surely that's a good enough excuse to destroy some brain cells . . .'

I sighed loudly, then said,

'Will you provide the aspirin tomorrow?'

'You have my word as a patriotic American.'

So I reluctantly put my coat back on, headed downstairs, hailed a cab, and within five minutes, found myself smack dab in the middle of Eric's party. The place was packed. There was loud dance music on the Victrola. A low cloud of cigarette smoke bathed his tiny apartment in a fuggy haze. Someone pushed a bottle of beer into my hand. I turned around. And that's when I saw him. A fellow around twenty-five, dressed in a dark khaki Army uniform, with a narrow face with sharply etched cheekbones. His eyes were also scanning the room. They suddenly happened upon me. I met his gaze. Only for a second. Or maybe two. He looked at me. I looked at him. He smiled. I smiled back. He turned away. And that was it. Just a simple glance.

I shouldn't have been there. I should have been home, fast asleep. And I've often wondered: had I not turned around at that very moment, would we have missed each other completely?

Fate is such an accidental thing, isn't it?

CHAPTER 2

The front door suddenly flew open. Ten more folk tumbled into the apartment. They were all very loud, very boisterous, and very well lubricated. The room was now so crowded it was impossible to move. I still couldn't see my brother – and was beginning to get a little cross about being talked into coming to this absurd party. I loved Eric's friends, but not en masse. Eric knew this – and often teased me about being anti-social.

'I'm not anti-social,' I'd retort. 'I'm just anti-crowds.'

Especially – I could have added – crowds in tiny apartments. My brother, on the other hand, adored mob scenes, and being part of a pack. He always had tons of friends. A quiet night at home was never pondered. He had to be meeting pals at bars, or finding a party to crash, or hitting jazz joints, or (at the very worst) squandering the evening in one of those all-night movie houses that lined 42nd Street – and showed triple features for twenty-five cents. Since his return from South America, his talent for gregariousness had reached new heights – to the point where I was beginning to wonder if he was ever finding time to sleep. He'd also reluctantly changed his appearance to get that job as a gag writer for Joe E. Brown. He'd trimmed his hair and stopped dressing like Trotsky – because he knew he wouldn't be hired unless he conformed to the buttoned-down sartorial norm that was demanded back then.

'I bet Father's rolling with laughter in his grave,' he said to me late one evening, 'knowing that his redder-than-Red son now buys his clothes at Brooks Brothers.'

'Clothes mean nothing,' I said.

'Stop trying to sweeten the pill. They mean *every-thing*. Everyone who knows me understands what these clothes mean: *I've failed.*'

'You're not a failure.'

'Anyone who starts off thinking he's the next Bertolt Brecht – but finally ends up churning out jokes for a quiz show – is allowed to call himself a failure.'

'You'll write another great play,' I said.

He smiled sadly.

'S – I've never written a *great* play. You know that. I've never even written a *good* play. And you know that too.'

Yes, I did know that – though I would never have said so. Just as I also knew that Eric's increasingly manic social life was a form of anaesthetic. It deadened the ache of disappointment. I knew he was blocked. And I also knew what was causing the block: a total collapse of confidence in his talent. But Eric refused to let me sympathize with him – always changing the subject whenever I brought it up. I finally took the hint and dropped the matter completely – ruing the fact that I couldn't get him to talk about his obvious distress, and feeling rather helpless as I watched him obsessively fill every waking moment with a binge of diversions . . . of which this party was yet another syndrome.

As the noise level in his living room reached the level of uproar, I quickly decided to make an exit if I didn't see my brother in the next sixty seconds.

Then I felt a hand lightly touch my shoulder, and heard a male voice in my ear.

'You look like someone who's looking for an escape hatch.'

I spun around. It was the fellow in the Army uniform. He was standing inches away from me, a glass of something in one hand, a bottle of beer in the other. Up close, he looked even more damn Irish. It was something about the ruddiness of his skin, the squareness of his jaw, the touch of mischief in his eyes, the fallen angel face which hinted at both innocence and experience. He was a less pugnacious version of Jimmy Cagney. Had he been an actor, he would have been perfect casting as the sort of idealistic young neighborhood priest who gave Cagney last rites after some rival gangster peppered him with lead.

'Did you hear me the first time?' he shouted over the roar of the party. 'You look like someone who's looking for an escape hatch.'

'Yes, I did hear you. And yes, you're very perceptive,' I said.

'And you're blushing.'

I suddenly felt my cheeks redden a little more. 'It must be the heat in here.'

'Or the fact that I am the most handsome guy you've ever seen.'

I looked at him with care, and noted that he was raising his eyebrows playfully.

'You're handsome, all right . . . but not drop-dead handsome.'

He studied me admiringly for a moment, then said, 'Nice counterpunch. Didn't I see you fight Max Schelling at the Garden?'

'Would you be talking about the Bronx Botanical Gardens?'

'Your name wouldn't happen to be Dorothy Parker, would it?'

'Flattery will get you nowhere, soldier.'

'Then I'll have to try getting you drunk,' he said, pushing a bottle into my empty hand. 'Have a beer,' he said.

'I already have a beer,' I said, raising the bottle of Schlitz in my other hand.

'A two-fisted drinker. I like that. You also wouldn't happen to be Irish, would you?'

'I'm afraid not.'

'Surprise, surprise. I was certain you were an

O'Sullivan from Limerick . . . and not some horsey Kate Hepburn type . . .'

'I don't ride horses,' I said, interrupting him.

'But you're still a WASP, right?'

I scowled at him.

'That's a WASP smile, right?'

I tried not to laugh. I failed.

'Hey! She has a sense of humor. I thought that didn't come with the WASP package.'

'There are always exceptions to the rule.'

'Delighted to hear it. So . . . are we getting out of here?'

'Sorry?'

'You said you were looking for a way out of here. I'm offering you one. With me.'

'But why should I go with you?'

'Because you find me funny, charming, absorbing, alluring, appealing . . .'

'No, I don't.'

'Liar. Anyway, here's another reason why you should leave with me. Because we've clicked.'

'Says who?'

'Says me. And says you.'

'I've said nothing.'

I heard myself saying, 'I don't even know you.'

'Does that matter?'

Of course it didn't. Because I was already smitten. But I certainly wasn't going to let on just how smitten I was.

'A name might help,' I said.

'Jack Malone. Or Sergeant Jack Malone, if you want to get official about it.'

'And where are you from, Sergeant?'

'A paradise, a Valhalla, a place where White Anglo-Saxon Protestants fear to tread . . .'

'Known as?'

'Brooklyn. Flatbush, to be exact.'

'I don't know Flatbush.'

'See! My point exactly. When it comes to WASPs, Brooklyn has always been a no-go zone.'

'Well, I have been to Brooklyn Heights.'

'But have you been to the Depths?'

'Is that where you're bringing me tonight?'

His face brightened.

'Game, set, match *already*?'

'I never concede that easily. Especially when the opponent in question has forgotten to ask me my name.'

'Whoops!'

'So go on – pop the question.'

'Vat ist your name?' he asked in a mock German accent.

I told him. He pursed his lips.

'That's Smythe with a *y* and an *e*?'

'I am impressed.'

'Oh, we're taught how to spell in Brooklyn. *Smythe* . . .'

He rolled the name around on his tongue, pronouncing it again in an arch English accent.

'*Smythe* . . . I bet you anything that, once upon a time, it was good old plain *Smith*. But then one of your hoity-toity New England forebears decided it was far too common, so he changed it to *Smythe* . . .'

'How do you know I'm from New England?'

'You've got to be kidding. And if I was a betting man, I'd put a ten-spot on the fact that you probably spell Sara without an *h*.'

'And you'd win the bet.'

'I told you I was a sharp cookie. *Sara*. Very pretty . . . if you like New England Puritans.'

I heard Eric's voice behind me.

'You mean, like me?'

'And who the hell are you?' Jack asked, sounding a little annoyed at having our banter interrupted.

'I'm her puritanical brother,' Eric said, putting his arm around my shoulder. 'More to the point: who the hell are you?'

'I'm Ulysses S. Grant.'

'Very funny,' Eric said.

'Does it matter who I am?'

'I just don't remember inviting you to this party, that's all,' Eric said, all smiles.

'This is your place?' Jack asked pleasantly, without a hint of embarrassment.

'Excellent deduction, Dr Watson,' Eric said. 'Mind telling me how you ended up here?'

'A guy I met at the USO club near Times Square told me he had this friend who had a friend who had another friend who knew of this bash on Sullivan Street. But listen, I don't want to make any trouble, so I'll leave now, if that's okay.'

'Why should you leave?' I said so quickly that Eric gave me a questioning, wry smile.

'Yes,' Eric said, 'why should you leave when certain people obviously want you to stay.'

'You sure you don't mind?'

'Any friend of Sara's . . .'

'I really appreciate it.'

'Where were you serving?'

'Germany. And I wasn't serving exactly. I was reporting.'

'For *Stars and Stripes*?' Eric asked, mentioning the official newspaper of the United States Army.

'How did you *ever* guess?' Jack Malone asked.

'I think the uniform tipped me off. Whereabouts were you stationed?'

'England for a while. Then, after the Nazi surrender, I was in Munich. Or, at least, what was left of Munich.'

'Did you ever get to the Eastern Front?'

'I write for *Stars and Stripes* . . . not the *Daily Worker.*'

'I'll have you know that I read the *Daily Worker* for ten years,' Eric said, sounding a little too self-important.

'Congratulations,' Jack said. 'I used to read the funnies every day as well.'

'I don't get the connection,' Eric said.

'We all outgrow the juvenile.'

'The *Daily Worker* is your idea of juvenilia?'

'*Badly written* juvenilia . . . like most propaganda sheets. I mean, if you're going to write a daily jeremiad on class warfare, at least write it well.'

'A *jeremiad*,' Eric said, sounding arch. 'My, my. We do know some big words, don't we?'

'Eric . . .' I said, glowering at him.

'Have I said something wrong?' he said, the words slightly slurred. That's when I realized he was drunk.

'Not wrong,' Jack said. 'Just *classist*. Then again, talking as an illiterate Brooklyn mick . . .'

'I never said that,' Eric said.

'No – you simply implied it. But, hey, I'm well used to *parvenus* making fun of my inelegant vowels.'

'We are hardly parvenus,' Eric said.

'But you are impressed with my command of French, *n'est-ce pas?*'

'Your accent could use some work.'

'Just like your sense of humor. Of course, speaking as one of your intellectual inferiors from the wrong side of the Manhattan Bridge, I always find it amusing that the biggest snobs in the world also happen to whistle the "Internationale" through their Ivy League teeth. Or maybe you read *Pravda* in the original Russian, comrade?'

'And I bet you're one of Father Coughlin's most devoted admirers.'

'Eric, for God's sake,' I said, appalled that he would make such an inflammatory comment – as Father Charles E. Coughlin was an infamous right-wing priest; a precursor of McCarthy who had a weekly radio broadcast, in which he hectored on

160

against communists and all foreigners and anyone who didn't bow down and kiss the flag. Anyone with an ounce of intelligence hated him. But I was relieved to see that this Jack Malone fellow wasn't rising to my brother's bait.

His voice still calm, he said, 'Consider yourself fortunate that I'm going to file that one away under *banter.*'

I nudged my brother with my elbow. 'Apologize,' I said.

After a moment's hesitation, Eric spoke.

'That was an inappropriate thing to say. I apologize.'

Instantly, Jack's face broke into a mild smile.

'Then we leave friends, right?' he asked.

'Uh . . . sure.'

'So . . . Happy Thanksgiving.'

Eric reluctantly took Jack's outstretched hand.

'Yes. Happy Thanksgiving.'

'And sorry for playing the gate-crasher,' Jack said.

'No need. Make yourself at home.'

With that, Eric beat a hasty retreat across the room. Jack turned to me.

'I kind of enjoyed that,' he said.

'*Really?*' I said.

'Damn right. I mean, the Army isn't exactly brimming with erudite types. And it's been a long time since I've been insulted in such a literate way.'

'I really do apologize. He can get awfully grand when he's had ten too many.'

'Like I said, it was fun. And I now know where

161

you get the hefty left hook. It's obviously a family specialty.'

'I never knew we came across as heavy hitters.'

'And you're just being modest. Anyway, Sara-without-an-h-Smythe . . . it's time for me to make an exit, as I have to report for duty at oh-nine-hundred tomorrow morning.'

'Then let's go,' I said.

'But I thought . . . ?'

'What?'

'I don't know. After the show I put on with your brother, you wouldn't want anything more to do with me.'

'You thought wrong. Unless, of course, you've changed your mind?'

'No, no . . . we're out of here.'

Taking me by the elbow, he led me towards the door. As we were halfway into the hall, I turned back and caught Eric's eye.

'You're leaving already?' he shouted over the din, looking appalled that I was being escorted off by Jack.

'Thanksgiving lunch tomorrow at Luchows?' I shouted back.

'If you ever get there,' he said.

'Believe me, she will,' Jack said, and we headed down the stairs. As soon as we reached the front door of the house, he pulled me towards him, and kissed me deeply. The kiss lasted a long time. When it was finished, I said,

'You didn't ask my permission to do that.'

'You're right. I didn't. May I kiss you, Sara-without-an-h?'

'Only if you drop that *without-an-h* line.'

'Done deal.'

This time the kiss seemed to last about an hour. When I finally broke it, my head was whirling like a roulette wheel. Jack also looked punch-drunk. He took my face in his hands.

'Hello there,' he said.

'Yes. Hello there.'

'You know I have to be at the Navy Yards . . .'

'You told me: by oh-nine-hundred sharp. But it's now, what? Just before one.'

'So, factor in travel time to Brooklyn, and we've got . . .'

'Seven hours.'

'Yeah – just seven hours.'

'It'll have to do,' I said, then kissed him again. 'Now buy me a drink somewhere.'

CHAPTER 3

We ended up at The Lion's Head on Sheridan Square. As it was Thanksgiving Eve, there wasn't much of a late-night crowd – which meant we could find a quiet table in an alcove. I drank two Manhattans quickly, and let myself be talked into a third. Jack threw back boilermakers: neat shots of bourbon, followed by steins of beer. The lights were always dimmed down low in The Lion's Head. There were candles on the tables. Ours had a flame that kept flicking back and forth, like an illuminated metronome. The glow repeatedly danced off Jack's face. I couldn't take my eyes off him. He was becoming more handsome by the second. Perhaps because – as I was also discovering – he was smart as hell. A great talker. Better yet, a great listener. And men are always ten times more attractive when they just listen.

He got me talking about myself. He seemed to want to know everything – about my parents, my childhood, my school days in Hartford, my time at Bryn Mawr, my job at *Life*, my thwarted literary ambitions, my brother Eric.

'Did he really read the *Daily Worker* for ten years?'

'I'm afraid so.'

'Is he a fellow traveler?'

'Well, he was a member of the Party for a couple of years. But that's when he was writing plays for the Federal Theater Project, and rebelling against everything he was brought up to be. And though I'd never tell him this, I really think the Party was nothing more than fashion to him. It was this year's color, or a certain style of suit that all his friends were wearing at a certain time . . . but one which he happily outgrew.'

'So he's no longer a member?'

'Not since forty-one.'

'That's something, I guess. But does he still sympathize with Uncle Joe?'

'Loss of faith doesn't always mean instant atheism, does it?'

He beamed at me. 'You really are a writer.'

'On the basis of one clever sentence? I don't think so.'

'I know it.'

'No, you don't – because you've never seen anything I've written.'

'Will you show me some stuff?'

'It's not very good.'

'O ye of little faith in yourself.'

'Oh, I have faith in myself. But not as a writer.'

'And what's the basis of that faith?'

'The basis?'

'Yes – as in, what do you believe in?'

165

'That's a big question.'

'Give it a shot.'

'Well, let's see . . .' I said, suddenly feeling expansive (courtesy of all those Manhattans). 'Right . . . first and foremost, I don't believe in God, or Jehovah, or Allah, or the Angel Moroni, or even Donald Duck.'

He laughed.

'Okay,' he said, 'we've got that one cleared up.'

'And, much as I love this damn country of ours, I really don't believe in wrapping yourself up in the flag. Rabid patriotism is like Bible-thumping: it scares me because it's so doctrinaire. Real patriotism is quiet, understated, thoughtful.'

'Especially if you're a New England WASP.'

I punched his arm. 'Will you stop that!'

'No, I won't. And you're still dodging the question.'

'That's because the question's far too big to answer . . . and I've had far too much to drink.'

'I'm not letting you off on a self-inflicted technicality like too much booze. State your case, Miss Smythe. What the hell do you believe in?'

After a moment's pause, I heard myself say, 'Responsibility.'

Jack appeared bemused. 'What did you just say?'

'Responsibility. You asked me what I believed in. I'm telling you: responsibility.'

'Oh, got it now,' he said with a smile. '*Responsibility*. Admirable concept. One of the cornerstones of our nation.'

'If you're a patriot.'

'I am.'

'Yeah, I figured that. And respect that. *Honestly.* But . . . how can I put this without sounding dumb? The responsibility I'm talking about, the responsibility which I actually believe in . . . well, I guess it all comes down to the responsibility you have to yourself. Because I really don't know much about life, and I haven't traveled or done anything really interesting . . . but when I look around me, and listen to my contemporaries talking, all I hear is stuff about how other people will work out life's problems for you. How getting married by the time you're twenty-three is a good thing, because you're suddenly relieved of the burden of making a living, or dealing with personal choice, or even spending time by yourself. Whereas I'm rather scared of the idea of entrusting my entire future to another person. Because, hell, aren't they as fallible as I am? And just as scared?'

I cut myself off. 'Am I ranting here?'

Jack threw back his shot of bourbon, and motioned to the bartender for more drinks. 'You're doing fine,' he said. 'Keep going.'

'Well, there's not a lot else to say, except that the moment you entrust your happiness to another person, you endanger the very possibility of happiness. Because you remove personal responsibility from the equation. You say to the other person, *make me feel whole, complete, wanted.* But the fact is: only you can make yourself feel whole or complete.'

He looked at me straight in the eye.

'So love is not a factor in this equation?'

I met his stare.

'Love shouldn't be about dependency, or *what you can do for me*, or *I need you/you need me*. Love should be about . . .'

I was suddenly at a loss for words. Jack threaded his fingers through mine.

'Love should be about love.'

'That'll do,' I said, then added, 'Kiss me.'

And he did.

'Now you've got to tell me something about yourself,' I said.

'Like what? My favorite color? My star sign? Whether I prefer Fitzgerald or Hemingway?'

'Well?'

'Fitzgerald any time.'

'I concur – but why?'

'It's an Irish thing.'

'Now it's you who's dodging the question.'

'There's not much to say about me. I'm just a guy from Brooklyn. That's about it.'

'You mean, there's *nothing* else about you I should know?'

'Not really.'

'Your parents might be a bit offended to hear you say that.'

'They're both dead.'

'I'm sorry.'

'Don't be. My mom died twelve years ago – just before my thirteenth birthday. An embolism. Very fast. Very nasty. And yeah, she was a saint . . . but I would say that.'

'And your father?'

'Dad went while I was overseas in the Army. He was a cop, and a professional hot-head who liked to pick arguments with everyone. Especially me. He also liked to drink. As in: a fifth of whiskey a day. Suicide on the installment plan. Eventually he got his wish. So did I – as I spent much of my childhood dodging his belt whenever he was drunk . . . which was all the time.'

'That must have been awful.'

He rubbed his thumb and forefinger together.

'This is the world's smallest violin.'

'So you're all alone in the world?'

'No, there's a kid sister, Meg. She's the real brains of the family: a senior now at Barnard. Full scholarship too. Pretty damn impressive for someone from a family of ignorant micks.'

'Didn't you go to college too?'

'No – I went to the *Brooklyn Eagle*. They took me on as a copy boy right after high school. And I was a junior reporter there by the time I enlisted. That's how I found my way on to *Stars and Stripes*. End of story.'

'Oh, come on. You're not going to stop there, are you?'

'I'm not that interesting.'

'I smell a whiff of false modesty – and I don't buy it. Everyone's got a story to tell. Even guys from Brooklyn.'

'You really want a long story?'

'Absolutely.'

'A war story?'

'If it's about you.'

He reached for his cigarettes, and lit one up.

'For the first two years of the war, I was behind a desk at the *Stars and Stripes* office in Washington. I begged for an overseas transfer. So they sent me to London – and a desk job covering stuff in Allied HQ. I kept screaming to be sent out into the field, but I was told I'd have to wait my turn. So I missed the Normandy landings, and the liberation of Paris, and the fall of Berlin, and us Yanks liberating Italy, and all those big sexy stories which went to the paper's senior writers – college guys mainly; all second lieutenants upwards. But, after a lot of wangling, I did get myself attached to the Seventh Army, as they marched into Munich. It was a real eye-opener. Because as soon as we arrived there, a battalion was dispatched to a village about eight miles outside of the city. I decided to go along for the ride. The village was called Dachau. The mission was a simple one: to liberate a penal camp there. The town of Dachau was actually rather sweet. It hadn't taken too many hits from our Air Force or the RAF, so the center of the village was pretty much intact. Nice gingerbready houses. Well-tended gardens. Clean streets. And then, this camp. Have you read anything about that camp?'

'Yes. I have.'

'I tell you, every member of the battalion went silent as soon as they'd marched through the gates. They'd expected to meet armed resistance from the camp guards – but the last of them had fled just twenty minutes before we showed up. And what they . . . *we* . . . found . . .'

He paused for a moment, as if censoring himself.

'What we found was . . . unspeakable. Because it defied description. Or comprehension. Or simple basic human reason. It was so *evil* – such an outrage – that it actually seemed unreal . . . to the point where even talking about it now almost cheapens it . . .

'Anyway, around an hour after we marched into the camp, the order came from Allied HQ to round up every adult resident of Dachau. The company's captain – a real hard-assed Southern boy named Dupree from New Orleans – gave the job to two sergeants. I'd only spent a few hours with this battalion, but had already reached the conclusion that Dupree was the world's biggest loudmouth – a graduate of The Citadel ('The Confederate West Point,' as he kept reminding us Yankees), and the original Mr Gung Ho. But after taking an inspection tour of Dachau, he was the color of chalk. And his voice just about made it to a whisper.

'"Take four men each," he told the sergeants, "and knock on every door of every house and shop in the village. Everyone over the age of sixteen – men *and* women, no exceptions – is to be ordered

171

into the street. Once you have rounded up every adult resident of Dachau, I want them marched up here in a perfectly ordered single line. Is that clear, gentlemen?'

'One sergeant raised his hand. Dupree nodded for him to speak.

'"Say they show any resistance, sir?" he asked.

'His eyes narrowed. "Make certain they don't, Davis – by whatever means necessary."

'But none of the good people of Dachau resisted the US Army. When our boys showed up at their front door, they all came out meekly – hands above or behind their heads, a few of the women gesturing wildly towards their children, pleading in a language they didn't understand . . . although it was pretty damn clear what they thought we might do. One young mother – she couldn't have been more than seventeen, with a tiny infant in her arms – saw my uniform and my gun, and literally fell at my feet, screaming in horror. I tried to reason with her, saying over and over again, "*We're not going to hurt you . . . we're not going to hurt you*" . . . but she was hysterical. Who could blame her? Eventually, an older woman in the line grabbed hold of her, slapped her hard on the face, then whispered fiercely into her ear. The young woman struggled to calm down – and clutching her baby to her chest, she joined the line, sobbing quietly. The older woman then looked towards me with fearful respect, giving me a submissive nod, as if to say: *She's under control now. Please don't do us harm.*

172

'*Harm you! Harm you!* I felt like shouting. *We're Americans. We're the good guys here. We are not you.*

'But I said nothing. I just curtly nodded back, and returned to my observer status.

'It took nearly an hour to round up every adult present in Dachau. There must have been over four hundred people in that line. As they began the slow march toward the camp, many of them began to weep. Because I'm certain they thought they were going to be shot.

'It was only a ten-minute walk from the middle of town to the gates of the camp. Ten minutes. Maybe half-a-mile at most. Ten minutes separating this cozy little village – where everything was neat and tidy and so damn manicured – from an atrocity. That's what made Dachau about ten times even more extraordinary and terrible: the knowledge that normal life was going on just a half-mile down the street.

'When we got to the gates of the camp, Captain Dupree was waiting for us.

'"What do you want us to do with the townspeople, sir?" Sergeant Davis asked him.

'"Just march them through the camp. The *entire* camp. That's the order from Allied Command – rumor has it, from Ike himself. They're to see *everything*. Spare 'em nothing."

'"And after they've seen the camp, sir?"

'"Let 'em go."

'They did as ordered. They marched those four hundred townspeople through every damn corner

173

of the camp. The barracks, with human waste piled up on the floors. The ovens. The dissecting tables. The mountain of bones and skulls piled up right near the crematorium. As they took them on this guided tour, the camp survivors – there must have been a couple of hundred of them – stood silently in the courtyard. Most of them were so emaciated they looked like the walking dead. I tell you, not one of the townspeople looked a survivor in the face. In fact, most of them kept their eyes fixed firmly on the ground. They were just as silent as the survivors.

'But then, this one guy lost it. He was a well-dressed, well-fed banker type. He must have been in his late fifties: good suit, well-polished shoes, gold watch in his vest pocket. Out of nowhere, he suddenly started to cry. Uncontrollably. The next thing we knew, he broke out of the line, and went staggering towards Captain Dupree. Immediately, two of our guys had their guns drawn. But Dupree waved them away. The banker type fell to his knees in front of the Captain, sobbing wildly. And he kept saying this one thing over and over again. He said it so much I remembered it:

'"*Ich habe nichts davon gewußt. . . . Ich habe nichts davon gewußt . . . Ich habe nichts davon gewußt.*"

'Dupree looked down at him, really puzzled. Then he called for Garrison – the translator who'd been assigned to our battalion. He was this shy, bookish type, who never looked directly at anyone. He stood by the Captain and stared wide-eyed at the weeping banker.

'"The hell is he saying, Garrison?" Dupree asked him. The banker's words were now so garbled that Garrison had to crouch down beside him.

'After a moment he stood up again.

'"Sir, he's saying – *I didn't know . . . I didn't know.*"

'Dupree's eyes went white. Then, suddenly, he reached down and pulled up the banker by the lapels of his suit, until they were face-to-face.

'"The fuck you didn't know," Dupree hissed at him, then spat in his face and pushed him away.

'The banker staggered back to the line. As the townspeople continued to be marched through the camp, I kept my eye on the guy. Never once did he try to wipe Dupree's spit off his face. Over and over again, he kept mumbling that phrase, *Ich habe nichts davon gewußt . . . Ich habe nichts davon gewußt.* A soldier standing near me said, "Listen to that kraut sonofabitch. He's gone off his rocker."

'But all I could think was: it sounds like an act of contrition. Or a Hail Mary. Or anything you say again and again to yourself, in an attempt to do penance, seek forgiveness, whatever. And I actually felt for the guy. Because I sensed what he was really saying was, *Yes, I knew what was going on in this camp. But I could do nothing about it. So I shut my eyes . . . and convinced myself that life in my village was as normal as ever.*'

He paused for a moment.

'I tell you, I don't think I'll ever shake the memory of that fat little man in a suit, saying *Ich habe nichts*

175

davon gewußt again and again and again. Because it was such a plea for forgiveness. And the basis of the plea was so frighteningly goddamn human: we all do what we have to do to get through the day.'

Jack reached for his cigarette. It was dead, so he fished out another Chesterfield and lit it up. After he took a puff, I pulled it out of his lips and took a long, deep drag.

'I didn't know you smoked,' he said.

'I don't. I dabble. Especially when I'm pensive.'

'You're feeling pensive?'

'You've given me a lot to think about.'

We fell silent for a moment, passing the cigarette back and forth between us.

'Did you forgive that German banker?' I finally asked.

'Forgive him? Hell, no. He deserved his guilt.'

'But you sympathized with his predicament, didn't you?'

'Sure, I sympathized. But I wouldn't have offered him absolution.'

'But say you had been him. Say you were the manager of the local bank, and you had a wife and kids and a nice secure life. But say you also knew that, just down the street from your nice little house, there was the slaughterhouse, in which innocent men, women and children were being butchered – all because your government had decided that they were enemies of the state. Would you have raised your voice in protest? Or would you have done what he did – keep your head down, get on with your life, pretend not to notice?'

Jack took a final drag on the cigarette, then stubbed it into the ashtray. 'You want an honest answer?' he asked.

'Of course.'

'Then the honest answer is: I don't know what I would have done.'

'That *is* an honest answer,' I said.

'Everyone talks about doing "the right thing", taking a stand, thinking about the so-called *greater good*. But talk like that is cheap. When we find ourselves on the front line – with flak coming at us – most of us decide we're not the heroic type. We duck.'

I stroked his cheek with my hand. 'So you wouldn't call yourself a hero?'

'Nah – a romantic.'

He kissed me deeply. When he ended it, I pulled him back towards me and whispered, 'Let's get out of here.'

He hesitated. I said, 'Is anything wrong?'

'I have to come clean on something,' he said. 'I'm not just going to the Brooklyn Navy Yards today.'

'Where are you going?'

'Europe.'

'Europe? But the war's over. Why are you going to Europe?'

'I volunteered . . .'

'*Volunteered?* There's no war to fight, so what's to volunteer for . . . ?'

'There may be no more war, but there's still a big US Army presence on the continent, helping handle stuff like refugees, bomb clearance, repatriation of POWs. And *Stars and Stripes* asked if I wanted to sign on to cover the postwar clean-up. In my case, it also meant instant promotion to the rank of lieutenant, not to mention another stint overseas. So . . .'

'And how long is this additional tour of duty?'

He lowered his eyes, avoiding mine.

'Nine months.'

I said nothing . . . even though nine months suddenly seemed like an epoch.

'When did you sign up for this tour?' I asked quietly.

'Two days ago.'

Oh God, no . . .

'Just my luck,' I said.

'Just my luck too.'

He kissed me again. Then whispered, 'I'd better say goodbye then.'

I felt my heart miss a beat . . . or three. For a moment I found myself wondering what sort of madness I was getting myself into. But that moment vanished. All I could think was: *this is it.*

'No,' I said. 'Don't say goodbye. Not yet anyway. Not until oh-nine-hundred.'

'Are you sure?'

'Yes. I'm sure.'

It was only a five-minute walk from Sheridan Square to my apartment on Bedford Street. We said nothing en route, just silently clutching on to each other as we negotiated the empty city streets. We said nothing as we climbed the stairs. I opened the door. We stepped inside. I didn't offer him a drink or coffee. He didn't ask. He didn't look around. He didn't make admiring noises about the apartment. There was no nervous small talk. Because, for the moment, there was nothing more either of us wanted to say. And because – as soon as the door shut behind us – we began to pull each other's clothes off.

He never asked me if it was my first time. He was just so exceptionally gentle. And passionate. And a little clumsy . . . though hardly as clumsy as me.

Afterwards, he was a little aloof. Almost shy. As if he had revealed too much.

I lay against him, amidst the now tangled, damp sheets. My arms were entwined around his chest. I let my lips linger on the nape of his neck. Then, for the first time in around an hour, I spoke.

'I'm never allowing you out of this bed.'

'Is that a promise?' he asked.

'Worse,' I said. 'It's a vow.'

'Now that *is* serious.'

'Love is a serious business, Mr Malone.'

He turned around and faced me.

'Is that a declaration of sorts, Miss Smythe?'

'Yes, Mr Malone. It is a declaration. My cards are – as they say – on the table. Does that scare you?'

'On the contrary . . . I'm not going to let *you* out of this bed.'

'Is that a promise?'

'For the next four hours, yes.'

'And then?'

'And then, once again, I become the property of the United States Army – who, for the time being, dictate the course of my life.'

'Even in matters of love?'

'No – love is the one area over which they have no control.'

We fell silent again. 'I will come back,' he finally said.

'I know that,' I said. 'If you survived the war, you'll definitely survive the peace over there. The thing is: will you come back for *me*?'

As soon as I uttered that sentence, I hated myself for saying it.

'Will you listen to me,' I said. 'I sound like I have some sort of proprietorial hold on you. I'm sorry – I'm being deeply silly.'

He held me tighter. 'You're not being deeply silly,' he said. 'Just *nominally* silly.'

'Don't you make light of this, Brooklyn boy,' I said, gently poking him in the chest with my finger. 'I don't give up my heart that easily.'

'Of that I am absolutely certain,' he said, kissing my face. 'And, believe it or not, nor do I.'

'There's not a girl stashed away over in Brooklyn?'

'Nope. Promise.'

'Or some Fräulein waiting for you in Munich?'

'There is no one.'

'Well, I'm sure you'll still find Europe very romantic . . .'

Silence. I felt like kicking myself for sounding so astringent. Jack smiled at me.

'Sara . . .'

'I know, I know. It's just . . . Damn it, it's not fair, you going away tomorrow.'

'Listen, had I met you two days ago, I would never have volunteered for this tour . . .'

'But we didn't meet two days ago. We met tonight. And now . . .'

'We're talking nine months, no more. September first, nineteen forty-six – I'm home.'

'But will you come looking for me?'

'Sara, I'm planning to write you every day of those nine months . . .'

'Don't get too ambitious. Every other day will do.'

'If I want to write you every day, I'll write you every day.'

'Promise?'

'I promise,' he said. 'And will you be here when I get back?'

'You know I will.'

'You are wonderful, Miss Smythe.'

'Ditto, Mr Malone.'

I pushed him down against the mattress, then climbed on top of him. This time, we were less shy, less clumsy. And totally unbridled. Even though I was scared to death. Because I'd just lost my heart to a stranger . . . who was about to vanish across the ocean for nine months. No matter how hard I tried to avoid it, this was going to hurt.

Night ended. Light seeped in through the blinds. I peered at the bedside clock. Seven forty. Instinctively I clutched him closer to me.

'I've decided something,' I said.

'What?'

'To keep you prisoner here for the next nine months.'

'And then, when you release me, the Army can keep me prisoner in some brig for the next two years.'

'At least I'd have you to myself for nine straight months.'

'Nine months from now, you'll have me to yourself for as long as you want me.'

'I want to believe that.'

'Believe it.'

He got up and began to pick up his uniform off the floor. 'I'd better make tracks.'

'I'm coming with you to the Navy Yards,' I said.

'There's no need . . .'

'There's every need. It gives me another hour with you.'

He reached back and took my hand.

'It's a long subway ride,' he said. 'And it is Brooklyn.'

'You might just be worth the trip to Brooklyn,' I said.

We dressed. I filled my little tin percolator with

Maxwell House and put it on the stove. When brown liquid began to splash upwards into its dome, I poured out two cups. We raised one each, clinking them together, but said nothing. The coffee tasted weak, anaemic. It only took a minute or two to slurp it down. Jack looked at me.

'It's time,' he said.

We left the apartment. Thanksgiving morning 1945 was cold and bright. Far too bright for two people who'd been up all night. We squinted all the way to Sheridan Square station. The train to Brooklyn was deserted. As we barreled through Lower Manhattan, we remained silent, clinging on to each other tightly. As we crossed under the East River, I said, 'I don't have your address.'

Jack pulled out two matchbooks from his pocket. He handed one to me. Then he dug out a pencil stub from the breast pocket of his uniform. Licking it, he opened his book of matches and scribbled a US Army postal address on the inside cover. He gave me the matches. I clutched them in one hand, then relieved him of the pencil and scribbled my address on the inside flap of my matchbook. When I handed it back to him, he instantly put it into his shirt pocket, buttoning the flap for safe keeping.

'Don't you dare lose that book of matches,' I said.

'They have just become my most prized possession. And you'll write me too?'

'Constantly.'

The train continued its headlong plunge under the river and through subterranean Brooklyn. When it jerked to a halt at Borough Hall, Jack said, 'We're here.'

We climbed back up into the Thanksgiving light, emerging right near a dockyards. It was a grim industrial landscape, with half-a-dozen naval frigates and troop ships berthed in a series of docks. They were all painted battleship grey. We were not the only couple approaching the gates of the Navy Yards. There must have been six or seven others, embracing against a lamp post, or whispering final declarations of love to each other, or just looking at each other.

'Looks like we've got company,' I said.

'That's the problem with Army life,' he said. 'There's never any privacy.'

We stopped walking. I turned him towards me.

'Let's get this over with, Jack.'

'You sound like Barbara Stanwyck – the original tough dame.'

'I think it's called – in war movie parlance – "trying to be brave".'

'There's no easy way to do this, is there?'

'No, there isn't. So kiss me. And tell me you love me.'

He kissed me. He told me he loved me. I whispered the same thing back to him. Then I yanked him by the lapels.

'One last thing,' I said. 'Don't you dare break my heart, Malone.'

I released him.

'Now go get on that ship,' I said.

'Aye-aye, sir.'

He turned and walked to the gates. I stood on the sidewalk, frozen to the spot, forcing myself to remain stoic, controlled, *sensible*. The guard at the gates swung them open. Jack spun around and shouted to me, 'September first.'

I bit down hard on my lip and shouted back: 'Yes. September first . . . without fail.'

He snapped to attention and executed a crisp salute. I managed a smile. Then he turned and marched into the Yards.

For a moment or two I couldn't move. I simply stared ahead, until Jack vanished from view. I felt as if I was in freefall – as if I had just walked into an empty elevator shaft. Eventually, I forced myself back to the subway station, down the stairs, and on to a Manhattan-bound train. One of the women at the Navy Yards gates sat opposite me in the same car. She couldn't have been more than eighteen. As soon as the train lurched out of the station, she fell apart, her heartbreak loud and unrestrained.

Being my father's daughter, I would never have dreamed of crying in public. Grief, affliction, heartache were all to be suffered in silence: that was the Smythe family rule. If you wanted to break down, you had to do it behind closed doors, in the privacy of your own room.

So I kept myself in check all the way back to Bedford Street. As soon as my apartment door closed behind me, I fell on the bed and let go.

I wept. And wept. And wept some more. All the time thinking: *you are a fool.*

CHAPTER 4

'You really want my opinion?' Eric asked me.
'Of course I do,' I said.
'My completely *honest* opinion.'
I nodded nervously.
'Okay then, here it is: you're an idiot.'
I gulped, reached for the bottle of wine, refilled my glass, and drank half of it in one go.
'Thank you, Eric,' I finally said.
'You asked me for an honest reaction, S.'
'Yes. That is true. And you certainly gave me one.'
I finished the glass of wine, reached again for the bottle (our second of the afternoon), and refilled my glass.
'Apologies for the bluntness, S,' he said. 'But it's still no excuse to hit the bottle.'
'Everyone occasionally deserves a glass or two more than usual. Especially when there's something to celebrate.'
Eric looked at me with amused scepticism.
'And what are we celebrating here?'
I raised my glass.
'Thanksgiving, of course.'

'Well, Happy Thanksgiving,' he said wryly, clinking his glass against mine.

'And I'll have you know that, on this Thanksgiving Day, I am happier than I ever have been. In fact, I am so damn happy I am delirious.'

'Yes, delirium is the operative word here.'

All right, I was feeling a little cockeyed. Not to mention emotionally overwhelmed, spent, and exhausted. Especially since, once I finally brought my crying under control, I only had an hour or so before I had to meet Eric at Luchows for Thanksgiving lunch. Which gave me no time to do anything restorative (like sleep). So I had a fast bath, heated up the remnants of the coffee I'd made earlier that morning, and tried not to cry when I saw the cup Jack drank from, sitting forlornly in the sink. Then, after I finished the pot of now-acidic coffee, I caught a taxi over to Luchows on 14th Street.

Luchows was a great New York institution: a vast German-American restaurant, which was allegedly modeled after the Hofbräuhaus in Munich – though, to me, it always looked like the extravagant interior of some Erich von Stroheim movie. Germanic art deco . . . and just a little over the top. I think it appealed to Eric's sense of the absurd. He also had a soft spot (as I did) for Luchows' schnitzels and wursts and *Frankenwein* . . . though the management deliberately stopped serving German-produced wine during the war.

I was a little late, so Eric was already seated at our table when I arrived. He was puffing away on a cigarette, buried in that morning's edition of the *New York Times*. He looked up as I approached, and seemed a little stunned.

'Oh my God,' he said melodramatically. 'Love at first sight.'

'It's not that obvious, is it?' I said, sitting down.

'Oh no . . . not at all. Your eyes are only redder than your lipstick, and you have that post-coital *glow* . . .'

'Shhh,' I hissed. 'People might hear you . . .'

'They don't need to hear me. One look at you, and they'd know in a minute. You've got it bad, haven't you?'

'Yes. I do.'

'And where, pray tell, is your uniformed Don Giovanni now?'

'On a troop ship, bound for Europe.'

'Oh, wonderful. So not only do we have love, we also have instant heartache. Perfect. Just perfect. Waiter! A bottle of something sparkling, please. We need urgent lubrication.'

Then he looked at me and said, 'Okay. I'm all ears. Tell me everything.'

Fool that I am, I did – and worked my way through nearly two bottles of wine in the process. I always told Eric everything. He was the person I was closest to in the world. He knew me better than anybody. Which is why I dreaded telling him about the night with Jack. Because I knew Eric had my best interests at heart. Which meant that I also knew how he'd interpret this story. Which, in turn, was one of the reasons I was drinking far too quickly and far too much.

'You really want my opinion?' Eric asked me when I finished.

'Of course I do,' I said.

'My completely *honest* opinion.'

That's when he told me I was an idiot. I drank a little more wine, and toasted Thanksgiving, and made that ludicrous comment about being deliriously happy.

'Yes, delirium is the operative word here,' Eric said.

'I know this all sounds mad. And I also know you think I'm acting like an adolescent . . .'

'This sort of thing makes everyone revert to being fifteen years old. Which makes it both wonderful and dangerous. Wonderful because . . . well, let's face it, there is nothing more blissfully confusing than really falling for someone.'

I decided to venture into tricky territory. 'Have you known that confusion?'

He reached for his cigarettes and matches. 'Yes. I have.'

'Often?'

'Hardly,' he said, lighting up. 'Just once or twice. And though, at first, it's exhilarating, the big danger is the hope that there might be a life beyond this initial intoxication. That's when you can really do yourself some damage.'

'Did you get hurt?'

'If, during the course of your life, you've fallen hard for someone, then you've undoubtedly been hurt.'

'Does it always work that way?'

He began to tap the table with his right index finger – a sure sign that he was feeling nervous.

'In my experience, yes – it does work that way.'

Then he looked up at me with an expression on his face which basically said, *don't ask me anymore.* So, yet again, that section of his life was ruled off-limits to me.

'I just don't want to see you get injured,' he said. 'Especially, as . . . uh . . . I presume it was the first time . . .'

I quickly nodded my head, then added, 'But say you felt so certain about this . . .'

'Excuse me for sounding pedantic, but certainty is an empirical concept. And empiricism, as you well know, isn't rooted in theory . . . but wholly in fact. For example, there is certainty that the sun will rise in the East and set in the West. Just as there is certainty that liquid will freeze below thirty-two degrees Fahrenheit, and that if you throw yourself out a high window, you will land on the ground. But there's no certainty that you will be killed from that fall. Probability, yes. Certainty? Who's to know? It's the same with love . . .'

'You're saying, love's like throwing yourself out a window?'

'Come to think of it, that's not a bad analogy.

Especially when it's a *coup de foudre*. You're having a relatively normal day, romance is about the last thing on your mind, you show up somewhere you didn't expect to be, there's this person on the other side of the room, and . . . *splat.*'

'Splat? What a charming word.'

'Well, that's always the end result of a free-fall. The initial plunge is totally intoxicating. But then, inevitably, you go *splat*. Otherwise known as: coming back down to earth.'

'But say . . . just say . . . that this was truly meant to be?'

'Once again, we're entering the realm of the non-empirical. You want to *believe* that this man is the love of your life – and that you were fated to meet. But all belief is theoretical. It's not grounded in fact, let alone logic. There's no empirical proof that this Jack Malone guy is the preordained man destined for you. Only the *hope* that he is. And in purely theoretical terms, hope is an even shakier concept than belief.'

I was about to reach for the wine bottle, but thought better of it.

'You really are a pedant, aren't you?' I said.

'When necessary. I am also your brother who loves you. Which is why I am counseling caution here.'

'You didn't like Jack.'

'That's not really the issue, S . . .'

'But had you liked him, you might not be so sceptical.'

'I met him for . . . what? . . . five minutes. We had an unfortunate exchange. End of story.'

'When you get to know him . . .'

'*When?*'

'He'll be back on September first.'

'Oh my God, listen to you . . .'

'He promised he'd be back. He swore . . .'

'S, have you lost all reason? Or judgment? From what you've told me, this guy sounds like a total fantasist . . . and something of an operator to boot. A classic Irish combination.'

'That's not fair . . .'

'Hear me out. He's on shore leave, right? He crashes my party. He meets you – probably the best educated, most elegant woman he's ever encountered. He turns on the blarney, the mick charm. Before you can say "hokum", he's telling you you're the girl of his dreams: *The one I knew was meant for me.* But, all the time, he knows that he can say these things without commitment – because, come nine a.m. this morning, he's out of here. And sweetheart, unless I've got this all wrong, you're not going to be hearing from him again.'

I said nothing for a very long time. I just stared down at the table. Eric tried to adopt a more comforting tone.

'At worst, chalk the whole thing up to experience. In some ways, him vanishing out of your life now is probably the best outcome. Because he will always be "that boy" with whom you had one wildly romantic evening. So the shine will never go off him. Whereas if you married the guy, you'd probably discover that he likes to cut his toenails in bed, or gargles too loudly, or clears his throat through his nostrils . . .'

'*Splat.* You've brought me back down to earth.'

'What else is a brother to do? Anyway, I bet you anything that after you get a really good night's sleep, a little perspective will sneak up on you.'

But it didn't. Oh yes, I did sleep wonderfully that night. Nearly ten hours. But when I woke late the next morning, I was instantly consumed by thoughts of Jack. He took up residence in my mind within seconds of my eyes blinking open . . . and then refused to go away. I sat up in bed, and replayed – frame by frame – our entire night together. I had total recall – to the point where I could perfectly conjure up his voice, the contours of his face, his touch. Though I tried to heed my brother's advice – telling myself over and over that this was nothing more than a fanciful brief encounter – my arguments didn't sway me.

Or, to put it another way, I could see all the reasons why I should be sceptical and dubious about Jack Malone. The problem was: I didn't want to accept any of them.

That was the most unsettling aspect of all this – the way I refused to accede to logic, reason, good old New England common sense. I was like an attorney trying to contest a case she really didn't believe in. Whenever I thought I might just be on the verge of rational judgment, Jack would come flooding back into my mind again . . . and I'd be lost.

Was this, verily, love? In its most pure, undistilled form? I couldn't attach any other meaning to what I was feeling – except that it was as all-consuming, debilitating, and dizzying as a serious bout of flu.

The only problem was: unlike the flu, the fever wasn't breaking. If anything, it got worse with every passing day.

Jack Malone would not leave me be. The ache I felt for him was huge.

On the Sunday morning of Thanksgiving weekend, Eric phoned me at home. It was the first time we'd spoken since lunch at Luchows.

'Oh, hi there,' I said flatly.

'Oh dear . . .'

'Oh dear *what?*' I said, sounding cross.

'Oh dear, you don't sound pleased to hear from me.'

'I am pleased to hear from you.'

'Yes – and your exuberance is noted. I was just calling to see if the Gods of Balance and Proportion had landed on your shoulder?'

'No. They haven't. Anything else?'

'I detect a certain brusqueness to your tone. Want me to come over?'

'No!'

'Fine.'

Then I suddenly heard myself saying, 'Yes. Come over. *Now.*'

'It's that bad, is it?'

I swallowed hard. 'Yes – it's that bad.'

It got worse. My sleep began to fracture. Every night – somewhere between the hours of two and four – I'd snap awake. I'd stare up at the ceiling, feeling empty and full of the most overpowering sense of longing. There was nothing reasonable or clearheaded about this need I had for Jack Malone. It was just always there. Omnipresent. Irrational. Absurd.

I'd finally surrender to my insomnia, and get out of bed, and go to my desk and write Jack. I wrote him every day. Usually I'd restrict myself to a postcard – but I might spend up to an hour drafting and redrafting a five-line epistle on a legal pad.

I kept carbons of every letter I wrote Jack. Sometimes I would dig out the manila file in which I kept the copies, and read through this ever-expanding volume of lovesick missives. Whenever I closed the file, I'd always find myself thinking: *this is preposterous*.

After a few weeks, it became even more preposterous. Because I'd yet to receive one letter from Jack.

Initially, I tried to rationalize away the absence of news from my beloved. I would work out schedules in my head, figuring: it must have taken him nearly five days to reach Europe by ship, another couple of days to make his way to wherever he was being stationed in Germany, and then at least two weeks for his first letter to cross back the

Atlantic to me (this was, after all, well before the days of Air Mail). Factor in the strain put on the postal system during Christmas – and the fact that there were still hundreds of thousands of GIs stationed around the globe . . . and it was suddenly clear why I hadn't heard from him by Christmas.

But then the New Year arrived. And there was still no word from Jack . . . even though I continued to write him every day.

I waited. No response. January ebbed into February. I became obsessed with the daily delivery of mail to my apartment building. It would arrive in a bundle around ten thirty. It took the super-intendent around two hours to sort through it all, and place it outside each apartment door. I began to devise my work schedule at *Life* so I could get home by twelve thirty and collect my mail, then race back to the subway and return to my office by one fifteen (the end of my lunch hour). For two weeks I rigorously stuck to this routine, hoping against hope that, this day, the long-awaited letter from Jack would finally arrive.

But I kept returning to the office empty-handed. And feeling a little more bereft with each passing day. Especially as my sleeplessness was beginning to escalate.

One afternoon Leland McGuire stuck his head into the tiny cubicle where I worked.

'I am about to give you the plum assignment of the week,' he said.

'Oh, really,' I said, sounding a little distracted.

'What do you think about John Garfield?'

'Wonderful actor. Easy on the eye. Somewhat to the left politically . . .'

'Yes, well, regarding that last aspect, we'll want to play down the political stuff completely. I don't think Mr Luce would appreciate reading about Garfield's socialist ideologies in the pages of his magazine. Garfield's a hunk. Women like him. So I want you to play up his "brawny, but sensitive" side . . .'

'Sorry, Leland – I'm not following you here. Am I going to be writing something about John Garfield?'

'Not only are you going to be writing about Garfield – you're going to be interviewing him. He's in town, and he's agreed to give us an hour of his time. So be there at eleven thirty to watch an hour of the filming, then you'll get a chance to talk with him around twelve thirty.'

I suddenly felt a stab of panic. 'I can't do twelve thirty tomorrow.'

'Pardon?'

'I'm sorry, but I just can't do twelve thirty tomorrow.'

'You already have plans?'

I heard myself say, 'I'm expecting a letter . . .' God, how I instantly regretted uttering that sentence. Leland looked at me incredulously.

'You're expecting a letter? I don't quite understand what that has to do with meeting John Garfield at twelve thirty?'

197

'Nothing, Mr McGuire. Nothing. I'll be happy to do the interview.'

He regarded me warily.

'Are you sure about that, Sara?'

'Absolutely, sir.'

'Right then,' he said. 'I'll ask Garfield's press agent to call you after lunch, and give you a briefing. Unless, of course, you're busy after lunch, expecting a letter . . .'

I met his stare. 'I'll look forward to his call, sir.'

As soon as Leland left my cubicle, I careened down to the ladies' room, locked myself in a cubicle, and sobbed like a fool. Then I checked my watch. Twelve ten. I bolted out of the Ladies', out of the Time and Life building, then over to the subway. With several changes of train – and a quick dash from Sheridan Square – I made it to my apartment by twelve forty. There was no mail outside my door. Instantly I dashed down the stairs to the basement, and banged on the door of the super-intendent's apartment. His name was Mr Kocsis – a tiny Hungarian in his fifties (he couldn't have been more than 4'11", who always made a point of being surly . . . except around the holiday season, when he was expecting his annual Christmas tip. But this was mid-February, so he wasn't putting on the charm.

'What you want, Miss Smythe?' he said in brittle English after opening his door.

'My mail, Mr Kocsis.'

'You get no mail today.'

I suddenly felt jittery. 'That can't be true,' I said.
'Is true, is true.'
'Are you absolutely certain?'
'You say I lie?'
'There has to be a letter. There has to be . . .'
'If I tell you "no letter", it's "no letter". Hokay?'

He slammed the door on me. I made it back upstairs to my apartment, collapsed across the bed, and lay there staring at the ceiling . . . for what only seemed like a couple of minutes. After a while, I glanced at the clock by my bed. Two forty-eight. *Oh God, oh God*, I thought. *I am cracking up.*

I leapt off the bed, ran out of the apartment, and into the first available cab. I made it to the Time and Life building just after three fifteen. When I reached my cubicle, there were four pink 'While You Were Out' slips on my typewriter. The first three were all messages from a 'Mr Tommy Glick – press agent for John Garfield'. The times of the messages were one thirty, two, and two thirty. The final message – logged in at two fifty – was from Leland: 'Come to my office as soon as you're back.'

I sat down at my desk. I put my head in my hands. I had missed the press agent's calls. We had lost the interview with Garfield. And now I was about to be fired.

I knew this was going to happen. Now it *had* happened. I'd let irrationality triumph – and I was about to pay a huge price for it. Yet again, I heard my father's voice in my head: *There's no use crying*

*over a mistake, young lady. Simply accept the conse-
quences with dignity and grace – and learn from your
infraction.*

So I stood up, and smoothed out my hair, and
took a deep breath, and walked slowly down the
corridor, ready to face my punishment. I knocked
twice on the door. *Leland McGuire: Features Editor*
was stenciled on to the frosted glass.

'Come in,' he said.

As soon as I was halfway through the door, I
was already talking.

'Mr McGuire, I am so terribly sorry . . .'

'Please shut the door behind you, Sara, and sit
down.'

His tone was cool, detached. I did as ordered,
sitting in the hard wood chair facing his desk, my
hands neatly folded in my lap – like a recalcitrant
schoolgirl called into the headmistress's study. Only
in this instance, the authority figure sitting in judgment of me could destroy my livelihood, my career.

'Are you all right, Sara?' he asked.

'I'm fine, Mr McGuire. Just fine. If I could simply
explain . . .'

'You are not fine, Sara. In fact, you haven't been
fine for weeks, have you?'

'I cannot tell you how sorry I am about missing
Mr Glick's calls. But it's only three thirty. I can
ring him right back, and get all the info on
Garfield . . .'

Leland cut me off.

'I've reassigned the Garfield interview. Lois

Rudkin will be handling it. Do you know Lois?'

I nodded. Lois was a recent graduate of Mount Holyoke, who'd joined our department in September. She was also quite the ambitious young journalist. I knew she looked upon me as her direct inter-office competition . . . even though I refused to play those games (believing, perhaps foolishly, that good work would always win out). I realized what was coming next: Leland had decided that there was need for only one woman writer in Features, and Lois was that writer.

'Yes,' I said quietly, 'I know Lois.'

'Talented writer.'

Had I wanted to be fired on the spot, I could have said, And I've seen the charm offensive she's launched on you. Instead, I just nodded.

'Do you want to tell me what's going on, Sara?' he asked.

'Have you not been happy with my work, Mr McGuire?'

'I have no serious complaints. You write reasonably well. You are prompt. Barring today, you are basically reliable. But you also look exhausted all the time, and completely distracted – to the point where, work-wise, you appear to be just going through the motions. And I'm not the only one in the office who's noticed . . .'

'I see,' I said, sounding non-committal.

'Has something terrible happened?'

'No – nothing terrible.'

'Is it . . . a matter of the heart?'

201

'It could be.'

'You obviously don't want to talk about this . . .'

'I'm sorry . . .'

'Apologies are not necessary. Your private life is your private life. Until it begins to affect your working life. And though the old newspaperman in me rebels against the idea of company boosterism, my superiors at *Time and Life* believe that everyone who works here should be a "team player", with a real commitment to the magazine. And in your case, I'm afraid that you are widely regarded as somewhat remote – to the point where certain people also consider you haughty and patrician.'

This was news to me – and I was deeply distressed by it.

'I certainly do not try to be haughty, sir.'

'Perception is everything, Sara – especially within a company environment. And the perception among your colleagues at *Life* is that you'd rather be elsewhere.'

'Are you going to fire me, Mr McGuire?'

'I'm not that brutal, Sara. Nor have you done anything that merits the ax. At the same time, however, I would like you to consider working for us independently . . . from home, perhaps.'

Later that night – drinking rough red wine with Eric in his apartment – I filled my brother in on the remainder of my conversation with Leland McGuire.

'So after he dropped that bombshell about thinking I should work from home, he offered me his terms. He'd keep me on full salary for six months – for which I'd be required to write a story every two weeks. I would no longer be considered a *Time and Life* staffer – just a freelance, so I'd have no benefits.'

'Believe me, there are huge benefits in not having to go to an office in the morning.'

'That thought has crossed my mind. But I've also been wondering how I'd adjust to working on my own.'

'You've said you wanted to write fiction for a long time. Surely, this would now give you the chance . . .'

'I've given up on that idea. I'm not a writer . . .'

'You've just twenty-four years old. Don't dismiss yourself as a lost literary cause. Especially when you haven't really tried.'

'Well, there's a little problem with my fiction writing career: I can't get started.'

'You could sing that.'

'Very funny . . . But not only am I a failed writer; I am also – according to Leland McGuire – something of a failure as a team player.'

'Who wants to be a "team player"?'

'It's easier than being considered *haughty* or *detached* or *patrician*. I'm not really that patrician, am I?'

Eric laughed.

'Put it this way: you wouldn't be mistaken as a Brooklynite.'

I gave him a sour smile. 'Thanks for that.'

203

'I'm sorry. That was thoughtless.'

'Yes. It was.'

'Still no news from him?'

'You know I would have said something . . .'

'I know. And I haven't wanted to ask you . . .'

'Because . . . let me guess . . . you think I'm a romantic fathead – who's lost her heart to a rogue after just one night of dumb passion.'

'True – but I would actually thank your Brooklyn Irish rogue for forcing you out of *Time and Life*. Neither of us is a team player, S. Which means we'll always be outside of the mainstream. And, believe me, that's no bad thing . . . if you can handle that. So, consider this an opportunity to discover if you are your own best company. My hunch is: you'll really take to working by yourself. You have that *remote* temperament, after all.'

I punched him lightly in the shoulder.

'You are impossible,' I said.

'But you give me such wonderful opportunities to be impossible.'

I breathed a sad sigh.

'I'm not going to hear from him again, am I?'

'Reality finally dawns.'

'I keep wondering if . . . I don't know . . . maybe he had an accident, or was transferred to somewhere so remote that he can't be contacted.'

'Then again, he could be on a top-secret spying assignment with Mata Hari – even though the French took the liberty of shooting her in nineteen seventeen.'

'All right, all right.'

'Get over him, S. *Please*. For your own sake.'

'God knows I want to. It's just . . . he won't go away. Something happened that night. Something so inexplicable, yet fundamental. And though I keep trying to convince myself that it's all folly, I simply know: he was it.'

The next morning, I cleared out my desk at *Life*. I walked down the corridor and popped my head into Leland's office.

'I just came to say goodbye,' I said.

He didn't motion for me to come in or sit down, nor did he stand up. He seemed a bit nervous in my presence.

'Well, it's not really a goodbye, Sara. We'll still be working together.'

'Have you thought about my first freelance assignment?'

He avoided my eyes. 'Not yet – but I will be in touch within a couple of days to discuss a few things with you.'

'So I should expect a call from you?'

'Of course, of course – as soon as we've put this week's issue to bed. Meanwhile, you might as well enjoy a couple of days off.'

He reached for a pile of papers and went back to work. It was my cue to leave. So I collected the cardboard box on my desk which contained the meagre contents of my cubicle, then walked to the elevator. As the door opened, I felt a tap on my shoulder. It was Lorraine Tewksberry. She worked as a layout designer in the art department, and was the acknowledged office gossip. She was a tall, narrow woman in her thirties, with a beak-like face and bobbed black hair. She got on the elevator with me. As the door closed behind us, she leaned over and whispered into my ear (out of range of the uniformed elevator operator), 'Meet me at the Chock Full O'Nuts on Forty-sixth and Madison in five minutes.'

I looked at her quizzically. She merely winked, put her index finger to her lips, then hurried out of the elevator as soon as we reached the lobby.

I deposited my box with the concierge at the reception desk, and walked around the corner to Chock Full O'Nuts. Lorraine was seated at a booth in the back.

'This will just take a minute, because a minute's all I've got. It's production day.'

'Is something wrong?' I asked.

'Only from where you're sitting. I just want you to know that there are a lot of us on the magazine who are sorry to see you go.'

'That's surprising – considering that Mr McGuire told me everyone thought I was aloof and haughty.'

'Of course he'd tell you that – because from the moment you refused to go out with him, he had it in for you.'

'How did you know he asked me out?'

Lorraine cast her eyes heavenwards. 'It's not that big an office,' she said.

'But he only asked me out once . . . and I was rather polite about turning him down.'

'The fact is, though – you did turn him down. And since then, he's been looking for a way of getting rid of you.'

'All this happened almost two years ago.'

'He's just been waiting for you to slip up. And, sorry to say this, but you have seemed a little off-beam for the last couple of months. If you don't mind me asking, is it guy trouble?'

'I'm afraid so.'

'Get over him, honey. All men are jerks.'

'You may have a point.'

'Believe me, I am a world-class expert on this subject. I also know this: Leland won't be giving you a single assignment from now on. He set up this freelance idea for you as a way of easing you out of the office, and giving all the plum soft assignments to Miss Lois Rudkin . . . who, as you may have heard, isn't merely Leland's favorite writer of the moment, but also his occasional bedfellow.'

'I had wondered . . .'

'You wondered right. Because unlike you, the smarmy little Miss Rudkin did take up the very married Mr McGuire's offer of a date. From what I heard, one thing led to another, and now . . . shazam, you're out of a job.'

I swallowed hard. 'What should I do?'

'If you want my honest opinion . . . you should say nothing and do nothing. Just take Mr Luce's money for the next six months, and go write the

Great American Novel if you feel like it. Or move to Paris. Or take some classes. Or just sleep late until the paychecks stop. But know this: there's no way you're going to be writing anything for *Life* again. He's made sure of that. And in six months' time, he'll officially fire you.'

Some years later, I heard that, in Chinese, the symbol for the word 'crisis' has two meanings: danger and opportunity. I wish I'd known that at the time – because my initial reaction to Lorraine's news was one of utter panic, utter crisis. I picked up my office box from the concierge, I took a taxi downtown to my apartment, I slammed the door behind me, I sat down on my bed, I put my head in my hands, thinking that my world was completely falling apart. Yet again, I found myself mourning the loss of Jack – as if he had died. Because for all I knew, he was, indeed, dead.

The next morning, I made a trunk call to the Department of the Army in Washington, DC. The switchboard operator finally put me through to *Stars and Stripes*. I explained to a receptionist that I was trying to locate one of their journalists – a certain Sergeant John Joseph Malone, currently on assignment somewhere in Europe.

'We can't give out such information on the phone,' the woman said. 'You'll have to put your request in writing to the Department of Enlisted Personnel.'

'But surely, there aren't that many journalists named Jack Malone writing for you.'

'Army rules are Army rules.'

So I called the Department of Enlisted Personnel. A clerk gave me the address to write for a Search for Personnel form. Once they received the completed form back from me, I should expect a reply back from the Department within six to eight weeks.

'Six to eight weeks! Isn't there anything I can do to speed up the process?'

'Ma'am, there are still something like four hundred thousand men stationed overseas. These things take time.'

I sent off for the form that afternoon. I also had a brainstorm, and paid a visit to my local news stand, right near the Sheridan Square subway station. After explaining my problem, the guy who ran it said, 'Sure, I can get you *Stars and Stripes* starting tomorrow. But back issues? This I'm gonna have to work on.'

The next morning, I stopped by the news stand at nine in the morning.

'You're in luck,' the newsie told me. 'My distributor can get me a month's back copies. That's thirty copies in all.'

'I'll take them all.'

They arrived two days later. I scoured each edition. There wasn't one byline under the name of Jack Malone. I continued to pick up the daily edition of *Stars and Stripes*. Still no sign of a Jack Malone story. Maybe he didn't write under his own name, I told myself. Maybe he was on a top-secret special assignment, and wasn't having anything published just now. Maybe he'd been lying to me all along – and wasn't a journalist at all.

The search form from the Department of Enlisted Personnel arrived a week later. I mailed it back the next morning. As I returned to my apartment from the postbox, I stared at the small stack of mail on the mat outside my door. Surely, it would be romantic justice if a letter from Jack was in that pile.

It wasn't.

I tried to remain controlled. I tried to invent yet another rationalization for his lack of response. But all I could think was: *why can't you answer me?*

The next morning – despite another night of splintered sleep – I jumped out of bed, feeling deeply decisive. The moment had come to reclaim my self-respect and put this entire moonstruck episode behind me. What's more, I would take Lorraine and Eric's advice, and use the time to make a serious attempt at writing fiction.

And I would begin this morning.

I had a fast shower. I dressed. I brewed up a pot of coffee. I drank two cups. I sat down in front of my Remington. I rolled a blank sheet of paper into the machine. I took a deep breath, my fingers hovering over the keys. I exhaled. My fingers slipped down to the table. Inadvertently, they began to tap its flat surface. I took another deep breath, and forced my fingers back over the typewriter keys. That's when I suddenly felt myself seize up

– as if a nerve had been pinched in my back, throttling all movement in my fingers.

I shuddered. I tried to move my hands – to make them type a simple sentence. I couldn't get them to work. Eventually I managed to force them away from the keys. My fingers gripped the edges of the table-top tightly. I was in need of some sort of ballast, as I felt as if I was about to lose all sense of equilibrium. My head was whirling. I felt vertiginous, muddled, frightened. The next thing I knew, I was in the bathroom, getting ill. When the entire ghastly business was over, I forced myself up off the floor and to the phone. I called my brother.

'Eric,' I said in a near-whisper. 'I think I am in a spot of bother.'

In our family, going to the doctor was always considered a sign of weakness. Even admitting that you were unwell – or feeling a little fragile – was frowned upon. Resilience was considered a crucial virtue – a sign of fortitude and self-sufficiency. *Never complain* was another of my father's stoic principles – and one to which I still tried to adhere. Which is why Eric knew immediately that my *spot of bother* was an understated, but definite plea for help.

'I'll be right over,' he said, sounding worried.

He *was* right over. He must have dashed across the Village – because less than ten minutes after I called, he was knocking on the door of my apartment.

'It's open,' I said, my voice barely audible.

I was seated in front of the typewriter. My fingers continued to grip the side of the table. Because I felt that the table was the only thing keeping me steady right now.

'Good God, S,' Eric said, his face registering alarm, 'what's happened?'

'I don't know. I can't move.'

'You're paralyzed?'

'I just cannot move.'

He came over and touched my shoulders. It felt as if someone had goaded me with an electric cattle prod. I jumped, and let out a shrill cry, and gripped the table even tighter.

'Sorry, sorry,' Eric said, looking even more stunned by my response.

'Don't apologize. It's me who should be apologizing . . .'

'At least we know you're not physically paralyzed. Are you sure you can't get up?'

'I'm scared . . .' I whispered.

'That's pretty understandable. But let's just try to get you out of that chair and on to the bed. Okay?'

I said nothing. Eric came over and placed his hands on mine.

'Try to let go of the table, S.'

'I can't.'

'Yes. You can.'

'Please, Eric . . .'

He gripped my fingers. I resisted at first, but his

212

grip tightened. With one pull, he lifted my hands off the table. They fell heavily into my lap. I stared down at them, blankly.

'Good,' he said. 'That's a start. Now I'm going to lift you out of the chair and on to the bed.'

'Eric, I'm so sorry . . .'

'Shaddup,' he said, suddenly grabbing me around the back with one arm and under my knees with the other. Then, taking a deep breath, he lifted me straight up out of the chair.

'Thank God you haven't put on weight,' he said.

'Very unlikely, under the circumstances.'

'You're going to be fine. S. Here we go . . .'

With that he carried me the six steps from my desk to my bed. Lowering me on to the mattress, he walked over to my closet, found the spare blanket, and draped it over me. I suddenly felt chilled to the bone. I crossed my arms, clutching my shoulders. My teeth began to chatter. Eric picked up the phone, dialed a number, then spoke quietly into the receiver. When he hung up, he turned to me and said, 'I just spoke to Dr Ballensweig's nurse. He's got an hour free at lunchtime, so he's agreed to make a house call . . .'

'I don't need a doctor,' I said. 'I just need sleep.'

'You'll get some sleep. But you really need a doctor first.'

Eric had discovered Dr Ballensweig shortly after he graduated from Columbia. Since he swore by him, he also became my doctor when I moved to the city. We liked him because he was completely no-nonsense (the antithesis of Manhattan medical omnipotence), and because his slight stature, his hunched shoulders, and his quiet deadpan delivery put us both in mind of an old-style country GP.

He arrived at my apartment a few hours later. He was wearing an old worsted suit and half-moon glasses, and carried an ancient black medical bag. Eric let him in. He immediately approached the bed, sizing me up.

'Hello, Sara,' he said calmly. 'You look tired.'

'I am,' I managed to say in a near-whisper.

'You've also lost some weight. Any idea why?'

I clutched myself tighter.

'Are you cold?' he asked.

I nodded.

'And you find it difficult to move?'

I nodded again.

'That's fine. I just want to speak with your brother for a few minutes. Would you excuse us?'

He motioned for Eric to step outside the apartment with him. When he returned, he was alone.

'I've asked Eric to take a walk while I examine you.'

He opened his case. 'Now let's see what the problem is.'

He got me to sit up. It took some work. He used a pocket light to look into my eyes. He checked my ears, my nose, my throat. He took my pulse and blood pressure. He tested my reflexes. He asked me a long list of questions about my general health, my diet, my inability to sleep, and the seizure

214

that had me clutching the table for an hour. Then he pulled up a chair by the bed and sat down.

'Well, there's nothing physically wrong with you.'

'I see.'

'I could dispatch you to New York Hospital for a battery of neurological tests – but I think they would show nothing. Just as I could have you admitted to Bellevue for psychiatric observation. But, once again, I think it would prove clinically pointless, and deeply distressing for you. Because I sense that you have suffered a minor breakdown . . .'

I said nothing.

'It's less of a nervous-based breakdown, and more of a physical one – brought on by lack of sleep and serious emotional distress. Your brother did mention that you've been having a rather difficult time of it recently.'

'It's all just a silly business . . .'

'If it's brought you to this juncture, then it's certainly not silly . . .'

'I've just allowed things to get out of hand. A complete romantic over-reaction on my part.'

'We all over-react to those sort of things. Even the most level-headed people, like yourself. It's the nature of the condition.'

'What's the cure?'

He gave me a paternal smile. 'If I knew that, I'd probably be the richest doctor in America. But . . . you know what I'm going to tell you: there is no cure. Except, perhaps, time. Which, of course, is about the last thing someone in the throes of that condition wants to hear. In your case, however, I think rest is crucial. A very long rest. Preferably somewhere out of your normal surroundings. Eric told me you're on a leave-of-absence from work . . .'

'More like a permanent leave-of-absence, Doctor.'

'Then take the opportunity to go away. Not to another city – but some place where you can walk a great deal. The seashore always works. Believe me, in my book, a walk on a beach is worth five hours on a psychiatrist's couch . . . though I'm probably the only doctor in this city who would tell you that. Will you give serious consideration to leaving town for a while?'

I nodded.

'Good. Meanwhile – though I understand your wish to avoid sedatives – I am worried about your lack of sleep. And I want to give you an injection now that will knock you out for a while.'

'For how long?'

'Just until tomorrow morning.'

'That's a long time.'

'You need it. The world always looks a little more manageable after a long rest.'

He opened his bag.

'Now roll up your sleeve.'

I smelled the sharp medicinal scent of rubbing alcohol as he poured it on the cotton, then swabbed it on my arm. Then I felt the sharp prick of a hypodermic needle, and another swab of the cotton after the needle was withdrawn. I lay back down on the bed. Within a moment, the world blacked out.

When it came back into focus again, it was morning. First light was seeping through the blinds. My head felt murky – as if a gauze had been placed in front of my eyes. For a moment or two I didn't know where I was. Everything seemed fine with the world. Until thoughts of Jack came flooding back – and a residual sadness enveloped me again.

But, at least, I had slept. For what? I reached over to the wind-up alarm clock on my bedside table. Six fourteen. Good God, I had been out for almost eighteen hours. Just as the good doctor promised. No wonder I was feeling so fogged in. I managed to sit up in bed. The thought struck me: I can actually sit up. Now that's an improvement over yesterday. Then I realized I was under the covers, and in a nightgown. It didn't take too long to work out who had undressed me and tucked me in, as Eric was asleep on my sofa, curled up beneath a blanket, snoring sonorously. I lifted back the bedclothes and gently put my feet to the floor. Then, taking one careful step at a time, I managed to make it into the bathroom.

I ran a very hot bath. I took off my nightgown and slid into the steamy water. Gradually, the fog around my brain lifted. I sat in the tub for the better part of an hour, staring at the ceiling, steaming away the strange interlude that had been the last day. Eighteen hours of drugged dormancy hadn't suddenly calmed my jagged nerves overnight.

I still felt an intense sense of loss – not just for Jack, but for the job I had failed to keep. But Dr Ballensweig was right: the world did seem more tangible after an extended period of unconsciousness. And I was simply grateful to be functioning normally again.

Eventually I forced myself out of the bath. I dried myself off. I wrapped my hair in a towel. I put on a bathrobe. I opened the door as quietly as possible. But as I started tiptoeing back towards my bed, I heard the sharp crack of a Zippo lighter being closed. Eric was propped up on the sofa, puffing away on the first cigarette of the morning.

'So . . . the dead do walk,' he said with a sleepy smile.

'Eric, you really didn't have to spend the night . . .'

'Of course I did. I certainly wasn't going to leave you alone after yesterday.'

'I am so sorry.'

'For what? As breakdowns go, yours was about as genteel as they get. Especially as it all happened out of public view.'

'I still feel so ashamed . . .'

'Why? Because things overwhelmed you? Because, for one day, you couldn't cope? Give yourself a break, S . . . and make us some coffee.'

'Of course, of course,' I said, going over to the kitchen area and turning on the hotplate.

'You were really down for the count. After Doc Ballensweig gave you the needle, you didn't stir once. Getting you into bed was like undressing a rag doll. But you don't want to hear about that, do you?'

'No. I really don't.'

'I did leave you alone for around an hour, while I popped out to the pharmacy and got a prescription filled for you. The bottle's on your bedside table. Dr Ballensweig wants you to take two of those pills just before bedtime, to make certain you sleep through the night. Once your sleep begins to stabilize again, you can throw them away.'

'They're not sedatives, are they? I don't need sedatives.'

'They are sleeping pills. Which help you sleep. Which you desperately need if you want to avoid a repeat of yesterday. So, stop sounding like a convert to Christian Science . . .'

'Point taken,' I said, filling the percolator with ground coffee.

'There's another thing I did while you were sleeping. I called your boss at *Life* . . .'

'You did what?'

'I phoned Leland McGuire, and explained that you were unwell. And under doctor's orders to take a sabbatical from New York . . .'

'Oh my God, Eric – you shouldn't have done that.'

'Of course I should have. Otherwise you would have sat here for the next ten weeks, waiting for McGuire to phone you with a freelance assignment . . . even though whatshername, the office gossip, told you that wasn't going to happen. I mean, doctor's orders are doctor's orders. You need an extended rest in somewhere wild and wooly. Which is why you're going to Maine.'

I blinked with shock. 'I'm going to Maine?'

'Remember the cottage Mother and Father used to rent near Popham Beach?'

I certainly did. It was a small two-bedroom shingle cottage, located within a summer colony of houses which fronted one of the most expansive corners of the Maine coast. For ten consecutive summers, our parents rented this cottage for an annual two-week vacation in July. We knew the owners – a now-elderly couple in Hartford called the Daniels. When I was in a drug-induced trance yesterday, Eric had called Mr Daniels and explained that I was taking a leave of absence from *Life* to do some writing, and wanted to hole up in somewhere nice and quiet.

'Without me saying another word,' Eric explained, 'Old Man Daniels offered you the cottage on the spot – telling me how pleased and proud he was of the fact that you were a staff writer at *Life*.'

'If only he knew the truth.'

'Anyway, I asked him how much he wanted in rent. He almost sounded offended by the question. "I wouldn't dream of charging Biddy Smythe's daughter rent . . . especially in the off-season".'

'He actually called Father "Biddy"?' I said with a laugh.

'WASP informality is a wonder to behold, isn't it? Anyway, the cottage is yours free of charge . . . until the first of May if you like.'

'That's an awfully long time in an awfully isolated spot.'

'Try it for two weeks. If you don't like it – if it gets too lonely – come home. The only cost you'll have is the housekeeper. Her name's Mrs Reynolds. She lives locally. For five dollars, she'll come in twice a week to clean the place for you, and she also has a car, so she'll pick you up at the train station in Brunswick on Monday evening. I've booked you on the train leaving Penn Station at nine a.m. You get to Boston just before three, and change there for the train to Brunswick, which arrives at seven twenty that night. Mrs Reynolds will be waiting for you at the station.'

'You really have me organized, don't you?'

'It's called forcing your hand. You need this time off. Left to your own devices, you wouldn't take it.'

My brother was right. Had he not taken charge, I would have stayed in Manhattan, waiting for word from Jack, word from Leland, word from the Department of Enlisted Personnel. And waiting desperately for something that might not come is never good for one's well-being. So I let myself be talked into this retreat. I packed a trunk with old clothes and lots of books. Against Eric's protest, I insisted on lugging my Remington typewriter with me.

'You shouldn't even be thinking about trying to write,' he said.

'I'm just going to bring it along in case inspiration hits . . . though I'd say that's about as likely as an asteroid hitting Popham Beach.'

'Promise me you won't even think about writing for at least two weeks.'

I promised Eric that. I kept the promise. Because as soon as I reached Maine, I gave in to indolence. The cottage was pleasant, in a shabby genteel sort of way. It was also still suffering from late winter damp – but several days of constant wood-burning in the fireplace (coupled with the judicious use of two smelly, but effective kerosene heaters) dried it out and made it supremely cozy. I spent the days doing very little. After sleeping late, I might lounge all morning in bed with a novel, or collapse into the saggy, comfortable easy-chair by the fireplace, and leaf through ten years of *Saturday Night/Sunday Morning* back issues – which I discovered stacked inside a wooden chest that also served as a coffee table. At night, I might listen to the radio – especially if Toscanini and the NBC Symphony were playing – while reading into the early hours of the morning. Every time I got the urge to write Jack, I resisted it. My typewriter remained closed, and hidden from view in a closet in the bedroom.

But, of course, the centerpiece of every day was the long walk I took down Popham Beach.

The beach was three miles long. The summer

colony was at its most northerly end – a cluster of weatherbeaten clapboard and shingle houses, set back a good half-mile from the water's edge. The colony was the only hint of habitation in the area. Because once you walked out of its beach-front gates and turned right, all you could see was a vast open vista of sea, sky and pure white sand.

It was April – so the beach was totally deserted. It was also that seasonal interregnum between winter and spring, marked by hard blue skies and a bracing chill. I'd bundle up against the cold, step out on to the sand, and would immediately feel something close to exhilaration. The wind was sharp, the air briny, the horizon limitless. I'd walk the three miles to that extreme southerly point where the sand ended. Then I'd turn around and head for home. On average, this round trip would take me two hours. During the course of this hike, my mind would inevitably empty. Maybe it was the epic grandeur of the Maine coast. Maybe it was the sense of isolation, the primal force of wind and water, the total lack of another human voice. Whatever the reason, Dr Ballensweig was right. Walking a beach was a restorative act. The sadness I felt – the sense of loss – didn't suddenly evaporate. But gradually, a certain equilibrium returned. With it came the dissipation of the emotional fever that had vexed me for the past few months. No, I didn't suddenly feel wise, knowing and sage about the febrile foolishness of all-consuming love. Rather, I felt blessedly flat, tired, and pleased to be free of life's ongoing eventfulness. For the first juncture in my life, I was spending an extended period of time by myself – and I liked it.

I had no contact with anyone – except the housekeeper, Ruth Reynolds. She was a large, cheerful woman in her late thirties. Her husband, Roy, was a welder at the nearby Bath Iron Works, they had a gaggle of kids, and in between keeping her large family organized, she picked up a little extra money as caretaker of the half-dozen cottages at Popham Beach. I was the only resident in the colony at this time of year, so Ruth lavished attention on me. The cottage had a bicycle – which I'd occasionally use to get to the nearest shop (a hilly five-mile pedal down a back road). Most of the time, however, Ruth insisted on driving me to the town of Bath to get groceries. And every Thursday night, I had a standing invitation to eat dinner with her family.

Their house was around a mile down the road from the colony – a different world from the battered gentility of this patrician enclave. Ruth and Roy lived with their five children in a cramped, tumbledown three-bedroom Cape Codder. It needed a paint job – both inside and out. Roy – a big bear of a man, with biceps like the steel girders he spent the day welding – was friendly in a shy sort of way. Their kids – ranging in ages from seventeen to five – generated extraordinary amounts of spirited chaos, yet Ruth was a real master at keeping their collective domestic life in order.

Dinner was always at five thirty. The young kids were in bed by seven. The two teenage boys then huddled in front of the radio in the kitchen, listening to Buck Rogers or The Shadow. Roy would excuse himself to start his night shift at the Iron Works. Ruth would dig out a bottle of Christian Brothers Port from the breakfront, pour out two glasses, then sit opposite me in a big squishy armchair.

It became a weekly ritual, this Thursday dinner.

'You know why I like to have you over on Thursday nights?' Ruth said to me as we settled into our chairs and sipped the sweet sticky port. 'Because it's the only day of the week when Roy works the eight-to-four a.m. shift. Which means it's the only time I have the chance to sit down with a girlfriend and natter.'

'I'm glad you consider me a girlfriend.'

'Of course I do. And I tell you, I wish I could see more of you. But five kids and a house to run leaves me just about enough time every day to sleep six hours – and not much more.'

'Well, you'll be seeing a bit more of me, as I've decided to extend my stay at the cottage for a few more weeks.'

Ruth clinked her glass against mine.

'Glad you're sticking around for a while,' she said.

'Well, it's not as if anyone's desperate for my presence at *Life*.'

'You don't know that.'

'Yes, I do' – and I explained that, a few days

earlier, I telegrammed my boss, Leland McGuire, explaining that I wanted to remain on in Maine, but would return to New York instantly if a free-lance assignment came up. Twenty-four hours later came his reply, via Western Union:

We know where you are if we need you.
Stop. Leland.

'That's kind of a terse answer, isn't it?' Ruth said.

'But wholly expected. Around six months from now, I fully expect to be out of a job.'

'If I were you, I wouldn't be worried.'

'Why not?'

'Because you're obviously smart, and you've also got a lot of poise.'

'I'm hardly poised. If you only knew the mistakes I've made recently . . .'

'I bet they weren't really big mistakes.'

'Believe me, they were big. I let something fool-ishly overwhelm me.'

'Something?'

'No . . . someone.'

'I did wonder if that was the case . . .'

'Is it that obvious?'

'No one comes to Maine at this time of year unless they're really trying to put some distance between themselves and a problem.'

'It wasn't a problem. Just the height of foolish-ness. Especially as it lasted just one night. And like an idiot, I allowed myself to believe it was true love.'

'But if you *thought* that, then maybe it was.'

'Or maybe it was just pure fantasy on my part. Falling in love with love.'

'Where is he now?'

'In Europe – with the Army. I've written to him so many damn times . . . but so far, there's been no reply.'

'You know what you have to do, don't you?'

'Forget him, I suppose.'

'Oh, you'll never do that. He'll always be there – because he made such an impact on you.'

'So what do I do?'

'It's simple: tell yourself it wasn't meant to be.'

'You know what you have to do, don't you?' That sentence stuck with me – because it summed up one of life's ongoing dilemmas: how do you reconcile the head with the heart? My rational brain told me to accept the reality that Jack Malone had come and gone out of my life within twelve hours. My irrational heart said otherwise. What astounded me was how persuasive the heart could be – especially since, before that Thanksgiving night, I considered myself immune to all things illogical. But now . . .

Now I knew otherwise.

The morning after that talk with Ruth, I was up at dawn. I ate a light breakfast. I walked the beach. I was back in the cottage by nine. I put a pot of coffee on the stove. While it percolated, I went into the bedroom and removed my Remington typewriter from the closet. I hauled it over to the kitchen table. I removed its cover. A thin packet of typing paper was stored on the inside cover. I opened the packet, and fed a sheet of paper into the roller. The coffee pot began to jerk spasmodically back and forth on the stove. I turned down the flame and poured myself a thick black cup of steaming Chock Full O' Nuts. I set the cup next to the typewriter. I sat down. I blew on the coffee, then took a long, steadying sip. I put the cup down. I placed my fingers over the keys. They immediately clenched up into fists. I forced myself to unclench them. Before I could think further about it, I suddenly typed a sentence:

I hadn't planned to be at that party.

My hands left the keys. They ended up on the table, my fingers drumming its stripped pine surface as I read that sentence again and again. After a few minutes, I decided to try a second sentence.

I had planned to be elsewhere.

My fingers jumped away from the typewriter and continued their rat-a-tat hammering on the table-top. I sipped the coffee. I stared at the two sentences emblazoned on the otherwise empty page. I decided to risk a third sentence:

Because that was the night I had promised to treat myself to that rarest of Manhattan pleasures: eight unbroken hours in bed.

Three sentences. Thirty-six words. I read through them again. Punchy. Direct. A hint of wryness creeping into the last line. The language was simple, with no excess verbal baggage. Not a bad start. Not bad at all.

I reached for the coffee cup. I downed the remaining contents in one go. I went over to the stove and refilled the cup. I fought the momentary urge to run out the door. I forced myself back to the kitchen table. I sat down. My fingers recommenced their manic rat-a-tat drumming on the table.

Three sentences. Thirty-six words. A full double-spaced typed page usually contained around two hundred words.

Well, go on, finish the page. It's just another one hundred and sixty-four words. Hell, you wrote those thirty-six words in ten minutes. An additional one hundred and sixty-four words should only take you . . .

Four hours. That's how long it took. Four long, dreadful hours – during which time I ripped out five sheets of paper from the roller, drank another pot of coffee, paced the floor, chewed on a pencil, made notes in the margins, and eventually, *miraculously*, made it to the bottom of the damn page.

Later that night, after supper, I nursed a glass of red wine while re-reading what I had written. It flowed reasonably well. The voice seemed approachable (or, at least, not off-putting). Stylistically, it had a bit of bite (without sounding too smartypants for its own good). Most importantly, the narrative took off quickly. The story had momentum. It was a plausible start.

But it was only one page.

The next morning, I was up again at sunrise. A fast breakfast, a brisk hike down the beach, a pot of coffee on the stove, and I was sitting in front of the typewriter by eight thirty.

By noon, I had the second page written. Later that night – just before slipping into bed – I re-read my two finished pages. I excised around thirty extraneous words. I tightened up several descriptive passages. I rewrote an awkward sentence, and eliminated one clunker of a metaphor ('His eyes had the seductive glow of a Broadway marquee' . . . changing it to: 'He had bedroom eyes').

Then, before I could start having a crisis of confidence, I placed the pages face down on the desk.

Up again with the sun. Grapefruit, toast, coffee. The beach. More coffee. The desk.

And I remained at the desk until I finished that day's page.

A work pattern was emerging. My day now had a structure; a purpose. As long as I got a page written, I would feel as if something had been accomplished. Everyone talks about the heady creative pleasures of writing – everyone except those who've actually tried to do it. There's nothing heady about the process. It is a task. Like all tasks, it is only pleasurable in retrospect. You are relieved to have met your daily quota. You hope the work you did today is of a satisfactory nature. Because, come tomorrow, you have to blacken another page at the typewriter. Willfulness is required to get the job done. Willfulness . . . and a strange sense of confidence. As I was discovering, writing was a confidence trick you played on yourself.

A page a day, six days a week. After the second week of work, I sent a telegram to Eric:

> Have decided splendid isolation suits me. Stop. Will be here for another few weeks. Stop. Am doing some writing. Stop. Don't be horrified. Stop. It actually goes well. Stop. Please keep checking my mail for news from Europe or the Department of Enlisted Personnel. Stop. Love, S.

Forty-eight hours later, a Western Union man showed up at the door of the cottage, with Eric's reply:

> If you're happy doing something masochistic like writing, then this fellow masochist is happy for you. Stop. I've been checking your mail twice a week. Stop. Nothing from Europe or Washington. Stop. File him away under 'mirage' and move on. Stop. I hate Joe E. Brown. Stop. And I miss you.

For the first time in months, I didn't feel a sharp stab of sadness about Jack. More of a dull discomfort. *Tell yourself it wasn't meant to be.* And while you're at it, get that next page written.

Another week. Another six pages. As usual, I took Sunday off. I returned to work on Monday. Having spent the first three weeks eking out every page – spending an hour worrying about the construction of a sentence, or scrapping one hundred and fifty words right when I neared the end of a page – I started sprinting at the type-writer. I pounded out three pages on Monday, four on Tuesday. I was no longer obsessively worrying about form, structure, rhythm. I was simply running with the material. It had taken over. It was writing itself.

And then, at 4.02 p.m. (I glanced at my watch) on Wednesday afternoon, April 20th 1946, I came to a halt. For a moment or two, I simply sat bemused in my desk chair, staring at the half-blackened page in the typewriter. The realization dawned.

I had just finished my first short story.

Another few minutes passed. Then I forced myself up, grabbed my coat, and hiked down to the water's edge. I squatted down in the sand, and stared out at the metronomic rhythm of the Atlantic surf. I didn't know if the story was good or bad. My self-deprecating Smythe family instincts told me to accept the fact that it probably wasn't worthy of publication. But, at least, it was completed. And I would revel in that achievement – for a moment or two anyway.

The next morning, I sat down at the kitchen table and read through the twenty-four-page story.

It was called 'Shore Leave' – and, yes, it was a fictional reworking of the night I met Jack. Only in this instance, it was set in 1941, and the narrator was a thirty-year-old book publisher named Hannah: a single woman who has always been unlucky with men, and has started to write herself off as someone who will never bump into love. Until she meets Richard Ryan – a Navy lieutenant, on shore leave for one night in Manhattan before shipping out to the Pacific. They meet at a party, the attraction is instantaneous, they spend the night walking the city, they fall into each other's arms, they take a room for a couple of hours at a cheap hotel, there is a stoic goodbye at the Brooklyn Navy Yards, and though he promises his heart to her, Hannah knows that she'll never see him again. Because the timing is all wrong. He's off to war – and she senses that this night in Manhattan will soon be forgotten by him. So she's left with the knowledge that, having bumped into her destiny, she's lost him within twelve hours of finding him.

I spent the next three days editing the story, making certain that the language was spare and devoid of mawkishness. What was it that Puccini said to his librettist when they were working on *La Bohème*? 'Sentiment . . . but no sentimentality.' That's what I was striving for – a certain poignancy that didn't edge into schmaltz. On Sunday, using carbon paper, I typed two clean copies of the edited story. Late that night, I read it through for a final time. I really didn't know what to think of it. It seemed to move along, and evoke a certain bitter-sweet mood . . . but I was too close to the story to discern whether it was any damn good. So I took the top copy of 'Shore Leave', folded it in half, and placed it in a manila envelope, along with the following note:

Eric:
   Here it is – the first out of the bottle. And I want you to be dead honest with me about its lack of literary merit.
   Expect me in Manhattan in around ten days. Dinner on me at Luchows the night I'm back.
   Love,
   S

I cycled to the local post office the next morning, and paid an extra dollar to have this envelope sent Express to Eric's apartment. Then I used the post office phone for a trunk call to Boston. I spoke with a college friend – Marge Kennicott – who was working as a junior book editor at Houghton Mifflin, and living on Commonwealth Avenue. She seemed delighted by the idea of putting me up for a week or so ('. . . if you don't mind sleeping on the world's lumpiest sofa'). I told her to expect me in forty-eight hours. As soon as I hung up, I called the railway station in Brunswick, and reserved a seat on the train to Boston for Wednesday morning. Then I cycled over to Ruth's house and told her I was leaving in two days' time.

234

'I'm going to miss you,' she said. 'But you look ready to go back.'

'Do I really look cured?' I said with a laugh.

'Like I've told you before, you'll never be cured of him. But I bet you now see it for what it was.'

'Put it this way,' I said. 'I'll never let myself fall so hard again.'

'Someone will come along and change your mind about that.'

'I won't let them. Romance is a game for saps.'

I truly meant that. Because what so unnerved me about this entire episode was how it undermined all sense of control – to the point where I could think of little else but the object of my infatuation. In my short story, Hannah comes away from her night of accidental passion feeling bereft – but also with the realization that she can fall in love. I knew that now too . . . and it bothered me. Because what I now realized was that I hadn't really been in love with Jack Malone. I had been in love with the *idea* of Jack. I had been in love with love. And I vowed never to make such a misjudgment again.

I packed up my trunk and typewriter, and had them shipped on ahead of me to New York. I took a final walk on Popham Beach. Ruth insisted on driving me to the train station in Brunswick. We embraced on the platform.

'I'm going to expect a copy of whatever you've been writing when it gets published.'

'It'll never get published,' I said.

'Sara – one of these days you're going to actually start liking yourself.'

I spent a perfectly pleasant week in Boston. Marge Kennicott lived in a perfectly pleasant apartment in Back Bay. She had perfectly pleasant friends. She had a perfectly pleasant fiancé named George Stafford, Jr – who was the heir apparent in his family's stockbroking firm. As always, Boston was a perfectly pleasant city – pretty, snobbish, dull. I resisted all of Marge's attempts to fix me up with perfectly pleasant eligible bachelors. I said nothing about the events that had driven me to Maine for seven weeks. After seven days of austere Brahman gentility, I was longing for the jangled disorder and chaotic exuberance of Manhattan. So I was relieved when I finally boarded the train back to Penn Station.

The day before I left Boston, I'd phoned Eric at home. He said he was going to be at work when my train arrived, but would meet me at Luchows for dinner that night.

'Did you get the envelope I sent you?' I asked nervously.

'Oh yes,' he said.

'And?'

'I'll tell you when I see you.'

There was a huge pile of mail on the doormat outside my apartment. I sorted through it, expecting nothing from Jack. My expectations were met. But there was a letter from the Department of the Army/Office of Enlisted Personnel, informing

236

me that Lieutenant John Joseph Malone was now stationed at Allied HQ in England. They also enclosed a postal address at which he could be reached.

I only read through the letter once. Then I dropped it in the trash basket by my desk, thinking: misjudgments are best tossed out of your life.

There was another letter in that pile of mail which caught my immediate attention – because the return address on the envelope said *Saturday Night/Sunday Morning*: a well-known magazine with which I had never corresponded, nor knew anyone who worked there. I tore back the flap. I pulled out the letter.

April 28th, 1946
Dear Miss Smythe,

I am pleased to inform you that your short story, 'Shore Leave', has been accepted for publication by *Saturday Night/Sunday Morning*. I have tentatively scheduled it for our first September '46 issue, and will pay you a fee of $125 for first publication rights.

Though I would like to run the story largely uncut, I have one or two editorial suggestions that you might be willing to consider. Please call my secretary at your convenience to set up a meeting.

I look forward to meeting you, and am delighted your fiction will be appearing in our magazine.

Sincerely yours,
Nathaniel Hunter
Fiction Editor

Three hours later – as I sat nursing a glass of champagne with Eric in Luchows – I was still in shock.

'Try to look pleased, for God's sakes,' Eric said.

'I *am* pleased. But I'm also a little stunned that you engineered all this.'

'As I told you before, I engineered nothing. I read the story. I liked the story. I called my old Columbia friend, Nat Hunter, at *Saturday Night/Sunday Morning* and told him I'd just read a story which struck me as perfect *Saturday/Sunday* material . . . and which just happened to have been written by my sister. He asked me to send it over. He liked it. He's publishing it. Had I not liked it, I wouldn't have sent it to Nat. Had Nat not liked it, he wouldn't be publishing it. So your story's acceptance was completely free of nepotism. I engineered nothing.'

'Without you, however, I wouldn't have had direct access to the fiction editor.'

'Welcome to the way the world works.'

I reached over and clasped his hand.

'Thank you,' I said.

'Much obliged. But, hey, it's a good story. You can write.'

'Well, dinner's on me tonight.'

'Damn right it is.'

238

'I missed you, Eric.'

'Ditto, S. And you're looking so much better.'

'I am better.'

'As good as new?'

I clinked my glass against his. 'Absolutely,' I said.

The next morning, I called *Saturday Night/Sunday Morning*. Nathaniel Hunter's secretary was exceedingly friendly, and said that Mr Hunter would be delighted to take me out to lunch in two days' time, my schedule permitting.

'My schedule permits,' I said, trying to sound blasé.

I also checked in with Leland McGuire at *Life*. His assistant answered the phone, then put me on hold after I asked to speak directly with my erstwhile boss. After a moment she came back on the line.

'Leland asked me to welcome you back to New York, and to say he'll be in touch as soon as he has an assignment for you.'

It was the reply I expected. I now knew for certain that, a few months from now, the dismissal notice from *Life* would land on my doormat. But with that $125 in my pocket from *Saturday Night/Sunday Morning*, I'd be able to survive for a month or so beyond that time. And maybe I could convince this Nat Hunter to give me a journalistic assignment or two.

Naturally, I was nervous on the morning of my lunch with Mr Hunter. By eleven I was tired of pacing my little apartment – so I decided to kill the remaining hour and a half before our meeting by walking all the way uptown to *Saturday/Sunday*'s offices on Madison and 47th Street. As I was locking my apartment door behind me, Mr Kocsis walked up the stair, a stack of letters in his hand.

'Mail early today,' he said, handing me a single postcard, then heading down the corridor, depositing letters on my neighbors' mats. I stared down at the card. Though the stamp was American, it was franked 'US Army/American Occupation Zone, Berlin'. My stomach was suddenly in knots. Quickly I turned the card over. Three words were scrawled on the reverse side.

I'm sorry.
Jack

I stared at this message for a very long time. Then I forced myself to head downstairs and out into the bright spring sunshine. I turned left outside my front door, and started heading north. The card was still clutched in my hand. Crossing Greenwich Avenue, I walked by a garbage can. Without a moment's thought, I tossed the card away. I didn't look back to see if it landed in the can. I just kept walking.

CHAPTER 5

The lunch with Nathaniel Hunter went well. So well that he offered me a job: assistant fiction editor of *Saturday Night/Sunday Morning*. I couldn't believe my luck. I accepted on the spot. Mr Hunter seemed surprised by my immediate answer.

'You can think about it for a day or two, if you want,' he said, lighting up one of the endless chain of Camels he smoked.

'My mind's made up. When do I start?'

'Monday, if you like. But Sara – do realize that, by accepting this job, you're not going to have much time for your own writing.'

'I'll find the time.'

'I've heard that before from many a promising writer. They get a story accepted by a magazine. But instead of trying to write fiction full time, they take on a position in advertising or public relations. Which inevitably means that they are too exhausted by the end of the day to do any writing whatsoever. As you well know, a nine-to-five job takes its toll.'

'I need to pay the rent.'

'You're young, you're single, you have no responsibilities. This is the time you should take a shot at a novel . . .'

'If you're so certain I should be at home writing, then why are you offering me this job?'

'Because, (a) you strike me as smart – and I need a smart assistant; and (b) as someone who gave up a promising literary career to be a wage-slave and edit other people's work, I consider it my duty to corrupt another promising young writer with a Faustian Bargain they really should refuse . . .'

I laughed.

'Well, you're certainly direct, Mr Hunter.'

'Make you no promises, tell you no lies – that's my credo. But do yourself a favor, Sara: *don't* take this job.'

But I wouldn't listen to his advice. Because I didn't have enough faith in my own talent to set up as a full-time writer. Because I was scared of failing. Because everything in my background told me to grab the secure job option. And because I also knew that Nathaniel Hunter was good news.

Like Eric, he was in his thirties: a tall, wiry fellow with thick graying hair, horn-rimmed glasses, a permanent self-deprecating scowl on his face. He was rather handsome in a tweedy academic sort of way – and endlessly amusing. He told me he'd been married for twelve years to a woman named Rose, who taught part-time in the Art History department at Barnard. They had two young boys, and lived on Riverside Drive and 108th Street.

From everything he said, it was clear that he was devoted to his wife and children (even though, when discussing his family, he would always cloak his comments in cynicism . . . which, as I came to realize, was his tentative way of expressing affection). This made me instantly comfortable with him, as I sensed there would be none of the flirtatious pressure I experienced while working with Leland McGuire. I also liked the fact that, during this first meeting, he never once made any enquiries about my private life. He wanted to hear my views on writing, on writers, on working for magazines, on Harry S. Truman, and whether I supported the Dodgers or the Yankees (the Bronx Bombers, of course). He never even asked if 'Shore Leave' was, in any way, autobiographical. He simply told me it was a very good story – and was surprised to hear that it was my first stab at fiction.

'Ten years ago, I was exactly where you are now,' he said. 'I'd just had a short story accepted by *The New Yorker*, and I was halfway through a novel I was certain would make me the John P. Marquand of my generation.'

'Who ended up publishing the novel?' I asked.

'No one – because I never finished the damn thing. And why didn't I finish it? Because I started doing foolish, time-consuming things like having children, and taking an editorial job at Harper and Brothers to meet the cost of having children, and then moving to the higher-paid echelons of *Saturday Night/Sunday Morning* to pay for private schools, and a bigger apartment, and a summer rental on the Cape, and all those other necessities of family life. So look to this shining example of squandered promise . . . and turn me down. Don't Take This Job.'

Eric concurred. 'Nat is absolutely right,' he said when I called him at *The Quiz Bang Show* to tell him about the job offer. 'You're commitment-free. This is the time to gamble a bit, and avoid all the usual bourgeois traps . . .'

'*Bourgeois traps?*' I said with a giggle. 'You can take the boy out of the Party, but you can't take the Party out of . . .'

He cut me off. 'That's not funny. Especially since you never know who's listening in.'

I felt awful. 'Eric, I'm sorry. That was dumb.'

'We'll continue this conversation later,' he said.

We met up that evening at McSorley's Ale House off the Bowery. Eric was seated at a booth in the rear of the bar, a stein of dark ale in front of him. I handed him a large square package.

'What's this?' he asked.

'A *mea culpa* for speaking before thinking on the phone.'

He tore off the brown wrapping paper. His face immediately brightened as he looked down at a recording of the Beethoven *Missa Solemnis*, conducted by Toscanini.

'I must encourage you to feel guilty more often,' he said. He leaned over and kissed me on the cheek. 'Thanks.'

'I was utterly indiscreet.'

'And I was probably being a little too paranoid. But –' he lowered his voice '– some of my former, uh, *friends* from that era have been having difficulties recently.'

'What kind of difficulties?' I said, whispering back.

'Questions from employers – especially those in the entertainment industries – about past political allegiances. And there are rumors that the Feds are starting to snoop around anyone who was once a member of that funny little party to which I used to belong.'

'But you left in, what, nineteen forty?'

'Forty-one.'

'That's five years ago. Ancient history. Surely, no one's going to care that, once upon a time, you were a fellow traveler. I mean, look at John Dos Passos. Wasn't he a big-deal Party member in the thirties?'

'Yes, but now he's righter than Right.'

'My point exactly – Hoover and his guys wouldn't now accuse Dos Passos of being a . . .'

'*Subversive*,' Eric said quickly, making certain I didn't use the 'C' word.

'Yes, *subversive*. My point is: it doesn't matter if you were once a member of that *club*, as long as it's clear you're no longer affiliated to it. I mean, if an atheist becomes a Christian, is he always considered a "former atheist", or someone who has finally seen the light?'

'The latter, I guess.'

'Exactly. So stop worrying. You've seen the light. You're a "good American". You're in the clear.'

'I hope you're right.'

'But I promise not to make jokes like that on your office phone again.'

'Are you really going to take this job with Nat?'

'I'm afraid so. And yes, I know all the logical reasons why I should dodge it. But I'm a coward. I need to know where the next paycheck is coming from. I also believe in the mysteries of timing . . .'

'How do you mean?'

That's when I told him about the postcard I'd received that morning from Jack.

'All he said was, *I'm sorry*?' Eric said.

'Yes – it was short and not so sweet.'

'No wonder you're taking the job.'

'I would have accepted Nat's offer, no matter what.'

'But Lover Boy's goodbye note clinched the matter?'

'Please don't call him Lover Boy.'

'Sorry. I'm simply angry on your behalf.'

'Like I told you weeks ago, I'm cured.'

'So you said.'

'Eric, I threw his card away.'

'And accepted Nat's job offer a couple of hours later.'

'One door shuts, one door opens.'

'Is that an original line?'

'Go to hell,' I said with a smile.

The beers arrived. Eric raised his stein. 'To the new assistant fiction editor of *Saturday Night/ Sunday Morning*. Please keep writing.'

'I promise I will.'

Six months later, I found myself replaying that conversation in my head on a snowy December afternoon, just before Christmas. I was in my cubbyhole office on the twenty-third floor of the *Saturday/Sunday* offices in Rockefeller Center. My small grimy window gave me a picturesque view of a back alleyway. There were a pile of unsolicited short stories on my desk. As usual, I had sifted through ten manuscripts that day – none of which were remotely publishable. As usual, I had written a report of varying length on each story. As usual, I had attached standard rejection letters to every story. As usual, I bemoaned the fact that I wasn't getting any of my own writing done.

The job had proved far more laborious than expected. It also had virtually nothing to do with editing. Rather, I was employed (along with two of Nat's other assistants) to work my way through the three hundred or so manuscripts that arrived at *Saturday/Sunday* each month by unknown writers. The editorial board of the magazine prided itself on the fact that every unsolicited manuscript was 'given due consideration' – but it was pretty clear to me after eight weeks there that, by and large, my job was to say no. Occasionally, I would bump into a story that showed promise – or even real talent. But I had no power to get it into print.

Rather, all I could do was 'send it upstairs' to Nat Hunter with an enthusiastic recommendation – knowing full well that the chances of him running it were negligible. Because the magazine only reserved four of its fifty-two annual issues for stories by unknown writers. The remaining forty-eight weeks were given over to established names – and *Saturday/Sunday* prided itself on its weekly offering of fiction by the most prestigious writers of the day: Hemingway, O'Hara, Steinbeck, Somerset Maugham, Waugh, Pearl Buck. The list was formidable, and made me realize just how absurdly lucky I was to be one of the four unknown writers to be plucked out of obscurity during 1946 for publication in the magazine.

As scheduled, 'Shore Leave' did appear in the September 6th edition of *Saturday/Sunday*. Several of my colleagues in the office complimented me on the writing. An editor at Harper and Brothers dropped me a nice note, saying that if and/or when I had amassed a book-length collection of stories, he'd be interested in considering them for publication. Someone from RKO Pictures made a tentative telephone inquiry about the rights to the story, but then sent a letter, explaining that 'wartime romances are now passé'. As promised, I did despatch a copy of the magazine to Ruth in Maine, and received a cheery card back in return ('You really have it as a writer . . . and this reader wants to read more!'). Eric squandered a significant portion of his weekly salary on a celebratory dinner at 21. And Nat Hunter also marked the occasion by taking me to lunch at Longchamps.

'So do you regret taking the job?' he asked as our drinks arrived.

'Hardly,' I lied. 'Do I seem like I regret it?'

'You're far too well-mannered and polite to ever openly express dissatisfaction. But – as I know you've discovered – yours is not the most fulfilling of jobs. Nor, for that matter, is mine – but at least I have the fringe benefit of an expense account, which allows me to lunch writers . . . like your good self. On which note: where's the next story?'

'I'm working on it,' I said. 'It's taking a little longer than I expected.'

'You are a terrible liar, Miss Smythe.'

He was right, of course. I was utterly transparent. And I was getting nowhere with my next story . . . even though I knew what I was going to write. It was a tale of an eight-year-old girl on summer vacation in Maine with her parents. She's their only child: over-protected, over-pampered, over-indulged . . . but also deeply aware of the fact that her parents don't like each other very much, and that she is the glue which is holding them together. One afternoon, her parents get into a horrendous argument, and she wanders off out of their rented beach house. She leaves the beach, takes a wrong turn and finds herself in a deep set of woods. She remains lost there overnight, and is found the next morning by the police. She's in shock, but basically unscathed. She has a tearful reunion with her parents. For a day or so afterwards, harmony reigns within the family. But then the parental fights start again, and she runs off into the woods. Because now she realizes that, as long as she's in jeopardy, her parents will cling to each other and get along.

I had a title for the story: 'Getting Lost'. I had the basic narrative structure worked out in my mind. What I didn't have was the will to sit down and write it. The *Saturday/Sunday* job was enervating. I'd arrive home at seven each night, sapped. After eight hours of reading other people's stories I felt like doing anything else but tackling my own work. So I began to play the postponement game – as in, *I'm just too depleted to open my typewriter, so I'll wake up at six a.m. tomorrow and crank out three hundred words before heading to the office.* But then, when the alarm went off the next morning, I'd roll over and sleep on until eight thirty. When I got back home that night, I'd be feeling as devitalized as ever, unable to think about my short story. On the nights when my energy level was high, I'd find other things to do. Like heading off to see a great Howard Hawks double bill at the Academy of Music on 14th Street. Or I'd squander the evening with an enjoyably pulpy William Irish novel. Or I'd decide that this was the moment the bathroom needed cleaning . . .

The weekends were worse. I'd wake up Saturday morning, determined to put in four hours at the typewriter. I'd sit down. I'd type a sentence. I'd hate the sentence. I'd yank the paper out of the typewriter. I'd roll in another piece of paper. This time I would get two, maybe even three sentences on paper before ripping it from the Remington.

And then I would decide it was time for a walk. Or a coffee at the Café Reggio on Bleecker Street. Or a trip uptown to the Metropolitan Museum. Or a late morning foreign movie at the Apollo on 42nd Street. Or a trip to the laundromat. Or any other piece of busy work which would help me dodge writing.

This went on for months. Whenever Eric asked how the new story was going, I'd tell him that I was making slow, steady progress. He'd say nothing, but the sceptical glint in his eye let it be known that he realized I was lying. Which made me feel around ten times more guilty, as I hated deceiving my brother. But what could I tell him? That I had lost all confidence in my ability to string a sentence together, let alone a story? Or that I now knew I was a one-off writer – someone with only a single story to tell.

Eventually, I confessed this to Eric. It was Thanksgiving Day 1946. Like the previous year, I met my brother for lunch at Luchows. Unlike the previous year, I wasn't in love. Instead, I was enveloped by disappointment: with my work, with the circumstances of my life . . . but, most tellingly, with myself.

Like the previous year, Eric ordered a bottle of sparkling wine to celebrate. After the waiter poured out two glasses, Eric raised his and said, 'To your next story.'

I lowered my glass and heard myself saying: 'There is no story, Eric. And you know that.'

'Yes. I know that.'

'You've known that for a long time.'

He nodded.

'Then why didn't you say anything?'

'Because all writers know what it's like to have a block. It's something you really don't want to talk about with anybody.'

'I feel like a failure,' I said, swallowing hard.

'That's dumb, S.'

'It may be dumb, but it's the truth. I messed up at *Life*. I should never have taken that job at *Saturday/Sunday*. Now I'm unable to write. Which means my entire literary output will end up being one forgotten story, published when I was twenty-four.'

Eric sipped his wine and smiled. 'Don't you think you're being just a tad melodramatic?'

'I *want* to be melodramatic.'

'Good. I prefer you when you're Bette Davis, not Katharine Hepburn.'

'God, you sound like *him.*'

'Is he still on the brain?'

'Only today.'

'It being your anniversary, I suppose.'

I winced. And said, 'That wasn't nice.'

'You're right. It wasn't. I'm sorry.'

'You're very hard on me sometimes.'

'Only because you're so hard on yourself. Anyway, it's not criticism. Just constructive *teasing*: an attempt to get you to lighten up. So stop torturing yourself about not being able to work. If you have a story to tell, you'll tell it. If you don't . . . it's not the end of the world. Or, at least, that's what I've decided recently.'

'You haven't given up on your play, have you?'

He stared down into his glass for a moment, then reached (as always) for his cigarettes and matches. He lit one, but didn't look back up at me.

'There is no play,' he said quietly.

'I don't understand . . . ?'

'It's simple, really. The play I've been writing for the last two years doesn't exist.'

'But why doesn't it exist?'

'Because I never wrote anything.'

I tried to disguise my shock. I failed. 'Nothing at all?' I said quietly.

He bit his lip. 'Not a word,' he said.

'What happened?'

He shrugged. 'There's only so much rejection one can take. Seven unproduced plays is enough for me.'

'Things change. Tastes change. You've got to travel hopefully.'

'And while you're at it, *physician heal thyself*.'

'You know how impossible it is to heed one's own advice.'

'Okay – then listen to mine. End the self-flagellation. Put the typewriter away until you're really ready to use it again.'

253

'I'll never use it again.'

'Stop sounding like me, for Christ's sakes. Especially as you *will* use it again.'

'How can you be so sure?'

'Because you'll want to. I'm sure of it. And because you will get over him.'

'I am *definitely* over him.'

'No, S. He's still around, nagging you. I can tell.'

Was I that transparent? Was it *that* obvious? Ever since I'd received that card from Jack, I had resolved to expunge him from my head; to file him away, and slam the cabinet door shut. Initially, I was so angry and hurt by his terse reply that it was easy for me to write him off as a delusional mistake. I mean, how dare he only write three lousy words in response to the three dozen or so letters and cards I sent him? He'd made me feel like a chump, a dupe. Over and over I heard myself at the gates of the Brooklyn Navy Yards, telling him he'd better not break my heart. Over and over I heard Jack say that he loved me. How could I have been so naive, so damn green?

Anger is always a sensible antidote to heartache – especially if you have very good reasons for feeling aggrieved. For months I held on to that sense of intense rancor. It helped me deal with his whole-sale rejection of me. I had made a massive mistake. As Eric predicted, Jack Malone turned out to be a fly-by-night artist; a Don Giovanni in Army khaki. If only he'd had the decency (or the courage) to write me straight away, telling me that there was no future between us. If only he hadn't kept me dangling for so long. If only I hadn't been such a romantic sap.

After anger comes resentment. After resentment, bitterness. And when that acrid aftertaste finally diminishes, what you are usually left with is wistfulness. A rueful cocktail of acceptance and regret. The *sadder but wiser* school of needlepoint mottos.

But by the time of my Thanksgiving lunch with Eric, I wasn't merely wistful. Naturally, the day in question (my so-called *anniversary* with Jack, as Eric so tartly noted) made me reflect on all that had happened to me during the past chaotic year. But it also brought home something which I kept trying to deny (but which Eric, damn him as usual) quickly detected: I still missed the guy.

And I still couldn't work out why one single night with someone had made such a resounding, lasting impact.

Unless . . .

Unless he was *it*.

But I tried not to dwell on this thought. Because it meant dwelling on Jack. And I didn't want to dwell on Jack because, in turn, it meant wondering if there was a thing called destiny – a thought which rekindled the residual grief I still felt about losing Jack.

A few days after Thanksgiving, however, a little perspective returned – and, once again, I retired Mr Malone to that drawer of my mental filing cabinet marked 'Romantic Mistakes'.

During that same week, I also took Eric's advice and put my Remington typewriter into hibernation at the back of my closet. Initially I felt a considerable degree of guilt at giving up the idea of writing. But by mid-December, the constant stab of angst had receded. And, rationalizing like crazy, I was able to convince myself that my writing career hadn't crashed and burned. Rather, it had decided to take an extended sabbatical.

'Am I ever going to see that new short story?' Nathaniel Hunter asked me at our Christmas lunch.

'Not for a while, I'm afraid.'

He looked at me quizzically. 'And why is that, Sara?'

I met his gaze directly. 'Because I never wrote it, Mr Hunter.'

He grimaced. 'That's a damn shame.'

'It's just a story.'

'You have a lot of promise, Sara.'

'That's very kind of you, but if I can't get the story written, then promise means nothing, does it?'

'I feel bad. Responsible.'

'Why? You did warn me. But it's not the job that stopped me from writing it. It's me.'

'Don't you want to be a writer?'

'I think so. But . . . I can't really figure anything out anymore.'

'It's a common complaint, I'm afraid.'

'Tell me about it. Especially since I have learned one basic rule of life over the last year.'

'Enlighten me.'

'Every time you think you know what you want, you bump into someone who alters your perspective completely.'

'Some people would call that "keeping your options open".'

'I would call it an ongoing recipe for unhappiness,' I said.

'But maybe some people *do* bump into what they want.'

'Without question. The problem is: having found what you want, can you actually hold on to it? And the terrible thing is: the answer to that question all comes down to things like luck, timing, maybe even a pinch or two of serendipity. Stuff over which we have such little control.'

'Take it from a guy who's compromised himself into a corner – we have control over *nothing*. We think we do, but the truth is: most of the big decisions we make in life are never thought out properly. They're all done quickly, instinctively, and usually out of fear. The next thing you know, you've boxed yourself into a situation you don't want to be in. And you find yourself asking, "how the hell did I get here?" But we all know the answer: we *wanted* to be here . . . even though we might spend the rest of our lives denying it.'

'So what you're saying is: we trap ourselves.'

'Absolutely. You know that old line from Voltaire: *man is born free, but everywhere in chains*. Well, in America today, most of the chains are self-imposed . . . courtesy of marriage.'

'I'm never getting married.'

'I've heard that one before. But, believe me, you will. And probably without even thinking too much about it.'

I laughed and said, 'How on earth can you *know* that?'

'Because it's the way it always happens.'

At the time, I dismissed Nathaniel Hunter's comments as those of a metropolitan cynic – and one who was ruing the approach of middle-age and the loss of his literary prospects. But I also knew of his devotion to his family – and how that probably tempered any professional disappointments he might be bearing. He might be 'in chains', but he secretly liked the chains.

Then, two weeks after Christmas, I came to work one morning to discover a notice posted on the door of the literary department, asking all staff members to attend an urgent meeting in the managing editor's office at ten that morning. Everyone from the department was already gathered by Mr Hunter's desk, speaking in low conspiratorial tones. But Mr Hunter wasn't there.

'What's happened?' I asked as I joined my colleagues.

'You mean you haven't heard?' asked Emily Flouton, one of the other assistant fiction editors.

'Heard what?'

'That our happily married boss just ran off with Jane Yates.'

I blanched with shock. Jane Yates was a quiet,

angular-faced woman in her late twenties who worked in *Saturday/Sunday's* art department. With her sharp features, her long braided hair, and her rimless round glasses, she always looked like the sort of New England librarian who was destined to end up a spinster.

'Mr Hunter ran off with *her*?' I heard myself saying.

'It's something, isn't it?' Emily said. 'Not only that – he's also quit his job. Rumor has it that he and Jane are planning to move to New Hampshire or Vermont, so he can write full time.'

'But I thought he was happily married.'

Emily rolled her eyes and said, 'Honey, what man is ever happily married? Even if you give the guy complete freedom, he'll still end up feeling trapped.'

I never saw Nat Hunter again. Because he never showed his face again in the offices of *Saturday/Sunday*. With good reason. In 1947, running out on your marriage was considered a major misdemeanor . . . and one which was punishable by professional demotion, if not ostracization. Had he just continued cheating on his wife, there would have been no problem – as adultery was tolerated (so long as you were never caught). But abandoning your family back then was regarded as immoral and downright unAmerican. In the case of Nat Hunter, it was also mind-boggling. Especially given that the object of his desire was a woman who reminded me of Mrs Danvers in *Rebecca*.

Most of the big decisions we make in life are never thought out properly. They're all done quickly, instinctively, and usually out of fear. The next thing you know, you've boxed yourself into a situation you don't want to be in.

For months after Mr Hunter's abrupt departure, I kept hearing him make that statement. I myself kept wondering: was the decision to upend his life also made quickly, instinctively, and out of fear? Fear, perhaps, of growing older, and feeling trapped, and never writing the novel he promised himself he'd write?

To the best of my knowledge, even after he vanished to New Hampshire with Jane Yates, he never got his novel published. Word had it he ended up teaching English composition at a small junior college near Franconia – until his death in 1960. 'Liver failure' was the cause given in the short *New York Times* obituary. He was only fifty-two years old.

But in the immediate aftermath of his departure from *Saturday/Sunday*, I held in constant remembrance his comments about how we never think through the big things in life. And I vowed to myself: I'll *never* make that mistake.

Then, in the early spring of 1947, I met a man named George Grey. He was a twenty-eight-year-old investment banker with Lehmann Brothers. Princeton-educated, erudite, courtly, handsome in a square-jawed sort of way, and a good companion. We were introduced at the wedding of one of my

Bryn Mawr friends. He asked me out. I accepted. The evening went well. He asked me out again. I accepted again. The evening was even more of a success. George Grey, I decided, was good news. And, much to my surprise, he admitted (after just two dates) that he was besotted with me.

So besotted that – a month after we met – he asked me to marry him.

Did I ponder this decision? Did I ask for time to reflect, contemplate, or muse about the ramifications of this momentous question?

Of course not.

I said yes. Without a moment's thought.

CHAPTER 6

Everyone was surprised by my news. No one more so than me.

'You're actually marrying a man named *Grey?*' Eric asked me when I told him about the engagement.

'I knew this is how you'd react,' I said.

'I'm not reacting. I'm just asking a question.'

'Yes, Eric. His name is Grey. Happy now?'

'Thrilled. And . . . let me work this out . . . the first time you mentioned him to me was around two weeks ago. At that point you'd been seeing him for . . . how long was it exactly?'

'Around two weeks,' I said sheepishly.

'So – just one month from the first date to the engagement announcement. He's obviously a fast worker . . . though nothing compared to the Brooklyn Boy.'

'I was just waiting for you to bring him up.'

'That's because he's still lurking around . . .'

'That is *not* true, damn it.'

'Of course it's true. Why else would you be marrying this other guy?'

'Maybe because I am in love with him.'

'You're talking crap – and you know it. You are not the sort of woman who falls for an investment banker named Grey.'

'I wish you would please stop telling me my own mind. George is a wonderful man. He will make me very happy.'

'He will turn you into somebody you don't want to be.'

'How the hell can you say that, when you've never even met him?'

'Because he's called *George Grey*, that's how. It's a name that conjures up a pipe and slippers . . . which he'll be asking you to fetch before you know it.'

'I am not a dog,' I said, my voice tightening. 'I fetch things for no one.'

'We all end up doing things we vow never to do . . . especially when we're chasing the illusion of love.'

'This is not a goddamn illusion, Eric!'

'Illusion, delusion, confusion – you could describe your condition in any number of ways . . .'

'I am not suffering from a condition . . .'

'Yes, you are. And it's called "trapping yourself . . . in the name of security".'

'Thank you for crediting me with knowing my own mind.'

'No one knows their own mind, S. *No one*. It's the main reason why we all make such an ongoing mess of things.'

Well, I certainly knew why I was marrying George

Grey. Because he was so decent, so dependable, and so enamored of me. We all adore being flattered. Or – better yet – being told that we are special, unique, the best thing that ever happened to somebody. George did this constantly. And I couldn't resist it. Because it was exactly what I wanted to hear.

He was also supportive – especially when it came to the issue of my stalled writing career. Shortly after our engagement was announced, we went out one night with Emily Flouton – who had become one of my good friends at *Saturday/Sunday* in the wake of Nathaniel Hunter's departure. Emily had just been dumped by her boyfriend of two years – and when I mentioned to George that she was feeling a little fragile, he insisted that she join us for a concert at Carnegie Hall and a late supper afterwards at the Algonquin. Emily and I spent much of the meal discussing Mr Hunter's replacement – a small, angular woman in her early forties named Ida Spenser. She'd been hired away from *Collier's* as our new boss, and quickly established a reputation within our department for deporting herself like a perpetually inflexible headmistress (of the *old-maidish* variety), and for slapping down anyone who dared to contradict her rigid way of doing things. We all hated her. As we waited for our food in the Grill Room of the Algonquin, Emily and I engaged in an extended rant about Miss Spenser. George listened with rapt attention ... even though our office politics were of absolutely no interest to him. But he was always solicitous.

'. . . and then she told me that I had no right to encourage any new authors without her approval,' Emily said. 'Only she can decide whether or not a writer gets a personalized letter of encouragement.'

'She must be a very insecure woman,' George said.

Emily looked at him admiringly. 'How did you know that?' she asked.

'Because George is very insightful about people,' I said.

'Stop flattering me,' he said, squeezing my hand. 'You'll give me a swelled head.'

'You with a swelled head?' I said. 'Not a chance. You're far too nice for that.'

'Now you are going to really make me feel stuck-up,' he said, lightly kissing me on the lips. 'Anyway, the only reason I said that your boss might be insecure is because I used to work for someone like that at the bank. He had to control everything. Every letter to a client, every inter-departmental memorandum had to be personally vetted by him. He was obsessive. Because he was about the most scared person I'd ever met. He lived in terror of delegating to anyone; he felt he could trust no one. And for a very simple reason: he couldn't trust himself.'

'That's our Miss Spenser to a *T*,' Emily said. 'She's so uncertain about herself that she thinks we're all out to get her. Which, of course, now we all are. What eventually happened to your boss?'

'He was kicked upstairs, and made a director of the company. Which was a blessing – because, quite frankly, I was on the verge of quitting my job.'

'I don't believe that for a moment,' I said, nudging him playfully. 'You'd never quit a job. It would contravene every notion you have about duty and accountability.'

'Now you're making me sound all stuffy, darling.'

'Not stuffy. Just responsible. *Very* responsible.'

'You make it sound like a personal defect,' he said with mock melodrama.

'Hardly, my love. I think responsibility is a great virtue – especially in a husband.'

'I'd drink to that,' Emily said grimly. 'Every guy I get involved with seems to have been born with the irresponsibility gene.'

'You'll get lucky,' I said.

'Not as lucky as you,' Emily said.

'Hey, I'm the real lucky one here,' George said. 'I mean, I'm marrying one of the most promising writers in America.'

'Oh, please . . .' I said, turning beet red. 'I've only published one story.'

'But *what* a story,' George said. 'Don't you agree, Emily?'

'Absolutely,' she said. 'Everyone in the department thought it was one of the top three or four stories we published last year. And considering that Faulkner, Hemingway and J.T. Farrell were the other three writers . . .'

'Stop!' I said. 'Or I'll crawl under the table.'

Emily groaned. And said, 'What this woman needs, George, is a massive dose of self-confidence.'

'Well, I'm the man for the job,' he said with a smile.

'And you must convince her to leave *Saturday/Sunday* before it kills her talent.'

'It was just one damn story,' I said. 'I doubt I'll ever write another.'

'Of course you will,' George said. 'Because after we're married, you won't have to worry about paying the rent anymore, or even having to put up with the dreadful Miss Spenser at *Saturday/ Sunday*. You'll be free of all that, and able to concentrate full time on your fiction.'

'Sounds great to me,' Emily said.

'I'm not at all sure if I'll be leaving *Saturday/ Sunday* right away,' I said.

'Of course you will,' George said sweetly. 'It's the ideal moment to make the break.'

'But it's my job . . .'

'Writing's your real job . . . and I want to give you the opportunity to do it full time.'

He leaned over and kissed me on the forehead. Then he stood up and excused himself.

'Nature calls,' he said with a chuckle. 'How about getting another couple of drinks. Being in love is thirsty work.'

I smiled. Tightly. And found myself thinking, *what a dumb line*. Instantly, my mind replayed some of our lovey-dovey conversation ('*Hey, I'm the real lucky one here . . . I mean, I'm marrying one of the most promising writers in America*'). I couldn't believe that we were already exchanging 'settled married couple' epithets like *darling* and *my love*. I felt myself flinch. It was just a minor contraction of the shoulders. It couldn't have lasted more than a nanosecond. But in the aftermath of that tiny shudder came a question: was that the first twinge of doubt?

Before I had time to consider that query, Emily said, 'Boy, are you one lucky girl.'

'Do you think so?'

'*Think so?* He's wonderful.'

'Yes. I guess he is.'

'Guess? *Guess?* Don't you see what you've landed?'

'A very nice man.'

'*Nice?* What's happened to you tonight? Did you take "understatement" tablets or something?'

'I'm just . . . I don't know . . . a little nervous, that's all. And I could really use another martini. Waiter!'

I caught the eye of a passing man with a tray, and motioned for a refill.

'Of course you're nervous,' Emily said. 'You're getting married. But, at least, you're marrying someone who clearly adores you.'

'I suppose so . . .'

'*Suppose?* He worships the ground you walk on.'

'Wouldn't you find it a bit worrying if you were the object of such adoration?'

Emily rolled her eyes and gave me a dark frown. 'Will you listen to yourself,' she said. 'Here you are – a published writer, engaged to a man who actually believes in your talent, who's going to free you from the worry of earning a living so you can dedicate yourself completely to your "art", and who also considers you the most wonderful person on the planet. And all you can talk about is your fear of being adored. I mean, *really*.'

'Everyone's entitled to a few last-minute doubts, aren't they?'

'Not when they've landed the catch of the year.'

'He's not a fish, Emily.'

'There you go again!'

'All right, all right . . .'

'Tell you what: if you really don't want to marry George, I'm happy to take your place. In the meantime, try to accept the fact that you've struck it lucky in love. I know it's difficult for you to admit such a *terrible* thing . . .'

'Emily: I *am* in love. I'm just . . . anxious, that's all.'

'I wish I had your problems.'

'Hey there!'

We both looked up. George was approaching the table, his mouth frozen in an expansive grin. People were always describing him as 'boyish' – and with good reason. With his perfectly parted sandy hair, his heavy horn-rimmed glasses, his slightly chubby freckled face, and his ability to look a little disheveled (even when dressed in one of the made-to-measure

Brooks Brothers suits he favored), he always had a certain schoolboyish demeanor: someone who, even at the age of twenty-eight, would still appear at home on a soccer field at Exeter (his prep school alma mater).

But as he came and sat down with us, I found myself looking beyond his current adolescent veneer, and seeing what he would become twelve years from now: a portly middle-aged banker whose youthful countenance had been replaced by a staid stoutness. A man of bulk and leaden gravity, with no lightness of touch, no animating spirit.

'Something the matter, darling?'

His voice registered concern. I snapped out of my anxious trance, and gave him a warm, loving smile.

'Just a little far away, dear.'

'I bet she's plotting her next story,' he said to Emily.

'Or dreaming about the wedding,' Emily said, with more than a hint of irony which my fiancé failed to pick up.

'Oh, so that's what you girls were talking about!'

Ugh.

Yes, I knew that George Grey was a deeply conventional man. And yes, I knew that he was someone who would always have his feet firmly planted on *terra firma*. There was nothing fanciful or capricious about George. When he tried to be passionately romantic, he often came across as downright silly. But he also had the disarming (and rather attractive) ability to admit that he lacked imagination, and couldn't really engage in flights of fancy. On our third date, he confessed:

'Give me a set of company accounts, and I can be engrossed for hours – like someone turning the pages of a really good novel. But play me a Mozart symphony, and I'm lost. I really don't know what to listen for.'

'You don't have to listen for anything in particular. You just have to like what you hear. It's what Duke Ellington once said, "If it sounds good, it *is* good."'

He stared at me with wide-eyed admiration. 'You are so damn smart.'

'Hardly,' I said.

'You're cultured.'

'You're not exactly from the Bronx, George. I mean, you did go to Princeton.'

'That's certainly no guarantee of ending up cultured,' he said – and we both laughed like hell.

I liked his self-deprecatory humor. Just as I also liked the way he showered me with books and records and nights at the theater and Sunday afternoon New York Philharmonic concerts – even though I knew that, for George, listening to Rodzinski conduct an all-Prokofiev program was the musical equivalent of two hours in a dentist's chair. But he would never let on that he was bored. He was so eager to please; to learn.

He was also a voracious reader – largely of hefty factual books. I think he was the only man I ever met who'd actually read all four volumes of Churchill's *The World Crisis*. Fiction, he admitted, was not one of his great interests. 'But you can teach me what to read.'

So I gave him a present of Hemingway's *A Farewell to Arms*. The morning after, he called me at *Saturday/Sunday*.

'God, what a book,' he said.

'You've finished it already?'

'You bet. He can really tell a story, can't he?'

'Yes, Mr Hemingway does have that ability.'

'And the stuff about the war . . . it's real sad.'

'Were you moved by the love story between Frederic and Catherine?'

'I had tears running down my face during that final scene in the hospital.'

'I'm glad to hear that.'

'But you know what I was thinking after I put the book down?'

'What, my love?'

'If only she'd had a good American doctor looking after her, she would have probably pulled through.'

'Uh . . . I'd never thought that. But, yes, I'm sure that's true.'

'I mean, I'm not knocking Swiss doctors.'

'I don't think that was Hemingway's idea either.'

'Well, after reading his book, I certainly wouldn't want you to have a baby in Switzerland.'

'I'm touched,' I said.

All right, so he was rather *literal*. But I decided I could live with such artlessness because of his decency, his obliging nature – and because I was so overwhelmed by his devoted attention. In the weeks running up to the wedding, I would silence any of my nagging doubts about my future with George by reminding myself: *he's so nice*.

'Yeah, all right, I'll admit it,' Eric said after he finally met George. 'He is a perfectly affable guy. Too affable, if you want my honest opinion.'

'How can anybody be *too affable*?' I asked.

'He's so damn eager to please. He wants to be liked at all costs.'

'That's not the worst thing in the world, is it? Anyway, he was understandably nervous about meeting you.'

'Why on earth would anybody be nervous of meeting me?' Eric asked sweetly.

'Because, to George, meeting you was like meeting Father. He felt that if you didn't approve of him, the marriage might not happen.'

'That's the dumbest thing I've heard in years.'

'He is a little old-fashioned . . .'

'Old fashioned? Try Paleozoic. But it really doesn't matter what I think – since there's absolutely no way you'd ever listen to my advice.'

'That's not true.'

'Then answer me this: if I told you I thought he was a disaster, a huge mistake, would you have agreed with me?'

'Of course not.'

'The defense rests.'

'But you *don't* think that, do you?'

'Like I said, he's a perfectly okay guy.'

'Just okay?'

'We had a pleasant chat, didn't we?'

Actually, that was true. We all met for an after-work drink at the bar of the Astor Hotel on Broadway – as it was right around the corner from the radio studios where Eric still turned out gags for *The Quiz Bang Show*. George was nervous as hell. I was nervous as hell. Eric was calm as hell. I had warned George that my brother could be a little idiosyncratic, and had somewhat left-of-center political views.

'Then I shouldn't tell him I'm on the campaign committee to get Governor Dewey the Republican nomination for President?'

'It's a free country – you can tell Eric whatever you like. But know this – he's a real Henry Wallace Democrat, and he hates the Republican Party and everything it stands for. Still, I'll never, *ever* dictate what you should say or do. So, it's your call entirely.'

He thought about this for a moment, then said, 'Maybe I'll sidestep politics.'

He managed to do this during our hour with Eric. Just as he also managed to talk in a surprisingly informed manner about the current state of Broadway, about the work of the Federal Theater Project (he got Eric to reminisce about his years with Orson Welles), and to ask a few intelligent questions about whether this new-fangled medium called television was going to undermine radio (to which my brother mordantly replied: 'Not only will it kill radio as we know it . . . it will also reduce the public's general level of intelligence by at least twenty-five per cent').

I was impressed (and rather touched) by how well George had briefed himself on subjects of interest to my brother . . . especially as I'd only mentioned to him in passing Eric's years with the Federal Theater Project. But George was like that – always meticulous, always well prepared, always wanting to get on the right side of someone. Listening to him talk intelligently about the forth-coming Broadway season – knowing full well that the theater actually bored George, and that he must have been studying *Variety* and the other showbiz magazines for the week before this drink – made me feel real love for him. Because I knew he was doing this for me.

Towards the end of our hour together, George excused himself to call his office. As soon as he was out of earshot, Eric said, 'Well, you certainly primed him well.'

'Actually, I told him very little about you.'

'Then I am impressed.'

'Really?'

'For a Republican, he's reasonably cultured.'

'How do you know he's a Republican?'

'Oh come on. He so looks the part. I bet you anything he's backing Dewey for the nomination.'

'I wouldn't know . . .'

'Yes, you would. And I'd lay money on the fact that Daddy Grey is a big cheese in the Westchester County Republican Party.'

Damn my brother for being so perceptive. Only he was wrong about one thing: Edwin Grey, Sr, was actually the chairman of the entire New York State Republican Party – a man who considered Governor Dewey his closest friend, and who acted as an unofficial adviser to a young, upcoming politican named Nelson Rockefeller.

Yes, my future father-in-law was something of a power broker, not to mention a serious white-shoe lawyer – a senior partner at a major Wall Street firm – and a man with the same stern Victorian countenance as Father. His wife, Julia, was a tall, contained woman with a decidedly aristocratic mien, and an unspoken (but readily discernible) belief that the world was divided into two groups: the ghastly hoi polloi, and a small number of people she would deign to find interesting.

The Greys were Presbyterian – both in faith and temperament. They lived like frugal members of the squirearchy in that corner of Greenwich, Connecticut, which, back in the forties, was still deep country. Their house – a fourteen-room mock-Tudor manse – was situated on a seven-acre parcel of woodlands, bisected by a stream. It was bucolic. Shortly before George popped the question, he brought me up for a weekend.

'I know they are going to love you,' he said on the train north from Grand Central Station. 'But I hope you won't be put off by the way they do things. They are formal kind of people.'

'Sounds just like my parents,' I said.

As it turned out, the Greys made my late parents look like mad bohemians. Though they treated me with courtesy and a relative degree of interest, they were deeply absorbed in their own rigid domestic protocol. They dressed for dinner. Drinks were served by a liveried manservant in the living room. All meals took place in a formal dining room. Mrs Grey deferred to her husband in all conversational matters. He was the one who voiced the opinions, whereas Mrs Grey either made small talk, or posed questions to me. Hers was a polite, but skillful interrogation, during which she got me talking about my parents, my education, my professional resumé, my overall world-view. I knew what she was really doing: probing my suitability for her son. I answered her questions in a pleasant, unadorned manner. I tried not to sound either too nervous or too ingratiating. My answers were always met by a tight smile – which meant that I couldn't read her reaction to me. George stared down at his plate during these Q&A sessions. Daddy Grey also detached himself from the interrogation – though he was still listening intently to everything I said . . . something I noticed when I glanced away from Mrs Grey for a second and saw him assessing me with care, his fingers interlocked and propped under his chin like a judge on the bench. Only once did he interrupt his wife – to ask me if my father had been a member of the Hartford Club: the very starched, very WASP meeting place for Hartford's captains of commerce.

'He was its president for two years,' I said quietly. I glanced quickly across the table at George. He was trying to suppress a grin. When I glanced back at Daddy Grey, he gave me the slightest of approving nods: as if to say, *if your father was president of the Hartford Club, you can't be all that bad.* Taking a cue from her husband, Mrs Grey afforded me another of her tight smiles – slightly wider than usual, but constrained nonetheless. I smiled back, secretly thinking: formality is always a way of defending a narrow view of the world; a belief that you can categorize people simply by the schools and colleges they attended, their political allegiances, the clubs to which their parents belonged. My parents also operated according to this rigid principle – and I suddenly felt this wave of sympathy for George, as I realized he too was raised in an emotionally arid household.

Unlike me, however, he didn't have an Eric to counterbalance his parents. Of course, I knew all about his older brother, Edwin. He was the family star. The valedictorian of his class at Exeter. Captain of the school's lacrosse team. A brilliant student at Harvard, from which he graduated *summa cum laude* in 1940. And though he was accepted at Harvard Law, he decided to accept an Army commission as second lieutenant. So he deferred his admission to Harvard Law and went off to war – where he was killed during the invasion of Normandy.

'I don't think my parents have ever really recovered from his death,' George told me on our second date. 'He was the repository of all their hopes, their ambitions. They adored him.'

'I'm sure they adore you too,' I said.

He just shrugged sadly, then said, 'I've never really been much of a jock or an academic whizkid.'

'You got into Princeton.'

'Yes – but only because my dad went there . . . as he still often reminds me. My grades at Exeter weren't up to much. And at college, I didn't make any of the Varsity teams, nor did I graduate with honors. I was a B minus student. I did all right – but for my parents, "all right" was a synonym for "failure". They expected excellence. I didn't deliver.'

'There's a lot more to life than good grades or making the lacrosse team. But my parents were the same way. Their social benchmarks were all to do with an extreme form of rectitude. Probity at all costs.'

George later told me that that was the moment he fell in love with me – because I was somebody who, thanks to my own background, so understood the milieu which shaped him . . . and also because I used words like *rectitude* and *probity*.

'You're not just beautiful,' he said later that night. 'You also have one hell of a vocabulary.'

Now, seated across the table from his profoundly constrained parents, I felt this immense kinship with George. We were cut from the same austere, uncomfortable cloth. We were both – in our own quiet way – trying to break away from the limitations of WASP-dom. We understood each other.

Like me, George had been hurt in love. Though he didn't tell me much about it, he mentioned that there had been a two-year romance with a woman named Virginia: the daughter of some well-known Wall Street lawyer, thereby garnering her 'high approval status' in the eyes of his parents. When she broke off the engagement (because she had fallen for the son of a Pennsylvania senator), George's parents took the news badly – considering it yet another failure on the part of their son when it came to achieving anything. He'd asked me about Jack – but I supplied him with scant details, except to say that it was a bit of 'romantic silliness' that amounted to nothing, especially as he disappeared back off to Europe before it could develop into anything substantial.

'He was a fool to lose you,' George said.

'And she you,' I replied immediately.

'I doubt she thinks that.'

'Well, *I* do. And that's what counts.'

He actually blushed, then reached over across the table and took my hand. 'At least I got lucky this time around,' he said.

'Timing is everything, I guess.'

Without question, the timing was definitely on our side. We shared similar family backgrounds, educational levels, social perspectives. Most importantly, we were both ready to get married (despite all my private protestations, I knew this to be true). George was sound. He was balanced, responsible. He loved me without reservation. Though I didn't feel any grand passion for him, I convinced myself that the absence of ardor wasn't truly important. After all, I had lost my heart to Jack and ended up feeling like a sap. Passion – as I had come to conclude – was for fools. It fogged the brain. It muddled rational thought. It led you down all the wrong paths. It was a mistake – and one which I would never make again.

And so, catching his eye across his parents' dining room table – seeing him gaze at me with such unconditional fondness – I made a decision. If he proposed marriage, I'd accept.

The rest of the dinner was a reasonable success. We made polite chit-chat. I told a few anodyne anecdotes about my work at *Saturday/Sunday*. I said nothing when Daddy Grey went into a tirade about how Harry S. Truman was nothing but a socialist haberdasher (if only my father had been alive to meet Daddy Grey – it would have been love at first sight). I feigned interest as Daddy Grey engaged George in a discussion about a pressing issue of the day: a new set of rules for Princeton's eating clubs which compelled them to accept members of all religious persuasions ('It's the Jewish lobby that's forced this issue,' Daddy Grey thundered; a comment which George shrugged off with a non-committal nod of the head). I smiled a lot and didn't speak unless spoken to.

After dinner, we retired to the library. Though I really felt in need of a brandy, I didn't ask for one. Then again, I wasn't offered one – as Daddy

Grey poured out a measure for George and himself. A fire was blazing in the hearth. I sipped a demitasse of coffee. An entire wall of the library was devoted to framed photographs of Edwin at assorted junctures in his life. The end table next to the sofa was also filled with additional portraits of Edwin – all in Army uniform. He did look exceptionally dashing. The room was a shrine – and my eyes scanned all additional walls and table-tops for any photos of George. There were none.

As if reading my mind, Mrs Grey said, 'We have plenty of pictures of George elsewhere in the house. The library is for Edwin.'

'Of course,' I said quietly, then added: 'I don't how anyone could cope with such a loss.'

'We're not the only family who lost a son,' Daddy Grey said, his voice betraying a slight tremor.

'I didn't mean to imply . . .'

'Grief is a private matter, don't you think?' he said, turning away from me to refill his brandy glass.

'I apologize if I said something wrong,' I said.

Silence. A silence that must have lasted a full minute. It was finally broken by Mrs Grey. Her voice was hushed.

'You are right. The sense of loss will never end. Because Edwin was exceptional. A man of astonishing gifts.'

She glanced briefly at George, then stared down at her hands, threaded tightly together in her lap.

'He was utterly irreplaceable.'

Another long silence. George stared into the fire, saying nothing, his eyes full.

I excused myself shortly thereafter, and went up to the guest room in which I was being billeted. I undressed, put on my nightgown, and got into bed, pulling the blankets over my head. Sleep did not arrive – which was not a surprise, considering that I was still trying to make sense of the dinner, the scene in the library, and the way in which George's parents were subtly making him pay for Edwin's death.

The sense of loss will never end. Because Edwin was exceptional. A man of astonishing gifts . . .

Had she not turned towards George at that moment, I would have thought that she was simply attempting to express a mother's inexpressible grief. But by narrowing George in her sights, and saying that his brother was irreplaceable, she was letting him (and me) know: *if I had to lose one child, it should have been you.*

I couldn't believe her cruelty. It made me feel intensely protective towards George. It also gave me a project: to emancipate this man from his family by loving him.

And I was certain that, in time, I would love him.

I stared at the ceiling of the bedroom for nearly an hour. Then I heard footsteps on the stairs, followed by the door of George's room (located directly opposite mine) opening and closing. I waited five minutes. Then I got up, left my room, and tiptoed quickly across the corridor. Without knocking, I quietly opened George's door. He was already in bed, reading. He looked up at me, startled. I put my finger to my lips, shut the door behind me, and walked over to the bed, sitting down next to him. I noticed that he was wearing striped pajamas. I stroked his hair. He was wide-eyed with bemusement. I leaned down and kissed him deeply. He returned the kiss – nervously at first, but then with considerable ardor. After a moment, I gently broke away. Standing up, I pulled my nightgown over my head. The chill of the room made me shiver. I crawled under the covers next to him. I took his head in my hands and began to kiss him gently on the face. He was tense.

'This is crazy,' he whispered. 'My parents . . .'

'Shh,' I said, putting a finger to my lips. Then I climbed on top of him.

It was the first time we'd made love. Unlike Jack, George played according to the carnal rules of the day – when sex before marriage was still considered foreign, perilous territory, to be traversed only after a sizeable amount of time had been spent with the other person. Though we'd kissed, George's natural tendency towards circumspection meant that he'd yet to make a proper move. By the way he'd asked me about my involvement with Jack (and whether 'Shore Leave' was auto-biographical), I sensed that he knew I was no virgin. But now, sharing a bed with him for the first time, I realized that he was.

He was anxious. He was awkward. He was fast. So fast that, afterwards, he lay slumped against me and whispered, 'I'm so sorry.'

'Don't be,' I said, my voice as hushed as his. 'There'll be other times.'

'Will there?'

'Yes. There will. If you want.'

'I want.'

'Good. Because I was starting to wonder . . .'

'Wonder what?'

'Wonder when on earth this was going to finally occur.'

'Seduction has never been one of my great skills.'

'Never?'

He turned away from me. 'Never.'

'Not even with Virginia?'

'She wasn't interested.'

'That happens, I suppose.'

'Yes – but usually not with someone you're engaged to.'

'Then you had a lucky escape. Think of what an arid marriage that might have been.'

'The best bit of luck I've ever had is meeting you.'

'I'm flattered.'

'Don't be. You're wonderful. My parents thought so too.'

'Really?'

'They were impressed with you. I could tell.'

'Well, personally, I found it very hard to guess what they were thinking.'

'It's just their manner. They have two religions: Presbyterianism and diffidence.'

'That still doesn't give them the right to be diffident towards you.'

'It's all to do with Edwin's death.'

'His death should make them value you even more.'

'They do value me. They just have difficulty expressing such things.'

'They undervalue you. They shouldn't.'

He looked at me with amazement. 'Do you really think that, Sara?'

I ran my index finger down along his face. 'Yes,' I said. 'I really do think that.'

I sneaked out of his room just before daybreak. I fell into bed for around an hour, but couldn't sleep. So I had a bath. Then I dressed and went downstairs, deciding to head out for a walk. En route to the front door, I passed by the dining room, and heard a voice: 'You must have slept badly, Miss Smythe.'

I stopped and saw Mrs Grey seated at the end of the dining table. She was already dressed and coiffed for the day, a cup of coffee in front of her.

'Not that badly.'

She gave me a look of ironic disdain. 'If you say so. Is George still asleep?'

I tried to fight off a blush. I don't think I succeeded as she arched her eyebrows.

'I wouldn't really know,' I said.

'Of course you wouldn't. Coffee?'

'I don't want to disturb you . . .'

'If you were disturbing me, I wouldn't ask you to join me in a cup of coffee, now would I?'

'Coffee would be lovely,' I said, sitting down. She got up and went over to a banquette, on which sat a sterling silver coffee pot and the appropriate china. She poured me a cup, returned to the table and set it in front of me.

'I'm certain the coffee will be most welcome after your restive night,' she said.

Oh God . . . I lifted the coffee cup up to my lips and took a quick sip. Then I set it down again. In the space of that simple movement, I'd decided to ignore her last comment. Instead I asked: 'Did you yourself sleep badly?'

'I always sleep badly. And you're dodging my question.'

I met her gaze. 'Had you asked me a question, Mrs Grey, I would have promptly answered it. Because it would have been impolite otherwise. But you *didn't* ask me a question. You simply made an observation.'

Another of her tight smiles. 'I can see now why you are a writer. Your powers of observation are formidable.'

'I'm not a writer.'

'You're not?' she said. 'Then what about that story in *Saturday Night/Sunday Morning*?'

'One published story doesn't make someone a writer.'

'Such modesty . . . especially given the immodesty of the story. Were you in love with that Navy boy?'

'It was a story, Mrs Grey, not a personal remembrance.'

'Of course it was, dear. Twenty-four-year-old women writers always invent stories about the love of their life.'

'There is something called imagination . . .'

'Not when it comes to a story like yours. It's a common enough genre: *romantic confessional box*; the sort of thing one usually finds in the *Ladies' Home Companion* . . .'

'If you are trying to insult me, Mrs Grey . . .'

'Hardly, dear. But do answer me this . . . and note that I am phrasing this *as* a question: did you actually spend the night with your sailor in a cheap hotel?'

I narrowed her in my sights. 'No, he actually spent the night at my apartment. And he wasn't a sailor. He was in the Army.'

There was a pause, during which she raised her coffee cup and took a sip. 'Thank you for clarifying matters.'

'You're welcome.'

'And if you think I am going to tell George about this, you are mistaken.'

'I sense George already knows.'

'Don't be so certain of that. When it comes to women, men only hear what they want to hear. It's one of the many failures of their sex.'

'You think your son George is a failure, don't you?'

'George is a well-meaning boy. Not one of life's

natural leaders, but modest and humane. For the life of me, I don't know what a smart girl like you sees in him. Your marriage will fail. Because, eventually, he will bore you.'

'Who says we will marry?'

'Trust me: you will. *C'est le moment juste.* It's how it happens. But it will be a ghastly mistake.'

'May I ask *you* a question, Mrs Grey?'

'Of course, dear.'

'Did your son's death transform you into a misanthrope, or were you always so bitter and joyless?'

She pursed her lips, and considered her reflection in the black sheen surface of her coffee. After a moment, she looked back up at me. 'I've enjoyed our conversation enormously, dear. It has been most enlightening.'

'For me as well.'

'I'm so glad. And I must say I'll come away from our little talk with a splendid realization . . . what I think you writers call *an epiphany.*'

'Which is what, Mrs Grey?'

'We are never going to like each other.'

Later that morning, I boarded a train back to Manhattan with George. We sat in the Club Car. He insisted on buying us a bottle of champagne (which turned out to be New York State sparkling wine). He insisted on holding my hand all the way to Grand Central Station. He could not take his adoring eyes off me. He looked love-sick – that same *morning-after* glow which I must have radiated on that Thanksgiving morning eighteen months ago.

Somewhere south of Port Chester, he said, 'Marry me.'

I heard myself reply, 'All right.'

He appeared stunned. 'What?'

'All right, I'll marry you.'

'You mean it?'

'Yes. I mean it.'

His stunned expression quickly gave way to elation. 'I don't believe it,' he said.

'Believe it,' I said.

'I'll have to call my parents as soon as we get to Manhattan. They'll be so thrilled. My mother especially.'

'Of course they will,' I said quietly.

I didn't say a word to George about the little chat that his mother and I had had over breakfast that morning. Nor did I relate its contents to Eric. Because I knew that – had I described the conversation with Mrs Grey, or told him about the extraordinary stiffness of the family into which I was marrying – he would have tried to talk me out of the engagement.

So I said nothing – except that I was happy as hell, and knew I was making the right decision. He met George for that drink at the Astor Hotel. He found him benignly pleasant. Afterwards, when George asked me if he'd made a reasonable impression on my brother, I said, 'He thought you were great.'

Just like your mother thought I was wonderful. Oh, the lies we tell each other to dodge everything we don't want to face.

Of course, immediately after accepting George's proposal, a doubting voice began to amplify inside my head. More troubling was the discovery that, the more time I spent with George, the louder that voice became. Eventually – after a few weeks – it was so omnipresent that I started to think: I must bail out. Quickly.

But then, a day or so later, I woke up to discover myself violently ill. For the remainder of the week, my morning would begin with a manic dash to the bathroom. Certain that I had been felled with some amoebic bug, I made an appointment to see Dr Ballensweig. He ran a few tests. When he gave me the results, I felt as if I had been hit by a car.

As soon as I got home, I phoned George at the bank.

'Hello, my darling,' he said.

'We need to talk,' I said.

'What's happened?' he said, suddenly worried.

I took a deep breath.

'Is it something terrible?'

'That depends on how you look at it.'

'Tell me, darling. Tell me.'

Another deep breath. Then I said, 'I'm pregnant.'

CHAPTER 7

A few terrible days later, I went over to Eric's apartment and told him my news. He flinched, then fell silent. Finally, he asked me a question. 'Are you happy about this?'

That's when I burst into tears, burying my head in my brother's shoulder. He held me and rocked me. 'You don't have to go through with this if you don't want to,' he whispered.

I pulled my head off his shoulder. 'What are you suggesting?'

'I'm just saying: if you want out, I can probably help you.'

'Medically, you mean?'

He nodded. 'An actress friend knows of this doctor . . .'

I held up my hand. 'I couldn't do that.'

'Fine,' he said. 'I was only offering . . .'

'I know, I know – and I appreciate . . .'

I broke off and buried my head in his shoulder again. 'I really don't know what the hell to do,' I said.

'Let me ask you this: do you really want to marry this guy?'

292

'No. It's a mistake. His mother even said that to me.'

'When?'

'After that night I spent at their house in Greenwich.'

'Was that the night you and George . . . ?'

I nodded. And blushed. 'Somehow she knew.'

'She was probably standing outside the door, listening in. Anyway, if she says it's a mistake, then she wouldn't be too shocked if you decided not to go through with the wedding.'

'You cannot be serious. George knows I'm pregnant. His parents know I'm pregnant. There is absolutely no way that I am going to be allowed out of this.'

'This is not a feudal state – despite the best efforts of the Republican Party. You are not chattel. You can do whatever the hell you want.'

'You mean, raise this child on my own?'

'Yes. In fact, we could do it together.'

It took a moment or two for this to register. 'I'm touched. Deeply touched. But it's an insane idea. And you know it. I couldn't raise this child on my own.'

'I would be there.'

'That's not what I'm talking about.'

'You're worried about what other people would think.'

'I'm worried about being completely marginalized. You've said it over and over: at heart, we're a puritan country. We ostracize anyone who commits a sexual transgression. And having a child out of wedlock – then raising it on your own – is considered a very big sin.'

'So being in a terrible marriage is a better alternative?'

'I'm sure I can make it work. George is not a bad man.'

'*Not a bad man.* That's one hell of an endorsement, S.'

'I know, I know. But . . . what can I do?'

'Make the tough call. Tell him you'll have the kid, but you won't have him.'

'I'm not that brave, Eric. I'm too damn conventional.'

'Well, by the time Georgie-boy and his parents are finished with you, you're going to feel like a character in an Ibsen play.'

'Thanks a lot.'

'How did they take the news?'

I considered this question, and finally answered, 'They took it reflectively.'

'*Reflectively?* What the hell do you mean by that?'

'They had a measured response to the news.'

'They're WASPs, for God's sake, not Italians of course they'd be measured. But I bet they were a bit glacial as well.'

I said nothing. Because *glacial* was the right word. Though George had informed his parents of our engagement on the afternoon I accepted his proposal, it was agreed that we'd wait at least a month or two before deciding on a date for the wedding.

Then I got the news from Dr Ballensweig, and had to pass it on to George. He took it pretty well, telling me how much he wanted children with me. I did point out that a child might put a strain on a new marriage – especially one where the two people involved had only known each other for a month before getting engaged. But George re-assured me that all would be fine.

'We're going to be just hunky-dory,' he said. 'Because when we're as much in love as we are, all problems are easily solvable.'

Hunky-dory. Wonderful.

'Naturally,' he said, 'Mother and Father might be a tad concerned about the fact that the wedding will now have to be brought a little forward.'

'You'll break the news to them, won't you?'

There was a long silence on the phone. When he spoke again, he sounded like a man who had just been 'volunteered' into leading the advance party into Injun Country.

'Of course I'll tell them,' he said, his nervous-ness so apparent. 'And I know they are going to be thrilled to be grandparents.'

He went up to Connecticut the following night. Early the next morning, the phone rang at my office. It was my future mother-in-law.

'Julia Grey here,' she said crisply.

'Oh, hello,' I said, sounding seriously thrown.

'I am planning to be in the city tomorrow. It is

important that we meet. Say four p.m. in the Palm Court of the Plaza. All right?'

Before I had time to reply, she had put down the receiver – making it very clear that she didn't care whether or not that time was suitable for me. I was being summoned. I would be there.

Instantly I picked up the phone and called George at his office.

'Darling, I was just about to call you,' he said.

'Your mother pre-empted you.'

'Oh. I see.'

'And from her brusque tone, it's pretty clear how she took the news.'

He cleared his throat. Loudly. Then said, 'Naturally, it came as a surprise to them. But after the initial . . . uh . . .'

'Shock?'

'Yes, well, uh, they were, truth be told, quite shocked. But that only lasted a moment or two. After which they became . . .'

'Furious?'

'Reflective.'

'Now they really hate me.'

'Darling, they don't hate you at all. On the contrary . . .'

'They think *what*? That I am a great social catch? The perfect banker's wife?'

I could almost hear him squirming at the other end of the phone.

'Darling, everything will be fine. Just fine. Trust me.'

'I have no choice, do I?'

'And don't worry about Mother's brusqueness. It's just . . .'

'Her style, I suppose?'

'Gosh, we're already completing each other's sentences.'

I put down the phone. I put my head in my hands. I felt cornered, trapped. There was no way out.

The next afternoon, I left my office at three thirty and walked up Fifth Avenue, full of dread. I entered the Plaza Hotel at the appointed time. Mrs Grey was seated at a table in the Palm Court. She saw me approach. She did not smile. She did not proffer her hand. She simply motioned to the chair beside her and said, 'Sit down, Sara.'

I did as ordered. She stared at me for a long time, her lips pinched, turning them into a fine inflexible line that bisected her face. I tried to meet her disdainful stare. I began to knead my hands together. Naturally she noticed this.

'Are you feeling anxious, Sara?' she asked mildly.

My hands froze. 'Yes. I am feeling anxious.'

'I suppose, were I in your situation, I would feel anxious as well. The fact is, though – I would never have landed myself in such a situation. One always pays a huge price for impulsiveness.'

'And, I suppose, you've never been guilty of impulsiveness?'

Her lips expanded into her telltale tight smile. 'No,' she said.

'Not a single act of rashness in your entire life?'

'I'm afraid not.'

'How controlled of you.'

'I will take that as a compliment, Sara. But back to business . . .'

'I didn't realize we were talking business.'

'Oh yes. This is, without question, a business conversation. Because, as far as I'm concerned, we have nothing else to talk about but the practical matter of arranging a wedding post haste. We don't want you walking down the aisle visibly *enceinte*, now do we?'

Another of her narrow smiles. I said nothing.

'Of course, everyone at the wedding will naturally know why we have so expedited the scheduling of the ceremony. Which, in turn, means that we will want to keep the event small and discreet. No doubt, this will not tally with your childhood fantasies of a big all-white wedding . . .'

'How do you know *what* my childhood fantasies were?' I asked, the anger showing.

'Don't all girls dream of a big wedding?'

'No.'

'Of course I forgot – you and your brother were always a little out of step with things, much to the distress of your very nice parents.'

I glared at her, wide-eyed.

'How dare you make such an assumption . . .'

'I'm not making an assumption, dear. I am simply reporting established fact. We have these very old friends in Hartford – the Montgomerys.

298

They were your parents' neighbors, *n'est-ce pas?*'

'Yes. They lived a few houses away from us.'

'Well, when Mr Grey and I discovered – somewhat abruptly, I should add – that you were to be our daughter-in-law, we decided to do a little checking into your background. It turned out Mr Grey knew Mr Montgomery from Princeton. Class of nineteen oh eight. And Mr Montgomery and his wife, Miriam, were exceedingly informative about your family. I never knew, for example, that your brother is a Communist.'

'He is *not* a Communist.'

'He joined the Party, didn't he?'

'Yes . . . but that was during the thirties, when it was fashionable . . .'

'Fashionable? To the best of my knowledge the Communist Party wishes to overthrow the government of this country. Is that your idea of *chic*, Sara?'

'He left the Party in forty-one. He made a mistake. He's the first to admit that now.'

'What a pity your poor parents aren't around to hear his renunciation.'

I felt myself getting very angry.

'Eric mightn't be the most conventional of men, but he was always a good son to our parents . . . and he is the best brother imaginable.'

'I do so admire familial loyalty. Especially in the face of such *unconventionality*.'

'I don't know what you are talking about.'

'Oh yes you do. So too, I gather, did your late

parents. In fact, word has it that your brother's *unconventionality* so upset your father that it hastened the stroke which killed him.'

'It's outrageous to blame Eric . . .'

'No one is apportioning blame, Sara. I'm just reporting what I heard from others. Just as I also heard that you directly contravened your father's wishes by moving to New York after Bryn Mawr. And shortly thereafter, the stroke felled him . . .'

I was on the verge of screaming at her. Or slapping her. Or spitting in her face. My heart was pounding, my rage immense. She saw this, and responded by affording me another of her little smiles. A smile which invited me to do something reprehensible . . . and pay an even bigger price than the one I was paying now. A smile which forced me to remain in control.

So, taking several deep steadying breaths, I simply stood up and said, 'We have nothing more to say to each other, Mrs Grey.'

Her tone remained temperate, steady.

'If you walk out of here now, dear, you will be creating enormous problems for yourself.'

'I don't care.'

'Oh yes you do. After all, I can't imagine a respectable family magazine like *Saturday Night/ Sunday Morning* allowing an unwed mother to remain in their employment. And once *Saturday/ Sunday* dismisses you on moral grounds, who on earth will hire you? Then there's the matter of your apartment. Isn't there some clause in the

standard New York City tenancy lease . . . Mr
Grey mentioned this to me *en passant* . . . about
landlords being able to evict tenants who have
committed acts of *moral turpitude*? Granted, having
a child out of wedlock might not fit the letter of
the law . . . but could you afford to fight such an
eviction in court?'

I sat down again. I said nothing. Mrs Grey
lowered her head for a moment. When she raised
it again, she was the picture of civility.

'I knew that, at heart, you were a sensible girl,
Sara. I'm certain that, from this moment forward,
we will get along just fine. Tea?'

I didn't respond. Possibly because I felt the way
a convicted felon must feel when he's been
sentenced to life imprisonment. This was the abyss.
And I was in it.

'I'll take your silence as a yes,' she said, motioning
towards a waiter. 'Now then, back to business. The
wedding . . .'

She outlined the plans. Under the hasty circumstances, a wedding at the family parish church in
Connecticut was out of the question ('one simply
does not organize such an event with two weeks'
notice'). Instead, there would be a simple straightforward service at the Marble Collegiate Church
in Manhattan – to which I would be allowed to
invite four guests, including my brother ('I presume
he will be giving you away?' she asked dryly).
There would be a simple, straightforward reception
afterwards here at the Plaza. George would be

organizing 'the honeymoon details', though Mrs Grey had suggested to him 'a nice, modest hotel' in Provincetown, into which he had subsequently booked us for a week. After the honeymoon, we would be moving into our new home . . . in Old Greenwich, Connecticut.

It took a moment for this news to register. 'George and I are moving *where*?' I asked.

'To Old Greenwich, Connecticut. You mean, he hasn't yet told you . . . ?'

'Considering that he only informed you of our news last night . . .'

'Of course, of course. The poor boy's had so much on his mind. Anyway, when he did tell us your *wonderful* news yesterday evening, Mr Grey gave him the most marvelous surprise. As our wedding gift to you both, we're letting you have a little house we bought as an investment a year or so ago in Old Greenwich. Do understand – it's hardly a mansion. But it's the perfect starter house for a young family. And it's only five minutes' walk to the railway station, so it will be very handy for George's commute to Manhattan. Do you know Old Greenwich? Very sweet little town . . . and right near Long Island Sound, so it will be perfect for . . .'

Drowning myself.

'. . . outings with other young mothers. After the baby arrives I'm sure you'll find so much to do up there. Coffee mornings. Church socials. Charity yard sales. The PTA . . .'

As I listened to her delineate, with relish, my prosaic future, all I could think was: this is a master-class in how to twist the knife.

I finally interrupted her.

'Why can't we live in George's apartment for a while?'

'That dreadful place? I wouldn't allow it, Sara.'

It wasn't that dreadful: a serviced one-bedroom flat in a residential hotel, the Mayflower, on 61st Street and Central Park West.

'We could always find a bigger place in the city,' I said.

'The city is no place to raise children.'

'But the baby's not due for around seven months. I don't want to be commuting back and forth to Connecticut to my job . . .'

'Your job?' she said, sounding amused. 'What job?'

'My job at *Saturday/Sunday*, of course.'

'Oh, *that* job. You'll be resigning at the end of next week.'

'No I won't.'

'Of course you will. Because a week later you will be married. And married women do not work.'

'I was planning to be the exception.'

'Sorry, dear. It cannot be. Anyway, given your condition, you'd have to give up work in a few months. It's the way motherhood works.'

I tried to remain rational, reasoned, in control.

'Say I refused? Say I simply walked out of this hotel right now and didn't go through with any of this?'

'I have already outlined the consequences to you. I do believe in individual free will – so, as far as I'm concerned, you may do whatever you want to do. Sadly, the outcome of such a decision may not be to your liking – as raising a child on your own without a job or a decent place to live may be a little difficult. But we would never dream of stopping you . . .'

My eyes began to water. I felt tears cascading down my face. 'Why are you doing this?' I whispered.

Mrs Grey looked at me, baffled. 'Doing what, dear?'

'Ruining my life.'

'*Ruining your life?* Please spare me the cheap melodrama, Sara. I certainly didn't force you to get pregnant, now did I?'

I said nothing.

'Anyway, if I was in your position, I would be positively delighted with the way everything's been arranged. After all, it's not many girls who get given a house in a desirable suburb as a wedding gift.'

A final tight smile. I stared down at the table. There was a lengthy silence.

'Cat got your tongue, dear? Or have you simply seen the logic of my arguments?'

My gaze remained fixed on the table.

'Splendid,' she finally said. 'Our plans will proceed as agreed. Oh . . . and look who's here to see us. What marvelous timing the boy has.'

I looked up. George was standing at the entrance of the Palm Court, hesitantly awaiting the wave of his mother's hand that would beckon him to the table. No doubt, she had given him an appointed time at which to arrive at the Plaza. Just as she had told him last night exactly how she was going to stage manage our life from this day forward. Because, in the world according to Mrs Grey, this was the price one paid for transgressing her sense of order and decorum and social standing.

Mrs Grey used her right index finger to beckon George forward. He approached our table shyly, like a schoolboy being called into the principal's office.

'Hi there,' he said, trying to sound cheery. 'Everyone happy?'

He glanced at me and saw that I had been crying. Immediately, he tensed. His mother said, 'Sara and I have been discussing future plans, and we're in agreement on everything.'

I said nothing. I continued to stare at the table-top. Her voice became testy. 'Aren't we, dear?'

I didn't raise my gaze, but I did say, 'Yes. Everything is fine.'

'And we now so understand each other, don't we?'

I nodded.

'So you see, George – everything is working out splendidly . . . as I told you it would. As I'm sure you well know, Sara – the poor boy is a bit of a worrier. Aren't you, George?'

'I guess so,' he said nervously. Sitting down next to me, he tried to take my hand. But I pulled it away before he clutched it. Mrs Grey caught sight of this little drama and smiled.

'I think I'll go powder my nose, and let you love-birds have a moment or two alone.'

As soon as she was out of earshot, George said, 'Darling, don't be upset . . .'

'I didn't realize I was marrying your mother.'

'You're not.'

'Oh yes I am . . . as it seems that she is calling all the shots here.'

'After the wedding, we can block her right out of our lives . . .'

'After the wedding we will be living in Old Greenwich, Connecticut. How nice of you to discuss this little change of address with me . . .'

'The offer of the house only came last night.'

'So you naturally decided to accept it without consulting me.'

'I meant to call you at work this morning.'

'But you didn't.'

'I was tied up in meetings.'

'Liar. You were afraid what my reaction might be.'

He lowered his head. 'Yes. I was afraid how you might react. But, look, the house in Old Greenwich was just a really generous offer from my parents. We don't have to accept it.'

I stared at him with utter contempt. 'Yes we do,' I said, 'and you know it.'

A pause. He squirmed in his chair. And finally said, 'You'll really like Old Greenwich.'

'I'm so glad you think so,' I said.

'And if you don't like it . . .'

'Then *what*?'

'Then . . .' He squirmed again. 'I promise you, it will all work out. Let's just get through the wedding . . .'

'And then – let me guess – you're going to tell her to stay out of our lives forever?'

Another uncomfortable pause. 'I'll try,' he said, his voice a near whisper. He then made a loud coughing noise to indicate that his mother was returning. When she approached our table, George instantly stood up and held her chair. After she sat down, she nodded to indicate that he could be seated. Then she turned her gaze to me.

'So,' she asked, 'did you have a nice chat about things?'

Had I been the fearless sort, I would have stood up and walked out of the Plaza, and accepted my fate. But to do that, in 1947, would have meant taking the most enormous personal gamble. And yes, as much as I loathed her, Mrs Grey was right about one thing: deciding to be a single mother would have meant instant unemployment, instant social ostracization. Back then, only widows and abandoned women were allowed to be single mothers. To decide to have a child outside of wedlock – or, worse yet, to reject an offer of marriage by the child's father – would have been considered, at best, deeply

307

reprehensible; at worst, deranged. And I didn't posses the *don't give a damn* mentality needed to buck conventionality. I longed to have Eric's seditious streak, but knew I couldn't pull it off. Like it or not, I was a small-c conservative. My parents may have despaired at my minor acts of rebellion – like moving to Manhattan after college. But they instilled in me such a fear of authority – and such deeply engrained notions of respectability – that I felt unable to do the impossible, awkward thing: telling George Grey and his godawful parent to go to hell.

I certainly wasn't going to tell Eric about my conversation with Mrs Grey (or the way I was being railroaded into a life in Old Greenwich, Connecticut), because I knew he would have gone berserk. At best, I would have to listen to his very impassioned, very persuasive arguments, pleading with me to bail out of this future domestic night-mare while there was still a chance. At worst, he would have done something melodramatic . . . like spiriting me out of the country to Paris or Mexico City until the baby was born.

But my mind was made up. I was going to marry George. I was going to move to the Connecticut suburbs. I was going to have the child. I had landed myself in this mess. I was going to accept my fate. Because I deserved my fate.

I also began to rationalize like crazy. All right, George was dwarfed by his mother – but once we were married, I would be able to gradually excise her from our lives. All right, I would hate leaving

New York – but maybe Old Greenwich would give me the peace and quiet I needed to try writing again. All right, my husband-to-be was the emotional equivalent of vanilla ice cream – but hadn't I vowed never to fall victim to wayward passion again? Hadn't I vowed to avoid another . . .

Jack.

Jack. Jack. Damn you, Jack. That night – that one absurd night – led me right into the dull, worthy arms of George Grey.

In the two weeks running up to the wedding, I assented to everything. I let Mrs Grey make all the arrangements for the ceremony and the party. I let her book me a rushed appointment at a dress-maker, who whipped up a standard-issue white wedding dress for $85 ('Of course we wouldn't dream of letting you pay, dear,' Mrs Grey said at the fitting). I let her choose the order of the service, the menu at the reception, the centerpiece on the cake. I accompanied George by train to Old Greenwich to inspect our new house. It was a small two-storey Cape Codder, located on a road called Park Avenue, within a five-minute walk from the railway station. Park Avenue was very leafy, very residential. Each house had a substantial front yard, with a very green lawn. They were all immaculately manicured. Just as all the houses showed no signs of wear-and-tear: no peeling paint, or decrepit roofs, or smudged windows. From my first stroll down Park Avenue, I knew immediately that this was a community which did not tolerate such sins against the body politic as unmowed grass or badly graveled drive-ways.

The houses along Park Avenue were New England in character – testaments to Poe-style Gothic rubbing shoulders with white clapboard, and Federalist red brick. Ours was one of the smallest properties, with low ceilings and small, cramped rooms. They were papered in discreet floral prints or tiny red-and-blue checks – the sort of old Americana patterns that put me in mind of the inside of a Whitman's chocolate box. The furniture was spartan in char-acter and size – cramped, narrow sofas; hard wooden armchairs, a pair of narrow single beds in the master bedroom. There was a plain wooden table in the other bedroom with a bentwood chair.

'This will be the perfect place to write your novel,' George said, trying to sound cheerful.

'So where will the baby sleep?' I asked quietly.

'In our room for the first few months. Anyway, we should look on this place as nothing more than a starter house. Once we have a couple of kids, we'll definitely need . . .'

I cut him off.

'One child at a time, okay?'

'Fine, fine,' he said, sounding anxious at my testy tone. 'I didn't mean to be pushing things . . .'

'I know you didn't.'

I moved back down the corridor to the master bedroom, and sat on one of the single beds. The mattress felt like a concrete slab. George sat down beside me. He took my hand.

'We can get a proper double bed if you like.'

I shrugged.

'And anything you want to do to this place is fine by me.'

How about burning it to the ground, darling?

'It'll be fine,' I said, my voice toneless.

'Of course it will. And we'll be happy here, right?'

I nodded.

'And I know you're going to grow to love it here. Heck, Old Greenwich is a great place to raise a family.'

Heck. I was marrying a man who used the word *heck*.

But I still didn't attempt to bail out of the wedding. Instead, I calmly upended my life. I handed in my resignation at *Saturday/Sunday*. I informed my landlord that I would be vacating my apartment. As I had rented it furnished, there was little to pack up. Just some books, my Victrola and my collection of records, a few family photos, three suitcases' worth of clothing, my typewriter. Looking at my small pile of possessions made me think, I travel light.

Finally, three days before the ceremony, I conjured up the nerve to tell Eric about my impending move to Old Greenwich. My delay in informing him of this news was a strategic one – as I knew he would become vehement as soon as he heard.

Which, of course, he did.

'Have they railroaded you into this move?' he asked angrily, pacing my packed-up apartment.

'George's parents simply offered us this charming little house as a wedding gift, and I thought: why not?'

'That's all there was to it?'

'Yes.'

He looked at me with deep scepticism. 'You – the most die-hard New Yorker imaginable – simply decided to close down your existence in Manhattan and move to goddamn Old Greenwich just because Georgie-boy's parents gave you a house? I don't believe it.'

'I thought it was time for a change,' I said, trying to sound calm. 'And I am looking forward to the peace and quiet.'

'Oh please, S – cut the serenity crap. You don't want to be in Connecticut. I know that. You know that.'

'It's a gamble, but it could turn out wonderfully.'

'I said it once. I said it before. You can walk away now, and I will support you in every way I can.'

I touched my stomach. 'I don't have a choice in the matter.'

'You do. You just don't see it.'

'Believe me, I see it. But I just can't make that leap of imagination. I have to do what's expected of me.'

'Even if it ruins your life?'

I bit hard on my lip and turned away, my eyes hot with tears.

'Please stop,' I said.

He came over and put his hand on my shoulder. For the first time ever, I shrugged him off.

'I'm sorry,' he said.

'Not as sorry as me.'

'We all ruin our lives in some way, I guess . . .'

'Is that supposed to make me feel better?'

'No. It's supposed to make *me* feel better.'

I managed a laugh. 'You're right,' I finally said. 'In some way or another, we all mess things up. Only some of us do it more comprehensively than others.'

To Eric's infinite credit, he never again reproached me about marrying George and moving to Connecticut. Three days after that difficult conversation in my apartment, he put on his only suit, a clean white shirt, and (for him) a subdued tie, and walked me down the aisle at the Marble Collegiate Church. George was in an ill-fitting cutaway (with a high-collar shirt) that accented his schoolboy chubbiness. The minister was a bored man with thinning hair and bad dandruff. He read the service in a reedy monotone, and at speed. From start to finish, the entire ceremony took fifteen minutes. As there were only twelve invited guests, the church seemed very cavernous – our vows echoing through the rows of empty pews. It was very lonely indeed.

The reception afterwards was also a rushed affair.

It was held in a private dining room at the Plaza. Mr and Mrs Grey weren't exactly the most welcoming of hosts. They didn't try to make conversation with Eric, or with my friends from *Saturday/Sunday*. George's chums from the bank were also exceptionally stiff. Before the dinner, they huddled together in a corner, talking quietly among themselves, occasionally emitting a sharp communal snigger of laughter. I was certain they were articulating what everyone at this joyless event was thinking, *so this is what's known as a shotgun marriage.*

Only, of course, this being a WASP shotgun marriage, everyone was carrying on as if it was a perfectly straightforward event.

There was a sit-down meal. There was a toast from Mr Grey. Like everything else that day, it was emotionless and brisk: 'Please raise your glasses to welcome Sara to our family. We hope that she and George will be happy.'

That was it. George's toast was almost as phlegmatic: 'I just want to say that I am the luckiest man in the world, and I know that Sara and I will make a great team. And I want you all to know that we're operating an open-door policy in Old Greenwich – so we're going to expect lots of visitors real soon.'

I glanced across the table and saw my brother roll his eyes. Then he realized that I saw him being caustic, and he gave me a guilty smile. That one small private moment aside, he really had been a model of tact and diplomacy all afternoon. Even though he looked utterly respectable in his black

314

suit, Mr and Mrs Grey still eyed him with anxious distaste – as if he was some sort of strange left-wing alien, about to jump on a table and hector us with passages from *Das Kapital*. At the reception, however, he made a point of chatting with my parents-in-law, and even managed to wangle a small laugh or two from them. This was an astonishing phenomenon – discovering that the Greys had a sense of humor – and I cornered Eric as he crossed the room en route to the bar for fresh drinks, whispering:

'What did you slip into their wine?'

'I was simply telling them how much they reminded me of *The Magnificent Ambersons*.'

I stifled a laugh.

'I'm glad to see you still have a sense of the comedic,' he said. 'You're going to need it.'

'It'll be fine,' I said, sounding unconvinced.

'And if it's not fine, you can always run back to me.'

I clutched his hands in mine. 'You're the best.'

He arched his eyebrows. 'I'm glad you finally figured that out.'

Eric did have one slight moment of mischief, when George called upon him 'to speak for the bride's family'. Standing up, he raised his glass and said, 'The best quote about *domicile conjugale* came from that very short Frenchman, Toulouse-Lautrec, who said that "marriage is a dull meal, preceded by dessert". I'm certain this will *not* be the case with George and Sara.'

Well, I thought it was witty – though most of the other guests coughed nervously after Eric sat down again. Then George and I cut the cake. We posed for a few photographs. The cake was served with coffee. Ten minutes later, Mr and Mrs Grey stood up, indicating it was time to draw things to a close. So we said our goodbyes. My father-in-law gave me a fast peck on the forehead, but had no words of luck or farewell for me. Mrs Grey air-kissed my cheeks, and said, 'You did fine, dear. Keep doing fine, and we will get along very well.'

Then Eric came over, embraced me, and whispered, 'Don't let the bastards get you down.'

He left. The room emptied out. The reception had started at 5.30 p.m. It was now eight o'clock, and it was over. There was nothing left for us to do but retreat upstairs to the 'honeymoon suite' which George had booked for us that night.

So upstairs we went. George disappeared into the bathroom and emerged in his pajamas. I disappeared into the bathroom and undressed, then slipped on a robe. I re-entered the room to find George already in bed. I unfastened the robe and slid into bed next to him, naked. He pulled me close to him. He began to kiss my face, my neck, my breasts. He unfastened the fly of his pajamas. He spread my legs and climbed on top of me. A minute later, he emitted a small groan and rolled off me. Then he tucked himself back into his pajama bottom, kissed the back of my neck, and wished me 'good night'.

It took a moment or two for me to realize that he had passed out. I glanced at the clock on the bedside table. Eight forty. *Eight forty on a Saturday night – my damn wedding night – and my husband is already asleep?*

I shut my eyes and tried to join him in early-to-bed unconsciousness. I failed. Opening my eyes again, I got out of bed and went into the bathroom, shutting the door behind me. I ran a bath. As the water cascaded out of the tap, I suddenly did something I had been threatening to do for the past few hours: I started to weep.

Within moments, the weeping became uncontrollable, and so loud that it must have been discernible over the sound of running water. But there was no sudden knock at the bathroom door, followed by a huge reassuring hug from George, telling me everything was going to be all right.

Because, of course, George was a very deep sleeper. If the loud Niagara of open taps didn't wake him, then why should he even hear his wife sobbing?

Eventually, I managed to regain control of myself. I turned off the taps. I caught sight of myself in the bathroom mirror. My eyes were red, my wedding makeup was streaked. I slid into the bath. I took a wash towel, dipped it in the hot water, then draped it over my face. I stared up into its white emptiness. Thinking, *I have made the worst mistake of my life.*

Too fast, too fast. Everything happened too fast.

He made love too fast. We got engaged too fast. I agreed to this wedding too fast. He fell asleep too fast.

And now . . .

Now I was trapped . . . though, of course, it was me who had trapped myself.

The honeymoon wasn't a great success either. The hotel which Mrs Grey had suggested in Provincetown was an elderly inn, run by an elderly couple and catering largely for elderly visitors. It was shabby genteel. Our bed had a sagging mattress. The sheets stank of mildew. The bathroom was down the hall from our room. There were rust stains in the bathtub, and the sink had chipped enamel. As it was the off-season there were few places open in Provincetown for dinner, so we were forced to make do with the food at the inn – all of which was heavily boiled. It rained for three of the five days we were there – but we did manage to get a few walks in on the beach. Otherwise, we sat in the lounge of the inn, reading. George tried to be cheerful. I tried to be cheerful. I also managed to get him to make love to me without his pajamas. It was still over within a minute. I asked him not to roll over and play dead afterwards. He apologized. Profusely. Instead he put his arms around me, holding me tight. Within moments, he was fast asleep – and I was trapped in his arms. I did not sleep well that night. Nor, for that matter, did I sleep well any night in Provincetown, thanks to the droopy bed, the bad food, the charmless atmosphere of the inn, and the fact that the true reality of marriage to George was beginning to hit.

The five nights came to an end. We boarded a bus which took five hours to drive the length of Cape Cod to Boston. We caught a train south. We arrived into Old Greenwich just before midnight. At that hour, there were no cabs at the station, so we had to carry our bags the ten minutes it took to walk up Park Avenue. As we approached our house, all I could think was, *I will die here*.

All right, I was being a little melodramatic. But the house seemed so drab, so poky, so damn cheerless. Inside, assorted boxes and suitcases from our respective New York apartments lay piled up in the living room. I looked at them and thought, *I could call the movers tomorrow and have all my stuff picked up while George was at work, and be gone before he arrived home that night.*

But where was I going to go?

In our bedroom, the two single beds were separated by a bedside table. When I first saw the house with George, he said that our first order of business upon moving in was to remove that table and push the beds together. But we were so tired after the twelve-hour journey from Provincetown that we simply slipped into our respective beds and fell asleep instantly. When I woke the next morning, there was a note awaiting me on the table:

Darling:

Off to the city to bring in the bacon. And as you were sleeping so peacefully, I decided I could fry the bacon myself. Back on the 6.12.

Love and kisses . . .

Off to the city to bring in the bacon. Did this man have no sense of irony whatsoever?

I spent the day unpacking. I took a walk over to Sound Beach Avenue – Old Greenwich's Main Street – and did some shopping. Back in '47, this corner of Connecticut had yet to become a busy dormitory community for Manhattan, so Old Greenwich still retained a small-town atmosphere. As befitting all small towns, all the shopkeepers quickly gauged that I was a newcomer, and turned on the communal charm.

'Oh, you're the gal who married Old Man Grey's son, and is living on Park Avenue,' said the woman in Cuff's – the local stationery shop, and the only place in town that sold the *New York Times*.

'Yes, I'm Sara Grey,' I said, stumbling over my new last name.

'Nice having you in town. Hope you'll be real happy here.'

'Well, it's certainly a friendly place,' I said, hoping I sounded sincere.

'Friendly it is. And great for raising kids.' She glanced at my midsection, which had yet to show a telltale bulge. She tried to repress a smirk. 'If,

320

of course,' you're planning to have kids so soon after the wedding.'

'You never know,' I said quietly.

In every shop on Sound Beach Avenue, I was greeted with the same question: 'New in town?' When I explained who I was, a knowing smile would follow, along with a pleasantly pointed comment like: 'Heard you had a real nice little wedding.'

Or: 'My, that was a whirlwind romance you and George had.'

By the end of this first shopping expedition, I felt as if I should wear a sign around my neck which read: *Just Married and Pregnant*. More worryingly, I had a stab of despair as I thought that the eight stores which lined Sound Beach Avenue would be my world.

George arrived home off the 6.12 from Grand Central Station, bearing flowers. After giving me a kiss on the lips, he noticed that half the boxes and suitcases on the living room floor had been cleared.

'Been unpacking already?' he asked.

'Yes – I put most of my things away.'

'Good work,' he said. 'And you can tackle all of my clothes tomorrow. And honey, if you wouldn't mind giving the suits a light pressing . . .'

'Oh, sure, I guess.'

'Great, great. Listen, I'm going upstairs to change. How about making us a celebratory martini for our first full evening in at our new house.'

'A martini? Okay.'

'Not too dry. My sweet tooth is partial to vermouth. And four olives, if we've got any.'

'We don't, I'm afraid.'

'Hey, no problem. Just add them to your shopping list tomorrow. And hey – forgot to ask . . . what's for dinner?'

'Uh, I bought some lamb chops and broccoli . . .'

'Oh heck, meant to tell you – I really hate broccoli . . .'

'Uh, sorry . . .'

'Hey, how were you to know? Meat and potatoes – that's my style. You know how to make a meatloaf?'

'Not really.'

'Oh, it's a cinch. I'll have Bea – Mom's cook – give you a call tomorrow, and tell you her top-secret meatloaf recipe. And hon . . .'

'Yes?' I said, my voice now muffled.

'If I eat after seven at night, I just don't sleep real good. So if you could aim to have dinner on the table no later than six forty-five, well that would be great.'

'I'll do my best.'

He leaned over and kissed my forehead. 'A guy can't ask for anything more than that.'

He went upstairs to change. I retreated to the kitchen and assumed my new role as housewife. I put the lamb chops in the oven to broil. I peeled the potatoes and plunged them into a pot of boiling water. I found a glass pitcher, a bottle of Gilbey's Gin and one of vermouth. I mixed a large pitcher of martinis. I suddenly felt the need for strong alcohol.

George complimented me on my cocktails, gently reminding me again to 'get those olives' in the morning. He liked the lamb chops, but hinted they could be a little more well-done ('I really like my meat scorched'). My mashed potatoes, however, didn't pass muster ('A little lumpy, don't you think, hon? Anyway, I'm really a roasted potato guy'). I hadn't done anything for dessert, which disappointed him . . . 'but hey, it's the first time you've cooked for me as man and wife, so gosh, why should I expect you to know my likes and dislikes. It's a learning curve, right?'

I smiled. Tightly. Just like George's mother.

'Get a chance to look around Old Greenwich?' he asked.

'Yes. It's very . . . quaint.'

'*Quaint*,' he said, rolling the word around his tongue. 'That's the perfect word, all right. I told you you'd like it up here.'

'Everyone in town seemed to know who I was.'

'Well, it is a small place. Word travels fast.'

'Evidently – as everyone also seemed to know that I was pregnant.'

'Oh,' he said, worried.

'Now I wonder how that little titbit of news got around the community.'

'I don't know.'

'Don't you?'

'What are you implying?'

'I'm implying nothing. I'm just wondering . . .'

'I'll tell you what probably happened. People

heard about us getting married so quickly, so they just put two and two together.'

'Unless, of course, somebody let slip with our little secret.'

'Who would do that?'

'Your mother.'

'That's a horrible thing to say.'

'It's just a speculation . . .'

'Why on earth would she be so vindictive?'

'It's her style . . . not to mention her way of putting me in my place. In fact, if I had the money, I'd put a thousand dollars on the fact that she tipped someone in town off about my pregnancy, knowing full well that it would spread like cancer . . .'

'Why are you doing this?' he said, his tone now sharp.

'Like I said before, I'm just speculating . . .'

'Well stop speculating *now*. I won't allow it.'

I stared at him, wide-eyed. 'You won't *what*?'

He took a deep breath, and tried diplomacy. 'All I'm saying here is this: Mother may have her difficult side, but she is not hateful. Anyway, she loves you . . .'

'Now that's funny.'

'I didn't know I was marrying a cynic.'

'And I didn't know I was marrying a momma's boy.'

He turned away, as if slapped.

'I'm sorry,' I said.

'That's okay,' he said.

But we both knew it really wasn't.

When I woke the next morning at nine, there was a note on my pillow:

Hey, sleepy head!

Am I going to be cooking bacon every morning?

Bea will be calling this morning with that recipe for meatloaf. Really look forward to sampling yours tonight. Hugs and kisses . . .

Yes, you are going to be frying your own bacon every morning. Because there's no way I'm getting up early just to be your very own short order cook.

Bea called later that morning . . . right after I had finished putting away the last of George's clothes. She sounded like a woman in her fifties – with a heavy Southern accent and the sort of deferential manners that put me in mind of Hattie McDaniel in *Gone With the Wind*. She called me 'Miz Grey'. She referred to my husband as 'Mistah George'. She told me that she'd been 'cookin' for Mistah George ever since he was a li'l child', and how he had 'the biggest darn sweet tooth' she'd ever seen. She also informed me that as long as I kept that sweet tooth of his happy, I'd keep Mistah George real happy. I promised her I'd try my best.

Then she gave me her meatloaf recipe. It was long and involved. It necessitated the use of several cans of Campbell's Condensed Tomato Soup, and at least two pounds of ground beef. I'd always hated meatloaf. I now knew I would grow to loathe it.

After taking down the recipe, I walked into the village and dropped all of George's suits at the local cleaners – because there was no way I was also going to be his valet. Then I bought all the necessary ingredients for the meatloaf, not to mention a jar of olives, and a seven-layer cake at the local bakery. Walking back to the house, I passed a garage which was also selling bicycles. There was a used ladies' Schwinn – painted black with high handlebars. There were a pair of wicker panniers on either side of the back wheel – making it the perfect bike for shopping. It was in good shape – and though twenty dollars wasn't a cheap price for a used bike, I still felt I was getting a reasonable deal, especially as the garage owner assured me he would service the bike himself. So I handed him the money, loaded my groceries into both panniers, and cycled off down Sound Beach Avenue.

Instead of heading for home, I biked to the end of the main street – past the local high school, the local small hospital, and several substantial houses – then turned left and pushed on for over a mile until I came to a set of gates which announced my arrival at Todd's Point Beach: *Residents Only*.

As it was late April, the guard at the gate wasn't on duty, so I cycled right on, past a parking lot, and then turned left. Instantly I braked. Instantly I felt the first smile cross my lips in days. Because there, in front of me, was a long smooth strip of white sand, and the deep blue waters of Long Island Sound.

I parked the bike against a wooden fence, pulled off my shoes, and felt the sand creep between my toes. It was a mild day, the sun was at full altitude, the sky was clear. I took in several deep lungfuls of sea air, then began to hike down the beach. It was about a mile long. I meandered slowly, emptying my brain, enjoying the first moments of calm I'd felt ever since the discovery that I was pregnant. At the far end of the beach, I sat down in the sand and spent around a half-hour doing nothing but staring out at the tidal waters of the Sound – the metronomic ebb-and-flow of the surf lulling me into a temporary state of placidity. Thinking:

This beach will be my safety valve, my escape hatch. This beach will be the way I survive George, his family, Old Greenwich, meatloaf.

I returned to the house and followed Bea's recipe to the letter: take two pounds of ground beef, mix it by hand with one minced onion, salt, pepper, and finely crushed cornflakes (yes: *cornflakes*), and one third of a can of Campbell's Condensed Tomato Soup. Shape it into a loaf. Place it inside a baking pan. Use the remaining two thirds of a can of soup to coat it completely. Then bake in an oven for thirty-five minutes.

Knowing that George would be arriving home on the 6.12, I put the meatloaf in the oven at 6.05

. . . which would give me ample time to meet my husband's 'Dinner before Seven' deadline. He walked in through the door at 6.20. He was carrying flowers. He gave me a peck on the cheek.

'Something smells good,' he said. 'Bea must have called.'

'She did,' I said, handing him a martini.

'You got the olives!' he said, his voice fulsome – as if I'd done something extraordinary, like splitting the atom.

'Your wish is my command,' I said lightly.

He looked at me carefully. 'That's a joke, right?'

'Yes, George – that's a joke.'

'Just making sure. You're a gal full of surprises.'

'Oh really?' I said. 'What kind of surprises?'

He took a sip of his martini, then said, 'Like the new bicycle out front.'

'It's not new, George. It's second-hand.'

'It's new to me, because I haven't seen it before.'

He smiled. Now it was my turn to take a long sip of my martini.

'I only bought it today.'

'Obviously. Was it expensive?'

'Twenty dollars.'

'That's not cheap.'

'It's a good bicycle. You want me to be riding something safe, don't you?'

'That's not the issue.'

'So what *is* the issue?'

'The fact that you bought it without consulting me.'

I looked at him with something approaching shock. 'You're kidding me?' I said.

His smile remained fixed. 'All I'm saying is, if you're going to go out and make a major household purchase like a bicycle, I'd like to be told . . .'

'It was a spur-of-the-moment decision. I saw the bicycle in Flannery's Garage, the price was right, so I bought it. Anyway, I need a bicycle to get around town . . .'

'I'm not disputing that.'

'Then what are you disputing?'

'Twenty dollars of household money was spent by you without . . .'

I cut him off. 'Do you hear what you are saying?'

'There's no need for that tone, Sara.'

'Yes, there is. Because you are being absurd. Listen to yourself. You sound so generous, so benevolent, such a *loving* husband . . .'

His face fell. 'I didn't know you had such a cruel streak,' he said.

'Cruel streak! All I'm doing is responding to you saying dumb things like I need to have your written approval before I dare bankrupt us by spending an extravagant twenty dollars on a bicycle . . .'

Silence. Finally, he said, 'I never asked for written approval.'

That's when I threw back the rest of my drink and stormed off to the bedroom, slamming the door behind me, and falling face down on the bed. After a minute there was a tentative knock on the door.

'You're not crying, are you?' he asked, sounding anxious.

'Of course I'm not crying. I'm too angry.'

'Can I come in?'

'It's your room too.'

The door opened. He tentatively came over to the bed. He had my martini glass in his right hand. It had been refilled.

'A peace offering,' he said, holding it out to me. I sat up and took it. He crouched down next to me, and touched his glass against mine. 'Everyone says the first decade of marriage is always the worst.'

I tried to smile.

'That was meant as a joke,' he said.

'I know.'

'We're not getting off to a very good start, are we?'

'No, we're not.'

'How can I make things better?'

'Stop treating me like your housekeeper, for a start. Yes, I am at home, which means I will take care of things like the shopping and the overall management of the house. But just because I am now financially dependent on you doesn't automatically mean that it is my duty to serve you.'

'I'd never treat you like a servant.'

'Believe me, you were. And I want it to stop now.'

'Fine,' he said, looking away like a child who'd just been reprimanded.

'And as regards the issue of money . . . you will discover that, when it comes to spending, I am true to my New England roots, in that I'm not interested in furs, diamonds, staterooms on the *Queen Mary*, or keeping up with the Joneses. And I don't think a bicycle exactly qualifies as a frivolous luxury, especially as I'll be using it to get groceries.'

He took my hand. 'You're right. I'm wrong. And I'm sorry.'

'You really mean that?'

'Of course I do. I'm just not used to living with a wife.'

'I'm not *a wife*. I am Sara Smythe. There is a difference. Work it out.'

'Sure, sure,' he said.

We both sipped our martinis.

'I want this to work, Sara.'

I touched my midsection. 'It has to work. For obvious reasons.'

'We'll make it work. I promise.'

He kissed me lightly on the lips, and stroked my hair.

'Good,' I said, caressing his cheek with my hand. 'I'm glad we had this talk.'

'Me too.'

He pulled me towards him, and held me tight. Then he said, 'So, is the meatloaf just about done?'

It was. We went downstairs and ate. He approved of my meatloaf. He was pleased with the seven-layer cake, and laughed when I informed him of

Bea's comments about his sweet tooth. We went to bed. We made love. This time he managed to hold on for almost two minutes. He seemed genuinely pleased about this. Then he kissed me fully on the lips, got up and bumped against the bedside table that separated our two beds. As he slipped beneath his blankets, he said, 'I must move that damn thing sometime.'

I slept well that night. But early the next morning, George shook me awake. As I came to, I could see he looked deeply upset about something.

'What's happened, darling?' I asked.

'My suits . . .'

'What?'

'My suits. Where have you put my suits?'

'I took them to the cleaner's.'

'You *what*?'

I was now awake. 'You asked me to get them pressed, so I took them to the cleaner's . . .'

'I asked you to press them yourself.'

'I don't know how to press suits.'

'You don't? Really?'

'Sorry – they didn't teach me such fundamental things at Bryn Mawr.'

'There you go again, with that nasty tongue of yours.'

'I'm only being nasty because you are being so incredibly thoughtless.'

'*Thoughtless?* What the hell am I going to wear today to the office?'

'What about the suit you were wearing yesterday?'

'It's wrinkled.'

'Then press it yourself.'

He went to the closet and angrily pulled it off the rail. 'All right then, I will,' he said. 'Because, at least, *I* know how to press a suit.'

'Well, it's great to discover that a Princeton education taught you something.'

I fell back on my pillow, pulling the blankets over my head. I stayed in that position for nearly half-an-hour – until I heard the front door slam, as George went off to work. As I lay there, my stomach did somersaults. I felt sick. But it wasn't morning sickness from which I was suffering. It was despair.

Naturally, George was guilty as hell about this early morning exchange – and a large bouquet of flowers arrived by messenger early that afternoon, accompanied by a card:

I am a well-pressed fool.
And I love you.

At least it was moderately witty.

When George came home that night, he acted as if he had gone through a Pauline conversion. Naturally he brought another peace offering of flowers, augmented by a big box of chocolates . . . indicating just how guilty he was feeling.

'Two bouquets in one day?' I said, nodding towards the twelve long-stemmed roses which had arrived that morning. 'It's starting looking like a mob funeral around here.'

His face fell. 'You don't like the flowers?'

'I was just trying to be funny.'

'Of course, of course,' he said. 'I was just checking.'

'Thank you.'

'No – thank you.'

'For what?'

'For putting up with me. I know it can't be easy.'

'All I want is a degree of equitableness between us.'

'You've got it. I promise.'

'Honestly?'

He took me in his arms.

'I've gotten this all wrong. And I'm going to change that.'

'Good,' I said, and kissed his forehead.

'I love you.'

'You too,' I said quickly, hoping I didn't sound unconvincing. But George had his mind on other things, as he asked, 'Is that meatloaf I smell?'

I nodded.

'You *are* wonderful.'

For the next few weeks, George really did make an effort to establish an *entente cordiale* between us. He excised all domestic demands from his conversation. He didn't ask Bea to call me with more of his favorite recipes. He accepted the fact that I couldn't iron a suit. He agreed when I suggested we start spending five dollars twice a week for a cleaning woman. He tried to be attentive – especially as my pregnancy had now become visible, and I was starting to tire easily. He tried to be loving and considerate.

In short, he tried. And I tried too. I tried to adjust to a life at home; a life away from the edgy rhythms and manic diversity of a great city. I tried to adjust to the business of running a house; to being that creature I always secretly vowed never to become: a homemaker in the suburbs.

Most of all, I tried to adjust to marriage – to that sense of shared space, shared preoccupations, shared purpose and destiny. Only I knew deep down that there was no real sense of shared anything. Had it not been for our little biological accident, our engagement would have collapsed within months (especially after I'd gotten a whiff of just how controlling his mother could be). But now, here we were, playing house, trying to pretend that we were happy newlyweds, yet also secretly knowing that all this was fraudulent. Because there was no real basis between us – no solid foundation of camaraderie or true rapport. Let alone love.

I sensed that George knew this too. Within a month of our wedding, we started to run out of things to say to each other. Yes, we made conversation, but it was forced, labored, prone to longueurs. We didn't share each other's interests. His Connecticut friends were country club types. The men all seemed to talk about golf, the Dow Jones average, and the ongoing horror that was Harry S. Truman. The women traded recipes and maternity tips, and planned coffee mornings, and looked upon me with great suspicion. Not that I was flashing my former Greenwich Village credentials in their face. I went to three coffee mornings, and tried to join in the conversations about the perils of stretch marks and the impossibility of making a really moist Angel Food cake. But I know that they smelled my disinterest. I wasn't 'one of them'. I struck them as bookish, and reserved, and not at all enthralled by my newfound status as a kept woman. I really did work hard at 'fitting in', but ambivalence is always sniffed out. Especially when it's a clique that's doing the sniffing.

Eric insisted on paying me a visit once a week. He'd catch a late morning train up from Grand Central, and spend the entire day with me, grabbing the 6.08 that night back to the city . . . just in time to avoid having to deal with George. I'd make us lunch. Then, if the weather was good, I'd arrange for him to have use of a bicycle from Flannery's Garage (the owner, Joe Flannery, and I had become friends), and we'd head off to Todd's Point, squandering the entire afternoon at the beach.

'I'll tell you something, S,' he said one balmy Thursday afternoon in mid-May, while we were sprawled on the blanket, staring up at an early summer sun. 'Old Greenwich may be the most white-bread place on earth . . . but I sure as hell could get used to the beach.'

'This beach is my sanity,' I said.

'It's that bad, is it?'

'Well, he's not beating me with a lead pipe or chaining me to a radiator . . .'

'At least that would be colorful . . .'

I laughed loudly. 'You have a serious sick streak, Eric.'

'You've only figured that out now?'

'No – but maybe when I was in the Sodom and Gomorrah of Manhattan, your wit didn't seem so extreme.'

'Whereas here, in *WASP Central* . . .'

'Oh, if you lived here, you'd be considered the Antichrist. They'd probably have you in the stocks on the village green.'

'How do you stand it?'

'I come to this beach a lot.'

'Do you miss the city?'

'Only five times an hour.'

'Then tell him you want to move back.'

'I might as well say that I want to move to Moscow. Anyway, his mother wouldn't hear of it. And if Julia Grey won't hear of something, then the matter is closed.'

'I bet she's subtly meddlesome.'

'Not subtly. *Unapologetically.* For the first two weeks or so, she left us alone. But now that the honeymoon is well and truly over, she calls me up at least once a day.'

'Lucky you.'

'I've never said this about somebody before . . . but I actually hate her.'

'It's that bad?'

'Yes – it's really that bad.'

From all indications, it was going to get worse. Because now that I was legally ensconced with her son, Mrs Grey felt it her right to direct all aspects of my life. She also made it very clear that her only real interest in me was in my role as the Grey Family Breeder.

The daily phone call would come promptly every morning at nine a.m.

'Hello, dear,' she'd say briskly. Then, without any of the usual pleasantries, she'd immediately launch into her agenda *du jour*.

'I've made an appointment for you with an excellent obstetrician in Greenwich.'

'But I like the doctor I've been seeing locally.'

'You mean Dr Reid?'

'Yes, I mean Peter Reid. His office is a five-minute walk from my house – and, more to the point, I'm really comfortable with him.'

'I'm sure he's very *nice*. But do you know where he went to medical school? McGill in Montreal.'

'McGill is an excellent university. And, to the best of my knowledge, babies *are* born in Canada. So I'm certain Dr Reid . . .'

She cut me off.

'My dear, McGill may be a good university, but it is not an *American* university. Whereas the specialist I'm sending you to – Dr Eisenberg – went to Harvard. You have heard of Harvard, haven't you, dear?'

I said nothing.

'He also happens to be chief of obstetrics at Doctors Hospital, with practices both in Manhattan and Greenwich. And he's Jewish.'

'Why should that matter?'

'Jews always make the best doctors. It's something about their innate sense of social inferiority: it makes them far more conscientious and rigorous. Because, of course, they always feel the need to try harder and prove a point. Especially in the case of Dr Eisenberg – who's still trying to gain membership of the Greenwich Country Club. You don't have any objections about being attended to by a Jew, do you, dear?'

'Of course not. What I object to is being told which doctor I will be attending.'

'But dear, we are paying for your care . . .'

'It's my husband who's paying . . .'

'No, dear. George's salary at the bank might stretch to cover the services of Dr Reid, but it certainly wouldn't pay for an eminent man like Milton Eisenberg.'

'Then I won't go to Dr Eisenberg.'

'Yes you will, dear. Because it is our grandchild. And we must have the best for him.'

'Let me be the judge of which doctor is the best for . . .'

'The matter is closed, dear. The appointment with Dr Eisenberg is at ten thirty tomorrow morning. I will send a taxi to collect you at ten.'

Then she put down the phone without saying goodbye. When I vented my anger that night at

George, he just shrugged and said, 'But she means well.'

'No, she doesn't.'

'She wants you to be seen by the best doctor imaginable.'

'She wants to manipulate everything.'

'That's unfair . . .'

'Unfair? *Unfair!* Don't you dare talk to me about *unfair.*'

'Humor her, *please*. It will make everyone's life easier.'

So I found myself transferred over to Dr Eisenberg – a curt, gruff man in his early sixties, devoid of any warmth, yet brimming with his own self-importance. No wonder Mrs Grey approved of him.

Every day there was a phone call. Every day there was some new matter that Mrs Grey needed to discuss with me. Most of the time, the subject of the call was meaningless.

'Hello, dear. I want you to go to Cuff's on Sound Beach Avenue and buy your husband this morning's edition of the *Wall Street Journal*. There's a story about a Princeton classmate of his, Prescott Lawrence, who is doing marvelous things on Wall Street.'

'I know George gets the *Wall Street Journal* at the bank.'

'But maybe he won't get it *today*. So be a good girl and pop round to Cuff's, and get the paper.'

'Fine, fine,' I said, then completely ignored the

directive. Later that afternoon, there was a knock on the door. It was a paperboy, with a copy of the *Wall Street Journal* in his hand.

'Here's the paper you ordered,' he said.

'I didn't order it.'

'Well, someone did.'

An hour later, the phone call came. 'Dear – did you get the paper?'

I held my tongue.

'Do make certain George reads that piece about Prescott Lawrence. And please don't make a fuss about such a simple little request in the future.'

Day in, day out the calls came. Eventually, around four months into my pregnancy, I snapped. It was a hot day in July – the temperature inching towards ninety, the humidity touching similar figures. The house was stifling. I was feeling top-heavy and bloated. Our bedroom had become a sweat box. I hadn't slept well for days.

Then the morning phone call came from Mrs Grey.

'Morning, dear . . .'

Before she had time to launch into this morning's demand, I hung up. The phone rang again a few seconds later. I ignored it. Five minutes later, it rang again – but I didn't pick it up. In fact, I didn't answer it for the balance of the day – even though it continued to clang into life every twenty minutes or so.

Around three that afternoon, the constant ringing finally stopped. I felt enormous relief. I had won a small victory. She'd finally got the point. From now on, she wouldn't badger me.

Around six twenty that night, the phone clanged back into life. Thinking it might be George, calling to say he was delayed at the office, I answered it. That was a mistake.

'Hello, dear.'

Her voice was as composed as ever.

'Would you mind explaining to me why you hung up on me this morning?'

'Because I didn't want to talk to you.'

There was a pause. I could sense that she was a little stunned by that statement. Finally she said, 'That is not acceptable.'

'I don't care if it is acceptable or not. I will simply not deal with your appalling behavior towards me anymore.'

She let out a small, low laugh.

'My, my, we are feeling emboldened tonight, aren't we?'

'Not emboldened. Just fed up.'

'Well, alas, I am afraid you will simply have to put up with my alleged meddlesome nature. Because you have married my son and . . .'

'Marrying your son doesn't give you the right to tell me what to do.'

'On the contrary, I have every right. You are carrying our grandchild . . .'

'He or she is *my* child.'

'Try fleeing this marriage and you will discover quick enough whose child he is.'

'I am not planning to flee this marriage.'

'Yes, you are. Why else is your brother visiting you at least once a week?'

'Because he's my brother, that's why. Because I'm lonely here.'

'That's because nobody likes you, dear. You don't fit in . . . something I'm certain you've complained about to your very dear brother during those long afternoons you spend together at Todd's Point . . .'

'How the hell do you know about my brother's visits . . .'

'It's a small town. People talk. Most especially, they talk to me. And dear, never use profanity with me again. I won't stand for it.'

'I don't give a damn what you will or will not stand for . . .'

'Oh yes you do,' she said mildly. 'Because know this: if you want to leave this marriage, that is fine by me, and it's also fine by Mr Grey. Just leave us the child . . .'

It took a moment for this to register.

'What did you just say?' I said, hushed.

Her tone remained cordial, mild. 'I said, I am very happy for you to leave this marriage after the birth of your child . . . on the condition, of course, that we retain custody of the child.'

'*We?*'

'George, of course . . . legally speaking.'

The phone trembled in my hand. I took a deep breath, trying to steady myself.

'Do you hear what you're saying?' I asked.

'What an extraordinary question,' she said with a mock laugh. 'Of course I *hear* what I'm saying. The real question is: do *you*, dear?'

'Say I simply vanished . . .'

'To where? A cabin in the woods? Some one-room apartment in a big city? You know we'd spare no expense finding you. And we would most certainly find you. When we did, the very fact of your disappearance would strengthen our legal case against you. Of course, you might consider waiting until the child is born, and then suing George for divorce. But before you choose that route, do remember this: Mr Grey is a partner in one of Wall Street's most venerable law firms. If necessary, the full legal artillery of that firm can be turned against you. Believe me, a divorce court would have you declared an unfit mother before you had a chance to exhale.'

The phone began to tremble again. I suddenly felt ill.

'Still there, dear?' she asked.

I couldn't speak.

'Have I upset you, dear?'

Silence.

'Oh my, I sense that I have. Whereas my purpose was simply to point out the stark alternatives should you attempt to do anything silly. But you're not planning to do anything silly, are you, dear?'

Silence.

'I want an answer.'

Silence. I couldn't open my mouth.

'An answer. *Now.*'

'No,' I whispered, 'I won't do anything silly.' Then I put down the phone.

When George came home that night, he found me curled up in bed, a blanket pulled tight around me. He looked alarmed.

'Darling? Darling?'

He shook me by the shoulder. I looked at him blankly.

'Darling, what's happened?'

I didn't answer him. Because I didn't feel able to answer him. The ability to speak had left me. I was here, but I was not here.

'Darling, *please*, tell me what's wrong.'

I keep staring at him. My mind felt curiously empty. A void.

'Oh God . . .' George said and ran out of the room. I nodded off. When I came to, help had arrived – in the form of my mother-in-law. She was standing at the edge of my bed, George at her side. As I came to, George was kneeling by my side, stroking my head.

'Are you better, darling?' he asked.

I still felt unable to respond. He turned back to his mother, looking deeply worried. She nodded her head towards the door, motioning for him to leave. As soon as he was gone, she walked over and sat down on George's bed. She looked at me for a very long time. Her gaze was dispassionate.

'I suppose I am to blame for all this,' she said, her voice as temperate as ever.

I turned my eyes downwards. I couldn't bear looking at her.

'I do know you are there, dear,' she said. 'Just as I also know that these sorts of little afflictions are usually a sign of deep personal weakness, and are often self-inflicted. So please understand: you are not fooling me. Not at all.'

I closed my eyes.

'Go on, feign sleep,' she said. 'Just as you're feigning this breakdown. Of course, if it was something to do with your pregnancy, I might have a certain sympathy. Mind you, I loathed being pregnant. Loathed every minute of it. I suppose you must hate it too. Especially given how much you hate the family into which you've married.'

She was right about my contempt for her family. However, she was so wrong about my feelings towards my pregnancy. I despised the circumstances in which I had landed myself. The absurdity of my marriage, the abhorrent nature of Mrs Grey . . . The one thing – the *only* thing – that was maintaining my sanity was the child I was carrying. I didn't know who or what this child would be. All I knew was that I felt a deep, absolute, unconditional love for him or her. I didn't totally understand this love. If asked, I probably wouldn't have been able to explain it in a rational, straightforward way. Because it wasn't rational or straightforward. It was just all-encompassing. The child was my future, my *raison d'être*.

But now, Mrs Grey had blanketed that future with a dark specter.

If you want to leave this marriage, that is fine by me, and it's also fine by Mr Grey. Just leave us the child . . .

A scenario began to unspool inside my head. The baby is born. I am allowed to hold him for a few minutes. A nurse comes and says that she's bringing him back to the nursery. As soon as he is out of my hands, a bailiff arrives bearing a writ. Mrs Grey has made good on her threat.

Believe me, a divorce court would have you declared an unfit mother before you had a chance to exhale.

A shudder ran through me. I felt as if I had touched a live wire. I clutched myself.

'Feeling cold, dear?' Mrs Grey said. 'Or are you just playacting for my benefit?'

I shut my eyes again.

'All right – be that way. A doctor should be here shortly. But I'm certain he should confirm what I already know: there is nothing physically wrong with you. Still, if you persist in continuing in this absent state, I'm certain there are several good sanitoriums in Fairfield County, where you'd be looked after until the baby arrives . . . and maybe even afterwards, if your mental state remained unchanged. I'm told that getting someone committed isn't that difficult. Especially if, like you, they are showing all the usual signs of mental distress . . .'

There was a knock on the door.

'Ah, that must be the doctor.'

The doctor was a solemn, taciturn man in his fifties. He introduced himself to me as Dr Rutan and explained that he was dealing with Dr Eisenberg's house calls this evening. He had all of Eisenberg's warmth and charm. When I didn't answer his first few questions – because I still felt incapable of speech – he didn't express concern or worry. He simply got down to business. He took my pulse, my blood pressure. He listened to my heart. He placed the stethoscope on my expanded abdomen, and listened there too. He did some prodding and poking with his hands. He opened my mouth and – using a tongue depressor and a penlight – he gazed inside. Then he pulled out a small penlight, and shined it in my eyes. Turning towards my husband and mother-in-law, he said, 'Everything is working fine. So either she is having a minor breakdown, or what could best be described as a very big sulk. It's not uncommon during pregnancy. If the woman is of the delicate sort, the whole experience can overwhelm them, throwing everything out of proportion. And so, like little children, they retreat into themselves. And sulk.'

'How long might this go on?' George asked.

'I don't know. Try to keep her fed and quiet. She should pull out of it in a day or two.'

'And if she doesn't?' Mrs Grey asked.

'Then,' the doctor said, 'we will consider other medical options.'

I shut my eyes again. Only this time the desired effect happened. I fell into nothingness.

When I opened my eyes again, I knew immediately that something was very wrong. It was the middle of the night. I could hear George snoring softly in the adjoining bed. The room was black. And hot. So hot that I felt sodden. Sodden to the skin. I also felt in urgent need of a toilet. But when I tried to sit up, I felt lightheaded, vertiginous, woozy. Eventually I managed to put my feet on the floor. Standing up took some effort. I tried to take a step and had to steady myself. My little episode earlier in the evening – my absent state, as Mrs Grey called it – must have been more serious than I realized. Because I felt truly weak.

I staggered across the darkened room, feeling my way to the bathroom door with outstretched hands. Reaching it, I stepped inside and flipped the switch. The room convulsed into light.

And I screamed.

Because there – in the bathroom mirror – was a reflection of myself. My face was the color of chalk. My eyes were yellow. And the bottom half of my white nightgown was red. Crimson red. Drenched in blood.

Then I felt as if I was falling into nothingness again. Only this time the plunge was accompanied by a nasty thud. Then the world went dark.

When I snapped back to consciousness, I was in a white room. With harsh white light. And an elderly man in a stiff white jacket beaming a penlight into my eyes. My left arm was strapped to the bed. I noticed a tube protruding from the arm, then a bottle of plasma hanging beside the bed.

'Welcome back,' he said.

'Oh . . . right,' I said, utterly incoherent.

'Do you know where you are?'

'Uh . . . what?'

He spoke loudly, as if I was deaf. '*Do you know where you are?*'

'Uh . . . well . . . no.'

'You are at Greenwich Hospital.'

This took a moment to sink in.

'Okay.'

'Do you know who I am?' the man asked.

'Should I?'

'We have met before. I am Dr Eisenberg – your obstetrician. Do you know why you're here, Sara?'

'Where am I?'

'As I said before: you are at Greenwich Hospital. Your husband found you on the floor of your bathroom, covered in blood.'

'I remember . . .'

'You're a very lucky young woman. You went into a dead faint. Had you fallen the wrong way, you could have broken your neck. As it turned out, you just have some minor bruising.'

Clarity was beginning to return. I suddenly felt scared.

'Am I all right?' I asked quietly.

He looked at me carefully.

'As I said, you only suffered some superficial bruising. And you lost quite a bit of blood . . .'

Now I was scared. And very conscious. 'Doctor, am I *all right*?'

Eisenberg met my stare. 'You lost the baby.'

I closed my eyes. I felt as if I was falling again. 'I'm sorry,' he said.

I had my right hand to my mouth. I bit hard on a knuckle. I didn't want to cry in front of this man.

'I'll come back later,' he said and headed towards the door.

Suddenly I asked, 'Was it a boy or a girl?'

He turned around. 'The foetus was only partially formed.'

'Answer me: was it a boy or a girl?'

'A boy.'

I blinked. I bit down on my knuckle again.

'I have some other difficult news,' he said. 'Because the foetus was only partially formed, we had to operate to remove it from your womb. During surgery, we discovered that part of the wall of your womb had been badly damaged by the abnormal pregnancy. So damaged, in fact, that it is highly unlikely you'll ever be able to conceive, let alone carry another pregnancy to full term. Understand: this is not a finite diagnosis. But from my clinical experience, the chances of you now being able to have a baby are, I'm afraid, improbable.'

There was a very long silence. He stared down

351

at his shoes. 'Do you have any questions?' he finally asked.

I put the palms of my hands against my eyes, and pressed hard, wanting to black out the world. After a moment, Eisenberg said, 'I'm sure you'd like to be on your own for a while.'

I heard the door shut. I kept my palms pressed against my eyes. Because I couldn't face opening them. I couldn't face anything right now. I was in a nose dive.

The door opened again. I heard George softly say my name. I removed my hands. He came into focus. He was very pale, and looked like he hadn't slept for days. Standing next to him was his mother. I suddenly heard myself say: 'I don't want her here.'

Mrs Grey blanched. 'What was that you said?' she asked.

'Mother . . .' George said, putting a hand on her arm – a hand which she immediately brushed away.

'Get her the hell out of here *now*,' I shouted.

She calmly approached the bed. 'I will forgive that comment on the grounds that you have been through a traumatic experience.'

'I don't want your forgiveness. Just go.'

Her face flexed into one of her tight little smiles. She bent down close to me. 'Let me ask you something, Sara. Having self-induced this tragedy, are you now using disrespect as a way of dodging the fact that you've become damaged goods?'

That's when I hit her. Using my free hand, I

slapped her hard across the face. It caught her off-balance, sending her to the floor. She let out a scream. George came rushing forward, yelling something incoherent. He helped his mother back to her feet, whispering, 'I'm sorry, I'm sorry . . .' in her ear. She turned and faced me, looking disoriented, dumbfounded, robbed of her triumphant malice. George put an arm around her and helped her out the door. A few minutes later, he came back in as rattled as someone who had just walked away from a car wreck.

'One of the nurses is looking after her,' he said. 'I said that she took a turn and fell.'

I turned away from him.

'I'm so sorry,' he said, approaching me. 'I can't begin to tell you how sorry . . .'

I cut him off. 'We have nothing more to say to each other.'

He tried to reach for me. I put my arm up to fend him off.

'Darling . . .' he said.

'Please leave, George.'

'You were right to hit her. She deserved . . .'

'George, I don't want to talk right now.'

'Fine, fine. I'll come back later. But darling, know this: we're going to be fine. I don't care what Dr Eisenberg says. It's just an opinion. Worst comes to worst, we can always adopt. But, really . . .'

'George – there's the door. Please use it.'

He heaved a deep sigh. He looked rattled. And scared.

'All right, I'll be back first thing tomorrow.'

'No, George. I don't want to see you tomorrow.'

'Well, I can come back the day after . . .'

'I don't want to see you again.'

'Don't say that.'

'I'm saying it.'

'I'll do anything . . .'

'Anything?'

'Yes, darling. *Anything.*'

'Then I want you to do two things. The first is, call my brother. Tell him what's happened. Tell him everything.'

'Of course, of course. I'll call him as soon as I get home. And the second request?'

'Stay away from me.'

This took a moment to sink in. 'You don't really mean that,' he said.

'Yes – I really mean that.'

Silence. I finally looked at him. He was crying.

'I'm sorry,' I said.

He rubbed his eyes with his hands. 'I'll do as you ask,' he said.

'Thank you.'

He was frozen to the spot, unable to move.

'Goodbye, George,' I whispered, then turned away.

After he left, a nurse came in, carrying a small ceramic bowl, containing a syringe and a vial. She placed the bowl on the bedside table, inserted the needle into the rubber top of the vial, inverted it and filled part of the syringe with a viscous fluid.

'What's that?' I asked.

'Something to help you sleep.'

'I don't want to sleep.'

'Doctor's orders.'

Before I could object further, I felt a quick jab in the arm. I was under within seconds. When I came to again, it was morning. Eric was sitting on the edge of my bed. He gave me a sad smile.

'Hi there,' he said.

I reached for his hand. He moved closer down the bed, and threaded his fingers through mine. 'Did George call you?' I asked.

'Yes. He did.'

'And did he tell you . . . ?'

'Yes. He told me.'

Suddenly I was sobbing. Immediately Eric put his arms around me. I buried my head in his shoulder. My sobs quickly escalated. He held me tighter as I cried. I was inconsolable. I had never known such wild, unbridled grief. And I couldn't stop.

I don't know how long I carried on crying. Eric said nothing. No words of consolation or condolence. Because words were meaningless at this moment. I would never have children. That was the terrible fact of the matter. Nothing anyone said could change that. Tragedy renders language impotent.

Eventually I subsided. I let go of Eric and fell back against the pillows. Eric reached out and stroked my face. We said nothing for a long time.

I was still in shock. Finally, he broke our silence.

'So . . .' he said.

'So . . .' I said.

'My sofa's not the most comfortable bed in the world, but . . .'

'It will do fine.'

'That's settled then. While I was waiting for you to wake up, I spoke with one of the nurses. They think you'll be ready to leave in about three days. So – if it's okay with you – I'll call George and arrange a time to go to your house in Old Greenwich and pack up your things.'

'It was never my house.'

'George was pretty emotional on the phone. He begged me to get you to reconsider.'

'There is absolutely no chance of that.'

'I intimated that to him.'

'He should marry his mother and get it over with.'

'Why didn't I think of that line?'

I almost managed a small smile.

'It will be good to have you back, S. I've missed you.'

'I've fucked it up, Eric. I've fucked everything up.'

'Don't think that,' he said. 'Because it's not true. But do keep using language like that. It dents your refined image. And I approve.'

'I landed myself in this entire disaster.'

'That's an interpretation – and one which is guaranteed to cause you a lot of useless grief.'

'I deserve the grief . . .'

'Stop it! You deserve none of this. But it's happened. And, in time, you will find a way of dealing with it.'

'I'll never deal with it.'

'You will. Because you have to deal with it. You have no choice.'

'I suppose I could jump out a window.'

'But think of all the bad movies you'd miss.'

This time, I nearly managed a laugh. 'I missed you too, Eric. More than I can say.'

'Give us two weeks together as roommates, and I'm sure we'll end up never talking again.'

'An asteroid will hit Manhattan before that happens. There's a pair of us in it.'

'Nice expression.'

'Yes. The Irish have all the right lines.'

He rolled his eyes and said, '*Yez lives and yez learns*.'

'Too damn true.'

I glanced out the window. It was a perfect summer day. A hard blue sky. An incandescent sun. Not a single hint of an inclement future. It was a day when everything should have seemed limitless, possible.

'Tell me something, Eric . . .'

'Yeah?'

'Is it always so hard?'

'Is *what* always so hard?'

'Everything.'

He laughed. 'Of course. Haven't you figured that out yet?'

'Sometimes I wonder: will I ever figure anything out?'

He laughed again. 'You know the answer to that question, don't you?'

I kept my gaze on the world beyond. And said, 'Yes, I'm afraid I do.'

PART THREE

SARA

CHAPTER 1

The first thing I noticed about Dudley Thomson were his fingers. They were short, stubby, fleshy – like a link of Polish sausages. He had a large oval face. His chin was augmented by two tiers of fat. He had thinning hair, round horn-rimmed glasses, and a very expensive three-piece suit. It was dark grey with a thick chalk pinstripe. I guessed that it was made-to-measure, as it carefully encased his bulky frame. His office was wood paneled, with heavy green velvet curtains, deep leather chairs, a large mahogany desk. It struck me as a small-scale approximation of a London gentlemen's club. In fact, everything about Dudley Thomson reeked of Anglophilia. He looked like an overweight version of T.S. Eliot. Only unlike Mr Eliot he wasn't a poet, dressed in the raiments of an English banker. Rather, he was a divorce lawyer – a partner at Potholm, Grey and Connell; the white-shoe Wall Street firm of which Edwin Grey, Sr, was a senior partner.

I had been summoned by Dudley Thomson to a meeting at his office. It was three weeks after I had been discharged from Greenwich Hospital. I was staying with my brother at his apartment on Sullivan Street, curling up every night on his lumpy sofa. As one of the senior nurses at the hospital had warned me, I would probably go through a period of depression and grief after my release. She was right. I had spent most of the three weeks inside Eric's apartment, only occasionally venturing outside for groceries or an afternoon double feature at the Academy of Music on 14th Street. I really didn't want to be around many people – especially those friends of mine who were married with children. The sight of a baby carriage on the street chilled me. So too did passing a shop which sold maternity outfits or infant paraphernalia. Curiously, I hadn't cried since that outburst in Greenwich Hospital. Instead, I had felt constantly numb, and wanted to do nothing more than sequester myself within the four walls of Eric's place. Which, with my brother's tolerant encouragement, was exactly what I had been doing – squandering the days with a stack of pulp thrillers, and working my way through Eric's extensive record collection. I rarely turned on the radio. I didn't buy a newspaper. I didn't answer the phone (not that it rang very much anyway). Eric – the most patient man on the planet – didn't worry out loud about my solipsism. Though he made subtle enquiries about my well-being, he never once suggested a night out. Nor did he pass a comment about my dazed gloom. He knew what was going on. He knew it had to run its course.

Three weeks into this period of self-incarceration, I received a letter from Dudley Thomson. He explained that he would be representing the Grey family in the divorce settlement and asked me to arrange an appointment with him at my earliest possible convenience. He said I could have my own legal counsel present at this meeting – but suggested that I not go to the expense of hiring a lawyer for this preliminary discussion, as the Greys wanted to settle matters as quickly as possible.

'Hire a lawyer,' Eric said after I showed him this letter. 'They want to settle for as little as they can.'

'But I really don't want anything from them.'

'You're entitled to alimony . . . or at least a sizeable settlement. That's the very least those bastards owe you.'

'I'd rather just walk away . . .'

'They exploited you . . .'

'No, they didn't.'

'They used you as a battery hen and . . .'

'Eric, stop turning this into a class warfare drama. Especially as the Greys and ourselves are basically from the same damn class.'

'You should still take them for every penny possible.'

'No – because that would be unethical. And that's not my style. I know what I want from the Greys. If they give it to me, then this entire matter can be settled without further grief. Believe me, what I want more than anything right now is no further grief.'

'At least find some tough divorce lawyer to have in your corner . . .'

'I need nobody. That's my new credo, Eric. From now on, I'm depending on no one.'

And so, I made an appointment to see Mr Thomson, and walked into his office without a legal entourage. He was rather surprised by that.

'I actually expected to see you here today with at least one legal counselor,' he said.

'Really?' I said. 'After advising me that I needed no counsel present at this interview?'

He flashed me a smile, showing bad dental work (a true sign of his deep Anglophilia). 'I expect no one to really follow my advice,' he said.

'Well, I have. So – let's get this over with. Tell me what you are proposing.'

He coughed a bit, and shuffled through a few papers, trying to mask his surprise at my directness. 'The Greys want to be as generous as possible . . .'

'You mean, *George* Grey wants to be as generous as possible. I was – *am still* – married to him, not his family.'

'Yes, yes, of course,' he said, sounding a little flustered. 'George Grey wants to offer you a most reasonable settlement.'

'What's his – and *your* – idea of a "most reasonable settlement"?'

'We were thinking of something in the region of two hundred dollars a month . . . payable up until the time you remarry.'

'I'm never getting married again.'

He attempted a benevolent smile. He failed. 'I can understand you're upset, Mrs Grey, given the circumstances. But I'm certain an attractive, intelligent woman like yourself will have no trouble finding another husband . . .'

'Except that I'm not in the market for another husband. Anyway, even if I was, I am now, medically speaking, *damaged goods* – to use my mother-in-law's kind words.'

He looked deeply embarrassed. 'Yes, I heard about your . . . medical difficulties. I am dreadfully sorry.'

'Thank you. But back to business. I'm afraid two hundred dollars a month is unacceptable. My salary at *Saturday Night/Sunday Morning* was three hundred a month. I think I deserve that.'

'I'm certain three hundred dollars a month would be agreeable.'

'Good. Now I have a proposal to put to you. When I told you that I am never planning to marry again, I'm certain you realized that George will, in effect, be paying me alimony for the rest of my life.'

'Yes, that thought did cross my mind.'

'I would like to simplify matters in that regard. I am willing to accept a one-off payment from George. Once that is made, I will ask for no further financial maintenance from him.'

He pursed his lips. 'And what sort of sum were you considering?'

'I was married to George for almost five months.

I was with him for two months before then. Let's call it a total of seven months. I would like a year's alimony for each of those months. That works out at . . .'

He was already scribbling figures on his desk blotter. 'Twenty-five thousand two hundred dollars,' he said.

'Precisely.'

'It's a large sum.'

'Not if you consider that, all going well, I should be alive for another forty-five or fifty years.'

'That is a point. And is that sum simply an opening offer?'

'No – it's the final offer. Either George agrees to pay me that amount up-front, or he can support me until the day I die. Are we clear about that, Mr Thomson?'

'Exceedingly. Naturally, I will have to discuss this with the Greys . . . sorry, with George.'

'Well, you know where to find me,' I said, standing up.

He proffered his hand. I took it. It was soft and spongy. 'May I ask you something, Mrs Grey?'

'Of course.'

'This may sound strange, given that I am representing your husband, but I am nonetheless curious to know one thing: why on earth don't you want ongoing alimony?'

'Because I want nothing to do with the Greys ever again. And you can convey my feelings to your clients, should you so wish.'

He let go of my hand. 'I sense they know that already. Goodbye, Mrs Grey.'

On the way out of the offices of Potholm, Grey and Connell, I saw Edwin Grey, Sr, walking towards me in the corridor. Immediately, he lowered his eyes to avoid meeting mine. Then he passed by me without saying a word.

As soon as I was out of the building, I hailed a taxi and headed back to Sullivan Street. The meeting had drained me. I wasn't used to playing the role of the hard negotiator. But I was pleased with the way I had handled things. Just as I had surprised myself with the statement that I would never marry again. It was said off the top of my head, without premeditation. I hadn't considered the matter before making this declaration. But it evidently reflected what I was thinking right now. Whether I would still be thinking this same way about marriage several years from now was another matter. What I did know was this: it didn't work when your heart led your head. It didn't work when your head led your heart. Which, in turn, meant . . .

What?

Maybe that we never get it right. We just muddle through.

Which is perhaps one of the great reasons why love always disappoints. We enter it hoping it will make us whole – that it will shore up our foundations, end our sense of incompleteness, give us the stability we crave. Then we discover that, on the contrary, it is a deeply exposing experience. Because it is so charged with ambivalence. We seek certainty in another person. We discover doubt – both in the object of our affection and in ourselves.

So perhaps the trick of it is to recognize the fundamental ambivalence lurking behind every form of human endeavor. Because once you recognize that – once you grasp the flawed nature of *everything* – you can move forward without disappointment.

Until, of course, you fall in love again.

Two days after my meeting with Dudley Thomson, a letter from him arrived in the mail. In it, he informed me that George Grey had accepted my proposal of a once-off payment of $25,200 – on the condition that I would *abnegate* (his word) any further claims to alimony and/or other forms of financial maintenance. He also suggested that fifty per cent of this sum would be payable to me on signature of a legally binding agreement (which he would draw up once I informed him that, in principle, I accepted these terms), and fifty per cent when the official divorce decree came through twenty-four months from now (New York State was *very* reluctant back then to issue divorces with ease).

I picked up the phone and called Mr Thomson, informing him that I agreed to these terms. Within a week of that call, a legal agreement arrived through the mail. It was lengthy and semantically challenging for anyone like myself who hadn't been to law school. Eric also read it and decided it was labyrinthine. So, that day, he found me a local attorney in the neighborhood. His name was Joel Eberts. He was a beefy man in his late fifties, built like a stevedore. He had his office on the corner of Thompson and Prince Streets. It was one room, with scuffed linoleum and fluorescent lighting. His handshake was like a vise. But I liked his blunt style.

After briefly perusing the contract, he whistled through his blackened teeth and said, 'You were actually married to Edwin Grey's son?'

'I'm afraid so. Do you know the Greys?'

'I think I'm a little too Semitic for their social tastes. But in my younger days, I used to practice labor law, and for a while I represented the dockers over at the Brooklyn Navy Yards. You ever been over to the Navy Yards?'

'Yes,' I said quietly. 'Once.'

'Anyway, Old Man Grey's firm made a lot of money representing the private contractors at the Navy Yards. Grey himself had this really fearsome reputation for actually taking pleasure in screwing the workers, especially when it came to negotiating contracts. And the thing was: the guy always won. I hated the sonofabitch – 'scuse my French – so I'll be happy to look this over for you. Six bucks an hour is what I charge. Is that okay?'

'Very reasonable. Too reasonable, in fact. Shouldn't I be paying you more?'

'This is the Village, not Wall Street. Six bucks an hour is my rate, and I'm not going to jack it up just because you're dealing with Potholm, Grey and Connell. But lemme ask you something: why just accept a one-off payment from the bastards?'

'I have my reasons.'

'As I am representing you, you'd better tell me them.'

Hesitantly, I informed him about the awfulness of the marriage, the nightmare that was my mother-in-law, and the miscarriage – with all its permanent implications. When I finished, he leaned over his desk and quickly squeezed my hand.

'That's a tough call, Miss Smythe. I'm really sorry.'

'Thank you.'

'Listen, I'll have all this sorted out in a couple of days. It shouldn't take more than around ten to twelve hours of my time, max.'

'That's fine,' I said.

A week later, Mr Eberts called me at Eric's apartment.

'Sorry it took me some time to get back to you, but this took a little longer to negotiate than expected.'

'I thought it was all pretty straightforward.'

'Miss Smythe – when it comes to law, nothing's straightforward. Anyway, here's the deal. First the Bad News: I ended up spending twenty hours on this agreement, so it's gonna cost you a hundred and twenty dollars . . . which I know is twice the originally quoted price, but that's how these things go. Especially since the Good News is really *Good News*. They're now gonna pay you a one-off settlement of thirty-five grand.'

'Thirty-five thousand dollars? But Mr Thomson and I had agreed twenty-five thousand.'

'Yeah – but I always like to get my clients a little more than they bargained for. Anyway, I spoke to a doctor friend of mine, who told me that we could have a case against that quack specialist your mother-in-law imposed on you. What was his name again?'

'Dr Eisenberg.'

'Yeah, that's the gonif. Anyway, according to my doc friend, Eisenberg was negligent in not detecting the catastrophic nature of your pregnancy – and therefore could be held responsible for the permanent damage you suffered. Of course, that jerk Dudley Thomson at Potholm, Grey and Connell tried to pooh-pooh the idea of medical negligence – until I told him that if the Greys really wanted a nasty public divorce case, we were prepared to give them one.'

'But I would never have agreed to that.'

'Believe me, I was aware of that. All I was doing was playing Call My Bluff. And then I told them we now wanted a settlement of fifty grand . . .'

'Good God.'

'Of course I knew they'd never agree to that. But it did scare the pants off them – because within a day they came back with a counter-offer of thirty-five. Thompson says it's their absolutely final offer, but I'm pretty sure I can get them up to forty . . .'

'Thirty-five will do just fine,' I said. 'Very honestly,

I don't think I should accept this new sum at all.'

'Why the hell not? The Greys have got the money. Medically speaking, they're partially to blame for what happened to you. More to the point, this is a good deal for them. Once they pay you off, they'll never have another responsibility towards you again . . . which is how you wanted it, right?'

'Yes, but . . . I had agreed to the sum of twenty-five.'

'That's until you hired a lawyer. And trust me on this one: *they owe you.*'

'I don't know what to say.'

'Say nothing. Just take the money . . . and don't feel any guilt about it.'

'At least let me pay you more than a hundred and twenty dollars.'

'Why? That's my fee.'

'Thank you.'

'No, thank you. I had great fun finally winning one against Edwin-goddamn-Grey. The agreement should be here tomorrow, so I'll call you when it's ready for signature. And here's another little bit of good news: they're gonna give you the entire thirty-five grand right now, on the condition that you don't contest the divorce.'

'Why on earth would I want to do that?'

'That's what I told him. So, there we go. Happy?'

'Overwhelmed.'

'Don't be. But if you wouldn't mind a small piece of advice, Miss Smythe?'

'Please.'

'As we used to say in Brooklyn, *spend the money smart.*'

I heeded that advice. When the payment came through a month later, I put it in the bank and went shopping. For an apartment. It only took a week to find what I was looking for: a sunny one-bedroom place on the first floor of a turn-of-the-century brownstone on West 77th Street off Riverside Drive. The apartment was spacious, with three bright rooms, high ceilings, hardwood floors. There was a small alcove area off the living room which would make a perfect study. But the best selling point – the thing that made me want the place immediately – was the fact that it had its own private garden. All right, it was only a ten by ten patch of cracked paving stones and dead grass – but I knew I could do wonderful things with it. More tellingly, I would have my own private garden in the center of Manhattan – a little dash of green in the middle of all that high-rise concrete and brick. True, the walls of the apartment were covered in heavy brown floral wallpaper. And yes, the kitchen was a little old-fashioned – it had an anti-quated ice box that actually required regular deliveries from the local ice man. But the real-estate broker said that she'd be willing to shave $300 off the asking price of $8000 to compensate for the renovations I would need to make. I told her to add another $200 to that figure, and we'd have a deal. She agreed. As it was a brownstone, I didn't have to be vetted by the board of the co-operative.

There was just a monthly maintenance fee of $20. I used Joel Eberts again to handle the legal work. I paid cash. I owned the apartment a week after I saw it.

'My sister the property owner,' Eric said archly while looking around the apartment only a few days before I closed the deal.

'Next thing I know, you'll be calling me a bourgeois capitalist.'

'I'm not being ideological – just wry. There is a difference, you know.'

'Really? I never realized that, comrade.'

'Shhh . . .'

'Stop being paranoid. I doubt Mr Hoover's bugged this apartment. I mean, the previous owner was a little old Latvian lady . . .'

'To Hoover, everyone's a possible subversive. Haven't you read what's been going on in Washington? A bunch of congressmen are screaming about Reds under the Bed in Hollywood. Calling for a committee to investigate Communist infiltration of the entertainment industry.'

'That's just Hollywood.'

'Believe me, if the Congress starts trying to dig up Commies in LA, then it'll just be a matter of time before they turn their attention to New York.'

'Like I told you before – if that happens, all you'll have to tell them is that you left the Party in forty-one, and you'll be in the clear. Anyway, you can always tell the Feds you have this *arch-capitalist, property-owning* sister . . .'

'Very funny.'

'Give it to me straight, Eric: do you like the place?'

He glanced again around the empty living room.

'Yeah – it's got great potential. Especially once you get rid of that Eastern European wallpaper. What do you think it's depicting? Springtime in Riga?'

'I don't know – but along with the kitchen, it's going before I set foot in here.'

'Are you sure about living on the Upper West Side? I mean, it's kind of quiet up here in the Dakotas.'

'I'll tell you, the only thing I miss about Old Greenwich is the sense of open space. That's why I like it up here. I'm a minute from Riverside Park. I've got the Hudson. I've got my garden . . .'

'Stop it, or you're going to start sounding like Thoreau at Walden Pond.'

I laughed, then said, 'After I pay for this place and do it up, I should still have around thirty-two thousand in the bank – that's including the inheritance money from Mother and Father, which I put into government bonds.'

'Unlike your profligate brother.'

'Well, that's what I wanted to talk to you about. The real-estate agent who sold me this place told me there was another apartment going on the third floor. So why don't you let me buy it for you and . . .'

He cut me off. 'No way,' he said.

'Don't be so dismissive of the idea. I mean, that place of yours on Sullivan Street really isn't the best . . .'

'It suits me fine. It's all I need.'

'Come on, Eric – it's a student place. It's like bad *La Bohème* – and you're nearly thirty-five years old.'

'I know *exactly* how old I am, S,' he said crossly. 'Just as I also know what I need or don't need. What I don't need is your damn charity, understand?'

His harsh tone stunned me.

'I was only making a suggestion. I mean, I know you don't like the Upper West Side, so if you saw a place downtown you wanted to buy . . .'

'I want nothing from you, S.'

'But why? I can *help* you.'

'Because I don't want help. Because needing help makes me feel like a loser.'

'You know I don't think that about you.'

'But *I* think that. So . . . thanks but no thanks.'

'At least consider it.'

'No. Case closed. But here's a practical tip from an impractical guy: find yourself a smart stockbroker and let him invest that thirty-two grand in blue chips: GE, General Motors, RCA, that kind of thing. Rumor has it IBM is also a smart bet – although they're still finding their feet as a company.'

'I didn't know you followed the market, Eric.'

'Sure – former Marxist-Leninists always pick the best stocks.'

When the apartment became mine a few days later, I hired a decorator to strip the wallpaper, replaster the walls and paint them a plain flat white. I also had him design a simple modern kitchen, featuring a new Amana refrigerator. All the work cost $600 – and for that all-inclusive price, he also agreed to sand and revarnish the hardwood floors, build two floor-to-ceiling bookshelves in the living room, and retile the bathroom. Like the rest of the apartment, it too went white. The remaining $400 of my decorating budget was spent on furniture: an antique brass bed, a tall ash chest of drawers, a simple Knoll sofa upholstered in a neutral beige fabric, a big cushy easy chair (also covered in the same fabric), a large pine table which would serve as a desk. It was amazing what you could buy with $400 back then – my budget also stretched to a couple of throw rugs, a few table lights, and a chrome kitchen table with two matching chairs.

The redecoration took around a month. All the furniture arrived on the morning the painters finally moved out. By nightfall – thanks to Eric's assistance – I had the place set up. I spent the next few days buying essentials like plates and glasses and cutlery and towels. I also exceeded my budget by a hundred and fifty dollars to invest in a state-of-the-art RCA radio and phonograph – all housed in one large mahogany cabinet. It was an indulgence, but a necessary one.

There were very few material things I craved. After reading in *Life* about the RCA Home Concert

Hall (yes, that was its actual name), I knew I was going to buy it . . . even though it cost a ferocious $149.95. And now here it was – sitting in a corner of an apartment I owned outright, blaring the opening movement of Brahms's 3rd Symphony. I was surrounded by the first furniture I had ever bought in my life. Suddenly I had possessions. Suddenly I felt very grown up – and very empty.

'Penny for them,' Eric said, handing me a glass of celebratory fizzy wine.

'I'm just a little bemused, that's all.'

'Bemused that you are the mistress of all you survey?'

'Bemused that I've ended up here, with all this.'

'It could be worse. You could still be a resident of the Grey Penal Colony in Old Greenwich.'

'Yes – divorce does have its rewards, I guess.'

'You're feeling guilty about all this. I can tell.'

'I know this sounds stupid, but I keep telling myself that it's not right I've been handed this without . . .'

'What? Suffering? Martyrdom? Crucifixion?'

I laughed. 'Yes,' I said. 'Something extreme and punitive like that.'

'I love a masochist. Anyway, S – as far as I'm concerned, thirty-five grand doesn't even begin to compensate you for the fact that you'll never . . .'

'Stop,' I said.

'I'm sorry.'

'Don't be. It's my problem. I will come to terms with it.'

He put an arm around my shoulder.

'You don't have to come to terms with it,' he said.

'Yes. I do. Otherwise . . .'

'What?'

'Otherwise I'll do something very stupid . . . like turning this into the central tragedy of my life. Which I don't want it to be. I'm not cut out to play the lamentable heroine. It's simply not my style.'

'At least give yourself some time to come to terms with things. It's only been two months.'

'I'm doing fine,' I lied. 'I'm doing just fine.'

In truth, I wasn't doing badly. Because I was also working hard at filling every hour of the day. After moving into the apartment, I set up meetings with half-a-dozen different stockbrokers, before settling on Lawrence Braun – the husband of an old Bryn Mawr friend, Virginia Sweet. She'd married Lawrence straight out of college, and was now coping with three under-fives in a rambling colonial house in Ossining. But it wasn't the connection with Virginia that made me give Lawrence my business – rather, the fact that he was the only stockbroker I met who didn't patronize me, or say things like: '*Now I know you ladies really don't have much of a head for figures . . . except when it comes to girdle sizes, ha! ha!*' (yes, that really was commonplace male wit in 1947). On the contrary, Lawrence questioned me carefully about my long-term financial goals (*Security, security, and more security*), and my attitude towards risk (*to be avoided at all costs*).

'Do you want this money to provide an immediate income for you?' he asked.

'Absolutely not,' I said. 'I'm planning to go back to work as soon as possible. I refuse to be the so-called lady of leisure. It's a waste of a life.'

'And if marriage happens again for you?'

'It won't. Ever.'

He thought about that one for a moment, then said, 'Fine. Then let's think very long term.'

His financial plan was a straightforward one. My five thousand dollars in government bonds would be moved into a pension plan that would mature when I was sixty. Twenty thousand dollars would be used to acquire a portfolio of blue-chip stocks – with the aim of achieving at least six per cent growth per annum. The remaining five thousand would be mine to play with – or to live on while I found work.

'All going well, you will have quite a substantial war chest behind you by the time you're into middle age. Add to this the fact that you will be sitting on an appreciable asset – a completely paid-off apartment – and it looks like you will be financially dependent on no one.'

That was what I wanted – complete independence. Never again would I allow myself to be dependent on someone else. I wasn't slamming the door on men, or sex, or the possibility of falling in love. But there was no damn way I was going

380

to stumble into a situation where I would be reliant on a man for my sense of self, my social status, or the cash in my pocket. From now on, I would be an autonomous unit: self-sufficient, unimpeded, unattached.

So I agreed to Lawrence's financial plan. Checks were written, investments made. Though I now had five thousand dollars in my bank account – to spend however I wanted – I forced myself to be prudent, determined not to squander it on frivolities. Because money now meant independence. Or, at least, the illusion of independence.

After sorting out my financial situation, I paid a call to *Saturday Night/Sunday Morning*. Nathaniel Hunter's appalling successor had only lasted a few months in the job. She'd been replaced by a tiny, impish woman named Imogen Woods – a real Dorothy Parker type who was known for her long lunches, her perpetual hangovers, and her spot-on taste in fiction. When I called her office, she told me to drop by the next afternoon around five. She was sitting in an armchair next to her desk, correcting some proof pages from the magazine. A Pall Mall was smoldering in an already brimming ashtray. A highball was in one hand, a pencil in the other. She had a pair of half-moon glasses on the end of her nose, through which she studied me with care.

'So – another refugee from married life,' she said.

'News obviously travels fast.'

'Hey – it's a magazine. Which, in turn, means it's filled with people who think they're doing something important, but secretly know they're doing nothing of importance, and therefore like nothing better than gossiping about other people's more interesting lives.'

'My life isn't particularly interesting.'

'A marriage that only lasts five months is *always* interesting. The shortest of my three marital disasters lasted six months.'

'And the longest?'

'A year and a half.'

'Impressive.'

She cackled loudly, exhaling a lungful of smoke. 'Yeah – like hell. So, tell me – when are you going to write another story for us? I dug your first one out of the file. Pretty damn good. Where's the next one?'

I explained that I considered myself a one-hit wonder – that I had tried writing fiction again, but found that I had nothing to say.

'So that's really going to be your only story?' she asked.

'I think so, yes.'

'He must have been quite a guy, your sailor.'

'*He* was fictitious.'

She threw back her highball.

'Yeah – and I'm Rita Hayworth. Anyway, I'm not going to pry, much as I'd like to. How can I help?'

'I know my old job is filled, but I was wondering

if I might be able to do a little freelance reading for you . . .'

'No problem,' she said. 'Ever since the goddamn war ended, everyone in America's decided they're a writer. We're deluged with unsolicited crap. So we'd be happy to throw around twenty manuscripts your way each week. We pay three bucks a report. It ain't a fortune, but it should pay for some groceries. Your friend Emily Flouton was telling me that you've just moved into your own place.'

'That's right,' I said.

'So tell me about it,' she said.

I did as instructed, explaining a bit about how I threw myself into apartment hunting after leaving George, how I'd found this place on West 77th Street, and had stripped the apartment bare, redecorating it in neutral tones.

'That'll work,' she said.

'What will work?'

'Your story about the apartment. We'll call it "Act Two" or "Starting Over" or something goddamn similar. What I want from you is a smart, funny account of finding your own place after your marriage got torpedoed.'

'But, like I told you, I'm not writing fiction anymore.'

'And I'm not asking you to write fiction. I'm asking you to be the first contributor to a new slot His Godship the Editor has asked me to develop. He wants to call it "Slice of Life" – which shows you the sort of imagination he's got. But that's the gist of it – a quick, elegant dispatch from that battlefront called "real life". A thousand words, no more, the fee is forty bucks, and to make sure you don't spend too much time sweating over it, I'm going to expect it on my desk five days from now. That's start of business Monday. Are you clear on that, Smythe?'

I gulped. Loudly. 'Are you sure you want me to write this?' I said.

'No – I always waste my time commissioning stuff I really don't want. Come on, Smythe: are you going to do this or what?'

After a nervous pause, I said, 'Yes – I'll do it.'

'That's settled then. Meanwhile, I'll have one of my lackeys dig out twenty new arrivals from the slush pile of The Great Unsolicited Short Story and have them sent over to your place. But do your own story first. And Monday *means* Monday. Okay?'

'I'll do my best.'

'No – you'll do it *very well*. Because that's what I'm expecting from you. One final thing – write sharp. I like sharp. Sharp always works.'

Naturally enough, by ten that Sunday night, I had given up hope of making the deadline the next morning. The area around my desk looked like a do-it-yourself snowfall, as it was knee-deep in balled-up typing paper. I was blocked, congealed, mentally barricaded. Over the previous four days, I had tried dozens of different openings to the piece. Each time, I had thrown my hands up in despair, ripped the paper from my Remington, and cursed myself for accepting this commission. I wasn't a writer – I was a fraud. Someone who'd gotten lucky the first time around, but had been a muse-free zone since then. Worse yet, I knew full well that inspiration only constituted around fifteen per cent of the ingredients needed for writing. Craft, diligence, and sheer obstinacy made up the rest of the equation – and I was certainly lacking in all these departments. Because if I didn't possess the stubbornness – and self-assurance – required to toss off a dumb thousand-word feature about redecorating my new apartment, then how would I ever do this sort of thing professionally?

I now knew the answer to that question: I didn't have the skill, the rigor, the sheer moxie required to get on with the job of writing. I didn't trust myself enough.

Just before midnight, I picked up the phone and called Eric, repeating this self-pitying rant to him. I ended with the plaintive comment: 'I suppose I can always stick to editing.'

'What a tragic denouement,' he said, with more than a hint of irony.

'I knew I could count on you for sympathy and understanding.'

'I simply don't understand why you can't just write the damn thing – and get it over with.'

'Because it's not that damn simple!' I said, adding: 'And yes, I do know I sound overwrought.'

'At least you haven't lost your capacity for self-knowledge.'

'Why do I ever tell you anything?'

'God knows – but if you want a piece of writerly advice, here it is: just sit down and punch it out. Don't think – just write.'

'Thanks a lot,' I said.

'Anytime,' he said. 'Good luck.'

I hung up the phone, I staggered into my bedroom, I fell on my bed, I nodded off (having hardly slept the previous night). When I came to again, the bedside clock read 5.12 a.m. I sat up, startled. Thinking: *I've got a deadline to make in less than five hours.*

I threw off all my clothes. I took a very hot shower, finishing it with a punishing thirty-second blast of ice-cold water. I dressed. I put a pot of coffee on the stove. I glanced at my watch. Five thirty-two a.m. The deadline was ten. When the coffee was ready, I poured myself a cup and carried it over to my desk. I rolled a piece of paper into my Remington. I took a fast sip of the still-scalding coffee. Then I took a very deep breath.

Don't think – just write.

All right, all right. I'll try . . .

Without thinking, I hammered out a paragraph:

The real-estate agent was a woman in her fifties. Her face was heavily rouged, her smile rigid, fixed. I saw her studying my ringless left hand, and the elaborate engagement ring which I had just recently transferred to my right hand.

'Was he a bum?' she said.

'No,' I said. 'It just didn't work out.'

I stopped for a moment. I took another gulp of coffee. I glanced at the six typed lines on the page. I started writing again.

'So you're looking for a fresh start?' she asked me.

'No,' I said. 'I'm just looking for an apartment.'

Not bad, not bad. Keep going. I downed the rest of the cup. I looked back down at the keyboard. I started typing again.

When I looked up again, it was 8.49 a.m. Morning light was flooding the living room. And four typed pages were stacked beside me at the desk. I pulled the final page from the Remington, and placed it at the bottom of the pile. Then, reaching for a pencil, I read through the feature – quickly excising a few clumsy phrases, tightening up the grammar, rewriting a small block of dialog. Another fast glance at my watch: 9.02 a.m. I reached for ten clean sheets of typing paper, one of carbon. I sandwiched the carbon paper between two sheets. I carefully rolled it into my Remington. I started retyping the story. It took just under forty minutes to finish the job. Nine forty-two a.m. No time to lose. I took the top copy of the story, tossed it into my briefcase, grabbed my coat and charged for the door. I hailed a cab going downtown on Riverside Drive, and told the driver I'd give him a hefty tip if he could get me to Rockefeller Center just before ten a.m.

'From here to Rockefeller Center in twelve minutes?' he said. 'Forgeddaboudit.'

387

'Just do your best, please.'

'Lady, that's all any of us can do.'

Besides being something of a philosopher, the cabbie was also a maniac behind the wheel. But he did get me to 50th and Fifth by 10.04. I gave him a buck-fifty, even though the meter only read eighty-five cents.

'Remind me to pick you up again,' he said when I told him to keep the change. 'I hope you get whatever you're rushing to get.'

I charged into the lobby of *Saturday/Sunday*. The elevator was crowded, and made a lot of stops before it reached the fifteenth floor. Ten eleven a.m. I walked briskly down the corridor. I knocked on Imogen Woods' door, fully expecting her secretary to greet me. But Miss Woods opened it herself.

'You're late,' she said.

'Just a few minutes.'

'And you look harassed as hell.'

'The traffic . . .'

'Yeah, yeah – I've heard that one before. And let me guess: your dog ate your copy.'

'No,' I said, fumbling with the clasps on my briefcase. 'I actually have it here.'

'Well, well – wonders do happen.'

I reached inside and handed over the five pages. She took them from me, then opened the door again.

'I'll call you when I've read it,' she said, 'which might take a couple of days, given how goddamn behind I am on everything. Meanwhile, go buy yourself a cup of coffee, Smythe. You look like you need one.'

I actually treated myself to breakfast at Lindy's: bagels and lox, accompanied by lots of black coffee. Then I walked one block uptown to the Colony Record Shop and dropped $2.49 on a new recording of *Don Giovanni*, featuring Ezio Pinza as the great womanizer. Feeling that I was being just a tad profligate, I opted for the subway home, kicked off my shoes, stacked the four new discs on my phonograph, pushed the lever marked *On*, flopped on my sofa, and spent the next few hours doing nothing but listening to Mozart and Da Ponte's sublime, dark tale of carnal crime and punishment. The music washed over me. I was exhausted, depleted. And totally bemused as to how the hell I had managed to get the story written. Though the carbon copy was on my desk, I didn't want to read through it right now. There was time enough to discover whether it was good or not.

Around three that afternoon – just as Don Giovanni was descending into hell – the phone rang. It was Imogen Woods.

'So,' she said, 'you *can* write.'

'Really?' I said, sounding uncertain.

'Yeah. *Really.*'

'You mean, you liked the piece?'

'Yes, Oh Unconfident One – I actually *did* like it. So much so that I'm going to commission another feature from you . . . if you're not too full of self-doubt to handle another commission.'

'I can handle another commission,' I said.

'That's what I like to hear,' she said.

The commission was for another 'Slice of Life' piece – only this time she wanted me to do something funny and smart on that most unnerving rite of passage: the first date. Once again, the length was a thousand words. Once again, she insisted it be in within a week. Once again, I pulled my hair out until – following Eric's advice – I sat down and simply wrote the thing straight through. Telling the silly story of the night that Dick Becker – one of my classmates at Hartford High; a tall, nervous science whiz with bad skin and an overbite – invited me to a Square Dance at the local Episcopalian church. It wasn't exactly the most lascivious first date in history. Rather, it was very awkward, very sweet. At the end of the evening (I had a curfew of nine thirty), he walked me to my door and chastely shook my hand.

Nothing terribly memorable happened, I wrote. *Neither of us did anything embarrassing, like clunking our heads together while attempting a kiss. Because there was no kiss. We were both terribly formal with each other. Formal and proper and oh-so-innocent. Which, after all, is the way a first date should be.*

This time I made the deadline with twenty minutes to spare. On my way back home from the *Saturday/Sunday* offices, I had breakfast again in Lindy's, then went to the Colony and bought a new recording of Horowitz playing three Mozart piano sonatas. As I walked back into my apartment, the phone started ringing.

'Now, in my jaundiced opinion,' Imogen Woods said, 'a first date should end with me waking up the next morning and discovering that I'm in bed with Robert Mitchum. But, of course, I'm not a nice girl like you.'

'I am not a nice girl,' I said.

'Oh yes you are. Which is why you're the perfect *Saturday/Sunday* writer.'

'So you liked the piece?'

'Yeah – give or take the occasional dumb line, I liked it. *Mucho.* So what next?'

'You want me to write something else for you?'

'I love a girl with impressive powers of deduction.'

My third commission was for a piece entitled 'When You Just Can't Get It Right', a moderately amusing thousand-word stroll through that perennial tonsorial problem called 'a bad hair day'. Yes, I knew this was lightweight stuff. Yes, I knew that this sort of thing would never win me a Pulitzer. But I also knew that I had a facility for wry observations on small domestic or personal subjects. I could – to quote Imogen Woods – *write sharp*. More importantly, I had discovered that I could actually write again . . . a discovery which astonished and delighted me. It wasn't fiction. It wasn't high art. But it was tightly constructed and had some wit. For the first time in years, I felt curiously confident. I had a talent. A small talent, perhaps – but a talent nonetheless.

I delivered 'When You Just Can't Get It Right' a day ahead of its due date. As always I celebrated with breakfast at Lindy's and the acquisition of a record at the Colony (a recording of Bach's *Goldberg Variations* for harpsichord, performed by Wanda Landowska – a bargain at eighty-nine cents). I heard nothing from Miss Woods for nearly forty-eight hours. By the time she called, I had convinced myself she'd so hated this new piece that my career at *Saturday/Sunday* was over.

'Well, His Godship the Editor and I have been having words about you,' she said as soon as I picked up the phone.

'Oh, really,' I said. 'Is something wrong?'

'Yeah – he hates your stuff and wanted me to break the news to you.'

After a long pause, I managed to say: 'Well, I guess that's to be expected.'

'Jesus Christ, will you listen to yourself. Little Miss Fatalistic.'

'So he . . . uh . . . wasn't asking you to fire me?'

'*Au contraire* – His Godship really likes those three pieces you wrote. So much so that he wants me to offer you a contract.'

'What kind of contract?'

'What kind of contract do you think? A *writing contract*, you dolt. You're going to have your own weekly column in the magazine.'

'You can't be serious.'

But she was. And during the first week of 1948, my column – 'Sara Smythe's Real Life' – made its first appearance in the magazine. It was, at heart, a continuation of the three 'Slice of Life' pieces I had already written for Miss Woods. Each week, I would take an incident or a minor problem – 'The Guy With Bad Breath', 'How I Can Never Boil Spaghetti Well', 'Why I Always Buy Stockings That Run' – and turn it into a light, fast divertissement. Without question, the column celebrated the trivial, the prosaic. But it was reasonably droll – and because it was rooted in the mundanity of day-to-day female existence, I never ran out of weekly ideas.

Initially I was paid fifty dollars a column for forty-eight columns per annum. To me, this was incredible money – considering that the piece never took more than a day to write. Within six months of its inauguration, however, His Godship renegotiated my contract – after the *Ladies' Home Journal* and *Woman's Home Companion* tried to poach me. Because, much to my complete surprise, 'Sara Smythe's Real Life' had become something of a success. I was getting around fifty letters a week from women readers across the country, telling me how much they enjoyed my allegedly funny observations on what Imogen Woods called 'girly stuff'. His Godship himself – Ralph J. Linklater – was also beginning to receive positive reader feedback about the column. Then two things happened which suddenly made me valuable – (a) four of *Saturday/Sunday*'s advertisers asked for their copy to be run alongside my column, and (b) I was approached by those two ladies' magazines, and offered a considerable raise in pay if I would defect to them.

I was astonished by these offers. So astonished that I mentioned them, en passant, to Imogen Woods – dropping it halfway into a phone conversation about my next column. She sounded instantly worried.

'Honestly, Imogen,' I assured her. 'I wouldn't dream of leaving the magazine. That wouldn't be ethical.'

'Well, God bless your George Washington conscience. But promise me this: don't respond to those letters until I've spoken to His Godship.'

Of course, I promised not to respond to the competing magazines. Call me naive – but I was perfectly happy being paid fifty dollars a column. Especially as it had become so straightforward to write. I didn't intend to use the other offers as a bargaining chip. When His Godship himself personally called me at home the next morning, I suddenly realized that that was what they had become.

I had met Mr Linklater just once before this conversation – when he invited me out to lunch (with Miss Woods) a few months after my column had started. He was a large, portly man who reminded me a lot of Charles Laughton. He liked to run the magazine in a grandfatherly way – but was notoriously harsh with anyone who contradicted him. As Miss Woods warned me before our lunch, 'Treat him like your favorite uncle, and he'll love you. But if you try to flash your smarts at him – not that you would – he won't respond to that at all.'

Of course, my Smythe family manners meant that I was instantly deferential to this man of authority. Afterwards, Miss Woods told me that His Godship thought I was 'just peachy' (an exact quote), and 'precisely the nice, clever sort of young woman we like writing for the magazine'.

His phone call came at eight a.m. I had been up late the night before, finishing next week's column – so I was still groggy when I reached for the phone.

'Sara – good morning! Ralph J. Linklater here. Haven't woken you, have I?'

I was instantly conscious. 'No, sir. It's nice to hear from you.'

'And it's wonderful to speak to our star columnist. You are still *our* star columnist, Sara . . . aren't you?'

'Of course, Mr Linklater. *Saturday/Sunday* has been so good to me.'

'Delighted to hear you say that, Sara. Because – as I'm sure you know – I like to think of all of us at *Saturday/Sunday* as family. You do consider us family, don't you, Sara?'

'Absolutely, Mr Linklater.'

'Wonderful. It's so good to know that. Because we consider you such a valuable part of our family. So valuable that we want to put you under an exclusive contract to us and increase your fee to eighty dollars a week.'

The word *exclusive* suddenly rang alarm bells in my head. I decided to tread carefully.

'Gosh, Mr Linklater, eighty dollars a week is really generous. And God knows, I really want to stay with *Saturday/Sunday* – but if I accept your offer, it means my income will *only* be eighty dollars a week. Which is kind of limiting, wouldn't you agree?'

'A hundred a week then.'

'That's very acceptable – but say someone else offers me a hundred and twenty dollars – and on a non-exclusive basis.'

'No one would do that,' he said, suddenly sounding a little irritated.

'You're probably right, sir,' I said, politeness itself. 'I guess the only thing that troubles me is the idea that I'd be closing off other options, other potential markets. Isn't making the best of your opportunities all part of the American Way?'

I couldn't believe I'd spoken that line (even though I knew that His Godship was always writing 'Thoughts from The Editor's Chair' pieces on *O.W.L.: Our Way of Life*). I couldn't believe I was suddenly in this high-stakes (for me) negotiation with our benevolent ruler, Ralph J. Linklater. But having entered into this negotiation, I knew I had to see it through.

'Yes, you're absolutely right, Sara,' His Godship said with reluctance, 'a competitive marketplace is one of the great glories of American democracy. And I really respect a young woman like yourself who understands the marketability of her talents. But one hundred and twenty a column is the absolute maximum I can pay. And yes, that would be for the exclusive use of your talents. However, here's what I'm also prepared to do. According to Miss Woods, you love classical music – and know lots about it. So say you also wrote an amusing monthly column for us about how to listen to Beethoven and Brahms, which record you should give your honey for Christmas . . . that kind of fun thing. We'll call the column . . . uhm . . . got any thoughts on the subject?'

'How about "Music for Middlebrows"?'

'Perfect. And I'll be willing to pay you sixty dollars per month for the column, in addition to the hundred and twenty you'll be getting for "Real Life". Does that sound like a peachy deal or what?'

'Very peachy.'

Within a few days, I had a contract from *Saturday/Sunday* for the terms agreed with His Godship. I paid Joel Eberts to look it over. He spoke to someone in the magazine's legal affairs department, and after a bit of horse trading, got them to include a clause which allowed both parties to renegotiate the terms in eighteen months' time. Once again, Mr Eberts only charged me six dollars an hour for his services. And when he handed me his bill for twenty-four dollars, he said, 'Sorry I took the extra hour, but . . .'

'Mr Eberts, *please*. I can well afford it. I'm now making more money than I know what to do with.'

'I'm sure you'll figure out ways of spending it.'

Actually, there was little I wanted to buy. My new music column meant that I was being inundated with free records from all the music companies. I had no mortgage, no rent. I had no dependents. I still had most of that five thousand dollars cash in the bank. Lawrence Braun seemed to be achieving reasonable growth on my twenty-thousand-dollar portfolio. I was suddenly earning seven thousand a year – giving me an after-tax income of five thousand dollars. Prudently, I started salting away two thousand per annum in my pension plan, but this still gave me nearly sixty dollars a week to live on. Back in 1948, a top-price ticket on Broadway or at Carnegie Hall was two dollars fifty. A movie was sixty cents. My weekly grocery bill was under ten dollars. Breakfast at my local Greek coffee shop was forty cents – and that included scrambled eggs, bacon, toast, orange juice, and bottomless coffee. A great meal at Luchows for two was no more than eight dollars tops.

Of course, I wanted to lavish as much money as possible on Eric. But he wouldn't let me do much more than pick up the occasional check for dinner or accept all the free surplus records I received from the record companies. Once or twice I made noises again about buying him an apartment, but these were always met with an instant 'No thanks.'

398

Though he kept telling me how thrilled he was with my success, it was clear that it made him a little anxious.

'I think I'll start introducing myself as Sara Smythe's brother,' he said one evening.

'But I always introduce myself as the sister of the funniest comedy writer in New York,' I countered.

'Nobody rates a comedy writer,' he said.

That wasn't totally true – because a few months after I signed my new contract with *Saturday/Sunday*, Eric called me early one morning in a state of high excitement. A young comedian named Marty Manning had been hired by NBC to create a show for the network's prime-time television schedule – due to go on the air in January 1949. Manning told Eric that he'd heard great things about him from his pal, Joe E. Brown – and, after a long lunch at the Friar's Club, offered Eric a contract as one of his show's top writers.

'Of course, I accepted on the spot – because Manning is a really hot talent: very smart, very innovative. The problem is, who the hell is going to watch television? I mean, do you know anyone who owns one?'

'Everyone says it's the coming thing.'

'Don't hold your breath.'

A few days later, one of NBC's lawyers contacted Eric to discuss his contract. The money was amazing: two hundred dollars per week, starting September 1st, 1948 – even though the show wasn't premiering until January twenty-eighth. There was a problem, however: the network had become aware of the fact that Eric was deeply involved in the Presidential campaign of Henry Wallace. He'd been Roosevelt's Vice President, until FDR dropped him from the 1944 ticket for being too radical, instead choosing the untried, universally disliked Harry S. Truman. Had FDR kept his nerve and retained Wallace as his VP, he'd be our president now – and, as Eric was fond of noting, we would have a proper democratic socialist in the White House. Instead, we ended up with 'that ward boss hack from Missouri' (Eric's words again) – a hack whom everyone was betting on to lose to Dewey in November. Especially since Wallace was now running as the candidate of his own Progressive Party, and was expected to rob Truman of many left-of-center voters.

Eric adored everything about Henry Wallace: his rigorous intelligence, his belief in social justice, his unwavering support for the working man and for the original principles of the New Deal. From the moment Wallace had announced his presidential candidacy – in spring of '48 – my brother had been a leading figure in the 'Show Business for Wallace' campaign, becoming one of the chief fundraisers in the Tri-State area, organizing benefit performances, soliciting contributions from the entertainment community in New York.

As Eric later described it to me, the NBC lawyer – Jerry Jameson – was a perfectly reasonable fellow, with a perfectly reasonable tone of voice, and a perfectly reasonable way of explaining why the network had a few problems with his political activism.

'God knows, the National Broadcasting Company is a staunch defender of First Amendment rights,' Jameson told him. 'And those rights, Eric, include supporting whatever political party or candidate you want – whether he's hard-left, hard-right, or just plain cuckoo.'

Jameson laughed at his own joke. Eric didn't join in. Instead he said, 'Let's get to the point here, Mr Jameson.'

'The point, Mr Smythe, is this: if you were simply supporting Wallace privately, there'd be no problem. But the fact that you're flashing your radical credentials for all to see is worrying some of the NBC brass. They know Manning wants you. He keeps telling everyone how good you are. And the way the brass see it is: if Marty wants you on the team, Marty should have you. All they're worried about is. . . .'

'What? That I might set up my own Politburo within NBC? Or maybe that I'll try to hire Laughing Joe Stalin as part of Marty's writing team?'

'I can see why Marty wants you. You really know how to turn out a one-liner . . .'

'I am not a Communist.'

'That's good to hear.'

'I am a loyal American. I have never supported a foreign power. I have never preached civil insurrection, or the overthrow of Congress, or come

401

out in favor of a Soviet as our next Commander in Chief.'

'Believe me, Mr Smythe – you don't have to convince me of your patriotism. All we're asking . . . *my* advice to you . . . is that you take a back seat in the Wallace campaign. Sure, you can attend fundraising stuff. Just don't be seen to be playing such an upfront role for the guy. Face fact, Wallace has absolutely *no* chance of being elected. Dewey's going to be our next president . . . and after November fifth, no one's going to give a damn about any of this. But Eric, take it from me – people are going to give a damn about television. Give it five, six years – and it will kill radio dead. You could be one of the pioneers of the medium. Someone, my friend, in the vanguard of an entire new revolution . . .'

'Cut the crap, Jameson. I'm a gag writer, not Tom Paine. And let's get one thing clear: I am *not* your friend.'

'All right. I'm very clear on that point. I am simply asking you to be realistic.'

'All right. I'll be completely realistic. If you want me to back out of the Wallace campaign, I want a two-year contract with Manning at three hundred dollars a week.'

'That's excessive.'

'"No, Jameson – that's the deal." And then I put down the phone.'

I poured Eric some more wine. He needed it.

'So what happened next?' I asked.

'An hour later, the sonofabitch came back and agreed to the three hundred bucks per week, the two-year contract, three weeks paid vacation, major medical, blah, blah, blah – on the condition that it would all be taken away from me if I was seen publicly raising funds for that bad Mr Wallace. They even added an extra proviso: they didn't want me near any Wallace rallies, campaign parties, whatever. "That's the price for your extra hundred a week," Jameson told me.'

'That's outrageous,' I said. 'Not to mention unconstitutional.'

'Well, as Jameson himself said, I didn't have to accept these terms – "because, after all, it is a free country".'

'So what are you going to do?'

'Oh, I've done it already. I said "yes" to NBC's terms.'

I said nothing.

'Do I detect a hint of reproach in your silence?' he asked.

'I'm just a little surprised by your decision, that's all.'

'I have to tell you, the Wallace people were very understanding. And supportive. And actually grateful.'

'Grateful? Why?'

'Because I'm giving them the extra five thousand dollars I'm making this year from NBC for agreeing to vanish from the Wallace campaign.'

I laughed loudly. 'That's brilliant,' I said. 'What a classy sting.'

He put his finger to his lips. 'It's obviously all Top Secret – because if NBC learned what I was doing with their hush money, the ax would fall on my head. There is a problem, though – I won't have the five grand until I start getting paid . . .'

'I'll write you a check,' I said.

'I promise it will be paid back in full by February first.'

'Whenever. I'm just so damn impressed, Mr Machiavelli. Do you always never let the right hand know what the left hand is doing?'

'Hey – it's the American Way.'

Wallace, as predicted, was trounced at the polls. Like the rest of the nation, Truman went to bed on the night of the election, fully expecting to wake up to Thomas Dewey's victory. But the math didn't work out that way – and Harry stayed put at the White House. On the morning of the election, I got cold feet. Fearing that a vote for Wallace was, in actuality, a vote for Dewey – I switched allegiance and voted for the President. When I later admitted this to Eric, he just shrugged and said, 'I guess somebody has to be sensible in this family.'

Two months later, *The Big Broadway Review* with Marty Manning premiered on NBC. It was an immediate, huge hit. Shortly thereafter, my banker rang me one morning to say that a check for five thousand dollars had just been lodged to my account. Eric was always a man of his word.

And now, *finally*, he was also a huge success.

The Big Broadway Review eventually turned into *The Marty Manning Show* – and became the talk of the town. Everyone adored it. I even went out and bought a television set – because, understandably, I had to see what my brother was cooking up each week. Marty Manning and his cohorts became overnight stars. But Eric and his writing team were also fêted. The *New York Times* ran a lengthy profile in its Sunday *Arts and Leisure* section on a day in the life of the *Marty Manning* writers – in which Eric featured prominently as the witty ringleader of this gang of paid gag men. Even Winchell mentioned him in his column:

Heard a good yuck the other day at the Stork Club from *Marty Manning* scribe, Eric Smythe: 'Where there's a will, there's always a relative!' Smythe – Marty Manning's major-domo for one-liners – also has a talented sis: Sara, whose ha-ha column in *Saturday Night/Sunday Morning* keeps the ladies laughing every week. Talented yucksters, them Smythes . . .

'Did you really tell Winchell that terrible joke?' I asked Eric after the column appeared.

'I was drunk at the time.'

'Well, he obviously thought it was funny.'

'Don't you know that rabid Republicans never have a sense of humor.'

'I love being referred to as a "yuckster".'

'What can I say, S? Fame at last.'

Not just fame – but also, for Eric, celebrity. Success transformed him. He reveled in his new-found professional esteem and prosperity. Finally, he cast off his aura of self-loathing, his need to play the failed writer-in-the-garret. Within a month of the show's premiere, he exchanged his down-at-heel atelier on Sullivan Street for an elegant furnished apartment at the Hampshire House on Central Park South. The rent was a staggering two hundred and fifty dollars a month – nearly four times that of his Greenwich Village place – but, as he was fond of saying, 'Hey, that's what the money's for.'

Besides his talent for comedy, Eric also discovered another interesting gift during that first heady year with Marty Manning: an ability to spend money recklessly. As soon as he moved to Central Park South, he revamped his entire wardrobe – and started favoring bespoke suits. Whereas Manning's other writers dressed like Damon Runyon characters – just back after a day at the track – Eric fancied himself a Noel Coward dandy: cravats, double-breasted suits in Prince of Wales check, hand-made brogues, expensive aftershave. But it wasn't just clothes that soaked up his money. He was out every night – a regular habitué at the Stork Club, or 21, or the Astor Bar, or the jazz clubs that lined 52nd Street. He would always pick up the tab. Just as he would insist on taking me on a week-long vacation to Cuba, staying at the ultra-expensive Hotel Naçional. Just as he would hire his own personal valet. Just as he would lend money to anyone who needed it. Just as he would always be broke at the end of every month . . . until the next pay check rolled in.

I tried to lecture him on financial restraint, and the virtue of putting a little bit aside every month. He didn't listen to me. He was having too good a time. And he was also in love – with a musician named Ronnie Garcia, who played sax for the Rainbow Room's resident band. Ronnie was a diminutive Cuban-American, raised on the Bronx's Grand Concourse; a high school dropout and self-taught musician who also managed to consume books at a ferocious rate. I'd never met a better-read person. As a musician, he'd backed the likes of Dick Haymes, Mel Torme, and Rosemary Clooney . . . but he could also carry on a very erudite conversation about Eliot's *Four Quartets* (in an authentic *dees-dems-and-does* Bronx accent). Eric had met him at a backstage Rainbow Room party for Artie Shaw in April of 1949 – and from that moment on, they were an item. Only, of course, they could never advertise that they were involved. Extreme discretion was demanded. Though the staff of the Hampshire House obviously knew that Ronnie was living with Eric, this was never mentioned. His fellow writers on *Marty Manning* never asked him about his private life – though they all knew he was the only member of the team who wasn't bragging about his skirt-chasing exploits. Ronnie and Eric never showed the slightest bit of physical affection towards each other in public. Even around me, their status as a couple was never acknowledged. Only once – over dinner alone with my brother in Chinatown – did Eric openly ask me if I liked Ronnie.

'I think he's wonderful. Smart as hell – and he plays a mean sax.'

'Good,' he said shyly. 'That really makes me happy. Because . . . well . . . uh . . . you know what I'm getting at, don't you?'

I put my hand on top of my brother's. 'Yes, Eric – I do. And it's fine.'

He looked at me warily. 'Are you sure?'

'If you're happy, I'm happy. That's all that matters.'

'Really?'

'Absolutely.'

He gripped my hand. 'Thank you,' he whispered. 'You don't know how much that means to me.'

I leaned over and kissed his head, then said, 'Shut up.'

'Now we just need to fix you up.'

'Forget it,' I said sharply. And I meant it. Because though I wasn't short of male company – let alone suitors – I deliberately sidestepped involvement. Yes, I did see a Random House editor, Donald Clark, for around four months. And yes, I did have a short-lived fling with a *Daily News* journalist named Gene Smadbeck. But I ended them both – possibly because Clark was too much of a pleasant stiff, whereas Smadbeck was, at the age of thirty, already trying to drink himself to death (though, when sober, he was a total charmer). When I told Gene that it was over, he didn't take the news very well – as he'd delusionally convinced himself he was in love with me.

'Lemme guess,' he said, 'you're dropping me for some corporate type, who will give you all the security I can't.'

'I was married to that sort of man – as you well know – and I left him after five months. So, believe me, I don't need a man to give me security. I've got enough of it myself.'

'Well, you've got to be leaving me for *someone*.'

'Why is it that men always have this preposterous idea that, if a woman doesn't want to see them anymore, it's because there *must* be someone else? Sorry to disappoint you – but I'm leaving you for no one. I'm leaving you because you're determined to self-destruct before the age of thirty-five . . . and I don't want a supporting role in your melodrama.'

'Christ, will you listen to the tough little broad.'

'I have to be tough,' I said. 'Because tough's the only way you hold your own . . . *as a broad.*'

This exchange took place in the bar of the New Yorker Hotel on 34th and Seventh. After finally extricating myself, I caught the subway home and spent the evening listening, yet again, to that amazing Ezio Pinza performance of *Don Giovanni*. Of all the records in my ever-growing collection, it was the one to which I kept returning. Tonight, however, I figured out why. In the opera, Donna

Elvira is swearing revenge against Giovanni – because he's robbed her of her virtue. In truth, however, Elvira's anguish is rooted in the fact that she fell head over heels for the Don who had seduced and abandoned her. Meanwhile Donna Anna is doing her damnedest to avoid the dull, cautious Don Ottavio who so desperately wants her as his wife.

For some curious reason, this story rang a bell with me.

I had surrendered to Don Giovanni. I had surrendered to Don Ottavio. But why surrender again to anyone when you're finding your own way in the world?

On New Year's Eve, 1949, Eric threw a bash at his Hampshire House apartment. There must have been forty people there, not to mention a five-piece band, featuring Ronnie (naturally) on sax. My contract with *Saturday/Sunday* had just been renewed for another two years. Thanks to Joel Eberts, my per column price had risen to a hundred and fifty dollars. The magazine had also just appointed me as their movie critic, at an additional hundred and fifty dollars per week. And I was still writing the monthly 'Music for Middlebrows' column. All told, I would be making sixteen grand in 1950 – crazy money for such easy, fun work. Meanwhile, Eric had also just finished an extended contractual renegotiation with NBC. Besides retaining his position as Marty Manning's chief writer, the network also wanted him to develop new ideas for other shows. To keep him sweet (and out of the prying hands of CBS), they upped his salary to four hundred dollars a week, and also handed him an annual twelve-thousand-dollar consultancy fee, along with his own office and a secretary.

And so, here we were, crammed in Eric's living room overlooking Central Park, shouting 'five-four-three-two-one' as the dying moments of the nineteen-forties vanished, and we all screamed 'Happy New Year' and embraced a new decade.

After being kissed by two dozen strangers, I managed to find my brother – standing near one of the windows. A fireworks display within the park was illuminating the midnight sky. Eric – giddy on too much champagne – grabbed me in a bear hug.

'Can you believe it?' he asked me.

'Believe what?'

'You. Me. This. *Everything.*'

'No. I can't believe it. Nor can I believe our luck.'

Outside, there was a rat-a-tat explosion, followed by a supernova flash of streaking red, white and blue light.

'This is it, S,' Eric said. 'This moment is defi-nitely *it*. So savor it. Because it might not last. It might vanish overnight. But now – right *now* – we're winning. We've won the fucking argument. For the time being, anyway.'

The party broke up at dawn. I greeted the first

sunrise of 1950 with bleary eyes. I was in desperate need of my bed. The doorman at the Hampshire House found me a cab. Back at my apartment, I fell asleep within seconds of climbing between the sheets. When I woke again, it was two in the afternoon. It was snowing outside. By night, that snowfall had upgraded itself into a major blizzard. It didn't stop until the morning of January third. The city was paralyzed by all the stacked-up snow. Venturing outside was virtually impossible for two more days. So I lived off assorted canned goods in my pantry, and managed to write a month's worth of 'Real Life' columns to make some reasonable use of this forced period of incarceration.

On the morning of January fifth, the radio reported that the city was getting back to normal. It was a bright, cold day. The streets had been cleared of snow; the sidewalks shoveled and salted. I stepped outside, and took a deep pleasing breath of bad Manhattan air. I knew I needed to do some serious grocery shopping (all my cupboards were now bare). But before I replenished my stocks, what I really craved – after five days indoors – was a long brisk walk. Riverside Park was my usual exercise yard – but this morning, I suddenly decided to head east.

So I turned right down 77th Street. I passed a series of local landmarks: the Collegiate School for Boys, Gitlitz's Delicatessen, the Belleclaire Hotel. I crossed Broadway. I walked by the shabby brownstones huddled together between Amsterdam and Columbus Avenues. I stared up at the gargantuan gothic splendour of the Museum of Natural History. I crossed Central Park West. I entered the park.

The footpaths in Central Park had yet to be cleared, so I had to negotiate the snow-bound road. Within moments of walking downhill, I was no longer in New York City – rather, in some wintry corner of backwoods New England: a white, frozen landscape, in which all sound had been absorbed by the sheer density of snow.

I made my way further down the hill, then crossed over to the path that ran by the lake. There was a narrow little laneway which led down to a gazebo. I took it. When I got there, I sat down on a bench. The lake was frozen. Above it loomed the midtown skyline: proud, lofty, impervious. Of all the vistas in Manhattan, this was my favorite – the pastoral stillness of the park overshadowed by the brash mercantile splendor of this mad island. No wonder I had headed here after five days indoors. A new decade had arrived – with all its edgy promise. This was my first proper chance to acknowledge it. Where better to do it but here?

After a few minutes, I heard murmurs in the distance. A woman my age entered the gazebo. She had a lean, patrician face – an attractive severity that made me instantly categorize her as a fellow New Englander. She was pushing a stroller. I smiled at her and looked inside. Wrapped up tightly against the cold was a little boy. I felt the usual stab of sadness that now hit me every time I saw a child. As always, I masked it with a tight smile and a platitude.

'He's beautiful,' I said.

'Thank you,' the woman said, smiling back at me. 'I agree.'

'What's his name?'

The question was answered by another voice. The voice of a man. It was a voice I had heard before.

'His name's Charlie,' the voice said.

The man – who had been two or three steps behind the woman and child – now joined us in the gazebo. Immediately, he put a proprietorial hand on the woman with the stroller. Then he turned towards me. And suddenly went white.

I felt a gasp well up in my throat. I managed to control it. Somehow – after a few seconds of shocked silence – I compelled myself to say, 'Hello.'

It also took Jack Malone a moment or two to regain his voice. Finally he forced himself to smile.

'Hello, Sara,' he said.

CHAPTER 2

'Hello, Sara.'

I stared at him without speaking. How long had it been? Thanksgiving Eve, 1945. Four years – give or take a month or two. Good God, *four years*. And somehow, some way, he'd haunted me all that time. Not a day went by when I didn't think of him. Always wondering where he was. If I would ever see him again. Or if that three-word postcard – *I'm sorry . . . Jack* – was his final statement on the matter.

Four years. Could it have evaporated so quickly? Blink once, you're a neophyte New Yorker, just out of college. Blink twice, you're a divorced woman of twenty-eight – suddenly face to face again with a man with whom you spent a night nearly fifty months ago . . . yet whose presence has loomed over everything since then.

I studied his face. Four years on, he still looked so damn Irish. His skin had remained ruddy, his jaw square. This altar boy was yet unlined. He was wearing a dark brown overcoat and thick leather gloves, and a flat cap. At first sight, Jack Malone was an exact fascimile of the man I'd met in 1945.

'Do you know each other?'

It was the woman talking. Check that: it was *his wife*. Her voice was pleasant, devoid of suspicion or mistrust – despite the evident shock experienced by myself and her husband only moments earlier. I looked at her again. Yes, she was definitely my contemporary – and pretty in a pinched sort of way. She was wearing a navy blue coat with a fur collar. She had matching gloves. Her short light brown hair was held in place by a black velvet band. She was as tall as Jack – nearly 5'10", I reckoned – but with no bulk whatsoever. Despite her heavy coat, you could still tell that she was angular, lean. She had one of those handsome, gaunt faces which called to mind portraits of the first settlers of the Massachusetts Bay Colony. I could have easily imagined her braving the hardships of 1630s Boston with steely resolve. Though she graced me with a pleasant smile, I sensed that, if necessary, she could be most formidable.

The baby was asleep. Not a baby, really – he must have been at least three years old. A little boy. And very cute, like all little boys. Swathed in a navy blue snowsuit, with little mittens that were attached to the snowsuit with metal clips. The color of his outfit matched his mother's coat. How sweet. How adorable – to be able to color-coordinate yourself and your child. What a nice privilege – though I was certain she didn't consider it a privilege. Why would she? She had a husband, a baby. She had *him*, damn her. *Him* . . . and a

416

womb that worked. Though I'm sure she probably considered that all to be her right. Her goddamn Divine Right to Motherhood, and to that Man. That loathsome, abominable, self-centered, handsome Irish . . .

Oh God, will you listen to me.

'Yes,' I heard him saying, 'of course we know each other. Don't we, Sara?'

I snapped back to Central Park.

'Yes, we do,' I managed to say.

'Sara Smythe . . . my wife Dorothy.'

She smiled and nodded at me. I did likewise.

'And our son Charlie, of course,' he said, patting the stroller.

'How old is he?'

'Just past the three-and-a-half-year mark,' Dorothy said.

I did some very fast math in my head, then gazed squarely at Jack. He averted his eyes.

'Three-and-a-half?' I said. 'A nice age, I bet.'

'Just wonderful,' Dorothy said, 'especially as he's now talking. A real little chatterbox, isn't he, dear?'

'Absolutely,' Jack said. 'How's your now-famous brother?'

'Flourishing,' I said.

'That's how Sara and I know each other,' he said to Dorothy. 'We met at a party her brother threw . . . when was it again?'

'Thanksgiving Eve, nineteen forty-five.'

'God, you've got a better memory than I have. And who was the guy you were with that night?'

Oh, you operator. Covering your tracks like a well-heeled thief.

'Dwight D. Eisenhower,' I answered.

There was a moment of stunned silence, followed by nervous laughter from Jack and Dorothy.

'You're still the fastest wit in the West,' Jack said.

'Hold on,' Dorothy said, 'you're not the Sara Smythe who writes for *Saturday Night/Sunday Morning*?'

'Yes – that's her,' Jack said.

'I love your column,' she said. 'I'm really a great fan.'

'Me too,' Jack added.

'Thank you,' I said, now staring at the ground.

She nudged her husband. 'You never told me you knew *the* Sara Smythe of "Sara Smythe's Real Life".'

Jack just shrugged.

'And didn't I read in Winchell,' Dorothy said, 'that your brother is one of Marty Manning's writers?'

'He's Manning's top banana,' Jack added. 'His head writer.'

Without meeting Jack's eye, I said, 'You've obviously been keeping tabs on us.'

'Hey, I just read the papers like the next guy. But it's great to see you both doing so well. Please say "hi" to Eric for me.'

I nodded. Thinking, don't you remember that he really didn't like you?

'You must come over and see us sometime,'

Dorothy said. 'Do you live in this neighborhood?'

'Nearby, yes.'

'Us too,' Jack said. 'Twenty West Eighty-Fourth Street – just off Central Park West.'

'Well, Jack and I would love to have you and your husband . . .'

'I'm not married,' I said. Once again, Jack averted his gaze.

'Please excuse me,' Dorothy said. 'That was very presumptuous of me.'

'Not at all,' I said. 'I *was* married.'

'Oh, really?' Jack said. 'For long?'

'No – not long at all.'

'I'm so sorry,' Dorothy said.

'Don't be. It was a mistake. A fast mistake.'

'Mistakes do happen,' Jack said.

'Yes,' I said. 'They do.'

I needed to end this conversation fast, so I glanced at my watch. 'God, look at the time,' I said. 'I must be getting back.'

'You will pay us a visit?' Dorothy asked.

'Sure,' I said.

'And if we wanted to get in touch with you?' Jack asked.

'I'm not in the phone book,' I said. 'My number's unlisted.'

'Of course it is,' Dorothy said. 'You being so famous . . .'

'I'm hardly famous.'

'Well, we're in the book,' Jack said. 'Or you can always find me at my office.'

'Jack's with Steele and Sherwood,' Dorothy said.

'The public relations agency?' I asked him. 'I thought you were a journalist?'

'I was – while there was a war to write about. Now, however, public relations is where the money is. And hey, keep this in mind: if you're ever looking for someone to bump up your public image . . . we're the company to do it.'

I couldn't believe his poise, the way he pretended that I was a mere casual acquaintance. Or maybe to him, I was always nothing more than that. Dorothy gave him another playful nudge.

'Will you listen to yourself,' she said. 'Constantly on the make.'

'I'm serious here. Our company could do a lot for a rising young columnist like Sara. We could give you a whole new profile.'

'With or without anaesthetic?' I said. Jack and Dorothy instantly laughed.

'God, you really are the fastest wit in the West,' he said. 'Nice seeing you again after so long.'

I stopped myself from saying, 'You too.'

'Nice meeting you, Dorothy,' I said.

'No – the pleasure was mine. You really are my favorite journalist.'

'I'm flattered,' I said.

Then, with a quick wave, I turned away and walked back toward the main footpath. When I got there, I leaned against a lamp post for a moment, and took a deep steadying breath. Then I heard their approaching voices as they too

420

started heading this way. Instantly, I dashed across the road, then marched with speed towards the 77th Street exit. I didn't turn back, for fear of finding them behind me. I wanted to get away. Fast.

When I reached Central Park West, I hailed a taxi to take me the four long crosstown blocks to Riverside Drive. As soon as I reached my building, I slammed my apartment door behind me, tossed my coat over the sofa, and began to pace my living room. Yes, I was manic. Yes, I was unnerved. Yes, I was deeply, deeply thrown.

That bastard. That heartbreaking bastard.

How old is he?

Just past the three-and-a-half-year mark.

Three-and-a-half. A nice age.

Three-and-a-half meant that Charlie was born in the early summer of '46. If he was 'just past' that mark, that meant conception would have taken place in . . .

I started ticking off the months on my fingers. June, May, April, March, February, January, December, November, October . . .

October, '45.

Oh, you complete, total s.o.b. She was already up the spout when you worked your gimcrack magic on me.

And to think – *to goddamn think* – of the idiotic, schoolgirl way I bought your act. The thousands of wasted words I poured out in letters to you. The absurd months of pining while I waited to hear from you. And then . . . *then!* . . . that one terse postcard.

I'm sorry.

And now I knew why. Just as I also knew that, for the past few years, he'd been tracking my career. He knew I'd been writing for *Saturday/Sunday*, just as he knew of Eric's success. He could have easily made contact with me through the magazine. Not, of course, that the charmer would have ever dreamed of doing something so upfront and straightforward.

I kicked a table. I cursed myself for being such a fool, for over-reacting, for still finding him so damn attractive. I went to the kitchen. I found a bottle of J&B Scotch in a cabinet. I poured myself a shot and threw it back, thinking: I never drink before sunset. But I was in need of something strong. Because of all the jumbled emotions whirling around my brain right now, the most predominant one was sheer, absolute longing for that bloody man. I wanted to hate him – to despise him for his dishonesty, and for the snow job he perpetrated on me. Better yet, I wanted to dismiss him from my thoughts with detached coolness – to shrug my shoulders and move on. But here I was – less than twenty minutes after seeing him – feeling simultaneously furious and covetous. I so loathed him. I so wanted him. For the life of me I couldn't fathom the instantaneous rush of shock, anger and desire when I first saw him in the park. All right, the shock and the anger I could comprehend. But that ardent surge of sheer want had thrown me completely. And left me in desperate need of another small Scotch.

After downing the second shot, I put away the bottle – and left the apartment. I forced myself to eat lunch at a local coffee shop, then decided to lose myself in a double feature at my neighborhood fleapit, the Beacon. The B-movie part of the program was some forgettable war picture with Cornell Wilde and Ward Bond. But the main feature – *Adam's Rib* with Hepburn and Tracey – was a complete delight: smart, sassy, and urbane (not to mention set in the world of magazines – which amused me no end). Not only do movie stars get the best lines, they also land themselves in on-screen romantic conundrums that are inevitably resolved . . . or which end with wonderful tragic gravitas. For the rest of us mere mortals, things never turn out so clearcut. It's always a state of ongoing mess.

I returned home around six. As soon as I walked through the door, the phone began to ring. I answered it.

'Hello there,' he said.

Immediately, my heart skipped a beat.

'Are you still on the line, Sara?' Jack asked.

'Yes. I'm still here.'

'So your number's not unlisted after all.'

I said nothing.

'Not that I blame you for telling me it was.'

'Jack – I really don't want to talk to you.'

'I know why. And I deserve that. But if I could just . . .'

'What? *Explain?*'

'Yes – I'd like to try to explain.'

'I don't want to hear your excuses.'

'Sara . . .'

'*No.* No excuses. No explanations. No justifications.'

'I'm sorry. You don't know how sorry . . .'

'Congratulations. You deserve to be sorry. Sorry for deceiving me. For deceiving *her*. She was part of your life when you met me, wasn't she?'

Silence.

'Well, *wasn't she?*'

'These things are never simple.'

'Oh, please . . .'

'When I met you, I didn't . . .'

'Jack, like I said, *I don't want to know*. So just go away. We have nothing to say to each other anymore.'

'Yes, we do . . .' he said with vehemence. 'Because for the last four years . . .'

'I'm putting the phone down now . . .'

'. . . for the last four years I have thought about you every hour of every day.'

Long silence.

'Why are you telling me this now?' I finally asked.

'Because it's the truth.'

'I don't believe you.'

'I'm not surprised. And yes, yes . . . I know I

should have written . . . Should have answered all those amazing letters you sent me. But . . .'

'I really don't want to hear any more of this, Jack.'

'Please meet me.'

'No way.'

'Look, I'm on Broadway and Eighty-Third Street. I could be at your place in five minutes.'

'How the hell do you know where I live?'

'The phone book.'

'And let me guess what you told your wife . . . that you were going out for a pack of cigarettes and a little fresh air. Right?'

'Yeah,' he said reluctantly. 'Something like that.'

'Surprise, surprise. More lies.'

'At least let me buy you a cup of coffee. Or a drink . . .'

'Goodbye.'

'Sara, please . . . give me a chance.'

'I did. Remember?'

I put down the phone. Instantly it rang again. I lifted the receiver.

'Just ten minutes of your time,' Jack said. 'That's all I ask.'

'I gave you eight months of *my* time . . . and what did you do with it?'

'I made a terrible mistake.'

'Finally – a hint of self-knowledge. I'm not interested. Just go away, and never call me again.'

I hung up, then took the phone off the hook.

I fought the temptation of another bracing shot

of Scotch. A few minutes later, my intercom rang. Oh Jesus, he was here. I went into the kitchen and lifted the intercom's earpiece, then shouted:

'I told you, I never want to see you again.'

'There's a coffee shop on the corner,' Jack said, his voice cracking on the bad line. 'I'll wait there for you.'

'Don't waste your time,' I said. 'I'm not coming.'

Then I hung up.

For the next half-an-hour I tried to do things. I dealt with a day's worth of dirty dishes in the sink. I made myself a cup of coffee. I brought it over to my desk. I sat down and attempted to proof-read the four columns I had written during the blizzard. Finally, I got up, grabbed my coat and headed out.

It was a two-minute walk from my building to Gitlitz's Delicatessen. He was sitting in a booth near the door. A cup of coffee was in front of him, as well as an ashtray with four stubbed-out butts. As I walked in, he was lighting up another Lucky Strike. He jumped to his feet, an anxious smile on his face.

'I was starting to give up hope . . .' he said.

'Give up hope,' I said, sliding into the booth. 'Because ten minutes from now, I'm walking out of here.'

'It is so wonderful to see you,' he said, sitting back down opposite me. 'You don't know how wonderful . . .'

I cut him off.

'I could use a cup of coffee,' I said.

'Of course, of course,' he said, motioning to the waitress. 'And what do you want to eat?'

'Nothing.'

'You sure?'

'I have no appetite.'

He reached for my hand. I pulled it away.

'You look so damn beautiful, Sara.'

I glanced at my watch. 'Nine minutes, fifteen seconds. Your time's running out, Jack.'

'You really hate me, don't you?'

I dodged that one by glancing back at my watch. 'Eight minutes, forty-five seconds.'

'I made a very bad call.'

'Words is cheap . . . as they say in Brooklyn.'

He winced, then took a deep drag on his cigarette. The waitress arrived with my coffee.

'You're right,' he said. 'What I did was inexcusable.'

'All you had to do was answer one of my letters. You got them all, didn't you?'

'Yes, all of them. They were fantastic, extraordinary. So extraordinary I've kept them all.'

'I'm touched. Next thing you're going to tell me is you showed them all to . . . what was her name again?'

'Dorothy.'

'Ah yes, Dorothy. Very *Wizard of Oz*. Let me guess: you met her in Kansas with her little dog Toto . . .'

I shut myself up. 'I think I should leave,' I said.

427

'Don't. Sara, I am so damn sorry . . .'

'I must have written you . . . what?'

'Thirty-two letters, forty-four postcards,' he said.

I looked at him carefully.

'That's a very precise inventory.'

'I prized each and every one of them.'

'Oh, *please*. Lies I can just about handle. But schmaltzy lies . . .'

'It's the truth.'

'I don't believe you.'

'She was pregnant, Sara. I didn't know that when I met you.'

'But you obviously knew *her*, some way or another, when you met me. Otherwise she couldn't have become pregnant by you. Or have I got that wrong too?'

He sighed heavily, exhaling a lungful of smoke.

'I met her in August forty-five. *Stars and Stripes* had just transferred me back to England after that assignment in Germany. I was doing a three-month stint at their main European bureau, which happened to be located at Allied HQ just outside of London. Dorothy was working at HQ as a typist. She'd just graduated from college – and had volunteered her services to the military. "I had this romantic idea of wanting to do my bit for the war effort," she later told me. "I saw myself as some Hemingway heroine, working in a field hospital." Instead, the Army made her a secretary in London. One day, during a coffee break in the canteen, we got talking. She was bored in the typing pool. I

428

was bored rewriting other journalists all day. We started seeing each other after work. We started sharing a bed. It wasn't love. It wasn't passion. It was just . . . something to do. A way of passing the time in the Ho-Hum capital of England. Sure, we liked each other. But we both knew that this was just one of those passing flings, with no future beyond our stint in England.

'A couple of months later, at the start of November, I was told I was going to cover the start of postwar reconstruction in Germany . . . but could first take some leave in the States. When I broke the news to her that I was departing, she was a little sad . . . but also realistic. It had been pleasant. We liked each other. And I thought she was really swank. Hell, I was a Catholic mick from Brooklyn, whereas she was this classy Episcopalian from Mount Kisco. I went to Erasmus High. She went to Rosemary Hall and Smith. She was way out of my league. She knew this too – though she was too damn nice to ever say that to me. Part of me was flattered that she'd even deigned to spend time with me. But stuff like this happens during wartime. She's there, you're there . . . so, why not?

'Anyway, I sailed from England on November tenth, never expecting to see Dorothy again. Two weeks later, I met you. And . . .'

He broke off, stubbing out his cigarette. Then he fished out another Chesterfield and lit it up.

'And what?' I asked quietly.

'I knew.'

Silence.

'It was immediate and instantaneous,' he said. 'A complete jolt. But I knew.'

I stared down into my coffee cup. I said nothing. He reached again for my hand. I kept it flat on the table. His fingers touched mine. I felt myself shudder. I wanted to pull my hand away again. I didn't move it. When he spoke again, his voice was a near-whisper:

'Everything I said to you that night, I meant. *Everything*, Sara.'

'I don't want to hear this.'

'Yes, you do.'

Now I pulled my hand away. 'No, I don't.'

'You knew, Sara.'

'Yes, of course I fucking knew,' I hissed. 'Thirty-two letters, forty-four postcards . . . and you ask me if I knew. I didn't simply miss you. I *longed* for you. I didn't want to, but I did. And when you didn't respond . . .'

He reached inside his overcoat and pulled out two envelopes. He placed them in front of me.

'What's this?' I asked.

'Two letters I wrote you, but never sent.'

I stared down at them. The envelopes were embossed with the US Army seal. They both looked worn and a little aged.

'The first letter was written on the ship back to Germany,' he said. 'I was planning to mail this to you as soon as we docked in Hamburg. But when I arrived there, a letter was waiting for me from Dorothy, telling me she was pregnant. I immediately requested a weekend leave, and took the boat-train to London. On the way there, I made up my mind to tell her that, much as I liked her, I couldn't marry her. Because . . .' another deep drag of his cigarette '. . . because I wasn't in love with her. And because I had met you. But when I got to England, she . . .'

'What? Fell into your arms? Cried? Said that she was so afraid you were going to abandon her? Then told you she loved you?'

'Yeah – all of the above. She also said her family would disown her if she had the child on her own. Having since met them, I know she was telling the truth. Don't blame her . . .'

'Why the hell would I blame her? Had I been in her position, I would have done exactly the same thing.'

'I felt I had no choice. The old Jesuit teaching kicked in: *you are accountable for your actions . . . you cannot escape the sins of the flesh* . . . all that enlightened Catholic guilt stuff compelled me to tell her that, yes, I would marry her.'

'That was very responsible of you.'

'She's a decent woman. We don't have major problems. We get along. It's . . . amiable, I guess.'

I made no comment. After a moment, he touched one of the envelopes and said, 'I wrote the second letter to you on my way back to Hamburg. In it, I explained . . .'

'I really don't want to know your explanations,'

431

I said, pushing both letters back towards him.

'At least take them home and read them . . .'

'What's the point? What happened happened . . . and over four years ago. We had a night together. I thought it might be the start of something. I was wrong. *C'est la vie*. End of story. I'm not angry at you for "doing your duty" and marrying Dorothy. It's just . . . you could have saved me a lot of grief and heartache had you just come clean with me, and told me what was going on.'

'I wanted to. That's what the second letter was about. I wrote it on the boat-train back to Hamburg. But when I arrived there, and found three of your letters waiting for me, I panicked. I didn't know what to do.'

'So you decided that the best approach was to do nothing. To refuse to answer my letters. To keep me dangling. Or maybe you just hoped I'd finally get the message and vanish?'

He stared down into his coffee cup, and fell silent. Eventually I spoke. '*Ego te absolvo* . . . is that what you want me to say? Shame I could have dealt with. Guilt I could have dealt with. *The truth* I could have dealt with. But you chose silence. After swearing love to me – which is a huge thing to swear to anybody – you couldn't face up to the simple ethical problem of coming clean with me.'

'I didn't want to hurt you . . .'

'Oh, Jesus Christ – don't feed me that dumb cliché,' I said, a wave of anger hitting me. 'You hurt me more by keeping me in the dark. And then when you deigned to send a postcard to me, what was your message? *"I'm sorry."* After eight months and all those letters, that's all you could say. How I despised you when that card arrived on my doormat.'

'Sometimes we do things we don't even understand ourselves.'

He stubbed out the cigarette. He was about to light up another one, but thought better of it. He looked disconcerted and sad – as if he didn't know what to do next.

'I really should go,' I said.

I started to stand up, but he took my hand.

'I've known exactly where you've lived for the past couple of years. I've read everything you've written in *Saturday Night/Sunday Morning*. I've wanted to call you every day.'

'But you didn't.'

'Because I *couldn't*. Until today. When I saw you in the park, I knew immediately that . . .'

I removed his hand from mine, and interrupted him. 'Jack, this is pointless.'

'Please let me see you again.'

'I don't go out with married men. And you *are* married, remember?'

I turned and moved quickly out the front door, not looking back to see if he was following me. The January night air was like a slap across the face. I was about to turn back west towards my apartment, but feared that he might come calling again. So I headed south down Broadway, ducking

433

into a bar in the lobby of the Ansonia Hotel. I sat at a table near the door. I downed a J&B. I called for one more.

'Sometimes we do things we don't even understand ourselves.'

Yes – like falling in love with you.

I threw some money on the table. I stood up and left. I hailed a cab. I told him to head downtown. When we reached 34th Street, I told him to head back uptown. The cabbie was bemused by this sudden change of direction.

'Lady, do you have any idea where you're going?' he asked.

'None at all,' I said.

I had the cab drop me in front of my apartment. Much to my relief, Jack wasn't loitering outside. But he had paid me a visit, as the two envelopes were waiting for me on the inside front door mat. I picked them up. I let myself into my apartment. I took off my coat. I went into the kitchen and put the kettle on the stove. I tossed both letters into the trash can. I made myself a cup of tea. I went into the living room. I put on a Budapest String Quartet recording of Mozart's K 421 quartet. I sat on the sofa and tried to listen to the music. After five minutes, I stood up, walked into the kitchen, and retrieved the letters from the trash. I sat down at the kitchen table. I laid the envelopes before me. I stared down at them for a long time, willing myself *not* to open them. The Mozart played on. Eventually, I picked up the first envelope. It was addressed to my old Bedford Street apartment. The address was smudged, as if it had been briefly exposed to rain. The envelope itself was crumpled, worn, aged. But it was still sealed. I tore it open. Inside was a single piece of *Stars and Stripes* stationery. Jack's handwriting was clear, fluent, easy to decipher.

November 27th, 1945
My beautiful Sara,

So here I am – somewhere off the coast of Nova Scotia. We've been at sea for two days now. Another week to go before we dock in Hamburg. My 'state room' could be politely called 'intimate' (it's 10'x6' – the size of a jail cell). It's also less than private, as I share it with five other guys, two of whom are congenital snorers. Leave it to the Army to figure out a way of fitting six soldiers into a broom closet. No wonder we won the War.

When we hoisted anchor in Brooklyn two days ago, I had to stop myself from jumping overboard, swimming to shore, hopping the subway back to Manhattan, and knocking on your Bedford Street door. But that would have cost me a year in the brig – whereas this current penal sentence is only nine more months. And you better be waiting for me at the Brooklyn Naval Yards when we dock in September . . . otherwise I might do something rash and self-destructive, like becoming a Christian Brother.

What can I say, Miss Smythe? Only this: people always talk about that thing called *at first sight*. I never believed in it myself . . . and always thought it was the stuff of bad movies (usually starring Jane Wyman).

But maybe the reason I didn't believe in it was because it didn't happen to me. Until you.

Isn't life wonderfully absurd? On my last night in New York I crash a party I shouldn't be at, and . . . there you are. And almost immediately, I thought: *I am going to marry her.*

And I will . . . if you'll have me.

All right, I'm being a little premature. All right, I'm probably getting a little carried away. But love is supposed to make you a little impetuous and daffy.

Our staff sergeant is calling us for mess duty, so I've got to end here. This gets mailed the moment I reach Hamburg. In the meantime, I will only think of you night-and-day.

Love,
Jack

As soon as I finished reading the letter, I read it again. And again after that. How I wanted to be distrustful, sceptical, hard-boiled. But instead all I could feel was sadness. A sense of what was there between us in the immediate aftermath of that night. A sense of what might have been.

I picked up the other envelope. Just as smudged, just as crumpled. A reminder that paper – like people – ages noticeably after four years.

January 3rd, 1946
Dear Sara,

I did some math today, and worked out that it has been thirty-seven days since I said goodbye to you in Brooklyn. I set sail that day, thinking: I have met the love of my life. All the way across the Atlantic, I started scheming of ways I could legally get myself out of being an Army journalist and back to you in Manhattan without facing a court martial.

Then, when we docked in Hamburg, there was a letter waiting for me. A letter which has turned my life upside down.

For the next five paragraphs, he told me the story of how he had met an American typist named Dorothy while stationed in England, how it had been a passing fling, and how it had ended in early November.

But then – upon docking last week in Hamburg – he had received word from her that she was pregnant. He'd visited her in London. Dorothy had cried with relief when he arrived – as she feared he might abandon her. But he wasn't the abandoning type.

All actions have a potential consequence.

Sometimes we get lucky and dodge the repercussions. Sometimes we pay the price. Which is what I am doing now.

This is the hardest letter I've ever written – because you are the woman I want to be with for the rest of my life. Yes, I feel that absolute, that certain. How do I know? I just know.

But there is nothing I can do to change the situation. I must do the responsible thing. I must marry Dorothy.

I want to beat my head against a wall, and curse myself for losing you. Because I know that, from this moment onwards, you will haunt my every move.

I love you.

I am so sorry.

Try, somehow, to forgive me.

Jack

Oh, you fool. You big dumb fool. Why the hell didn't you send this letter? I would have understood. I would have believed you. I would have forgiven you on the spot. I would have coped. I would have eventually gotten over it. And I would have never started hating you.

But you couldn't face . . . what? Hurting me? Letting me down? Or simply admitting the whole damn lousy business?

But the act of admission – of owning up to a mistake, an error of judgment, a bad call – is sometimes the hardest thing imaginable. Especially when, like Jack, you suddenly find yourself cornered by a biological accident.

'You really believe his story?' Eric asked me later that night on the phone.

'In a way, it makes sense, and explains . . .'

'What? The fact that he's a moral coward, who couldn't give you the benefit of the truth?'

'He did tell me that he'd made a terrible mistake.'

'We all make terrible mistakes. Sometimes they're forgiven, sometimes they're not. The question is: do you want to forgive him?'

Long pause. I finally said, 'Isn't forgiveness always easier for everyone involved?'

Eric sighed loudly.

'Sure – and while you're at it, why don't you shoot yourself in the foot with a tommy gun, pausing twice to reload.'

'Ouch.'

'You asked for my opinion, there it is. But, S – you're a big girl. Believe him if you want. You know what happened before. For your sake, I hope it doesn't happen again. So if you want a ten-cent piece of advice: *caveat emptor*.'

'There's nothing to *buy* here, Eric. He's married, for God's sakes.'

'Since when has "being married" ever stopped anyone from engaging in extra-marital stupidity?'

'I won't be stupid here, Eric.'

I really had no intention of being foolish. At three in the morning – having finally let insomnia win that night's war – I sat down at my desk and typed a letter.

January 6th, 1950
Dear Jack,

Who was it who said that hindsight was always 20/20? Or that if you come to a fork in the road, you should always take it? I'm glad I read your letters . . . which I am returning to you now. They explained a lot. They made me sad – because, like you, I too felt something close to certainty in the aftermath of that Thanksgiving night. But everyone comes equipped with a back story . . . and yours mitigated against any future between us. I don't feel rancor or animosity towards you because of Dorothy. I just wished you'd had the courage to mail those letters.

You intimated that you have a reasonably good marriage. Having myself made a very bad marriage, 'reasonably good' sounds more than reasonably good to me. You should consider yourself a lucky man.

In closing, may I wish you and your family all good things for the future.

Yours,

And I signed it *Sara Smythe*. Because I wanted to be doubly sure that he got the letter's underlying message: goodbye.

I looked up the address of Steele and Sherwood in the phone book. I found a large manila envelope and addressed the letter to him there. I threw on some clothes, dashed to the mailbox on the corner of Riverside Drive and 77th Street, then dashed back to my apartment. I got undressed and climbed back into bed. I could now sleep.

But I didn't sleep late. Because, at eight a.m., the intercom began to buzz. I staggered into the kitchen to answer it. It was someone from my local florist. My heart immediately sank. I answered the door. The delivery guy handed me a dozen red roses. Inside was a card:

I love you.
Jack

I put the flowers in water. I tore up the card. I spent the day away from my apartment – loitering with intent in a variety of midtown screening rooms, watching this month's releases for my movie column. When I got home that night, I was relieved to see no letters awaiting me on the inside doormat.

At eight the next morning, however, the intercom rang again.

'Handleman's Flowers.'

Oh, God . . .

This time, I received a dozen pink carnations. And, of course, a card:

Please forgive me. Please call me.
Love, Jack

I put the flowers in water. I tore up the card. I prayed that my letter would arrive at his office this morning, and that he would get the message and leave me be.

But, at eight the following morning . . . *buzz*.

'Handleman's Flowers.'

'What's it today?' I asked the delivery guy.

'A dozen lilies.'

'Take them back.'

'Sorry, lady,' he said, thrusting them into my hand. 'A delivery is a delivery.'

I found my third (and last) vase. I arranged the flowers. I opened the card.

I *am* taking the fork in the road.
And I still love you.
Jack

Damn him. Damn him. Damn him. I grabbed my coat and stormed off in the direction of Broadway – to a Western Union office on 72nd Street. Once there, I went over to the main counter and picked up a telegram form and a much-chewed pencil. I wrote:

No more flowers. No more platitudes. I do not love you.
Stay out of my life. Never see me again.
Sara

I walked over to a hatch in the wall, and handed

442

the form to a clerk. He read the message back to me in a deadpan voice, saying *Stop* every time I had indicated a period. When he was finished, he asked me if I wanted the regular or fast rate.

'As fast as possible.'

The charge was a dollar-fifteen. The telegram would be delivered to Jack at his office within two hours. As I reached into my purse to pay for the telegram, my hand began to shake. On the way home, I stopped in a luncheonette and stared down into a black cup of coffee, trying to convince myself that I had done the right thing. My life – I told myself – was finally going well. I was enjoying professional success. I was materially comfortable. I had gotten through the marital breakup as cleanly as could be expected. All right, the knowledge that I would never have children continued to haunt me . . . but it always would be there, no matter who I was with. And it would most certainly be there if I was involved with a married man. Especially one who already had a child of his own.

All right, all right, I still loved him. But love cannot succeed without a pragmatic foundation. And there was nothing pragmatic about Jack's situation. It would only lead us – *me* – to grief.

So, yes, I had done the right thing in sending that telegram. Hadn't I?

I was out for the rest of the day. When I got home that night, I opened the door and felt an acute stab of disappointment when there wasn't a telegram from Jack waiting for me. I slept until nearly noon the next morning. Waking up with a jolt, I immediately went downstairs to see if the mail yielded anything from Mr Malone. It didn't. The thought struck me: no flowers today. Maybe I was so asleep I didn't hear the intercom . . .

I made a call to Handleman's Flowers.

'Sorry, Miss Smythe,' Mr Handleman said, 'today wasn't your lucky day.'

Nor was the next day. Or the day after. Or the day after that.

A week went by without a word from Jack. *Stay out of my life. Never see me again.* Oh God, he'd taken me at my word.

Again and again, I told myself I had made a wise, sensible decision. Again and again, I longed for him.

And then, nine days after I sent that telegram, a letter finally arrived. It was short. It read:

Sara:
This is the second hardest letter I've ever written in my life. But unlike the first letter, I will mail this one.
I will respect your wishes. You won't hear from me again. But know this: you will always be with me – because I will never get you out of my head. And because you are the love of my life.

I didn't tear this letter up. Perhaps because I was too stunned at the time. Later that morning, I took a taxi to Penn Station and boarded the train to Chicago – where some local ladies' club had invited me to give a lunchtime talk to their members, and were paying me two hundred dollars, plus all my expenses, for an hour's work. I was supposed to have been away for four nights. Instead, I arrived in Chicago in time for the city's worst blizzard in thirty years. As I quickly discovered, a Chicago blizzard made the equivalent Manhattan climatic event look like a mild sprinkling of flurries. Chicago didn't simply come to a standstill – it became petrified. The mercury dipped to ten below zero. The wind off Lake Michigan sliced you like a scalpel. The snow kept falling. My talk was canceled. My train back east was canceled. Venturing outside was impossible. For eight days I was incarcerated within the Hotel Ambassador on North Michigan Avenue, passing the time by punching out a few more 'Real Life' columns on my Remington, and reading cheap mysteries. Thinking: this isn't the American Midwest. This is a bad Russian novel.

Every hour of every day, I kept trying to convince myself that sending that telegram to Jack was the correct decision. He'd fractured my heart once before. I was right not to let him do it again. Or, at least, that's the justification I kept repeating over and over, in an attempt to stop myself from thinking I had made the worst mistake of my life.

Eventually, the trains started running again. Getting a reservation back to New York was a nightmare. After forty-eight hours, the concierge at the Hotel Ambassador finally managed to wangle me a seat, but no berth. So I sat up all night in the bar car, drinking black coffee, trying to read the latest J.P. Marquand novel (and getting rather fed up with the alleged spiritual crisis suffered by his starchy Boston banker hero), nodding off, and waking up with a stiff neck to sunrise over beautiful Newark, New Jersey.

It was cold, but clear in Manhattan. I deposited myself in a taxi, and slept all the way up Broadway. There was a pile of mail on the mat outside my apartment door. I shuffled through it. Nothing with Jack's telltale scrawl. He was really taking me at my word. I went inside. I checked my ice box and cupboards, and noticed that, yet again, I was low on stocks. I picked up the phone, called Gristedes, and gave them a big order. Because it was still early in the morning, they said they would send a delivery boy around with the groceries in under an hour.

So I unpacked, then had a bath. As I was drying myself off, the intercom rang. I threw on a bathrobe, wrapped my hair in a towel, dashed into the kitchen, picked up the receiver, and said, 'Be there in a sec.'

I went out into the hallway. I opened the front door. Jack was standing there. My heart missed about four beats. He smiled one of his anxious smiles.

'Hello,' he said.

'Hello,' I said, sounding toneless.

'I got you out of the bath.'

'Yes. You did.'

'I'm sorry. I'll come back later.'

'No,' I said. 'Come in now.'

I led him into my apartment. As soon as he closed the door behind him, I turned to face him. Less than a second later, we were in each other's arms. The kiss went on for a very long time. When it ended, he said my name. I silenced the possibility of any further talk by putting my hand behind his head, and kissing him again. It was a deep, long kiss. There was no need for words. I just wanted to hold him. And not let go.

CHAPTER 3

L ater that morning, I turned to Jack and said, 'I want you to grant me one small wish.' 'I'll try.'

'Let me have you to myself all day.'

'Done deal,' he said, slipping out of my bed and walking naked into the kitchen. I heard him dial the phone, and make low muted conversation for a few minutes. Finally he returned to the bedroom, clutching two bottles of beer.

'I'm now officially out-of-town on business until Friday at five p.m.,' he said. 'That's three days, two nights. Tell me what you want to do, where you want to go . . .'

'I want to go nowhere. I just want to stay here with you.'

'Fine by me,' he said, crawling back into bed and kissing me deeply. 'Three days in bed with you sounds like the best idea imaginable. Especially as it also gives us the license to drink Schlitz at ten in the morning.'

'If I'd known you were coming, I'd have bought champagne.'

You always know when you have true rapport

with someone. When you're in each other's presence, you find you can't stop talking to each other. Or, at least that's how it was with us during those three days. We never left the apartment. We barricaded ourselves from the world. I didn't answer the phone. I didn't answer the door – except when I had arranged for a delivery of supplies. Groceries arrived from Gristedes. I called my local liquor store, and had them send over some wine and bourbon and beer. And Gitlitz's Delicatessen were willing to dispatch anything from their menu at short notice.

We locked ourselves away. We talked. We made love. We slept. We woke up. We started talking again. We actually knew so damn little about each other. We were both greedy for information. I wanted to learn everything – to pick up where we left off four years ago, and hear more about his childhood in Brooklyn, his tough-guy father, and his mother – who died when he was thirteen.

'It was the damnedest thing,' he told me. 'I was in the seventh grade. It was Easter Sunday nineteen thirty-five. We'd all just come back from Mass – Mom, Dad, Meg and me. I got out of my suit, and went out with a couple of pals in the neighborhood to play stickball in the next street. My mom told me to be back within an hour tops, as we had a bunch of relatives coming over for lunch. Anyway, there I was, playing with my pals, and Meg came charging down the street, tears running down her face . . . she was all of eleven at the time

. . . screaming, "Mom's real sick." All I remember after that was running like hell back towards our house. When we got there, an ambulance was out in front, along with the cops. And then, suddenly, these two guys came out of our front door, carrying a stretcher, with a body on it covered by a sheet. My dad was behind the stretcher, being supported by his brother Al. My dad never cried, but here he was sobbing like a kid. That's when I knew . . .

'An embolism is what caused it. Some artery to her heart got blocked, and . . . She was only thirty-five. No history of heart trouble. Nothing. Hell, Mom never got sick. She was too busy looking after all of us to even think of getting sick. But there she now was on that stretcher. Gone.

'I felt as if the bottom of my world had just been snatched from under me. That's what my mom's death taught me. You go out to play stickball, thinking your life is secure. You come back, and discover it's been permanently maimed.'

I ran my hand through his hair. 'You're right,' I said. 'Nothing's ever secure. And I don't think anyone gets through life without being dealt some truly bad cards.'

He touched my face. 'And the occasional four aces.'

I kissed him. Then said, 'You mean, I'm not a royal flush?'

'You're the best hand imaginable.'

Much later that night – after feasting on two of Gitlitz's famous corned beef on rye sandwiches,

450

and a few bottles of Budweiser – he got talking about his work in public relations.

'Naturally, I saw myself leaving *Stars and Stripes* and landing a big job on the *Journal-American* or even the *New York Times*. But when I found out I was about to be a dad, I decided to opt for something a little more lucrative than the usual sixty-dollar-a-week starting salary at one of the big papers . . . if, that is, they were even willing to take me on. More to the point, the London bureau chief on *Stars and Stripes* – Hank Dyer – had been working at Steele and Sherwood before the war, so I had a pretty easy entrée into a job. And I kind of like it – since most of the time, it's about three-martini lunches with journalists, and schmoozing the client. At first, I was doing all Manhattan-based stuff, but our business has really started to expand and we're now handling a lot of corporate accounts. So, for the moment, I'm the liaison with a string of insurance companies up and down the eastern seaboard. It's not as much fun as the early days, when I was looking after a fight promoter and a couple of mid-level Broadway producers. But they've upped my salary by seventy dollars a week, and the traveling expenses are good . . .'

'You should be well compensated for having to go to Albany and Harrisburg.'

'Believe me, I'm only going to keep with the insurance boys for another two years max. Then, if I can, I'm leaving PR and getting back into newspapers. My sis Meg tells me she expects me to win a Pulitzer by the time I'm thirty-five. I told her, "Only if you're editor-in-chief of McGraw-Hill by then." Mind you, she might just get there. McGraw-Hill have just made her a fully fledged editor . . . and she's only twenty-five.'

'Is she married yet?'

'No way. She thinks all men are bums,' he said.

'She's dead right.'

Jack looked at me warily. 'Do you really mean that?'

'Absolutely,' I said with a smile.

'Was your ex-husband a bum?'

'No – just a banker.'

'Something bad happened during the marriage, didn't it?'

'What makes you think that?'

'The way you've dodged telling me anything about him.'

'Like I said before, marrying George was a major error of judgment. But, at the time, I thought I had no choice. I got pregnant.'

Now I told him everything. The grim shotgun wedding. The appalling honeymoon. My circum-scribed life in Old Greenwich. My nightmare of a mother-in-law. Losing the baby. Losing my ability to have children. When I was finished, Jack reached over across my kitchen table and took both my hands.

'Oh, sweetheart,' he said. 'How do you deal with it?'

'The way you deal with any loss: you just do.

There's no other option, except excessive booze, alcohol, pills, nervous breakdowns, depression, or any of those other self-pitying options. But do you know what I sometimes wonder? Especially late at night, when I can't sleep. Was I to blame? Did I somehow will the miscarriage myself? Because, at the time, I kept thinking: if only I would miscarry, I'd be free of George . . .'

'That was a perfectly legitimate way to think, given that your wimp of a husband and his goddamn mother were making your life hell. Anyway, we all think dark stuff when we're scared or trapped . . .'

'The thing is: I got my wish. The miscarriage happened. And I also destroyed my chance to ever have children . . .'

'Will you listen to yourself. You didn't destroy *anything*. It was . . . I don't know . . . rotten goddamn luck. We think we have command over so much stuff. We don't. Sure, there are the really rare moments when we have to make a ethical call. But, by and large, we're victims to things over which we have little control. You had no control over this. *None*.'

I swallowed hard. I looked at him with care. His vehemence had surprised – and pleased – me.

'Thank you,' I finally said.

'For nothing.'

'I needed to hear that.'

'Then I needed to tell you that.'

'Stand up,' I said.

He did as ordered. I pulled him towards me. I kissed him deeply.

'Come back to bed,' I said.

Around nine p.m. on our second night together, he got up out of bed, and said he had to make a phone call. Pulling on his trousers and fastening a cigarette between his lips, he excused himself and walked into the kitchen. I heard him dial a number. He spoke in a pleasant, low voice for around ten minutes. I went into the bathroom, and tried to distract myself by having a shower. When I emerged ten minutes later – swathed in a robe – he was back sitting on the edge of my bed, lighting up a fresh cigarette. I smiled tightly, wondering if my sense of guilt and rivalry was apparent.

'Everything okay at home?' I asked mildly.

'Yeah, fine. Charlie's got a touch of flu, which means Dorothy had a bad night last night . . .'

'Poor Dorothy.'

He looked at me carefully. 'You're really not jealous?'

'Of course I'm goddamn jealous. I want you. I want to be with you day and night. But because you're married to Dorothy, that can't be. So, yes, I am jealous of the fact that Dorothy is your wife. But that doesn't mean I hate Dorothy. I'm just totally envious of her – which shows my bad taste, writ large. And you do love her, don't you?'

'Sara . . .'

'I'm not asking that in an accusatory manner. I'm just interested. For obvious reasons.'

He stubbed out his half-finished cigarette. He fished a fresh Chesterfield out of the pack and lit it. He took two deep drags before finally speaking. 'Yes,' he said. 'I do love her. But it is not *love*.'

'Meaning?'

'We got thrown together because of Charlie. We adore our little boy. We get on well with each other. Or, at least, we've worked out a way of getting on with each other. There's no . . . passion. There's a kind of amiability . . .'

'You never . . .'

'Once in a while, sure. But it doesn't seem to be that important to her.'

'Or to you?'

'Put it this way. With Dorothy, it's . . . I don't know . . . pleasant, I guess, nothing more. With you, it's . . . everything. If you know what I mean.'

I leaned over and kissed him. 'I know what you mean.'

'Do yourself a favor – throw me out now. Before it gets complicated.'

'The problem is: if I threw you out, you'd be back here in five minutes, begging to be let in.'

'You're right.'

'One day at a time, eh?' I said.

'Yeah: one day at a time. And we've still got all day tomorrow.'

'That's right. Nearly twenty-four hours.'

'Come here,' he said.

I walked over to where he stood. He began to

kiss my face, my neck. Whispering: 'Don't move.'

'I'm not going anywhere,' I said.

We slept late the next morning. It was snowing again. I made coffee and toast. We lounged on the bed, eating breakfast. For the first time in days, we said nothing for a while – the sort of pleasurable silence that usually exists between a long-established couple. We shared that morning's edition of the *New York Times*. The Pablo Casals recording of Bach's solo cello suites played on my Victrola. The snow kept coming down.

'I could get used to this,' he said.

'So could I.'

'Let me see your story,' he said.

'What story?' I said, suddenly thrown.

'The story you wrote about us.'

'How did you know about that?'

'Dorothy. As she told you in the park, she's a big fan. She's also been reading *Saturday Night/Sunday Morning* for years. So as we were walking home from the park, she told me that the first thing she ever read of yours was a short story you wrote for *Saturday/Sunday* in . . . when was it?'

'Nineteen forty-seven.'

'Well, when she told me what the story was about, I simply went: "Oh" . . . and hoped to hell she didn't see how damn shocked I looked.'

'She didn't suspect . . . ?'

'Hell no. I mean, she has no idea that we spent a night together. So show it to me.'

'I don't think I have a copy in the apartment.'

'Do you expect me to believe that?'

'All right,' I said. 'Wait here.'

I went out into the living room, rummaged around one of my file boxes, and found the magazine containing 'Shore Leave'. I went back into the bedroom and handed it to Jack. Then I headed towards the bathroom.

'I'm having a bath,' I said. 'Knock on the door when you've finished it.'

Fifteen minutes later, the knock came. Jack walked in, sat down on the edge of the tub, and lit up another cigarette.

'So?' I asked.

'Do you really think I kissed like a teenager?'

'No – but I think the guy in the story did.'

'But it's our story.'

'Yes. But it's also just *a* story.'

'A brilliantly written story.'

'You don't have to say that.'

'I wouldn't if it wasn't true. So where's the next one?'

'That is my entire literary output to date.'

'I'd like to read more by you.'

'You can – every week in *Saturday Night/Sunday Morning*.'

'You know what I'm saying here.'

I reached up with my wet soapy hand and rested it on his thigh.

'I really don't mind being trivial, minor, light-weight.'

'You're better than that.'

457

'That's your opinion – and I'm touched by it. But I also know my limitations.'

'You're a great writer.'

'Hardly. Anyway, I'm not remotely interested in being "great". I like what I write. I do it pretty well. Sure, it's inconsequential, left-handed stuff. But it pays the bills and lets me go to movies in the afternoon. What more could a girl ask for?'

'Literary fame, I guess,' he said.

'"Fame is a bee. It has a song. It has a sting. Ah too, it has a wing."'

'Emily Dickinson?'

I looked at him and smiled. 'You really know your stuff, Mr Malone.'

The day drifted by. Around five that afternoon, I pulled him back into bed. At six, he turned to me and said,

'I suppose I'd better be going.'

'Yes. I suppose you must.'

'I don't want to.'

'And I don't want you to either. But there we are.'

'Yep. There we are.'

He showered. He dressed.

'Now I'm going to leave,' he said. 'Before I start kissing you again.'

'Okay,' I said quietly. 'Leave.'

'Tomorrow?'

'Sorry?'

'Could I see you tomorrow?'

'Of course. Absolutely. But . . . will you have the time?'

'I'll find the time. Around five, if that's okay.'

'I'll be here.'

'Good.'

He leaned towards me. I put my hand against his chest, stopping him from coming closer.

'Tomorrow, Mr Malone.'

'Just one last kiss.'

'No.'

'Why?'

'Because we'll end up back in bed.'

'Point taken.'

I helped him on with his coat.

'I shouldn't be leaving,' he said.

'But you are.'

I opened the door.

'Sara, I . . .'

I put a finger to his lips. 'Say nothing.'

'But . . .'

'Tomorrow, my love. Tomorrow.'

He gripped my hand. He stared directly into my eyes. He smiled.

'Yes,' he said, 'tomorrow.'

CHAPTER 4

By five twenty the next afternoon, I was convinced he wouldn't be coming. I'd been pacing the floor since four fifty – certain that he'd had a change of heart, or had been found out by Dorothy, or had suddenly succumbed to guilt. But then the doorbell rang. I went dashing out of my apartment. And there he was – with a bottle of French fizz in one hand and a bouquet of lilies in the other.

'Sorry, darling,' he said. 'Stuck in a meet . . .'

I cut him off.

'You're here,' I said, grabbing him by the lapels and pulling him towards me. 'That's all that counts.'

An hour or so later, he turned to me in bed and asked, 'What happened to the champagne?'

I scoured the floor – covered with our discarded clothes. The champagne was lying on its side, atop Jack's overcoat. The flowers were strewn next to it.

'That's where it landed,' I said.

He jumped out of bed, picked up the bottle, ripped off the foil, and popped the cork. A geyser of foam baptised us both.

460

'Nice one,' I said, as champagne streamed down my face.

'Oops,' he said.

'You're lucky I love you,' I said.

He handed me the bottle. 'Bottoms up,' he said.

'I do have glasses in this house.'

'By ze neck, dahling,' he said. 'It's ze Muscovite vey.'

'Okay, comrade,' I said taking the bottle and tipping it back. 'And by the way, this champagne is from France, and far too expensive to be spraying around my bedroom. What is it, six or seven dollars a bottle?'

'Does it matter?'

'If you've got a family to support . . . then, yes, six dollars does matter.'

'God, you are deeply responsible.'

'Shut up,' I said, running my hand through his hair.

'With pleasure,' he said, and lowered me back down on the bed.

Afterwards, he lay against me, his arms curled around my chest. We fell into a silent reverie for a few moments. Then he said, 'Ever since I walked out of here last night, all I could think about was walking back in here again.'

'I was ticking off the hours too.'

'Around three last night, I couldn't sleep.'

'Join the club.'

'If I'd only known . . . because I was so tempted to call you.'

461

'You must never call me from your house.'

'I won't.'

'If this is going to work, we must be completely discreet. No phone calls from your house or your office. Use a pay phone when you want to call me. There can never be any correspondence between us. If I give you a gift, you keep it here. And no one can ever know about us. *No one.*'

'Why the great worry about secrecy?'

'Do you really think I want to be cast in the role of the Happy Homewrecker? Or the kept woman? *La maîtresse?* No way, soldier. I'll be your lover. I won't be your *femme fatale*. I want you . . . but I don't want the incumbent grief that comes with loving a married man. That's what I decided at three this morning. You'll have your life. I'll have my life. And you and I will have a life together . . . which no one else will know about.'

'Believe me, Dorothy doesn't suspect anything . . . though she was intrigued by the new after-shave I was wearing.'

'But I wasn't wearing any perfume yesterday.'

'Yeah – but I stopped in a pharmacy on the way home and bought two bottles of Mennen Skin Bracer, and splashed some on before walking in the door . . . just in case you were still lingering on my face.'

'Why two bottles?'

He reached down for his overcoat, and pulled out a little bag from a local pharmacy.

'A bottle for home, a bottle for here. I also bought

462

the same soap and deodorant and toothpaste I keep in my apartment.'

I looked at him warily. 'You're a quick worker, aren't you? Or maybe you'd done this sort of thing before.'

'I have never, *ever* done this sort of thing before.'

'I'm glad to hear that.'

'I just don't want to hurt Dorothy.'

'If you really don't want to hurt Dorothy, get dressed now and leave. Because this is definitely going to hurt Dorothy.'

'Not if she doesn't find out.'

'She will find out.'

'Only if I let her find out. I won't let her find out.'

'Are you that clever?'

'It's not a matter of cleverness . . . it's a matter of protecting her.'

'As in: *what she doesn't know won't hurt her*?'

'No . . . as in: I won't leave her . . . but I won't give you up either. Of course, you might not like this arrangement.'

'Oh, so that's what this is: an arrangement? *Cinq-à-sept*, as they say in jolly old Paree? You know your French literature, Jack. Who am I going to be? Emma Bovary?'

'Wasn't she married?'

'Touché.'

'Sara . . .'

'And how silly of me to think of myself as an adulterous woman, when I'm actually . . . what? . . .

a courtesan . . . isn't that the right term? Yes, *a courtesan* whose aristocratic lover leaves a bottle of Mennen aftershave in her *toilette*.'

Long silence. Jack tried to put his arms around me. I placed my hand against his chest and gently pushed him away.

'I'm not going to let myself get mangled again,' I said.

'I won't hurt you.'

'We'll see about that.' I glanced at my watch. 'You should head home to your wife.'

He left a few minutes later. 'I'm out of town on Monday and Tuesday, due back in New York midday on Wednesday,' he said, putting on his coat.

'Fine,' I said.

'But if I work it right, I should be able to rearrange my final meetings in Philadelphia, and get back here around eight in the evening on Tuesday . . . if you'd like a guest for the night.'

'I don't know. I'm really going to have to think this through, Jack.'

'Sara . . .'

'And don't forget to take your aftershave and toothbrush with you. I don't want them in the house.'

'I'll call you,' he said, kissing me on the forehead as he left the apartment.

But he didn't call over the weekend. Nor did he call on Monday. *Idiot, idiot*, I kept telling myself. *You've pushed him away.* By eight on Tuesday night,

I was bracing myself for the worst. *If you really don't want to hurt Dorothy, get dressed now and leave. Because this is definitely going to hurt Dorothy.* Why the hell had I said that? It had obviously sunk in. Why had I made such a big deal over the aftershave? Because I had to be Miss Sense and Sensibility, didn't I? *You should head home to your wife.* He'd taken me at my word. He'd gone home. Permanently.

Then, at eight ten, the doorbell rang. I stormed to the front door, and opened it angrily. Jack was dressed in his dark brown overcoat, and the sort of snap-brimmed brown felt hat favored by newspapermen. He had a suitcase in one hand, a bouquet in the other.

'Where the hell have you been?' I asked.

'Philadelphia,' he said, sounding taken aback by my anger. 'But you knew that.'

'And on Saturday and Sunday?'

'At home with my family, as you instructed me . . .'

'I know what I told you. That doesn't mean you have to follow my damn advice.'

He tried to suppress a smile. 'Come here, you kook,' he said.

Within seconds of falling backwards into my apartment, we had pulled off each other's clothes. We didn't get further than the carpet in my living room. When I felt myself on the verge of disturbing the neighbors, I engulfed his mouth with mine. Afterwards, we said nothing for a very long time.

'Hello,' he finally said.

'Hello,' I laughed.

'Four days was . . .'

'Too damn long,' I said. 'I can't tell you how much I missed you.'

'I would never have guessed.'

'Don't get cocky, soldier.'

I got up and disappeared into my bedroom. I put on a bathrobe. I reached inside my closet and brought out a shopping bag. When I returned to the living room, Jack was sitting on the sofa, pulling on his underwear.

'No need to get dressed,' I said.

'But I might freeze. You keep things on the chilly side here.'

'This might keep you warm,' I said, reaching into the bag and tossing him a large rectangular package, gift-wrapped in stern blue Brooks Brothers paper.

'A present?' he said.

'My, my – you are clever.'

He tore off the paper. He smiled – and immediately put on the blue linen bathrobe I'd bought him yesterday.

'You've got style, Miss Smythe,' he said.

'You like?'

'I love it. Brooks Brothers. Total class. I feel like I went to Princeton.'

'It suits you.'

He walked into the little entrance foyer off the living room, and sized himself up in the mirror.

'Yes,' he said. 'It really does.'

I reached into the shopping bag and handed him another wrapped package.

'Are you nuts?' he said.

'No. Just generous.'

'Too generous,' he said, kissing me on the lips.

'See if you like it first,' I said.

He opened the paper. He laughed. Inside were two bottles of Caswell and Massey's Bay Rum Aftershave.

'Two bottles?' he said, twisting off the top of one bottle.

'One for here, one for home.'

He gave me an amused smile, then took a long sniff of the scent. 'That's nice stuff,' he said. 'Are you trying to tell me something?'

'Yes. Mennen makes you smell like a bad locker room.'

'Oh, you snob. Brooks Brothers robes, now Caswell and Massey aftershave. Next thing it will be elocution lessons.'

'Is there anything wrong with me buying you nice things?'

He stroked my hair. 'Absolutely not. I approve. I'm just wondering how I'll explain the new aftershave to my wife.'

'You could always say you bought it yourself.'

'But I'm someone who never drops more than a buck on a bottle of aftershave.'

'Well, Brooklyn boy – here's a thought. Drop by Caswell and Massey tomorrow – they're on

Lexington and Forty-Sixth Street – and buy your wife a bottle of their eau de toilette. Then you can tell her that, while buying her this gift, you sampled their Bay Rum aftershave and decided you needed to graduate from Mennen. She'll approve, believe me.'

He splashed some of the aftershave into his hand, and on to his face.

'What do you think?' he asked.

I put my face close to his, then began to kiss his neck.

'It works.'

'You're wonderful. How portable is your type-writer?'

'Not very portable.'

He went over to my desk and lifted up my Remington. 'I could carry that,' he said.

'I'm sure you could. But why would you?'

'I have an idea.'

Two days later, I was on a morning train to Albany with Jack. We checked into the Capital Hotel as Mr and Mrs Jack Malone. While he went off to see his clients, I sat down at the desk in our room and punched out a 'Real Life' column on my Remington. Jack came back from his appointments around five. I had him undressed within a minute. Half an hour later, he lit up a cigarette and said, 'This is, without doubt, the sexiest thing that's ever happened to me in Albany.'

'I should hope so,' I said.

It was fifteen below in Albany, so we stayed in

468

that night and ordered room service. The next morning Jack braved the elements to deal with a few more clients. I took a brisk walk around downtown – and decided that I had seen enough of Albany for one morning. So I retreated back to our room, punched out half of my movie column on my Remington, then killed the afternoon at a wonderfully cheesy Victor Mature double-feature (*Samson and Deliah* and *Wabash Avenue*) at a nearby RKO fleapit. I was back at the hotel by five thirty. As I was about to open the door of our room, I could hear Jack on the phone.

'All right, all right – I know you're angry, but . . . what's one more night? . . . Yeah, yeah, yeah . . . you're right . . . but, hey, it's not like I want to be away . . . You know I love you . . . Look, an extra night in Albany probably means another ten bucks this week . . . Okay, okay . . . You too, darling . . . Tell Charlie I love him . . . and yeah, five o'clock tomorrow without fail . . . Okay, bye.'

I waited a moment, then opened the door. Jack was lighting up a cigarette and pouring a shot of Hiram Walker bourbon into a hotel tooth glass. He tried to force a smile, but looked strained. I came over, put my arms around his neck and said, 'Tell me.'

'It's nothing.'

'It's hardly nothing if it's making you look so tense.'

He shrugged. 'Just a bad business call, that's all.'

I let go of his neck, walked into the bathroom,

469

took the remaining tooth glass off the sink, returned to the room and poured myself two fingers of bourbon.

'What's wrong?' he asked.

'I hate being lied to.'

'How have I lied to you?'

'"*Just a bad business call.*" I heard who you were talking to on the phone.'

'What do you mean, you heard?'

'I mean, I was standing outside the door . . .'

'Eavesdropping?'

'I didn't want to walk in right when you were speaking with Dorothy.'

'Either that or you wanted to listen in . . .'

'Why the hell would I want to listen in, Jack?'

'I don't know. You were the one who was standing outside the door . . .'

'That's because I didn't want to put you in an uncomfortable position by bursting into the room . . .'

'I'm sorry,' he said suddenly.

'Never lie to me, Jack. *Never.*'

He turned away, looking out the grimy window at the dim lights of downtown Albany. 'I just thought . . . I don't know . . . the last thing you wanted to hear was that I'd had a fight with Dorothy.'

'You're a fool, Malone. I may not like the idea you're married, but that's the territory you occupy – and I accept that. But if this is going to continue, you'll have to keep lying to Dorothy. If you can handle that, fine. If you can't, I'll catch the last train back to Grand Central tonight.'

He turned and touched my arm. 'Don't catch that train.'

'What was the argument about?'

'She wanted me back tonight.'

'Then you should have gone home.'

'But I wanted to stay here with you.'

'Much appreciated – but not when you start lying to me, in order to cover up lying to Dorothy.'

'I'm a jerk.'

I managed a smile.

'No – you're a *married* jerk. Is she suspicious?'

'Not at all. Just lonely. And I'm so damn muddled. There are times when I wish Dorothy wasn't so decent and understanding. If she was a bitch . . .'

'Everything would be fine?'

'I wouldn't feel so bad.'

'Poor, poor you: she's not a bitch.'

'God, you can be a hard case, he said.

'That's because I have to be. It's not easy loving someone with divided loyalties.'

'They're not really that divided. I adore you.'

'But you are also committed to her.'

He shrugged. And said, 'I have no choice.'

'So, you're dealing with a conundrum. The question is: are you going to let the conundrum remain insoluble?'

'What do you suggest I do?'

'Work out a way of being with me and with Dorothy. Compartmentalize. Be French.'

'Can you handle that?'

'I don't know. Time will tell. The real question is: can you handle it, Jack?'

'I don't know either.'

'Well, I'd try to figure that one out, Jack. Because if this romance becomes one long exercise in bad conscience, I'll walk. I know what I can – and cannot – expect out of this. It's up to you, my love.'

We returned to Manhattan the next morning. At Grand Central Station, he held me tightly.

'I'd better stick close to home for the next few days,' he said.

'That's probably smart.'

'Can I call you?'

'Do you really have to ask that question?'

He kissed me lightly on the lips.

'Love you,' he said.

'You sound tentative.'

'I'm trying not to be.'

I didn't hear from him the next day. Or the day after. Or the day after that. Naturally, his silence drove me crazy. Because it could only mean one thing: it was over.

The weekend came and went. On Monday, I stayed by the phone all day, just in case. But he never called. Then, at six thirty on Tuesday morning, the doorbell rang. He was standing outside. Behind him, a taxi was waiting in the street. His face lit up when I answered the door – even though I was still in a nightgown and was the picture of post-sleep disarray.

472

'Are you ready?' he asked.

'Where the hell have you been?' I asked, groggily.

'I'll talk with you about that later. Right now, I want you to get dressed, get packed . . .'

'I'm not following you.'

'It's simple: we're booked on the eight forty-seven from Penn Station to Washington, DC. We're staying three days at the Mayflower Hotel, and . . .'

'Jack, I'd like an explanation . . .'

He leaned forward and kissed me.

'Later, darling. I've got to run to the office before we depart.'

'Who says I'm going. And why the hell are you suddenly springing this on me?'

'Because I just decided to spring this on you ten minutes ago. Track seventeen at Penn Station. Be there no later than eight thirty. Which gives you around ninety minutes to pack and get down there.'

'I don't know, Jack.'

'Yes, you do,' he said, kissing me again. 'Bye.'

Before I could say another word, he turned and headed into the taxi. When he got inside, he rolled down the window and shouted, 'Be there.'

Then the taxi headed off.

I went back inside. I kicked a chair. I made a fast, firm decision: I wouldn't be railroaded into running out of town with Jack – just because he'd suddenly decided I should accompany him. Hell, the bum hadn't called me in six whole days. So there was absolutely no way that I was going to capitulate to his demands.

473

Having reached this judgment, I went straight into my bedroom and packed a suitcase. Then I jumped into the shower, dressed hurriedly, grabbed my typewriter and found a taxi heading south on West End Avenue.

I made the train with around ten minutes to spare. As planned, Jack was waiting for me on the platform. A porter walked ahead of me, my suitcase and Remington balanced on his trolley. Seeing me approach, Jack whipped off his snap-brim hat and bowed with a flourish.

'I'm a fool to be doing this,' I said.

'Kiss me,' he said.

I gave him a fast buzz on the lips.

'That's not much of a kiss,' he said.

'I want some answers first.'

'You'll get them,' he said, handing the porter a tip.

We found our seats. As soon as the train pulled out of the station, Jack suggested we go to the dining car for breakfast. We ordered coffee. Jack made small talk – breezily asking me about the past six days, what movies I'd seen, how my work was going, and did I really think that Stevenson had a chance against Ike if (as expected) they did go head to head in the '52 election. Eventually, I cut him off.

'What the hell has you so happy this morning?'

'Oh, this and that,' he said, still sounding far too cheerful.

'Are you going to explain to me why you vanished for six days?'

'Yes, I will.'

The coffee arrived. We fell silent until the waiter left.

'Well, go on then,' I said.

The requisite cigarette was placed between his lips. After lighting it, he glanced around the car, noting that there wasn't anyone sitting directly next to us. Then he leaned forward and said, 'I told her.'

This took a moment to register.

'What did you just say?' I asked.

'I told her.'

'You told *Dorothy* . . . ?'

'Yes. I told Dorothy.'

My shock was deepening.

'What exactly did you say?'

'I told her everything.'

'Everything?'

'Yes,' he said. 'Everything.'

CHAPTER 5

The train was just emerging into New Jersey when I was able to speak again.

'When did you tell her?' I whispered.

'The night I got back from Albany with you.'

'How did you explain . . .'

'I gave her the whole story. How we met after I came back to the States in forty-five. How I knew instantly that you were . . .'

He stopped and took a deep drag on his cigarette. After a moment or two he started talking again.

'Dorothy is no fool. She got the entire gist of the story immediately. Then she said, "So you're going to leave us?" I said no, I wouldn't leave, because I had made a commitment . . . taken a vow . . . to her. And, of course, because we had Charlie. But I wouldn't give you up either. Of course, if she now wanted me to leave, I'd go. But it would have to be her choice, her decision.'

'So she threw you out?'

'No. She told me she needed time to think. And she made me promise *not* to contact you until she had considered all this. Which is why you didn't

476

hear from me for nearly a week. I respected her wishes – even though she froze me out for five straight days. Then, last night, she finally spoke to me.

"'I don't have much choice in the matter," she said. "But understand this: I *never* want to know. As far as I'm concerned, you're on the road a couple of days a week. You are *out of town*. But when you're home with Charlie and me, you're *completely* with us."'

I finally spoke again. 'Of course she has a choice. She could throw you out. If I was in her position, I would. In a heartbeat.'

'Yeah – I probably deserve that.'

I put down my coffee cup. I leaned forward and spoke quietly. 'You don't really think that, Jack. I mean, you should have seen your face ten minutes ago when you saw me walking down the platform. You looked like the cat who'd gotten the cream. For the life of me, I couldn't figure out why. Now, of course, I know exactly why you're so damn happy. What a fantastic position for a guy like you to be in: the loyal little wife at home with the baby . . . and then, there's *the other woman*, to whom the loyal little wife has suddenly decided to turn a blind eye, on the proviso that she's never referred to as anything but *out of town*. In fact, here's a thought: why don't you stop using my real name and start calling me by my new acronym: *O.O.T* . . . *out of town*.'

'I thought you'd be pleased with this news.'

'Of course you'd think that. After all, you're the one who's suddenly been transformed overnight from a guilt-laden Catholic to a happily poly-gamous Mormon. Because your poor wife has given you the license to have it your own damn way.'

'I am not being smug.'

'No – you're just totally pleased with yourself. Why shouldn't you be? You've confessed, you've been absolved. And now you can screw me two or three times a week, then waltz back home with a bouquet of roses, feeling irreproachable . . .'

'Shhh . . .' he said, nervously looking around the dining car.

'Never tell me to shut up,' I said, standing up.

'Where are you going?'

'Leaving.'

He was on his feet. 'What do you mean, *leaving*?'

I stormed off down the corridor. Jack threw some money down on the table, and chased after me. He caught me between coaches. I shrugged him off.

'I don't get this,' he said, yelling above the roar of the wheels.

'Of course you don't. That's because you never think about other people's feelings . . .'

'I told Dorothy because I couldn't lie . . .'

'No – you told Dorothy because you needed her to absorb the remorse that you felt about cheating on her. You gambled that she wouldn't throw you out. You gambled right. Now you have the ideal arrangement. Except there's one little problem: I want nothing to do with it.'

'If you'd just let me explain . . .'

'Goodbye,' I said.

'What?'

'I'm getting off at Newark.'

I moved into the next car. Jack followed me. 'Don't get off the train,' he said.

'I won't be part of an arrangement.'

'It is not an "arrangement".'

'Well, it sure as hell looks like that to me. Now if you'll excuse me . . .'

'Darling . . .' he said, lightly touching my shoulder.

'Get off!' I barked. Suddenly all eyes in the carriage were on us. I blushed deeply. Jack turned white.

'Fine, fine,' he whispered. 'Have it your way.'

With that, he turned and went back towards the dining car.

With my gaze firmly fixed on the ground – to avoid seeing the disapproving glances of my fellow passengers – I slunk back to my seat. I sat down. I stared out the window, feeling the sort of jumpy after-shock that always accompanies an *exchange of words*. A few moments later, a conductor wandered down the aisle, shouting, 'Newark. Next stop, Newark.'

I was about to stand up and grab my suitcase and typewriter. I didn't move. The train shunted into Newark. I remained seated. After a few minutes, the conductor blew his whistle, and we continued our journey south.

Around half an hour later, Jack came walking

down the aisle. He did a double-take when he saw me. But he did not smile.

'You're still here,' he said, sitting down opposite me.

'Clearly,' I said.

'I'm surprised.'

'So am I.'

'What made you change your mind?'

'Who said I've changed my mind?' I said. 'I might still get off at Philadelphia.'

'That's your choice, Sara. Just like it's also your choice whether . . .'

'I will not be cast in the role of *the other woman*.'

'But that is exactly *why* I told her,' he whispered. 'That's why I admitted to her that I loved you. Because I didn't want you to be forced into that *mistress* role. Because Dorothy had to know – no matter how painful it was – that I was in love with you. Because that, in turn, gave her some options – like throwing me out, if she wanted to.'

'Weren't you disappointed when she foolishly decided to keep you?'

'On one level, *yes* . . . I was disappointed. Because it would have freed me to be with you all the time. But it would have distressed the hell out of me as well. Because of Charlie, and because of Dorothy, who is too damn nice to be with a bum like me.'

I sighed loudly.

'I still wish you'd never told her. Because now, every time you're with me, I'll find myself thinking: *she knows.*'

'All right, now she knows. But it's not as if Dorothy and I were ever the love of each other's life. She wouldn't be with me if it hadn't been for that little accident. She knows that too. So, it's with her that I have the *arrangement*. Not you. *Never you*. Believe me: this is all going to work out fine.'

'I don't know . . .'

'It will. I promise.'

'Never promise anything.'

'Why not?'

'Because you open up the prospect of disappointment. And because – now that Dorothy knows – things will change between us. Change is always unsettling.'

'I won't let things change between us.'

'They will, my love. Because we'll be no longer living in fear of discovery.'

'But that's a good thing.'

'Agreed,' then I added: 'But it will never be as romantic, will it?'

At Washington, we immediately checked into a hotel and made love. We made love again late that night. And the next night in Baltimore. And the night after that in Wilmington. We returned to Manhattan. We shared a cab uptown. He dropped me at my apartment. He kissed me long and hard. He promised to call me tomorrow.

He kept his promise, phoning me the next afternoon from work. I asked him how he was greeted at home yesterday. I could hear him choose his words with care.

'She was happy to see me.'

'No questions asked about *out of town* . . . ?'

'None whatsoever.'

'How's Charlie?'

'Wonderful.'

'Did you sleep with her?' I suddenly heard myself asking.

'Sara . . .' he said, trying to sound patient.

'I need to know.'

'We shared the same bed.'

'Cut the crap, Jack.'

'She wanted to, so . . .'

'You had no choice. Oops! Miss Sarcastic strikes again.'

'You shouldn't ask me about that.'

'You're right. I shouldn't. It's self-injurious and self-defeating. Like being in love with a married man. Can you come over now?' I asked, cutting him off.

'Now?'

'Yes. *Now*. Because I need you *now*.'

He walked through my door thirty minutes later. An hour afterwards, he jumped up from my bed, and made a fast telephone call, informing some client that he was running ten minutes late. As he dressed, he said, 'I'm out of town tomorrow.'

'Whereabouts?'

'Hartford and Springfield, allegedly. But I could actually be here – if that fits in with your schedule.'

'I'll see if I can move a few things around.'

When he showed up the next night, he had a large suitcase with him.

'I just thought I might leave a few things here. If that's all right.'

'I suppose you'd like your very own closet.'

'That would be handy.'

That night, he unpacked two suits, two pairs of shoes, three shirts, and several changes of underclothes. His umbrella soon found a home next to mine in a stand by the front door. A spare overcoat ended up in his closet. So too did a raincoat and one of his favorite snap-brim hats. Gradually, a complete second wardrobe appeared in my spare closet. His bathrobe hung next to mine on the back of the bedroom door. His shaving cream, brush and razor monopolized a corner of the bathroom sink. His ties dangled off the closet doorknob (until I bought him a tie rack). There were two spare cartons of Chesterfields in a kitchen cabinet. There were bottles of Ballantine Ale (his favorite) in the ice box. There was always a fifth of Hiram Walker in the living room.

He now lived here.

Or, at least, he lived here two days a week. The other two days, he was legitimately *out of town*. Traveling north to the more dismal corners of New England (Worcester, Lowell, Manchester). Or west to the Rust Belt cities of Pennsylvania. Or south on the Philadelphia-Washington axis. Some weeks, I would pack my Remington and accompany him on these journeys (though, snob that I am, I generally stuck to the Washington or Philadelphia runs). On Friday night, he would return home to Dorothy and Charlie. Though he would make a point of calling me daily (always from a phone booth), I wouldn't see him again until Monday. Initially, I didn't like this long three-day absence. Within a month or so, however, I began to appreciate the symmetry of our domestic schedule. I loved being with Jack. I loved his camaraderie. I loved having him in my bed. I was never bored in his company. He made me happy.

But I also came to like the fact that, come the weekend, my privacy would be returned to me. As I had discovered during my brief, wretched marriage to George, I was not a natural cohabiter. Even with Jack – a man I adored – there was a part of me which was pleased to see him leave on Friday, because it meant that, for three entire days, my life would be unencumbered. I could move at my own speed, set my own schedule, not worry about the needs of someone else. Yet, by Sunday night, I'd be desperate to see him again. And, come Monday at six, I'd start listening for him – waiting to hear the front door open (he now had his own set of keys), and the key to turn in my lock.

I also came to accept that this was, verily, an *arrangement*. Because unlike a conventional marriage, our relationship was conducted within strict parameters. We knew when we could (and couldn't) see each other. I never called him at the office. I never called him at home. I had him for a set time each week. If I wanted, I could extend that time by accompanying him out of town. Come Friday, he was no longer mine. But rather than mourn his seventy-two-hour absence, I quickly recognized it as something of a gift. In many ways, the arrangement suited me perfectly – and afforded me benefits (in terms of personal latitude and basic time to myself) that eluded most married women. More tellingly, I didn't have to engage in the power struggle which so defines most marriages. Our arrangement – the deal we struck between ourselves (without ever properly verbalizing it) – operated according to a very simple prin-ciple: no one was in charge here. No one was the head of the household. No one played the role of the breadwinner and of the little woman at home. We were equals.

Of course, we both fought like hell. But as the arrangement deepened, the arguments shifted away from the emotional complexities of my truncated life with Jack. As I had told him that night in Albany (and as I well knew myself): the moment a romance becomes bogged down in endless discus-sions about its inherent problems is also the moment that it ends up being labeled *terminal*.

So, we steered clear of such issues. Naturally, I would always ask after Dorothy and Charlie. Every time his son was mentioned in conversation, I'd get that twinge of loss which accompanied all thoughts about my inability to have children. Jack was sensitive to this – and, on several occasions, deliberately dodged my questions about his son.

But I'd force the issue, telling him that I wanted to know about Charlie's progress . . . especially as he was everything to Jack.

Three months into our arrangement, the thought struck me one day that whenever we argued, it was usually about non-personal matters: like whether we really should be defending a police state like South Korea.

'Look,' Jack said, 'that sonofabitch who runs South Korea . . . what's his name?'

'Sygman Rhee.'

'Right – well, there's no doubt that Rhee is a complete totalitarian. But at least he's *our* totalitarian.'

'There, you admit it. He's a repressive dictator. And though I have nothing but contempt for Stalin and his North Korean stooge, should we really be propping up totalitarian regimes?'

'Will you *listen* to yourself. You sound like some Adlai Stevenson liberal . . .'

'I *am* an Adlai Stevenson liberal.'

'Which essentially means that you have a *nice* soft-centered view of the world. You should learn some basic *realpolitik*. As Chamberlain discovered to his horror, appeasement gets you nowhere.'

'Oh, please don't give me your tough-guy view of foreign policy. "Speak quietly, but carry a big stick" might have worked for Teddy Roosevelt – but these days, the big sticks are atomic bombs . . . which happen to scare the hell out of me.'

'Listen, force is the only thing that any aggressor

understands. General MacArthur's right: if we want to end the Korean conflict tomorrow, we should let North Korea and China sample our atomic bombs, then bring in Chiang Kaishek to run the whole show.'

'Well, thank God it's Harry Truman in the White House, rather than that lunatic MacArthur . . .'

'That man was a war hero.'

'True – but he's out of control.'

'Only if you're a Communist.'

'I am no Communist.'

'Maybe not – but given that it runs in your family . . .'

He cut himself off. 'Sorry,' he said instantly. 'That was dumb.'

'Yes it was. Very dumb.'

'Forgive me.'

'On one condition: you never bring that up again. I regret ever telling you about Eric's little past flirtation with that party.'

'I'll never say anything again about it.'

'That's a solemn promise?'

'Absolutely.'

'Good. Because I think it's about time I told my brother about us.'

'How do you think he'll take the news?'

I shrugged. But I knew the answer to that question: *not well.*

I wasn't seeing much of Eric that year – owing to the fact that he was in such demand. Between writing *The Marty Manning Show*, developing new program ideas for NBC, spending time with Ronnie, and generally living it up, his time was limited. Still, he never stopped being a loyal brother, calling me at least twice a week.

Then, shortly after Jack started to move some clothes into my apartment, Eric and Ronnie paid me a surprise visit one Sunday afternoon around five p.m. Standing on my doorstep, Eric informed me that they were whisking me out for drinks at the St Regis, dinner at 21, and a jam session at the Blue Note.

'Great,' I said. 'I'll just get my coat.'

Eric and Ronnie exchanged glances.

'You mean, you're not going to let us in?' Eric asked.

'Of course you can come in,' I said nervously. 'But what's the point, if we're leaving right away?'

Eric looked at me with deep scepticism. 'S, who the hell is in there?'

'No one. Why would there be anyone . . .'

'Fine then,' Eric said, 'we'll come in from the cold while you get ready.'

He pushed past me. Ronnie hovered on the doorstep, not wanting to appear rude.

'You might as well come on in, Ronnie,' I said. 'Because the cat is now definitely out of the bag.'

No, Jack hadn't paid me a surprise Sunday visit, and was not lurking inside. But evidence of his presence was everywhere in the apartment – evidence which I would have hidden had I known Eric was coming by.

'So,' Eric said, staring at the large pair of black wingtip shoes by my inside door, 'not only is there a mystery man, but he also has large feet.'

He wandered around the apartment, raising his eyebrows when he saw the collection of male toiletries in the bathroom, the slippers by my bed, the collection of paperbacks on the side table in the living room.

'I didn't realize you were a fan of Mickey Spillane,' Eric said, picking up a copy of *I, The Jury*.

'He's an acquired taste,' I said.

'I bet,' Eric said, 'along with Hiram Walker bourbon and Chesterfields. My, my, S – you are developing some seriously masculine habits. Next thing I know, you'll have installed a spittoon by your bed, and will be playing after-hours pinochle with the boys at the Twentieth Precinct.'

'Well . . . I was thinking of taking up bowling.'

Eric turned to Ronnie. 'Quite the wit, my little sister.'

'I've always thought that.'

'Thank you, Ronnie,' I said.

'Of course, you'd never think a man was living here, would you, Ronnie?' Eric asked.

'I see no sign of that,' Ronnie said, maintaining a straight face.

'Thank you again, Ronnie,' I said.

'Yes, thank you *so much*, Ronnie,' Eric said, 'for siding with my sister.'

'I'm not siding with her,' Ronnie said. 'I'm just respecting her privacy.'

'Touché, Ronnie,' Eric said. 'But as her older brother, I *don't* have to respect her privacy. So I'll just come straight out and ask her: why the hell didn't you tell me you were living with someone?'

'Because,' I said, 'I'm not living with someone.'

'Well, Dr Watson,' Eric said, 'all the evidence points to a male presence in this household. A *permanent* male presence.'

'Maybe she doesn't want to tell you,' Ronnie said.

'Yes,' I added, 'maybe she doesn't.'

'Fine, fine,' Eric said. 'I would never, *ever* dream of interfering in my sister's affairs. Does he have a name?'

'Interestingly enough, he does. But I'm not going to tell it to you yet.'

'Why the hell not?'

'Because I'm not ready to tell it to you.'

For the rest of the night, Eric plagued me with the same question: *who's the guy?* After his twentieth attempt to pry the information from me, Ronnie finally told him he was going to stand up and leave unless he got off the subject. Eric took the hint. But first thing the next morning, he was on the phone, demanding, yet again, to know the name of the gentleman in question.

'He must be bad news if you're refusing to tell me.'

'Be patient – when I'm ready to inform you, I will.'

'Why aren't you ready now?'

'Because I don't know whether it has a future.'

'Well, if it doesn't, then you might as well tell me now . . .'

'Can't you accept the fact that you don't need to know everything about me?'

'No.'

'Well, too bad. My lips remain sealed.'

For the next two weeks, Eric kept up the pressure – and enhanced my guilt. Because he was right: we'd always tried to be open with each other. Even Eric finally told me about his sexuality, a horribly difficult admission in those days, so surely I owed him a direct answer to his question . . . even though I dreaded his reaction. Finally, I suggested that Eric meet me for a drink at the Oak Room of the Plaza. We were working on our second martinis when I finally felt enough gin-fueled courage to say, 'The man's name is Jack Malone.'

Eric blanched. 'You cannot be serious,' he said.

'I'm completely serious.'

'*Him?*' he said.

'Yes. Him.'

'But that's unbelievable. Because he was gone with the wind. He messed up your life. And after you met him and his wife, didn't you tell me you'd given him the brush-off?'

'I know, I know, but . . .'

'So how long *exactly* has this been going on?'

'Over four months.'

Eric looked deeply shocked.

'*Four months*. Why on earth did you keep it a secret for so long?'

'Because I was terrified of your disapproval.'

'Oh for God's sakes, S – I might not have liked the guy when I first met him, and I certainly didn't like the way he ditched you, but . . .'

'After Jack vanished you told me, over and over again, that I was a fool to be expending so much emotional energy on such a no-hoper. So, naturally, when he came back into my life, I was really worried about your reaction.'

'I don't have fangs and I don't sleep in a coffin, S.'

'I know, I know. And I felt terrible about concealing this for so long. But I knew that, before I told you anything, I had to find out whether or not this had a future.'

'Which it evidently does – otherwise you wouldn't be telling me now.'

'I love him, Eric.'

'So I gather.'

'But I really mean it. This is not some dumb infatuation with a married man, some transient romance. This is it. And it's mutual.'

Eric went quiet. He sipped his martini. He smoked. Eventually, he shrugged and said, 'I suppose I should meet him again, shouldn't I?'

I set up a drink a few days later – late Friday afternoon in the bar of the St Moritz, one block east from where Eric lived on Central Park South. I was nervous as hell. So too was Jack – even though I assured him that my brother had promised me he would be on his best behavior. Things got off to a bad start when we were kept waiting thirty minutes. Then a bar-man came to our table to inform us that Eric had called and said he'd been stuck in a meeting, but would be with us in ten minutes.

Another forty minutes passed, during which time Jack drank another two bourbon and sodas, and smoked three more cigarettes.

'Is this your brother's idea of a joke?' he finally asked, sounding annoyed.

'I'm sure there's a very good reason . . .' I said, sounding nervous.

'Either that, or he believes that his time is more valuable than my own. Of course, I'm just some PR guy, whereas he's the great gag writer.'

'Jack, *please.*'

'You're right, you're right. I'm just being a hothead.'

'No – you should be annoyed. But there's nothing I can do . . .'

'So let's have another drink.'

'A *fourth* bourbon and soda?'

'Are you telling me I can't hold my liquor?'

'Waiter!' I said, catching him as he passed by our table. 'Another bourbon and soda for the gentleman, please.'

'Thank you,' Jack said dryly as the waiter moved off.

'I'd never stand between a man and his booze.'

'Is that your idea of irony?'

'No – that's me dropping a hint, which you won't take.'

'I know my limits.'

'Fine, fine.'

Jack glanced towards the door. 'But I don't think your brother does.'

I looked the same way. My heart instantly sank. Because Eric had just arrived – and he was drunk. He had a dead cigarette clamped between his teeth, his eyes were glazed, his gait unsteady. When he caught sight of us, he pulled off his hat with a flourish and bowed deeply. Then he stumbled over to our table, and planted a big wet kiss on my mouth.

'Blame it all on Mr Manning. He insisted on pouring two bottles of wine down my throat at lunch.'

'You're an hour and a quarter late,' I said.

'That's show business,' he said, falling into a chair.

'At least you could say you're sorry to Jack.'

Immediately, Eric was on his feet. He snapped to attention, and exercised a crisp military salute. I now wanted to kill him. Thankfully, Jack kept his cool. He threw back his bourbon and soda, and reached for the fresh drink the waiter had just deposited on our table. 'Nice to see you, Eric,' he said quietly.

'And top o' the morning to you, Mr Malone,' Eric said in a dreadful Pat O'Brien accent.

'Maybe we should do this another day,' I said.

'Yeah,' Jack said. 'That might be a good idea.'

'Nonsense, nonsense,' Eric said. 'One little drink and my equilibrium will be completely restored. Now, what are the lovebirds going to drink with me? But, of course . . . Waiter! A bottle of champagne.'

'I'll stick to bourbon,' Jack said.

'Bourbon?' Eric said. 'Come, come – there's no need to be proletarian . . .'

'Are you calling me a prole?' Jack said.

Eric switched into the Pat O'Brien accent again.

'Sure, behind every common man lurks a poet.'

'For God's sake, Eric,' I said.

'I am just joking,' he said in his normal voice. 'No offence intended.'

Jack nodded, but said nothing. Instead, he lifted his fresh drink and downed half of it.

'Ah,' Eric said, 'the strong silent type.'

'What is your problem?' Jack asked.

'I have no problems,' Eric said. 'None at all. In fact, I am as happy as an Irishman in a bog.'

'That's enough, Eric,' I said.

'You're absolutely right. I apologize profusely for my absurd reverie. Now, sir, let us mend fences over a glass of France's best fizz.'

'Like I told you, I'm sticking with bourbon.'

'Fine, fine. I do understand. And approve.'

'You *what*?' Jack asked.

'I approve. Of bourbon, I mean. Especially since bourbon is such a good solid American drink.'

'Is there anything wrong with an *American* drink?' Jack asked.

'Hell no, pardner,' he said, now doing John Wayne. 'It's just, bourbon ain't my firewater, son.'

'Yeah – I forgot. All Commies drink champagne.'

Eric looked as if he'd been slapped. I wanted to flee the room. After a moment's shock, Eric recovered face and put on a Scarlett O'Hara voice.

'Dear, oh dear, someone's been speaking a little too freely about my colorful past. Wouldn't be y'all, sis, would it?'

'Jack, let's go,' I said.

'But what about our champagne?' Eric asked.

'Shove it,' Jack said.

'I so love the lyrical patois of the Brooklyn-eze.'

'I talk American – though I'm sure talking American strikes you as far too patriotic.'

'Hardly. After all, wasn't it old Sam Johnson himself who said that patriotism is the last refuge of the scoundrel?'

'Fuck you,' Jack hissed, tossing the remainder of his drink into Eric's face. Then he turned and stormed out of the bar.

Eric sat there, with bourbon and soda cascading down his cheeks. He appeared perplexed by this baptism.

'Thank you,' I said, my voice shaky. 'Thank you so much.'

'Did I do something wrong?'

'Go to hell,' I said, and left.

496

I dashed through the lobby, and caught Jack just as he was walking out the door.

'Darling,' I said. 'I'm so sorry . . .'

'Not as sorry as I am. Why the hell did he do that?'

'I don't know. Nerves, I guess.'

'That wasn't nervousness – that was him being an asshole.'

'Please forgive me.'

'You're not at fault here, sweetheart. He's the guy with the problem. And the problem is me.'

He gave me a fast buzz on the cheek.

'Listen, I've got to get home,' he said. 'I'll call you over the weekend – when I've stopped wanting to punch a brick wall.'

He headed out into Central Park South. I wanted to chase after him, and reassure him that this whole incident meant nothing . . . even though I knew that wasn't true. The worst thing you can do when something goes really wrong is to insist that everything's just fine; that, come tomorrow, everyone will wake up as friends. If only life worked that way. If only we didn't complicate things so damn much.

So I didn't run after Jack, figuring it was best to talk to him once his emotional temperature was back to normal. Instead, I walked back to the bar, steeling myself for the confrontation I was about to have with my brother.

But when I entered the cocktail lounge, I now found Eric slumped in his chair, passed out. He was snoring loudly, much to the displeasure of the other patrons in the lounge, not to mention the bartender.

'Is that guy with you?' he asked as I crouched down beside Eric.

'I'm afraid so.'

'Well, get him out of here.'

It took a minute of constant shaking before Eric finally came around. He stared at me quizzically.

'What are you doing here?' he asked.

'Looking at a jerk,' I said.

The bartender found a member of the hotel staff to help me escort Eric out of the St Moritz and one block west to his apartment at Hampshire House. Thankfully, Ronnie was at home. He rolled his eyes when he saw Eric's less than sober state. We each took an arm and led him into the bedroom.

'I think I'm just a little tired,' Eric mumbled before falling face down on the bed and passing out. Ronnie relieved my brother of his shoes, then covered him with a blanket.

'Let's let him sleep it off,' he whispered, motioning for me to follow him back into the living room. 'I'm sure you could use a drink.'

'After what's happened, I think alcohol's about the last thing I'm interested in.' Then I filled him in on Eric's little performance in the bar of the St Moritz.

'Jesus,' Ronnie said when I finished. 'He really knows how to mess things up.'

'I just can't believe he acted that way . . . especially knowing how important it was to me that he got along with Jack.'

'He's jealous.'

'Of what?'

'Of your guy, of course.'

'But that's crazy. I mean, when I was married, he wasn't at all resentful of my husband . . .'

'But, from what I can gather, that's because he wasn't threatened by him. Whereas with this new guy . . .'

'But why the hell should he be threatened by Jack?'

'Because he means so damn much to you, that's why. And because he was really hurt by the fact that you kept it all from him for a couple of months.'

'How do you know that?'

'He told me, that's how.'

'I *had* to keep it from him. Until I was sure that . . .'

'Hey, I'm not criticizing you here. All I'm saying is that your crazy brother adores you more than anything in the world. You should hear how he talks about you. You're everything to him. And now along comes this guy – whom he met once before, right?'

'Yes – and they hated each other on sight.'

'There you go. So this Jack guy suddenly shows up again in your life – and it's obviously so damn serious that you keep it all a secret from your brother. For months. And now he's feeling anxious about losing you.'

'*Losing me?* That's the last thing that would ever happen.'

'You know that. I know that. But jealousy isn't exactly the most rational of emotions, is it?'

I sat around with Ronnie until about six, hoping Eric might wake up. But when it became apparent that he was out for the night, I headed back to my apartment. I desperately wanted to hear from Jack – but the phone remained silent. At eight the next morning, however, my doorbell rang. I jumped out of bed, flung on a robe, and raced to the front door. Standing there was Eric. His eyes were bloodshot, his face ashen. He was visibly nervous.

'Will you ever speak to me again?' he asked.

'I don't have many other options, do I?'

He came inside. I put a pot of coffee on the stove. He sat at the kitchen table, saying nothing. After a few minutes I spoke.

'So, let's hear the act of contrition.'

'I was wrong.'

'Incredibly wrong.'

'Now Jack hates me.'

'Do you really care whether he does or not?'

'Yes, I do. Because I know he means so much to you.'

'Then it isn't just me to whom you should be apologizing.'

'True,' he said. 'It won't happen again.'

'No, it won't. Because I don't want to be put in a position where I am forced to choose between you and Jack. There's no need for that choice to be made.'

'I know, I know. Ronnie told me the same thing last night . . . after giving me the hardest time imaginable for what I'd done. He told me I'd behaved like a thirteen-year-old.'

'That's giving a thirteen-year-old too much credit.'

'Do you think Jack will forgive me?'

'Try him.'

I didn't hear from Jack that weekend – which worried me, because he usually checked in at least once on Saturday. By late Sunday evening, I was wondering if, in the wake of Eric's little performance, he'd suffered a change of heart. By Monday morning, I was certain what was coming next: a tense phone call, during which he'd inform me that, after much reflection, he'd decided that he simply could no longer sustain such divided loyalties, and had to return permanently to the bosom of his family. Or maybe a Dear John letter would arrive in the morning mail, in which he would state that Eric's outburst on Friday had crystallized matters for him, and he now realized we had no future together. Or, worst yet, he'd resort to a telegram, with the same message that he sent me all those years ago:

I'm sorry.
Jack

It's amazing how silence brings out our most terrible fears – and makes us expect the worst.

But then he called me at nine on Monday morning.

'I thought I'd never hear from you again,' I said.

'I'm not that stupid.'

'But you were angry.'

'Yeah – I was angry. But not at you.'

'You still didn't call. And it got me worried.'

'I needed to calm down. Then the weekend at home went all wrong. Charlie came down with a temperature of a hundred and six . . .'

'Oh my God. Is he all right?'

'Yeah. We had to get a pediatrician to make a house call. It was just a viral thing. But we were up all night Friday. Then on Saturday morning, when we were having breakfast, Dorothy suddenly broke down and started crying. When I asked her what was wrong, she refused to say. Of course, I knew why she was so upset. But when I tried to get her to tell me what was bothering her, she clammed right up. That's when I asked, "Do you want me to leave?" Suddenly she wasn't crying anymore. She was just angry as hell.

'"Oh, that would suit you right down to the ground, wouldn't it?" she said.

'"No," I said, "it really wouldn't."

'"Well, I don't know if I can stand this anymore," she said, and went running into the bedroom. I decided it was best to leave her alone. Around a half-hour later, she came out, dressed, fully made up, looking completely calm. She gave me a kiss, asked me to forgive her for her outburst, and then told me that, since we were housebound today with Charlie, she was now going out to our local deli to buy us a big lunch. She was gone for around thirty minutes. When she came back, it was like nothing had happened. We sat down, we ate, Charlie's fever finally broke, we watched Milton Berle on TV . . . one big happy family. And for the rest of the weekend, she didn't say a thing about getting upset. This morning, I packed my suitcase, told her I'd be out of town until Thursday night. She kissed me goodbye, and said something cheerful like, "Don't forget to call." And I've got to tell you, Sara, I never felt like a bigger heel in my life.'

'Then end this, Jack.'

'You don't want that, do you?'

'Of course not,' I said. 'Do you?'

'I want you more than anything. If you weren't there, I don't know how I'd get through the day. Sorry . . . I'm starting to sound like a sentimental idiot.'

'That's quite all right by me. Keep sounding like a sentimental idiot.'

'I heard from your brother today.'

'You *what*?' I said, sounding shocked.

'There was a wrapped gift and a letter waiting for me here at the office when I walked in this morning. Want to hear what he wrote?'

'Of course.'

'It's short and sweet: "Dear Jack: I behaved like a child the other afternoon. A drunken child. I can't excuse my behavior. Sometimes we do dumb things in life. This was dumber than most. I know how much my sister loves you. I would never do anything to intentionally hurt her – but I know my actions on Friday have hurt her terribly, and for that I feel shame. Just as I also feel total shame for treating you with such contempt. If you don't want to forgive me for that outburst, I won't blame you. All I can say, in closing, is this: I was wrong. And I am so sorry."

'He added a PS – "Here's the bottle of champagne I was going to buy you the other night. I hope you and Sara will toast your happiness with it." I have to say, I was kind of touched. And I just wrote him back a note: "Thanks for the bubbly. No hard feelings. Jack." You think that's enough?'

'I think that's just fine,' I said. 'Thank you.'

'For what?'

'For being forgiving. It's not an easy thing to do sometimes.'

'I love you, Sara.'

'Ditto, ditto, Jack. Will I see you tonight?'

'Well, I'm not going to drink the champagne on my own.'

From that moment onwards, an *entente cordiale* was established between my brother and Jack. Though they hardly saw each other, each made a point of politely asking me about how the other was doing. Jack was a big fan of *The Marty Manning Show*, and frequently dropped Eric a card whenever he particularly liked one of his sketches. When Jack's next birthday came around, Eric made a point of sending him a beautiful Parker pen.

Of course, I was delighted that Eric and Jack had established an armistice between them. Because, at heart, they were such polar opposites with profoundly disparate world views. I knew they really didn't like each other – but, after that incident in the St Moritz, they both went out of their way to avoid saying anything to me that could be construed as a cutting comment. Perhaps both realized that it was foolish to vie for my affections, as such gamesmanship is inevitably alienating and self-destructive. Anyway, I didn't want to have to choose between them – because that would have been a horrible decision which would have left everyone bereft. As I said to Eric in the wake of his apologetic note to Jack:

'This isn't a popularity contest here. You're my much-adored brother. He's my much-adored guy. If it wasn't for me, you would never have known each other.'

'Yes,' Eric said, 'you've got a lot to answer for.'

'I know, I know. And I can perfectly understand why you mightn't see eye-to-eye on . . .'

'Everything.'

'You're right, you're right. He's an Eisenhower Republican and you're a liberal Democrat. You're showbiz, he's a company man. You're an atheist, he's still a serious Catholic.'

'Not to mention a firm upholder of the seventh commandment.'

'You can't stop, can you? When in doubt, spring a oneliner.'

'Sorry, sorry.'

'Please, Eric – don't make Jack a battleground between us. It'll end badly.'

'It will never be mentioned again.'

To his infinite credit, it wasn't. Nor did Jack ever utter a further disparaging word about my brother. Nor did Jack's wife have another outburst about his divided loyalties (or, at least, none that he reported to me). In true nineteen-fifties style, we all simply let the matter drop. Back then, everyone did their best to avoid frank discussions about anything that was potentially painful. The urge to over-analyze was one that we all dodged. Better to say nothing – and to accept the fact that certain things just couldn't be fixed.

So a status quo developed between us all. I saw my brother at the weekends. I saw Jack during the week. His wife never asked about me. I always let Jack bring up the subject of his family. It was all very civilized, very polite, very workable. And I also discovered a useful ally – in the shape of Jack's sister, Meg.

After the scene in the St Moritz, I was deeply hesitant about being finally introduced to Meg, fearing that she might dislike me on sight, or simply disapprove of my role as the other woman in her brother's life. Jack himself also seemed disinclined to confess all to his sister.

'I need to find the appropriate moment,' he told me. And though I knew what he was really saying – *I'm scared to death of what she might say* – I simply assured him that he should wait until the time was right.

So it was something of a surprise to pick up the phone one June morning at my apartment, around a month after I had first told Eric about Jack's re-emergence in my life, and be greeted by a sharp, sassy voice, identifying herself as:

'Meg Malone – the phantom sister.'

'Oh, hi there,' I said, sounding a little hesitant.

'You sound nervous,' she said.

'Well . . .'

'No need. Especially with a broad like me. You free for lunch today?'

'Uh, sure.'

'Good. One p.m. at Sardi's. One small thing: you do drink, don't you?'

'Uh, yes.'

'Then we'll get along fine.'

Despite Meg's assurances that I had no need to feel nervous about meeting her, I was still exceptionally tense when I walked into Sardi's that lunchtime. The maître d' escorted me to 'Miss Malone's usual table' – a banquette, in a prominent position on the restaurant's central side wall. She was already there when I arrived – a cigarette in one hand, a gimlet in the other, a copy of the *Atlantic Monthly* open on the table in front of her. Unlike Jack, she was diminutive, yet pretty in an ageing-tomboy sort of way. As I approached the table, she looked me up and down with care. Then, as I sat down, she pointed to her copy of the *Atlantic* and said, 'Has the thought ever struck you that Edmund Wilson is completely full of shit?'

'Full of shit . . . or just plain fat and pompous?'

That comment garnered a hint of a smile. 'What are you drinking?' she asked.

'If that's a gimlet, I'll take one.'

'Sold,' she said, and launched back into a diatribe against Wilson, Cyril Connolly, and all other would-be purveyors of literary criticism. By the time the second gimlet arrived, I was learning all about the internecine goings-on at McGraw-Hill. By the time lunch and the bottle of Soave arrived, she wanted to know everything about working for *Saturday Night/Sunday Morning*. By the time coffee showed, it was three p.m., we were both tight (in every sense of the word), and I was getting all the dirt on Meg's recent affair with a senior editor at Knopf.

'You know what I most like about married men?' she said, gesturing loosely with her wine glass. 'The fact that they think they are in control of the situation, whereas we're the ones with the real power. We can kick their ass out of the apartment whenever we're fed up with them. Of course, I'm a romantic about these things.'

'I can tell,' I said, laughing.

'Jack always said that I inherited the cynical genes in the family. Unlike himself – who, despite the tough Brooklyn mick exterior, is so damn soft about everything. You should hear how he talks about you. As far as he's concerned, you're his salvation, his redemption from everything that has trapped him in life. When he first tried to tell me about you, he was so damn jittery, so apprehensive. Finally I cut him off and said, "For Christ's sake, Jack – I'm not Father Gilhooey. Do you love the girl?" To which he said, "More than anything." And . . . will you look at that . . . you're blushing.'

'Yes,' I said. 'I am blushing.'

'Blush away. I'm just pleased for you both. As some guy in the Brill Building once wrote, "Love is a wonderful thing."'

'He was terrified of telling you.'

'That's because my brother is the worst kind of Irish Catholic. He really believes in Original Sin, Man's fall from grace, hellfire-and-damnation, and all the rest of that cheerful Old Testament crap. Whereas I told him, morality is bullshit. All that counts is a certain degree of decency between people. From what I gather, he's been pretty decent to Dorothy about the whole thing.'

'Maybe – but I sometimes feel guilty as hell about her.'

'Listen, he could have been a total bad guy and walked right out on her and Charlie. Face it, a lot of men would've done that. But he's loyal. Just as

509

Dorothy's loyal. I mean, I've always thought that Dorothy was basically a decent woman. Not exactly sparky, or a laugh-a-minute, but fundamentally all right. So what if their marriage isn't about grand passionate love – he's got that with you. With Dorothy, there's a basic, working comradeship – and that's no bad thing. Most marriages I know are based on mutual loathing.'

'Does that mean you'll never get married?'

'I'd never say *never*. But, at heart, I think I'm cut out for the single life. I like a guy around . . . but I also like when he leaves.'

'I can sympathize with that position.'

'So you can handle being "the other woman"?'

'It is amazing, discovering how much you can actually handle in life.'

After this lunch, Meg and I became firm friends, and made a point of having a Girls' Night Out every six weeks or so. Jack was delighted that we'd hit it off so well . . . even though he was always a little worried about what we talked about during these boozy dinners. One night at my apartment, curled up against him on the sofa, he started giving me the third degree about my recent conversations with his sister.

'What we talk about is none of your business,' I teased him.

'I bet it's all girls' talk,' he said.

'Girls' talk! Here we are – a pair of professional women, Bryn Mawr and Barnard educated – and you imagine us trading recipes for brownies.'

510

'No – but I could see you talking about nail polish or nylons.'

'If I didn't know you were winding me up, I'd let you have it.'

'So come on – what do you talk about?'

'Your performance in bed.'

He turned white. 'Are you serious?'

'Totally. And Meg wants to know every last detail.'

'Jesus God . . .'

'Well, what else do you expect us to talk about?'

'You are joking, right?'

'Why are men so dumb?'

'Because we make the mistake of falling for smart cookies like you.'

'Would you rather a dumb cookie?'

'Never.'

'That was a smart answer.'

'So you're not going to tell me . . .'

'No. Our conversations are private ones . . . as they should be. But I will let you in on a small thing I admitted to her yesterday: I'm happy.'

He looked at me with care. 'Really?'

'Don't sound so damn surprised.'

'I'm not *surprised*. Just pleased, that's all.'

'Believe me, so am I. Because everything is going so well.'

He leaned down and kissed me. 'Life can be sweet.'

'Yes,' I said, kissing him back. 'It can be that.'

And when life is sweet, time seems to pass at an accelerated rate. Perhaps because the days are marked by a certain euphonious rhythm – a sense of events moving at an easy, well-ordered pace; of circumstances working in everyone's favor. My columns were going well. Harper and Brothers paid me a whopping five thousand (big money in those days) to bring out a book of my 'Real Life' pieces in 1952. Jack was promoted. He became a Senior Account Executive – and though he was still handling all those insurance companies, at least his salary had doubled. Meanwhile, Eric had his contract renewed at NBC with a salary increase which inflated his bank balance even more. Meg was promoted to a senior editor's position at McGraw-Hill, and took up with a bassist in the Artie Shaw band (it lasted around six months – something of a romantic epic by normal Meg standards). Most tellingly, my life with Jack settled into a pleasant routine. From what I could glean, Dorothy too had adjusted to her husband's curious domestic arrangements – even though she still refused to refer to his days with me as anything but *out of town*.

It's a much-uttered truism that we never really recognize happiness until after it has passed us by. But during the last half of 1951, I was aware of the fact that this was, without doubt, a wonderful juncture in time.

Then it ended. I even remember the exact day: the eighth of March, 1952. At six in the morning. When I was woken out of bed by the repeated ringing of my doorbell. Jack was out of town in

Pittsburgh on business – so I couldn't imagine who the hell would be bothering me at this pre-dawn hour.

I opened the front door, and found Eric shivering outside. He looked like he'd been up all night. He also appeared spooked. I was instantly scared.

'What's happened?' I asked.

'They want me to name names,' he said.

CHAPTER 6

'They' were the network: the National Broadcasting Corporation. The afternoon before, a Senior Vice President for Corporate Affairs – a certain Mr Ira Ross – called Eric at his office on the thirty-second floor of Rockefeller Center, and asked if he had a moment or two to meet with him and a colleague. Eric wondered if the meeting could wait for tomorrow – as he was on deadline for next week's edition of The Marty Manning Show.

'Sorry,' Ross said, 'but we need to see you now.'

'*We*,' Eric said. 'As soon as that sonofabitch said *we*, I knew I was a dead man.'

Eric paused for a moment to sip his coffee. He asked if I had any whiskey in the house.

'Eric, it's six in the morning.'

'I know what time it is,' he said. 'But the coffee's a little weak, and a shot of rye would perk it up a bit.'

When I hesitated, he said, 'Please, S. This is not the moment to start arguing about the rights or wrongs of pre-dawn drinking.'

I stood up and retrieved a bottle of Hiram Walker from a kitchen cabinet.

'It's not rye, it's bourbon. Jack doesn't drink rye.'

'As long as it's over fifty proof, I don't give a damn what it is.'

He poured a large belt of bourbon into his coffee cup. Then he sipped it again, flinching slightly as the whiskey went down.

'That's better,' he said, then continued with the story.

'So up I went to Ross's office on the forty-third floor. Among the NBC writers, Ross has always been known as Himmler – because he's the guy who exterminates anyone the company wants out of the way. His secretary visibly paled when she saw me – a sure-fire sign that I was in deep shit. But instead of escorting me into his office, she brought me to an adjoining conference room. There were five guys sitting around a table. When I came in, all of them stared up at me, as if I was some death-row inmate who's been hauled in front of the appeals board for one final stab at clemency. There was a long tense silence. Idiot that I am, I tried to lighten things up by cracking a joke.

'"All this for me?" I said. But nobody laughed. Instead, Ross stood up. He's a real bloodless guy, Ross. The nondescript accountant type with thick glasses and greasy brown hair. No doubt he was bullied like hell at school – and has been getting his revenge ever since, as he so clearly delights in the small amount of power that his job gives him. Especially at a moment like this – when he was about to conduct his very own UnAmerican Activities investigation on the forty-third floor of Rockefeller Center.

'So up he stood and tonelessly introduced everyone at the table. There was Bert Schmidt, the network's head of Variety and Comedy. There were two guys – Golden and Frankel – from Legal Affairs. And there was this gentleman named Agent Brad Sweet from the Federal Bureau of Investigation. You should have seen this Sweet guy. He looked like he just walked out of Central Casting. A real big, square-jawed Midwestern type, with a crew cut and a short, thickening neck. I'm sure he played linebacker when he was at high school in Nebraska, married the girl he brought to the senior prom, and probably spent his entire four years at Wichita State dreaming of the moment he could go to work for Mr Hoover, and defend Mom and the American flag from dangerous gag-writing subversives like me. Got the picture?'

'Yes,' I said, pouring a small measure of bourbon into my coffee. 'I've got the picture.'

'What's with the whiskey?'

'I think I need it too.'

'Anyway, Ross motioned to a chair. I sat down. As I did, I noticed that, in front of Agent Sweet, was a big thick file with my name on it. I glanced over to the lawyers. They had my NBC contracts laid out on the table. I tried to make eye contact with Bert Schmidt – he's always been my biggest supporter within NBC – but he looked away. Scared shitless.

'Ross now got the inquisition going with that standard opening question: "I'm sure you know why you're here."

'"Not exactly," I said, "but if there are two lawyers involved, I must have done something pretty damn heinous. Let me guess? I pinched a couple of jokes from Ernie Kovaks, and now you've got me up on a plagiarism charge."

'Once again, the laugh quotient was less than zero. Instead, Ross got tetchy, and asked me to show everyone in the room a little respect. I said, "I'm not trying to be disrespectful. I'm just wondering what I'm doing here . . . and what the hell I've done wrong."

'That was when Agent Sweet stared at me with his fanatical Audie-Murphy-school-of-patriotism eyes, and uttered the question I knew I'd eventually be called upon to answer.

'"Mr Smythe, are you now or have you ever been a member of the Communist Party?"

'Without even thinking about it, I instantly said, "No." Agent Sweet tried to control a smirk as he opened my very substantial file, and said, "You're lying, Mr Smythe. If this was a court of law, you could be indicted for contempt."

'"But this isn't a court of law," I said. "It's a kangaroo court . . ."

'That really infuriated Ross. "Listen, smartass,"

517

he said in a low, threatening hiss, "you'd better cooperate here, or . . ."

'One of the lawyers – Frankel, I think it was – put a hand on his arm, as if to say: *no threats.* Then he turned to me and tried to sound all pleasant and reasonable.

'"You're absolutely right, Mr Smythe. This is not a court of law. This is not an investigation, or a congressional committee. This is simply a meeting convened for your benefit . . ."

'"*My benefit!*" I said, a little too loudly. "Now that's a good one."

'"All we're trying to do here," Frankel said, "is to help you avoid a potentially damaging situation."

'"Oh, so we're all friends here?" I said, looking straight at Bert Schmidt. "Well, golly gosh gosh, I never knew I had so many friends in high places . . ."

'"This is pointless," Ross said to his fellow inquisitors. At which point Schmidt tried to play good cop.

'"Eric, *please* – try to cooperate here."

'"All right, all right," I said. "Fire away."

'Agent Sweet turned back to the file. "As I said, Mr Smythe, we have evidence here that refutes your last statement. According to our records, you joined the Communist Party in March of nineteen thirty-six, and were a member of its New York cell for five years, resigning only in nineteen forty-one."

'"Okay, I confess. For a short period of my life,

518

just after I left college, I was a member of the Party. But that was ten long years ago . . ."

"'Why did you just lie to me about this past affiliation?" Agent Sweet asked me.

"'Would you want to admit to such a dumb old allegiance?"

"'Of course not – but if asked by a federal officer of the United States Government, I'd tell the truth. A mistake is a mistake. But a mistake can only be rectified if you own up to it, and try to put the matter right."

"'As I just told you, I quit the Party over a decade ago."

'The other lawyer, Golden, came in here, trying to sound friendly.

"'What made you leave the Party, Eric?"

"'I'd lost faith in the doctrines they were pushing. I thought they were ideologically wrong about a lot of things. And I also began to believe the rumors that were being spread about Stalin's repressive policies in Russia."

"'So," said the ever-helpful Counselor Golden, "you realized Communism was wrong."

'He didn't pose that sentence as a question – rather, as a statement. Bert Schmidt shot me this pleading, *don't be stupid here* look. I said, "That's right. I decided Communism was wrong. And evil."

'That was certainly the right answer – because immediately everyone at the table relaxed a little bit, though Ross himself looked disappointed that I had suddenly stopped playing the hostile witness.

No doubt he would have really enjoyed shining a bright lamp in my face and hitting me over the head with a phone book in an attempt to dredge the truth from me. Instead, everyone became sweetness and light. For a moment or two, anyway.

'"Given your admirable change of heart on the matter of Communism," Agent Sweet said, "would you call yourself a patriotic American?"

'I was also expecting this dumb question. And I knew I'd have to lie. So I assured Agent Sweet – and everyone else at the table – that I loved my country more than life itself, or some such crap. Sweet seemed pleased with my response.

'"Then you'd be willing to cooperate?" he asked me.

'"Cooperate? What do you mean by *cooperate*?"

'"I mean, helping us infiltrate the Communist network that is threatening the fundamental stability of the United States."

'"I wasn't aware of such a threat," I said.

'"Believe me, Mr Smythe," Agent Sweet said, "it is there and very formidable. But with the cooperation of former Party members like yourself, we can burrow deep into the heart of the Party and root out the real ringleaders."

'I tell you, S – at that precise moment, I almost lost it completely. I wanted to tell Agent Sweet that he sounded like one of the Hardy Boys, on the trail of the Big Bad Commies. *Help us infiltrate the Communist network that is threatening the fundamental stability of the United States.* Can you believe such garbage? As if there was ever a Communist network in this country to begin with.

'I tried to sound logical. "Listen, Mr Sweet – back in the nineteen thirties, a lot of people joined the Party because it was the thing to do at the time. It was a fad, like the hoola-hoop."

'Ross loved that comment: "You dare to equate an evil doctrine like Communism with something as benign as a hoola-hoop?"

'"My point, Mr Ross, is that I was a naive kid just out of Columbia who bought into the whole Rights-of-Man, equal-distribution-of-wealth claptrap that the Party peddled. But, when you get right down to it, the real reason I joined was because it was the thing to do. I was working in the Federal Theater Project . . ."

'"A hotbed of subversive activity," Ross said, cutting me off.

'"Mr Ross, when the hell have a bunch of actors and directors ever threatened the fundamental stability of any regime anywhere?"

'"Oh!" said Ross triumphantly. "You consider the US government to be a *regime*, do you?"

'"That's not what I was saying . . ."

'"A truly patriotic American would know that the Founding Fathers gave us the most democratic system of government this planet has ever seen."

'"I've read *The Federalist Papers*, Mr Ross. I fully understand the separation-of-powers doctrine, as hammered out by Hamilton, Madison and all those other enlightened men . . . who, quite frankly, would be appalled to see a citizen of this country being interrogated about his allegiance to the flag . . ."

"'This is not an interrogation," Ross barked, banging his fist on the table. Once again, Frankel put a steadying hand on his arm. Then he said, "Eric, I think all that Agent Sweet – and everyone here – is trying to establish is whether or not you are still tied to the Party."

"'Doesn't that big file of mine show that I quit over ten years ago?'

"'Indeed, it does," Sweet said. "But who's to say that your resignation from the Party wasn't a sham? For all we know, you could still be one of their covert operatives, masquerading as a former Communist . . ."

"'You're not being serious, are you?" I said.

"'Mr Smythe, the FBI is *always* serious. Especially when it comes to matters of national security."

"'I've said it once, I'll say it again: I quit the Party in nineteen forty-one. I've had no further associations with the Party. I don't like the goddamn Party, and I now rue the day I joined it. For God's sake, I'm just one of Marty Manning's writers. Since when has a gag man been considered a threat to national security?"

"'Mr Smythe," Agent Sweet said, "our files indicate that, over the past ten years, you have consorted with many Communists." Then he began to list a whole bunch of names – mainly other writers, with whom I had, at best, a passing professional connection. I tried to explain that, like me, most of the guys were of the generation which joined the Party. Do you know what Sweet said?

'"My brother's from your generation, and he didn't join the Party."

'Once again, I stopped myself from saying something like: "That's because your brother was probably a Midwest hick, and not some over-educated East Coast writer who was stupid enough to read Marx and buy into his Workers of the World Unite garbage." Instead, I attempted, yet again, to explain that I had made a youthful mistake, for which I was now deeply sorry. Yet again, Golden tried to lead me out of trouble.

'"Eric, I know that everyone at this table is very pleased to hear your admission of error. Like Agent Sweet said, we all make mistakes – especially when we're young. And though I personally believe you when you say that you've had no contact with the Party since nineteen forty-one, I'm sure that you can appreciate the fact that some further proof of your complete disengagement from the Party is necessary."

'I knew what was coming next – though I was still hoping against hope that I could somehow manage to dodge the question they were about to put to me.

'"Quite simply," Golden said, "all Agent Sweet needs to know are the names of the people who brought you into the Party, and those individuals who are still active Party members today."

"'And,' Agent Sweet added, "by naming these names, you will not only be demonstrating your complete lack of affiliation with present Communist activity . . . you will also be confirming your patriotism."

"'Since when has denouncing innocent people been considered an act of patriotism?' I asked.

"'Communists are not innocents,' Ross shouted at me.

"'The one-time Communists I know certainly are.'

"'Ah,' Agent Sweet said, "then you admit that you do know Communists."

"'*Former* Communists, like me.'

"'Eric,' Frankel said, "if you could just provide Agent Sweet with a few of their names . . .'"

"'And destroy their lives in the process?'

"'If they are as innocent as you claim to be, then they have nothing to fear.'

"'Unless, of course, they also refuse to name names. That's the game here, isn't it? You scare me into naming names. Then, after I commit an act of moral cowardice and shop a couple of people, you go to them and play the same game. *Give us names, and we'll leave you alone.* The problem is, after you leave me alone, I have to deal with myself. And I might not like the person with whom I am now left alone.'

"'Are you saying you won't name names?' Ross asked.

'"I am saying that, as I do not know any active Communists, giving you a bunch of names would be a pointless exercise."

'"Let us be the judge of that, Mr Smythe," Sweet said.

'"And if I refuse?"

'"You can kiss your job goodbye," Ross said. "Not just at NBC, but at every network, movie studio, advertising agency, or college across the country. You'll be completely unemployable. I'll make certain of that."

'I met his stare. "I'm sure you will," I said.

'Suddenly, Bert Schmidt entered this Socratic dialog. "Eric, hear me out. You're one of the most talented comedy writers in America today. In my book, you're one of NBC's great assets; a major player in our industry, with a great prosperous future ahead of you. Put baldly, we don't want to lose you. I know this is unpleasant stuff – but everyone here is being asked the same questions. So even if you refuse to name names, somebody else will give us those names. And, unlike you, they will still be in a job. What I'm saying here is: don't make things hard for yourself. Tell Agent Sweet what he needs to know, and you can put the whole business behind you. Anyway, no one will ever learn that it is you who gave the names . . . isn't that right, Agent Sweet?"

'"Absolutely. Your signed affidavit will be marked Confidential and will only be for the eyes of Bureau officers, and certain investigators working for HUAC – the House UnAmerican Activities Committee."

'"So I too will never know who exactly shopped me to the Feds?"

'"No one shopped you, Mr Smythe," Agent Sweet said. "They simply did the proper American thing. Which is all we ask of you now."

'"I have a contract with this network. You can't just fire me on the spot."

'Golden and Frankel both began to leaf through their copies of my contract. Frankel spoke first. "According to clause twenty-one (a) of Terms and Conditions of Employment, you can be dismissed from the National Broadcasting Corporation on the grounds of moral turpitude."

'"Now that is total crap."

'"It would be up to a court of law to decide that," Frankel said. "You'd have to sue us – which, as you well know, would cost you a lot of money. Though I don't want to sound threatening here, the fact is that our pockets are deeper than yours, Eric. And the case would drag on for years – during which time you'd still be out of a job . . . and, as Mr Ross pointed out, sadly unemployable."

'I couldn't fathom what I was hearing. Kafka comes to Rockefeller Center. I decided I had to stall for time. So I said, "I need to think about this carefully."

'"Of course," Agent Sweet said. "We're happy to give you seventy-two hours to contemplate your decision. Do understand, though – if you refuse to cooperate, not only will NBC have grounds for dismissal, but the Bureau will also be beholden to report you to HUAC. Without question, you will then be subpoenaed to testify in front of the committee. Should you refuse to do so – or should you go to Washington and refuse to answer any of the committee's questions under oath – you will be found in contempt of court, and sentenced to a term of imprisonment.'

'"My, what a pretty picture you paint of my future."

'"This doesn't have to be your future," Agent Sweet said, "as long as you cooperate."

'Then he played his trump card. Opening up his file, Sweet pulled out a picture of Ronnie and held it up. My stomach started doing backflips. I had to hide my hands below the table, because I didn't want anyone to see them shaking.

'"Do you know this man?" Sweet asked me.

'"Yes, I know him." My voice sounded jittery.

'"How do you know him?"

'"He's a friend."

'Sweet leaned forward. "What *kind* of friend?"

'You should have seen this asshole's judgmental gaze – as if I was Sodom *and* Gomorrah rolled into one. I looked over at Bert Schmidt for support, but once again, he gave me one of those desperate looks which said, *I can't help you here.*

'Sweet didn't like my silence. "Please answer the question, Mr Smythe. What kind of friendship do you have with this man?"

'All eyes at the table were on me. Ross was

smirking. I found it difficult to speak. "We're just friends," I finally said.

'Sweet let out this big sigh. Then he pulled a small file out of my big file, opened it up, and started reading from it:

'"Ronald Garcia. Born, Bronx, New York. Age: thirty-one. Profession: musician. No prior convictions, no criminal record. Current address: Suite 508, Hampshire House, 150 Central Park South, New York, New York. That also happens to be your address, Mr Smythe."

'"Yes, it's my address."

'"So Mr Garcia, in essence, lives with you."

'"As I said before, we are friends. We know each other through the entertainment business. Ronald was between apartments. Money was tight, so I offered him a place to stay for a while."

'"And where does he sleep in your apartment?"

'"On the sofa. It's one of those pull-out-into-a-bed jobs . . ."

'Sweet studied the file again. "According to two of the Hampshire House maids that we interviewed, your sofa bed has never been used. They both made statements, clearly stating that they had seen Mr Garcia's personal belongings on the table by your bed, his toiletries in your bathroom. What's more, the . . . uh . . . *condition* of the linen on your bed indicated that . . . uh . . . two people were definitely sharing the bed, and engaged in . . ."

'Frankel cut him off. "I think we've all heard

enough, Agent Sweet. And I'm certain Mr Smythe gets the point."

'I put my face in my hands. I really felt as if I was about to be sick. They had me in a corner. And the bastards knew it.

'A hand touched my shoulder. Then I heard Bert Schmidt's voice.

'"Come on, Eric – let's get a cup of coffee."

'He helped me up from the table. I was in shock. I couldn't bear to look at any of those shits again. But as we walked out, Agent Sweet said, "Seventy-two hours, Mr Smythe. No longer. And I do hope you'll do the right thing."

'Schmidt and I rode down in the elevator to the lobby. He got us a cab outside, and told the driver to take us to the Carnegie Deli on Fifty-Sixth and Seventh.

'"I'm not exactly hungry, Bert," I said.

'"I just want to get away from that fucking building," he said.

'At the Deli, we got ourselves a booth right at the back. After the waitress showed up with our coffee, Schmidt started talking to me in a low, conspiratorial voice.

'"I'm sorry," he said. "You don't know how sorry I am."

'"What did you tell them?"

'"They didn't investigate me."

'"Bullshit. Of course they questioned you. Because I've heard you brag about your days with Odets and Harold Clurman at the old Group

Theater . . . a real hive of *political subversion* if there ever was one . . ."

"'Unlike you, I wasn't a member of the goddamn Party . . .'"

"'But you still knew plenty of people who were. And I bet, when pressed, you had to give those fuckers a couple of names, didn't you?'"

"'I would never dream of . . .'"

"'Bullshit, Bert. You've got two ex-wives and three kids in private school. All you *kvetch* about is how you haven't got enough money to pay for those showgirls you like to bang . . .'"

"'Keep your fucking voice down . . .'"

"'They're destroying me, and you want me to fucking whisper?'"

"'All right, all right,' Bert said quietly. 'This is awful. This is shit. I can't agree with you more. But Eric, I have no influence with these assholes. Nobody does. They have their own rules . . .'"

"'*Unconstitutional* rules.'"

"'That may be . . . but everyone's too scared to say that.'"

"'Bert, you've got to tell me: did you give them my name?'"

"'Hand on my heart, on my children's lives, I swear to you: *no*, I didn't.'"

"'But you did cooperate with them, didn't you?'"

"'Eric, *please* . . .'"

"'Answer me.'"

'He pressed the heels of both hands against his eyes. When he pulled them away, his eyes were wet.

"Yeah," he said softly. "I gave them some names."

"'Some?"

"'Two or three . . . maybe four. But honestly, Eric – the names I gave . . . they were people who were going to get investigated no matter what. I mean, I was telling them stuff they already knew."

'He looked at me, begging for understanding, for absolution. I didn't know what to say. He saw this. "Don't give me that contemptuous silent shit," he said, suddenly angry. "I had no choice. I have mouths to feed, responsibilities to meet. If I'd refused to cooperate . . ."

"'I know: you would have lost everything. Now if the guys you named refuse to cooperate, they'll lose everything. I think it's called passing the buck."

"'Go on then," he hissed at me. "Play the goddamn saint. Win a fucking Oscar for virtue and nobility."

"'They're going to fire me anyway – now that they know my dirty little secret."

"'If you cooperate with the Feds, the network won't fire you."

"'You don't know that."

"'Yes, I do. Because Frankel and Golden in Legal Affairs assured me that, as long as you helped Agent Sweet, NBC would turn a blind eye to . . . uh . . . your domestic arrangements."

"'You have that in writing?"

"'Are you nuts? They're not going to put that in writing, because they're holding all the cards. But I know for a fact that if you help them out, they

531

won't fire you. As I said upstairs, no one wants to lose you. You're valuable to the network. And, personally speaking, I hope I can still call you my friend."

'That's when I stood up and walked right out of the deli. That was, what? Five yesterday afternoon. I've been walking ever since.'

I reached for the bottle of Hiram Walker and poured another slug into his coffee cup.

'You've not been home since?'

'Nah. I just kept walking around. Finally ended up in one of those all-night movie houses on Forty-Second Street. Trying to blot everything out.'

'Where's Ronnie?'

'Out of town for a couple of nights – as part of a band that's backing Rosemary Clooney down at Atlantic City. I was going to call him at his hotel . . . but I didn't want to upset him yet. There'll be time enough for that. Anyway, I couldn't bear going back to the apartment . . . knowing that the fucking Feds had actually gone to the trouble of interviewing a couple of maids about . . .'

He lifted his coffee cup and tossed back the bourbon.

'Am I that important, S? Am I such a threat to national security that they have to grill a couple of maids about who sleeps in my bed?'

'I can't believe it either.'

'Oh, believe it, S. Because these bastards are dead serious. It's cooperate with them, or commit professional suicide.'

'You need to get a lawyer.'

'Why? What's some overpriced legal eagle going to tell me that I don't already know? Anyway, even if the lawyer was able to work a miracle and somehow get the Feds off my back, the network would then be pressured into axing me on the grounds of "extreme moral turpitude". Once that was made public, my career would be beyond dead. I'd be finished.'

'You must find out who named you.'

'What good would that do?'

'Maybe you could exert some ethical pressure on them to retract their denunciation . . .'

'Ethical pressure. You're a bright lady, S . . . but right now, you sound like Pollyanna. There are *no* ethics to this game, S. None. It's every man for himself – and that's what Joe McCarthy and his asshole cronies are playing upon: that basic adult fear of losing everything you've worked so hard to achieve. Bert Schmidt is right: when faced with the choice of losing your livelihood, or shopping your friends, you're going to screw your friends.'

'So you're going to cooperate?'

'Don't look at me that way,' he said, suddenly hostile.

'I'm not looking at you any way, Eric. I was just asking . . .'

'I don't know. I've got . . . what? . . . two and a half days to make a decision. I've also got no money in the bank.'

'What do you mean, no money? You made over sixty thousand last year . . .'

'Yeah, and I spent over sixty thousand.'

'How the hell did you do that?'

'It's easy. So damn easy that I now also have something called debt.'

'Debt? On your paycheck? How much?'

'I don't know. Seven, eight thousand, maybe . . .'

'Oh my God . . .'

'Yeah: oh my God. So you see my problem here. If I don't cooperate, not only am I branded a Commie and a pervert, but NBC also turns off the money faucet. And I am bankrupt on all fronts.'

'So what are you going to do?'

'I haven't a fucking clue. What would *you* do?'

'Honestly?'

'Yes, honestly.'

'Honestly . . .' I said, 'I don't know.'

CHAPTER 7

The next two days were nightmarish. I insisted that Eric see a lawyer. Naturally enough, he turned out to be Joel Eberts. As soon as nine o'clock arrived, I called Eberts' office. He answered the phone himself, and told us to come downtown immediately. Given his union background, Mr Eberts was completely sympathetic with Eric's dilemma. But after trawling through his contract with NBC – and also hearing about the FBI's information on Ronnie – he said he could do nothing except offer moral support.

'Of course, we could fight this in court. But – as the NBC counsel told you – they can well afford to have this thing drag on for years. In the meantime, you'll be branded a Red. And – although I don't give a damn about who sleeps with whom – I'm afraid they can hang you on the morals clause. Worst yet, if you do take them on, they'll leak stuff to some slimeball like Winchell. Next thing you know, the dirt'll be dished in his column. You'll be through.'

'So what am I supposed to do?' Eric asked.

'My friend – that is completely your call. And I

don't envy you your options one bit. Because, either way, you lose. The real question here is: what do you want to lose *least*?'

Eric shifted anxiously in his chair.

'I simply cannot turn stool pigeon on people who were guilty of nothing more than the same dumb idealism which I once shared. Jesus Christ, even if these people were the Rosenbergs, I still couldn't turn them in. I'm probably not patriotic enough.'

'Patriotism isn't the issue here,' Joel Eberts said. 'Joe McCarthy and that clown Nixon are probably two of the biggest patriots imaginable. And they're both swine. No, the question here is a harder one: can you harm yourself to save others . . . even though you also know that, eventually, they're going to be harmed anyway. Of course, it's easy for me to sit here and tell you how I might react. But I'm not in your situation. I'm sure Hoover and his henchmen have a file on me as well, but they can't get me disbarred for my politics. Or, at least, not yet. They can't ruin my life. But they can ruin yours.'

I watched as Eric kneaded his hands together. Without realizing it, he kept rocking back and forth in his chair. His eyes seemed vacant, haunted. He desperately needed sleep – if only to escape this ordeal for a couple of hours. I so wanted to help. But I didn't know how to help him.

'There's only one piece of advice I can give you,' Joel Eberts said. 'And if I were in your position, it's the action I'd follow: leave the country.'

Eric considered this for a moment. 'But where would I go?' he asked.

'There are a lot of other places on this planet besides America.'

'I'm asking: where would I go to make a living?'

'How about London?' I said. 'They have TV in London, don't they?'

'Yeah – but they don't have my sense of humor. They're English, for Chrissakes.'

'I'm sure you'd find some niche for yourself. And if not London, then there's Paris or Rome . . .'

'Oh yeah, me writing gags for the French. What a swell idea that is . . .'

Joel Eberts came in here. 'Your sister's right. A talented guy like yourself will find work anywhere. But that's a secondary concern right now. What you should be focusing on is getting out of the country within forty-eight hours.'

'Won't the Feds come after me?'

'Probably not. The pattern so far is that, once they've frightened you overseas, they generally leave you alone . . . unless, of course, you try to come back home.'

'You mean, I'll never be allowed back to the States again?'

'Mark my words – within a couple of years, this whole *meshuga* blacklist business will be completely discredited.'

'*A couple of years*,' Eric said, sounding disconsolate. 'Who the fuck ever heard of an American having to go into exile?'

'What can I say? These are bad times.'

Eric reached out and took my hand. He squeezed it hard. 'I don't want to go. I like it here. It's all I know. And have.'

I swallowed hard and said, 'The other options are terrible ones. At least this way, you'll be able to get away as cleanly as possible.'

Silence. Eric continued to shift uneasily in his chair, struggling with the decision. 'Even if I did decide to leave, there's a problem. I don't have a passport.'

'That's not a problem,' Joel Eberts said.

He told us what to do. I insisted that we act on his advice immediately – because, as Eberts warned Eric, he could not afford the luxury of a reflective decision.

'Forty-eight hours from now, they're going to expect a list of names from you,' Eberts said. 'If you don't give it to them, that's it. The steamroller heads in your direction. You'll be out of a job. You'll get a subpoena from HUAC. From that moment on, the Department of State will block any passport applications until after you've testified. They did that to Paul Robeson. They'll certainly do it to you.'

The way around this, however, was to get Eric a passport within the next twenty-four hours. According to Eberts, it usually took two weeks to process an application . . . unless you had proof that you were traveling at the last minute. So, as soon as we left Eberts' office, we took a taxi uptown to a big branch of Thomas Cook's on Fifth Avenue and 43rd Street. After some checking around, one of the travel agents there found a single berth on the SS *Rotterdam* sailing for Hoek van Holland the following night. We bought the ticket, then raced uptown to the Passport Office on 51st and Fifth. The clerk inspected Eric's ticket to Europe, and told him that, in order to get the passport issued by five p.m. tomorrow (a mere two hours before the SS *Rotterdam* sailed), he'd need the proper photographs, a copy of his birth certificate, and assorted notarized signatures by close of business today.

It was a scramble – but Eric just managed to clear the deadline that afternoon. The clerk assured him that he'd have the passport by the end of tomorrow – which would give Eric an hour to dash across town and make it to the ship by six (he had to be on board at least an hour before it sailed). It would be tight, but he'd make it.

Once we were finished at the passport office, Eric suggested we head back to his apartment at the Hampshire House. Once there, I helped him winnow through his large wardrobe and choose just enough to fit into a single large suitcase. As he put the cover on his Remington typewriter, he suddenly sank into his desk chair.

'Don't make me get on that ship,' he said.

I tried to stay controlled. 'Eric, you have no choice.'

'I don't want to leave you. I don't want to leave Ronnie. I've got to see him tonight.'

'Then call him. See if he can get back here.'

He started to sob again. 'No. I couldn't bear the goodbye. The scene at the docks. All that heart-rending crap.'

'Yes,' I said quietly. 'I'd avoid that if I were you.'

'I'll write him a letter – which you can give him when he comes back here at the weekend.'

'He will understand. I'll make sure he does.'

'It's absurd, all this.'

'Yes,' I said. 'It is absurd.'

'I'm just a jokesmith. Why the hell are they treating me like Trotsky?'

'Because they're bullies. And because they've been given carte blanche to act like bullies.'

'Everything was going so well.'

'It will go well again.'

'I love what I do, S. I've found my niche. Not only does it pay me ridiculous amounts of money, but writing the show also happens to be a lot of fun. Which is something that work isn't supposed to be. That's what really hurts about having to run away – knowing that, for the first time in my life, everything is the way I want it to be. The job. The money. The success. Ronnie . . .'

He gently released himself from my arms, and walked over to the living room window. Night had fallen on Manhattan. Down below was the black interior of Central Park, flanked by the seductive glow of lit apartments along Fifth Avenue and Central Park West. What always struck me about this view was how perfectly it reflected the city's spirit of arrogant indifference. It was a skyline that issued a challenge: *try to conquer me.* But even if you did – even if, like Eric, you were fêted as a New York success – you still didn't ever really make your mark on the place. All that striving, all that ambition – and the moment after you'd had your moment, you were forgotten. Because there was always someone else in Manhattan coming up right behind you, battling to have their moment. Today, Eric was the hottest writer in television comedy. When the SS *Rotterdam* set sail tomorrow night, word would spread that he'd fled overseas rather than name names. Some people would applaud his actions, some would deplore them. By this time next week, however, he'd be a tertiary consideration in the minds of any of his professional colleagues. Because that's how things worked. His disappearance would be like a death. Only those who loved him would mourn his absence. For everyone else who knew him, the shock of his vanishing would be a temporary (and welcome) respite from all the incumbent pressures of work. For a few days, people would talk among themselves in hushed voices about the transitory nature of success; and the ethical rights or wrongs of Eric's choice to flee the country. Then the subject would be dropped. Because it was the start of another week and a new show had to be written.

Just as it always did.

Though I didn't ask him, I sensed that Eric was thinking what I was thinking, as we both looked out on the muted glow of that uptown skyline. Because he put his arm around my shoulders and said, 'People spend their entire damn lives chasing what I've had.'

'Stop talking about it in the past tense.'

'But it's over, S. It is over.'

We ordered in dinner from room service. We drank two bottles of champagne.

I slept on his sofa bed that night, wishing all the time that Jack was in town. The next morning, Eric drew up a list of his debts. He was nearly five thousand dollars in the red to places like Dunhill, and Brooks Brothers, and 21, and El Morocco – and assorted other watering holes and purveyors of luxury goods, with whom he maintained an account. He had less than a thousand dollars in the bank.

'How did you land yourself in this mess?' I asked.

'I always picked up the tab. And I also discovered a post-Marxist weakness for luxury items.'

'That's a dangerous failing. Especially when coupled with reckless generosity.'

'What can I say . . . except that, unlike you, I've never known the pleasures of thrift. Anyway, one good thing about leaving the country is that I'll be out of reach of the IRS.'

'Don't tell me you've got a tax problem too?'

'It's not a problem, actually. It's just that I haven't filed a return for . . . I don't know . . . maybe three years.'

'But you have been paying them some tax, haven't you?'

'Well, if I haven't taken the trouble of filing a return, why would I also bother sending them some money?'

'So you owe them . . .'

'Lots. I think it's something like thirty per cent of everything I've earned ever since I've joined NBC. Which is a sizeable chunk of change.'

'And you put *nothing* aside.'

'For God's sakes, S – when have I ever done anything sensible?'

I stared down at the list of debts, and resolved to settle them myself once Eric was on the far side of the Atlantic. In addition to my invested portion of the divorce settlement, I'd been saving consistently since writing for *Saturday/Sunday*, and I'd also just banked that five-thousand-dollar advance from Harper and Brothers. So I'd be able to clear my brother's name at assorted emporia around town. The IRS would be another matter. Maybe I could sell some stock, or get a mortgage on the apartment. For the moment, however, I just wanted to get Eric aboard that ship. Worried that he might suddenly lose his nerve and vanish for a few critical hours, I made him promise to stay in the apartment until four thirty . . . when we'd grab a cab to the passport office.

'But this could be my last-ever day in Manhattan. At least let me take you to lunch at 21.'

'I want you to lie low, Eric. Just in case . . .'

'What? That J. Edgar Hoover and his boyfriend have decided to tail me for the day?'

'Let's just get through this as cleanly as possible.'

'There's nothing at all clean about this. *Nothing.*'

Eric didn't like it – but he eventually did agree to stay put for the day while I did all the busy work. I got him to write me a check for the remaining thousand dollars in his bank account. I went to his branch of Manufacturers' Hanover, cashed it, and bought him the equivalent amount in traveler's checks. I paid a fast visit to Joel Eberts' office and collected a power-of-attorney document. Then I rushed uptown to Tiffany's and bought him a sterling silver fountain pen, and had it engraved: *From S to E. Always.*

I was back at his apartment by three. He signed the power-of-attorney form, giving me complete charge over all of his financial matters. We agreed that, come tomorrow, I'd find a storage depot, in which all his remaining clothes, papers, and personal effects would be lodged until he returned home. He handed me a thick envelope, addressed to Ronnie. I promised him I'd get it to him as soon as he was back in the city. Eric ducked into the bathroom for a moment, and I managed to slip the wrapped gift from Tiffany's into his suitcase. Then, just before four thirty, I looked at him and said, 'It's time.'

Once again, he went to the window, leaning his head against the glass, staring out at the city.

'I'll never have a view like this again.'

'I'm sure London has its moments.'

'But they're low-storey ones.'

He turned towards me. His face was wet. I bit my lip.

'Not yet,' I said. 'Don't get me crying yet.'

He wiped his eyes with the back of his sleeve. He took a deep breath. 'Okay,' he said. 'Let's go.'

We left quickly. The doorman hailed us a cab. We got stuck in godawful traffic on Fifth Avenue, and just made it to the passport office with two minutes to spare. Eric was the last customer of the day. When he approached the window, the clerk who had been dealing with his papers yesterday told him to take a seat for a moment.

'Is anything wrong?'

The clerk avoided eye contact with us. Instead, he picked up a phone, dialed a number, and spoke quickly into it. Putting it down, he said, 'Someone will be with you in a moment.'

'Is there a problem?' Eric asked.

'Just take a seat, please.'

He pointed to a bench on the opposite wall. We sat down. I glanced anxiously at the clock on the wall. With rush-hour traffic it would take, at best, forty minutes to get Eric to the 46th Street Pier. Time was of the essence.

'What do you think's going on?' I asked Eric.

'Nothing, I hope, except mindless bureaucracy.'

Suddenly a side door opened. Out walked two gentlemen in dark suits. When Eric saw them, he turned ashen.

'Oh shit,' he whispered.

'Good afternoon, Mr Smythe,' one of them said. 'I hope this isn't an unpleasant surprise.'

Eric said nothing.

'Aren't you going to introduce me?' the gentleman asked. Then he proffered his hand. 'Agent Brad Sweet of the Federal Bureau of Investigation. You must be Sara Smythe.'

'How do you know that?' I asked.

'The doorman at the Hampshire House knows you. And he informed us that you'd been with your brother in his apartment since yesterday evening. After, of course, your visit to the law offices of a certain . . .' He held out his hand. His associate put a file into it. He opened the file. He read aloud from it. 'The law offices of a certain Joel Eberts on Sullivan Street. He has impeccable subversive credentials, your lawyer – not to mention a file on him as thick as the Manhattan phone book. Then, after your little legal pow-wow, you headed to the offices of Thomas Cook at 511 Fifth Avenue and booked passage on the SS *Rotterdam*, departing this evening. Afterwards, of course, you came here to the passport office, hoping to pull that last-minute travel ruse, so beloved of individuals trying to leave the United States in a hurry.'

He shut the file.

'But, I'm afraid, you won't be leaving the country tonight – as the Department of State have put your passport application on hold, pending the outcome of the Bureau's investigation into your political allegiances.'

'That's outrageous,' I heard myself saying.

'No,' Agent Sweet said mildly. 'It's all perfectly legal. After all, why should the State Department issue a passport to someone whose presence overseas may be harmful to American interests . . .'

'Oh for God's sakes,' I said, 'what harm has he done to this country?'

Eric said nothing. He just sat on the bench, staring down at the fake marble floor.

'If he cooperates with us tomorrow, his passport will be issued within twenty-four hours. If, of course, he still wants to leave the country. Five p.m. tomorrow at NBC, Mr Smythe. I look forward to seeing you there.'

With a curt nod in my direction, Agent Sweet and his associate left. Eric and I sat motionless on the bench for a few minutes. Neither of us could move.

'I'm dead,' he said.

I stayed with him again that night. I tried to get him to talk things through – to work out some sort of strategy before facing Sweet and the NBC people tomorrow.

'There's nothing more to discuss,' Eric said.

'But what are you going to do?'

'I am going to get into bed, pull the covers over my head, and hide.'

I couldn't stop him from doing that. Nor did I want to – as, at least, I would know where he was. He was so exhausted, so stressed, that he fell asleep shortly after getting into bed. I tried to follow suit – but I spent much of the night staring at the living room ceiling, feeling both convulsed with rage and utterly helpless in the face of the FBI's onslaught on my brother. My mind was speeding, as I tried to figure some sort of possible way out for Eric. But I came up with nothing. He'd either have to name names, or suffer the consequences.

I wanted to believe that – if I was in his position – I'd play Joan of Arc, and refuse to co-operate. But everyone envisages themselves doing the heroic thing when sitting in an armchair. Brought face-to-face with the reality of the dilemma, however, things often turn out differently. You never really know what you're made of until you find yourself standing astride a precipice, looking down into a very deep void.

Sleep finally hit me around three that morning. When I jolted awake again, the sun was at full wattage. I glanced at my watch. Eleven twelve. Damn. Damn. Damn. I shouted for Eric. No reply. I got up from the sofa and went into his bedroom. He wasn't there. Nor was he in the bathroom, or the kitchen. Panicked, I scoured all surfaces for a note, telling me he'd gone out for a walk. Nothing. I picked up the house phone and spoke to the doorman.

'Yeah – Mr Smythe left around seven this morning. It was funny, though . . .'

'What was funny?'

'He called me before he came downstairs, and

asked me if I'd like to make ten bucks. Sure, says I. "Well, I'm gonna take the elevator down to the basement, and I'll give you ten bucks if you open the service entrance and let me out. Oh, and if anybody comes by looking for me this morning, just tell 'em I haven't left the apartment." No problem, I tell him. I mean, I can easily shaddup for ten bucks.'

'Did anyone come by?'

'Nah – but there's been these two guys in a car, parked across the street since I came on duty at six.'

'So they didn't see him leave?'

'How could they, when he went out the back.'

'He didn't tell you where he was going?'

'Nah – but he had a suitcase with him . . .'

Now I was alarmed.

'He what . . . ?'

'He had this big suitcase with him. Like he was goin' away somewhere.'

I thought fast.

'How'd you like to make another ten bucks?' I asked.

I threw on some clothes, I took the elevator down to the basement. I handed the doorman ten bucks. He opened the door to the service entrance.

'If those men come back asking either for Eric or me . . .' I said.

'You're still asleep upstairs, right?'

The service entrance led to an alleyway on West 56th Street. I hopped a cab, and took it down to

Joel Eberts' office. Because, quite frankly, I didn't know where else to go. As always, he was welcoming – and appalled when I told him what had happened at the passport office yesterday afternoon.

'I tell you,' he said, 'we're turning into a police state – and all in the name of the Red Menace.'

But he was even more alarmed by the news that Eric was last spotted sneaking out of the side entrance of the Hampshire House with a suitcase in hand.

'You can run, but you can't hide from these bastards. If he's not at NBC today, HUAC will instantly subpoena him. And the Feds will dream up some crime and misdemeanor in order to issue a warrant for his arrest. He should just face the music, no matter what happens.'

'I agree – but as I don't know where he's gone, I can't give him that advice.'

'You know, you don't need a passport for Canada,' Eberts said.

He made a fast call to Penn Station, asking to be put through to the reservations office. Yes, they told him, a train had left at ten that morning – but there were no passengers registered under the name of Eric Smythe. When he asked if they could check and see if he was registered on any other departing trains, they said that they didn't have the time or manpower to search through every passenger list of every train.

'You know what the guy in Reservations told me?' Eberts said after hanging up the phone. "If finding this guy is so important, call the Feds.'"

That was the only time I'd laughed in two days.

I suddenly had a brainstorm, and asked to use the phone. First I called the Rainbow Room and spoke to the receptionist and found out that the Rainbow Room band were staying at the Hotel Shoreham in Atlantic City. I got the number and got lucky: Ronnie – in true musician style – was still asleep at twelve thirty. But he woke up quickly after I told him about the events of the last two days.

'You have no idea where he is?' he asked, sounding genuinely worried.

'I was hoping that he might have come down to see you. But had he, he would have been there by now.'

'Look, I'll stay in the room all afternoon. If he's not here by four, I'll see if I can get out of tonight's gig and come back to Manhattan. I hope to hell he hasn't done something really stupid. I mean, if he loses his job, he loses his job. I'll make sure he's all right. As I know you will too.'

'I'm sure he just panicked,' I said, trying to convince myself this was true. 'I bet anything that he'll surface in a couple of hours. Which is why I'm heading back to his apartment straight away. You can reach me there all day.'

I was back at the Hampshire House by one. I used the service entrance, and took the elevator up to Eric's apartment. There was no sign of his return, and the switchboard operator had logged no calls for him. I used the house phone to call Sean, the doorman.

'Sorry, Miss Smythe. Your brother hasn't shown his face yet – but those two guys in the car are still out front.'

I worked the phones all afternoon, calling every possible bar, restaurant, or haunt that Eric frequented. I called the travel agent at Thomas Cook who'd booked Eric's passage to Europe, on the long shot that he might have asked her to dispatch him somewhere within the States. I checked in every hour with Ronnie. I phoned the superintendent of my building, wondering if he'd seen my brother loitering with intent outside. I knew that all my efforts at locating him were futile ones – but I had to keep busy.

At four, Ronnie phoned me, to say that he'd managed to find someone to cover him for tonight, and he was taking the next train back to Manhattan. He showed up at the apartment around six thirty. I was pacing the floor at that point, wondering why Agent Sweet hadn't phoned the apartment at five to enquire about Eric's whereabouts. After all, he was supposed to have been at NBC then. But now he was a fugitive; a man who had run away. Though I didn't want to articulate my deepest fear to Ronnie, I couldn't help but think: I may never see my brother again.

At eight, we called the Carnegie Deli and had them deliver sandwiches and beer. We settled down in the living room and continued the wait. The evening went by quickly. Ronnie was a great talker – with a huge cache of stories about growing up in Puerto Rico and earning his chops as a musician. He chatted on about all-night drinking sessions with Charlie Parker, and surviving as one of Artie Shaw's side men for seven months, and why Benny Goodman was the cheapest band leader in history. He kept me laughing. He helped numb the fear we were both feeling. Round about midnight, however, he started to admit his worry.

'If your dumb, crazy brother has done anything really self-destructive, I'll never forgive him.'

'That'll make two of us.'

'If I lost him, I'd . . .'

He shuddered a bit. I reached out and gripped his arm.

'He'll be back, Ronnie. I'm sure of it.'

By two that morning, however, there was still no sign of him. So Ronnie retired to the bedroom and I returned, once again, to the sofa bed. I was so drained that I was asleep within minutes. Then I smelled smoke. My eyes jumped open. It was early morning. This dawn light was creeping through the blinds. Groggy, I squinted at my watch. Six nineteen. Then I heard a voice.

'Good morning.'

It was Eric, sitting in an armchair near the sofa, taking a deep drag of his cigarette. His suitcase was on the floor next to him.

I leapt up from the bed. I threw my arms around him.

'Thank God . . .' I said.

Eric managed a tired smile. 'He had nothing to do with it,' he said.

'Where the hell have you been?'

'Here and there.'

'You had me frantic. I'd thought you'd left town.'

'I did. Sort of. At seven yesterday morning, I woke up and decided that the only thing I could do was get the next flight to Mexico City. Because, outside of Canada, Mexico's the only foreign country you can enter without a passport. And hell, I'd done time down there after Father died, so I figured it was a logical destination for me.

'Of course, I knew the Feds would be out in front of the building, so I tipped the doorman and had him slip me out of the side entrance. I hopped a cab, and told him to take me to Idlewild. Want to know something funny? If the cabbie hadn't taken the Fifty-Ninth Street Bridge, I'm sure I'd be on a flight to Mexico right now. But there we were, heading to Queens on that bridge. And I made the mistake of turning around in the back seat, and seeing that midtown skyline framed by the rear window. And before I had time to think about it, I told the cabbie, "Change of plan. As soon as you get off the bridge, turn around and bring me back to Manhattan."

'The driver didn't like this one bit. "You crazy or somethin'?" he asked me.

'"Yeah, I'm crazy. Crazy enough to stay here when I shouldn't."

'I got him to drop me off at Grand Central Station. I checked my bag at the left luggage place there – but it was raining, so before I turned the bag over to the guy, I opened it up to get a folding umbrella I'd packed away for London. That's when I found your gift. I tell you, I cried when I saw the inscription. Because I also knew that this was the pen I'd use to name names.'

I swallowed hard. And said nothing.

'That's what I had decided, halfway across the Fifty-Ninth Street Bridge. I was going to be a stoolie. I was going to sing like a canary. I was going to sell out several people who I hadn't seen in years, and who were as innocent as I was. I was going to keep my job, and keep my lifestyle, and keep being able to run a tab at 21. Yeah, I'd feel bad about it . . . but *dem's de breaks*, right? I mean, if the Feds knew I'd been a member of the Party, then they also knew that the people I'd be naming had been members too. So all I'd be doing is telling them stuff they already knew.

'Or, at least, that's how I rationalized it to myself.

'So I clipped the pen inside my jacket pocket, and decided that I'd celebrate my last eight hours as a man with a relatively clean conscience by doing whatever the hell I wanted to do. Especially since I had a thousand bucks in traveler's checks in my wallet. So I treated myself to a champagne breakfast at the Waldorf. Then I wandered into Tiffany's and dropped some serious cash on a sterling silver cigarette case for Ronnie and a little something for you.'

He reached into his jacket pocket and pulled out a small blue box marked *Tiffany's*. He tossed it over to me. I stared down at it.

'Are you crazy?' I asked.

'Absolutely. Well go on, open the damn thing.'

I lifted off the lid, and stared down at an absurdly dazzling pair of platinum teardrop earrings, studded with small, perfect diamonds. I was speechless.

'Does your silence indicate ambivalence?' he asked.

'They're beautiful. But you shouldn't have done this.'

'Of course I should have. Don't you know that the great American rule of thumb is – when committing an act of moral cowardice, always soften the blow for yourself by spending a lot of money?

'Anyway, after my little spree at Tiffany's I walked up Fifth Avenue and spent a few leisurely hours at the Metropolitan Museum, looking at Rembrandts. They've got *The Return of the Prodigal Son* on loan from Amsterdam. Helluva picture, as Jack Warner would say. The misery of family, the need for redemption, the tug between responsibility and desire – all wrapped up in one really dark canvas. I tell you, S – the only person to use black better than Rembrandt is Coco Chanel.

'After the Met, it was lunchtime. Off to 21. Two martinis, an entire Maine lobster, half a bottle of

Pouilly-Fumé . . . and I was ready for a little more *hoch kultur*. The New York Phil was doing a matinée at Carnegie Hall with your old favorite, Bruno Walter, on the podium. And the band were playing Bruckner's Ninth Symphony. Amazing stuff. A big cathedral of sound. A guided tour of heaven in the company of a devout believer – and a sense that there is something just a little grander and more all-encompassing than our trivial endeavors on Planet Stupid.

'The audience went nuts when the concert ended. I too was on my feet, cheering my lungs out. Until I glanced at my watch. Four thirty. Time to stroll down to Rockefeller Center and engage in some very dirty work.

'Agent Sweet and that shithead Ross were waiting for me on the forty-third floor. Once again, I was escorted into the conference room. Once again, Ross glowered at me.

'"So," he said, "you've decided to cooperate."

'"Yes," I said. "I'll give you some names."

'"Agent Sweet told me about your little escapade at the passport office yesterday."

'"I panicked," I said.

'"That's one way of describing your actions."

'"But if the passport had come through, you'd be out of the country by now," Sweet said.

'"And I would have rued that decision for the rest of my life," I said.

'"Liar," Ross said.

'"You mean, you've never heard of a Pauline conversion, Mr Ross?"

'"Didn't that happen on the road to Damascus?" Agent Sweet asked.

'"Yes – and it's about to happen here right now in Rockefeller Center," I said. "What do you want to know?"

'Sweet sat down opposite me. He was working hard at containing his excitement, knowing full well that I was about to inform on my friends.

'"We'd like to know," he said, "who brought you into the Party, who ran your cell, and who were the other members of the cell."

'"Fine," I said. "Would you mind if I wrote this down."

'Sweet handed me a yellow legal pad. I pulled out your beautiful new pen. I uncapped it. I took a deep troubled breath. And I wrote eight names. It took less than a minute – and the funny thing was, I remembered them all with ease.

'When I was finished, I recapped the pen, put it back in my pocket, then pushed the pad forward – as if I couldn't bear to look at it. Sweet came around and patted me on the shoulder. "I know this couldn't have been easy, Mr Smythe. But I'm glad you've done the proper, patriotic thing."

'Then he picked up the pad. He stared at it for a moment, then threw it back in front of me and said, "What the hell is this?"

'"You wanted names," I said. "I gave you names."

'"Names," he said, snatching up the pad again. "This is your idea of names?" Then he started reading them one by one.

'"Sleepy, Grumpy, Dopey, Bashful, Happy, Sneezy, Doc, and . . . who the fuck is SW?"

'"Snow White, of course," I said.

'Ross grabbed the pad from Sweet's hand. He glanced at it, then said, "You have just committed professional hara-kiri."

'"Didn't know you spoke Japanese, Ross. Maybe you were one of their spies during the last war."

'"Get out," he yelled at me. "You're dead here."

'As I left, Sweet told me to expect a subpoena from HUAC any day. "See you in Washington, asshole," he shouted as I left.'

I stared at Eric, wide-eyed. 'You *really* wrote the names of the Seven Dwarfs?' I asked.

'Well, they were the first Communists that came to mind. Because, let's face it, they lived collectively, they shared their communal wealth, they . . .'

His face fell. He started to shudder. I ran over and held him. 'It's okay, it's okay,' I said. 'You did wonderfully. I'm so damn proud of . . .'

'Proud of what? The fact that I killed my career this afternoon? The fact that I'm now unemployable? The fact that I'm about to lose everything?'

I suddenly heard Ronnie's voice. 'You haven't lost us,' he said.

I looked up. Ronnie was standing in the doorway of the bedroom. Eric glanced in his direction.

'What are you doing here?' he asked tonelessly. 'You're not due back till Monday.'

'Sara and I were just a little worried that you might have vanished into thin air.'

'I really think you both could spend your time worrying about more important matters.'

'Will you listen to Mr False Modesty,' Ronnie said. 'And where the fuck have you been since naming the Seven Dwarfs?'

'Oh, here and there. Mainly a bunch of seedy bars on Broadway, then an all-night movie theater on Forty-Second Street. Saw a honey of a new Robert Mitchum thriller: *His Kind of a Woman*. Howard Hughes produced. Jane Russell co-starred, natch. Pretty nifty script: "I was just taking my tie off, wondering if I should hang myself with it." Kind of summed up how I felt last night.'

'Mr Self-Pity,' Ronnie said. 'Too bad you couldn't have dropped a nickel and told us you were alive and well.'

'Oh – but that would have been easy. And I don't do easy.'

I tousled his hair.

'But you did good, Mr Smythe,' I said. 'Didn't he, Ronnie?'

'Yeah,' he said, coming over and taking his hand. 'He did real good.'

'This calls for a toast,' I said, picking up the phone. 'Will room service deliver champagne this early?'

'Sure,' Eric said. 'And while you're at it, tell them I want an arsenic chaser.'

'Eric, don't worry,' I said. 'You're going to survive this.'

He leaned his head on Ronnie's shoulder.

'I doubt it,' he said.

CHAPTER 8

The story broke in the papers the next morning. Predictably, it was that great patriot, Walter Winchell, who dished the dirt. It was just a five-line item in his *Daily Mirror* column. But it did a lot of damage.

> He may be Marty Manning's best scribe . . . but he used to be a Red. And now Eric Smythe's in nowheresville after taking the Fifth with the Feds. He may know how to crack a joke, but he doesn't know how to sing 'God Bless America'. And what about the romantic company the never-married Smythe is keeping at his swank Hampshire House pad? No wonder NBC showed him the door marked 'Get Lost'.

Winchell's column hit the streets at noon. An hour later, Eric called me at my apartment. I was still in deep shock from reading this decimation job on my brother, but I didn't know if he'd seen it yet. Until, of course, I heard his voice. He sounded dazed.

'You've read it?' he asked.

'Yes. I read it. And I'm sure you could sue that bastard Winchell for defamation of character.'

'I've just been handed an eviction notice,' he said.

'You *what*?'

'A letter was just pushed under my front door from the management of Hampshire House, informing me that I'm to vacate my apartment in forty-eight hours.'

'On what grounds?'

'What do you think? Winchell's line about the "romantic company" I'm keeping at my "swank Hampshire House pad".'

'But surely, the management knew that Ronnie was living there with you.'

'Sure. But the deal was, I didn't say anything and they didn't ask anything. But now, that shit Winchell has blown everyone's cover – and the Hampshire House management are being forced to do something public and noticeable . . . like evicting the pervert.'

'Don't call yourself that.'

'Why not? It's how everyone's going to see me now. After all, I'm the *never-married Smythe*, right? You don't have to be Lionel Trilling to grasp the underlying meaning of that sentence.'

'Call Joel Eberts – ask him to get an injunction blocking the eviction notice, then fight the bastards in the courts.'

'What's the point? They'll win anyway, and I'll be even deeper in debt.'

'I'll pay the legal bills. Anyway, Mr Eberts isn't that expensive . . .'

'But we're probably talking about a six-month battle . . . which I'll end up losing. I'm not going to drain your bank account on my behalf. Especially as you're going to need the money. Because, thanks to me, your position at *Saturday/Sunday* is probably now in jeopardy.'

'Don't be silly,' I said. 'They wouldn't play the guilt-by-association card.'

But they did. The morning after the Winchell piece appeared, I received a call from Imogen Woods, my editor at *Saturday/Sunday*. She was trying to sound calm and casual – but she was clearly nervous. She suggested we meet for a coffee. When I told her I was really behind in work – thanks to the chaotic events of this week – and couldn't see her until after the weekend, her tone changed.

'I'm afraid it's a matter of some urgency,' she said.

'Oh,' I said, suddenly nervous. 'Well, could we talk about it now?'

'No. I don't think this is something for the phone . . . if you take my meaning.'

I did. And I was now genuinely worried. 'Okay – where do you want to meet?' I asked.

She suggested the bar of the Roosevelt Hotel near Grand Central Station in an hour's time.

'But I have a deadline for you this afternoon,' I said.

'It can wait,' she said.

I reached the Roosevelt at the appointed hour of eleven. Imogen had a Manhattan on the table in front of her. She smiled tightly as I approached. She stood up and kissed me on the cheek. She offered me a drink. I said I'd prefer coffee at this hour of the morning.

'Have a drink, sweetheart,' she said, radiating uneasiness.

'Okay,' I said, now thinking that alcohol might be necessary. 'A Scotch and soda.'

She ordered the drink. She made small talk about attending the Broadway opening of a Garson Kanin play the previous night.

'Winchell was there too,' she said, studying my face for a reaction. I gave her none.

'I think he's a monster,' she said.

'So do I.'

'And I just want you to know that I really felt for you yesterday, after I saw that item in Winchell's column,' she said.

'Thank you – but it was my brother who was smeared . . .'

'Listen, I just want you to know that, personally speaking, I am completely behind you both . . .'

Alarm bells began to ring between my ears. 'That's nice to know,' I said, 'but, like I told you, it's Eric who's taking the heat right now, not me.'

'Sara . . .'

'What the hell is wrong, Imogen?'

'Early this morning, I got a call from His Godship the Editor. It seems the magazine's board had their monthly meeting last night, and one of the big topics of conversation was the controversy swirling around your brother. Because, let's face it, it's not just his past political associations that have upset them. It's also his private life.'

'That's right. It's *his* private life. *His* past political associations. Not mine.'

'We know you were never politically involved . . .'

'What do you mean, *we*?'

'His Godship, Ralph J. Linklater, had a visit yesterday morning from a guy named Sweet from the FBI. He told him that they had been running quite a substantial investigation into your brother's political past. It had been going on for a few months. Naturally enough, they also decided to run a background check on you.'

'I don't believe this. Why on earth would they be interested in me?'

'Because, like your brother, you have a certain public platform . . .'

'I write movie reviews and a completely frivolous column about completely frivolous things . . .'

'Sara, *please* . . . I'm just the messenger here.' Then after a quick scan around the bar, she leaned forward and whispered: 'Personally, I think these investigations are insane. And even more un-American than the un-American activities they're supposed to be rooting out. But I'm caught in the middle like everyone else.'

'I have never, *ever* been a Communist,' I hissed. 'Jesus Christ, I voted for Truman in forty-eight, not Wallace. I am about the most apolitical person imaginable.'

'That's what the Feds told Linklater.'

'Then what's the problem here?'

'There are two problems. The first is, your brother. If he had cooperated with NBC, there would have been no problem. The fact that he didn't means there is now a problem vis-à-vis you and *Saturday/Sunday*.'

'But *why*? I am not his keeper.'

'Listen, had Eric talked, the Winchell item would have never appeared, and all this would have been forgotten about. But now he's been exposed as a one-time Communist, and as a man who does not have . . . how can I say this? . . . a *typical* domestic home life. From what Linklater told me this morning, the board's great worry is that his problems will somehow cast a bad light on you . . .'

'Let's cut the crap, Imogen,' I said loudly. 'What you're really saying is that *Saturday/Sunday* is worried about having a columnist whose brother is a former Communist *and* a practicing homosexual . . .'

That brought the bar to a silent standstill. Imogen looked like she wanted to vanish into the floor.

'Yes,' she said quietly. 'That is the essence of their dilemma.' She motioned me towards her. 'But it's compounded by another problem. His Godship knows about you and the married man.'

I sat back in my chair, stunned.

'Who told him?' I finally said.

'The FBI guy.'

My shock deepened. 'But how the hell did he know?'

'I gather that when they decided to investigate your brother a couple of months ago, they also figured they should look into your background. And although they didn't find any political stuff, they did discover that you were having this thing with a married guy . . .'

'But the only way they could have done that was by spying on me. Or listening in on my phone calls. Or . . .'

'I don't know how they found out. All I know is: *they know*. And they've told Linklater . . . and Linklater has told the board.'

'But . . . but . . . it's my private life. It has no impact whatsoever on my column. I mean, I'm not exactly someone in the public eye. As you know, I even balked at having a photo of me in the magazine. No one knows who I am. I like it that way. So why . . . *why?* . . . should anyone worry about with whom I share my life?'

'Now that your brother's been exposed, I think Linklater is worried word might slip out about your own domestic arrangements. I mean, it's only a matter of time before Eric is subpoenaed by HUAC. His testimony will make the papers. If he still refuses to cooperate, he'll be cited for contempt, and he'll probably do time. This will mean even more publicity. Who's to say the Feds mightn't feed Winchell or some other hack a little tidbit about you and your married friend? And you know what that asshole would write: "*It isn't just Redder-than-Red Eric Smythe who's got an interesting private life. Single Sis Sara – she who writes that funny 'Real Life' column in* Saturday/Sunday *– has her own inter-esting set-up with a guy who's got a wedding band on his left finger. And I thought* Saturday/Sunday *called itself a family magazine.*'"

'But that's insane logic . . .'

'I know it's insane . . . but this is how people are thinking right now. I've got a brother, he's a professor of chemistry out at Berkeley. And the University Regents have just asked him to sign a loyalty oath – *yes*, an actual piece of paper, in which he swears that he's not a member of any subversive organization endangering the stability of the United States. Every faculty member at the university's been forced to do the same thing. To me, this sort of thing is repugnant. Just as I also think it's repugnant what's happening to your brother. And to you.'

'What *is* happening to me, Imogen?'

She met my gaze. 'They want to put both your columns on hold for a while.'

'In other words, you're firing me.'

'No, we are definitely *not* firing you.'

'What the hell do you call it then?'

'Hear me out. His Godship really likes you, Sara – as we all do. We don't want to lose you. We just think that, until this entire issue with your brother is resolved, it's best if you lie low for a while.'

'Better known as vanishing from view.'

'Here's the deal – and, under the circumstances, I don't think it's a bad one. We announce in the next issue of the magazine that you're taking a leave of absence for six months to do some other writing. We continue to pay you a retainer of two hundred dollars a week. Then, six months from now, we review the entire situation.'

'And if my brother's still in trouble then?'

'Let's cross that bridge when we come to it.'

'Say I decide to fight this? To go public about the way you are buckling to pressure from . . .'

'I really wouldn't do that if I were you. You can't win this one, Sara. If you try to fight it, they'll simply fire you, and you'll end up with nothing. At least this way you come out of the situation with no loss of face, no major loss of income. Consider it a paid sabbatical, courtesy of *Saturday/Sunday*. Go to Europe. Go write a novel. All His Godship asks for is . . .'

'I know – my complete and total silence.'

I stood up. 'I'm going now,' I said.

'Please don't do anything rash,' she said. 'Please think this all through.'

I nodded. Imogen stood up. She took my hand.

'I'm sorry,' she whispered.

I pulled my hand away.

'Shame on you,' I said.

I left the Roosevelt. I marched north up Madison Avenue, oblivious to the wave of pedestrians heading south. I was in something close to a rage, and would have chewed the head off of anybody

569

who dared to bump into me. I hated the world at that moment. I hated its pettiness – its malevolence and spite. More than anything, I hated the way people used fear as a way of gaining control over others. Right now I wanted to jump the next train to Washington, and walk straight into the office of J. Edgar Hoover, and ask him what he really felt could be achieved by persecuting my brother. *You say you're defending our way of life,* I'd tell him. *But all you're really doing is enhancing your power. Information is knowledge. Knowledge is control. Control is based on fear. Because you now have us all afraid, you win. And all we like sheep have no one but ourselves to blame for your power, because we've given it to you.*

I was so enraged that I ended up walking nearly twenty blocks before realizing where I was. I looked up and noticed a street sign saying *East 59th Street.* I was only five minutes away from Eric's apartment. But I knew I couldn't see him in the state I was in. Just as I knew that I couldn't really tell him about the conversation I'd just had with Imogen Woods . . . though I also realized that as soon as he saw the notice in *Saturday/Sunday* next week that I had 'gone on sabbatical', he'd blame himself.

I leaned against a phone booth, wondering what my next move should be. I answered that question immediately by stepping inside the booth, dropping a nickel in the slot, and doing something I vowed never to do: calling Jack at work.

He'd been due back from Boston this morning, and was planning to stop by and see me on his way home tonight. I needed to see him now. But when I rang his office, his secretary told me he was in a meeting.

'Would you let him know that Sara Smythe called.'

'Will he know what this is about?'

'Yeah – I'm an old friend from the neighborhood. Tell him I'm in Manhattan, and was hoping to take him to lunch at Lindy's. I'll be there at one, if he can make it. If not, ask him to phone me there.'

Jack walked into Lindy's exactly at one. He looked very nervous. As we never met during the day, let alone in a public place, he did not kiss me hello. Instead, he sat down opposite me, and took my hands under the table.

'I saw Winchell,' he said.

I took him through everything that had happened: Eric refusing to name names, the Winchell column, the eviction notice from Hampshire House, and my conversation with Imogen Woods. When I got to the part about the FBI informing *Saturday/Sunday* about my relationship with a married man, Jack tensed.

'Don't worry,' I said. 'I doubt any of this will ever go public. I won't let it go public.'

'I don't believe this,' he said. 'I can't fathom how . . .'

He broke off. He let go of my hands, and anxiously patted his jacket pockets for his cigarettes.

'Are you all right?'

'No,' he said, fishing out a Chesterfield and his lighter.

'I promise you, Jack – your name will never be linked with . . .'

'To hell with my name. Eric and you have been smeared. And that . . . those bastards . . . they . . .'

He broke off. His distress in the face of our predicament touched me beyond words. At that moment, I loved him unconditionally.

'I'm sorry,' he finally said. 'I am so goddamn sorry. How's Eric bearing up?'

'I think he's scrambling to find a new place to live. The eviction notice is six p.m. tomorrow.'

'Tell him if there's anything . . . *anything* . . . I can do . . .'

I suddenly leaned over and kissed him.

'You're a good man,' I said.

He had to run back to the office. But he promised to call me tonight before returning home to Dorothy. Not only did he phone – but he also rang Eric at his apartment that evening, offering support. The next day, he showed up at the Hampshire House at five to help my brother move his stuff to the Ansonia on Broadway and 74th Street. The Ansonia was a residential hotel, favored by people in the mid-to-lower echelons of show business. Eric's new apartment was a dark, one-bedroom suite, overlooking a back alley. It had peeling green floral wallpaper, a threadbare green carpet pockmarked by cigarette burns, and a tiny kitchenette, consisting of a hotplate and a faulty ice box. But the rent was cheap: twenty-five dollars a week. And the management didn't seem terribly concerned about the co-habiting arrangements of its residents. As long as the rent was paid on time – and you didn't disturb the peace – their attitude was: we don't want to know.

Eric hated the new apartment. He hated the grim, last-chance-saloon atmosphere of the Ansonia. But he had few options. Because he was so damn broke. After his little shopping spree, he had less than a hundred bucks in his pocket. With the eviction notice from the Hampshire House came a bill for four hundred dollars – covering assorted room service and hotel charges. When Eric told the hotel management that he wouldn't be able to settle the bill before his departure, they informed him that they would impound all his belongings. So Ronnie and I paid Tiffany's a visit, and collected a seven-hundred-and-twenty-dollar refund on the diamond earrings and the silver cigarette case. After settling his Hampshire House bill, the remaining three hundred and twenty dollars paid for a month's deposit and two months' rent at the Ansonia. Jack insisted on organizing the van which moved Eric's stuff to his new apartment. Just as he also arranged for two painters to strip the new apartment of its cheerless wallpaper, and brighten the place up with several coats of white emulsion.

Eric and I were both overwhelmed by Jack's generosity.

'You know, you really don't have to be doing this,' I told Jack as I cooked dinner at my place. It was the Monday after Eric moved apartments, and the painters had started work that day.

'Hiring a couple of painters for two days isn't exactly going to break the bank. Anyway, I had a bit of a bonus windfall. Out of nowhere, I was handed a check for over eight hundred dollars. It's Steele and Sherwood's way of saying thank you for bagging a new insurance client. When things are going well for you, you should help others, right?'

'Sure. But I always thought that, when it came to Eric . . .'

'Hell, that's all in the past. As far as I'm concerned, he's family. And he's in trouble. I know how I'd feel if I was forced to move from the Hampshire House to the Ansonia. So, if a coat of paint cheers the new place up a little bit for your brother, it's money well spent. I also hate what's happened to you.'

'I'll be okay,' I said, not exactly sounding convinced.

'Have you gotten back to *Saturday/Sunday* since the meeting with your editor?'

'No.'

'You have to accept their offer, Sara. Your editor's right – if you fight *Saturday/Sunday*, you'll lose. Take the money, darling. Take a break. In a month or two, all this naming names stuff should blow over. It's gotten way out of hand. It's gone crazy.'

I wanted to believe Jack that the nightmarish game called blacklisting would be over soon. Just as I wanted to reject *Saturday/Sunday*'s offer of two hundred dollars a week as a retainer fee. Because, after all, what they were offering me was a Faustian Bargain: money to balm their guilt at suspending me . . . out of the absurd fear that their so-called 'family magazine' mightn't look so 'family' if it was discovered that one of their columnists shared her bed with a married man, and had an ex-Communist brother who also practiced 'the love that dare not speak its name'.

His Godship really likes you, Sara – as we all do. We don't want to lose you. We just think that, until this entire issue with your brother is resolved, it's best if you lie low for a while.

God, Imogen looked so conscience-stricken when she hit me with that suggestion. But, of course, like everyone else, she too felt under threat. Had she not 'followed orders', she might have found her own position at the magazine in jeopardy. Or maybe questions would have been asked about her loyalty to God and Country. That was the worst thing about the blacklist – the way it scared everyone away from acts of common good, and appealed to the most basic of human instincts: personal survival . . . at all costs.

'Take the money, darling.'

In the end, I did. Because Jack was right: this

was a fight I could not win. And because I also knew that *Saturday/Sunday* could have simply dropped me without cause. At least this way, I would be guaranteed a salary for the next six months – and the money would be very useful in keeping Eric afloat.

The Winchell column about Eric's dismissal didn't just result in his eviction from the Hampshire House. One by one, every restaurant or emporium which once welcomed him as a great customer (and, noting his free-spending ways, granted him credit) slammed the door in his face. A few days after his move to the Ansonia, he arranged to meet Ronnie for an aftermidnight drink at the Stork Club. But when he showed up, the maître d' informed him that his presence wasn't desired. Eric knew the guy by name ('Hell, I used to give him a ten-buck tip every week'). He pleaded to be let in.

'Sorry, Mr Smythe,' the maître d' said. 'I don't make the rules. And I think the management is a little worried about the tab you owe us.'

The next day, the Stork Club tab arrived: seven hundred and forty-four dollars and thirty-eight cents. To be paid within twenty-eight days, or else.

This demand was quickly followed by similar ones from Alfred Dunhill, 21, El Morocco, and Saks Fifth Avenue – all of which asked that he settle up his accounts within four weeks or face legal proceedings.

'I never knew so many people read Walter

Winchell,' I said, sifting through this small stack of threatening letters.

'Oh, that bastard is enormously popular. Because, of course, he's such a great American.'

'Did you really spend a hundred and seventy-five dollars on a pair of hand-made brogues?' I asked, scanning one of the attached bills.

'A fool and his money are quickly parted.'

'Let me guess: Bud Abbott, or maybe it was Lou Costello? Of course, it wouldn't be Oscar Wilde.'

'I don't think so – though he's a gentleman with whom I am now feeling a growing rapport. Especially as I can write my own "Ballad of Reading Gaol" after HUAC finds me in contempt of court.'

'One drama at a time, please. You haven't been subpoenaed by the committee yet.'

'Oh yes I have,' he said, picking up a document off the chipped card table that he was now using as a makeshift desk. 'Good news comes in big bundles. This arrived this morning. A Federal official actually showed up here personally, and shoved it into my hand. I've even got a date for my appearance: July twenty-first. Washington's pretty humid in July, isn't it? So are most federal penitentiaries.'

'You're not going to jail, Eric.'

'Oh yes I am. Because the committee will demand names. Under oath, of course. When I refuse to provide them with this information, I will most definitely be going to jail. That's how it works.'

'We'll call Joel Eberts. You need some legal counsel.'

'No, I don't. Because the equation here is a

simple one: cooperate and avoid the slammer. Don't cooperate, and enjoy six months to a year as a guest of the United States government in one of their select prisons.'

'First things first, Eric. Give me all the bills.'

'No way.'

'I've got the cash in the bank. It's not a stretch . . .'

'I won't let you pay for my stupidity.'

'It's just money, Eric.'

'I was profligate.'

'Also known as *generous*. So let me be generous back. What's the total damage? About five grand?'

'I am ashamed of myself.'

'You'll be even more ashamed when you're hauled into court for non-payment of bills. This way, your debts are cleared. It's one less worry. You've got enough to deal with.'

'All right, all right,' he said, tossing me the pile of bills. 'Play Good Samaritan. But on one condition: that five grand is considered a loan. To be paid back as soon as I get some work.'

'If it makes you feel better, fine – call it a loan. But I'm never going to ask you for the money.'

'I can't stand all this generosity.'

I laughed. And said, 'Next thing you know, you might have to renounce misanthropy and start accepting that there are a few decent people out there who actually care about you.'

I paid off Eric's bills the next day. I also called Imogen Woods at *Saturday/Sunday* and informed her that I would accept the magazine's leave-of-absence offer. She assured me that, six months from now, I'd be back writing for them.

'Please don't hate me,' she said. 'I'm just caught in the middle like everyone else.'

'Everyone's caught in the middle, aren't they?'

'What are you going to do with the six months?'

'My first goal is trying to keep my brother out of jail.'

Actually, my first goal was trying to snap Eric out of the depression into which he quickly descended. A depression which deepened when Ronnie was offered an amazing job opportunity: a three-month nationwide tour as part of Count Basie's orchestra. The offer arrived a week after he moved into the Ansonia with Eric. Privately he told me that – though he was over the moon about the prospect of playing in Basie's big band – he was reluctant to take the gig. Because he was worried about Eric's mental stability.

Over coffee at Gitlitz's deli, Ronnie told me, 'He's not sleeping, and he's drinking a fifth of Canadian Club every night.'

'I'll talk to him,' I said.

'Good luck. He doesn't want to be talked to.'

'Have you let him know about the Basie offer?'

'Of course. "Go, go," he tells me. "I'll be fine without you."'

'You want to take the job, don't you?'

'It's a chance to play with the Count . . . of course I want it.'

'Then take it.'

'But . . . Eric needs me. And he's going to need me even more in the run-up to his Committee appearance.'

'I'll be here.'

'I'm scared for him.'

'Don't be,' I lied. 'Once he finds some new work, he'll settle back down again.'

To his credit, Eric did knock on a lot of doors after his dismissal from NBC. Initially, he was optimistic about his employment prospects. After all, he was Eric Smythe – the major-domo writer from *The Marty Manning Show*; a man who was widely regarded in New York as one of the true comedic innovators in that new-fangled medium called television. What's more, he also had the reputation for being a consummate pro. He was smart, mischievous, and fast. When it came to cranking out material, he always made a deadline – and it was constantly fresh and original. As everyone in the business acknowledged, he was good news.

But no one would now hire him. Nor would they even meet with him. As soon as he was settled at the Ansonia, he started working the phone, trying to line up appointments with assorted producers and agents around town.

'I must have made a dozen calls yesterday,' he said when I dropped by the apartment with a bag of groceries for him. 'The people I was calling were guys who'd been after me in the past to write for them. Not one of them was available to speak with me. Three were in meetings, four were at lunch, and the rest were out of town.'

'Well,' I said, 'maybe it was just your unlucky day.'

'Thank you, Louisa May Alcott, for looking on the bright side of life.'

'I'm just saying – don't panic yet.'

By five the next afternoon, however, complete panic had set in. Once again, Eric had called the same twelve producers and agents. Once again, none of them was available to speak to him.

'So, do you know what I decided to do?' he said on the phone to me. 'I decided to jump the Broadway local down to Fiftieth Street and pay a little speculative lunchtime visit to Jack Dempsey's – where half of the comedy agents in New York meet to talk shop every day. There must have been, I don't know, maybe six of these guys sitting around a table. All of them knew me. All of them, at one time or another, tried to get me as a client . . . although I was one of those proud bastards who always maintained that he never needed an agent. Anyway, in I saunter to Jack Dempsey's. As soon as the table sees me approaching, it's like the local leper has made an appearance. Half the guys wouldn't talk to me. The others suddenly had to be elsewhere. Within two minutes of me turning up, the table was cleared. With the exception of this one old guy, Moe Canter. He must be around seventy-two. He's been handling acts since the days of vaudeville. A straight shooter, Moe. As soon as everyone's fled the scene, he tells me to sit down and buys me a cup of coffee. And he gives it to me straight:

"'Eric, what can I tell you? People in our business are scared. Everyone's terrified of ending up on some congressman's shit list – and they will snub their own brother if it means staying alive professionally. So, for the moment, I think you should consider another line of work. Because – after the Winchell item – you're an untouchable in this town. I'm sorry – but that's how it is."

'He then told me how much he admired me for refusing to rat on my friends. Know what I said back? "Everyone loves a hero . . . as long as he's dead."'

I took a deep breath. I tried to sound reasonable. 'All right,' I said, 'this is bad, but . . .'

'*Bad?* It's a fucking catastrophe. My career is kaput. Yours too. And it's completely my fault.'

'Don't say that. And don't completely write yourself off as yet. Remember, the Winchell piece appeared only a week ago. So it's still fresh in everyone's memory. A month from now . . .'

'You're right. Everyone will have forgotten about the Winchell item. Instead, they'll be focusing on my contempt citation from the House Committee on UnAmerican Activities. And after my performance in front of the congressmen, I'm certain the employment opportunities will just keep rolling in.'

I could hear liquid being poured into a glass. 'What is that?'

'Canadian Club.'

'You now start drinking at three in the after-noon?'

'No, today I actually started drinking at two.'

'You have me worried.'

'There's nothing to worry about. Hell, I can always make a living churning out sonnets. Or maybe I'll corner the market in epic Norse verse. Now there's a section of the writing market that's probably blacklist-proof. All I need to do is brush up my Icelandic and . . .'

'I'm coming over,' I said.

'No need, S. I am feeling just hunky-dory.'

'I'll be there in five minutes.'

'I won't be. I have an important appointment this afternoon . . .'

'With whom?'

'With the Loew's Eighty-Fourth Street movie house. They're showing a helluva double feature: *Sudden Fear* with Joan Crawford, Gloria Graham and the delectable Jack Palance, followed by *The Steel Trap* with Joe Cotton. An afternoon of pure monochromatic bliss.'

'At least let Jack and me take you to dinner tonight.'

'Dinner? Hang on, I must consult my social diary . . . No, I'm afraid I'm otherwise engaged this evening.'

'What are you doing?'

'According to my calendar, I'm getting drunk. Alone.'

'Why are you avoiding me?'

'I *vant* to be alone, *dahling*.'

'Just meet me for a fast cup of coffee.'

'*Ve'll* talk tomorrow, *dahling*. And please, don't call back – because the phone will be off the hook.'

He hung up. Naturally I tried to phone right back. The line was busy. So I threw on my coat and dashed down the three blocks of Broadway which separated my apartment from the Ansonia Hotel. When I reached its seedy reception desk, the clerk told me that my brother had just left the building. So I hopped a cab north, and paid seventy-five cents for a ticket to the Loew's Eighty-Fourth Street. I scoured the orchestra, I scoured the loge, I scoured the balcony. No sign of my brother. *Sudden Fear* was playing as I conducted my search. When I realized that Eric was nowhere to be found, I slumped into a seat. On-screen Joan Crawford was having words with Jack Palance:

'*Remember what Nietzsche said – live dangerously.*'

'*You know what happened to Nietzsche?*'

'*What?*'

'*He died.*'

I left the movie house. I returned home. I called the Ansonia. There was no answer in Eric's room. Jack came home from work. He sat vigil with me all evening. Every half-hour I phoned the Ansonia. Still no answer from my brother. Around nine, Jack went out and did a search of local bars, while

I sat by the phone. Jack was back within an hour, having turned up no sign of Eric. At midnight, Jack called it quits and went to bed. I continued to sit by the phone in the living room. Eventually I nodded off. When I came to again, it was six thirty. Jack was dressed and handing me a cup of coffee.

'You must feel great,' he said.

'Try diabolical.'

I took a fast sip of the coffee, then dialed the Ansonia. 'Sorry,' the switchboard operator said after a dozen rings. 'No answer at that extension.'

I hung up. 'Maybe I should call the police,' I said.

'You last spoke to him yesterday afternoon, right?'

I nodded.

'Well, the cops aren't going to do anything about a guy who's been missing for less than twenty-four hours. Give it until this afternoon. If you haven't heard from him by then, we'll get worried. Okay?'

I let him pull me up and enfold me in a big hug. 'Try to get some proper sleep,' he said. 'And call me at the office if you need me.'

'Are you sure about that?'

'Tell them you're a Miss Olson from Standard Life in Hartford – and my nosy secretary won't think a thing about it.'

'Who's Miss Olson?'

'Someone I just made up. Try not to worry about Eric, eh? I'm sure he's fine.'

'You've been amazing through all this.'

He shook his head. 'I wish I could do more.'

I fell into bed. When I stirred again, it was just after twelve noon. I grabbed the bedside phone and called the Ansonia. This time I got lucky. Eric – sounding sleepy as hell – answered.

'Oh thank God,' I said.

'What the hell are you so thankful for?'

'Your safe return. Where have you been?'

'My usual all-night haunts – ending up at the New Liberty picture house on Forty-Second Street. Me and the local tramp fraternity – sleeping it off in the balcony.'

'You know, I did go searching for you at the Loew's Eighty-Fourth Street yesterday afternoon.'

'Figured you would do that – which is why I decided to catch a double bill at New Liberty.'

'Why are you avoiding me? You've never shut me out, Eric.'

'Well, there's a first time for everything. Listen, I'm going back to sleep now. And the phone is going off the hook. Don't call us. We'll call you . . . as everyone in New York now tells me.'

Naturally I did try to call him back. But the line was constantly busy. I fought the urge to march down to the Ansonia and confront him. Instead I used the Miss Olson alias and called Jack. He gave me sound advice: back right off. Give him a few days on his own.

'He has to come to terms with this stuff by himself,' Jack said.

'But he's in no fit condition to be left alone.'

'He hasn't gone mental yet, has he?'

'No – he's just drinking all the time, and staying out all night.'

'He's grieving. What's happened to him is like a death. You've got to let it run its course. Right now, nothing you say to him will make sense. Because he can't see sense.'

So I didn't call him for three days. I waited until five in the afternoon on Friday. He sounded reasonably awake and sober.

'I've got a new job,' he said.

'Really?' I said, suddenly excited.

'Absolutely. In fact, it's more than a job – it's a new-found vocation.'

'Tell me.'

'I am now a professional drifter.'

'Eric . . .'

'Hear me out. It's such fantastic work; the most productive way imaginable of squandering time. What I do all day is wander. Drifting from movie house to movie house. Grabbing a twenty-five-cent lunch at the Automat. Loitering in the Metropolitan and Natural History Museums, walking, walking, walking. Do you know that yesterday, I actually strolled right up from West Seventy-Fourth Street to Washington Heights? It only took me around three hours. Part of me wanted to keep on hiking north to the Cloisters, but as it was three in the morning . . .'

'You walked up to Washington Heights in the middle of the night? Are you nuts?'

'No – just fulfilling my role as a drifter.'

'Have you been drinking much?'

'Certainly not while I'm asleep. But I do have some additional news on the work front.'

'Really?' I said.

'Yes – splendid news. I decided to bypass the agent route and instead opened my telephone book and offered my services to five different comedians I know. Guess what? All of them turned me down. These aren't even top-echelon comics. These are the sort of mid-grade guys who play the mid-grade clubs in the Poconos and the Catskills and West Palm Beach. So my stock has sunk so low that even the second-raters don't want to know me.'

'As I've told you again and again, this initial period is going to be rough. Once you get the HUAC hearing out of the way . . .'

'And I serve my year behind bars . . .'

'All right, say it comes to that. Say you do go to jail. It will be terrible, but you'll get through it. When the blacklist ends, not only will you be respected for refusing to name names, but . . .'

'*When* the blacklist ends? Will you listen to yourself. The chances of the blacklist ending are currently up there with me becoming Secretary of State. Even if the whole damn thing ends up discredited, the mud will stick. I'll always be regarded as the *never-married one-time Communist*. No one will ever want to hire me again.'

He refused to be talked out of this bleak perspective. Just as he also refused to let me see him. Once again, I charged down to the Ansonia. Once again, he was gone by the time I got there. It was another twenty-four hours before I made telephone contact with him again. This time, I didn't ask for a lengthy explanation about his whereabouts over the last night and day. I tried to sound practical.

'How are you doing for money at the moment?' I asked.

'Rolling in it. Lighting Cuban cigars with five-dollar bills.'

'Delighted to hear it. I'll be leaving fifty dollars for you in an envelope in reception.'

'No thanks.'

'Eric, I know what your financial position is.'

'Ronnie gave me some cash before he left.'

'How much?'

'Plenty.'

'I don't believe you.'

'That's your problem, S.'

'Why won't you let me help you?'

'Because you've paid a high enough price for my idiocy. Got to go now.'

'Am I going to see you for dinner this weekend?'

'No,' he said – and put down the phone.

I placed fifty dollars in an envelope and handed it in to the Ansonia's reception. The next morning, I found it on my front doormat – the name Eric crossed out and Sara penciled over in my brother's distinctive scrawl. That day, I must have left a dozen messages for him. No reply. In despair, I managed to track Ronnie down to a hotel in Cleveland. He was shocked when I told him of Eric's increasingly erratic behavior.

'I phone him about twice a week,' Ronnie said, 'and he always sounds okay to me.'

'He said you left him some money . . .'

'Yeah, around thirty bucks.'

'But you went off on tour ten days ago. He must be broke. He's got to accept my money.'

'He won't – out of guilt for what happened to you at *Saturday/Sunday*.'

'But he knows they're paying me two hundred dollars a week as a retainer. And I've got no mortgage, no dependents. So why shouldn't he take fifty? It still leaves me plenty . . .'

'I don't have to tell you how your brother works, do I? The guy's got a huge conscience and a lousy streak of pigheadedness. It's a bad combination.'

'Would he accept the money from you?'

'Yeah – he might. But there's no way I could come up with fifty bucks a week.'

'I've got an idea.'

That afternoon, I walked down to Western Union and wired fifty dollars to Ronnie at his hotel in Cleveland. The next day, he wired it back to Eric at the Ansonia. I called Ronnie that night in his next port of call: Cincinnati.

'I had to feed Eric some crap about Basie giving everyone in the band a raise,' he said, 'but he didn't seem particularly suspicious. I think he really needs the cash. Because he told me he'd go straight down to Western Union with the wire and pick up the cash.'

'Well, at least we know that he'll now have enough money each week to keep himself fed. Now if I could just get him to see me.'

'He'll want to see you when he's ready to see you. I know he's missing you.'

'How do you know that?'

'Because he told me, that's how.'

As instructed, I kept my distance. I made my daily phone call to check up on his well-being. If I was lucky, I reached Eric when he was sober and reasonably lucid. Usually, however, he sounded either drunk or hungover, and basically dispirited. I stopped enquiring about whether he'd been exploring other possible work options. Instead, I listened to his monologues about the five movies he'd seen the previous day. Or the books he'd been reading at the Forty-Second Street Library (he'd become one of the habitués of its Reading Room). Or the Broadway show he'd 'second-acted' last night:

'Second-acting is such an easy thing to do,' he told me. 'You stand near the theater until the first intermission. When everyone comes pouring out for a cigarette, you mingle with the crowd, step inside and find yourself an empty seat at the back of the orchestra. And you get to see the next two acts free of charge. What a ruse, eh?'

'Absolutely,' I said, trying to sound cheerful, trying to pretend that sneaking into Broadway

591

shows was a perfectly acceptable activity for a man crowding forty.

What I really wanted to do was to intervene – to run down to the Ansonia, bundle Eric into a car, and take him up to Maine for a few weeks. I'd actually broached this idea with him on the phone – arguing that some time out of New York would be beneficial, and would give him some perspective.

'Oh I get it,' he said. 'After a week of walking along an empty beach, my equilibrium will be repaired, my faith in humanity restored, and I will be in tip-top shape to parry with all the delightful folk on the UnAmerican Affairs Committee.'

'I just think a change of scene might prove beneficial.'

'Sorry – no sale.'

I stopped begging to see him. Instead, I found a desk clerk at the Ansonia – Joey – who was happy to keep me informed about Eric's comings-and-goings for five bucks a week. I knew this was a form of surveillance – but I had to somehow keep tabs on his general mental and physical condition. Joey had my home number, in case of an emergency. A week before his HUAC appearance, the phone rang at three in the morning. Jack – asleep next to me – bolted upright. So did I. I reached for the receiver, expecting the worst.

'Miss Smythe, Joey here at the Ansonia. Sorry to call you in the middle of the night, but you did say I should phone anytime if there was a problem ...'

'What's happened?' I said, genuinely frightened.

'Don't worry – your brother's not hurt. But he showed up here around fifteen minutes ago, bombed out of his head. I tell you, he was so gone that myself and the night detective had to carry him in from the cab. As soon as we got him upstairs, he was sick everywhere. He was bringing up a lot of blood . . .'

'Call an ambulance.'

'It's already been done. They should be here in a couple of minutes.'

'I'm on my way.'

Jack and I were dressed and out the door in an instant. We grabbed a cab down to the Ansonia. An ambulance was parked out front. As we raced into the lobby, Eric was being brought downstairs on a stretcher. In the last three weeks since we met, he'd aged around ten years. His face seemed emaciated, skeletal. He had a scraggy beard, currently dappled in blood. His hair had become flimsy, his hands bony, his fingernails ravaged and dirty. He looked undernourished, cadaverous. But it was his eyes that scared me the most. Red, bloodshot, glassy – as if he had been permanently shellshocked by life. I took his hand. It felt so thin, so devoid of weight. I called his name. He just stared blankly at me. I started to cry. Jack – white with shock – held me as the ambulance men rolled him outside and loaded him into the back of their van.

We were allowed to ride with him. The ambulance

took off down Broadway at speed. I held Eric's hand during the five-minute ride to Roosevelt Hospital. My eyes were brimming. I kept shaking my head.

'I should never have left him on his own,' I said.

'You did everything you could.'

'*Everything?* Look at him, Jack. I failed him.'

'Stop that,' he said. 'You've failed nobody.'

At the hospital, Eric was rushed straight into the emergency room. An hour went by. Jack disappeared to an all-night coffee shop around the corner and came back with doughnuts and coffee. He smoked cigarette after cigarette. I kept pacing the floor of the waiting room, wondering why the hell we hadn't heard anything. Eventually, a tired-looking doctor in a white coat emerged through the swing doors of the ER. He was around thirty, and had a lit cigarette in a corner of his mouth.

'Someone here waiting for a Mr –' he glanced down at the chart in this hand '– Eric Smythe?'

Jack and I immediately approached the doctor. He asked me my relationship to Mr Smythe. I told him.

'Well, Miss Smythe – your brother is suffering from a combination of malnutrition, alcoholic poisoning, and a ruptured duodenal ulcer that would have probably killed him in another two hours if he hadn't been rushed here. How the hell did he get so undernourished?'

I heard myself say, 'It's my fault.' Immediately, Jack jumped in:

'Don't listen to her, Doctor. Mr Smythe has been having some serious professional career problems, and has essentially allowed himself to go to hell. His sister has done all she could . . .'

The doctor cut him off. 'I'm not trying to apportion blame here. I just want to know what brought him to the state he's in now. Because we've had to rush him up to operating theater . . .'

'Oh my God,' I said.

'When the duodenal gland ruptures, it's either surgery or death. But I think we got to him just in time. The next couple of hours will be crucial. Please feel free to make yourself at home. Or if you give us a number, we'll call . . .'

'I'm staying,' I said. Jack nodded in agreement.

The doctor left us. I sank into a waiting room seat, trying to keep my emotions in check. Jack sat down next to me. He put his arm around my shoulders.

'He's going to make it,' he said.

'This should never have happened . . .'

'It's not your fault.'

'Yes, it is. I shouldn't have left him to his own devices.'

'I'm not going to listen to you beat yourself up . . .'

'He's everything to me, Jack. *Everything*.'

I put my face into his shoulder. After a moment I said, 'That didn't come out the way I meant it to . . .'

'Sure. I understand.'

'Now I've hurt you.'

'Stop,' he said softly. 'You don't need to explain.'

By seven that morning, there was no further word on Eric's condition – except that he was out of the operating theater, and had been transferred to the intensive care unit. Jack offered to call in sick to work, but I insisted that he go to his office. He made me promise that I'd call him every hour with an update – even if there was no news.

As soon as he left, I stretched out on a sofa in the waiting room and passed right out. The next thing I knew, a nurse was shaking me. 'Miss Smythe, you can go see your brother now.'

I was instantly awake. 'Is he all right?'

'He lost a lot of blood, but he pulled through. Just.'

I was escorted through the emergency room to a dark, crowded public ward at the extreme rear of the hospital. Eric was in a bed at the end of a row of twenty beds. The noise was deafening – an endless discord of distressed patients, brusque orderlies, and people shouting to be heard over the ward's cavernous acoustic. Eric was groggy, but lucid. He was lying flat, a sheet pulled up to his neck, two large intravenous tubes of plasma and a clear viscous liquid disappearing under the covers. He said nothing for a moment or two. I kissed his forehead. I stroked his face. I tried not to cry. I failed.

'Now that's stupid,' he said in a thick, post-anaesthetic voice.

'What?'

'Crying – as if I was dead.'

'A couple of hours ago, you looked dead.'

'I feel it right now. Get me out of here, S.'

'In your dreams.'

'I mean . . . get me a room. NBC will pay . . .'

I didn't answer him – as it was pretty damn obvious that he was delirious.

'Get me a room,' he said again. 'NBC . . .'

'Let's not bring that up now,' I said, continuing to stroke his forehead.

'They never canceled my insurance . . .'

'What?'

'In my wallet . . .'

I nabbed a porter who found Eric's wallet (it had been locked away in the hospital safe after he was admitted – along with his watch and the seven dollars in cash that was his current net worth). In the wallet there was a Mutual Life card, on the back of which was a phone number. I called it – and discovered that Eric was still on the NBC corporate health and life plan.

'Yes, I have been able to dig out his file,' said the Mutual Life clerk with whom I spoke. 'And we are aware of the fact that Mr Smythe is no longer an NBC employee. But under the terms of this policy, his medical and life benefits remain in force until December thirty-first, nineteen fifty-two.'

'So I can have him moved to a private room in Roosevelt Hospital.'

'I'm afraid you can.'

Within an hour, Eric was relocated to a small, but reasonably pleasant room on an upper floor of the hospital. He was still deeply groggy.

'What? No view?' was his only comment about his new surroundings before he passed out again.

At four that afternoon, I called Jack and assured him that Eric was out of danger. Then I went home, and slept until morning. When I woke, I found Jack asleep beside me. I curled my arms around him. Tragedy had been averted. Eric had pulled through. And I had this extraordinary man in bed beside me.

'You are everything to me too,' I whispered. But he just snored on.

I got up, showered, dressed, and brought Jack breakfast in bed.

As always, he lit a cigarette after taking his first sip of coffee.

'How are you bearing up?' he asked.

'You know, the world always looks better after twelve hours of sleep.'

'Damn right. What time are you heading to the hospital?'

'In about a half-hour. Can you come with me?'

'I've got this early meeting in Newark . . .'

'No problem.'

'But give him my best. And tell him I'm here if he needs me for anything . . .'

On my way down to the hospital, the thought struck me that Jack had worked out his own way of dealing with my brother. Ever since the black-listing, he'd been scrupulously correct (and generous) towards Eric – but from a careful distance. He avoided having to deal with him face to face. I couldn't blame him . . . especially as he well knew that the FBI had his name as the man in my life. And I hugely admired the fact that he had, in his own quiet way, stuck by Eric throughout this crisis . . . whereas many people would have been terrified to even be vaguely associated with him.

Eric was awake when I reached the hospital. Though still gaunt and haggard, a minor hint of color had returned to his cheeks. And he was a bit more lucid than yesterday.

'Do I look as bad as I feel?'

'Yes. You do.'

'That's direct.'

'You deserve direct. What the hell were you trying to do?'

'Drink a lot.'

'And not eat at the same time?'

'Food takes up valuable boozing time.'

'You're lucky that Joey at the Ansonia was with you . . .'

'I really wanted to go, S.'

'Don't say that.'

'It's the truth. I couldn't see a way out . . .'

'I've told you over and over, you will get through this. But only if you let me help you through it.'

'I'm not worth the price you've paid . . .'

I rubbed my thumb and forefinger together.

'Know what this is? The world's smallest violin.'

He managed a smile. I took his hand. And said, 'What else do we have except life?'

'Booze.'

'Maybe – but I've got some bad news on that front. According to the doctor I spoke to on the way in here, your drinking days are over. Your duodenal is now hanging on by a thread. Given time, it should repair itself. But even after it heals, your stomach won't be able to handle booze anymore. Sorry to tell you this . . .'

'Not as sorry as me.'

'The doctor also said you're going to be in here for at least two weeks.'

'At least NBC has to pick up the tab.'

'Yes – that is rather gratifying'

'What about my little appearance in front of HUAC next week?'

'I'll get Joel Eberts to postpone it.'

'Permanently, if possible.'

As it turned out, Mr Eberts was only able to get a month-long postponement of the HUAC subpoena. During that time, Eric managed to dry out and recuperate. After his two-week stay at Roosevelt Hospital, I convinced him to let me rent us a cottage in Sagaponack. Back then, that corner of Long Island was still completely undeveloped. Sagaponack was a tiny fishing village – a real briny, ungentrified community of lobster boats and spit-on-the-floor bars and leathery-looking fishermen.

Even though it was only three hours by train from Manhattan, it felt completely remote. The place we rented was a simple weatherbeaten two-bedroom structure which fronted a vast empty beach. At first, Eric could only manage to sit in the sand, and stare out at the breaking waters of Long Island Sound. By the end of our two weeks there, he was walking a mile or so on the beach every day. Though he was on a strict bland diet (I became an expert at making macaroni-and-cheese), he still managed to put on a little weight. More tellingly, he started to sleep eight to ten hours a night. We did as little as possible during the day. There was a shelf of cheap detective novels in the cottage – which we devoured. There was no radio, no television. We didn't buy a newspaper during the entire two weeks of our stay. Eric let it be known that he wanted to cut himself off from the world beyond this beach. I had no objections to this plan. After the past few weeks, I too wanted to slam the door on that jumbled disorder called life. Of course, I missed Jack terribly. I'd invited him to come out for a few days – but he said he was currently overwhelmed at work . . . and the weekends were out because those days were sacrosanct for Dorothy and Charlie. There was no phone at the cottage. Instead, I would walk in to the village twice a week and wait in the post office for a call from Jack. The agreed time was three in the afternoon on Tuesdays and Thursdays. He was always prompt. The local postmistress also

601

ran the switchboard, and struck me as a deeply nosy type – so I was careful not to mention anything about the blacklist or Jack's family on the phone. If she was listening in (and I'm pretty sure she was), all she heard was two people missing each other terribly. But every time I suggested he try to pop out for just a day and a night, Jack was adamant that he was under far too much work pressure right now.

As it turned out, the two weeks passed in a delicious blur. On the night before we left, Eric and I planted ourselves on the beach to watch the sun dissolve into the Sound. As the beach was bathed in a malt whiskey haze of fading light, Eric said,

'At moments like this, I think to myself: it's cocktail time.'

'At least you're still here to see moments like this.'

'But moments like these are much better with a gin martini. In the coming weeks, I know I'm really going to miss alcohol.'

'Everything will be fine.'

'No. It won't. Four days from now, I face that fucking committee.'

'You'll survive it.'

'We'll see.'

The next morning we returned to the city. We reached Penn Station by noon and shared a cab uptown. I dropped Eric off at the Ansonia.

We agreed to meet for breakfast tomorrow at nine – after which I was going to accompany him downtown for a meeting with Joel Eberts.

'Do we really have to do this Eberts thing?' he asked me as the Ansonia's doorman took his bag out of the trunk.

'He's your lawyer. He's going to be with you when you face the committee on Friday. So it's best if he runs through with you some sort of strategy beforehand.'

'There's no strategy involved in taking the Fifth.'

'Let's worry about this tomorrow,' I said. 'Now go upstairs and call Ronnie. Where's he playing tonight?'

'I don't know. I've got his tour schedule buried somewhere.'

'Go find it – and make that call. I'm sure he's dying to hear from you.'

'Thank you for the last two weeks. We should do this more often.'

'We will.'

'You mean, after I get out of jail.'

I kissed him goodbye. I climbed back into the cab and rode the four blocks north to West 77th Street. I spent the afternoon sorting through my accumulated mail. There was a substantial package from *Saturday Night/Sunday Morning* – containing twenty letters from assorted readers, all of whom saw the notice in the magazine of my so-called sabbatical, and wished me a speedy return into print.

'I'm going to miss you,' a Miss M. Medford of South Falmouth, Maine, wrote me. I felt a sharp stab of loss when I read that. Because – though

I'd never say so in front of Eric or Jack – I desperately missed being in print.

Around four, I left the apartment and ran out for groceries. I was back just before five. Then minutes later, I heard a key turn in the front lock. I pulled open the door, I pulled Jack into the apartment. Within a minute, I had him in bed. Half an hour later, we finally spoke.

'I think I missed you,' I said.

'I think I missed you too.'

Eventually we got up. I made us dinner. We ate, we drank a bottle of Chianti, we went back to bed. I don't remember what time we fell asleep. I do remember waking with a jolt. Someone was ringing my doorbell. It took me a moment or two to realize that it was the middle of the night. Four eighteen, according to the bedside clock. The doorbell rang again. Jack stirred.

'What the hell . . .' he said groggily.

'I'll deal with it,' I said, putting on my robe and heading into the kitchen. I picked up the earpiece of the intercom. I pressed the talk button and muttered a sleepy 'Hello.'

'Is this Sara Smythe?' asked a gruff voice.

'Yes. Who are you?'

'Police. Could you please let us in.'

Oh no. Oh God, no.

For a moment or two, I was rooted to the spot, unable to move. Then I heard the gruff voice again in my ear.

'Miss Smythe . . . are you still there?'

I hit the button that opened the street door. A moment or two later, I heard a knock on my own door. But I couldn't bring myself to answer it. The knocking became louder. I heard Jack getting out of bed. He came into the kitchen, tying his robe around him He found me standing near the intercom, leaning my head against the wall.

'Jesus Christ, what's happened?' he said.

'Please answer the door,' I said.

The knocking was now insistent.

'Who the hell is there?'

'The police.'

He turned white. He walked out into the foyer. I heard him unlock the door.

'Is Sara Smythe here?' asked the same gruff voice I heard on the intercom.

'What's going on, officer?' asked Jack.

'We need to speak with Miss Smythe.'

A moment later, two uniformed policemen entered the kitchen. Jack was behind them. One of them approached me. He was around fifty, with a large soft face, and the vexed look of someone with bad news to impart.

'Are you Sara Smythe?' he asked.

I nodded.

'Do you have a brother named Eric?'

I didn't answer him. I just sank to the floor, crying.

CHAPTER 9

The police drove us downtown. I sat in the back of the car with Jack. My head was buried in his shoulder. He had both his arms around me. He held me so tightly it felt as if he was almost restraining me. I needed to be restrained – because I was on the verge of coming apart.

First light was creeping into the night sky as we headed east on 34th Street. No one in the car said anything. The two cops stared ahead at the rain-streaked windscreen, ignoring the crackling static of their two-way radio. Jack was doing his best to be silently supportive – but his sense of shock was palpable. I could hear the hammer-blow pounding of his heart against his chest. Maybe he was frightened I might start howling again – which is what I did with uncontrollable anguish after they told me the news. For around half an hour afterwards, I lay on my bed, the sheets gripped tightly against my chest. I was inconsolable. Whenever Jack tried to comfort me, I screamed at him to go away. I was so out of control – so desolate – that I could not bear the idea of anyone offering me comfort at a moment when I was beyond comfort, beyond solace. Eventually one of the cops asked me if I needed medical assistance. That's when I somehow managed to pull myself together, and got dressed. Jack and one of the cops each took an arm to help me out of the car – but I politely shrugged them off. As Eric himself would have said (wickedly imitating Father): a Smythe never falls apart in public. Even when she has just been given the worst possible news.

Now, I was too incapacitated to cry. The grief I felt was so infinite, so incalculable that it went beyond mere tears, or howls of anguish. I was devoid of speech, devoid of reason. All the way downtown, all I could do was lay my head against Jack, and try to force myself to remain contained.

We turned south on Second Avenue for two blocks, then headed east again on 32nd Street until we pulled up at the side entrance of a squat brick building. Chiseled above its front door were the words: 'Office of the Medical Examiner of the City of New York'.

The police escorted us through a side entrance, marked: 'Deliveries'. Inside, there was an elderly black gentleman sitting behind a desk. He was the morgue's St Peter. When one of the officers leaned forward and said, 'Smythe,' the gentleman opened a large ledger, and ran his finger down a page until he stopped at my brother's name. Then he picked up a phone and dialed a number.

'Smythe,' he said quietly into the receiver. 'Cabinet fifty-eight.'

I felt myself getting precarious again. Sensing this, Jack put his arm around my waist. After a moment, a white-coated attendant came into this waiting area. 'You here to identify Smythe?' he asked tonelessly.

One of the cops nodded. The attendant motioned with his thumb to follow him. We trooped down a narrow corridor, painted an institutional green and lit by fluorescent tubes. We stopped in front of a metal door. He opened it. We were now in a small room, as refrigerated as a meat locker. There was a wall of numbered stainless-steel cabinets. The attendant walked over to Cabinet 58. One of the officers gently nudged me forward. Jack stood by my side. He tightened his grip on my arm. There was a long silent moment. The officers glanced awkwardly at me. The attendant began to absently drum his fingers against the steel door. Finally I took a long deep breath and nodded at the attendant.

The cabinet slid open with a long whoosh. My eyes snapped shut. After a moment I forced them open. Eric was lying before me – covered from the neck down by a rough white sheet. His eyes were closed. His skin seemed bleached. His lips had turned blue. He didn't look at peace. He simply looked lifeless. An empty shell that once was my brother.

I stifled a sob. I snapped my eyes shut again – because I couldn't bear to see him. Because I didn't want this final glimpse to be the one that haunted my thoughts forever.

'Is this Eric Smythe?' asked the attendant.

I nodded.

He pulled the sheet up over Eric's face, then shoved the gurney back into the cabinet. It closed with a thud. The attendant reached for a clipboard, hanging from a wall by a nail. He flipped through a few forms, found what he was looking for, and handed the clipboard to me.

'Sign at the bottom of the page, please,' he said, pulling a chewed-up pencil out of the breast pocket of his grubby white coat.

I signed. I returned the clipboard to him.

'What undertaker are you using?' he asked.

'I've no idea,' I said.

He pulled off a perforated edge of the form. It had the name Smythe on it, followed by a serial number. He held it out towards me.

'When you know who you're using, tell 'em to call us and quote this number. They know the drill.'

Jack pulled the slip of paper out of the attendant's hand.

'Understood,' he said, shoving the slip into his jacket pocket. 'Are we done here?'

'Yeah, we're done.'

The cops escorted us out. 'Can we drop you home?' one of them asked.

'I want to go to the Ansonia,' I said.

'We can do that later,' Jack said. 'What you need now is rest.'

'I'm going to the Ansonia,' I said. 'I want to see his apartment.'

'Sara, I don't think . . .'

'I am going to his apartment,' I said, barely containing my anger.

'Fine, fine,' Jack said, nodding to the officers. We got back into the police car. I managed to keep myself contained on the drive uptown. Jack looked exhausted and deeply preoccupied. Though he held my hand, he seemed absent. Or maybe that was because I felt as if I was in some sort of horrible reverie; a walking nightmare from which there was no escape.

At the Ansonia, Joey the night porter was still on duty. He was immediately solicitous. He found someone to cover for him at the front desk – and brought us into the bar.

'I know it's kind of early, but could you use a drink?'

'That would be good,' I said.

'Whiskey?'

Jack nodded. Joey brought over a bottle of cheap Scotch and two shot glasses. He filled them to the brim. Jack downed his in one go. I took a sip and nearly gagged. I took a second sip. The whiskey burned the back of my throat – like harsh, essential medicine. By the fourth sip the glass was empty. Joey refilled it, then topped up Jack's drink.

'Was it you who found him?' I asked.

'Yeah,' Joey said quietly. 'I found him. And . . . if I'd known, I'd never have allowed the delivery guy to . . .'

'What delivery guy?' I asked.

'A guy from the local liquor store. From what I can work out, your brother called the store late yesterday afternoon and asked them to deliver a couple of bottles of Canadian Club to his room. At least this is what Phil, the day man, told me. He was on duty when the guy from the liquor store showed up, asking for the number of your brother's apartment. If it'd been me at the desk, I would've called you right away – 'cause, after what happened a couple weeks ago, I knew he had problems with booze. Anyway, I came on around seven. Didn't see or hear from your brother until just after midnight, when he called me, sounding completely out of it. Like he was so gone, he was slurring his words. Couldn't understand a thing he said. So I got someone to cover for me and went upstairs. Must've knocked for around five minutes. No answer. So I went downstairs, got the pass key. When I opened the door . . .'

He broke off, sucked in his chest, exhaled. 'I tell ya, Miss Smythe. It wasn't pretty. He'd collapsed on the floor. Blood pumping out of his mouth. There was blood all over the phone too, which means he was hemorrhaging pretty bad when he called me. I was gonna phone you – but the situation was so bad I really felt like I had to wait for the ambulance. It didn't take 'em long to get here – ten minutes max. But by the time they arrived, he was gone. Then the cops showed up – and they took over. Telling me I couldn't call you – 'cause they had to break the news to you themselves.'

611

He reached for a glass, filled it with Scotch. 'Think I need a drink too,' he said, throwing it back. 'I can't tell you how bad I feel about all this.'

'It's not your fault,' Jack said.

'The two bottles of Canadian Club . . . were they empty?' I asked.

'Yeah – completely,' Joey said.

My mind clicked back to that morning in Roosevelt Hospital, when I told Eric that the doctor said he'd never be able to drink again. He took the news philosophically. Though he didn't articulate it, he seemed quietly pleased to be back in the land of the living. During our two weeks in Sagaponack, he really started putting himself back together. Hell, when I dropped him off here less than twenty-four hours ago, he was . . .

I stifled a sob. I put my head in my hands. Jack stroked my hair.

'It's okay,' he said softly.

'No, it's not,' I shouted. 'He killed himself.'

'You don't know that,' Jack said.

'He drank two bottles of Canadian Club, knowing full well his ulcer couldn't handle it. I warned him. The doctors warned him. He seemed so good yesterday on the train in from the Island. He really didn't worry me at all. But I obviously misread . . .'

I broke off and started to sob again. Jack put his arms around me and rocked me. 'Sorry, sorry,' I said.

'Don't blame yourself,' Jack said.

Joey coughed nervously. 'There's something else I've gotta tell you, Miss Smythe. Something Phil told me. Around three yesterday afternoon, your brother had a visitor. A guy in a suit, carrying a briefcase. He flashed some ID at Phil and said he was a federal process server. He asked Phil to phone your brother and summon him to the lobby – but not say who was here. So Phil did as ordered. Your brother came into the lobby, and the process server stuck a document into his hand and said something official like, "You are hereby served notice that blah, blah, blah." Phil couldn't hear it all. But he did say that your brother looked pretty stunned by what the guy was saying.'

'What happened after Eric was served the papers?' I asked.

'The suit left, and your brother headed back to his room. Around ninety minutes later, the delivery guy from the liquor store showed up.'

'Eric definitely didn't go out at any time?'

'Not according to Phil.'

'Then the papers must still be upstairs. Let's go.'

Joey looked hesitant. 'It's still a real mess, Miss Smythe. Maybe you should wait . . .'

'I can handle it,' I said, standing up.

'This is not a good idea,' Jack said.

'I'll be the judge of that,' I said, and walked out of the bar. Joey and Jack followed behind me. Joey stopped by the front desk and got a key for Apartment 512 from the wall of letter boxes behind the counter. We took the elevator up to the fifth floor. We walked to a scuffed door marked 512. Joey paused before inserting the key. 'Are you sure you want to go in there, Miss Smythe?' he asked.

'I'll be fine.'

'Let me go in,' Jack said.

'No. I want to see it.'

Joey shrugged and sprung the lock. The door drifted open. I stepped inside. I sucked in my breath. I had expected a stained bloody carpet. I wasn't prepared for the protracted dimensions of that stain. The blood was still wet and glistening. It covered the phone and dappled the furniture. There was the bloody outline of a hand on two of the walls, and on a table near to where Eric fell. The whole horrible sequence of my brother's final minutes suddenly came together in my head. He'd been sitting on the broken-down sofa, drinking. An empty bottle of Canadian Club was on the floor by the cheap little television. The second bottle – drained, except for a finger or two of liquid – stood on the low wood-laminated coffee table. There was a blood-splattered glass on the sofa. Eric must have started hemorrhaging while finishing the final bottle. Frightened, he covered his mouth with his hand (the reason for all the bloody hand prints). Then he staggered to the phone, and called Joey. But he was too incoherent from the Canadian Club (and from the shock of bleeding) to say anything. He dropped the phone. He fell towards the folding card table that served as his desk. He leaned against it for support. He collapsed to the floor. And died immediately. Or, at least, that's what I desperately hoped. Because I couldn't bear the thought of Eric in extended pain.

I couldn't stare at the stain for long. My eyes moved towards the card table. An official-looking document was wedged under an ashtray. It too was speckled with blood. I pulled it out. I stared at it. It was a notice from the Internal Revenue Service, informing Eric that he was to be subjected to an audit – and that, based on the income information they had received from the National Broadcasting Company, they were now demanding an immediate payment of $43,545 to cover three years of back tax. The letter also stated that, if he wanted to contest this demand, he would have thirty days to present the proper certified accounts to his local IRS office, in order to appeal the specified sum. However, were he to ignore this deadline for appeal, and/or fail to pay the specified sum, he would be subject to criminal prosecution, imprisonment and confiscation of his property.

Forty-three thousand five hundred and forty-five dollars. No wonder he ordered in those two bottles of Canadian Club. If only he'd phoned me. I would have rented a car and driven him to Canada. Or I could have given him enough money to fly to Mexico and survive for a couple of months. But he panicked and succumbed to fear. Or maybe he just couldn't face the thought of another trial after the HUAC trial – followed by imprisonment, bankruptcy, and years thereafter of trying to chip away at that debt.

The letter shook in my hand. Jack was immediately at my side, steadying me. 'The bastards,' I said. 'The bastards.'

He took the paper from me and scanned it. 'God,' he said. 'How could they have done that?'

'How? How?' I said, sounding unhinged. 'It's easy. Had Eric cooperated and named names, this demand never would have been served on him. But if you don't play ball with those shits, they'll do everything possible to destroy you. *Everything*.'

I started to cry again. I buried my head in Jack's shoulder.

'I'm sorry,' he said. 'I'm so damn sorry . . .'

I felt another hand on my shoulder. It was Joey. 'Let's get you guys out of here,' he said softly. 'You don't want to look at this no more.'

We somehow made it to the elevator and back to the bar. Joey left us the whiskey and a couple of glasses. Jack poured us two shots. I was descending into deeper shock – to the point where my hands were starting to shake. The whiskey helped. For the eighth time that night, I pulled myself together. Jack was slumped in an armchair, staring ahead. I reached for his hand.

'Are you okay?' I asked.

'Just overwhelmed. And guilty that . . .'

He hesitated.

'Yes?'

'Guilty that I never really got on with Eric.'

'It happens.'

'I should've tried harder. I should've . . .'

He broke off, on the verge of sobbing. People always surprise you at the strangest moments. Here was Jack – who never really liked my brother – in tears over his death. That's the thing about a genuine tragedy. It reminds everyone that all the arguments we have with each other are ultimately pointless. Death silences the quarrel – and we're suddenly left with the realization that our dispute with the other person had a built-in obsolescence; that, like everything we do, it was of the moment. And that moment – that sliver of time we call life – counts for nothing. Yet we still have the arguments, the quarrels, the rancor, the anguish, the jealousy, the resentment . . . the splenetic underside which shadows everyone's existence. We live this way – even though we know it will all end; that, somehow, everything is doomed. Maybe that's the real point of anger – it's the way we rage against our complete insignificance. Anger gives consequence to that which is fundamentally inconsequential. Anger makes us believe we're not going to die.

We drank some more whiskey. It had its beneficial effects. We said nothing for a while. We just sat in that empty bar as it gradually became flooded with morning light. Eventually I spoke.

'I have to tell Ronnie.'

'Yeah,' Jack said. 'I was thinking that. Do you want me to handle it?'

617

'No. He has to hear it from me.'

I asked Joey to go upstairs and root around Eric's papers, to find Ronnie's touring schedule. He discovered it on the same table where I found the IRS demand. Ronnie was playing in Houston that night. I waited until noon to call him – by which time I was back in my apartment, and had already begun to make arrangements for the funeral in a few days' time. Ronnie was groggy when he answered the phone. He seemed surprised to hear from me, and instantly worried.

'You sound bad,' he said.

'I am bad, Ronnie.'

'It's Eric, isn't it?' he asked in a hushed voice.

And that's when I told him. I tried to keep it as simple as possible – because I knew I'd start falling apart again if I got into too much detail. There was a long silence when I finished.

'Ronnie . . . you okay?' I finally asked.

Another silence.

'Why didn't he call me?' he asked, his voice barely audible. 'Or you?'

'I don't know. Or maybe I do know, and I don't want to say . . .'

'He loved you more than . . .'

'Please, Ronnie. Stop. I can't deal with . . .'

'Okay, okay.'

Another silence.

'You still there?' I asked.

'Oh Jesus, Sara . . .'

He started crying. Suddenly, the phone went

dead. Half-an-hour later, he called back. He sounded shaky, but under control.

'Sorry I hung up,' he said. 'I just couldn't . . .'

'No need to explain,' I said. 'You better now?'

'No,' he said, sounding flat. 'I'll never get over this.'

'I know,' I said. 'I know.'

'I really did love him.'

'And he you, Ronnie.'

I could hear him swallowing hard, trying not to cry. Why is it that we always try to be brave at moments when bravery is futile?

'I don't know what to say,' Ronnie said. 'I can't make sense of this.'

'Then don't. The funeral's the day after tomorrow. Can you make it?'

'No way. Basie's a strict operator. He'd let you off work if it was your mother who died. But flying back to New York for a friend's funeral? No way. And people might start asking questions about the type of friend Eric was.'

'Don't worry about it.'

'I will worry about it. I want to be there. I should be there.'

'Call me when you're back in the city. Call me anytime.'

'Thanks.'

'You take care.'

'You too. Sara?'

'Yes?'

'What am I going to do?'

I knew what I was going to do. After I put down the phone, I careened into the bedroom, collapsed across the bed, and let go. I must have cried for a solid hour. Jack tried to comfort me, but I screamed at him to go away. I needed to do this – to weep my heart out; to surrender to the sheer terribleness of what had happened.

There are moments when you think you will cry forever. You never do. Eventually, sheer physical exhaustion forces you to stop, to settle, to becalm yourself amidst all the mad turbulence of bereavement. And so, after an hour (maybe even ninety minutes – I had lost all track of time), I forced myself up from the bed. I took off all my clothes, letting them drop to the floor. I ran a bath. I made it as hot as I could tolerate. Wincing as I slid into it, my body quickly adjusted to its warmth. I took a face cloth. I dunked it in the water. I wrung it out. I draped it across my face. I kept it there for the next hour, as I floated in the hot water and tried to empty my mind of everything. Jack wisely didn't come in to see how I was. He kept his distance. When I eventually emerged from the bath – covered in a robe, with a towel around my hair – he didn't try to hug me, nor did he say anything inane like, 'Feeling better, dear?' He was smart enough to realize that I shouldn't be crowded right now.

Instead, he asked, 'Hungry?'

I shook my head. I sat down on the sofa. 'Come here,' I said.

He joined me. I took his face in my hands. I said nothing. I simply looked at him for a very long time. He didn't say anything. He didn't ask what I was thinking. Maybe he knew. *You are everything I have now. Everything.*

Eric's funeral took place two days later. It was held at the Riverside Funeral Home on Amsterdam and 75th Street. Only a dozen people showed up: Jack and Meg, Joel Eberts, a handful of friends from Eric's theater days, a classmate or two from Columbia. Nobody from NBC made an appearance. Marty Manning did send a wreath, and a note to me, in which he said that Eric wasn't just a brilliant writer of comedy, but a true mensch . . . and someone who didn't deserve the fate that had befallen him:

'*We live in strange times,*' Manning wrote, '*when a man as funny and gentle as your brother is bullied into despair. Everyone on the show loved him. We all wish we could be there Monday to say a proper goodbye – but Monday is our big rehearsal day. And as Eric himself would have said, "The show must go on." Please know you're in our thoughts . . .*'

I knew full well (from Eric) that Monday was just the first readthrough of that week's script – and that it never really started until around eleven in the morning. Had Manning and Company wanted to, they could have easily made the ten a.m. service at the Riverside. But I understood their reluctance to make an appearance at the funeral. Just as I understood the subtext of the line about Eric being bullied into despair. Like everyone else, Manning and his team were terrified of the same fate befalling them. And I was pretty damn certain that a directive came from Ira Ross and the brass on the forty-third floor that no NBC personnel should attend the funeral, just in case the FBI had decided to post a man at the door to take down the names of anyone who dared to show solidarity with Eric.

As it turned out, Mr Hoover and his associates reckoned that my dead brother was no longer a threat to national security – so unless they had the Riverside Chapel covertly staked out, I could detect no sign of FBI presence. Instead, the dozen mourners who dared to show their faces sat together in the first two rows as a Unitarian minister made a series of telling comments about Eric's integrity, his sense of conscience, his courage. The minister's name was Roger Webb. The funeral home had recommended him when I said that Eric was, in essence, a non-believer ('Then this Unitarian reverend is the guy for you,' the funeral director told me). I had expected some bored man-of-the-cloth who would say a few prayers, mutter a couple of platitudes, and be glancing at his watch during the entire service. But Roger Webb was young, earnest and actually nice. He made a point of calling me a day before the funeral and asking a lot of questions about Eric. I suggested that he come over to my apartment to talk things through. He showed up a few hours later – a baby-faced thirty-year-old from Columbus, Ohio. From a few passing comments he made as we sipped a cup of coffee, I sensed that he was good news – and, like most Unitarians, liberal in temperament. So I opened up, telling him exactly what had befallen Eric – and the admirable, but self-destructive choice he made when he refused to name names. I also risked mentioning his involvement with Ronnie.

He listened in silence. Then he finally said, 'Your brother sounds like he was a remarkable man. And a total original.'

I felt my throat tightening. 'Yes,' I said. 'He was definitely that.'

'We're actually scared of originality in this country. Of course, we spout on about rugged individualism, and all that John Wayne nonsense. But, at heart, we're a nation of Babbitts. "Don't rock the boat, don't step outside the social norm, don't question the system, be a team player, a company man." If you don't conform, God help you.'

'You sound like Eric.'

'I'm certain your brother would have put it in a smarter, wittier fashion that I just did. I'm a huge fan of *The Marty Manning Show*.'

'I want you to speak your mind at the service, if that's all right with you.'

'No one can really speak their mind these days – because it may be taken down and used against you. But there are ways of getting the message across.'

The next morning, Roger Webb stood to the left of my brother's coffin and addressed the sparse assembly of twelve mourners. He talked about choice.

'Choice defines us. Choice forces us to confront our true nature – our aspirations, our fears, our ethical fibre. Often in life, we make the wrong choice. Or, in the case of Eric, we do something quietly heroic – we make the right choice, even though we know it is that choice which will undermine all that we have created in life. Eric was faced with an appalling decision. Should he harm others to save himself? It is the sort of choice that illuminates an individual's conscience. Had Eric opted to save himself, his would have been an understandable decision – because, after all, the instinct towards self-preservation is a huge one. And personally speaking, I don't know what I would have done if I had been presented with the choice Eric had to make. For that reason, I hope we can all find understanding in our hearts for those who have recently had to face such a choice – and, for whatever reason, could not sum up the same level of selflessness which Eric did. Forgiveness is one of the hardest things in life – and possibly the most crucial. Eric did something supremely courageous. But those who did otherwise should not be condemned outright. This is a curious moment in American life – and one which, I sense, will come to be viewed in retrospect as a foul, demagogic juncture in our collective history. I hope we can all find the courage to understand the moral pressures which have engulfed so many of us – to salute Eric Smythe's bravery and mettle, yet to also show empathy for those who felt it necessary to make equally difficult, but more self-preserving choices.

'Being a minister, I should probably underpin such a sermon with a line from the Bible. But being a Unitarian, I can also get away with invoking poetry – specifically, a few lines from Swinburne. "Sleep; and if life was bitter to thee, pardon, If sweet, give thanks; thou hast no more to live; And to give thanks is good, and to forgive."'

Next to me, Jack buried his face in his hands. Meg started to sob. So too did most of the other mourners. But I simply stared ahead at the coffin, appalled that this was actually happening. Maybe it was the stark sight of that simple pine box – and the realization that my brother was inside it. Or maybe it was the knowledge that everything you do in life is reduced to this – that this is your ultimate destiny. Whatever the reason, I was too numb to cry; too deadened by the shock of the past few days.

We said the Lord's Prayer. We asked that our trespasses be forgiven, as we (allegedly) forgave those who trespassed against us. We sang a single hymn, 'A Mighty Fortress Is Our God' – chosen not because of its uplifting Lutheran message, but because Eric once told me it was the one hymn he could never get out of his atheistic head from all those Sundays that our parents dragged us to church. Roger Webb gave a final benediction, asking us to go in peace. The undertakers wheeled the coffin down the aisle. We followed, streaming out into a perfect spring day. There was much hugging and dabbing of eyes among the mourners as the coffin was loaded into the back of the hearse. People began to say their goodbyes. Only four of us – Jack, Joel Eberts, Roger Webb and myself – were going to accompany Eric to the crematorium in Queens. I wanted it this way – because I knew that all eyes would be on me as the coffin disappeared into the furnace, and I needed these final moments to be private ones.

We traveled out in a long black limousine. It trailed the hearse. We got stuck in a massive traffic jam on the Queensboro Bridge. There had been an accident up ahead. Everyone began to lean on their horns. None of us had spoken since leaving the funeral home. Roger Webb broke the silence.

'Looks like we're going to be a little late,' he said absently.

'I think they'll wait for us,' Joel Eberts said, and I found myself giggling for the first time in days.

'Eric would have loved this,' I said over the din of car horns. 'The perfect New York send-off. Even though he never really liked Queens.'

'No one from Manhattan likes Queens, the Bronx or Brooklyn,' Joel Eberts said. 'The problem is, when you're dead – Manhattan doesn't want you anymore. So you inevitably end up being shipped to Queens, the Bronx or Brooklyn. I think that's called "irony".'

'Did your brother specify cremation in his will?' Roger Webb asked.

'There was no will,' Joel Eberts said.

'Predictably,' I said. 'Eric was anti-efficient. Not that there was any estate to speak of. Even if there was, those bastards in the IRS would swallow it whole. No doubt, they'll now try to put some sort of lien on the few odds-and-ends he left behind.'

'That's another day's work, Sara,' Joel Eberts said.

'Yeah, I guess it is,' I said wearily.

'Joel's right,' Jack said, squeezing my hand. 'One thing at a time. You've been through enough.'

'And it's not over yet,' I said bleakly.

'That was a hell of a good sermon, Reverend,' Joel Eberts said. 'But I've got to tell you something – though I think turning the other cheek is a noble, high-minded idea, putting it into practice is goddamn impossible . . . 'scuse my French.'

'I'm a Unitarian – so you can use "goddamn" all you like,' Roger Webb said with a smile. 'But you're right. "Turning the other cheek" is a Christian idea. And like most ideals – especially Christian ones – it's exceptionally difficult to live up to. But we must try.'

'Even in the face of out-and-out betrayal?' Joel Eberts asked. 'Sorry – but I believe there's a cause-and-effect to our actions. If you risk doing *a*, then *b* will inevitably happen. The problem is – most people think that they can dodge the consequences of *b*. They can't. Things always catch up with you.'

'Isn't that a rather Old Testament view of morality?' Roger Webb asked.

'Hey – I'm Jewish,' Joel Eberts said. 'Of course I take an Old Testament line on such things. You make a choice, you make a decision. You live with the ramifications.'

'So, in your book, there's no such thing as absolution?' Jack asked.

'Spoken like a good Catholic,' Joel Eberts said. 'That's the big difference between the Irish and the Jews. Though we both wallow in guilt, you guys are always chasing absolution. You're always working the forgiveness angle. Whereas we Jews go to our graves blaming ourselves for *everything*.'

The traffic eventually started moving. Within ten minutes, we were at the gates of the cemetery. We all fell silent again. We followed the paved road, past row after row of graves. Finally, after acres of headstones, we reached a squat stone building, topped by a long narrow chimney. The hearse bypassed the front entrance, and headed toward the rear of the crematorium. We stopped by the entrance. The limousine driver turned back to us and said, 'We'll wait here until somebody comes out and tells us they're ready.'

Ten minutes later, a greying gentleman in a dark suit emerged from the doors of the crematorium and nodded towards us. We went inside. The chapel was a small, simple room – with five rows of pews. Eric's coffin was on a bier, to the right of the altar. We filed down to the front row. As previously agreed between us, Roger Webb did not offer a final prayer. Or a final benediction. He simply read a single passage from the Book of Revelations:

And God shall wipe away all tears from their eyes; and there shall be no more death, neither sorrow, nor crying, neither shall there be any more pain: for the former things are passed away.

I didn't believe a word of that Biblical passage. Nor did my late brother. Nor, I sensed, did Roger Webb. But I'd always loved the sentiment behind those lines: the idea of an eternity without anguish or adversity; a celestial pay-off for the vicissitudes of life. Roger Webb spoke the lines beautifully. So beautifully that I felt a small sob catch in my throat. A moment later, I heard the clank of machinery. A curtain behind the bier opened, and a belt beneath the coffin rolled it towards the furnace. Immediately, I stiffened. Immediately, Jack took my hand. And held it tightly.

The curtains closed. The funeral director opened the chapel doors. We left – and rode back to the city in silence.

When we reached my apartment, Jack offered to stay with me for another night. But that would have made five nights in a row – and though he didn't say anything, I was certain that Dorothy was getting rather anxious about his extended absence from home. I didn't want to do anything that upset the equilibrium which had been established between his two households, so I insisted he return to his family.

'I'll tell you what,' he said. 'I'll take the rest of the week off work, and be with you all day tomorrow.'

'You can't do that,' I said. 'And you know it. You've already taken half of last week off.'

'You are more important.'

'No,' I said, taking him in my arms. 'I'm not. You've got a job to be getting on with. Don't risk it for me. I'll be all right.'

He promised to call me twice a day, every day. The first call of the next morning, however, came from the Riverside Funeral Home. Eric's ashes had arrived back from the crematorium. Would I be home this morning to receive them?

An hour later, the doorbell rang. It was a gentleman in a dark suit and a Homburg. With a slight bow, he asked me my name, then handed me a small box, wrapped in brown paper. I brought it inside, placed it on my kitchen table, and stared at it for a very long time, not wanting to open it. Eventually, I got up enough nerve to tear off the paper. I hadn't requested an urn – so the remains of my brother were returned to me in a square cardboard box. The box was painted grey, with a marbleized finish. A simple white card adorned its cover. On it was written: *Eric Smythe*. I admired the calligraphy. It was most impressive.

I stopped myself from raising the cover and peeking inside. Instead, I stood up, grabbed my raincoat, and placed the box in one of its pockets. Then I left my apartment and walked down Broadway to the 72nd Street subway station.

I knew where I was going. I had chosen the venue days earlier – when pondering (in the few lucid moments I'd had since Eric's death) where he might like his ashes sprinkled. Though the Hudson River was convenient to us, I knew he'd object to the idea of ending up anywhere in the vicinity of New Jersey – as he made ceaseless jokes about the Garden State (once when I suggested an outing to Princeton and environs, he tartly said, 'Sorry – I don't do Jersey').

The East River was also struck off my list of possibilities – as it had no associations for him whatsoever. Nor did Central Park – because, at heart, my ultra-urban and urbane brother didn't really think much of greenery or wide open spaces. He loved the jangled chaos of city streets, the snarled traffic, the edgy ambulation of crowds, the sheer manic brio of Manhattan. Part of me wanted to scatter him on 42nd Street – but that seemed just a little too bleak. Then the idea hit me. Though Eric had no affinity with verdancy or lush terrain, he did spend a considerable amount of time in that most citified and gritty of public spaces: Washington Square Park. During all those years he lived in the Village, it was his outer office: a place in which he'd loiter for hours on a park bench with a novel, or take on the chess hustlers who occupied the northeastern corner of the park.

631

He often spoke about how much he loved the park's egalitarian rough-and-tumble, not to mention the ragtag collection of New York characters who gathered within its confines every day.

'I sit in this park,' he once told me, 'and I know why the hell I walked out of Hartford and never looked back.'

So now he would permanently commingle with the habitués of his favorite open-air bolthole.

Of course, I couldn't take a cab downtown. Though Eric might have gotten very free and easy with money in his final years, he would have loved the idea of heading to his final resting place for a nickel on the subway. Nor was I going to bring anyone along to help me scatter the ashes. This was my last moment with my brother. I wanted it to be a private one.

So I slipped a token in the turnstile on 72nd Street, and caught the No. 1 train south. It was ten o'clock. Rush hour was over – but it was still crowded. There were no seats, so I stood, holding on to a strap. Someone bumped into me. Instantly, my hand went down to my pocket. A wicked thought crossed my mind: imagine if it had been a pickpocket, and he had stolen the box. The poor thief would have suffered a coronary when he saw what he'd lifted.

I stood all the way downtown. I got off at Sheridan Square, and started heading east. I made a detour down Bedford Street – the location of my first apartment in Manhattan. I strolled on to Sullivan

Street, and walked past the door of the brownstone in which Eric had lived for over a decade. I thought back to those years in the Village. I wondered if Eric would still be alive if he hadn't achieved such esteem. If he hadn't been such a high-profile writer in such a high-profile new medium, would the Feds have ignored him? No amount of success was worth the price my brother had paid. None at all.

When I reached Washington Square Park, the sun was at full wattage. There were a couple of drunks asleep on the benches. There were two young sharpies hustling chess. There were a couple of NYU students breaking the 'Don't Sit on the Grass' rules. There was an organ grinder, with a pet monkey on his shoulder. As he cranked his machine, it churned out a honky-tonk version of 'La donna è mobile' from *Rigoletto*. Eric would have approved – both of the Verdi and the eccentric instrumentalist churning out this final musical send-off. I looked up into the cloudless sky, and was pleased that the wind had decided to absent itself today. I took the box out of my pocket. I removed the cover. I stared down into the chalky white powder. I started to walk around the little path that circumnavigated the entire park – a ten-minute journey at the absolute maximum. Every few yards, I took a handful of ashes and scattered them on the path. I didn't look up to see if anyone was noticing what I was doing. I paced myself, making certain that I did the complete circuit of the park. When I reached the Fifth Avenue gate again, the box was empty. Eric was gone. Then I turned north and started walking uptown.

I walked all the way home. The next day I walked down Broadway straight to Battery Park. A day or so later (my calendrical sense had vanished), I headed north, ending up at the Cloisters in Fort George Park. As promised, Jack called twice a day, deeply concerned about my emotional state. I told him I was fine. He had been called out of town to Wilmington and Baltimore – and felt guilty about not being there with me.

'You don't have to worry about me at all,' I said. 'I'm coping.'

'Are you sure?'

'There's nothing to worry about,' I lied.

'I miss you. Desperately.'

'You're the best, Jack. I couldn't have gotten through this without you.'

But I wasn't getting through this. I'd stopped sleeping. My diet consisted of saltines, tins of Campbell's Tomato Soup, and non-stop coffee. And I was spending eight hours a day walking, killing the rest of the time at double-features in the big picture palaces that lined Broadway. Like my brother in the weeks after he was fired, I too had become a professional drifter.

A week after the funeral, I received a phone call from Joel Eberts. He sounded preoccupied.

'You free this morning?' he asked.

'Since being suspended with pay, I'm a woman of leisure.'

'Then drop by the office. There are one or two things I need to go over with you.'

I was there an hour later. Joel seemed unusually edgy. He gave me a fast paternal hug, and told me I looked tired. Then he motioned for me to sit in the chair opposite his desk. He picked up a file marked 'Eric Smythe' and started rifling through it.

'There are a couple of things we need to discuss. The first is – the matter of his insurance policy.'

'His *what*?'

'Eric, as it turns out, had his life insured by NBC. It was part of the medical cover which paid for his bills after his hospitalization last month. As we know, the network hadn't canceled his medical policy after sacking him. What I've since discovered is that the bastards also never canceled his life cover. What's more, last year, when everyone at NBC thought he was the best thing since sliced bread – and, more to the point, commercially valuable – they upped his life insurance to seventy-five thousand dollars.'

'Good God.'

'Yeah – it's a hell of a chunk of change. And it all goes to you.'

'You can't be serious.'

'Well, let's say around half of it will end up in your bank. The other half, I'm afraid, will fall into the hands of the IRS. I know their actual demand is around forty-three thousand . . . but I've got a good tax guy I use – a tough s.o.b. I've talked through this case with him, and he's pretty sure he can get their demand shaved down by around seven to ten grand. Still, that's around thirty-five thousand to you . . . which ain't bad.'

'I don't believe it.'

'Eric would've been pleased, knowing it was going to you.'

'But without a will, who's to say it will go to me?'

'You're his only extant family member. There are no other siblings, right? We'll have to jump a few standard legal hurdles. But, trust me, it'll be a cinch. The money is yours.'

I sat there, saying nothing. Because I didn't know what to say. Joel Eberts sat opposite me, studying me with care.

'So that's the good news,' he said.

'By which you mean . . .'

He hesitated, then said, 'There is something else I want to talk with you about.'

I was worried by his tone. 'Something serious?' I asked.

'I'm afraid so, yes.'

Another apprehensive pause. Joel Eberts was never apprehensive.

'Sara,' he said, leaning forward. 'I need to ask you a question.'

'All right,' I said, my anxiety rising. 'Ask.'

'Say I told you . . .'

He broke off. He looked supremely uncomfortable.

'What's wrong, Joel?'

'Part of me doesn't really want to go into this.'

'Go into *what*?'

'The question I have to ask you.'

'Ask it.'

He paused.

'All right. Here it is. Say I told you that I knew the name of the individual who named your brother to the FBI . . .'

'You *do*?' I said loudly.

He held his hand up.

'One thing at a time. Say I did know. The question is . . . and I really think you should consider this carefully: would you want to know that individual's name?'

'Are you kidding me? *Absolutely*. So tell me. Who was the shit . . . ?'

'Sara . . . are you sure? Really sure?'

I suddenly felt very cold. But I still nodded. And said, 'I want to know.'

He stared directly at me, fixing me in his gaze.

'It was Jack Malone.'

CHAPTER 10

I couldn't move. I sat rigid in the chair, staring down at my hands. I felt as if I had just been kicked in the face.

Though I wasn't looking at him directly, I could feel Joel Eberts' gaze on me.

'Are you all right?' he asked.

I shook my head.

'I'm so damn sorry,' he said.

'You've known about this since . . . ?'

'The day after the funeral.'

'You waited this long to tell me?'

'I needed to check a lot of things out first. I really didn't want to hit you with this, until I was absolutely certain that it was true. Even then, I debated for days about whether to tell you . . .'

'You were right to tell me. I had to know this.'

He sighed a tired sigh.

'Yeah – I guess you did,' he said.

'How did you find out?'

'Lawyers talk to other lawyers who talk to other lawyers who talk to . . .'

'I don't follow you.'

'Ever heard of Marty Morrison?'

I shook my head.

'One of the biggest corporate lawyers in the city. Ever since this blacklist crap started, Marty's firm has handled a lot of people who've been called to testify by HUAC. 'Cause it's not just the entertainment business that's been investigated. The Feds have also been poking their noses into schools, colleges, even some of the biggest companies in America. As far as they're concerned, there's a Red under every bed.

'Anyway, Marty and I have known each other since Adam. He grew up two blocks from me in Flatbush. We were at Brooklyn Law together. Though he went the Wall Street way, we've always maintained the friendship. Of course, we're constantly giving each other crap about our political differences. I always say he's the only Republican I will ever break bread with. He still calls me Eugene Debs. But he's a straight shooter. Very well connected. Someone who knows where all the bodies are buried.

'He also happens to be a big Marty Manning fan. Around a year ago, we're having lunch one day, he gets talking about some sketch he saw the previous night on Manning's show. That's when I do a little bragging and tell him that Manning's head writer – Eric Smythe – happens to be my client. Marty was actually impressed . . . though, of course, he had to make a joke about it: "Since when the hell has a stevedore lawyer like you been representing writers?"

'That was the only mention of your brother. A year goes by. The stuff hits the fan with NBC. Eric refuses to do the dirty on his friends. He ends getting slimed in Winchell's column. The next day, Marty rings me here. "Saw the item about your client in Winchell," he tells me. "Tough call." Then he asks if there's anything he can do to help, because he knows all those assholes on the HUAC committee. He also thinks they're opportunistic trash – not that he'd ever admit that publicly.

'Anyway, I thanked Marty for the offer of help – but told him that your brother wasn't looking for a deal . . . and certainly wouldn't suddenly become a stoolie after all the damage that the Winchell piece had done. So, unfortunately, there was nothing he could do.

'Then, of course, four weeks later, Eric was dead. And . . .'

He stopped. He twitched his lips. He avoided my stare. 'What I'm about to say to you might really anger you. Because it was none of my business. But . . .'

He stopped again.

'Go on,' I said.

'I was so goddamn upset . . . *enraged* . . . after Eric died that I made a call to Marty. "You can do me a favor," I said. "Get me the name of the bastard who shopped my client." And he did.'

'Jack Malone?'

'Yeah: Jack Malone.'

'How did your friend find out?'

640

'It wasn't hard. According to Federal law, anything revealed under testimony at a HUAC hearing – or during an interview with an agent of the FBI – cannot be printed or publicly disseminated. But there are three former G-men – backed by this right-wing supermarket magnate named Alfred Kohlberg and some super-patriotic priest called Father John F. Cronin – who have set up a company called American Business Consultants. Their principle job – if you can believe this – is to scrutinize employees in major corporations, making sure they're not Reds. But they also publish two newsletters – *Counterattack* and *Red Channels*. These rags exist for one purpose only – to list the names of everyone who's been accused of being a Communist in a closed executive session of HUAC. Those two newsletters are the Blacklister's Bible: they're the place corporate America and the entertainment industry look to see who's been named. Naturally enough, Marty Morrison has a subscription to both of these shit sheets. He discovered that your brother had been listed in *Red Channels* – which is also how Eric's employers at NBC learned that he'd been named during testimony in front of HUAC.

'From there it was easy for Marty to call a couple of lawyers he knows around town – guys who've cornered the blacklisting market, making very big bucks representing people who've been dragged in front of HUAC. Of course, lawyers being lawyers, they're always exchanging notes with each other.

Marty hit pay dirt on the third call. A big white-shoe attorney named Bradford Ames – who, among other things, looks after the legal side of Steele and Sherwood. Ames owed Marty a favor. Marty cashed it in now.

'"Between ourselves, do you have any idea who might have named Eric Smythe?" Marty asked him. Of course, Ames had heard of your brother – because his blacklisting and his death had been all over the papers. "Between ourselves," he told Marty, "I know exactly the guy who shopped Smythe. Because I represented him when he testified in executive session at HUAC. The funny thing about this guy was that he wasn't in showbiz. He was a public relations guy with Steele and Sherwood. Jack Malone."'

My mind was reeling. 'Jack testified in front of HUAC?' I asked Joel.

'That's what appears to have happened.'

'I don't believe it, Jack's about the most loyal American imaginable.'

'According to Marty, he had a skeleton in his closet. A really small one – but even tiny skeletons get used against you nowadays. It turns out that, right before the war, Mr Malone put his name down for some Joint Anti-Fascist Refugee Committee . . . which was one of those organizations that was helping people fleeing from Nazi Germany and Italy and the Balkans. Anyway, as it turns out, the committee that Malone was associated with had direct links with the American Communist Party.

Brad Ames said that Malone swore up on a stack of Bibles that he was never a member of the Party . . . that a couple of Brooklyn friends of his had finagled him on to the committee . . . that he'd only gone to a couple of meetings, nothing more. The problem was – one of the guys who allegedly finagled him on to the committee had been sub-poenaed by HUAC. And he'd named Malone during his testimony. Which is how Jack Malone also ended up in the pages of *Red Channels* – and how his bosses at Steele and Sherwood found out about his accidental flirtation with subversion.

'Naturally enough, Malone sang "Yankee Doodle Dandy" in front of his employers – and said he'd do anything required to clear his name. They called their corporate attorney, Bradford Ames. He met Malone – and they talked things through. Ames then went to some guy on the committee – and did a bit of bartering. Which is how things work at HUAC. If the witness isn't hostile, the number of names – and the actual names them-selves – are agreed beforehand between the committee and the witness's attorney. Malone offered to name the same guy who named him. That wasn't enough for the committee. So he also offered to name three other people he knew on the committee. But the committee said, 'No sale' – as the guy who named Malone had also named those names as well.

'You've got to give them one new name,' Ames told him. 'Just one. Afterwards you tell them it was all a youthful mistake, and how you love America more than Kate Smith, blah, blah, blah. Then they'll exonerate you.'

'So that's when Malone said, "Eric Smythe." Naturally, Ames knew the name immediately – 'cause he too watched *Marty Manning*. He told Malone that he thought the committee would be satisfied with that name. Because Eric Smythe was a relatively big fish.

'A week later, Malone went down to Washington and testified in front of HUAC. It was an executive session – which meant that it was all behind closed doors, and not for the public record. So I suppose Malone thought that no one would ever know.

'But lawyers always talk.'

'*I'm sorry*,' Jack said when I first told him about Eric being named. '*I am so goddamn sorry . . . Tell him if there's anything . . . anything . . . I can do . . .*'

I remember leaning over to kiss him, and saying: '*You're a good man.*'

I saw him after Eric's death standing in that godawful room at the Ansonia, looking down at the bloodstain, then sobbing into my shoulder. Once again, he said, '*I'm sorry. I'm so damn sorry . . .*' Once again, I was so touched by his sense of emotional solidarity, of shared grief. *He was crying for Eric, for me – for the tragedy of it all*, I remember thinking later.

But now, it turns out it was guilt that was making him cry. Guilt and shame and remorse and . . .

I swallowed hard. My hands tightened into fists. Not only did he betray us . . . he cried about it.

'Did the committee exonerate Malone?' I asked.

Malone. Not Jack. He would never be Jack again. He'd now be *Malone*. The man who destroyed my brother.

'Of course,' Joel Eberts said. 'He was cleared completely. According to Marty, Steele and Sherwood was so pleased with the way he handled everything with HUAC, they slipped him a bonus.'

'You know, you really don't have to be doing this,' I'd said after he'd insisted on paying to have Eric's belongings moved, and for the paint job at the Ansonia.

'Hiring a couple of painters for two days isn't exactly going to break the bank,' he'd said. *'Anyway, I had a bit of a bonus windfall. Out of nowhere I was handed a commission check for over eight hundred dollars. It's Steele and Sherwood's way of saying thank you . . .'*

For naming names. For saving your own skin. For decimating Eric's life. For killing any love or trust between us. For ruining everything. All that for eight hundred dollars. At today's exchange rates, would that be the equivalent of thirty pieces of silver?

'So Malone doesn't have a clue that anyone knows he fingered Eric?' I asked.

'I doubt it. Sara, I said it once, I'll say it again: you don't know how bad I feel about this . . .'

'Why should you feel guilty?' I said, standing up. 'I thank you.'

'For what?'

'For telling me the truth. It couldn't have been an easy decision. But it was the right one.'

'What are you going to do about this, Sara?'

'There is nothing *to do*,' I said. 'It's *done*.'

I left his office. I stepped out into the street. I took two steps, then reached out for a nearby lamp post and held it tightly. No, I didn't break down. Or let out a scream of anguish. Instead, a second wave of shock ran through me. I gulped for air. My stomach heaved. I bent over and was sick in the street.

I retched until there was nothing left to retch. My body was drenched in sweat. I managed to right myself up. I found a tissue in my jacket pocket, and used it to dab my mouth. Then I worked up the strength to raise my right hand and hail a cab home.

When I reached my apartment, I walked into the living room, and sat down in an armchair. I stayed seated for what only seemed like minutes. When I glanced at my watch, however, I realized that more than an hour had gone by. The shock was still so penetrating that I wasn't conscious of time. Instead, I felt glazed, hollow – to the point where standard emotional responses seemed futile. I just sat there, blankly. Not knowing what to do.

Another hour went by. Then I heard a key in the lock. Jack walked in. He was fresh from a road trip, with a suitcase in one hand and a bouquet of flowers in the other.

'Hey there!' he said, putting down his suitcase and approaching me. I stared down at the floor. I suddenly couldn't stand the idea of looking at him. Instantly, he sensed that something was very wrong.

'Sara, darling . . .' he said.

I said nothing. He leaned over and tried to touch me. I shrugged him off. He now looked alarmed.

'What's happened?' he whispered, crouching down beside me.

'I want you to leave, Jack. Leave and never come back.'

He dropped the flowers. 'I don't understand,' he said, his voice now barely a whisper.

'Yes you do,' I said, standing up. 'Now go.'

'Sara, please,' he said. As I turned towards the bedroom, he put his hand on my shoulder. I turned on him.

'Never, *never* touch me again.'

'Why are you . . .'

'*Why? Why?* You know *why*, Jack. You just thought I would never find out.'

His face crumpled. He sat down on the sofa. He put his face in his hands. He didn't say anything for a very long time.

'Can I explain?' he finally asked.

'No. Because nothing you say matters anymore.'

'Sara, my love . . .'

'No terms of endearment. No explanations. No rationalizations. We have nothing to say to each other anymore.'

'You've got to hear me out.'

647

'No. I don't. There's the door. Use it.'

'Who told you?'

'Joel Eberts. He knew someone who knew the guy who represented you when you went in front of the committee. Joel said that – according to his lawyer friend – you put up no resistance. You sang on the spot.'

'I had no choice. *None.*'

'Everyone has a choice. You made yours. Now you have to live with it.'

'They had me in a corner, Sara. I was going to lose . . .'

'What? Your job? Your income? Your professional standing?'

'I have a kid. I have to pay the rent. I have to put food on the table.'

'Everyone has to do that. Eric had to do that.'

'Look, the last thing I wanted to do was hurt your brother.'

'But you still gave his name to the FBI and the House UnAmerican Activities Committee.'

'I thought . . .'

'What? That the Feds would let him off with a warning?'

'Someone gave them my name. They insisted I give them names.'

'You could have said no.'

'Don't you think I wanted to?'

'But you didn't.'

'There was no way out. If I refused to give names, I'd lose my job. But then someone else would come along and name the people I named.'

'But that would have been someone else, *not you.*'

'I had to put my responsibilities first . . .'

'Responsibilities to whom, Jack?'

'To Dorothy and Charlie.'

'But not to me? Or to my completely innocent brother? Or were we simply expendable?'

'You know I don't think that.'

'I don't know you anymore.'

'Don't say that, Sara.'

'Why not? It's the truth. You've destroyed everything.'

My voice remained somehow controlled. Jack buried his head deeper in his hands. He fell silent again. When he finally spoke, his voice sounded diminished, small.

'Please try to understand: they insisted, *demanded*, that I give them a name. Believe me, I tried to explain that I had never been a Communist; that I had joined that anti-Fascist committee when I was a kid of eighteen, and only because I believed it was making a principled stand against Hitler, Mussolini and Franco. The FBI guys said they understood that. Just as they also knew that I had served my country in the war – and hadn't dabbled in politics since then. As far as they were concerned, I was a "good American" who'd made a small youthful mistake. Other people who were on that committee had also made mistakes – and in a demonstration of their patriotism, they had given the names of those who were associated with this group at the time, or had once had Communist sympathies.

'"They're probably as innocent as you are," one of the Fed guys told me. "But you must understand: we are investigating a vast conspiracy which poses a threat to national security. We simply need to discover who is at the heart of the conspiracy. Which is why we need names. By giving us information not only are you doing a service to your country; you are also eliminating yourself from our investigations. But by refusing to assist us, the cloud of suspicion still hovers over you. Face fact, anyone who's been a Communist in the past is going to get found out. So you might as well make a clean breast of everything . . . while you still can."'

Jack paused again. He lifted his head up, attempting to look me in the eye. But I turned away.

'Their argument had a ruthless logic to it. Someone had named me. I would prove my innocence by naming someone else. They, in turn, would prove their innocence by naming someone else. Everyone was betraying each other. But the thing about this betrayal was – no one had a choice.'

'Yes, they did,' I said, suddenly angry. 'The Hollywood Ten had a choice – they all went to jail. Arthur Miller had a choice: he refused to name names. *My brother* had a choice . . . and he lost his life.'

Jack's head went back into his hands.

'I tried to give them just the names of the other people on the committee. "That's not good enough," they told me. "We already know everyone who was with you back then. What we need is someone else." I told them I didn't know any other Communists. They wouldn't buy that. "Everyone knows a one-time Commie." I said I hated the idea of hurting someone else. "You're hurting nobody," they told me. "As long as he owns up to his past and agrees to cooperate with us, no harm will come to him." Again, I tried to convince them that the only Communists I knew were on that committee, and that was over a decade ago. But they were adamant. I had to give them one new name. Otherwise . . .

'So, I had a problem. I had to give them an ex-Communist. But I didn't know any ex-Communists.'

'Except my brother.'

'I was desperate. But the way I put it to the Feds, I told them: "Look, the only guy I know who may have a connection with the Party quit so long ago, it's irrelevant." They said, "Then he can exonerate himself, just like you're about to do."'

'So, that's when you gave them Eric's name.'

'Sara, *darling* . . . given his high-profile status in the television business, he was bound to get rumbled for his political past sooner or later. Surely you can see that.'

'Oh yes – I do see that. And, quite frankly, ever since all this godawful blacklisting business started,

I knew that, eventually, Eric's very brief flirtation with the Party would catch up with him. What I did not expect was that the man I once loved would turn out to be the snitch, the Judas.'

Long pause.

'*Once loved?* he asked.

'Yes. Once. No more.'

He looked up at me, devastated.

'Never for a moment did I want to harm him,' he said. 'And I figured that, like everybody else, he'd also play the game.'

'Fortunately, Eric had something called *a conscience.*'

'You don't think I don't have a conscience?' he said, now on his feet, his voice loud with edgy despair. 'You don't think I haven't been haunted by what happened to Eric?'

'You played along so brilliantly after he was fired, didn't you? You should have been an actor. You were so utterly sympathetic and supportive. You couldn't do enough for the guy.'

'That wasn't playing along. That was . . .'

'I know. Guilt and anguish and penitential shame. You're the perfect Catholic. I bet you even went to confession after you shopped him.'

'I never, *never* expected him to fall apart . . .'

'So that made it all right to name him?'

'Please try to understand . . .'

'There is *nothing* to understand . . .'

'I didn't mean harm.'

'But you *did* harm.'

'I just didn't know . . .'

I stared at him.

'What did you just say?' I asked quietly.

He took a short intake of breath.

'I said, "I didn't know".'

'*Ich habe nichts davon gewußt*,' I said.

'What?'

'*Ich habe nichts davon gewußt*. I didn't know.'

'I don't understand . . .'

'Yes, you do. Dachau, nineteen forty-five. You were with the Army battalion that liberated the camp. Ike ordered that all the townspeople be marched through the barracks and crematoria, so they could see the horror that had been perpetrated in their names. And there was this one fat, well-dressed banker who broke down and kept telling you . . . *Ich habe nichts davon gewußt* . . . *Ich habe nichts davon gewußt*. Remember?'

He nodded.

'That did happen, didn't it?' I asked. 'Or is it just another of your lies?'

'No,' he said, 'it did happen.'

'*Ich habe nichts davon gewußt*. You told me that story on my first evening with you. I was already in love with you before you told it to me. Afterwards –' I gulped hard '– afterwards, I thought you were the most remarkable man I had ever met. Wasn't I a fool? Especially given your little disappearing act. I should have known better. But you had my heart, you shit . . .'

'You still have my heart, Sara . . .'

653

'Liar.'

'It's the truth.'

'If that was the truth, you would have never named Eric. But you thought you could get away with it. You thought I'd never find out.'

He started to weep. 'I'm sorry,' he said.

'Apology not accepted. You and Eric were my entire world. Now that's gone.'

'Darling, I'm still here.'

'No, you're not.'

'Sara, *please*, I beg you . . .'

'Get out.'

'Don't do this.'

'Get out.'

He staggered towards me, his arms open. 'I love you,' he said.

'Don't you dare say that word.'

'I love you.'

'Out now!'

'I . . .'

He tried to hold me. I screamed at him to go away. Then I began to hit him. I slapped him around the face and the head. He put up no resistance, no defence. Suddenly, I too was crying. Weeping uncontrollably. My blows were ineffectual. I collapsed to the floor, bawling my eyes out. Once again, he tried to reach for me. This time, I used my right fist and caught him in the mouth. He reeled backwards, colliding with an end-table. It fell over, smashing a lamp to the ground. He followed it, landing on his knees. My crying jerked

654

to a halt. We stared at each other, wide-eyed. He touched his lips. They were bleeding. He stood up and staggered into the bathroom. I couldn't move. A minute went by. He came out, holding a handkerchief against his mouth. It was reddened with blood. He said nothing. I started getting to my feet. He proffered his free hand to help me. I declined it. I went into the kitchen. I found a dish towel. I took out a block of ice from the ice-box. I put it into the sink and used an ice pick to chip away at it. I wrapped a baseball-sized chunk of ice in the dish towel, and returned to the living room.

'Here,' I said, handing it to him. 'This will keep the swelling down.'

He took it and put it to his mouth.

'I want you to leave now, Jack.'

'All right,' he mumbled.

'I'll pack up your things tomorrow. I'll leave a message at your office, telling you when I'm not here, so you can collect them.'

'Let's talk tomorrow . . .'

'No.'

'Sara . . .'

'Never call me again.'

'Sara . . .'

'Give me your keys for here.'

'Let's wait until tomorrow before . . .'

'The keys!' I said, my voice loud again. With reluctance, he fished out his key ring, unfastened the top clasp, and took off two keys. Then he dumped them into my outstretched hand.

'Now let yourself out,' I said, and walked into the bedroom, locking the door behind me.

I fell on to the bed. Jack rapped on the door several times, begging to be let in. I pulled a pillow over my head to block out his voice. Eventually, after a few minutes, the banging stopped.

'I'll call you later,' he said through the door. 'Please try to forgive me.'

I didn't reply. I simply pulled the pillow tighter around my head.

I remained on the bed after I heard the front door close. My anguish was soon replaced by a numb clarity. There would be no forgiveness, no absolution. What Jack had done was so grievous – such a complete breach of trust – that I could never excuse it. He had betrayed Eric. He had betrayed me. Yes, I understood the reasons why he named my brother. Yes, I understood the pressures he was under. But I still couldn't pardon him. Though you might be able to forgive stupidity or lack of thought, it's impossible to condone a cynical, calculated action. All right, it might have only been a matter of time before Eric was accused by somebody of having former Communist sympathies. But how could I ever sleep again next to the man who made the accusation? That's what so astonished me about Jack's decision – his inability to fathom the fact that the moment he pointed the finger at my brother, he killed our life together. He knew just how inseparable Eric and I were. He knew that he was the only family

656

I had left. He was, I always sensed, silently jealous of our devotion to each other. Is that why he undermined everything? Or was there a deeper, even more disturbing truth lurking behind his action: Jack Malone was a moral coward. A man who refused to face the music – and who, when presented with a critical choice, would always grab the expedient, self-serving option. He couldn't face writing me after discovering that Dorothy was pregnant. Years later, when he accidentally barged back into my life, he pleaded with me to understand the shame that made him vanish for so long. Fool that I was, I eventually bought his excuse, his passionate apologies. By letting him back into my life, I began the process that eventually led to my brother's death.

Now, sprawled across my bed, I heard the voice of my brother echoing in my head: 'Forget him,' he told me repeatedly during that year when I so openly pined for Jack. 'He's a bum.'

Just as I also remembered that disastrous meeting I organized in the bar of the St Moritz – when Eric showed up drunk and became so insulting that Jack threw his drink in his face.

They always hated each other . . . even though they both denied it. When that Fed turned to Jack and asked him for the name of a Communist, did he perhaps think: *now I can finally nail that bastard*?

But such speculation was now pointless. Because one simple fact stared me in the face: I would never again have anything to do with Jack Malone.

The phone began to ring. I ignored it. An hour later, flowers arrived. I refused to accept them – telling the delivery man to throw them in the nearest trash can. Later that afternoon, a telegram arrived. I tore it up without opening it. At six that night, the doorbell began to ring. It kept ringing for fifteen minutes. When it finally stopped, I waited another fifteen minutes before opening my front door and peering out into the lobby. There was a letter waiting by the main door. I went out and retrieved it. I recognized the handwriting on the envelope. I went back into my apartment and tossed the letter into the trash. Then I put on my coat. I picked up my typewriter and the suitcase I had packed earlier that afternoon. I locked my apartment door behind me, and struggled with the bags to the front door.

As soon as I stepped out into the street, Jack was there – huddled in my doorway, looking ashen, manic, and sodden from the rain.

'Go away,' I shouted.

He eyed the luggage with alarm. 'What are you doing?'

'Leaving.'

'For where?'

'None of your business,' I said, heading down the steps.

'Please don't go . . .'

I said nothing. I turned right towards West End Avenue. He followed behind.

'You can't leave. You are *everything* to me.'

I kept walking.

'I will be lost if you go.'

I kept walking. He suddenly dashed in front of me and fell to his knees.

'You are the love of my life.'

I looked down at him. Not with anger or pity. Rather, with total dispassion.

'No,' I said quietly. '*You* are the love of your life.'

He reached for the hem of my raincoat. 'Sara, darling . . .' he said, tears rolling down his cheeks.

'Please get out of my way, Jack.'

He grabbed the hem and held on. 'No,' he said. 'Not until you hear me out.'

'I'm going, Jack.'

I tried to move. He held on tightly.

'Jack – it's over.'

'Don't say that.'

'It's over.'

'You have to hear me out.'

'It is *over*. Now let go . . .'

I was interrupted by a voice.

'You got a problem here, lady?'

I turned around. A cop approached us.

'Ask him,' I said, nodding toward Jack, still on his knees. The cop looked down at him with disdained amusement.

'So what's the problem, fella?' the cop asked him.

Jack let go of my hem. 'No problem,' he said. 'I was just . . .'

'Beggin' forgiveness is what it looks like to me,' the cop said.

Jack stared down at the pavement. The cop turned to me. 'Was he botherin' you?'

'I just wanted to get into a cab. He thought otherwise.'

'You gonna let her get into a cab, fella?'

Jack hesitated for a moment, then nodded slowly.

'Good call. Now what I want you to do is stand up and sit on the stoop there while I help your lady friend into a taxi. You gonna do that like a smart guy?'

Jack got to his feet, walked over to a nearby stoop, and sat down – looking totally defeated. The cop picked up my bags and walked me to the corner of 77th Street and West End Avenue. He put out his hand. A cab stopped within seconds. The driver came out and put my bags in the trunk.

'Thank you,' I said to the cop.

'No problem. That guy didn't do anything stupid to you, did he?'

'Nothing criminal, if that's what you mean.'

'Okay then. Have a good trip – wherever you're going. I'll keep an eye on lover boy for a couple of minutes, so he doesn't go chasing after you.'

I got into the cab. I said 'Penn Station' to the driver. We pulled out into the traffic. I looked back and saw Jack still sitting on the stoop, crying uncontrollably.

At Penn Station, I collected a ticket I had reserved that afternoon, and had a porter bring my bags to the sleeping compartment I had booked on the night train to Boston. I'd paid a supplement to ensure that I had a single compartment. I needed to be alone tonight. After I settled in, a steward knocked on my door. I told him I wouldn't be eating, but a double whiskey and soda would be most welcome. I changed into a nightgown and a robe. I lowered the bed. The steward returned with my whiskey. I drank it slowly. Once or twice the glass began to shake in my hand. I finished the whiskey. I climbed in between the stiff sheets. I turned off the light. The train shunted out of the station. I fell asleep.

I awoke again to a knock on the door. The steward entered, bearing toast and coffee. We were half-an-hour outside Boston. First light was bleaching the night sky. I sat up in bed, sipping the coffee, watching the emergence of a New England dawn. I had slept deeply, without dreams. My stomach felt taut with sadness. But no tears stung my eyes. My decision had been made; my heart hardened. It was morning. I was on the move. And the steward's coffee was actually drinkable.

At South Station in Boston, I switched trains. By noon that day, I had arrived in Brunswick, Maine. As arranged, Ruth Reynolds was at the station to collect me. It had been over five years since I'd fled to Maine in the spring of 1946 after everything went wrong in the wake of Jack's disappearance. Yesterday afternoon, when I felt myself hitting bottom again, I decided that the only thing to do was to leave town; to disappear without trace for a while. Had I stayed in Manhattan, Jack would have constantly bombarded me with phone calls, flowers, telegrams, and late-night appearances on my doorstep. More tellingly, I needed to go somewhere away from everything to do with the blacklist, NBC, *Saturday Night/Sunday Morning*, Walter Winchell, and all the painful resonances which I now associated with Manhattan. So that's when I reached for my address book and found the phone number of Ruth Reynolds in Bath, Maine. She remembered me immediately ('Hell, I am one of the biggest fans of your column. Why aren't you writing it anymore?'). And yes, she had a couple of summer cottages for rent right now. There would be no problem accommodating me as of tomorrow, if need be.

So I reserved a seat on the first train out of town, packed a suitcase, and fled . . . leaving Jack crying on a doorstep. Now, here I was, back in Maine. Being enveloped in one of Ruth Reynolds' bear hugs.

'Well, don't you look great,' she lied.

'You too,' I said, even though I blanched when I first saw her on the station platform – and noted that she had put on at least thirty pounds in the intervening years.

'No need to fib, honey,' she said. 'I'm fat.'

'No, you're not.'

'You're a nice girl, Sara – but a terrible liar.'

We drove north out of Brunswick towards Bath. 'So . . . how's it feel being a journalistic star?' she asked me.

'I'm hardly a star. Anyway, I'm on leave of absence from *Saturday/Sunday*.'

'Is that why you decided to come back to Maine?'

'Yeah,' I lied. 'There's some stuff I want to get down on paper.'

'Well, you picked the perfect place for peace and quiet. I'm afraid I couldn't get you your old cottage, because Mr and Mrs Daniels sold their place years ago. You still in touch with them?'

I shook my head.

'Anyway, I found you something very cute. And it's got an extra bedroom if you want a guest . . . or if your brother pays you a visit.'

I stiffened. Ruth noticed this. 'Something wrong?' she asked.

'No,' I said – as I vowed to myself I would remain tight-lipped about events of the past few months.

'How is that brother of yours?'

'Fine, fine.'

'Nice to hear it.'

We made small talk for the rest of the drive. When we reached Bath, we turned right down Rt. 209, stopping in the general store at a village called Winnegance to pick up supplies. Then we continued along the lonely two-lane blacktop that snaked its way down the spindly peninsula which ended at Popham Beach. The beach was as empty as ever.

'Nothing ever changes around here, does it?' I said.

'That's Maine.'

Ruth told me I was welcome at her house that night for dinner. But I begged off, saying I was tired.

'How about tomorrow then?' she asked.

'Let's talk in a couple of days,' I said, 'after I've settled in.'

'You sure everything's all right?'

'Of course. The house suits me just fine.'

'I was talking about you, Sara. Is everything okay with you?'

'You said how good I looked, didn't you?'

She was taken aback by the sharp tone. 'And I was telling the truth. But . . .'

Before she could pose another question, I cut her off.

'It's been a difficult few months, all right?'

'Sara, I do apologize. I didn't mean to pry.'

'You're not prying. And excuse my tone. It's just . . . I need time by myself.'

'Well, up here in Maine, we never crowd anyone. So when you want company, you know where to find it.'

I didn't want company. Or conversation. Or any form of human contact. I wanted to shut down; to close myself off from everyone. I did just that. I wrote a letter to the accounts department of *Saturday/Sunday*, informing them that I wanted all pay checks to be dispatched directly to my bank. I wrote Joel Eberts, authorizing him (when Eric's insurance check came through) to pay off the IRS and then deposit the remainder of the payment in my stock market fund. I also sent him a set of keys to my apartment and asked if (for a fee) he would hire someone to collect my mail; to hold all correspondence and pay all bills . . . on the condition that he kept my whereabouts private from anyone who was trying to contact me. A few days later, he wrote back, agreeing to get his part-time secretary to drop by once a week and gather up all correspondence. He also enclosed power-of-attorney forms, allowing him to write checks from my account to cover all bills.

'But are you sure,' he said in his covering letter to me, 'that you don't want me to forward on any personal letters?'

'Absolutely sure,' I wrote back. 'And you must keep my forwarding address a secret – especially from Jack Malone, should he contact you. More specifically, I do not want to know if he does contact you. So you must also keep this informa-tion from me.'

I was determined to kill all potential contact between myself and Jack. Not just because I refused to budge from my irreconcilable position, but also because I was terrified that, were I to read one of his pleading letters (or, worse yet, allow myself to encounter him face to face), I would crumble on the spot . . . as I had done all those years ago when he had accidentally barged back into my life. We were finished together. Nothing he said or did would change that. He was gone from my life. I was alone now. I wanted it that way.

I didn't make contact with Ruth for the first three weeks I was at the cottage. Of course, she did come down twice a week to clean the place and change the sheets. But I made certain I was out walking on the beach when she arrived. She accepted my aloofness – and left me notes asking if she could run any errands for me. I drew up lists for her – for groceries and for books I asked her to borrow from the local library. Besides leaving her cash for these essentials, I always ended my list with an apology for my aloofness: 'Sorry for being so distant. One day, when I am back on Planet Earth, I will come over with a bottle of something strong and Scottish, and explain all. But for the moment, let me wallow in my solipsism . . . a big dumb word meaning "self-pity".'

A few days later, I came back from my morning stroll to find all the groceries I requested, and three thick novels I'd always dodged reading (Mann's *The Magic Mountain*, James's *The Wings of a Dove*, and – as my popcorn antidote to all that serious literature – Thomas Heggen's wonderful Second World War yarn, *Mister Roberts*). There was also a bottle of J&B. A note was enclosed:

Sara:
No need for apologies. Just know we're here when you need us. As it's still kind of nippy at night, I thought the bottle of Scotch might

be effective heating . . . especially if you get bored lighting fires every evening.

A week slipped by. Then another. Then another. I read. I walked. I slept. I received one letter – from Joel Eberts, informing me that the seventy-five-thousand-dollar insurance check had cleared. Through his 'tax guy', he had also cut a deal with the IRS on the matter of Eric's back payments.

They settled for $32,500. I wanted to push them lower, but as my tax guy pointed out, we still managed to haul them down quite a bit. So we have to be grateful for that. I had a chat with Lawrence Braun – your stockbroker. He plans to invest the balance in solid blue-chip companies – unless (as he put it) 'Miss Smythe has suddenly become adventurous'. I told him that, unless I heard otherwise from you, blue chips were the way to go.

That's all my news from this end, except to say that you do have a stack of private correspondence here. I'm happy to keep it in storage. When you want it, just say the word.

In closing, Sara – let me add this one personal hope: that you are somehow coming to terms with all that has happened. No one deserves what you had to face in the past couple of months. By its very nature, life is unfair. But it has been, of late, mercilessly unfair to you. This will change. You may never get over the loss of your brother. Just as you may never get over Mr Malone's act of betrayal. But I know you will eventually come to terms with both events. Because to move forward, we all must somehow come to terms with every damn thing that life throws in our path.

For now, however, take your time. Put the world on hold. Find your way through this difficult juncture. And do know that I am here, whenever you need me.

But I needed no one. Until the beginning of my fourth week at the cottage. It was a Tuesday morning. I woke up feeling odd. Two minutes later, I was violently ill. I spent a ghastly quarter-of-an-hour in the toilet. The next morning I was sick again. On Thursday, the dawn chorus of nausea passed me by. But it returned again on Friday, and hit me throughout the weekend.

I needed to see a doctor. Especially as my period was also two weeks late. So I made contact with Ruth again. I didn't go into the nature of my complaint. I simply told her it was a medical problem. She dispatched me to her family doctor – a severe-looking man in his fifties named Grayson. He wore a crisp white shirt, a crisp white medical jacket, rimless glasses, and a permanent scowl. He looked like a mean-minded druggist. His offices were on Center Street in Bath. His patients were the men employed at Bath Iron Works and their families. He had no bedside manner whatsoever.

668

I told him the nature of my problem, and the fact that my period was so late.

'Sounds like you could be pregnant,' he said tonelessly.

'That's impossible,' I said.

'You mean, you and your husband haven't been having . . .'

He paused, then uttered the word '*relations*' with considerable distaste.

'I'm not married,' I said.

His eyes flickered down to my left hand. He noticed the absence of a wedding ring. He hesitated, then said, 'But you have been having *relations* with . . .'

'With someone, yes. But there is no medical way I could be pregnant.'

Then I explained about my earlier failed pregnancy and how the obstetrician at Greenwich Hospital told me I could never have children.

'Maybe he was wrong,' Dr Grayson said, then asked me to roll up my sleeve. He drew some blood. He handed me a glass vial and directed me towards the toilet. When I returned with the urine sample, he told me to come back two days later for the results.

'But I already know the outcome,' I said. 'I can't be pregnant. It's an impossibility.'

But I kept getting sick every morning. When I returned to Dr Grayson's office two days later, he looked up briefly from my file and said, 'The test was positive.'

I was dazed beyond belief. I didn't know what to say. Except, 'That can't be.'

'These tests are rarely wrong.'

'In this instance, I'm certain it's mistaken.'

The doctor shrugged with disinterest.

'If you want to be delusional, that's your choice.'

'What a horrible thing to say.'

'You are pregnant, *Miss* Smythe,' he said, putting particular emphasis on my single status. 'That is what the test said – so that is my clinical diagnosis. Choose to believe it or not.'

'May I have a second test?'

'You can have as many tests as you want – as long as you are willing to pay for them. But I would also advise you to see an obstetrician as soon as possible. You're staying locally, yes?'

I nodded.

'The nearest obstetrician is Dr Bolduck in Brunswick. He's located off Maine Street, right near the college. I'll give you his number.'

He scratched a few numbers on to a prescription pad, then tore it off and handed it to me. 'You can settle with my receptionist on the way out.' I stood up. 'One last thing, Miss Smythe,' he said.

'Yes?'

'Congratulations.'

Ruth was waiting for me in the lobby. I paid my bill, then nodded that I was ready to leave. Prior to this, I hadn't told her about the pregnancy test. I certainly wasn't going to tell her now. But my face betrayed my worries. Because, as soon as we were outside, she touched my arm and said, 'It isn't anything fatal, is it?'

I nearly managed a laugh. 'I wish it was.'

'Oh dear,' she said. And I instantly realized that I had given the game away. Suddenly I put my head against her shoulder. I felt stunned, stupefied.

'How about a nice breakfast somewhere?' she asked.

'I might throw it all up.'

'Then again, you might not.'

She brought me to a little diner near the Iron Works. She insisted that I eat scrambled eggs and home fries and two thick buttery slices of toast. I was reluctant at first – but quickly dug in. After three days of nausea, the food tasted wonderful. It also helped dull the shock of my news.

'I know you're a private kind of person,' Ruth said, 'so I'm not gonna pry. But if you want to talk about it . . .'

I suddenly found myself telling her everything that had happened to me since my last stay at the cottage. It all came pouring out. She blanched when I told her about losing the baby and being told I would never conceive again. She took my arm when I informed her about Eric – and Jack's role in my brother's collapse.

'Oh, Sara,' she whispered. 'I wish to God I'd known about your brother.'

'I doubt his death made the Maine papers.'

'I never read 'em anyway. No time.'

'Believe me, you're better off.'

671

'What a terrible year for you.'

'I have known better ones,' I said. 'And now, just to unhinge things completely, it turns out I'm pregnant.'

'I can only begin to imagine the sort of shock you're feeling.'

'About a ten on the Richter scale.'

'Are you pleased?'

'I've never been in a train wreck – but I think I now understand what it feels like.'

'I don't blame you.'

'But once the after-shock wears off . . . yeah, I'm going to feel pretty damn pleased.'

'That's good.'

'This is like news from outer space. I had accepted the fact that I would never have kids.'

'That must have been hard.'

'Very.'

'Doctors often get things wrong.'

'Thankfully.'

'May I ask you something?'

'Of course.'

'Are you going to tell him?'

'No way.'

'Don't you think he deserves to know?'

'No.'

'I'm sorry – it's none of my business.'

'I can't . . . *won't* . . . tell him. Because I can't forgive him.'

'I could see how that would be hard.'

I heard the ambivalence in her voice.

'But . . . ?' I asked.

'Like I said, Sara – it's not for me to be sticking my nose into some tough stuff.'

'Go on – say what you want to say.'

'It's his kid too.'

'And Eric was my brother.'

Silence.

'You've got a point there. Matter dropped.'

'Thank you.'

I raised my coffee cup. And said, 'But it's good news.'

She raised her cup and clinked it against mine. 'It's great news,' she said. 'The best news.'

'And totally unbelievable.'

Ruth laughed.

'Honey,' she said, 'all good news is unbelievable. For a lot of very obvious reasons.'

CHAPTER 11

I went to see Dr Bolduck a few days later. I braced myself for another flinty, stern medic – who would glare at my ringless finger and play the New England Puritan. But Bolduck was a pleasant, genial man in his late thirties – a Bowdoin graduate who'd returned to his college town after medical school to set up practice. He put me at my ease immediately.

'So, Dr Grayson referred you to me?' he asked. I nodded. 'Has he been your doctor for long?'

'I'm new to the area. And I'm already on the lookout for a new GP.'

'Really?'

'I don't think we hit it off too well.'

'But Dr Grayson is such a delightful man,' he said, arching his eyebrows in Groucho Marx style. 'With the most wonderful bedside manner.'

I laughed, then said, 'I don't think he liked the fact that I wasn't married. Does that bother you, Doctor?'

He shrugged. 'Your private life is your private life, Miss Smythe. All I care about is getting you and your baby through the pregnancy safely.'

674

'I still don't believe I'm pregnant.'

He smiled. 'That's a common complaint.'

'What I mean is: medically speaking, I cannot be pregnant.'

Then I took him through everything that had happened five years ago at Greenwich Hospital. Unlike Dr Grayson, he expressed immediate interest, and asked for the name of the obstetrician who'd dealt with me then.

'I'll write to him and request your medical records. In the meantime, I agree with you: a second pregnancy test would be prudent.'

He took a blood sample. I filled a vial with urine. I arranged to see Dr Bolduck in a week's time. I returned to the cottage at Popham Beach. I tried to come to terms with my news. I had craved a child. I had quietly mourned my inability to have one. When Jack came back into my life, this grief intensified – though I refused to articulate it in front of him. Now I *was* pregnant (unless, of course, that test was very wrong). Had I been a Christian I would have called it a miracle. Had I still been with Jack, I would have been thrilled beyond belief. Instead, I felt a curious mixture of elation and despondency. Elation because I would finally have a child. Despondency because I would never speak with the child's father again. As bad ironies go, this one was particularly grim.

My mind was constantly haunted by thoughts of Eric and Jack. My grief overtook me without warning. One moment I would be reasonably collected; the next, I would be transported to the edge of the abyss. I remembered the distress I felt in the months after I'd miscarried – how grief became a shadowy companion, stalking me unawares. This time, its presence was more acute, more constant. Because Jack had decimated everything. That knowledge strengthened my resolve to make no contact with him about my pregnancy. He could not be trusted. He was beneath contempt. He would have nothing to do with this child.

Yes, I was being hard, steely. But the hardness was necessary – a means by which to cope with the all-permeating sense of loss. Initially it gave me a *modus vivendi* to get me through days which often seemed bottomless. But now there was the astonishing prospect of a baby. And though that prospect wouldn't soften my stance towards Jack, I knew it would give me a sense of possibility; a destination at the end of all this anguish.

I kept my appointment with Dr Bolduck seven days later. He was as genial as ever.

'I'm afraid the delightful Dr Grayson was right: pregnancy tests rarely lie. You are definitely going to have a baby.'

I smiled.

'Well, at least you seem pleased with the news,' he said.

'Believe me, I am. And flabbergasted.'

'That's understandable. Especially as I've just been reading your file from Greenwich Hospital . . . which only arrived yesterday. The doctor attending you was, in my opinion, wrong to inform you that your damaged womb ruled out all possibilities of carrying a child to term. Yes, one of your fallopian tubes was badly damaged, which does significantly lessen the potential for conception. And yes, the internal injury that the wall of your womb suffered also decreases the possibility of a pregnancy. But it doesn't rule it out altogether. I personally know of several cases where conception happened after this sort of medical event, and the pregnancy was carried to full term. Which, in plain language, means that your doctor at Greenwich Hospital may have just been a tad pessimistic about your chances of having a baby. Personally, I think what he did was shameful, because it caused you years of unnecessary distress. But don't quote me on that. Part of the Hippocratic oath has a clause saying you can never censure another doctor . . . especially in front of one of his patients.'

'Don't worry – I'll censure him myself. He was an awful man. So awful he made Dr Grayson look like Albert Schweitzer.'

Now it was Dr Bolduck's turn to laugh. 'I might use that,' he said.

'Be my guest.'

His smile changed into a look of professional seriousness. 'Though this is wonderful news, I really am going to want you to take it easy. *Very* easy. Because of the previous internal damage, this will be a delicate, finely balanced pregnancy.'

'Is there a chance that I might lose it?'

'There is always a one-in-six chance of miscarrying in the first three months of term.'

'But with my previous history . . . ?'

'The odds might be as low as one-in-three . . . but they're still in your favor. You will simply have to be as careful as possible. As long as you don't go climbing Mount Kathadin or decide to play ice hockey for Bowdoin, you should have a good shot at holding on to it. I'm afraid luck also has a lot to do with these things too. Are you planning to stay around here?'

I had nowhere else to go. And since rest and lack of anxiety were going to be crucial over the next eight months, there was no way I would be returning to Manhattan.

'Yes, I'm staying in Maine.'

'Again, this is none of my business . . . but do you really think it's a good idea being alone in an isolated place like Popham Beach?'

I had to admit that it wasn't. So – as much as I rued the loss of that extraordinary sweep of sand, sky and ocean – I moved a week later into Brunswick. After scanning the Classifieds in the *Maine Gazette* for a few days, I managed to find a pleasant, if somewhat rustic apartment on Federal Street. It was a one-bedroom unit in an unprepossessing white clapboard house. The decor could have been politely described as 'tired': yellowing walls, cast-off furniture, a basic kitchen, a brass bed in urgent need of a polish. But the morning light flooded the living room. There was a large mahogany roll-top desk and a wonderful old-style editor's chair (the desk and chair were actually what sold me on the place). And it was close to the college, the town, and the offices of Dr Bolduck – so I could walk everywhere.

Ruth helped me move. I set up an account with the Casco National Bank on Maine Street, and (via Joel Eberts) arranged to have my weekly *Saturday Night/Sunday Morning* checks dispatched there. I had another four months to go on my alleged 'leave of absence'. The weekly retainer easily covered my eighteen-dollar weekly rent and all basic necessities. It even left me enough over to buy a radio, a Victrola, and a steady supply of books and records. I also started reading newspapers again: the local *Maine Gazette* and the *Boston Globe* (as it took three days for the *New York Times* to reach Brunswick). Joe McCarthy and his band of cronies were in full demagogic flight. The Rosenbergs were entering the final appeal process against their death sentence for allegedly smuggling atomic bomb secrets to the Soviets. Eisenhower was looking a dead cert to beat Adlai Stevenson for the presidency in the coming November election. And the blacklist seemed to get longer with every new Associated Press wire report from Washington. On a minor personal level, I knew that this ever-deepening Red scare meant that there was no way I'd be welcomed back to *Saturday/Sunday* after my residency in purdah was over. Eric's death had been all over the papers – and his Godship the Editor would be far too nervous about upsetting the board by reinstating me. After all, I was the sister of a deceased man who had the unpatriotic nerve *not to* rat on others. Surely that made me damaged, unAmerican goods . . . and unworthy of access to the precious column inches of *Saturday Night/Sunday Morning*.

So I figured that, halfway through my pregnancy, the guilt money from *Saturday/Sunday* would run out, after which I would have to start tapping into the insurance cash from NBC or my stock port-folio . . . though a certain corner of my frugal puritan brain fretted about the idea of raiding my capital at such a young age. Especially as I would definitely need that money to help bring this child up on my own. I also worried about the fact that – thanks to the Winchell piece and my reluctant furlough from *Saturday/Sunday* – the word around town was that I was politically suspect and best left unemployed.

But every time I started to have one of these nervy reveries about my future employment prospects (or lack thereof), I managed to calm myself down with the thought that, one way or another, I'd find a way of making a living. More tellingly, I was luckier than most. I had money in the bank and an apartment in Manhattan which I owned outright. They might take my career away from me . . . but they couldn't snatch the roof over my head.

Anyway, there was no chance I'd be back in Manhattan for some time. Just as there was also no chance that I'd be telling anyone about my pregnancy. Ruth was the only person who knew – and she promised to keep quiet on the subject.

'Trust me,' she said, 'I know how small towns work. The moment word gets out is the moment you'll start getting interested stares on the street.'

'But won't I begin to get those stares once I start to show?'

'It really depends how high a profile you choose to adopt; how many people you get to know, and what you tell them. I promise you – if you let it be known that you're the Sara Smythe who writes for *Saturday Night/Sunday Morning*, your social diary is going to get very full. Half the English department at Bowdoin will probably want to meet you – because new people in town are few and far between. And new people who are nationally prominent columnists . . .'

'I'm hardly Walter Lippmann, Ruth. I'm a very minor figure who writes very minor stuff.'

'Listen to Miss Modesty.'

'It's the truth. And, believe me, I'm telling no one about what I did in Manhattan. I've had enough intrusiveness – courtesy of the FBI – to last me for the rest of the decade.'

So I maintained a very low profile. Following Dr Bolduck's advice, I did nothing strenuous – limiting my exercise to walks in the Bowdoin Pines behind the campus, or to the college's library (where I managed to wangle a Brunswick resident's reader's ticket), and to the shops that lined Maine Street. I found a grocer who delivered, and a newspaper shop which agreed to order the Sunday edition of the *New York Times* for me. I became a good customer of the town's main book and record shop. I was soon on first-name basis with the librarians at Bowdoin, Mr Cole at the grocer's, Thelma the chief cashier at Casco National Bank, and Mr Mullin, the druggist. Though everyone initially asked me my name – and whether I was new in town – the line of enquiry stopped there. There were never sly questions about what I was doing in Brunswick, or whether I had a husband, or how I was supporting myself. As I came to discover, this lack of obtrusive curiosity was the Maine way. People respected your privacy . . . because they wanted you to respect theirs. More tellingly, in true Maine style, the state's unspoken social code was a fiercely independent one: *your business is your own damn business, not mine.* Even if they were interested in your back story, they forced themselves to appear disinterested . . . out of fear of being labeled meddlesome, or the village gossip. Maine was probably one of the few places in America where taciturnity and reserve were considered civic virtues.

Brunswick, therefore, was an easy place to live. After five years of turning out journalistic copy week after week, it was pleasant to take a sabbatical from my typewriter. I caught up with reading.

I audited a conversational French course at the college, and spent at least three hours a day studying verb conjugations and vocabulary. Once a week, Ruth insisted on picking me up in her Studebaker and bringing me to her house for dinner. Once a week, I would walk the three blocks to Dr Bolduck's office, and submit myself to an examination. Six weeks into the pregnancy, he pronounced himself pleased with my progress to date.

'So far so good,' he said after I got dressed and sat down in the chair opposite his desk. 'As long as we get you to the second trimester without complications, you really should have a good chance of seeing this all the way through. You are taking it easy, right?'

'Brunswick isn't exactly a strenuous town.'

Dr Bolduck winced. 'Do I take that as a back-handed compliment?'

'I'm sorry. That came out all the wrong way.'

'No – you're right. This is a pretty quiet place.'

'Which makes it the right place for me at this moment in time.'

'I've been meaning to ask you: are you doing any writing while you're here?'

I went white. He immediately looked apologetic.

'I'm sorry,' he said. 'That was intrusive of me.'

'How did you know I was a writer?'

'I do subscribe to *Saturday Night/Sunday Morning*, Sara. Just as I also read the *Maine Gazette* every afternoon. Your brother's death made the paper up here, you know.'

'I don't believe it.'

'It was a wire service report: a short piece about his sudden death, and his earlier dismissal from NBC after Winchell exposed his past. And how Sara Smythe of *Saturday Night/Sunday Morning* was his sister.'

'Why didn't you mention this before?'

'Because that would have been nosy. In fact, now I feel like a right fool for that slip of the tongue. I really would never have mentioned anything.'

'Do you think other people in Brunswick know who I am?' He shifted uneasily in his chair. 'They do, don't they?'

'Well . . .' he said hesitantly. 'It is a small place. And though no one would directly ask questions to your face, they do talk among themselves. The other night, for example, I was at a dinner with a couple of college people and Duncan Howell – the editor of the *Maine Gazette*. I don't know how your name came up in conversation, but Duncan turned to me and said, "Do you know who I hear is living in Brunswick? Sara Smythe – who wrote that really smart column in *Saturday/Sunday*. I'd love to approach her about maybe writing something for us . . . but I don't want to intrude. Especially as I gather she's up here to get away from New York and that whole business with her brother . . ."'

I suddenly felt ill.

'Dr Bolduck, you didn't say anything about me being a patient of yours?'

'God, no. That would have been completely unethical. I'd never, *never* dream of . . .'

'Fine, fine,' I said weakly.

'I now feel terrible. But I promise you this: Maine being Maine, people will never let on they know who you are.'

'Who I am is completely inconsequential. What worries me is the stares in the street I'll begin to get once my pregnancy is apparent.'

'Once again, no one will ever shun you because of your marital status.'

'They'll just gossip behind my back.'

'As small towns go, this is a pretty tolerant place. I think you'll find more sympathy than anything else. And I tell you this: everyone at that dinner the other night said what happened to your brother was an awful thing . . . and wasn't he a brave man to stand up for what he believed.'

'So you don't think he was a Communist stooge? A flunky of Stalin, disguised as Marty Manning's top banana? You're smiling. Why?'

'Because encountering Manhattan wit, face to face, in Brunswick is a rare thing. But can I say something? Like a lot of people I know around here, I have great doubts about what McCarthy and his ilk are up to. Especially as they are supposedly running this witch hunt in our name . . . which makes me very uncomfortable. And I just want to say: I am truly sorry for your loss. Do you have other siblings?'

'He was my only family.'

685

Dr Bolduck said nothing . . . and I was grateful for that. I quickly changed the subject back to medical matters, asking whether my need to urinate every half-hour was particularly worrisome.

'I'm afraid it's a common complaint during pregnancy,' he said. 'And one which medical science has no answer for.'

'Until next week then?' I asked, standing up.

Bolduck got up from his chair. 'Once again, I am sorry for that faux pas.'

'No . . . it's better to know these things.'

'Would you mind if I told you something else then?'

'Go ahead.'

'I know that Duncan Howell, being the decent guy that he is, would never dream of calling you to see if you want to write for the *Maine Gazette*. But from the way he sounded, I'm sure he'd be thrilled to bits if you were interested.'

'I'm taking a break from the word business,' I said. 'But thanks for the tip.'

Naturally, two days later, I picked up the phone and called Duncan Howell at the *Maine Gazette*. I was put through to him immediately.

'Well, this is an honor,' he said.

'You are about the first editor in history who's ever said that.'

'Glad to hear that. It's nice to have you in Brunswick.'

'It's nice to be here.'

'How about letting me buy you lunch, Miss Smythe?'

'That would be fine.'

'Now we have two choices of venue. I could take you to the Brunswick version of posh – which means the dining room of our best inn, the Stowe House. Or I could introduce you to some proper local color, in the form of our best diner: the Miss Brunswick.'

'Oh, the diner without question,' I said.

Duncan Howell was a pleasant, portly man in his early thirties. He dressed like a college professor: tweed jacket, v-neck sweater, knit tie. He wore horn-rimmed glasses. He smoked a pipe. He was a son of Brunswick. He'd grown up knowing he'd go to Bowdoin and eventually work for the paper his family had owned for the past seventy-five years. He spoke with the slow, no-rush, back-country cadences that defined the Maine inflection. But like everyone else I'd met in the state, he was anything but a hick.

He was already seated at a booth in the Miss Brunswick when I entered. It was a proper diner: a prefabricated corrugated aluminum structure with a laminated vinyl lunch counter, and six booths, and a clientele of truckers and soldiers from the local naval air station, and a short order cook with a lit cigarette in his mouth, and waitresses who used pencils as bobby pins. I liked it immediately. Just as I also liked Duncan Howell.

He stood up as I entered. He waited until I sat down opposite him before taking his seat again.

The waitress called him 'Duncan'. He insisted on referring to me as Miss Smythe. He suggested I try The Trucker's Special: a steak, a stack of pancakes, three eggs, home fries, six pieces of toast, bottomless coffee. When I said that I might stick to a modest hamburger and a cup of Joe, he said that I'd never have a future driving a rig.

We ordered. We made small talk. He talked a bit about local politics, about the expansion of the local paper mill, and regional worries that the Boston train might soon be canceled, due to lack of economic viability. He told me a bit about the *Maine Gazette*: how his great-grandfather founded it in 1875, how it maintained an independent political stance, and (like most of Maine) refused to slavishly back a specific political party.

'By inclination, this is a Republican state,' he explained. 'But that doesn't mean that we've always supported Republican candidates for national or state office. We always came out in favor of Roosevelt. Twice, we supported Democrats in our senate races . . .'

'And what do you think of Joe McCarthy?' I asked.

He didn't seemed disconcerted by my challenging tone . . . though, frankly, I was surprised that I popped that question so directly.

'I'll be entirely straight with you, Miss Smythe. I do take the idea of a Communist menace seriously. I do think, for example, that all the evidence points to the guilt of the Rosenbergs, and that treason is a capital offence. But on the subject of Mr McCarthy . . . well, he genuinely worries me. Because (a) I consider him a complete opportunist who is using this Communist issue as a way of wielding power, and (b) because he has destroyed a lot of innocent people in the process.'

He looked at me directly. 'And, in my book, destroying innocent people is unforgivable.'

I met his gaze. 'I'm glad you think that way.'

He shifted the conversation towards my 'work' at the moment.

'I'm *not* working at the moment. No doubt, you know why.'

'We did run a piece about your brother. I'm very sorry. Is that why you came to Maine?'

'I needed to get away for a while, yes.'

'I presume *Saturday/Sunday* were very under-standing about giving you leave.'

'Oh, they certainly wanted me on leave. Because, as far as they were concerned, my brother's refusal to play ball with HUAC meant that I was now a liability to them.'

Duncan Howell actually looked shocked. 'Tell me they didn't do that.'

'I was as stunned as you were. Especially as they knew I was about the most apolitical person imaginable. Even my poor brother had completely renounced his brief fling with Communism during the thirties.'

'But he still refused to name names.'

'Quite rightly, in my opinion.'

'It's a tough call, any way you look at it. And I can see why certain people probably thought naming names was a patriotic gesture . . . and why others saw it as a self-serving one. But I certainly respect your brother's high principles.'

'Look where it got him. I'll be honest with you, Mr Howell. There are times when I wish to God he'd just named names like everybody else. Because he'd still be here. And because, quite honestly, if history teaches us anything it's that today's life-or-death argument becomes a lot less consequential as years go by. What I'm saying is: sooner or later, the country will wise up and the blacklisting will end. In time, historians will probably write about this period as a political aberration; a shameful blight in our national life. And they'll be right. But my brother will still be dead and gone.'

'I'm sure he'd still want you to be writing.'

'But – haven't you heard? – I've been blacklisted too.'

'Only by *Saturday/Sunday*. And they haven't officially terminated you.'

'As soon as this paid leave-of-absence is over, they will. And word travels fast in Manhattan. Once *Saturday/Sunday* fires me, I'm definitely going to be declared a journalistic untouchable.'

'Not in Brunswick, Maine, you won't.'

'Well, that's nice to know,' I said with a laugh.

'And I bet one of the hardest things about your enforced sabbatical is being "out of print", so to speak.'

'How did you guess that?'

'Because I've been around journalists all my life. If there's one thing they can't live without, it's an audience. I'm offering you an audience, Sara. A *small* audience. But an audience nonetheless.'

'Aren't you worried about employing a political hot potato like me?'

'No,' he said directly.

'And what sort of thing would you want me to be writing?'

'Probably something similar to your "Real Life" column. We'd talk that through.'

'*Saturday/Sunday* might get a little upset, were they to discover that I was working for someone else while collecting their paycheck.'

'Did you sign a contract with them, granting them complete exclusivity to your work?'

I shook my head.

'Did they insist that you didn't write for anyone else while on leave?'

'No.'

'Then there's no problem.'

'I guess there isn't.'

'But there is, of course, the matter of money. Now, if you wouldn't mind a private question, what did they pay you weekly for your column?'

'One hundred and eighty dollars.'

Duncan Howell gulped. 'I don't even make that much,' he said. 'And there's no way I could ever come near matching that. We are a small town, after all.'

'I'm not saying you have to match that. How's fifty bucks a column sound to you? That's about what I spend a week on rent and basic items.'

'It's still far more than I pay any other columnist on the paper.'

I arched my eyebrows. Duncan Howell took the hint. 'Fine, fine,' he said, proffering his hand. 'Fifty a week it is.'

I took his hand. 'Nice to be back on the job,' I said.

Of course, Duncan Howell was right. Though I wasn't admitting it (and kept telling myself that I really wanted a break from my typewriter), I was desperately missing my weekly fix in print. And yes, he was so damn shrewd to glean that off me. Just as he probably sensed that what I needed more than anything was work. I wasn't good at being slothful, unproductive. I needed direction, focus; a shape and a purpose to the day. Like anyone who was used to having an audience, I really craved one again. Even if my audience was no longer a national one, but the eight thousand daily readers of the *Maine Gazette*.

The column premiered a week after the Miss Brunswick Diner meeting. We agreed to call it 'Day-to-Day Stuff'. Like the old column, it was a gently satirical commentary on prosaic matters. Only now I lost some of my usual metropolitan slant, and focused in on somewhat more homey, parochial matters: like 'Twenty-Three Dumb Uses for Kraft Velveeta Cheese'. . . . or 'Why Leg Waxing

Makes Me Always Feel Inadequate' . . . or (my personal favorite) 'Why Women Just Can't Relate to Beer'.

Duncan Howell insisted that I keep the flip tone which so characterized my *Saturday/Sunday* columns. 'Don't feel you have to write down for your audience. Mainers always know when someone's condescending to them . . . and they don't like it. They might take some time getting used to your style . . . but, eventually, you'll win them over.'

Certainly, the first few weeks of 'Day-to-Day Stuff' didn't win anybody over.

'What are you doing, employing such a wiseguy gal to write such a wiseguy column in a decent, respectable paper like yours?' ran one of the first Letters to the Editor.

A week later, another torpedo landed in the Letters column. *'Maybe this sort of thing plays well in Manhattan, but Miss Smythe's world view certainly doesn't seem to have the slightest bearing on life as we live it up here. Maybe she should think about heading back south.'*

Ouch.

'Don't take those letters personally,' Duncan Howell said when we met again at the Miss Brunswick for a little tête-à-tête a month after the column started.

'How can I *not* take it personally, Mr Howell? After all, if I'm not connecting with your readers . . .'

'But you *are* connecting,' he said. 'Most of the

newsroom really like you. And every time I go to a dinner around town, at least one or two of the Bowdoin or local business people tell me how much they enjoy your take on things, and what a coup it was to get you for the paper. We always expect a couple of nay-sayers to complain about anything new and a little different. That's par for the course. So, *please*, don't fret: you're doing just fine. So fine that I was wondering . . . might you be willing to start writing two columns a week for us?'

'That's a joke, right?'

'No – I'm absolutely serious. I really want to get "Day-to-Day Stuff" established – and I think the best way to do this is to up the ante, so to speak . . . and make them read you every Monday and Friday. You game?'

'Sure, I guess. Can you afford it?'

'I'll work it out somehow.'

He held out his hand again. 'Do we have a deal?'

'And I came to Maine thinking about a life of leisure.'

'Once a journalist . . .'

I took his hand and shook it. 'Right – it's a deal.'

'Glad to hear it. One final thing . . . there are a lot of people around town who would love to meet you. I don't know what your social calendar is like these days . . .'

'It's completely empty, by choice. I'm still not in a particularly sociable frame of mind.'

'Understood completely. These things do take

694

time. But if you're ever feeling in the need of company, do know that there are plenty of opportunities. You have fans.'

Like Dr Bolduck. Not only was he chuffed that, by calling Duncan Howell, I took the bait he dangled in front of me . . . but also that I had just passed the first trimester mark without problems.

'No worrying discharges, no constant cramps, no ominous discomfort?'

'Nothing ominous whatsoever. In fact, this has all been far simpler than my last pregnancy.'

'Well, what can I say except: good stuff. Fingers crossed. And keep taking it as easy as possible.'

'Not with Duncan Howell now insisting on two columns a week.'

'Oh yes, I heard about that. Congratulations. You're becoming a local name.'

'And I'll be even more of a name three months from now, when everyone on Maine Street sees the bump in the belly.'

'Like I said before, it will not be as big a deal as you imagine. Anyway, why should you care what people think around here?'

'Because I live here now, that's why.'

Dr Bolduck didn't have an answer to that. Except: 'Fair enough.'

The following week, I began to be published every Monday and Friday. There was another spate of letters in the paper, bemoaning my smarty-pants style. But Duncan Howell called me weekly for an impromptu editorial conference on the next week's copy – and he constantly sounded enthu-siastic about the way the column was progressing. He also said that he was getting terrific feedback about its twice-weekly appearance. So much so that he had some good news: the two largest papers in Maine – the *Portland Press Herald* and the *Bangor Daily News* – had both enquired about perhaps picking up serialization rights for the column.

'The money they're offering isn't great: about sixty dollars each per week for the two columns,' Mr Howell said.

'Of which I'd receive how much?'

'Well, this is new territory for me. Because the *Maine Gazette* has never really been in a situation where one of our columnists has ended up being syndicated. But I spoke with someone at our lawyers, and they said that a sixty/forty split between the writer and the originating newspaper was commonplace.'

'Try eighty/twenty,' I said.

'That's awfully steep, Miss Smythe.'

'I'm worth it,' I said.

'Of course, you are . . . but how about seventy/thirty?'

'I'll settle for seventy-five/twenty-five, nothing less.'

'You drive a tough bargain.'

'Yes. I do. Seventy-five/twenty-five, Mr Howell. And that covers this, and all future serializations. Fair enough?'

A pause.

'Fair enough,' he said. 'I'll have our lawyers draft an agreement for you to sign.'

'I'll look forward to receiving it. And thanks for getting me into Portland and Bangor.'

'Am I ever going to get you over to dinner? My wife is really dying to meet you.'

'In time, Mr Howell. In time.'

I knew I was probably coming across as some affected solipsist . . . but the combination of my pregnancy and my ongoing grief made me shy away from any social gatherings. I could handle my weekly dinner with Ruth, but the idea of making polite conversation over a dinner table – and answering well-meaning questions like, "So, what brought you to Brunswick?" – made me want to steer clear of all social possibilities. I was still succumbing to outbursts of despair. I preferred to keep them private ones. So I kept refusing all invitations.

But when Jim Carpenter suddenly asked me out one afternoon, I surprised myself by saying yes. Jim was an instructor in French at Bowdoin. He taught the class I was auditing. He was in his late twenties – a tall, gangly fellow with sandy hair, rimless glasses, and a retiring, somewhat shy demeanour that masked a mischievous streak. Like everyone else at Bowdoin (the students included), he dressed in the standard New England academic garb: tweed jacket, grey flannels, button-down shirts, a college tie. But, in the course of our conversational lessons,

697

he dropped the fact that Bowdoin was his first teaching job – and that he'd landed in Maine after two years of work on his doctorate at the Sorbonne. I was the only auditor in the class. Though I was also the only woman student (Bowdoin was resolutely all-male back then), Jim remained quite formal and distant with me for the first two months of the course. He asked a few basic questions – *en français* – about my work (*'Je suis journaliste, mais maintenant je prends une periode sabbatique de mon travail'* was all I'd say about it). He made discreet enquiries about my marital status, and whether I was enjoying my time in Maine. Otherwise, he maintained a professional stance of complete disinterest. Until one afternoon – a few weeks after the column started – he caught me on the way out of class. And said, 'I'm enjoying your column enormously, Miss Smythe.'

'Oh, thanks,' I said, feeling slightly embarrassed.

'One of my colleagues in the department said you used to write for *Saturday Night/Sunday Morning*. Is that true?'

'I'm afraid so.'

'I never knew I had a celebrity in my class.'

'You don't.'

'Modesty is an overrated virtue,' he said with a slight smile.

'But immodesty is always boring, don't you think?'

'Perhaps . . . but after a couple of months in Maine, I really wouldn't mind a dose of good old-fashioned Parisian arrogance. Everyone is so polite and self-effacing here.'

'Maybe that's why I like it. Especially after Manhattan, where everyone's always selling themselves. There's something rather pleasant about a place where, five seconds after being introduced, you *don't* know what the person does, how much they earn, and how many times they've been divorced.'

'But I *want* to know that stuff. Maybe that's because I'm still trying to shake off my Hoosier roots.'

'You're actually from Indiana?'

'It happens.'

'Paris really must have been an eye-opener then.'

'Well . . . the wine is better there than in Indianapolis.'

I laughed. 'I think I'll use that line,' I said.

'Be my guest. But on one condition: you let me take you out for dinner one evening.'

I must have looked surprised, because Jim instantly blushed, then said, 'Of course, you're under no obligation . . .'

'No,' I said, interrupting him. 'Dinner one night would be fine.'

We arranged the date for three days' time. Twice before then, I thought about calling up and canceling. Because going out with anybody was the last thing I was interested in at this moment. Because I didn't want to have to do a lot of explaining about everything that had happened to me over the last six months. And because I was pregnant, damn it.

But another voice within my head told me to stop being such a cautious stiff. It was only a dinner, after all. He didn't seem like the sort of guy who had fangs and slept in a coffin. Though I was eschewing social gatherings, I was suddenly beginning to rue the absence of company. So I put on a decent dress and a spot of make-up, and let him take me to the dining room of the Stowe House for dinner. He was somewhat nervous and hesitant at first – which was both endearing and annoying, as I had to work hard initially at making conversation. But after the second cocktail, he started loosening up a bit. By the time he had most of a bottle of wine in him (I restricted myself to two glasses), he began to show flashes of a genuinely amusing mind . . . albeit one forced to hide behind a button-down countenance.

'You know what I loved most about Paris?' he said. 'Besides, of course, the sheer absurd beauty of the place? The ability to walk until dawn. I must have squandered half my time there, staying up all night, wandering from café to café, or just meandering for miles. I had this tiny room in the Fifth, right off the rue des Ecoles. I could pay my rent and stuff my face for fifty dollars a month. I could spend all day reading at this great brasserie – Le Balzar – just around the corner from my garret. And I had a librarian girlfriend named Stephanie who moved in with me for the last four months of my stay . . . and couldn't understand why the hell I wanted to exchange Paris for a teaching post in Brunswick, Maine.'

He paused for a moment, suddenly looking embarrassed. 'And that's the last glass of wine I'm drinking tonight – otherwise I'll start sounding like a walking edition of *True Confessions*.'

'Go on, *encore un verre*,' I said, tipping the rest of the bottle into his glass.

'Only if you join me.'

'I'm a cheap date. Two glasses is my limit.'

'Have you always been that way?'

I was about to say something foolish and revealing like, 'I'm under doctor's orders to drink no more than a glass or two a day.' Instead, I kept it simple: 'It always goes to my head.'

'Nothing wrong with that,' he said, raising his glass. '*Santé.*'

'So why did you throw away Stephanie and *la vie parisienne* for Bowdoin College?'

'Don't get me started. I might commit an act of self-revulsion.'

'Sounds like a grisly prospect. But you still haven't answered my question.'

'What can I say . . . except that I'm the son of an ultra-conservative, ultra-safe insurance executive from Indianapolis. And if you're brought up in the insurance world, you always think cautiously. So, though Paris was a great dream, when the job offer from Bowdoin came through . . . well, it's a salary, right? And the potential for tenure, security, professional prestige. All that boring, cautionary stuff . . . about which I'm sure you happily know nothing.'

'On the contrary, my father was a big cog in the Hartford insurance machine. And my guy did public relations for . . .'

I suddenly cut myself off.

'Oh, there's a guy in your life?' he asked, attempting to sound as nonchalant as possible.

'There *was* a guy. It's over.'

He tried to stop himself from beaming. He failed. 'I'm sorry,' he said.

'It all happened around the same time as my brother . . . You know about my brother?'

He put on a serious face again. 'Yes. When I mentioned you were auditing my course to a colleague at the college, he said that he read a news story about him . . .'

'Dying.'

'Yes. Dying. I really am sorry. It must have been . . .'

'It was.'

'And that's why you moved to Maine?'

'One of the reasons.'

'Was your former guy another reason?'

'He added to the mess, yes.'

'God, what a tough year you've . . .'

'Stop right there . . .'

'Sorry, have I . . . ?'

'No, you've been very sweet. It's just . . . I really can't take much in the way of sympathy . . .'

'Okay,' he said. 'Then I'll play tough and cynical.'

'You can't – you're from Indiana.'

'Is everyone from Manhattan as smart as you are?'

'Is everyone from Indianapolis as fulsome as you are?'

'Ouch.'

'That wasn't meant in a derogatory way.'

'But it wasn't exactly *fulsome* either.'

'Touché. You are quick.'

'For a guy from Indianapolis.'

'It could be worse.'

'How's that?'

'You could be from Omaha.'

He shot me one of his mischievous smiles. And said, 'I like your style.'

Truth be told, I liked his too. When he walked me back to my front door that night, he asked if I might be willing to risk life and limb by taking a day-trip in his car this coming Saturday.

'What's so dangerous about your car?' I asked.

'The driver,' he said.

His car was a two-seater, soft-top Alfa-Romeo, in bright tomato red. I did a double-take when he pulled up in it outside my house that Saturday morning.

'Aren't you a bit young for a mid-life crisis?' I asked, sliding into one of the low bucket seats.

'Believe it or not, it was a gift from my father.'

'Your dad, Mr Indianapolis Insurance King? I don't believe it.'

'I think it was his way of applauding my decision to return home and take the job here.'

'Oh, I get it. It's a variation on How You Gonna Keep 'Em Down On the Farm After They've Seen Paree? With a sportscar, naturally.'

'A *heavily insured* sportscar.'

'Surprise, surprise.'

We spent the day zooming north on Route 1. Past Bath. Past splendidly atmospheric small towns like Wiscasset and Damriscotta and Rockland, eventually reaching Camden around lunchtime. We killed an hour or so in a wonderful used bookshop on Bayview Street. Then we walked down to a little waterfront joint, and ate steamers, washed down with beer. Afterwards, Jim lit up a Gauloise. I declined his offer of a cigarette.

'Good God,' he said. 'A low alcohol tolerance, and an aversion to cigarettes. You must be a secret Mormon in disguise.'

'I tried to be a smoker in college. I failed. I don't think I ever got the knack of inhaling.'

'It's an easy knack to master.'

'One of my many lapses in talent. But answer me this: how the hell can you smoke those Frenchie butts? They smell like an exhaust pipe.'

'Ah, but they taste like . . .'

'. . . a French exhaust pipe. I bet you're the only guy in Maine who smokes them.'

'Should I take that as a compliment?' he asked.

Jim was great fun. We kept up an entertaining banter all day. He had wit. He was ferociously literate. He could also mock himself. I liked him enormously . . . as a pal, a chum, *un bon copain.* Nothing more. Even if I'd been in the market for romance, he wouldn't have fit the bill. Too gawky. Too doting. Too needy. I wanted his company, but I didn't want to fuel his hopes that this might lead to anything more than camaraderie. So – when he suggested a date a few days later – I pleaded work.

'Oh, come on,' he said lightly. 'Surely you could manage a movie and a cheeseburger one night this week.'

'I'm really trying to focus on my column,' I said, and instantly hated myself for sounding like a precious prig. To his credit, Jim laughed. And said,

'You know, as kiss-off lines go, that stinks.'

'You're right. It does stink. What's the movie?'

'*Ace in the Hole,* directed by the very great Billy Wilder.'

'I saw it last year in Manhattan.'

'Any good?'

'The nastiest movie about journalism ever made.'

'Then you'll see it again.'

'Yeah. I guess I will.'

So much for trying to put Jim off. But, to his infinite credit, he never hinted at a romantic subtext to our nights out. Like me, he was new in Brunswick. He craved company. And – though I didn't like admitting it – so did I. Which made it very hard to refuse his offer of a movie, or a chamber music concert in Portland, or an evening with a few of his faculty friends (yes, I was finally becoming sociable). Even after a month of seeing each other, the goodnight kiss was always planted on my cheek. There was (dare I say it) a part of me that wondered: why the hell isn't he making a move? Even though I sensed that his reticence in that department came from the fact that he knew I wasn't interested.

I also knew that, eventually, I would have to own up about my pregnancy. Because – now nearly five months on – I was beginning to develop a telltale bulge in my belly. But I kept putting off this revelation. Because, coward that I am, I feared the effect it might have on our friendship. I so liked him. So wanted him to continue being my pal . . . and sensed that it would all fall apart when he discovered my news.

I resolved to tell him, however, after one of my weekly appointments with Dr Bolduck.

'Once again, everything seems to be going according to the usual pregnancy plan,' he said.

'I am following your orders to the letter, Doc.'

'But I hear you're at least getting out and about a bit . . . which is a good thing.'

'How did you hear that?'

'It's a small town, remember?'

'And what else did you hear?'

'Just that you'd been seen around at a couple of Bowdoin faculty dinners.'

'In the company of Jim Carpenter, right?'

'Yes, I did hear that. But . . .'

'He's just a friend.'

'Fine.'

'I mean that. I am not stringing him along.'

'Hold on here. No one's saying you're stringing him along. Or that you're an item. Or anything like that.'

'But people have noted we've been seeing each other. Well, haven't they?'

'Welcome to Brunswick, Maine. Where everyone knows everyone else's business. In a non-malicious way, of course. Don't let it bother you.'

But it did – because I knew that Jim would publicly look like a fool as soon as my pregnancy became around-town news. So I resolved to tell him the next day.

It was a Saturday. We had arranged to drive out to Reid State Park for the afternoon. But that morning I woke up feeling a little nauseous: a condition I blamed on some tinned salmon I had eaten the night before. So I called up Jim and begged off the afternoon. When he heard I was feeling poorly, he instantly offered to call a doctor, rush to my bedside, and play Florence Nightingale . . .

'It's just an upset stomach,' I said.

'That could mean a variety of things.'

'It means I ate a can of bad Canadian fish last night, and now I am paying for it.'

'At least let me drop by later on and check in on you.'

'Fine, fine,' I said, suddenly too weary to argue.

Moments after I put down the phone, the nausea

actually hit. I raced to the bathroom. I became very sick. When the worst was over, I rinsed out my mouth and staggered back to bed. My night-gown was soaked with sweat. I felt chilled. But, at least, the vomiting had stopped.

It started again five minutes later. This time there was nothing to come up. I hung over the toilet, retching wildly, suddenly feeling ill beyond belief. After this bout of the dry heaves, I made it back to bed . . . and was up a few moments later, hugging the toilet bowl for ballast.

On and on this went for an hour. Finally, my stomach could heave no more. I collapsed into bed. My body finally surrendered to exhaustion. I passed out.

In Brunswick during the 1950s, nobody ever locked their doors. Initially when I moved into my apartment, I always threw the latch. Until the woman who cleaned the place left me a note saying that I didn't need to maintain this security-conscious habit – as the last house robbery in town was around four years ago . . . and the guy was drunk at the time.

I hadn't locked my front door since then. Without question the fact that my door was left open that Saturday afternoon saved my life. Because, around three p.m., Jim showed up at my apartment and knocked on the door for five minutes. I didn't hear his persistent knocking, as I was unconscious at the time. Knowing I was unwell, he decided to enter the apartment. He kept calling out my name.

He got no response. Then he entered my bedroom. As he later told me:

'I thought you were dead.'

Because he found me in a pool of blood.

The sheets were crimson, sodden. I was insensible. Jim couldn't get a word out of me. He dashed to the phone. He called an ambulance.

I briefly came round in the hospital. I was on a gurney, surrounded by doctors and nurses. I heard one of the doctors speaking to Jim.

'How long has your wife been pregnant?' he asked.

'She's pregnant?'

'Yes. Didn't you know . . . ?'

'She's not my wife.'

'What's her first name?'

'Sara.'

The doctor began to snap his fingers in front of my face. 'Sara, Sara . . . are you there? Can you hear me?' I managed to mutter three words: 'The baby is . . .' Then the world went dark again.

When it came back into focus, it was the middle of the night. I was alone in a small empty ward. I had drips and tubes in my arms. My vision was blurred. My head had been cleaved by an ax. But it was nothing compared to the pain in my abdomen. I felt splayed, eviscerated. My flesh was raw, on fire. I wanted to scream. I couldn't scream. My vocal cords appeared frozen. I fumbled for the call button dangling by my side. I held it down for a very long time. I heard brisk footsteps down the corridor. A nurse approached my bedside. She looked down at me. Again I tried to speak. Again I failed. But my face told her everything.

'The pain . . . ?' she asked.

I nodded my head wildly. She put a small plunger in my hand.

'You're on a morphine drip,' she said.

Morphine? Oh God . . .

'So every time the pain gets too much, just press down on this plunger. And . . .'

She demonstrated it for me. Immediately a surge of narcotic warmth spread across my body. And I vanished from consciousness.

Then it was light again. Another nurse was standing over me. The bedclothes had been pulled down. My hospital nightgown was over my belly. A bloody bandage was being yanked off my skin. I shuddered in pain.

'I wouldn't look at that, if I was you,' the nurse said to me.

But I did look – and shuddered again when I saw the horrendous railroad track of stitches across my abdomen. I managed a word:

'What . . . ?'

The pain kicked in again. I fumbled for the plunger. The nurse put it in my hand. I pressed down on it. Darkness.

Light again. Now I saw a familiar face above me: Dr Bolduck. He had a stethoscope on my chest. His finger was on my left wrist, checking my pulse.

'Hi there,' he said. His voice was quiet, subdued. I knew immediately what had happened. 'How's the pain?'

'Bad.'

'I bet. But this is the worst you should experience.'

'I lost it, didn't I?'

'Yes. You did. I am so sorry.'

'What happened?'

'You were suffering from a clinical condition known as an "incompetent cervix"; a condition which is virtually impossible to diagnose until it's too late. Essentially, your cervix couldn't handle the weight of the baby once it passed the five-month mark. So, when the cervix failed, you hemorrhaged. You're lucky your friend Jim found you. You would have died.'

'You operated?'

'We had no choice. Your womb was ruptured. Irreparably. If we hadn't operated . . .'

'I've had a hysterectomy?'

Silence. Then, 'Yes, Sara. A hysterectomy.'

I fumbled for the plunger. I pushed it down. I went under.

Then it was night. The overhead lights were off. It was raining outside. A major thunderstorm. Howling winds. Rattling glass. Celestial tympani. The occasional flash of lightning. It took a few minutes for the morphine fog to lift. The pain was still there, but it was no longer acute. It had become a dull, persistent ache. I stared out the window. I thought back to five years ago in Greenwich. How

I buried my head in Eric's arms and fell apart. How – at the time – it seemed like the world had ended. Six months ago in New York – staring at the bloodstains in my brother's apartment – I too thought that life could not go on.

And then Jack. And now this.

I swallowed hard. I resisted the temptations of the morphine plunger. The rain was now splattering across the window, like liquid buckshot. I wanted to cry. I could not. All I could do was look out into the dark, blank night. And think: *so this is what happened.* Maybe it was the residue of the narcotics. Maybe it was post-operative shock. Or maybe there comes a point when you simply can no longer grieve for everything that life throws at you. It's not that you suddenly accept your fate. Rather, that you now understand a central truth: there is a thing called tragedy, and it shadows us all. We live in fear of it. We try to keep it at bay. But, like death, it is omnipresent. It permeates everything we do. We spend a lifetime building a fortress against its onslaught. But it still triumphs. Because tragedy is so casual, aimless, indiscriminate. When it does hit us, we look for reasons, justifications, messages from on high. I get pregnant. I lose the baby. I am told I will never have another. I get pregnant again. I lose the baby again. What does this mean? Is somebody trying to tell me something? Or is this just how things are?

Later that day, Jim showed up. He was looking

uneasy. He carried a small bouquet of flowers. They were already half-wilted.

'I brought you these,' he said, putting them on the little table by my bed. As soon as he set them down, he immediately backed away to the other side of the room. Either he didn't want to crowd me, or he was uneasy about being within my close proximity.

'Thank you,' I said.

He positioned himself against the wall near the door. 'How are you feeling now?' he asked.

'I really recommend morphine.'

'You must have been in agony.'

'Nothing a hysterectomy can't cure.'

The color was bleached from his face.

'I didn't know. I'm so . . .'

'I am the one who should apologize. I should have told you about this from the start. But I was a coward . . .'

He held his hand up. 'No need to explain,' he said.

'The doctor said that if you hadn't found me . . .'

There was an awkward pause.

'I'd better go,' he said.

'Thank you for the visit. Thank you for . . .'

'May I ask you something?' he said, cutting me off.

I nodded.

'The guy who got you pregnant . . . are you in love with him?'

'*Was*. Very deeply.'

'It's over?'

'Completely.'

'No,' he said, 'it's not.'

I had no answer to that. Except something lame like: 'Let's talk when I finally get out of here.'

'Uh, sure,' he said.

'I am sorry, Jim. Very sorry.'

'That's okay.'

But I knew that it wasn't okay. Just as I also realized that news of my hospitalization would disseminate quickly through Brunswick. Certainly, Duncan Howell knew that I had been rushed to the Brunswick Hospital – as a big floral arrangement arrived that same afternoon. It was accompanied by a card:

Get well soon . . . From the staff of the Maine Gazette.

I didn't expect an effusive note. But the generic quality of the message made me wonder whether Mr Howell had discovered the real reason behind my medical emergency.

Dr Bolduck informed me that – due to my surgical wounds and the amount of blood I had lost – I could expect to spend ten more days in the care of Brunswick Hospital. I was anxious about missing my forthcoming deadlines for the column – and put a call through to the editor's office. For the first time since I started writing for the *Maine*

Gazette, Mr Howell didn't take my call. Instead his secretary got on the line – and informed me that the editor was 'in a meeting', but that he wanted me to have the next two weeks off, 'at full pay'.

'That's very generous of Mr Howell,' I said. 'Please thank him for me.'

I spent much of the next ten days in a post-operative blur. Even though the worst of the pain had dissipated, I let it be known that I was in serious physical discomfort. I must have sounded convincing to Dr Bolduck and the nursing staff, as they kept my morphine bag topped up. There are moments in life when certain things shouldn't be confronted; when you don't want clarity, forth-rightness, the truth. This was one of them. Every time I felt myself veering towards terrible lucidity, I reached for the morphine plunger. I knew that, at the end of ten days, I would have to get out of this bed, and continue my life. Until then, however, I craved chemical denial.

Ruth dropped in every other day. She brought home-made oatmeal cookies, and magazines, and a bottle of Christian Brothers brandy.

'Who needs brandy when you've got this?' I said, brandishing the morphine plunger.

'Whatever works,' she said with a worried smile.

She offered to collect my mail for me. 'No mail, no newspapers, nothing tangible. I'm on a vacation from everything.'

I could see her eyeing the plunger in my hand. 'Is that stuff helping things?' she asked.

715

'You bet,' I said. 'In fact, I might get it installed on tap in my apartment.'

'What a wonderful idea,' she said. Her tone was so pleasant that I knew she was humoring me. 'You sure you don't need anything?'

'I do need something.'

'Tell me.'

'A complete memory loss.'

Two days before I was discharged, one of the nurses rolled away the morphine drip.

'Hey! I need that,' I said.

'Not anymore,' she said.

'Says who?'

'Dr Bolduck.'

'But what about the pain?'

'We'll be giving you some pills . . .'

'Pills aren't the same.'

'They do the job.'

'Not as well as the morphine.'

'You don't need the morphine.'

'Oh yes I do.'

'Then take it up with the doctor.'

The pills diminished the pain, but they certainly didn't dispatch me to Never-Never Land like the morphine. I couldn't sleep. I spent the night watching the hospital ward ceiling. Somewhere near dawn, I decided that I hated this life. It was too agonizing, too appallingly fragile. Everything hurt too much. It was best to make an exit now. Because I knew full well that once the morphine had drained out of my system, I would enter a realm beyond endurance. All reserves of strength, stoicism, resilience had been depleted. I didn't want to grapple anymore with such ruthless sorrow. I couldn't face the idea of living in a state of permanent anguish. So the alternative was a simple one: permanent escape.

The nurse had left two painkillers by my bedside if I needed them during the night. I would ask Dr Bolduck for an extra-large prescription to take with me when I checked out of here. I would go home. I would open a bottle of decent whiskey. I would chase all the pills with copious amounts of J&B. Then I would tie a bag round my head, sealing all potential air leaks with tape. I'd get into bed. The pill-and-Scotch cocktail would knock me out. I'd quietly smother to death in my sleep.

I reached for the two pills. I swallowed them. I continued to stare at the ceiling. I suddenly felt rather wonderful, knowing that I would only have to cope with forty-eight hours more of life. I began to organize to-do lists in my mind. I would have to make certain my will was up-to-date. No doubt, there would be a local lawyer in town who could offer me express service . . . as long as I didn't let on that the new will would be in probate only a day after I signed it. I would have to decide on funeral arrangements. No religious send-off. No memorials. Maybe a listing in the *New York Times* obituary, so a few people back in Manhattan would be informed of my demise. But definitely no organized memorial service. Just a local cremation here in Maine, and the local undertakers could do what the hell they wanted with my ashes. And my money? My so-called estate? Leave it all to . . .

Who?

There was no one. No husband. No family. No child. No loved ones.

Loved ones. What a facile expression to describe the most central need in life. But who were my loved ones? To whom would I bequeath my estate? I was flying solo. My death would mean nothing. It would hurt no one . . . so my suicide would not be a selfish or vengeful act. It would simply be a drastic, but necessary from of pain relief.

The painkillers kicked in. I fell into a deep sleep. I woke sometime during mid-morning. I felt curiously calm, almost elated. I had a plan, a future, a destination.

Dr Bolduck came around that afternoon. He checked my war wounds. He seemed pleased with the healing process. He asked me about the pain. I complained of a constant nasty ache.

'How are those pills working?' he asked.

'I miss the morphine.'

'I bet you do. Which is why there's no way I'm letting you near it again. I don't want you leaving here thinking you're Thomas de Quincey.'

'I think opium was his substance of choice.'

'Hey, I'm a doctor, not a literary critic. But I do know morphine is addictive.'

'You will give me something for the pain.'

'Sure. I'll give you a week's supply of those pills.

Within three or four days, the pain should finally vanish, so I doubt you'll need them all.'

'That's good to know.'

'How are you faring otherwise?'

'Surprisingly all right.'

'Really?'

'It's a difficult time, but I'm coping.'

'Don't be surprised if you feel depressed. It's a common reaction.'

'I'll be vigilant,' I said.

He then said that I could go home tomorrow. I called Ruth and asked if she could pick me up in the morning. She was there at nine. She helped me into her car. She brought me back to my apartment. It had been cleaned the day before. There were fresh sheets on the bed. Ruth had gone shopping, and the larder was stocked with basic provisions. A small pile of mail was on my kitchen table. I decided it could all remain unopened.

Ruth asked me if there was anything else she could do for me.

'There's a prescription from Dr Bolduck . . .'

'No problem,' she said, taking the scrawled form from my hand. 'I'll just pop down to the druggist on Maine Street and get it filled right away. Don't want you in pain, after all.'

While she was out, I made a phone call to the first attorney-at-law in the Brunswick phone book. His name was Alan Bourgeois. He answered the phone himself. I explained that I had a will on file with my lawyer in New York, but it had left my entire estate to my brother, who was now deceased. How could I change it? He said he'd be happy to draw up a new will – which would supercede the old one. Might I stop down tomorrow? Or if I was free this afternoon, he could make time for me. It was a slow day.

I arranged to see him at two p.m. Ruth returned an hour later with the filled prescription. 'The druggist said you're to take no more than two every three hours. There's a week's supply.'

Forty-two pills. That should be enough to do the job.

'I can't thank you enough for everything,' I said to Ruth. 'You've been a great friend.'

'I'll check in tomorrow, if that's okay.'

'No need,' I said. 'I'll be fine.'

She looked at me with care. 'I'll still stick my head in,' she said.

That afternoon, I called a cab to take me down Maine Street to the office of Alan Bourgeois. His office was a room over a haberdasher's. He was a small man in his mid-fifties, dressed in a nondescript grey suit, beneath which was a v-neck sweater. A pen holder adorned his breast pocket. He looked like the perfect country lawyer: quiet, direct, businesslike. He took down all my personal details. He asked for the name of my New York lawyer. He then asked how I wanted to divide up my estate.

'Fifty per cent should go to Ruth Reynolds of Bath, Maine,' I said.

'And the remaining half?'

I drew a breath. 'The remaining half should be left in trust for Charles Malone until his twenty-first birthday.'

'Is Charles Malone a nephew?'

'The son of a friend.'

Mr Bourgeois said that the will would be a straightforward document, and he would have it ready tomorrow.

'Is there no chance we could finalize it all today?' I asked.

'Well, I suppose I could take care of it before close-of-business. But it would mean you having to come back in a few hours.'

'That's not a problem,' I said. 'I have some errands I have to run.'

'Fine by me,' he said, and we arranged to meet again just before five.

I wasn't able to walk very far – so I called a cab again. I asked the driver to wait while I made a trip to a hardware store, where I bought some bags and a wide roll of packing tape. I moved on to the bank, where I withdrew fifty dollars to cover the cost of Mr Bourgeois's legal fees. Then the cabbie drove me up to the Maine State Liquor Store near the college. I was about to buy a fifth of J&B when I saw a bottle of Glenfiddich next to it. The difference in price was six dollars. I decided to splurge.

I was dropped off home. I arranged for the cabbie to collect me again just before five. I had ninety minutes. I used them productively. I gathered up all check books and deposit books, and assembled them on the table. I found my few pieces of jewelry, and placed them alongside the bank stuff. I rolled a piece of paper in my typewriter and punched out a fast letter to Joel Eberts, explaining about the new will. I gave him the name of Alan Bourgeois, and told him I'd arrange for a copy of the document to be mailed to him.

By the time the will reaches you, I will have left this life. I am not going to offer a great defense for my decision to put an end to things. Except this: I simply know I can't go on.

In the new will, you have been listed as my executor, so I'll trust you to sell the apartment, liquidate the stock, and set up a trust for Charles Malone – to whom half of my estate is being left. I'm certain you find it strange that I am making him such a major beneficiary. My rationale is a simple one: Jack Malone was the man I loved most in my life. Yes, he destroyed that love by betraying Eric, but that betrayal doesn't negate his central role in the final part of my life. I always wanted children, but I didn't get that wish. Malone has a son. Let him benefit from the love I once had for his father . . . but please make certain that under no circumstances can Malone himself have any access to the trust.

In closing, let me say that you have always been a great friend to me. Do understand: I know this is the right choice. I look upon it as something akin to the breakdown of a protracted negotiation. I've fought my corner to the best of my ability – yet I find myself constantly overwhelmed, constantly defeated. It's time to surrender to the inevitable – and admit that the negotiation should come to an end.

I wish you well. I thank you for everything.

I signed the letter. I folded it and placed it in an envelope. I addressed the envelope, and attached a stamp to it. Then I rolled another sheet of paper into my Remington and typed a short note that I planned to leave in an envelope on my front doormat:

Dear Ruth:

Don't go inside. Do call the police. Do accept my apologies for landing you with this unpleasant chore. Do contact Alan Bourgeois at his office on Maine Street in Brunswick. Do know that I think you were about the best ally imaginable.

Love,

I scrawled my signature. I placed the note in the envelope. I wrote *Ruth* on its front. I left it on the dining table, to be placed outside later this evening.

A knock came at the door. It was the taxi. I picked up my coat and the letter to Joel Eberts.

I posted it in the mail box near my front door. Then I climbed into the cab and returned to the office of Alan Bourgeois. He greeted me with a stern nod, and motioned for me to sit in the steel chair which faced his desk. Then he picked up a legal document on his desk, and handed it to me.

'Here it is,' he said. 'Read through it carefully – because if there are any amendments or codicils, now's the time to get them done.'

I studied the document. Everything seemed to be in order. I said so.

'You left the funeral arrangements section somewhat vague,' Mr Bourgeois said.

'I want a vague funeral,' I said lightly. Immediately, Mr Bourgeois looked at me with concern, so I added: 'Fifty years from now, of course.'

He pursed his lips and said nothing. I returned the document to his desk.

'It all seems just fine. Shall I sign it now?'

He reached into his pocket and produced a fountain pen. Unscrewing the cap he handed it to me.

'I've made three copies of the will. One for your records, one for your lawyer in New York, and one for my files. You'll need to sign them all, then I'll put on my notary public hat and notarize the lot. By the way, I meant to tell you: the notary charge is two dollars per document. I hope that isn't too exorbitant.'

'No problem,' I said, scribbling my signature in the appropriate place on all three documents. As

I handed them back, Mr Bourgeois used an old-fashioned engraver to stamp his seal on each of the signed pages. Then he added his own signature below the seal.

'You now have a new will,' he said. Then he reached over to his in-tray and handed me a bill for forty-one dollars. I took out my purse, counted out the money and put it on his desk. He put my copy of the will into a thick manila envelope and, with a hint of ceremony, placed it in my hands.

'Thank you for the speedy service,' I said, standing up to leave.

'Anytime, Miss Smythe. I hope I can be of service to you again.'

I said nothing. I headed towards the door. Mr Bourgeois said, 'Mind if I ask you a nosy question?'

'Go ahead.'

'Why did you need this will so quickly?'

I had already anticipated this question, and had prepared a reasonable answer. 'I'm going away on a trip tomorrow.'

'But I thought you just got out of the hospital today?'

'How on earth did you know that?' I asked, my tone sharp.

'I know your column from the paper, and I also heard you'd been unwell.'

'From whom?'

He looked taken aback by my stridency. 'From . . . uh . . . just around Brunswick. It's a small town, you know. I was just curious, that's all.'

'I'm taking a trip. I wanted to have my will in order, especially as my brother . . .'

'I do understand. No offence meant, Miss Smythe.'

'None taken, Mr Bourgeois. Nice doing business with you.'

'And you, ma'am. Going anywhere nice?'

'Sorry?'

'I was just wondering if the place you were going is nice.'

'I don't know. I've never been there before.'

I took the taxi back to my house, determined to get this over with as soon as possible . . . just in case Mr Bourgeois had sensed that I was up to something self-destructive and dispatched the police over to my apartment. I stared out at the now-dark streets of Brunswick, thinking: this will be my last glimpse of the outside world. When the cab pulled up in front of my house, I tipped the driver ten dollars. He was stunned, and thanked me profusely. *Well, it's my last cab ride*, I felt like saying. *Anyway, come tomorrow, I won't have any use for money.*

I went inside. I retrieved the letter to Ruth and placed it on my outside mat. Then I bolted the door behind me. I took off my coat. The cleaner had laid a fire in the grate. I touched the kindling with a match. It ignited instantly. I went into the bathroom. I retrieved the bottle of painkillers. I walked into the kitchen. I pulled out a bag, a roll of tape and a pair of scissors. I went to the bedroom.

I placed the bag on my pillow, then I cut off four long strips of tape and attached them to the bedside table. I picked up the bottle of Glenfiddich and a glass. I went into the living room. I sat down on the sofa. My hands began to shake. I poured a slug of Glenfiddich into the glass. I downed it. My hands were still trembling. I poured myself another finger of whiskey. Down it went in one go. I took a deep breath and felt the glow of the whiskey spread across my body. My plan was straightforward. I would down all the pills in clusters of five, chasing each handful with a large glass of Glenfiddich. When the bottle was empty, I'd move quickly into the bedroom, get the bag taped around my head, and lie down on the bed. The combination of Scotch and painkillers would ensure unconsciousness within minutes. I'd never wake up again.

I pulled the bottle of pills out of my skirt pocket. I popped off the cap. I counted out five pills into my hand. The phone began to ring. I ignored it. The phone continued to ring. I poured a very large glass of whiskey. The phone wouldn't stop ringing. I began to fear that Alan Bourgeois might have been checking up on me – and that if I didn't answer it, he'd think the worst. It was best to answer it, and assure him I was just fine. I put the pills back into the bottle. I reached for the phone.

'Sara, Duncan Howell here.'

Damn. Damn. Damn. I tried to sound agreeable.

'Hi, Duncan.'

'Am I calling you at a bad moment?'

'No,' I said, taking another swig of Scotch. 'Go ahead.'

'I heard you were discharged from Brunswick Regional today. How are you faring?'

'I'm just fine.'

'You've had us all worried. And I must have had at least a dozen letters from readers, wondering when your column would be returning.'

'That's very nice,' I said, the bottle of pills rattling in my hand. 'But . . . might I call you later? Or tomorrow perhaps? It's just . . . I am still rather drained, and . . .'

'Believe me, Sara – knowing how sick you've been, I really didn't want to call tonight. But I felt I should talk to you before you found out . . .'

'Found out what?'

'You mean, no one from New York has been on to you this afternoon?'

'I was out. But why would anyone from New York get on to me?'

'Because you were prominently featured in Walter Winchell's column today.'

'*What?*'

'Would you like me to read it to you?'

'Absolutely.'

'It's not exactly flattering . . .'

'Read it, please.'

'All right, here we go. It was the fourth item from the top: "*She used to be a hot-shot columnist with* Saturday Night/Sunday Morning, *but now she's*

728

doing time in Hicksville. Sara Smythe – the yuck-yuck dame behind the popular 'Real Life' column – vanished from print a couple of months ago . . . right after her Redder-than-Red brother, Eric, was booted from his job as Marty Manning's head scribe. Seems that Eric wouldn't sing about his Commie past . . . a major unpatriotic no-no which also made Saturday/Sunday *nervous about keeping Sister Sara in print. A month later, the ole demon rum sent Eric to an early grave, and Sara disappeared into thin air. Until one of my spies – on vacation in the great state of Maine – picked up a little local rag called the* Maine Gazette *. . . and guess who was churning out words in its big-deal pages? You got it: the once-famous Sara Smythe. Oh, how the mighty do fall when they forget a little tune called 'The Star Spangled Banner'."'*

Duncan Howell paused for a moment, nervously clearing his throat.

'Like I said, it's hardly nice. And I certainly took umbrage at our paper being called "a little local rag".'

'That son of a bitch.'

'My conclusion entirely. And we're standing right behind you in all of this.'

I rattled the pills in my hand again, saying nothing.

'There's something else you need to know,' Duncan Howell said. 'Two things, actually. Neither pleasant. The first is that I received a call this afternoon from a man named Platt. He said he was in the legal affairs department of *Saturday Night/Sunday Morning*. He'd been trying to track you

729

down . . . but as he didn't have any idea of your whereabouts, he'd decided to call me – having discovered, from Winchell's column, that you were writing for us. Anyway, he asked me to inform you that, by writing for us, you were in breach of contract . . .'

'That's total garbage,' I said, my voice surprisingly loud.

'I'm just passing on what he told me. He also wanted you to know that he was stopping your leave-of-absence payments from this moment on.'

'That's all right. There were only a few more weeks to go. Any other good news?'

'I'm afraid there have been some repercussions from the Winchell column.'

'What kind of repercussions?'

'I received two phone calls late this afternoon from the editors of the *Portland Press Herald* and the *Bangor Daily News*. They both expressed grave concern about the anti-American allegations in the Winchell item . . .'

'I am not anti-American. Nor was my late brother.'

'Sara, I assured them of that. But like so many people these days, they're scared of being associated with anything or anyone who has even the slightest Communist taint.'

'I am not a goddamn Communist,' I shouted, then suddenly hurled the bottle of painkillers across the room. The bottle smashed into the fireplace, fragmenting into pieces.

'No one from the *Maine Gazette* is saying that. And I want to be very clear about something: we are completely behind you. I've spoken with half the members of our board this afternoon, and everyone agrees with me: you are an asset to the paper, and we will certainly not be intimidated by a yellow journalist like Mr Winchell. So you have our complete support, Sara.'

I said nothing. I was still watching the painkillers melt against the wooden logs in the fireplace. My suicide had gone up in smoke. But so too had the desire to take my life. Had I killed myself, it would have been interpreted as a capitulation to Winchell, McCarthy, and every other bully who used patriotism as a weapon; a means to wield power. Now I wouldn't give those bastards the satisfaction of my death. Now . . .

'Are you still there, Sara?'

'Yes. I'm here.'

CHAPTER 12

I put a call in to Joel Eberts the next morning.
'Now before you tell me anything,' he said,
'know this: I'm sure we could sue that shit
Winchell for libel, defamation of character . . .'

'I don't want to sue him.'

'I heard about *Saturday/Sunday* too. We could
definitely squeeze them for the remaining few weeks
of your leave . . . and probably more.'

'I couldn't be bothered.'

'You've *got* to be bothered. If people like you
don't fight back . . .'

'I'm in no mood for a fight. Because you know,
and I know, that it's a fight I won't win. Anyway,
I'm leaving the country.'

'When did you decide that?'

'Late last night. Actually, around five this
morning.'

'Personally, I think it's a good idea. Can I help
in any way?'

'I need a passport. Do you think they'll grant
me one?'

'I don't see why not. You haven't been subpoenaed
by HUAC. You aren't under investigation by the

Feds. There'll be no problem – though I'd probably move quickly, just in case someone in DC read that Winchell piece and decides you're worth scrutinizing. When are you coming back to New York?'

'I should be there tomorrow evening.'

'I still have power-of-attorney on your bank accounts. Want me to book you passage on a boat this weekend?'

'Absolutely.'

'I'll get to work on it now.'

'One final thing. I sent you a letter yesterday afternoon. It was written under considerable duress . . . and at a moment when I really wasn't thinking clearly at all. You must promise me that you won't read it . . . that you'll tear it up and throw it away as soon as it arrives.'

'It must be some letter.'

'Do I have your word?'

'Scout's Honor. Call me as soon as you arrive. Are you going to be staying at the apartment?'

'Where else?'

'Well, if you do, you might have a visitor . . .'

'Oh no . . .'

'Oh yes . . .'

'Has he been bothering you much about me?'

'You told me not to tell you anything . . .'

'I'm asking now.'

'I have a stack of letters from him. According to the super in your building, he's been dropping around every other day, on the off-chance you might have come back.'

I felt a stab of guilt and remorse. It passed quickly. 'I'll find a hotel,' I said.

'That might be wise . . . if you really don't want to see him.'

'I really don't want to see him.'

'It's your call, Sara. Phone me when you get into town.'

After I finished talking with Joel Eberts, I put a call in to Dr Bolduck. When I explained that I was planning to leave town tomorrow, he expressed concern.

'It's only two weeks since the operation. The stitches have just come out. I would be much happier if you were resting for at least another week.'

'A transatlantic crossing isn't exactly strenuous physical activity.'

'Yes – but you'll be in the middle of the ocean for five days. Say you need medical attention?'

'I'm sure most ships travel with a doctor or two.'

'I really wish you'd stay.'

'I can't. I won't.'

He heard the adamancy in my voice. 'I do understand your need to get away,' he said. 'It's not unusual after . . .'

'So, in your clinical opinion, I'm not putting my health in jeopardy by traveling.'

'Physically, it's a little risky . . . but not impossibly so. Mentally, it's a smart idea. You know what my advice is to people who've been through a bereavement? Keep moving.'

I did just that. Ruth came over that afternoon and helped me pack up the apartment. I wrote a letter to Duncan Howell, resigning my column.

Please understand: I haven't been cowed by Walter Winchell. I just need a complete break from all things journalistic. After the last year, anonymity seems like a very good thing. I thank you for your ethical stance after the Winchell column. Many an editor would have taken the easy way out and defenestrated me. You didn't – and I will always remember that.

I also wrote a quick note to Jim:

If I was you, I wouldn't forgive me. I played fast-and-loose with the truth – which was both unfair and unscrupulous. All I can offer in my defence is the fact that – for all the obvious reasons – I was apprehensive of talking about my pregnancy. That doesn't excuse my behavior. The worst thing you can do in life is hurt another person . . . and I sense that I have hurt you.

The two letters were mailed the next morning from the Brunswick railway station. I was traveling light – a suitcase and my typewriter. I hadn't bought much in the way of clothes since coming to Maine, and any books and records I'd acquired were being donated to the local library. The station

735

porter checked my bags straight through to Penn Station. Ruth – who'd driven me to the station – hugged me goodbye.

'I hope the next time you come back to Maine, you won't be fleeing something.'

I laughed. 'But it's such a good place to slam the door on the rest of the country.'

'Then why on earth do you have to go overseas?'

'Because, thanks to Mr Winchell, I find myself abroad at home. So I'm now going to find out whether I'm at home abroad.'

I slept most of the way to New York. I was still feeling depleted. And I was still in a certain amount of pain – thanks to the way that my supply of painkillers had ended up in the fire. I hadn't dared asked Dr Bolduck for a new prescription, so I was now using aspirin to deaden the discomfort. Every time I saw myself sitting on that sofa with the bottle of pills and the whiskey, I shuddered. Because for the two days before, the decision to take my life had seemed so logical, so reasonable . . . to the point where I actually felt rather elated by the prospect of terminating everything. But now, as the train snaked its way down the eastern seaboard, I couldn't help but think: *if that phone call hadn't come, this is a day I wouldn't have seen*. It wasn't even a particularly nice day – as it was overcast and gloomy. But it was *a day*. I was still here to look at it. I was grateful for that.

I arrived at Penn Station around nine that night.

I had a porter help me with my bags across the street to the Hotel Pennsylvania. They had a vacancy. I paid for one night, with an option to extend for a second. I didn't want to be in this town for long. Upstairs in my room, I stared out at the midtown skyline, then closed the blinds to block out its audacious glow. I unpacked, undressed, climbed into bed and was asleep within minutes. I woke at eight, feeling rested for the first time in months. I had a bath, I got dressed, I called Joel Eberts. He told me to come right over. On the way downtown in a taxi, I read the *New York Times*. On page eleven, there was a small story at the bottom of the page about the suicide yesterday afternoon of a Hollywood actor named Max Monroe, aged forty-six, known for his roles in a variety of RKO and Republic B-movies. He was found dead yesterday afternoon at his apartment in West Hollywood from a self-inflicted gunshot wound.

According to his agent, Mr Monroe had been suffering from depression for the past two years – ever since work opportunities dried up after he was branded a hostile witness by the House Committee on UnAmerican Activities.

I put down the paper, unable to finish the story. I glanced out the window of the taxi. New York was as frantic and self-obsessed as ever. Everyone rushing somewhere. Everyone so preoccupied, so busy that they probably weren't even aware of the deeds being perpetrated in their name – the careers crushed, the trusts betrayed, the lives destroyed.

That was the thing about the blacklist – unless it touched you personally, you could carry on as if nothing dark was happening around you. I couldn't fathom how we had allowed ourselves to be cowed by such patriotic demagogs. All I knew was: I had to leave. To put an ocean between myself and my country. Until the madness ended.

Joel Eberts greeted me with a paternal hug and a considerable amount of news. He'd booked me passage on the SS *Corinthia*, sailing that night, docking seven days later in Le Havre. He'd secured me a single inside cabin: nothing fancy, but at least I'd have the place to myself. He had all the forms ready for my passport.

'It's the same deal as your brother – you run up to the passport office at Rockefeller Center, you hand in all the forms and a check for twelve dollars, you show them your transatlantic boat ticket, and they should have a passport for you by five this evening. But you better hurry. The deadline for one-day processing is ten thirty. That now gives you a half-hour to get there, tops.'

Forms in hand, I grabbed a cab. It raced uptown. I made the passport office at ten twenty-five. The clerk vetted all the forms, and told me to be back at the office by close of business today. As I came out of the office, I noticed that I was opposite the *Saturday Night/Sunday Morning* building. I didn't give it a second glance. I just hailed a cab and headed downtown again.

Joel Eberts had offered to bring me to lunch at

a little Italian place near his office. We sat down. We ordered. The boss – a friend of Joel's – insisted on bringing us each a glass of Spumante. We toasted my journey to foreign parts.

'Have you thought about what you are going to do over there?'

'No. I don't even know where I'll end up . . . though, initially, I'll probably head to Paris.'

'You will write me as soon as you've gotten settled somewhere?'

'I'll wire you. Because I'll also need to set up bank transfer facilities.'

'No problem. I'll handle all that.'

'And you will give me a bill for all that you've been doing on my behalf?'

'Call it a friendly favor.'

'I would really rather pay you properly, Joel.'

'That's one of the many things I like about you, Sara – you're completely ethical.'

'Look where it's gotten me.'

He paused for a moment, abstractedly rubbing the rim of his glass with his stubby index finger. 'Do you mind if I ask you something?'

'Yes – I still think about him a lot.'

He smiled. 'Are my thoughts that transparent?' he asked.

'No – I am.'

'As I told you on the phone, there must be fifteen, twenty letters from him, stacked up in my office. He also called me around four times. Begging me to tell him where you were.'

'What did you say?'

'What you told me to say: that you had left New York and were living in an undisclosed location. Then he asked if I was forwarding on his letters. I said that you instructed me to hold all personal mail until you returned.'

'Did he leave you alone after that?'

Another pause. 'Do you really want to know this?' I nodded. 'He came to see me personally. Around six weeks ago. He sat in the chair opposite my desk, and . . .'

'Yes?'

'He started to cry.'

'I don't want to hear this.'

'Fine,' he said, reaching for the menu. 'Shall we order?'

'What did he say?'

'You said you *don't* want to hear this . . .'

'You're right,' I said, reaching for the menu. 'I don't. Tell me what he said.'

Joel put down the menu. 'He told me you were the best thing that ever happened to him; the center of his life. And he tried to explain . . .'

'How he killed my brother?'

'You know that's not true.'

'All right, all right – he didn't *physically* end his life. But he certainly got the ball rolling in that direction. He pointed the finger. He handed Eric to the Feds on a plate. How can I forgive that? *How?*'

Joel drummed his fingers on the table. 'Forgiveness

is the hardest thing in life . . . and the most necessary. But it's still the hardest.'

'That's easy for you to say.'

'You're right. It is. Eric wasn't my brother.'

'Exactly,' I said, reaching for the menu. 'And yes, I will have the veal *piccata.*'

'Good choice,' Joel said, motioning towards the waiter. We ordered. Then Joel reached into his pocket. He pulled out an envelope, and handed it to me. I saw that it was postmarked *Brunswick, Me.*

'Here's the letter you sent me,' he said.

'Oh,' I said, suddenly uneasy. 'You didn't read it, did you?'

'It's unopened, Sara – at your request. As long as it's legal, I always follow my clients' instructions.'

'Thank you,' I said, tucking the letter into my bag. He looked at me carefully. I sensed that he knew what was in that letter – and how close I had skirted the precipice.

'I hope you'll get some rest during the trans-atlantic crossing,' he said. 'You look tired, Sara.'

'I am tired. And yes, I do plan to spend most of the next seven days on the SS *Corinthia* fast asleep. If they allow me on the boat, that is.'

'Why wouldn't they?'

'You can't board a transatlantic ship without a passport, can you? And if the Department of State stopped Eric from getting a passport . . .'

'Don't worry – they'll issue you a passport.'

Joel was right. At five that afternoon, the clerk

at the Rockefeller Center passport office handed me a spanking new green travel document, valid for five years. My lawyer accompanied me to the office, just in case my application had run into difficulties. But no questions were asked, no objections raised. The clerk even wished me 'Bon Voyage.'

We managed to find a taxi amidst the rush-hour madness on Fifth Avenue. I had just under forty-five minutes to make it to Pier 76, where the SS *Corinthia* was docked and setting sail that night at seven thirty. I started out of the cab window as night fell on Manhattan. I suddenly wanted to jump out, run to the nearest phone booth, and call Jack. But what would I have said?

'Do you believe things happen for a reason?' I heard myself saying.

Joel looked at me with care. 'You're talking to the original Jewish agnostic, Sara. I don't believe in some Almighty plan, or even that dumb thing called "destiny". I believe you should try to live your life ethically, and otherwise hope for the best. What else can we do?'

'I wish I knew, Joel. I wish . . .'

'What?'

Silence.

'If only Eric had gotten his passport . . .'

'Sara . . .'

'Or if he'd gone to Mexico the next day . . . If he hadn't looked back in that taxi on the way to the airport, and seen the midtown skyline . . . If only . . .'

'Don't play the *if only* game, Sara. You can never win it.'

We inched our way west on 50th Street. We reached Twelfth Avenue. We turned south towards 48th Street. We pulled into the gates of Pier 76. We got out of the cab. The driver handed my suitcase and typewriter to a porter. He lurked nearby. I suddenly found myself clutching on to Joel's coat sleeves.

'What am I doing here?' I asked.

'Getting on that boat.'

'I'm scared.'

'You're leaving the country for the first time. It's only natural to be anxious.'

'I'm making the wrong call.'

'You can always turn around and come back. It's not a life sentence, you know.'

'Tell me I'm crazy.'

He kissed me gently on the head – like a father giving his daughter his blessing.

'Bon voyage, Sara. Wire me when you find your footing.'

The porter cleared his throat, hinting that it was time to get aboard. I hugged Joel. Gently, he detached my hands from his sleeves.

'What will I do over there?' I said.

'At the very worst, you'll survive. Which is what we all do.'

I turned and followed the porter up the gang-plank. Just before we reached the main deck, I spun around. The taxi carrying Joel Eberts was pulling out of the gate. I kept my eyes at street level. To look up would have meant paying a final mournful tribute to the Manhattan skyline. I didn't want a long goodbye. I just wanted to leave town as quietly as possible.

CHAPTER 13

Seven days after slinking out of New York Harbor, the SS Corinthia docked in Le Havre. I stepped on to French soil, my equilibrium still wobbly after all that time at sea. I immediately took a taxi to the railway station, and caught the express to Paris.

A week later, I checked out of my hotel on the rue de Sevres and moved into a small *atelier* on rue Cassette in the Sixth. I lived there for the next four years. Initially I took French lessons and squandered the days in cinemas and brasseries. Then I found a job in a small Franco-American advertising agency on the Champs-Elysées. Through colleagues at work, I was parachuted into the center of Paris's burgeoning American community – for this was the time when the weakness of the franc, the luxury of the GI bill, and the ongoing witch hunt back home meant that the French capital was heaving with expats. Initially, I resisted mingling with my compatriots. Inevitably, though, I found myself getting more and more tangled in the American community. Especially after I met Mort Goodman – the executive editor of the *Paris Herald-Tribune* – at a party.

'I'm sure I know your name from somewhere,' he said after we were introduced.

'Did you ever work in New York?' I asked.

'Sure,' he said. 'I was with *Collier's* for three years before getting the job over here.'

'Well, I used to write a bit for *Saturday/Sunday*.'

'Oh hell, you're *that* Sara Smythe,' he said, then insisted on taking me out to lunch the next day. By the end of that lunch, he offered me the chance to contribute the occasional feature to the paper. I kept on churning out copy for the advertising agency, but started having my by-line appear every few weeks in the *Herald-Tribune*. Three months after I started getting published in that paper, Mort Goodman took me out for another lunch and asked if I'd like to try my hand at a column.

'Traditionally, we've always had a resident American-in-Paris write a weekly piece on life in the capital, local color, *la mode du moment* . . . whatever. Now the guy who's been doing it for the past two years has just got himself fired for missing four deadlines in a row, due to his little love affair with the bottle. Which means the position is open. Interested?'

Of course, I said yes. My first column appeared on November seventh, 1952 . . . three days after Eisenhower beat Stevenson for the presidency. That election – and McCarthy's accelerating hearings in Washington – hardened my conviction that the best place for me at the moment was right here in Paris. And I liked the place. No, I wasn't one of those dumb romantics who swooned every time I smelled the aroma of a freshly baked baguette in my local *boulangerie*. Paris to me was a complex, contradictory entity – simultaneously rude and gracious, erudite and banal. Like anyone interesting, it was deeply contradictory. Its epic grandeur – its sense of self-importance – meant that Paris saw itself as a unique entity within which you, the resident, were privileged to dwell. In this sense, it reminded me of New York, as it was totally indifferent to its citizenry. The Americans I met who hated Paris – and railed against its arrogance – were usually people from smaller, more intimate cities like Boston or San Francisco, where the local *beau monde* stroked each other's ego, and anyone in a position of power or authority felt as if they counted. Parisian arrogance meant that nobody was important, nobody counted. It's what I loved most about the city. As an expat, you didn't try to be ambitious in Paris. You tried to live well. You always felt as if you were an outsider . . . but, after everything that had happened in New York, I embraced that *étranger* role with relief.

And Paris, in turn, embraced me. The column gave me a profile there. But so too, I discovered, did the circumstances surrounding my expatriatism. I never mentioned anything about my brother. Much to my surprise, however, many members of the American community knew about Eric's death, just as they had also heard how I'd been dropped from *Saturday/Sunday*. I avoided talking about such matters – because I didn't like the idea of using the blacklist as a form of social currency . . . and also because, according to Smythe family values, there was something deeply gauche about seeking sympathy for any personal misfortune. But I still found myself being made a member of an eclectic, raffish community. Having lived a rather singular life in New York (and having never been the most gregarious of people), it was liberating to find myself now plunged into something of a social whirl. I was out on the town at least five nights a week. I drank with the likes of Irwin Shaw and James Baldwin and Richard Wright and many of the other American writers who were living in Paris. I heard Boris Vian sing songs in some St Germain *cave*, and actually attended a reading given by Camus at a St Germain bookshop. I became a habitué of late-night jazz haunts. I indulged in long lunches with friends at Le Balzar (my favorite brasserie). I developed a taste for Ricard and casual affairs. Paris treated me well.

I was kept in regular contact with things New York, courtesy of Joel Eberts. We wrote each other once a week – generally to discuss financial matters (when it became clear that I was going to be staying in Paris for a while, he found someone to sublet my apartment), and also for Joel to forward any mail that came my way.

In June of 1953, his weekly update ended with the following paragraph:

There is only one personal letter in the batch of mail I'm enclosing this week. I know who it's from – because it was hand-delivered to me by its author: Meg Malone. She waltzed in here a few days ago, unannounced, insisting I tell her where she could find you. All I said was that you had left the country. Then she handed me the enclosed envelope, and insisted that I forward it to you. I told her what I told her brother: that you had specifically requested that any mail from Jack be held by me. 'I'm not Jack,' she countered – and lawyer that I am, I had to concede she had an argument there. She said nothing else – except that, if I didn't forward the letter, I'd be her sworn enemy for life. The fact that she said this with a smile made me like her . . . and also made me honor her request. So here's the letter. Read it if you wish. Throw it away if you don't want to. The choice is your own.

Timing is everything in life. This letter arrived at the wrong moment. It was the night after the Rosenbergs had been executed at Sing-Sing for allegedly selling atomic bomb secrets to the Soviets. Like just about every American I knew in Paris (even those who usually voted Republican), I was horrified by this despotic act – and one which, yet again, made me despise the forces which had destroyed my brother. For the first time in my life, I had actually done something vaguely political –

attending a candlelight vigil in front of our Embassy (along with around three thousand Parisians, led by notables like Sartre and de Beauvoir), signing a petition condemning this act of state murder, and feeling completely ineffectual and furious when the word came through (around two that morning, Paris time) that the executions had gone ahead. The next day, Meg Malone's letter arrived courtesy of Joel. My first thought was: *tear it up . . . I don't need to hear any apologias for Jack Malone.* Instead, I ripped open the envelope and read:

Dear Sara,

I don't know where you are, or what you're thinking. But I do know that Jack loves you more than anything, and has been in something approaching constant agony since you disappeared. He told me everything that happened. I was horrified by what he had done. I can fully understand your grief and fury. But . . . yes, here comes the but . . . he is as much a victim of the insanity that has gripped our country as your brother. This is not to condone his choice, or to excuse an action which many would interpret as self-serving. Faced with an appalling choice, he panicked. In doing so, he knows he killed your love for him. He has been trying to make contact with you for nearly a year, but has failed. Your lawyer informed him that you were refusing to read his letters. Once again, I

750

cannot blame you for feeling that way. And, believe me, the only reason I am writing to you now is because Jack is currently suffering from something akin to a nervous breakdown – which is related entirely to the overwhelming guilt he feels about naming your brother and losing you.

What can I say, Sara? Except this: I know how deeply you once loved him. I don't ask for a miraculous reconciliation. All I ask is that, somehow, you find a way to forgive him – and to communicate your forgiveness to him. I think it would mean an enormous amount to him. He is now a deeply unhappy man. He needs your help to find his way back to himself. I hope you can put the tragedy you suffered to one side, and write him.

Yours,

Meg Malone

I was suddenly angry. All the pain I had put away suddenly came roaring back. I rolled a piece of paper into my Remington. I typed:

Dear Meg,

I think it was George Orwell once who wrote that all clichés are true. With that in mind, here's my response to your plea on behalf of your brother:

Jack has made his own bed. He can lie in it. Alone.

751

Yours,
Sara Smythe

I pulled the letter out of the machine. Within a minute I had signed it, folded it, shoved it into an envelope, addressed it to Meg, and affixed the appropriate stamps and air-mail sticker to its front.

Two weeks after I mailed that letter, a telegram arrived for me at the offices of the *Herald-Tribune*. It contained four words:

Shame on you.
Meg

As soon as I read it, I balled up the telegram and threw it away. If Meg's reply was designed to make me feel awful, it succeeded. So much so that I ended up going out with a new friend from the *Herald-Tribune* – Isabel van Arnsdale – and drinking too much vin rouge, and telling her the entire damn story. Isabel was the paper's chief sub-editor – a stocky Chicago woman in her late forties. She'd moved over to Paris in '47, right after her third marriage collapsed. She was known to be a consummate journalistic pro, and someone who could put away a bottle of whiskey, yet still seem sober.

'Jesus Christ,' she said when I finished telling her the tale of the past year. 'Correction: Jesus-*fucking*-Christ.'

752

'Yeah – I could use a spell of boredom,' I said, sounding deeply tipsy.

'No – what you could use is a life without encumbrance.'

'There's no such thing.'

'True – but take it from a veteran of three crap marriages: there are ways of insulating yourself against further pain.'

'What's the secret?'

'Don't fall in love.'

'I've only done that once.'

'And, from what you said, it ruined your life.'

'Perhaps. But . . .'

'Let me guess: when it was right, it was . . . I dunno . . . *Transcendental? Incomparable? Peerless?* Am I getting warm?'

'I just loved him. That's all.'

'And now?'

'Now I wish he'd leave me alone.'

'What you mean is: you wish you could stop thinking about him.'

'Yes. That is what I mean. I still hate him. I still love him.'

'Do you want to forgive him?'

'Yes I do. But I can't.'

'There's your answer, Sara. From where I sit, it's the right answer. Most women would never have had anything to do with him after the way he initially disappeared on you. To then betray you and your brother . . .'

'You're right, you're right.'

'Your response to his sister's letter was the proper one. It's finished, over, *kaput*. Don't look back. He's a bad piece of work.'

I nodded.

'Anyway, as you already know, this town is crawling with interesting guys. Not to mention a lot of uninteresting guys who are still *baisable*, if you catch my drift. Go out, have some more adventures. Believe me, in a couple of months, you'll have gotten over him.'

I wanted to believe that. And to accelerate this distancing process, I continued my series of cavalier flings. No, I didn't turn into a *femme fatale*, with three guys on the go at once. I was an old-fashioned serial monogamist. I met someone. I took up with them for a little while. I let the thing run its course. When it started getting serious, or tiresome, or simply routine, I'd jump ship. I became an expert at disentangling myself from a relationship with the minimum of fuss. Men were useful for companionship, for occasional acts of tenderness, and for the ephemeral pleasures of sex. Anytime I found someone getting too dependent on me, I'd end it quickly. Anytime a guy started trying to change me – to wonder out loud what on earth I was doing living in a small *atelier*, and why I favored Colette-style pants suits over more 'feminine' apparel – they'd be politely shown the door. In the four years I resided in Paris, I had three marriage proposals – all of which I turned down. None of the men in question was wildly inappropriate. On the contrary, the first was a successful merchant banker; the second, a lecturer in literature at the Sorbonne; and the third, a would-be novelist, living on Daddy's trust fund. All of them were, in their own way, thoroughly charming and intelligent and emotionally stable. But each of them was on the lookout for a wife. That was a role I wasn't interested in ever playing again.

The years in Paris evaporated far too quickly. On December thirty-first, 1954, I stood on a balcony overlooking the avenue Georges V in the company of Isabel van Arnsdale, and assorted other *Herald-Tribune* reprobates. As car horns sounded – and a fireworks display illuminated the winter sky – I hoisted my glass towards Isabel and said, 'Here's to my last year in Paris.'

'Stop talking crap,' she said.

'It's not crap: it's the truth. By this time next year, I want to be on my way back to the States.'

'But you've got a great life here.'

'Don't I know it.'

'Then why the hell throw it all away?'

'Because I'm not a professional expatriate. Because I miss baseball, and bagels, and Barney Greengrass the Sturgeon King, and Gitlitz's delicatessen, and showers that work, and a grocery store that delivers, and speaking my own language, and . . .'

'*Him?*'

'No goddamn way.'

'You promise?'

'When have you last heard me speak about him?'

'Can't remember.'

'There you go.'

'Then when are you going to do something stupid, like fall in love again?'

'Hang on – you told me that the only way to get through life was by *never* falling in love.'

'Jesus Christ, you really don't think I'd expect anyone to follow that advice?'

But the thing was: I had followed her counsel. Not intentionally. Rather, because, after Jack, no one I met ever triggered that wonderfully strange, deranged, dangerous surge of . . . what do you call it? Desire? Delirium? Passion? Completeness? Stupidity? Self-delusion?

Now I knew something else: I couldn't be with him, and I couldn't get over him. Time may have numbed the ache – but like any anaesthetic, it didn't heal the wound. I kept waiting for the day when I would wake up and Jack would have finally fled my thoughts. That morning had yet to arrive. An ongoing thought had started to unsettle me: say I never came to terms with this loss? Say it was always there? Say it defined me?

When I articulated this fear to Isabel, she laughed. 'Honey, loss is an essential component of life. In many ways, *c'est notre destin*. And yes, there are certain things you never really get over. But what's wrong with that?'

'It's so damn painful . . . that's what's wrong with it.'

'But living *is* painful . . . *n'est-ce pas?*'

'Cut the existential crap, Isabel.'

'I promise you this – the moment you begin to accept that you're *not* going to get over it . . . you might just get over it.'

I kept that thought in mind during the next twelve months – when I drifted into a brief fling with a Danish jazz bassist, and wrote my weekly column, and spent long afternoons at the Cinémathèque Française, and (if the weather was clement) read for an hour each morning on a bench in the Luxembourg Gardens, and celebrated my thirty-third birthday by giving notice at the *Herald-Tribune*, and writing Joel Eberts that the sublet of my apartment should end by December thirty-first, 1955. Because I was coming home.

And on January tenth, 1956, I found myself back at Pier 76 on West 48th Street, stepping off the SS *Corinthia*. Joel Eberts was there to meet me.

'You haven't aged one damn bit, counselor,' I said after giving him a hug. 'What's your secret?'

'Constant litigation. But hey, you look wonderful too.'

'But older.'

'I'd say, "exceedingly elegant".'

'That's a synonym for "older".'

We took a taxi uptown to my apartment. As per my instructions, he'd arranged with the janitor to have it repainted when the tenants moved out before Christmas. It still reeked of turpentine and fresh emulsion – but the whitewash of the walls was a cheering antidote to the ashen January morning.

'Only a crazy person decides to return to New York in the thick of winter,' Joel said.

'I like murk.'

'You must have been a Russian in a former life.'

'Or maybe I'm just someone who has always responded well to gloom.'

'What a lot of dreck you talk. You're a survivor, kiddo. And a canny one at that. If you don't believe me, check out the pile of bank and investment statements I've left in a folder on your kitchen table. You hardly touched a cent of your capital while you were in France. And the rent from the sublet built up rather nicely. Also: your stock-broker is one sharp operator. He's managed to add about thirty per cent value to both the divorce settlement fund and Eric's insurance payout. So if you don't want to work for the next decade . . .'

'Work is something I can't do without,' I said.

'I concur. But know this – financially speaking, you're damn comfortable.'

'What's in here?' I asked, kicking a cardboard box that was by the couch.

'It's all of the accumulated mail I didn't forward to you over the years. I had it sent up yesterday.'

'But you forwarded me just about everything, except . . .'

'That's right. His letters.'

'I told you to throw them out.'

'I decided that there was no harm keeping them

758

until your return . . . just in case you decided you did want to read them, after all.'

'I don't want to read them.'

'Well, your building gets its garbage collected once a day, so you can throw them out whenever you like.'

'Have you ever heard from Jack or his sister again?'

'Nope. Have you?'

I'd never told Joel about my reply to Meg's letter. I wasn't going to now.

'Never,' I said.

'He must have taken the hint. Anyway, it's all history now. Just like Joe McCarthy. I tell you, I'm no conventional patriot – but on that day in fifty-four when the Senate censured the bastard, I thought: unlike a lot of other places, this country has the reassuring habit of finally admitting that it got something wrong.'

'It's just too bad they didn't censure him three years earlier.'

'I know. Your brother was a great man.'

'No – he was simply a good man. Too good. Had he been less good, he'd still be alive. That's the hardest thing about coming back to Manhattan – knowing that every time I walk by the Ansonia or the Hampshire House . . .'

'I'm sure that, even after four years, it still hurts like hell.'

'Losing your brother never gets easier.'

'And losing Jack?'

I shrugged. 'Ancient history.'

He studied my face carefully. I wondered if he saw I was lying.

'Well that's something, I guess,' he said.

I changed the subject. Quickly.

'How about letting me buy us lunch at Gitlitz's?' I said. 'I haven't had a pastrami on rye and a celery soda in five years.'

'That's because the French know nothing about food.'

I hoisted the box of Jack's letters. We left the apartment. Once we were outside, I tossed the box into the back of a garbage truck that was emptying cans on West 77th Street. Joel's eyes showed disapproval, but he said nothing. As the jaws of the truck closed around the box, I wondered: *why did you do that?* But I covered my remorse by linking my arm through Joel's, and saying, 'Let's eat.'

Gitlitz's hadn't changed in the years I had been away. Nor had most of the Upper West Side. I slotted back into Manhattan life with thankful ease. The bumpy readjustment I had been dreading never materialized. I looked up old friends. I went to Broadway shows and Friday matinées at the New York Philharmonic and the occasional evening at the Metropolitan Opera. I became a habitué once again of the Met and the Frick and the 42nd Street branch of the Public Library, and my two local fleapit movie houses: the Beacon and the Loew's 84th Street. And every other week, I punched out a 'Letter from New York' – which was then dispatched, courtesy of Western Union, to the offices of the *Paris Herald-Tribune*. This bi-monthly column was Mort Goodman's farewell present to me.

'If I can't get you to stay and write for me in Paris, then I better get you writing for me from New York.'

So now I was a foreign correspondent. Only the country I was covering was my own.

'*In the four years I was loitering with intent on the rue Cassette* (I wrote in a column, datemarked March 20th, 1956), *something curious happened to Americans: after all the years of economic depression and wartime rationing, they woke up one morning to discover that they now lived in an affluent society. And for the first time since the Roaring Twenties, they're engaged on a massive spending spree. Only unlike the hedonistic twenties, this oh-so-sensible Eisenhower era is centered around the home – a happy, reasonably affluent God-fearing place, where there are two cars in every garage, a brand new Amana refrigerator in the kitchen, a Philco TV in the living room, a subscription to the* Reader's Digest, *and where grace is said before every TV dinner. What? You expatriates haven't heard of a TV dinner? Well, just when you thought American cuisine couldn't get more bland . . .*'

That column (written in one of my flippant H.L. Menckenesque moods) caused my phone to ring off the hook for a few days – as it was picked up by the Paris correspondent of the very conservative *San Francisco Chronicle*, who used large quotes from it in a piece he wrote about the sort of anti-American rubbish that was being printed in an allegedly respectable paper like the *Paris Herald-Tribune*. Before I knew it, I was back in Walter Winchell's column:

> News Flash: Sara Smythe, one-time yuckster for *Saturday Night/Sunday Morning* and recent professional American-in-Paris, is back in Gotham City . . . but not too happily. According to our spies, she's churning out a column featuring a lot of cheap cracks about Our Way of Life for all those bitter expats who choose to live away from these great shores. Memo to Miss Smythe: if you don't like it here, why not try Moscow?

Four years earlier, Winchell's smear would have killed all potential employment prospects in New York. How times had changed – for now, I received a series of calls from editors whom I used to know around town during the late forties and early fifties, asking if I'd like to have lunch and talk things over.

'But, according to Winchell,' I told Imogen Woods, my former editor at *Saturday/Sunday* (now the number two at *Harper's*), 'I'm still the Emma Goldman of West Seventy-Seventh Street.'

'Honey,' Imogen said, digging into her Biltmore Hotel cobb salad, and simultaneously signaling to the waiter for more drinks, 'Walter Winchell is yesterday's chopped liver. In fact, you should be pleased Winchell took another swing at you. Because it's how I found out you were back in New York.'

'I was surprised to get your call,' I said carefully.

'I was really glad you agreed to meet me. Because . . . and I'm being totally honest here . . . I was ashamed of myself when *Saturday/Sunday* let you go. I should have stuck up for you. I should have insisted that someone else give you the news. But I was scared. Terrified of losing my lousy little job. And I hated myself for being such a coward. But I still went along with them. And that will always weigh on my conscience.'

'Don't let it.'

'It will. And when I read about your brother's death . . .'

I cut her off before she could say anything more.

'We're here now,' I said. 'And we're talking. That's what counts.'

By the end of that lunch, I was the new *Harper's* film critic. The phone continued to ring at home. The book editor of the *New York Times* offered me reviewing work. So too did his counterpart at the *New Republic.* And a commissioning editor at *Cosmopolitan* arranged a lunch meeting, telling me she'd love to revive the 'Real Life' column – 'only tailored to today's sophisticated fifties woman'.

I accepted the reviewing work. I turned down the *Cosmopolitan* offer, on the grounds that my erstwhile column was erstwhile. But when the editor asked if I'd like to do a lucrative six-month stint as the magazine's agony aunt – I accepted on the spot. Because I was about the last person in the world who should be giving out sensible advice.

The *Cosmopolitan* editor – Alison Finney – took me to lunch at the Stork Club. While we were eating, Winchell came in. The Stork Club had always been his haunt, his outer office – and though everyone in New York now considered Winchell's power to be on the wane (as Imogen Woods had told me), he still commanded the most highly visible of all corner tables, furnished with its very own telephone. Alison nudged me and said, 'There's your greatest fan.' I shrugged. We finished our lunch. Alison excused herself and disappeared off to the Ladies'. Without thinking about what I was doing, I suddenly stood up and walked towards Winchell's table. He was correcting some copy, so he didn't see me approach.

'Mr Winchell?' I said pleasantly.

He looked up and quickly scrutinized my face. When it was clear I wasn't worth his attention, he picked up his pencil and glanced back down at his copy.

'Do I know you, young lady?' he said, a hint of gruffness in his voice.

'Actually you do,' I said. 'But you know my brother even better.'

'Oh yeah? What's his name?'

'Eric Smythe.'

I could tell that the name didn't register, as he pursed his lips for a second, then continued making a correction.

'And how's Eric?' he asked.

'He's dead, Mr Winchell.'

His pencil stopped for a moment, but his eyes remained fixed on his copy.

'Sorry to hear that,' he said, sounding dismissive. 'My condolences.'

'You don't know who I'm talking about, do you?'

He said nothing. He continued to ignore me.

'"*He may be Marty Manning's best scribe . . . but he used to be a Red.*" You wrote that about my brother, Mr Winchell. He lost his job after that, and ended up drinking himself to death. And you don't even remember his name.'

Winchell now glanced up – in the direction of the maître d'.

'Sam,' he shouted, pointing towards me. I continued speaking – the tone of my voice remaining conversational, strangely calm.

'And I bet you don't even remember *me*, do you? Even though you wrote about me just a week ago. I'm the Sara Smythe who, "*according to our spies, is churning out a column featuring a lot of cheap cracks about Our Way of Life for all those bitter expats who choose to live away from these great shores. Memo to Miss Smythe: if you don't like it here, why not try Moscow?*" Amazing how I can quote you chapter and verse, Mr Winchell.'

I felt a hand touch my arm. It was Sam, the maître d'.

'Miss, would you mind going back to your table, please?' he asked.

'I was just leaving,' I said, then turned back to Winchell. 'I just wanted to thank you for that recent mention, Mr Winchell. You wouldn't believe how many work offers I've had since you wrote about me. It just shows how much clout you still wield these days.'

Then I turned and headed back to my table. I said nothing to Alison about what had just happened when she returned from the Ladies'. I just suggested we order a final round of drinks. Alison agreed, and motioned to the waiter to freshen up our gimlets. Then she said, 'I bet you Winchell will now write something about you drinking too much at lunchtime.'

'That man can write whatever the hell he wants,' I said. 'He can't hurt me anymore.'

But, after our one and only meeting, Walter Winchell never mentioned me in his column again.

Still, he really had been most useful on the professional front. I now had so much work on hand that I was pleased when the phone eventually went quiet again. It allowed me to get on with a large backlog of assignments. As always, I especially liked writing over the weekends – as it was a time when all my assorted editors weren't working, and when the vast majority of my friends were with their families. Sunday, in fact, was the one day I was assured of never getting a single call – which also made it the perfect day to work straight through without distraction.

Until the phone rang one Sunday morning in May at the early hour of nine. I reached for it.

'Sara?'

My pulse spiked. The phone shook in my hand. I had been wondering if this call would ever come. Now it had.

'Are you still there?' the voice asked.

A long pause. I wanted to hang up. I didn't.

'I'm here, Jack.'

CHAPTER 14

' o,' he said.
'So,' I said.
'It's been a while.'
'Yes, it has.'
'How are you?'
'Fine. You?'
'Fine.'
He didn't sound fine. His voice was constricted, diminished. He was as nervous as I was. I heard street noises in the background.
'Where are you?' I asked.
'The corner of Seventy-Seventh and Broadway.'
Just like old times, I thought. Sneaking out of the house to phone me.
'Are you busy right now?' he asked.
'Kind of. I've got a deadline . . .'
'Oh. Too bad.'
'Sorry. It's just . . . well, work.'
'I understand,' he said.
'How did you know I was back in town?'
'Walter Winchell.'
'My biggest admirer.'
He laughed – but the laugh quickly transformed

into a cough. It took him a moment to bring it under control.

'Are you okay?' I asked

'Yeah,' he said. 'I've got a little bronchial infection . . .'

'You shouldn't be standing on a cold street corner . . .'

'Well, it was my turn to take the baby out.'

That took a minute to sink in.

'You have a baby?' I asked.

'Yes. A daughter. Kate.'

'How old?'

'Seventeen months.'

'Congratulations,' I said.

'Thanks,' he said.

Another pause.

'Well . . .' he said. 'I just wanted to say hello.'

'Hello.'

'Sara . . . Meet me. Please.'

'Jack, I really don't think that's a good idea.'

'It's been four years.'

'I know, but . . .'

'Four years. That's a long time. I'm asking for nothing. I just want to see you. Half an hour of your time. No more.'

The phone started shaking again in my hand. I finally said, 'Gitlitz's in ten minutes.'

I hung up. I stood by the phone, unable to move. A baby. A daughter. Kate. No . . .

I wanted to flee. To pack a bag, and run to Penn Station, and catch the next train to . . .

Where?

Where could I run to this time? And even when I got there, he'd still be with me. As always.

I resisted the temptation of a steadying slug of Scotch. I forced myself into the bathroom. I stared at myself in the mirror. He'll think I look older . . . because I am older. I brushed my teeth. I quickly applied lipstick. I brushed my hair. I put down the brush. I gripped the sink, trying to steady myself. The urge to flee hit me again. I forced myself out of the bathroom. I put on my coat. I left the apartment. It had started to snow outside. I turned my collar up against the cold. I lowered my head. I marched the two blocks east to Gitlitz's.

When I entered the deli, the first thing I saw was a large blue baby carriage parked by a booth. I approached the booth. Jack was sitting there, both hands wrapped around a cup of coffee, staring down into its black surface. He didn't notice my initial arrival. This was fortunate – as it gave me a moment to absorb the shock of his appearance. He had lost a frightening amount of weight. His cheeks were hollow, his skin pasty. His hair had thinned. His eyes radiated fatigue. He did not look well. He had aged twenty years since I'd last seen him.

He glanced up. His eyes met mine. He attempted a smile, but he couldn't bring it off. I tried to smile back – but I could see that he registered my alarm at his condition. Instantly, he slid out of the booth and got to his feet. Standing up, the severity of his weight loss was even more disturbing. He reached for me with both hands, then thought better of it, and proffered his right one. I took it. It felt thin, emaciated. His eyes were locked on me. I found it difficult to meet his gaze.

'Hi,' he said.

'Hi.'

'You look wonderful.'

I didn't supply the normal refrain – 'You do too' – because it was impossible to do so. Instead, I looked down into the baby carriage. Kate was asleep – a pretty, chubby baby in a snowsuit, covered by a thick plaid blanket. I reached into the carriage. I stroked one of her hands. Instinctively, it opened. Her tiny finger closed around my pinky. I stood there, trying to hold everything in check.

'She's beautiful,' I said.

He stood by my side and looked down with me.

'Yes,' he said, 'she is that.'

'Dorothy and you must be very pleased.'

He nodded, then motioned for me to take a seat. I gently disengaged my pinky from her hand. I slid into the booth. He sat down opposite me. He ordered more coffee. His hands curved around his cup again. We said nothing for a while. He finally spoke, his eyes focused on the table.

'This is . . . I was always wondering . . . I . . . I'm glad to see you, Sara.'

I didn't know what to say. So I stayed quiet.

'I don't blame you for hating me,' he said.

'I don't hate you.'

'You did.'

'Maybe. For a while. But . . . hate is a hard thing to sustain. Grief isn't. Grief is something that can stay with you for a very long time.'

'I know,' he said. 'There have been periods over the last four years when I thought: will it ever get bearable?'

'Did it?'

'No. Never. I missed you every hour of every day.'

'I see.'

'And your grief for Eric. Did it ever . . . ?

'Dissipate? No. But I learned to live with it. Just as I learned to live with my grief for you.'

He looked up at me again.

'You grieved for *me*?' he asked.

'Of course,' I said. 'Endlessly.'

He stared at me with wounded bemusement.

'But . . . you refused to talk to me.'

'Yes. I did.'

'And you never read my letters?'

'That's right, they were never opened.'

'Then how can you say . . .'

'That I missed you all the time? Because I did. Because I loved you. More than anyone.'

He put his head in his hands. 'Then why the hell didn't you let me make contact, Sara?'

'Because . . . I couldn't. The grief was too big. I loved you so damn much that, when you betrayed Eric and me . . . when Eric died . . . I couldn't

772

face you. What had happened was just too terrible. What made it even more terrible was . . . the fact that I understood why you had to do what you did. How you'd been put in an appalling situation; a situation in which it would have been easy to panic, to make a very wrong call. But that still . . . *still* . . . didn't lessen the repercussions of your choice. Because it took away the two people I valued most.'

The coffee arrived. He continued looking down at the table. He said, 'Do you know how often I've replayed that scene in my head?'

'What scene?' I asked.

'The scene where the two Feds were interviewing me in a conference room at Steele and Sherwood. The company's lawyer was with me. The interview had gone on all morning. I kept ducking and diving the question of the Communists I knew. For three hours, I stuck to my guns – and just named the people who had already named me. Finally, the Feds got frustrated – and asked to see the company lawyer in private. They must have been gone around twenty minutes. He came back alone. And said, "Jack: if you don't give them another name, you're going to be called in front of the Committee as a hostile witness. And your career at Steele and Sherwood will be finished."

'All I had to do was say no. That's all that was required. All right, I might have lost my job, but . . . I would have found a way of putting bread on the table. But they had me in a corner. And

773

those Feds – they were so good at sniffing out your weaknesses. Jesus, did they play on mine. They knew all about us, of course – and they kept dropping hints about how, if I didn't cooperate, not only would I be fired from Steele and Sherwood, but word would probably get around about my complicated domestic arrangements. Not only would I be branded a pinko sympathizer, but Mr Flexible Morality. I remember exactly what one of the Feds told me: "Pal, if you were running two households in Paris, no one would give a shit. But in America, we operate according to a slightly harsher moral code: *get found out, get fucked over*. You'll be lucky to end up shining shoes somewhere."

'That's when I gave them Eric's name. As soon as it was out of my mouth, I knew I had killed everything. It was just a matter of time before you found out. And when Dorothy found out, she told me I was beneath contempt.'

'But didn't she understand that you did it for her and Charlie?'

'Oh, she got that all right. But she still saw it as another of my betrayals. She kicked me out for a while after that. Told me that she'd give me the divorce I'd always wanted . . . that I'd now be free to be with you . . .'

It took me a moment or two to speak.

'I didn't know,' I said.

'If only you'd read my letters . . . if only you'd let me contact you . . . I kept thinking: this is the shittiest irony imaginable. And it's my own fault . . .'

He broke off, reached into his overcoat pocket, and fumbled around until he found a cigarette. He screwed it into a corner of his mouth. He picked up a book of matches off the table. He lit his cigarette with shaking hands. The light of the match cast his face in a gaunt glow. He looked so shrunken, so denuded, so defeated by everything. I saw myself throwing out his box of letters. Letters which he must have spent hours writing. As I spent hours writing him throughout the winter of '46 . . . when I simply couldn't believe the wonderfully delirious love I felt for him. For four years, his letters sat gathering dust in Joel's office. Four years. I let them sit there. And then, on the day I returned to New York, I simply tossed them away – as a final act of reprisal. Why didn't I read them when he first sent them? Why did I have this need to punish him? A punishment which would now haunt me. Because I would always wonder: had I read those letters in the months after Eric's death, might I have understood? Might I have found a way of forgiving him? Might we have discovered a way back to each other?

'What happened after Dorothy threw you out?'

'I spent around six months on a fold-out couch in Meg's apartment.'

Meg. Her letter to me in the winter of '53:

What can I say, Sara? Except this. I know how deeply you once loved him. I don't ask for a miraculous reconciliation. All I ask is that, somehow, you find a way to forgive him – and to communicate your forgiveness to him. I think it would mean an enormous amount to him. He is now a deeply unhappy man. He needs your help to find his way back to himself.

But, oh no, I couldn't be seen to weaken from my position. I had self-righteousness on my side. He had to be permanently condemned. He'd made his bed (as I so caustically wrote back to Meg). Now he could lie in it. Alone.

'Eventually, Meg engaged in some delicate diplomacy with Dorothy,' Jack said. 'At heart, my wife has always been a complete pragmatist. And the reason she took me back was an utterly pragmatic one: living alone with a small child was difficult. "As far as I'm concerned," she told me, "you're a second pair of hands, nothing more. Except, of course, to Charlie. He needs a father. It might as well be you."'

'And you still went back after she said that?' I asked.

'Yes. I went back. To a loveless marriage. But I'd made a vow, a commitment. I tell you, Catholic guilt is something to behold. But the real reason I went back was Charlie. I couldn't stand to be apart from Charlie.'

'I'm sure he needs you very much.'

'And I him. Without Charlie, I don't think I would have made it through the last couple of years.'

He suddenly shook his head, with annoyance.

'Sorry, sorry – that sounds melodramatic.'

'Are you all right?'

'Never better,' he said, taking a nervous drag on his cigarette.

'You look a little . . . wan.'

'No. I look like shit.'

'You're not well, are you?'

His fingers closed around the coffee cup again. He continued to avoid looking at me.

'I wasn't well. A bad bout of hepatitis. Word of advice: never eat cherrystones at City Island.'

'It was just hepatitis?' I asked, trying not to sound overtly sceptical.

Another fast drag of his cigarette.

'Do I look that bad?'

'Well . . .'

'Don't answer that. But yeah – hepatitis can really kick the crap out of you.'

'You've been off work?'

'For six months.'

'Good God . . .'

'Steele and Sherwood have been pretty understanding. Full pay for the first three months, half pay since then. It's meant things have been a little tight, especially with the beautiful Kate now in our lives. But we've managed.'

'Are things now better between you and Dorothy?'

'Kate's made a difference. It's given us something to talk about. Other than Charlie, that is.'

'There must have been some sort of thaw between the two of you before then,' I said, nodding towards the baby carriage.

'Not really. Just a night when we both had four Scotches too many, and Dorothy momentarily forgot that, at heart, she didn't like me.'

'I hope Kate makes you both very . . .'

He cut me off. His tone was suddenly harsh.

'Yeah, thanks for the Hallmark Cards sentiment.'

'I mean that, Jack. I don't wish you any ill.'

'You sure?'

'I never did.'

'But you didn't forgive me either.'

'You're right. For a long time, I found it very hard to forgive what you'd done.'

'And now?'

'The past is the past.'

'I can't undo what happened.'

'I know.'

He reached over to where my right hand was resting on the table. He covered it with his own. As soon as he touched me, I felt something akin to a small electrical charge course up my arm . . . the same charge I'd felt on that first night in 1945. After a moment, I moved my left hand on top of his.

'I'm so sorry,' he said.

'It's okay,' I said.

'No,' he said quietly, 'it will never be okay.'

I suddenly heard myself say, 'I forgive you.'

Silence. We said nothing for a very long time.

Then Kate began to stir – some quiet burbling sounds quickly escalating into a full-scale lament. Jack stood up and hunted around the baby carriage until he found the pacifier she had spit out. As soon as it was back between her lips, she ejected it again and continued crying.

'She's in the market for a bottle, I'm afraid,' Jack said. 'I'd better get home.'

'Okay,' I said.

He sat down quickly again opposite me.

'Can I see you again?' he asked.

'I don't know.'

'I understand . . .'

'There's no one else.'

'That's not what I was implying.'

'It's just . . . well . . . I guess I don't know what I think right now.'

'No rush,' he said. 'Anyway, I have to go out of town for a week or so. It's a business thing. Up in Boston. Some account Steele and Sherwood wants me to handle when I go back to work next month.'

'Are you well enough to travel?'

'I look worse than I am.'

Kate's crying now escalated.

'You'd better go,' I said.

He squeezed my hand one last time.

'I'll call you from Boston,' he said.

'Okay,' I said. 'Call me.'

He stood up. He rearranged the blanket around Kate. He turned towards me again. I stood up.

Suddenly he pulled me towards him – and kissed me. I met his kiss. And held it. It only lasted a moment. When he ended it, he whispered:

'Goodbye.'

Then he put both hands on the baby carriage and pushed it forward.

I sat down in the booth. I crossed my arms on the table. I laid my head atop them. I sat that way for a very long time.

For the next week, the shock lingered. I did my work. I saw movies. I saw friends. I kept replaying that kiss in my head. I didn't know what to make of it. I didn't know anything anymore.

He said he would call. He didn't call. But he did write. A short card, with a Boston postmark. It was scribbled in a shaky hand.

I'm still here. It should be over soon.
I love you.
Jack

I read that card over and over, trying to decipher its underlying meaning. Eventually I decided there was no underlying meaning. He was still in Boston. Whatever he was doing would end shortly. He loved me.

And I still loved him.

But I expected nothing. Because – as I had learned – if you expect nothing, then anything is a surprise.

Another week went by. No calls. No cards. I

remained calm. On Monday morning, April fifteenth, I was running out the door, en route to a press screening of some film. I was late, the traffic on Broadway was grim, so I decided to skip the bus and grab the subway downtown. I walked briskly to the 79th Street station, buying a *New York Times* from the newsie who was always out in front. I climbed aboard the downtown train. I did my usual quick scan of the paper. When I reached the Obituary page, I noticed that the lead death of the day was a Hartford insurance executive who once worked with my father. I quickly read his obituary, and was about to move on to the opposite page when my gaze stumbled on a short listing amidst the page-wide columns of Deaths:

MALONE, John Joseph, age 33, at Massachusetts General Hospital, Boston, on April 14th. Husband of Dorothy, father of Charles and Katherine. Formerly of Steele and Sherwood Public Relations Inc., New York. Will be much mourned by family and friends. Funeral Mass, Wednesday, April 17th, Holy Trinity Church, West 82nd Street, Manhattan. House private. No flowers please.

I only read it once. Then I lowered the paper on to my lap. I stared ahead of me. I saw nothing. I heard nothing. I didn't notice the passage of time. Until a man in a uniform came over to me and said, 'You okay, lady?'

I now realized that the train had stopped. The carriage was empty.

'Where are we?' I managed to ask.

'The end of the line.'

CHAPTER 15

Two days later, I went to the funeral. The church – Holy Trinity – wasn't large, but it still seemed cavernous. There were only twenty or so mourners in attendance. They all sat in the front two pews – directly facing the casket. It was surrounded by four lit candles, and draped in an American flag – because, as befitting any veteran of the Armed Forces, Jack was entitled to a funeral with full military honors. Two soldiers in dress uniform stood at attention on either side of the coffin. The service began with the tolling of a bell. A priest and two altar boys marched down the aisle. One of the boys held a smoking censer of incense. The other carried a large gold cross. The priest – a short, greying man with a hard face – walked around the coffin, sprinkling it with holy water. Then he mounted the pulpit and began the Latin Mass. His voice was tough, no-nonsense. Like the man he was burying, the priest was a Brooklyn boy. I kept wondering if he had ever heard Jack's confession.

A baby began to cry in the front row. It was Kate. She was being held by her mother. Dorothy's face was drawn and tired. Next to her sat Charlie – in a blazer and a pair of flannel pants. He was the image of his father. So much so that I found it hard to look at him.

The priest moved briskly through the Latin prayers of the Mass. Whenever he reverted back to English and spoke about 'our dear departed brother, Jack', I felt my eyes sting. There were a few muffled sobs – largely from Meg, who sat on the other side of Charlie, her arm around his shoulders. I didn't recognize any of the other mourners. I sat in the back row of the church, far away from the assembled crowd. I mixed in with a few local parishioners who had wandered in to say prayers, or simply seek shelter from the wet April day.

I had to be here. I had to say goodbye. But I also knew that I belonged in the back of the church – away from Dorothy and the children; away from Meg. I had caused enough grief within this family. I didn't want to cause more by making an appearance. So I arrived at the church fifteen minutes before the funeral, and waited in a doorway on the opposite side of 82nd Street. I watched as two limousines pulled up out front, and the family entered the church. I loitered opposite for another five minutes – until I was certain that all the other mourners had entered. Then, wrapping a scarf tightly around my head, I crossed the street, climbed the church stairs and – with my head lowered – slipped quickly into the back row. The sight of the coffin was like a kick in the stomach.

Up until this moment, the idea that Jack was dead seemed absurd, inconceivable. After reading his obituary in the *New York Times*, I forgot all about the screening I was supposed to attend, and instead found myself wandering aimlessly around the city for the balance of the day. At some juncture, I made my way home. It was dark. I opened the door. I let myself inside. I took off my coat. I sat down in an armchair. I remained in that armchair for a very long time. Only after an hour or so did I notice that I had failed to turn a light on in the apartment; that I was sitting alone in the dark. The phone started to ring. I ignored it. I went into my bedroom. I undressed and got into bed. I pulled the covers tight over me. I stared up at the ceiling. I kept expecting to fall apart, to come asunder and weep uncontrollably. But I was too concussed to cry. The enormity of it all – the terrible realization that I would never talk to him again – rendered me insensible. I couldn't fathom his loss. Nor could I now fathom why I had spent four years being so stubborn, so intractable, so unforgiving. Four years separated from the man I loved – a separation sparked by his dire mistake . . . but then fueled by my inability to be understanding, to show mercy. By punishing him I had punished myself. Four years. How could I have squandered those four years?

I didn't sleep that night. At some point I got out of bed, I got dressed. I left the apartment and sat for two hours in an all-night coffee shop on

Broadway and 76th Street. Dawn arrived. I stood up. I paid my bill. I walked over to Riverside Park. I walked down to the river. I sat on a bench. I stared out at the Hudson. I kept willing myself to break down – to have that big cathartic moment. But all I could do was look out blankly at the water and wonder whether I had, in my own way, killed him.

I finally returned to the apartment. The clock in the kitchen read nine fifteen a.m. The phone rang. This time I answered it. It was Joel Eberts.

'Thank God,' he said, after I picked up. 'I called all day yesterday. You had me worried.'

'No need,' I said.

'You sound tired.'

'I had a bad night.'

'I'm not surprised,' he said. 'After I saw the announcement in the *Times* yesterday, I wondered . . .'

'I'm handling it,' I said quietly.

'Do you have any idea about the cause of death?'

'No.'

'He didn't try to make contact since you were back in the city?'

'No, never,' I lied, unable to talk about anything right now.

'That was probably for the best.'

I said nothing.

'You sure you're okay, Sara?'

'It's just a shock, that's all.'

'Well, if you're not okay, I just want you to know that I'm here. Call me anytime.'

'Thanks.'

'And whatever you do . . . don't feel guilty. It was all a long time ago.'

But I did blame myself. Totally.

Sheer exhaustion forced me into bed at seven that evening. I woke just after five. It was still dark outside – but I had slept deeply, so I felt curiously rested. I knew that the funeral would begin in just over four hours. I dreaded going. I had no choice but to go.

Now, sitting in the rear of the church, I kept my head lowered as the words of the Mass reverberated around my ears.

Agnus Dei, qui tollis peccata mundi: dona eis requiem.

Lamb of God, thou takest away the sins of the world, grant them rest.

Or, even more piercing:

Lacrimosa dies illa, qua resurget ex favilla judicandus homo reus; huic ergo parce, Deus.

On this day full of tears, when from the ashes arises guilty man, to be judged: Oh Lord, have mercy upon him.

I pressed my fingers hard against my eyes. I had judged him. And yes, I had finally forgiven him. Far too late.

Kate started to cry again. Only this time she

could not be consoled. After a few minutes, she was wailing. I had been keeping my head bowed – but I raised it just as Meg was coming up the aisle. She had obviously decided to relieve Dorothy of the baby, as she had her niece in her arms, and was heading for the door. She saw me and froze – her face initially registering shock. Then it hardened into something approaching pure cold contempt. I quickly lowered my head again. I wanted to flee – but I knew she would be outside with the baby. I sat there for ten minutes, feeling total shame. The Mass forged on – the priest asking us again to pray for the soul of 'a good husband, a good father, a fine responsible man'. As he fell silent for a moment, I heard footsteps. I stole a quick glance, and saw Meg already halfway down the central aisle, carrying a now-subdued Kate back towards the front row. Immediately, I ducked out of the pew and moved quickly through the front door, down the steps, and into the first cab I could hail.

'Where you going?' the driver asked.

'I don't know. Just drive.'

He headed down Broadway. At 42nd Street, I left the cab and ducked into the first movie house I could find. I sat through a double-feature. Then I moved on to the next movie house, and sat through another double-feature. Then I walked to the Automat and drank a cup of coffee. While there, I reached a decision that had been formulating in my brain during all those hours of non-stop movies. I finished the coffee. I checked my watch. It was just after seven p.m. I went back out on to 42nd Street and hailed a cab going east. At First Avenue, I asked the taxi to pull up in front of an apartment complex called Tudor City. There was a doorman on duty. He was busy with a delivery of groceries. I told him I was here to see Margaret Malone. He looked me over and decided I didn't appear sinister.

'Is she expecting you?'

I nodded.

'Apartment Seven E. Go right on up.'

I took the elevator to the seventh floor. I marched straight down the corridor to Apartment E. Before I lost my nerve, I rang the bell. After a moment, the door opened. Meg was standing there, still dressed in the black suit she had worn to the funeral. She looked drained, exhausted. A lit cigarette was in her left hand. She flinched when she saw me. Her lips tightened.

'You've got to be kidding,' she said.

'Meg, can I . . . ?'

'No. You can't. Now get lost.'

'If you'd just hear me out . . .'

'You mean, the way you heard my brother out? Go fuck yourself.'

With that, she slammed the door. I put a hand against the wall for support, until I stopped shaking. After a moment, the door opened again. Meg suddenly looked crushed, heartbroken. I took a step towards her. She buried her head in my shoulder. She wept loudly. I put my arms around her – and finally cried too.

When we both calmed down, she brought me into her living room and motioned me towards an armchair. The apartment was a small one-bedroom efficiency – indifferently furnished, crammed with books and periodicals and overflowing ashtrays. Meg disappeared into the kitchen and returned with a bottle of Scotch and two glasses.

'Medicine,' she said, pouring out two shots. She handed me a glass, collapsed into an armchair opposite mine, and lit a fresh cigarette. After two deep drags, she finally spoke.

'I really never wanted to see you again.'

'I don't blame you,' I said.

'But I also understood you. If it had been Jack, instead of Eric, I would have been merciless.'

'I was too merciless.'

Another deep drag on her cigarette. 'Yeah,' she said. 'You were. But . . . he told me you forgave him.'

'He said that?'

'Yeah. Around a week before he died. He knew he was going for over a year.'

'A year?'

'At least. Leukemia is pretty damn remorseless. Once you've got it, you know the jig is up.'

'Leukemia?' I said, sounding shocked. 'But he had no history . . .'

'Yeah – it just came out of nowhere. Like most catastrophes.'

'So Jack wasn't in Boston on business?'

'No – he was at Mass General Hospital, under the care of some big-cheese blood specialist – one of the best in the country. He was trying some last-ditch treatment to save him. But as the doc told me around a week before Jack went, he was beyond treatment.'

'At least Steele and Sherwood was picking up the bill.'

'Are you kidding me? Steele and Sherwood didn't pay a penny of his medical costs.'

'But he told me he was going back to work for them . . . that they had him on sick leave.'

'That's because he didn't want to tell you the truth.'

'What truth?'

'They fired him two years ago.'

I reached for the whiskey glass and took a long drink.

'But he was one of their star executives,' I said.

'Yeah,' Meg said. '*Was*. Until he fell apart after . . .'

She hesitated a minute.

'All right: I'll give it to you straight, Sara. After Eric died and you refused to deal with him, Jack had something of a breakdown. He stopped sleeping, he lost a lot of weight, he started showing up for meetings looking unshaven and sloppy. Once or twice – he actually broke down in front of clients. To their credit, Steele and Sherwood were pretty understanding. After around eight months of this kind of wayward behavior, they put him on sick leave, and actually dispatched him to a psychiatrist at the company's expense. Everyone thought he was getting better. But we were wrong.'

'Was that when you wrote me in Paris?'

'Yes. That is when I wrote you.'

One letter. One short, generous letter was all that was asked of me. And I couldn't bring myself even to do that. Pride is the most blinding and self-indulgent of all emotions.

'Anyway,' Meg said, 'during his few weeks back at work, everyone thought that he was returning to his old self. But he couldn't pull it off. He started missing meetings, and seemed unable to close any deal. They put up with him for another six months, then finally called him in one day and asked him to clear his desk. Again, they were decent with him: six months' severance pay, and health care benefits for a year. But he was now completely unemployable – especially as he sank back into a depression after they laid him off. At least Kate's birth picked him up a bit – but right after she came along, he started looking very anemic, and the lymph nodes in his neck began to bulge. I kept telling him that he shouldn't worry – that his body was reacting to all the stress he'd been under. But personally, I feared the worst. So did Jack. And when the diagnosis finally came . . .'

She broke off and reached for the Scotch bottle. Both our glasses were topped up.

'I have to tell you,' she said, 'that Dorothy was

amazing through most of this. Given that she really couldn't stand my brother – that the whole marriage was a massive mistake, and she truly loathed everything about his life with you – she still stuck by him. Right to the end.'

'He told me that she threw him out after he testified in Washington.'

'Yes – she was pretty appalled at him for co-operating with the Committee . . . especially when she found out how it triggered your brother's death. Worst yet, she couldn't stomach seeing him so broken by the fact that he'd lost you. Not that I could blame her. But eventually – after a lot of talking from me – she let him come home. Because, deep down, I think she hated being on her own. Not that she would have anything to do with him in a "marital" way again – except for one drunken night, which is how Kate appeared on the scene.'

'He did mention that.'

'Well, what he probably didn't mention was that his severance pay was all spent after six months. Then Kate arrived, then the leukemia was diagnosed – but by that time, his health insurance had run out. So the last year of his life was a complete financial disaster. He had a little stock – but he had to sell all that to pay his doctor's bills. It really got bad for a while. So bad that I've been paying their rent for the last three months. And – between the Mass General Hospital tab and the funeral – Dorothy's looking at about eight thousand dollars' worth of debt . . . not to mention the little problem of now raising two kids on her own.'

I took another needed sip of whiskey.

'I feel this is all my fault,' I said.

'That's dumb – and you know it.'

'But I should have written him that letter you wanted me to write.'

'Yes – you should have done that. But would it have stopped him from falling apart again? Who the hell knows? He still blamed himself for Eric. And as for his illness . . . Sara, despite what some dimestore romantic novelists might like to think, a broken heart has never caused leukemia. Jack collided with his genetic fate. It's as simple as that.'

'But if I had forgiven him years ago . . .'

'Now is it you who wants absolution?'

'I was wrong.'

'I'll agree with that. But so was Jack. And yeah – for a while I really loathed you for not helping him when he needed you.'

'Not now?'

She crushed out her cigarette, and instantly lit up another. 'I've lost my brother, my only sibling. Just like you've lost yours. So hate's rather point-less under the circumstances, isn't it? Anyway, you meeting him a couple of weeks ago meant a lot to him.'

'If only he'd told me exactly how sick he was.'

'What good would that have done? Anyway, he was right not to tell you. Just as I also know that, in all those letters he wrote to you, he never once mentioned his breakdown, or getting fired. He had his dignity, Jack. More to the point, he felt he'd burdened you enough – and that he didn't want to make you feel guilty. All he kept telling me – over and over again – was how much he missed you, and how sorry he was.'

'I never read the letters.'

'You could now.'

'I threw them out.'

Meg shrugged.

'He loved you, Sara. You should have seen his face whenever he talked about you. It was goddamn incandescent. I'd never seen anything like it. Didn't understand it, to be honest – because I'd never felt that way about anyone. All right, he could be something of a fuck-up, my brother. He made some terrible calls. He didn't know how to face up to big decisions. He had an awful habit of losing his nerve. And God, how he hated himself for failing you twice. And for failing Eric. Just as he also hated himself for failing Dorothy and the kids. But I also know that, at heart, he was just stumbling through like the rest of us. Trying his best. It may not have amounted to much. But, *at least*, he truly loved you. Without condition. And how often in life does that ever happen?'

I knew the answer to that question – but I didn't articulate it. Because I just couldn't.

'Would you do something for me?' I finally asked.

'I doubt it. But, go on – try me.'

'I want you to ask Dorothy to meet me.'

'Forget it. I may not hate you anymore. She *does*. She always has. And now . . . now the lady's got enough problems to handle without trying to forgive you. Which – I promise you – she never will.'

'I don't want her forgiveness. I just want to . . .'

'I don't care what you want to do. There is absolutely no way that my sister-in-law will ever agree to meet you.'

'Hear me out,' I said.

Meg did just that. And sat quietly for a moment or so after I finished talking with her.

'All right,' she said. 'I'll see what I can do.'

A few days later, she called me at home.

'I've spoken with Dorothy. It took some work – but she's agreed to see you. I didn't explain much to her. In fact, I kept it all very vague – except to say that I thought it was important you met. Believe me, she was *very* reluctant. But I brought her around – telling her that you had a crucial matter you needed to discuss with her. Don't expect this to be pleasant, Sara. She feels you're responsible for many of her problems.'

'She's right. I am.'

'There's a coffee shop on the corner of Amsterdam and Eighty-Sixth. Can you make tomorrow at four? I've arranged to leave work early, so I can stay with Charlie and Kate while she meets you.'

I agreed. The next afternoon, I got to the coffee shop just before four. I found a booth at the back.

I ordered tea, and found myself stirring it constantly as I waited for Dorothy to arrive. She showed up ten minutes late. She was dressed in a simple tweed skirt and a Peck and Peck blouse. She looked very tired – the dark moons under her eyes accentuated by the way her hair was pulled back in a tightly woven bun. She sat down opposite me. She did not exchange a greeting. She simply said, 'You wanted to see me.'

'Thanks for coming,' I said, sounding deeply tense. 'Coffee?'

She shook her head.

'Anything else. Tea? Hot chocolate? A sandwich?'

'Nothing. You wanted to see me. Here I am. I have about twenty minutes, no more.'

'Isn't Meg with the kids?'

'Yes, but Charlie's got tonsillitis – and we're expecting the pediatrician to make a house call around four thirty. So this will have to be fast.'

'Well . . .' I said, clearing my throat, really not knowing how to broach the subject I was about to bring up. 'Meg was telling me you were having some difficulties.'

'My sister-in-law has a big mouth. My difficulties are my business, not yours.'

'I wasn't trying to pry or be nosy. It's just . . . I would like to try to help.'

'*Help?*' she said with a hollow laugh. 'You *help* me? No thanks.'

'I can understand why you might feel . . .'

'Don't patronize me, Miss Smythe.'

797

'I'm not patronizing you.'

'Then don't tell me how I feel. I *know* how I feel – which is angry. Angry that I didn't have the courage, ten years ago, to tell Jack that we didn't have to get married, just because I was pregnant. Angry that I stayed in a marriage when there was no love between us. And angry that I didn't have the guts to end it when he first told me about you.'

'I never pushed him to leave you.'

'Oh, I was well aware of that. He told me that you refused to play the happy home-wrecker; that you were *oh-so-understanding* of his need to keep his family together – even though you *oh-so-adored* him.'

'I did adore him.'

'Congratulations. He was just as gooey about you. It was like living with a lovesick adolescent. I don't know why the hell I put up with it.'

'Why *did* you put up with it?'

'Because there was a child. Because I was brought up to believe that you lived with your mistakes. Because I was also brought up to believe that respectability meant everything. And because I'm a stupid, weak woman who didn't have the courage to realize that she *could* live without a husband. And then, of course, it turned out that my husband was a stupid, weak man who also ratted on others.'

'He only did that because he was terrified of losing his job, and undermining his ability to support you and Charlie.'

'Don't tell me you're defending him now? Especially after you emotionally crippled the fool by rejecting him. Anyway, the great dumb irony of the situation was that, by turning snitch, he lost everything: you, the job, me for a while . . .'

'You took him back, though . . .'

'More weakness on my part. Charlie missed him desperately. I decided that he needed his father.'

'But you didn't?'

Long silence.

'Of course I needed him. I didn't love him . . . but I still needed him. And then, after he got sick . . . it's a strange thing, isn't it, how we sometimes discover our real feelings about people a little too late. It was awful watching him go. Awful. And I was suddenly desperate to keep him. At any cost. That's why he went to Boston – because I'd heard of this specialist at Mass General who was trying a new sort of treatment for leukemia. Jack didn't want to go – mainly because he knew how much it was going to cost, and because we didn't have the money. But I insisted. Because I so wanted him to live.'

'Then you did love him.'

She shrugged. 'Eventually. Yes. When he was finally free of you.'

I said nothing.

'He never made contact with you after you came back to the city?' she asked.

'No.'

'Are you telling me the truth?'

'Yes, I am,' I said, trying my best to look truthful.

'I'm glad to hear that. Because I didn't want him to see you again. Because you didn't deserve . . .'

She broke off, and absently began to shred the paper napkin on the table.

'How I hated you,' she whispered. 'And the reason I so hated you is because: you had his love.'

'But then I threw it away.'

'Yes, you did. And I'll admit something rather ugly: I was so pleased when you did that. Because I thought: she will come to regret this. Which you have.'

She tossed away the shredded napkin. We fell silent again. I said, 'I know that you now have financial problems.'

'What concern is that of yours?'

'I'd like to help you.'

'No way.'

'Please hear me out. When Eric died, there was an insurance policy from NBC which was worth forty-two thousand dollars. I had it invested. It's now worth almost sixty-five thousand. What I'd like to propose is this: I give you eight thousand straight away to settle all the medical and funeral debts. Then I take the remaining fifty-seven thousand, and set up a trust for Kate and Charlie. The trust will generate an income which you can use for their school and eventually college, and anything else you think . . .'

She cut me off.

'And what do you want out of this?'

'Nothing.'

'I don't believe that.'

'It's the truth.'

'You're actually willing to give me and my children nearly sixty grand ... with no strings attached?'

'That's right.'

'Why?'

'Because it's the right thing to do.'

'Or maybe because it's a way for you to salve your conscience.'

'Yes, maybe it is.'

She reached for another napkin, and began to shred it.

'No strings?' she asked.

'None,' I said.

'I am not a charity case.'

'This is a gift, not charity.'

'And what will you live on when you're old and no longer writing columns?'

'I had quite a reasonable divorce settlement. It's all invested. One day, it will turn into a very nice pension.'

The napkin came apart in her fingers.

'You couldn't have children, could you?' she asked.

I met her gaze.

'That's right: I couldn't have children. He told you that?'

'Yes, he did – as a way of assuaging my fears that he'd start a second family with you, and then disappear. At the time, I was really *pleased* that you'd never have children. Isn't that terrible? But that's how much I hated you. In my mind, you threatened everything I had.'

'Isn't that always the basis of hate?'

'I guess it is.'

Pause.

'I want you to take the money, Dorothy.'

'And if I did . . . ?'

'It's the end of the matter. The money is yours.'

'This . . . *gift* . . . will never, *never* give you any entitlement to Kate or Charlie . . .'

'I expect nothing in return.'

'You will get nothing in return. That's the one string *I* will attach to this gift: I will accept it only if you agree that, as long as I'm alive, you will never make contact with my children. And one more thing: after today, I never want to see or hear from you ever again.'

Without hesitating, I said, 'Fine.'

'I have your word?'

'You have my word.'

Silence. She reached into her handbag and pulled out a little notebook and a pen. She wrote a name and a number on a leaf of paper, then tore it out and handed it to me.

'This is the phone number for my lawyer. You can talk to him about setting up the trust.'

'I'll get on to it tomorrow morning.'

Silence. Then she said, 'You know what I think sometimes? How if he hadn't run into you again that afternoon in Central Park . . . I remember that afternoon so clearly. We were out walking. He was tired. He wanted to go home. But it was such a beautiful day I insisted we stop by the gazebo next to the lake. Suddenly, there you were . . . and everything changed. All because I asked him to loiter for a bit by the lake.'

'It's the way things work, isn't it? Chance, happenstance . . .'

'And choice. Things might happen accidentally – like me getting pregnant, or you meeting an old lover and his family in the park. But then we make choices. That's what we have to live with: not the accident, the *fluke* – but the choices we make in the wake of it. Because they really determine our destiny.'

She glanced at her watch. 'I must go.'

She stood up. I did so too.

'Goodbye then,' I said.

'Goodbye,' she said.

Then she quickly touched my sleeve and said two words: 'Thank you.'

I never saw her again. I never spoke with her again. I never came near her children. I honored the conditions she demanded. I kept my word.

Until she died.

PART FOUR

KATE

CHAPTER 1

'Until she died.'

The manuscript ended there. I held the last page in my hand, staring down at that final line. After a moment, I let it drop on to the hefty pile of pages scattered on the floor by the sofa. I sat back. I gazed blankly out the window, trying to think, not knowing what to think. Dawn's early light was cleaving the dark sky. I glanced at my watch. Six fifteen. I had been reading all night.

Eventually, I forced myself to stand up. I walked into the bedroom. I stripped off my clothes. I stood under a shower for a very long time. I got dressed. I made coffee. While it percolated, I gathered up the manuscript pages and returned them to the box in which they came. I drank the coffee. I picked up my coat and the manuscript box. I left the apartment. The doorman hailed me a taxi. I told the driver I was heading to 42nd Street and First Avenue. As we cruised downtown, I turned on my cellphone and made a call. Meg answered, her 'Hello' accompanied by a bronchial wheeze.

'I'm coming over,' I said. 'Now.'

'What the hell time is it?' she said.

'Just after seven.'

'Jesus Christ. Has something happened?'

'Yes. I've been up all night. Reading.'

'Reading what?'

'I think you know.'

Silence. I broke it. 'Just as I think you know where I was yesterday evening.'

'Haven't a clue,' she said.

'Liar.'

'I've been called worse. Should I put on a flame-retardant dress before you get here?'

'Yes,' I said, and hung up.

She was actually dressed in a pair of men's pajamas and an old bathrobe when I arrived. The requisite two cigarettes were already burning in an ashtray. The television was tuned to CNN, the volume far too loud. As always, there was a pile of books and periodicals by an armchair. The remnants of a recent supper – a half-eaten Chinese take-out – had yet to be cleared off the little table that doubled as a desk and dining area. The apartment was the same as I'd always known it all my life. It was just as Sara must have seen it – when she came here on the night of my father's funeral in 1956.

'I'm never talking to you again,' I said, as I walked in and tossed the manuscript box on her sofa.

'Glad to hear it,' she said, clicking off the television. 'Coffee or coffee?'

'Coffee. And an explanation.'

'For what?' she asked, pouring me a cup from her old electric percolator.

'Don't go coy on me, Meg. It doesn't suit you.'

'And there I was, thinking that I might try "coy" for Christmas.'

'Quite a book,' I said, nodding towards the manuscript box. 'I presume you've read it?'

'Yes,' she said. 'I've read it.'

'She didn't hire you as her editor, did she?'

'I read it as a friend.'

'Oh yes, I forgot. You and Mystery Woman just happened to have been bosom buddies for the last four decades. And now I suppose you're going to help her get her book published?'

'She doesn't want it published. She wrote it for herself.'

'Then why did she want *me* to read it?'

'It's part of your life. You needed to know.'

'I needed to know *now*? Right after my mother's funeral?'

She just shrugged and said nothing. I said, 'You should have told me, Meg. You should have told me *everything* years ago.'

'You're right, I should have. But Dorothy was very insistent. Because she made it very clear that she wouldn't touch the trust if either of you found out.'

'She *should* never have touched the trust.'

'If she hadn't, you would never have had that fancy private school education of yours . . .'

'Big deal.'

'It *was* a big deal . . . and you know it. Because it took a lot of guts for Dorothy to do what she did. Jesus, imagine it: having to rely on money from your late husband's lover to get your kids through school.'

'But I thought Uncle Ray paid for our school and college.'

'Ray never gave your mom a dime. He was the original WASP tightwad. No kids, a big white-shoe practice in Boston, an even bigger bank account. But when his sister and her husband were in dire straits – after Jack lost his job at Steele and Sherwood – Ray pleaded poverty. Even when Jack was dying at Mass General, that asshole didn't once pay him a visit . . . even though the hospital was only a ten-minute walk from his Beacon Hill townhouse. Worse yet, he didn't exactly spend a lot of time comforting his sister during that time. One lunch on the afternoon before Jack died, during which he told his sister that she should never have married "that Brooklyn mick". Dorothy hardly spoke to him after that. Then again, I don't think they ever really liked each other anyway. He always disapproved of *everything* to do with Dorothy. Especially when it came to my brother.'

'But I was still told that Ray was my great benefactor.'

'Your mom had to find some story to tell you about the money. God knows, it sickened her to accept Sara's gift. And though she never said much about it, I know that it ate away at her. But she was the ultimate pragmatist. She couldn't afford your education on what she made as a librarian.

So she was going to swallow her pride – as she always did, the fool – and do what was best for the two of you.'

'You mean, like keeping all this from me until my mid-forties?'

'She was adamant that neither of you knew. Because I think she feared what you both might think. Anyway, a week before she died, I went to see her at New York Hospital. She knew she only had a couple more days. And she asked me: "Once I'm no longer around, are you going to tell her?" I said I'd stay schtum if that's what she wanted. "It's your call," she told me. "But if you do decide she should know, let *her* tell Kate. It's her story as much as mine."'

'But how did she know even where Sara was?'

'From time to time, she'd ask me about her. She knew that Sara and I had become good pals, that we were in pretty regular contact. Just as she also knew that, through me, Sara was keeping tabs on you.'

'*Keeping tabs on me?* Judging by that photo gallery by her door, not to mention the album she sent me, she was doing a little more than that. With your help.'

'You're right. I gave her all the photographs. I supplied her with all the newspaper clippings. I kept her abreast of all that was happening to you. Because she wanted to know. Because she genuinely cared about you. And because I felt she deserved to follow your progress.'

'Mom didn't mind that?'

'She didn't say. But, about ten years after Jack's death, she did make this passing comment about how "that woman has been very good about staying away from us". A couple of years later – when you were in *Guys and Dolls* at school – Sara showed up at a performance. I was with your mom, and I know that Dorothy saw her. But she said nothing. Just as she said nothing when she showed up at your graduations from Brearley and Smith. Again, Dorothy knew she was there – but she also saw that Sara was playing by the rules. And I think, in her own curious way, she liked the fact that she was so interested in you, and how you were doing. Remember: by the time you graduated from Smith, your dad was dead for twenty years. And Dorothy realized that the trust had made all the difference when it came to raising you and Charlie. So, in her own unspoken way, she was grateful.'

'But they never met again?'

'Nope. It was a four-decade silence . . . and they only lived seven blocks from each other. But you know what your mom was like. A cupcake with a reinforced steel filling.'

'Tell me about it. Negotiating with her was like taking on Jimmy Hoffa.'

'There you go. But though she was a hard ass, she was also pretty damn ethical. That's why she hinted to me that, if the story was going to be told to you, Sara would have to do it. Because it was her own unstated way of letting Sara know that she didn't go to her grave angry at her. It was a gesture, a *mitzvah*. I think Dorothy's final thought on the subject was: if I'm no longer here to worry about it, why not let her finally meet you.'

'Then why didn't you just come out and introduce us . . .'

'Your hard-ass mom had the last word on that. "If that woman decides she does want to meet Kate, you must promise me that you'll say nothing to Kate in advance. In fact, I want you to deny all knowledge of that woman. Let *her* figure out a way of getting in touch with Kate . . . and then see if Kate will listen to her."'

I shook my head in stunned incredulity. It was a classic Mom move. Forgiveness . . . but with a little *get-the-message* sting as part of the overall absolution package. She always knew how to ram home a moral point – yet to mask it behind a lily-scented smokescreen of decorum and propriety. This was, without question, her final masterstroke. She understood me better than anyone. She knew – *damn her* – that I'd play the hard bitch and resist all attempts to meet up with some old lady I'd initially file under *dotty*. Just as she also knew that Sara was strong-willed enough to finally get her own way, and force a meeting. And then? Then I'd be in possession of the story – but only Sara's *version* of events. Had Mom wanted to put across her point of view, she herself would have told me everything before she died. Or she would have left a long letter of explanation. Instead, for reasons I still couldn't fathom, she chose silence . . . and the risk that I would only hear Sara's side of the story. And this decision baffled me completely.

'You still should have warned me that a bomb-shell was en route in my direction,' I said.

'A promise is a promise,' Meg said. 'Your mom made me swear on a stack of Gideons not to say a damn word to you. I knew you weren't going to be a member of my fan club after Sara finally met you. But . . . what can I say? If there's one worth-while thing that Catholicism taught me, it was how to keep a secret.'

'Are you sure Charlie never knew?'

'Mr Self-Pity? Even as a kid, he was too absorbed in feeling sorry for himself to ever notice anything going on around him. And since he didn't deign to see your mom for the last fifteen years . . . Nah, Charlie-boy was way in the dark about this. And always will be. Unless you tell him now.'

'Why would I do that? Especially as it would just reinforce all of Charlie's beliefs about his dysfunctional heritage. And when he learned that Daddy was a rat . . .'

She suddenly turned on me. 'Never, *never* call him that again.' Her voice was hard, angry.

'Why the hell not?' I said. 'He only destroyed a couple of lives. And now – hey, presto! – back he comes to haunt mine.'

'Well, *honey bun*, I am so desperately sorry to hear that your fragile psyche was undermined by the discovery that your father was one complicated guy . . .'

'*Complicated?* He did some terrible things.'

'Yes he did. And God, how he paid for it. Just as Sara paid for her bad calls. You don't get through life without paying big time for getting it wrong.'

'Tell me about it. I'm the poster child for Getting It Wrong.'

'No – you're the poster child for self-flagellation. Which is so dumb.'

'That's me: Ms-Refuses-to-be-Happy. It's a great Malone family tradition.'

'What family isn't screwy? What family doesn't have some shit hidden in the attic? Big deal. But what saddens the hell out of me . . . what neither your mother nor I could ever work out . . . was why, over the past ten years, you always seemed so damn disappointed in everything. Especially yourself.'

'Because I *am* disappointing.'

'Don't say that.'

'Why not? I've failed everybody: my mom, my son. Even that shit, my ex-husband. And me. I've really failed me.'

'You are so wrong there,' she said, trying to take my hand. I pulled it away.

'No. I'm not.'

'You know what I discovered some time ago? Everything in life is fundamentally catastrophic. But the thing is, most stories don't end happily or tragically. They just *end*. And usually in something

815

of a muddle. So as long as you know that it's all a shambles with a definite terminus, well . . .'

'Oh I get it. Try to be happy within the shambles?'

'Hey, is happiness a federal offence?'

'I don't do happy.'

'You used to, you know.'

'Yeah, but that was before I started making mistakes . . .'

'With guys, you mean?'

'Perhaps.'

'Listen, I could write chapter and verse on every damn disappointment and sadness and failure I've suffered. So what? Terrible stuff happens to everyone. It's the basic law of living. But so is one simple fact: you have no choice but to keep going. Am I happy? Not particularly. But I'm not unhappy either.'

I stared down into my drink. I didn't know what to say, think, or feel anymore.

'Go home, Kate,' Meg said gently. 'You need some sleep.'

'Understatement of the year,' I said, picking myself up out of the chair. She stood up as well.

'I think I'll phone Mom's lawyer tomorrow,' I said. 'It's time to get the will probated. Not that there's much to probate. The way I figure it, the trust was virtually depleted by the time I finished college.'

'She used the money wisely – for you guys.'

'I never wanted anything from her.'

'Yes, you did. Like every kid, you wanted a perfect,

unflawed parent. Instead, you discovered that she was a mess. Just like the rest of us.'

I put on my coat. She picked up the manuscript box and said, 'Don't forget your book.'

'It's not *my* book. And how about you giving it back to her?'

'Oh no,' she said, dropping the box in my hands. 'I'm not playing mailman for you.'

'I don't want to see her.'

'Then take it to a post office and send it to her.'

'Fine, fine,' I said wearily. I hoisted the box. I reached for the front door. 'I'll call you tomorrow,' I said.

'So we *are* going to talk again?'

'Do we have a choice?' I said.

'Go to hell,' she said, giving me a fast, no-nonsense kiss on the cheek.

Outside Meg's building, I hailed a cab. I gave the driver my home address. Halfway there, I told him that I had decided to change destination. We were now heading to West 77th Street.

I reached her building just after eight. I pressed her bell on the front door intercom. She answered, sounding very awake.

When she heard my voice, she buzzed me in immediately. She was waiting for me in the open door of her apartment. She was as carefully dressed and poised as before.

'This is a lovely surprise,' she said.

'I'm not staying. I simply wanted to give you this.'

I handed over the box.

'You've read it already?' she asked.

'Yes. I've read it.'

We stood there, not knowing what to say next.

'Please come in,' she finally said.

I shook my head.

'Please,' she said. 'Just for a moment.'

I went inside. I didn't take off my coat. I sat down in one of her armchairs. I didn't accept her offer of coffee or tea. I didn't say anything for a while. And she shrewdly didn't attempt to draw me into a conversation. She just sat opposite me, waiting for me to speak.

'I wish I hadn't read your book,' I finally said.

'I understand.'

'No, you don't,' I said quietly. 'You can't begin to understand.'

Another silence. Then I said, 'The Jack Malone in your book . . . that's not the dad my mom told me about. I mean, he was Mr Morality, Mr Good Irish-Catholic. I always felt . . . I don't know . . . as if, compared to him, my mom was the lesser person. Some lowly school librarian who lived this tedious life with two kids in a cramped apartment, and who was so damn constrained that no other man would ever dream of marrying her.'

'Meg told me she did go out with the occasional fellow . . .'

'Yeah – when I was growing up, she dated one or two guys. But from the mid-seventies onwards, I don't think there was anyone. Maybe she'd been betrayed enough by dear old Dad.'

'You might be right.'

'You screwed up her life.'

She shrugged. And said, 'That's an interpretation. But it was her choice to stay with him. And that choice shaped the way her life ensued. Was it the right choice? I wouldn't have put up with such an arrangement. I would have thrown him out. But that's me – not your mother. So who's to say if it was the right choice or the wrong choice. It was just *a* choice.'

'Just like it was your choice to be my guardian angel. "Someone to watch over me." Didn't you have anything better to do with *your* life, Miss Smythe? Or were you so completely incapable of getting over the wonderful Jack Malone that you had to turn your attention to his daughter? Or, let me guess, I was your way of doing penance.'

She looked at me with a steady gaze. Her voice remained calm.

'Meg did warn me you took no prisoners . . .'

'I think I am a bit upset,' I said. 'I'm sorry.'

'You have a right to be. It's a lot to take in. But just for the record: after your father died, I left journalism . . .'

'You? The writer who always needed an audience? I don't believe it.'

'I got sick of the sound of my own typewriter . . . and my own frothy shallowness. So I moved into publishing. I was an editor at Random House for thirty-five years.'

'You never married again?'

819

'No – but I was never short of male company. When *I* wanted it.'

'So you never got over my father?'

'No one ever matched Jack. But I came to terms with it . . . because I had to. Of course, I think about your father every day. Just as I think about Eric every day. But Jack's been dead for . . . what is it? . . . God, so many years. Eric even longer. It's the past.'

'No, it's *your* past.'

'Exactly. My past. My choices. And do you want to know something rather amusing? When I die, all that past will vanish with me. It's the most astonishing thing about getting old: discovering that all the pain, all the drama, is so completely transitory. You carry it with you. Then, one day, you're gone – and nobody knows about the narrative that was your life.'

'Unless you've told it to somebody. Or written it down.'

She smiled a small smile. 'I suppose that's true.'

'Was that the object of getting me to read this literary exercise the day after I buried my mom?' I said, pointing towards the manuscript box. 'To finally let me in on a few sordid family secrets – and, in the process, *share your pain?*'

Oh God, listen to me. She dismissed my sarcasm with a light shrug.

'Meg and I both felt that you should read this.'

'Why did you write it?'

'I wrote it for myself. And maybe for you too . . .

though I didn't know if I'd live long enough for you to read this, and for us finally to meet.'

'You have some way of engineering a meeting, Miss Smythe. Couldn't you have waited a bit? I mean, I only buried my mother two days ago.'

Another patrician shrug.

'I'm sorry if . . .'

'And why did you have to stalk me?'

'That wasn't stalking. I came to the funeral because I felt I should be there, and pay my respects . . .'

'And I suppose that was you who called me at my mother's place after the funeral . . .'

'Yes, that was me. But Meg told me you'd decided to sleep there, and I just wanted to hear your voice and make certain you were all right.'

'You expect me to believe that?'

'It's the truth.'

'Just like you expect me to believe that, while we were growing up, you really never once saw me or my brother – even though, to all intents and purposes, you were funding our education?'

'I said, I didn't come near you. That doesn't mean that I didn't attend your graduation from Smith or Brearley.'

'Or didn't see me play Sister Sarah in my school production of *Guys and Dolls*?'

'Yes,' she said with a slight smile. 'I was there.'

'And were you sneaking glimpses at Charlie throughout his childhood as well?'

She shook her head.

'Naturally, I was pleased that the trust helped pay for his education. But I really didn't follow his progress as closely.'

'Because he was the child who kept you from my dad?'

'Perhaps. Or maybe because you were the child I was supposed to have with your father.'

Silence. My head was swimming. I suddenly craved sleep.

'I've got to go. I'm very tired . . .'

'Of course you are,' she said.

I stood up. She followed.

'I'm glad we finally met, Kate,' she said.

'I'm sure you are. But I want you to know something: this is the last time we will ever do so. You're to stay away from Ethan and myself. Is that clear?'

She remained impassive. How the hell did she manage that?

'Whatever you want, Kate,' she said.

I headed towards the door. She walked ahead of me and opened it. She touched my arm and held it.

'You're just like him, you know.'

'You know nothing about me . . .'

'I think I do. Because I also know that, unlike your brother, you were always there for Dorothy. Just as you are still there for Meg – who utterly adores you. She just wishes you were happier.'

I gently disengaged my arm from her grip.

'I wish that too,' I said. Then I left.

CHAPTER 2

As soon as I was outside her building, I walked halfway up the street. Then I suddenly sat down on the steps of a brownstone until I had composed myself. A thousand and one chaotic thoughts went swirling around my brain – all of them skewed, troubled. And I couldn't help but wonder: were these the same steps upon which my father sat down and wept when Sara told him it was over?

Another thought preoccupied me: the urgent need for sleep. I forced myself up. I found a taxi. I went home. I called Matt at his office. We had a civilized, neutral conversation. He told me that he'd taken Ethan to a Knicks game last night, and that our son was longing to see me this afternoon. I thanked Matt for looking after Ethan during the past few days. He asked me how I was doing.

I said, 'It's been a curious time.' He said, 'You sound tired.' I said, 'I am tired,' and mentioned that I appreciated his thoughtfulness over the past week. Matt started to say something along the lines of how he hoped we could be friends again. I said nothing, except: 'No doubt we'll be in touch

823

about Ethan stuff.' Then I hung up the phone and climbed into bed. As I closed my eyes and waited for sleep, I thought about that wartime photo of my dad, taken by my mom when they were both stationed in England. He was young, he was smiling, he was probably thinking: *in a couple of weeks, I'll never again see the woman taking this picture*. No doubt, similar thoughts were shared by that woman as she peered through the viewfinder. *Here's one for the scrapbook: my wartime fling*. That's what now so haunted me about that photo: the fact that an entire story was about to engulf the man in the picture and the woman behind the camera. But how could they have known? How can any of us recognize that inexplicable moment which seals our fate?

The image vanished. I slept. The alarm clock woke me just before three. I got dressed and walked over to collect Ethan from school. En route, I found myself once again trying to make sense of Sara's story. Once again, I failed – and instead started feeling overwhelmed by just about everything. When Ethan came bounding out of Allan-Stevenson's front door, he quickly searched the crowd of parents and nannies. Finding me, he smiled his shy smile. I bent down to kiss him. He looked up at me with worry.

'What's wrong, Ethan?' I asked.

'Your eyes are all red,' he said.

I heard myself say: 'Really?'

'Have you been crying?'

'It's Grandma, that's all.'

We started walking towards Lexington Avenue.

'You'll be home tonight?' he asked me. I could hear the anxious edge to his voice.

'Not just tonight. I told Claire she didn't have to come in until Monday. So I'll also be picking you up at school tomorrow. Then we'll have the whole weekend to hang out, and do whatever you want.'

'Good,' he said, taking my hand.

We stayed in that night. I helped Ethan with his homework. I made hamburgers. We horse traded: after he agreed to play two games of Snakes and Ladders with me, I granted him thirty minutes on his Game Boy. We popped popcorn and watched a video. I unwound for the first time in weeks. Only once was there a moment of sadness . . . when Ethan, snuggled up against me on the sofa, turned and said, 'Can we go see the dinosaurs after school tomorrow at the Museum?'

'Whatever you want.'

'Then can we all watch a movie here tomorrow night?'

'You mean, you and me? Sure.'

'And Daddy too?'

'I can invite him over, if you want.'

'And then on Saturday, we'll all get up and . . .'

'If I invite him over, Ethan, you know he won't be staying here. But I will ask him over if you want.'

He didn't answer me, and I didn't push the issue.

As if by silent mutual agreement, we let the matter drop and returned our attention to the television screen. A few minutes later, he pulled my arms more tightly around him . . . his own unspoken way of telling me just how difficult he found this world of divided parents.

The next morning, after dropping Ethan off at school, I returned to the apartment and phoned Peter Tougas. Though I knew he had been my mother's lawyer for the past thirty years, I never had any dealings with him (I'd used an old Amherst friend, Mark Palmer, to handle my divorce and other judicial pleasantries). Mom didn't see much of Mr Tougas either. With the exception of her will, there was little in her life that had required legal counsel. When I called, his secretary put me straight through.

'Great minds think alike,' he said. 'I had it down to call you in the next day or so. It's time to get things rolling on the probate front.'

'Could you fit me in around noon today? I'm out of the office until Monday, so I figured we might as well get together now, when there's no work pressure on me.'

'Noon is no problem,' he said. 'You know the address?'

I didn't. Because I only met Peter Tougas for the first time at Mom's funeral. As it turned out, his office was in one of those venerable 1930s buildings that still line Madison Avenue in the lower fifties. His was a small-time legal practice, operating out of a three-roomed no-frills office, with just a secretary and a part-time book keeper as staff. Mr Tougas must have been around sixty. A man of medium height, with thinning grey hair, heavy black glasses, and a nondescript grey suit which looked about twenty years old. He was the antithesis of my uncle Ray, and his white-shoe patrician lawyer credentials. No doubt, Mom chose him exactly for that reason . . . not to mention the fact that his rates were reasonable.

Mr Tougas came out to greet me himself in the little anteroom where his secretary worked. Then he ushered me into his own office. He had a beat-up steel-and-wood desk, an old-style steel office chair, and two brown vinyl armchairs which faced each other over a cheap teak-veneered coffee table. The office looked like it had been furnished from a Green Stamps catalog. No doubt, this sort of frugality also appealed to Mom. It reflected the no-frills way she lived her own life.

He motioned me to sit in one of the armchairs. He took the other. A file marked 'Mrs Dorothy Malone' was already in position on the coffee table. It was surprisingly thick.

'So, Kate,' he said in an accent with distinct Brooklyn cadences, 'you holding up?'

'I've had better weeks. It's been a strange time.'

'That it is. And excuse my directness – but it'll probably take you longer than you think to get back to normal. Losing a parent . . . *your mother* . . . is a very big deal. And never straightforward.'

'Yes,' I said. 'I'm finding that out.'

'How's your son . . . Ethan, isn't it?'

'He's fine, thanks. And I'm very impressed you know his name.'

'Whenever I saw your mother, she always talked about him. Her only grandchild . . .' He stopped, knowing he'd made a gaffe. 'Or, at least, the only one she saw regularly.'

'You know that my brother's wife didn't . . . ?'

'Yes, Dorothy did tell me about all that. Though she didn't come right out and say it, I could tell just how much it upset her.'

'My brother is a very weak man.'

'At least he came to the funeral. He seemed very upset.'

'He deserved to be upset. "Better late than never" doesn't work as an excuse when the mother you virtually ignored for years is now dead. Still . . . I actually felt sorry for him. Which rather surprised me – given that I'm not exactly known for my benevolence.'

'That's not what your mother said.'

'Oh please . . .'

'I'm serious. The way she talked about you . . . well, I could tell that she considered you a very loyal daughter.'

'Mom often got things wrong.'

Mr Tougas smiled. 'She also said that you were very hard on yourself.'

'That she got right.'

'Well,' he said, picking up the folder, 'shall we make a start?'

828

I nodded. He opened the folder, withdrew a thick document, and handed it to me.

'Here's a copy of your mother's will. I've got the original in the office safe, and will be sending it to Probate Court tonight – as long as you, the sole executor, approve it. Do you want to take a moment to read through it, or should I summarize everything?'

'Is there anything personal in the document I should know about?'

'No. It's all very straightforward, very clean. Your mother left everything to you. She put no stipulation on how you should disburse her estate. She did tell me, in our conversations, that she knew you'd be sensible about how you dealt with the trust. Were you ever aware of the trust's existence before your mom's death?'

I shook my head, then said, 'I've been finding out about a lot of things over the past couple of days.'

'Who told you about it? Miss Smythe?'

I flinched. 'You know her?'

'Personally? No. But your mother did tell me all about her.'

'So you knew about Miss Smythe and my father?'

'I was your mother's lawyer, Kate. So, yes, I did know about the background to the trust. Do you mind if I take you through its financial history?'

'Fine by me.'

'Well,' he said, pulling out another batch of documents, 'the trust was created in nineteen fifty-six, with . . .' he flicked through a bunch of pages '. . . an opening capitalization of fifty-seven thousand dollars. Now your mom drew down the interest from the principal for twenty years. But then, in nineteen seventy-six . . .'

'The year I graduated from college.'

'That's right. Dorothy once mentioned that to me. Anyway, in seventy-six, she stopped drawing any income from the trust.'

'Because the trust fund was depleted, right?'

'Hardly,' he said, looking at me with a certain paternal amusement. 'If your mother was only drawing down interest from the trust for twenty years, it means she never dug into the principal. In other words, the principal remained intact.'

'I don't understand . . .'

'It's very simple. After nineteen seventy-six, your mother never touched the trust again.'

'So what happened to it?'

'What happened to it?' he said with a laugh. 'Like the rest of us, it matured. And, fortunately, the people handling it . . .' (he mentioned the name of a big brokerage house) . . . 'they invested wisely on your mother's behalf. A largely conservative portfolio, with a small amount of adventurous stocks that paid off very nicely indeed.'

I was still finding all this difficult to comprehend. 'So, what you're saying is – after I left college, my mom left the trust alone?'

'That's right. She never touched a penny of it . . . even though her investment guy and myself

830

both encouraged her to draw down some sort of income from it. But she always maintained that she was perfectly fine on what she had to live on.'

'That's not true,' I heard myself saying. 'Money was always tight for her.'

'I kind of sensed that,' he said. 'Which, quite frankly, made her decision never to invade the trust rather baffling. Especially as – given the way her portfolio was structured – the principal doubled itself every seven years. So, by ninety-five, the trust had grown to . . .' He peered down at some figures. 'Three hundred and fifty-two thousand dollars, and a couple of pennies.'

'Good God.'

'Hang on, I'm not done yet. Now in ninety-five, her investment guys took a couple of smart positions on all these new information technology companies, not to mention one or two emerging web browsers. And, of course, from ninety-six onwards, the market has been non-stop bullish. Which, in turn, means that they actually doubled the existing principal in five years.'

'Doubled?' I whispered.

'That's right. And, at close of business last Friday . . . which was the last time I asked them to give me an update . . . the trust stood at . . .'

Another squint at a column of figures.

'Right, here we are . . . Seven hundred and forty-nine thousand, six hundred and twelve dollars.'

Silence.

'That can't be right,' I said.

'I can show you the computer print-out of the current balance. Your mother had money, all right. A lot of money. She just chose not to touch it.'

I was going to blurt out: '*Why didn't she?*' But I knew the answer to that question. She chose not to touch it – because she was saving the money for me. Not that she would ever have even hinted at such a legacy. Because (and I could almost hear her telling this to Mr Tougas), '*I know far too many perfectly nice young people who have been ruined by a little too much money a little early in life. So I don't want Kate to know about this until after my death – at which point she should have already learned a thing or two about the value of money, and about making her own way in the world.*'

Always one for the big moral lesson, my mom. Always one for denying herself everything. Always refusing to buy new clothes, new furniture, even a couple of reasonably modern, modest appliances. Even though – as I now knew – she could have afforded herself so much material comfort, so much that would have made her life that little bit gentler. But, oh no, always the stoic. Always the proper puritan who answered each one of her difficult daughter's entreaties with: '*I really do have enough, dear . . . I need so little . . . you must put yourself first, dear.*'

And knowing the way her mind operated, I also understood the logic of her decision. Meg was right: she was the ultimate pragmatist . . . yet one with a deeply ethical streak. So though she might have felt compelled to accept *that woman's money* to pay for her children's education, there was no way that she was ever going to use a penny of the trust for her own needs. Because that would have undermined her complex sense of pride. Perhaps (as Meg had intimated) she did eventually forgive Sara Smythe . . . but once Charlie and I were no longer her dependents, she decided to act as if the trust no longer existed. Instead, she concealed it like buried treasure, to be discovered after her death. The last of the big bombshells to be landed on my doorstep in the days after her funeral.

Seven hundred and forty-nine thousand, six hundred and twelve dollars. It made no sense. No sense at all.

'Kate?'

I snapped back to the here and now. Mr Tougas was reaching over to his desk and retrieving a box of Kleenex. He put it on the coffee table, gesturing towards it. That's when I realized that my face was wet. I pulled a tissue from the box. I dabbed my eyes. I muttered, 'Sorry.'

'No need to be,' Mr Tougas said. 'I'm sure it's all a bit of a shock.'

'I don't deserve it.'

He allowed himself a small laugh. 'Sure you do, Kate. You and Ethan. It'll make things a lot easier.'

'And Charlie?' I said.

'What about Charlie?'

'I was just wondering: what's his share in all this?'

'His share? As I explained earlier, he has no share. Your mother cut him out of the will. Didn't she tell you . . . ?'

'Oh, she told me that Charlie was not going to be inheriting anything. But she also said that there was virtually nothing in her estate.'

'I guess she wanted to surprise you.'

'She succeeded.'

'Anyway, your mother was very specific about the fact that the trust was yours, and yours alone.'

'Poor Charlie,' I said.

Mr Tougas shrugged. 'You reap what you sow.'

'I guess that's true,' I said and stood up. 'Is there anything else we need to discuss today?'

'Well, there are still a couple of small points about the probate. But if you'd rather wait until next week . . .'

'Yes, I would like to wait. I need time to . . .'

'You don't have to explain,' he said. 'Give me a call whenever.'

I headed out to the street. I turned right and started walking north. I walked slowly, oblivious to my fellow pedestrians, to the traffic, to the din of the city. As if on auto-pilot, I made a reflexive right on 74th Street. I let myself back into my apartment, and began to act on the temporary escape plan I had been hatching in my head all the way uptown.

Picking up the phone I called Avis, and arranged to pick up a car that afternoon at their East 64th Street depot. Then I booked a room for that night at a hotel in Sarasota Springs. Powering up Ethan's computer, I sent an e-mail to Matt:

Ethan and I are going to be out-of-town until late Monday night. You can reach me on my cellphone at all times.

I paused for a moment, then quickly typed:

Once again, thank you for your kindness during the last awful week. It was much appreciated.

Then I wrote my name and hit the Send button.

At three that afternoon, I was standing outside the Allan-Stevenson School on East 78th Street. As Ethan emerged through the front door, he was a little bemused to see me standing there . . . with two small duffel bags parked by my feet.

'We're not going to the dinosaurs?' he asked, sounding disappointed.

'I have a better idea. A more fun idea.'

'What kind of fun?'

'Want to run away for the weekend?'

His eyes flickered with excitement. 'You bet.'

I handed him an envelope, addressed to his home room teacher, Mr Mitchell.

'Run on inside with this – it's a note to Mr Mitchell, telling him we're going to be far away from school until Tuesday.'

'How far?'

'Real far.'

'Wow.'

He grabbed the note and dashed back inside the school building, handing it to the receptionist at the front desk. An hour later, we were driving up the East Side Drive, heading west on the Cross Bronx Expressway, hitting the 287, crossing the Hudson just south of Tarrytown, then joining the 87 towards the depths of upstate New York.

'Where's Canada, Mommy?' Ethan asked me after I revealed our final destination.

'Canada's up above us.'

'Above us, like the North Pole where Santa lives?'

'That's right.'

'But we won't see Santa?'

'No. We'll see . . . uh, Canadians.'

'Oh,' Ethan said, sounding rightfully bemused.

Why had I chosen Canada as a run-away destination? No real reason – except that it was the first place that came into my head when I suddenly decided to get out of Dodge with Ethan. Also, it was the first time I had crossed the border since 1976 – when I ran off for a pseudo-romantic weekend in Quebec City with a then-boyfriend named Brad Bingham (well, he did go to Amherst). If I remember correctly, Brad was the deputy editor of the Amherst literary magazine, and was something of a Thomas Pynchon fanatic who harbored dreams about running off to Mexico and writing some big abstract novel. In college, we all entertain such quixotic fantasies about a future-without-responsibilities. Until we are shoved into the workaday world, and we accept our destiny, and conform to the social norm. Last I heard, Brad was a big-deal attorney in Chicago. There was a picture of him in the *Times* when he represented some sleaze-ball multi-national corporation in an anti-trust case that was being argued in front of the Supreme Court. He'd put on thirty pounds and lost most of his hair and looked so depressingly middle-aged. Like the rest of us.

But, hey, he introduced me to Quebec City, and he was pretty gracious when, a week or so later, I decided that we should just be pals. Thanks to him, I was now heading north to Canada with my son.

'Does Daddy know where we're going?' Ethan asked.

'I sent him a message.'

'He was going to bring me to a hockey game on Saturday.'

Oh God, I'd forgotten he'd mentioned this night-time outing to me weeks ago (as the Saturday in question fell out of the usual two weekends a month which Ethan spent with his father). I reached over to the dashboard, and grabbed my cellphone.

'I could have you up for kidnapping,' Matt said after I reached him at the office. His tone, thankfully, was ironic. Mine was instantly sheepish.

'It was a last-minute idea,' I said. 'I'm really sorry. We can turn right around again if . . .'

'That's okay. I think Quebec City sounds great. You will have him back in time for school on Tuesday?'

'Absolutely.'

'And you told the school he'd be out on Monday?'

'Of course. I'm not that irresponsible.'

'No one's saying you're irresponsible, Kate.'

'That's your implication . . .'

'It isn't.'

'Fine, fine, fine. Look, I'm sorry if I screwed up your hockey game plans.'

'That's not the point . . .'

'Then what is the point, Matt?'

'You can never stop, can you?'

'I'm not trying to *start* anything.'

'All right, all right, *you win*. Happy now?'

'I'm not trying to *win* anything, Matt.'

'This conversation's closed.'

'Fine,' I said, now appalled by the senseless stupidity of this exchange. Would I never get *anything* right? After a moment's silence, I asked, 'Do you want to speak to Ethan?'

'Please.'

I handed the phone to my son.

'Your dad,' I said.

I listened in while Ethan spoke to Matt. He sounded a little tentative, a little shy – and certainly cowed by the argument he'd just overheard. I felt a horrible stab of guilt, and wondered if he'd end up hating us for fracturing his life; for squandering his stability at a premature age.

'Yeah, Dad . . . yeah, I'd like that . . . the circus would be great . . . Yeah, I'll be a good boy for Mommy . . . yeah, bye . . .'

He handed me the phone. We didn't speak for a long time. Finally he said, 'I'm hungry.'

We stopped at a McDonald's outside of New Paltz. Ethan sat quietly, eating his Chicken McNuggets and french fries, fingering the cheap plastic toy that accompanied his kiddie meal. I sipped a styrofoam cup of rancid coffee, looking at him anxiously, wishing I could somehow make everything fine for him . . . and knowing that that was impossible.

I touched his face.

'Ethan, darling . . .'

He suddenly jerked his head away, and started to cry.

'I want you to live with Daddy,' he said between sobs.

Oh God . . .

I reached out for him, but he pulled away, his sobs escalating.

'I want my mommy and daddy to live together.'

His voice was now piercing – heartbreakingly so. An elderly couple at a nearby table glared at me as if I was the personification of everything that was wrong with contemporary womanhood. Ethan suddenly threw himself against me. I gathered him up in my arms, and rocked him until he calmed down.

When we finally got back on the road, Ethan promptly fell asleep. I stared ahead at the dark highway, trying to maintain my concentration, trying not to fall apart behind the wheel, my eyes clouding up, a low fog rolling in over the road, my headlights trying to pierce its cotton candy veil. I felt as if I was driving into a vacuum. A void to match my own.

When we reached the hotel I had booked in Sarasota Springs, Ethan was still conked out. So I carried him up to the room, got him into his pajamas, and tucked him into one of the room's two double beds. Then I sat in a bath for an hour, staring blankly at the ceiling.

Eventually I dragged myself out of the tub and ordered a Caesar salad and a half-bottle of red wine from room service. I picked at the romaine lettuce. I downed the Bordeaux. I attempted to read an Anne Tyler novel I'd thrown into my bag – but the words swam in front of me. I put down the book and stared out the window at cascading snow. As hard as I tried, my mind couldn't let go of one repetitive thought: *I have fucked it all up*.

The snow had stopped by the time I snapped awake. Morning dawned clear and cold – a promising day. I felt rested. Ethan seemed brighter, and excited about the trip north. He devoured a stack of pancakes. He asked all sorts of questions about the journey ahead. He wanted to know if we'd see bears in Canada. Or moose. Or wolves.

'Maybe a wolf, if we're lucky,' I said.

'But I want to see a bear too.'

'I'll see if that can be arranged.'

It took nearly seven hours to reach Quebec City – but Ethan seemed to enjoy the ride. Especially as I had thrown a Game Boy into his bag – and was relieved to discover that he could play it in a moving car without getting sick. He read books. We chatted about a wide variety of topics (whether Godzilla really was a good monster who'd simply lost his way in life; which Power Ranger Ethan planned to emulate when he grew up). He loved crossing the border – and charmed the woman customs inspector at Canada Douanes by asking her where we could buy a wolf. He was fascinated by all the road signs in French. We bypassed Montreal and took Highway 40 north. It followed the St Lawrence – and Ethan was riveted by the sight of a major river that had become a solid chunk of ice. Night was falling. It was another two hours to Quebec City. Ethan slipped off to sleep, but woke when we pulled into the driveway of the Château Frontenac. The cold air jolted him awake immediately. Our room was poky, but it had a fantastic view over the city. Ethan stared out at the fairytale lights of Vieux Quebec.

'I want to go downstairs,' Ethan said.

We threw our coats back on, and went out. A light snow was falling. The faux gas lamps of Old Quebec cast the cobbled streets in a spectral glow. The city's gingerbread architecture looked edible. Ethan held my hand, and was wide-eyed. Seeing his unalloyed pleasure lifted me for the first time in weeks.

'I want to live here,' Ethan said.

I laughed. 'But you'd have to learn French.'

'I can learn French. And you and Daddy can learn French.'

I tried to fight off a wave of sadness. 'Let's go back to the room, Ethan. It's cold.'

Back upstairs, we ordered room service. After Ethan finished off *le hot dog et pommes frites* (and I picked at a truly bland *coq au vin*), Ethan said, 'Next time we go away, Daddy will come with us.'

'Ethan, darling . . .'

'And then we can all go to DisneyWorld at Easter.'

'You and I are going to DisneyWorld, Ethan,' I said.

'And Daddy will come too.'

I took a deep, steadying breath. I reached for Ethan's hand.

'Ethan, you know that Daddy now lives with Blair . . .'

'But he'll live with you again.'

'No, Ethan, he won't be living with me again.'

'Don't say that.'

'Daddy and I have both told you this before.'

'But it's not fair . . .'

'You're right. It's not fair But it's what's happened. We can't live together.'

'You *can* . . .'

'No, Ethan, we can't. We never will again. I know it's sad, but it doesn't mean . . .'

I didn't get to finish that sentence, as Ethan went running into the bathroom, slamming the door after him. Then I heard him sobbing. I opened the door. He was sitting on the top of the toilet seat, his face in his hands.

'Go away,' he said.

'Ethan, let me try to explain . . .'

'Go away!'

I decided not to push the issue, so I returned to the bedroom, turned on the television, and aimlessly channel-surfed. My stomach was in chaos. I didn't know what to do or say to make the situation better. After two minutes I tiptoed back to the bathroom door and listened. His crying had subsided. I heard him lift up the toilet seat and pee. I heard him flush the john, then run some water. I heard him walking towards the door, so I dashed back to the armchair by the television. Ethan came out of the bathroom, his head bowed. He walked over to his bed and climbed in under the covers. I turned around to him and asked, 'Would you like to watch some cartoons?'

He nodded, so I flipped around stations until I found Cartoon Network. Only, of course, it was dubbed into French.

'Want me to change it?'

'No,' he said quietly. 'It's funny.'

So we sat watching Tom and Jerry *à la française*. Ethan remained lying on his side, huddled under the covers. After around five minutes he said, 'I want a cuddle.'

Instantly I went over and lay beside him on top of the covers. I put my arms around his shoulders and drew him close to me.

'I'm sorry, Ethan. I'm sorry.'

But Ethan didn't reply. He just stared straight ahead at the cat-and-mouse fight on the screen. His silence said it all. Though we'd never given him false hopes about a possible reconciliation, an ongoing fear of mine was now confirmed. The fear that, ever since he had been aware of his parents' separation, he had been convincing himself it was merely a temporary situation; that, one fine morning, Daddy would move back in with Mommy, and Ethan's once-secure world would be restored to him. But now, the reality had finally hit. As I held him tighter in my arms, I couldn't help but think that, thanks to the combined efforts of both his parents, Ethan had just been given a premature introduction to one of life's fundamental truisms: when it comes to giving you a sense of security, people always fail you.

Ethan didn't bring the subject up again for the rest of the trip. We spent the next day exploring Vieux Quebec's back streets. We took a cab to the rural outskirts of town and went on a horse-driven sleigh ride through snowbound woodlands. Early that evening, we attended a children's puppet show in a tiny theater. It was *Peter and the Wolf*, in French (*naturellement*), but Ethan knew the story by heart (he had the CD at home), and delighted in being able to follow it in a foreign language. We ate dinner in a restaurant that featured a wandering accordionist, playing what I gathered was old Quebec favorites. The music was deeply resistible, but Ethan seemed to enjoy the novelty of it – especially when the accordionist approached our table, asked Ethan what French songs he knew, and then serenaded him with *Frère Jacques*.

All in all, it was a good day. Ethan never appeared glum or preoccupied (and, believe me, I was monitoring his moods carefully). He fell into bed that night tired, but reasonably happy. He kissed me goodnight and told me he wished we could stay another day in Quebec.

'So do I,' I said, 'but Allan-Stevenson might object if I keep you out another day.'

'You could tell them I got sick.'

I laughed. 'My boss might also get a little grumpy with me if I didn't show up on Tuesday. But hey, Easter's not far off. And Easter means . . .'

'DisneyWorld!'

'You've got it. Now get some sleep.'

As soon as Ethan had conked out, I picked up the phone and called Meg.

'Where the hell are you?' she asked.

I told her.

'Quebec in the middle of January? You must be a masochist.'

'Hey, why should old habits die hard.'

She laughed. 'You sound a little better.'

'We had a good day. And since "good days" have been in short supply recently . . .'

'I hear you . . .'

'I also managed to see Mom's lawyer yesterday.'

'And?'

'Well, the trust didn't turn out to be depleted.'

'Really?'

'In fact . . .'

And then I told her the exact sum involved.

'You're kidding me,' she said.

'I'm not.'

'Jesus Christ. You're certainly buying lunch the next time.'

'It's quite something, isn't it?'

'*Quite something?* It's unbelievable.'

'Yes. I guess it is.'

'I tell you, sweetheart – your mother was some operator.'

'Yes,' I said quietly. 'I suppose she was.'

'Don't tell me you're unhappy about this windfall?'

'I'm just . . . I don't know . . . just bewildered. By everything.'

'I know. But don't be bewildered by this. It's good news.'

'Yes, I suppose it is . . . though I do feel kind of strange about Charlie . . .'

'Fuck him. You were the one who was there for your mom.'

'But he was the one who lost his father.'

'You did too.'

'But, unlike Charlie, I never knew my dad. And unlike Charlie, Mom never made me feel as if I had stood in the way of . . .'

'Hang on,' Meg said. 'She really did love Charlie.'

'I'm sure. But did she ever *like* him?'

'I don't know.'

'Face fact: if Charlie hadn't come along, she would never have married Jack Malone. And her life may have been happier.'

'Don't count on that. Your mother did have a talent for martyrdom.'

'Tell me about it. All that money sitting there, and she still had to nickel-and-dime herself.'

'She never got over it, Kate. *Never*. It was the great tragedy of her life.'

Unlike Sara Smythe. It may have been her great tragedy too . . . but at least she came to terms with it. Or, at least, she learned how to live with it. My mom also 'lived with it', but it haunted her every move. I saw that now. Just as I also saw that I never really understood her. When did I ever see her courage in raising two children alone? When did I ever glimpse the mettle with which she coped with life? Never. She cut corners and wore twenty-year-old dresses and refused to recover her threadbare sofa and lived in a cramped apartment – all so, one day, I wouldn't have to repeat her story . . . so the second half of my life would be comfortable, secure, well-upholstered. But I was too wrapped up in my own griefs; my own sense of having been betrayed by men, by circumstances, by life. Unlike my mother – who stayed silent for four decades about the betrayal that fractured her life and sent it on a difficult trajectory. No doubt, she also wanted to scream: *me, me, me, me, me*. But she never would have dreamed of articulating such a self-centered complaint. She remained silently stoical. Not realizing that, in her own undemonstrative way, she was heroic.

'You okay, Kate?' Meg asked, registering my silence.

'I'm trying to be.'

'You'll be fine. I know it. And if you're not, at least you can now be a rich, miserable pain-in-the-ass.'

I laughed. And said, 'I'm going to bed.'

'Lunch next week?'

'Of course. And this time, I really am picking up the tab.'

Ethan and I both slept well. I was relieved to see that the threat of a snowstorm failed to materialize in the morning. We were on the road by nine a.m. Three hours later – just after we had crossed the border back into New York – Ethan turned to me and said, 'I want to spend tonight with my daddy.'

I bit my lip and said nothing, except: 'Whatever you want, big guy. Let's call him right now.'

I reached for my cellphone and rang Matt's office. His secretary put me through. We had a reasonably civilized conversation. Then I turned the phone over to Ethan.

'Daddy, can I come and stay with you tonight?'

They chatted for a few minutes, Ethan sounding really enthusiastic as they bantered away. Of course, I felt envy. Of course, I knew this was wrong – but when a child is shared between two parents, there is always this ongoing worry that your ex is showing him the better time, or relating to him more positively than you. No matter how you try to dodge it, a competitive climate develops between you and your ex. You've taken him to the circus? I'm bringing him to *The Lion King* on Broadway. You've bought him Nikes? I'm getting him his first pair of Timberlands. It's grim, this aggressive game of *who's the better divorced parent?* And totally unavoidable.

Ethan finished talking to Matt, and handed the phone back to me.

'You sure you don't mind letting him stay with us tonight?' Matt asked.

Yes, I minded. But I knew that, somehow, I had to stop minding. Otherwise I would be flagellating myself forever.

'It's fine,' I said. 'Honestly.'

'Great,' he said, sounding surprised. 'Thank you.'

We sped south. With a stop for an early dinner, we arrived in northern Manhattan just before eight. I called Matt again and told him to expect us in around twenty minutes. As I'd had Ethan's school clothes cleaned at the Château Frontenac (and his bookbag was also in the trunk of the car), there was no need to stop by our apartment. Matt was waiting outside his building on West 20th Street. As soon as I'd stopped the car, Ethan was out the door and in his father's arms. I went around to the trunk. I opened the duffel bag containing Ethan's clothes. I transferred some toilet supplies and a clean set of underwear into his school bag. Then I lifted out the cleaned uniform (still wrapped in the hotel's dry-cleaning cellophane) and handed it to Matt. Ethan took his school bag.

'He's got a change of socks and jockeys in his bag, along with his toothbrush. And here's his school uniform.'

'You know, he does have a spare set of all that stuff here,' Matt said.

'I hadn't thought of that . . .'

'Doesn't matter,' he said, then nudged Ethan forward. 'Thank your mom for a great weekend.'

I bent down. Ethan planted a kiss on my right cheek. 'Thanks, Mom,' he said simply.

I stood back up.

'Well . . .' Matt said.

'Well . . .' I said, thinking how awkward we now were with each other. You meet. You couple. You get to know each other very, *very* intimately. You make a baby together. Then it all goes wrong. So wrong that it gets reduced to terse exchanges, terse handshakes, a child with divided loyalties.

Matt proffered his hand. I took it.

'That was a dumb argument the other day,' I said.

'Very dumb.'

'It's always been something of a specialty of ours, dumb arguments.'

'Yes,' he said with a light laugh. 'We definitely have a talent for fighting. But . . . it happens, I guess.'

'Yes,' I said quietly. 'It happens.'

A slight smile between us, then the handshake ended. I bent down and kissed Ethan, saying, 'See you tomorrow after school, darling. I'll be home from the office around seven.'

Ethan nodded, then turned with his dad and entered the building. I got the car back to Avis. Then I went home. The silence of the empty apartment was huge. But I reminded myself that it was just for tonight.

The next morning, I returned to the office. I had such a backlog of work that I had lunch sent in. But I did set aside a few minutes to call Peter Tougas.

'You feeling better, Kate?' he asked.

'A bit.'

'Like I said last week, it's going to take a lot of time.'

'Doesn't everything?'

'You might have a point there. So . . . are we ready to proceed with the probate?'

'Absolutely. But I first need to ask a question: as the sole beneficiary of the trust, I am free to do whatever I like with the money?'

'Yes,' he said, sounding wary. 'As I mentioned the other day, there were no stipulations in the will about the use of the funds.'

'Good. Because I've decided that my brother should be cut back in.'

'What?' Mr Tougas said, sounding genuinely shocked.

851

'I want Charlie to have half the trust.'

'Hang on a minute, Kate . . .'

'It's what . . . ? Nearly seven hundred and fifty thousand? Give him three seventy-five.'

'You don't have to do this.'

'I am aware of that.'

'At least take a couple of days to reflect . . .'

'I have taken a couple of days to reflect on it.'

'Take a couple more . . .'

'No. I've made my mind up. I want him to get half the trust.'

'Kate . . . you know how he treated your mother.'

'You're right. I do. But he still gets half the trust.'

'On what grounds?'

I didn't say. Even though I now knew the grounds, the reasons. My mother – the silent master strategist – had checkmated me. She'd set it all up: first getting Sara to tell me her story, then letting her lawyer floor me with the news about the trust. Nothing said, everything implied. Even though the implication was now clear as hell: when it comes to forgiveness, language may be important . . . but gesture is everything. Because gesture begets another gesture. Just as forgiving another allows you to forgive yourself. Sara and my mother didn't speak for decades, but the gestures were made, the forgiveness rendered. Now, in death, my mother was doing what she always did. She was asking me a question: *can you do the same with your brother? Even though you know he's so wrong?*

'Please, just give me one reason . . .' Mr Tougas said.

'Because it's what she would have wanted.'

Long silence.

'All right, Kate,' Mr Tougas said. 'I'll prepare the necessary paperwork. And would you like me to phone Charlie and break the news?'

'Please.'

'What should I tell him?' he asked me.

'Tell him to call me.'

I hung up the phone. I went back to work. I left the office around six thirty. En route home, I made a fast stop at F.A.O. Schwarz, picking up a motorized Lego robot. Yes, I knew it was a useless piece of plastic junk. But Ethan had seen it advertised on television, and had been dropping hints for weeks that he wanted one. I had it gift-wrapped. Then I caught a cab north, arriving home just after seven fifteen. Clare the nanny was tidying up the kitchen. She gave me a hug (she hadn't seen me since the funeral), and asked how I was doing.

'I'm coping,' I said. 'How's our guy?'

'In his room, waging intergalactic war on his computer.'

I poked my head into his room. He turned around from his computer screen. He caught sight of the F.A.O. Schwarz bag, and his face lit up.

'Can I see? Can I see?' he asked.

'Don't I get a "hello"?'

He ran over and gave me a fast kiss on the cheek. 'Hello. Can I see?'

I handed him the bag. 'Wow!' he said when he saw that it was the Lego he so craved. 'You knew.'

Yeah. Maybe for a change, I did.

He sat down on the floor and began to open the box, looking up at me to ask: 'Will you come put it together for me?'

'Of course . . . after one phone call.'

'Mom . . .' he said, sounding disappointed.

'Just one call, then I'm yours.'

I walked into the bedroom. I lifted the receiver. I took a deep breath. This was a call I had been postponing for days; a call I knew I had to make. I phoned Information. I got the number for a *Smythe, S.* on West 77th Street. I dialed it. She answered. I said, 'Hi. It's me. Kate.'

'Oh, hello,' she said, sounding surprised. 'How very nice to hear from you.'

Especially as, just a few days ago, I told you we'd never speak again.

'Yes, well, uh . . .' I was really being articulate.

'Is something the matter?'

'No. Not at all. I was just wondering . . .'

'Yes?'

'Well . . .'

Oh, go on. Spit it out.

'Well,' I said. 'I was thinking of taking Ethan to the Children's Zoo on Saturday. You know the Children's Zoo, don't you?'

'Yes. I do.'

'Anyway, we'll be going there around eleven. If

854

you wanted to meet us there . . . and, maybe, have lunch with us afterwards . . . ?'

A small pause.

'Yes,' she said. 'I would like that very much.'

'Good,' I said. 'We'll see you Saturday.'

I put down the phone. I was about to pick it up again to call Meg, but Ethan shouted, 'Mom, you've got to help me.'

I walked into his room. There, scattered across the floor, was a mosaic of useless plastic pieces. Ethan had the assembly instructions in his hand.

'Come on,' he said. 'Put it together.'

I groaned and sat down beside him. I groaned again when I glanced at the instructions. They were spread across ten pages and were written in six languages. You needed a degree from MIT to decipher them.

'Ethan, this is really hard.'

'You'll do it,' he said.

'Don't be so sure of that.'

'Come on. Try.'

Try. Ha. What do you think I do? All the damn time.

'Mom . . .' he said, trying to get me to focus on the matter at hand.

I looked up at him – and suddenly saw the resentful, pimply adolescent who would give me the cold shoulder while still desperately needing me. I saw the gangly, awkward college kid, making one mistake after another. I saw the young man, renting his first apartment in New York or Boston or Chicago or wherever – so sure of himself on the surface, yet so riddled with doubt like everyone else. And I wondered: when would it hit him? When would he realize that this is all such a deeply flawed business? That we never get it right? Most of us proceed forward with good intentions. We try our best. Yet so often we fail ourselves and others. What else can we do but try again? It's the only option open to us. Trying is the way we get through the day.

Ethan reached for the biggest piece of plastic on the floor. He held it out to me.

'Please. Make it work.'

'I don't know how to make it work, Ethan. I don't know how to make anything work.'

'You can try.'

I opened my hand. He handed me the lump of plastic. I thought: *I don't want to fail you . . . but I might.*

Then I looked up into his expectant eyes.

'Okay,' I said. 'I'll try.'